The critics love these bestselling books from

SUSAN SIZEMORE

PRIMAL HEAT

New York Times and *USA Today* bestseller

"An intriguing alternate reality with absorbing characters and touches of humor makes this series one of the best and most consistently appealing around."

—*Romantic Times*

"Passion, danger, and mystery fill the pages of *Primal Heat* . . . an intense and satisfying read."

—Romance Reviews Today

"This world grows more fascinating as each new chapter unfolds. Politics, power, mystery, and romance make for a heady combination . . ."

—Huntress Reviews

MASTER OF DARKNESS

New York Times and *USA Today* bestseller

"What a bad boy charmer! Definitely Sizemore's most fun and original hero to date. . . . Once again, Sizemore serves up a terrific blend of edgy humor, passionate romance, and thrilling danger."

—*Romantic Times*

"Great action, snappy dialogue and powerful prose. . . . Susan Sizemore's *Master of Darkness* is engaging from beginning to incredible end."

—A Romance Review

I HUNGER FOR YOU

USA Today bestseller

"Sizemore's sizzling series gets more intriguing. . . . Hot romance and intense passions fuel this book and make it a memorable read."

—*Romantic Times*

"An alluring plot, page-turning excitement, and scrumptious romance."

—Romance Reviews Today

"Sizemore's vampire world is among the best . . . out there . . . This is one book that belongs on your list of keepers."

—Huntress Reviews

"Plenty of vampires, sexual tension, and action to go around."

—A Romance Review

I THIRST FOR YOU

"Passion, betrayal, and fast-paced action abound in this sizzling tale. . . ."

—*Library Journal*

"Edge-of-your-seat thrills combine with hot romance and great vampire lore!"

—*Romantic Times*

"An action-packed, suspenseful roller-coaster ride that never slows. [Readers] will root for this passionate couple. Don't miss it!"

—Romance Reviews Today

I BURN FOR YOU

"With her new twist on ancient vampire lore, Sizemore creates an excellent and utterly engaging new world. *I Burn for You* is sexy, exciting, and just plain thrilling. It's the perfect start for a hot, new series."

—*Romantic Times*

"I adored *I Burn for You* and really hope it's the beginning of another wonderful vampire series from Ms. Sizemore."

—*Old Book Barn Gazette*

"[A] sexy read laced with laughter, the first in a burning new series."

—*Booklist*

"Sizemore's hunky vamps can visit me anytime! I was so sorry to see this book end. This one is a must buy."

—All About Romance

MORE RAVES FOR THE WORK OF SUSAN SIZEMORE

"Wicked sensuality."

—Christina Dodd

"Thrilling, sexually charged."

—*Booklist*

"Sizemore knows how to write realistic vampires."

—All About Romance

Also by Susan Sizemore

Primal Desires

Primal Heat

Master of Darkness

Crave the Night

I Hunger for You

I Thirst for You

I Burn for You

Anthologies

The Shadows of Christmas Past
(with Christine Feehan)

Moon Fever
(with Maggie Shayne, Lori Handeland,
and Caridad Piniero)

Primal Needs

Susan Sizemore

POCKET STAR BOOKS
New York London Toronto Sydney

Pocket Star Books
A Division of Simon & Schuster, Inc.
1230 Avenue of the Americas
New York, NY 10020

Cover design by Lisa Litwack. Photo of woman by Shirley Green.

Manufactured in the United States of America

ISBN-13: 978-1-60751-466-4

For Ethan Ellenberg

Chapter One

December 12
San Diego, CA
Clan Wolf Citadel

"Charles? What kind of name is Charles for a vampire?"

Sid knew that her brother was trying to distract her as they waited in Matri Juanita's moonwashed garden. A faint glow lit the sky to the east of San Diego, the result of another wildfire in the mountains. At least the wind was blowing the far-off ash and smoke away from the city.

To show she appreciated Laurent's effort, she went along with the distraction. "We've had this discussion for nearly two years. I like the name Charles. It's a nice, normal name."

"Laurent's a nice, normal name," Laurent said.

"No, it isn't."

"It is for a vampire."

"What would you prefer I named him?" she asked.

"Something with gravitas. Something suitable—"

"For melodrama?" she interrupted. "I'm sick of melodrama."

"Melodrama comes with the territory, kid. What about changing his name to Anthony?"

Sid laughed. "Oh, please! Our mother is named Antonia. My sire is named Anthony. Your own daughter is Antonia Junior."

"We call her Toni. Your kid's going to be called Chuck, you know. Chuck the Vampire. I shudder to think of it."

"What about Charlie the Vampire?" she asked.

"Almost as bad."

It had been a long time since Sid had been in this garden. The scent of night-blooming flowers brought back a lot of memories. She noticed that her fingers were twined tightly together in her lap and made a conscious effort to relax. She glanced at the house. "What's taking so long? Shouldn't they be ready by now? And why do we even have to do this in the first place?"

They were taking her baby from her, and she hated them.

Laurent put his hand over hers. "You know that this is for the best. You can't deal with Charles on your own once his fangs come out."

Mortals had no idea how terrible the terrible twos could really be. She wished she'd had a daughter. Not only did their kind need more females if they were going to remain a viable species, but young vampire females didn't turn into bloodlusting animals when their baby fangs first came in.

Testosterone poisoning started early among vampire males, and the aggression needed to be controlled, channeled. Young males needed to be civilized if they were to mature into sane Primes. They needed drill sergeants more than they did doting mothers. Or so Sid had always believed, until her own son came along. Generation upon generation of vampire mothers had been through this. The ceremony this evening was supposed to reassure her that the finest care would be taken of her baby, but . . .

"You weren't raised in a crèche," Sid reminded Laurent. "Mom dealt just fine with you. You turned out okay. Eventually."

"Eventually." There was no humor in the sound when he laughed. "Antonia did the best she could when she had the chance to be near me. But remember that she was a prisoner, and that I was mostly raised among a pack of Tribe young where the rule is kill or be killed. Sometimes I doubted I would make it out alive. The Clans created a safe, structured environment for our little monsters. This is best for Charles, and for you."

Sid sighed. "I'm not fighting the necessity of sending my baby away, but I hate it."

He patted her hand. "Every parent hates it."

This reminder didn't make the pain of loss any easier, but it did reinforce the necessity of this custom.

The sound of a door sliding open drew their attention and they both stood as Lady Juanita's bondmate gestured.

"Please come with me, Laurent," he said. "Please wait a few moments longer, Lady Sidonie." He bowed very formally to her, then disappeared back into the house.

"If he knew you better he wouldn't call you a lady," Laurent said.

It was the sort of lame joke brothers were supposed to make. She was called Lady Sidonie because providing the Wolf Clan with a child made her head of her own House.

"Go on in," she told Laurent. "Maybe you can get them to hurry up with this stupid ceremony.

Why does Lady Juanita have to be so damn formal anyway?"

He gave her a reassuring kiss on the cheek before he left her alone in the garden.

It was only after Sid was by herself that the memories of the last time she'd been by this bench, in front of this fountain, came rushing back.

Three Years Ago

"I've been looking for you, Sidonie," Joe Bleythin said.

Sid stood. The moment she'd dreaded had finally arrived. "I thought you might be."

Joe said, "Lucy, you got some 'splainin' to do."

If he could joke, maybe this wouldn't be as bad as she thought. The meeting of vampires and werefolk earlier in the evening had brought out some startling revelations about the entwined histories of their species. It had also left open questions about her and Joe's relationship that Sid was reluctant to discuss.

"What can I say?" Sid asked. "I'm as surprised as you are to find out that vampires and werewolves can mate."

"Do you know that you blink when you lie?"

"I do not!"

Joe gave a harsh laugh. The air around them seemed to grow colder. "So you are lying."

Her werewolf knew her too well—except for the things she'd made him forget. Sid turned away. "I do not want to have this conversation with you, Joseph Bleythin. At least not here and now."

"What do you know?" he demanded. "When did you know it? And for how long? And just what haven't you been telling me?"

"About the Hunyaras? I don't know any more than you do about the bad guy's claims about Cathy's family coming from a werewolf having children with a vampire." That much was true, even if . . .

"Your species didn't seem repulsed by the idea of mating with members of my species when the subject came up. Why was I the one who protested?"

Sid shrugged. "Well, you know Primes. Vampire males see it as their right to have sex with anything that takes their fancy. But—"

"What about vampire females? What about you?"

"What *about* me?"

"How much have you lied to me about us? Why?"

His anger was shredding her. "It's complicated." She sighed. "Maybe the lesson is to never do anything for anyone else's own good, because it'll only come back and bite you on the ass."

"Explain that to me."

"Okay." She looked up at the moon rather than at Joe. "I love you."

He was silent for a long time, and she couldn't bear to look at him. She heard him pace around the fountain, then come back to her.

"I don't love you," he said.

Sid made herself look him in the eye. "Yes, you do. You just don't remember."

"What are you talking about?"

"We've been lovers, Joe. I made you forget."

After that, the shouting started.

When it was over, her life might as well have been, too.

Chapter Two

Present Day

"You're thinking about Joe, aren't you?"

Sid didn't know when her sister-in-law had come to sit beside her. The former vampire hunter moved quietly for a mortal. "How can you tell? You're not telepathic, Eden."

"I know that miserable look. It's not Charles that was on your mind just now."

Eden was the only person to whom Sid had confided the details of the incredible disaster she'd made out of her relationship with Joe Bleythin. Even then, she'd only told Eden because her observant friend had guessed most of it. The other members of Wolf Clan and Bleythin Pack who worked together thought that Joe had left San Diego and the Bleythin detective agency because he craved even more adventure in his life.

He'd actually left because he hated Sid's guts and wanted absolutely no contact with her. She didn't blame him. In fact, she'd originally offered to leave, but he wouldn't hear of it. So now she bore the extra guilt of being responsible for a werewolf leaving his pack for a lone existence.

"Life sucks," Sid muttered.

"Don't it, though?" Eden answered. "Or were you voicing vampire philosophy?"

"You have no respect for my culture," Sid said.

"Just leavening your melodrama with a bit of humor. You supernatural sorts take yourself way too seriously sometimes. Look at you, for example: clinging to a lot of outmoded customs, when you're dying to break loose and live in the twenty-first century."

"Our customs help us survive," Sid answered. "I know how that sounds, after what I did to Joe and using a sperm donor to have Charles, but I do believe that our way of life mostly makes sense. I *have* to believe that," she added desperately. She looked toward the entrance of the house. The waiting was driving her crazy. "You didn't come here to try to talk me out of tonight's ceremony, did you?"

She half hoped that was why Eden had joined her in the garden, but the mortal shook her head.

"The crèche system is one that's worked very well for your people for centuries. Do you know that in all of the generations my people have hunted yours, we've never found the hiding place of a crèche? Charles is going to be perfectly safe during a time when he's most vulnerable."

"I know." Sidonie sighed. "But still—"

"I'm here for two reasons," Eden interrupted. She pointed toward the distant glow. "First, since you're going to need something to occupy you, how would you like to join a group of us that are going up to volunteer to fight the fire tomorrow?"

"Sure, why not?" Sid answered dispiritedly. "What's your second reason?"

Eden took Sid's hand and pulled her to her feet. "It's time for the ceremony. I'm here to fetch you."

There was a ceremony for every aspect of Clan and Family life. Sid understood the importance of rites of passage, but she wished they'd just let her kiss her baby good-bye and get the inevitable over with quickly.

When she came into the Wolf Clan Citadel's central gathering room, she saw Lady Juanita's bondmate holding Charles in his arms. Charles was enthusiastically gnawing on the wrist the Prime held to his mouth.

"Chuck the Vampire needs blood other than yours, mama Wolf," Laurent said, taking Sid's other hand.

"I know that," she answered miserablely.

An altar was set up in the center of the large room. Lady Juanita, the Clan Matri, stood on one side of it. Laurent led Sid to stand on the other side. Candles lent light to the windowless space, concentrated in a golden arc around the statues of the moon goddess and leaping wolf set on the altar. Clan members and friends, all either Primes or Householders, gathered in the shadows beyond the light. Sid watched the Matri, not knowing what would happen next, since you had to be a mother before you could attend a Severing.

Ugly word, that. *Severing.*

Laurent stepped behind Sid, and her mother, Lady Antonia, and her sire, Tony Crowe, came to stand beside her. Sid assumed that Charles would be brought up to the altar, but instead, Tony and Antonia grasped her arms as Laurent's fingers settled against her temples.

I just found out I have to do this, her brother's thought came to her. *I'm sorry.*

Sorry for what?

Instead of a coherent answer, the trap closed around her. Laurent's thoughts opened her mind but the vise that closed around it was made up of the telepathic power of everyone in the room.

They were going to take her baby from her! Not just physically, but in every possible way. They were going to make her forget Charles!

Of course not. Memory remains. Lady Juanita's words came to her. *This will protect you both. You won't be apart forever.*

Sid didn't believe the Matri. She didn't care even if it *was* the truth. She fought hard with every mental trick she knew to hold on to the awareness, the love they intended to steal from her.

How can you do this? she mentally screamed. *Please don't do this!*

But there was no mercy. Nothing could stop the overwhelming combined strength of those who loved her from doing what was best for her and her child.

When the darkness swept over her, Sid almost welcomed it. Knowing she'd lost, but already not remembering what she'd been fighting for, she prayed the darkness would last forever.

Chapter Three

December 12
Present Day

Joe Bleythin had no doubt that Dee McCoy was a mortal woman, but she was like no other mortal he'd ever met. For one thing, she was a full member of the Dark Angels, which meant she was tougher than nails and able to keep up with her supernatural comrades. For another, she was a witch. This didn't mean that she was just psychic, like many other mortal beings. Oh, no—Dee performed rituals and did spells, and they really worked. Joe found that very weird.

He liked to think there were scientific explanations for what happened in the world, even his werewolf ability to shape-shift. Dee had told him that magic was a combination of chemistry, physics, and biology blended with psychic energy, but he suspected she only told him that to calm him down.

He breathed deeply now to at least appear calm as Dee finished casting a protective circle around the campsite. Everyone in the Crew was tired from a day spent firefighting, but they'd agreed to go along with this ritual because Dee claimed this was the right place and the perfect time for it. Plus, Tobias had told them that he didn't want to hear any bitching; they could get some rest when it was over.

While he waited, Joe looked at the people gathered with him around the fire and wondered if he really wanted his memories back. Maybe Dee's magic wouldn't work. If it didn't, a vampire as powerful as Tobias could probably break through the blocks Sid Wolf had put in his mind. But the last thing Joe wanted was a vampire inside his head.

He'd once been violated, psychically raped by a vampire, and for a while he'd barely been able to be around any of her kind. But if you were going to be a Dark Angel, you had to be able to work with all kinds: vamps, werefolk, selkies, sorcerers—even Jerame, and nobody was quite sure what he was. Fallen angel, maybe? Elf? Anime hero brought to life? He wasn't telling, and in the Crew it was best not to ask personal questions. They were kind of like the foreign legion that way. Tobias Strahan led, the Crew followed, and nothing but getting the job done mattered.

On their off hours they partied. Or, on nights like this, they sat around and waited while one of their number submitted to a magical cleansing.

Joe drew his knees up and propped his chin on them. He sighed loudly, which got him a look from Joaquin the werejaguar.

"Feeling silly?" the other shifter asked.

"Completely." He noticed Dee moving in a slow circle around the edges of the camp. Curls of smoke rose from the clay bowl she carried. "I hate that incense she uses."

"Take a sniff," Joaquin advised. "For once, the firesmoke in the air is doing some good. It's completely covering Dee's herbs. Are we all going to have to get naked and dance around the fire this time?"

"Since when have you ever minded getting naked?" Joe asked.

"Our neighbors might mind."

Even though there were plenty of mortal firefighters and volunteers camped out well back from the fire line, too, Joe was confident of their privacy.

Dee finished warding the perimeter. She spoke to Tobias, who stood guard, then she turned toward Joe. He was on his feet waiting for her, tense with expectation. Or maybe he was just sick with dread.

"Is it too late to change my mind?" Joe asked the witch.

"After Tobias has agreed to it?" She jerked a thumb over her shoulder. "Why don't you go ask him?"

She knew he wouldn't. "What do you want me to do, Dee?"

She handed him a thermos cup of steaming liquid. "Drink it all."

Joe didn't look at it. He closed his eyes and chugged it down.

It tasted like strong black coffee.

"Uh, Dee, are you sure this—"

"Oh, please," she complained. "Why does everyone think magic has to be all that woo-woo stuff?" She had a fiery temper to go with her blazing red hair and snatched the cup out of his hands.

"What do I do now?"

"That's up to you," Dee said. "Do you want to remember or don't you?"

"Yes, but—"

She walked away before Joe could finish.

He sat back down and looked at Joaquin. "Mortals are nuts, have you noticed?"

Joaquin shrugged. "They have their uses."

"I don't know," Joe said, gazing into the campfire. He waited for something magical to happen, but time passed and all he was aware of was the hot wind and scent of smoke. He sighed. "Sometimes I think we should all just stick to dealing with our own species and avoid mortals altogether."

"Vampires can't do without mortals," Joaquin reminded him.

Doing without vampires might be a good idea for werefolk, Joe thought darkly. But there was only one vampire he really felt that way about.

He was relieved that Dee's magic hadn't worked. He could honestly claim that he'd given recovering his memories a try, which ought to keep Tobias off his back about the need for every member of the Crew to be psychically whole. Joe suspected that if that *was* absolutely necessary, half of them wouldn't even be here.

"Besides, hiding from mortals won't do us any good," Joaquin went on. "There's six billion of them, and they've got spy satellites and cell phones and Wi-Fi hotspots."

"We've got all that stuff," Joe pointed out.

"And we've got telepathy and all kinds of other

psychic crap," Joaquin added. "But we're still overrun by the mortals' population advantage. There's nowhere to hide because they're everywhere. Even if we did manage to isolate ourselves, the mortals would just find a way to screw the habitat even faster than they already are."

Joe pointed his chin toward the distant fire line. "Did they do that or did we?"

"That's what we're here to find out," Joaquin answered. "If we find out that the arson is our mess, we'll take down the ones responsible."

Joe couldn't fathom why any member of the supernatural community would deliberately destroy terrain—except maybe to drive out the mortals encroaching on the wild places. But figuring out the reason for any assignment wasn't his problem. His job was to kill whoever Tobias ordered them to kill.

Joaquin stood and yawned. "Been a hard day. If we're not going to get a decent show from Dee's potion, I'm going to sack out for a while before my watch."

"Sorry for the lack of entertainment." Joe got to his feet and stretched tired muscles. "Sleep sounds like a great idea."

Chapter Four

Five Years Ago

"The Carlisles' plane is now wheels up. Rejoice." Sid glanced up at the Mexican sky from the hotel balcony before she flipped shut her cell phone and turned to Joe with a dazzling smile. "We have returned a teenage runaway to the bosom of her family. Miranda is no longer our problem."

"Hallelujah and amen," Joe answered.

He saluted his partner with his beer bottle and she raised her margarita glass in response. For a few minutes, they gazed out at the beach and ocean from their third-floor balcony. Life was good without Miranda in it.

"Technically, this was an easy job," Sid said, breaking the contented silence.

"Technically," Joe said. And they both broke out laughing.

"You know, if I believed in demons I'd say Miranda was fathered by an incubus instead of doting daddy Carlisle," Sid said when she stopped laughing.

"She certainly has the sexual appetite of a succubus," Joe said.

"At sixteen, so did I."

"Yeah, but you're a vampire. You're supposed to be insatiable."

Sid fanned her face with her hand. "Why, Mr. Bleythin, you make me blush."

He looked closely at her face, lit by the setting sun. "No, I don't."

She might not have been blushing, but he did notice that his close scrutiny caused her nipples to pucker under her thin, aqua silk tank top.

"Oh, my," Joe murmured.

Sid took another sip of her drink, then ran her tongue slowly around her lips. Joe's entire body tightened, and the air between them sizzled with mutual desire.

They were partners. This was a professional relationship. He was a werewolf. She was a vampire.

But he'd been wanting to kiss her since the day they'd met.

She stood as he came around the small table. Her arms went around him as his mouth came down on hers.

Her mouth clung to his while her words came into his mind. *Do you have any idea how jealous I was when Miranda tried to seduce you?*

You were jealous of me? Joe was full of wonder. *I go green when anyone even* looks *at you.*

His hand slipped under her shirt to cup her breasts. He had every intention of kissing his way down her long, lovely neck, all the way down to the peaks of her nipples, to worship her breasts—and that was only the beginning.

Except that out here on the balcony probably wasn't a good place to do it.

Joe swung Sid into his arms and took her inside the suite. It was only a few steps to the bedroom but Joe stood in the sitting room for a while with his eyes closed, enjoying the weight of her in his arms, the warmth of her skin against his, the feel of her gold hair against his cheek, and all the marvelous scents that were the essence of Sidonie Wolf.

Her ear was pressed against his chest.

"Listening to my heartbeat?" he asked.

She stroked his neck. "Mmmmm . . . delicious."

He carried her into the bedroom and caught his breath at the way she slid slowly down his body when he set her down. Her tongue flicked across the base of his throat.

Joe groaned. "Are you going to bite me?"

Blue eyes full of mischief and desire gazed up at him. "Do you want me to?"

Good question. *Hard* question. Joe didn't want to think right now.

"Better not," he managed, though the decision was damned hard.

"Later."

Sid took his hand and led him to the bed. He wondered if she'd heard the promise in her voice and if the word frightened and thrilled her as much as it did him.

She unbuttoned his shirt and he savored every tiny touch of her fingers slowly working down his chest.

"Fuzzy," she said after his shirt dropped to the floor.

"Werefolk," he reminded her, and held his breath at the momentary fear that she'd reject him.

Instead, she spun him around and tossed him onto the bed. "Vampire," she reminded him at this feat of strength. Then she swiftly shed her clothes and straddled his hips. "*Insatiable* is the term you used, I believe? Darlin', you have no idea . . ."

She bent down for a swift kiss while he stroked her breasts. His cock strained upward against her belly, the throbbing heat and pressure driving him crazy. His hands stayed on her breasts as she sat up and she arched her back in response.

"I've waited a long time for this," he told her as he watched the pleasure on her face, the passion in her eyes.

"We both have. Joe, I—"

Chapter Five

December 13
Present Day

The raw hunger in Sid's voice still sounded in Joe's mind as he came up out of the dream. The same raw hunger echoed in his blood and bones and skin. He reached for her, knowing he'd find nothing but empty air, knowing he was alone in the dark. The pain of the memory brought him awake with tears in his eyes.

Acrid smoke in his nostrils and stinging the back of his throat reminded him of where he was. He lay on his back in the tent and swore to himself at the realization that Dee's memory potion had worked all too well.

Joe sat up and rubbed his throbbing temples. What had Dee put in that potion of hers?

Joe noted the distinct scents of the two other Crew members inside the tent. The night scents and sounds outside were less than they should be because the animals and people had fled the area of the fire. He heard the sounds of helicopters and planes in the distance as the night shift fought the blaze. He picked out the smells of fuel and fire retardant. Wind whipped and the night roared. The situation outside wasn't pleasant, but all was as it was supposed to be.

Inside the tent people slept, and that was as it was supposed to be. Outside people passed on guard duty or sat around talking, waiting for the day.

Everyone slept but him, because he'd been woken by a nightmare. That was all it was, he told himself, just a bad dream.

A bad dream about great sex.

He wiped the sweat off his brow and tried to think of something other than his erection. Dee had used the power of suggestion to put him in a mood where he expected to remember something and that had triggered the dream and—

Except that it had all happened. Every word. Every touch. Every smell and taste and sensation.

Joe couldn't deny the reality of it for more than a few seconds.

"Goddess damn it," he muttered.

He remembered tracking the runaway Miranda Carlisle from California to a resort town on the Baja peninsula. He could remember the taste of cold beer and the sparkle of light on the water. He wanted to remember anything but the things that demanded his attention.

Damn Dee.

Damn Sidonie Wolf.

The thought of her name opened the floodgates.

"What are you staring at?" Sid asked. "Are you peering into my soul? I think I should warn you that—"

"You have the most beautiful eyes I've ever seen."

He leaned up on one elbow and stroked her blushing cheek. The long length of her warm body pressed against his in the bed, every delicious curve so right against him. They'd been resting together for a long time. Days. They'd make love, they'd sleep, they'd talk a little then they'd make love again. He was hungry, but only for her.

"Everything about you is the most beautiful I've ever seen."

She ran her fingers through his hair, pressed her palm against the back of his neck. "You shouldn't be talking like this, Joe."

"Why not?"

A sad smile played across her lips. "Because it tempts me to say similar things."

"Like what?"

She gave in to his eagerness. "Well, like how I love how black and soft your hair is. And how your voice always turns me on even when you're just saying 'Do you want another cup of coffee?' Or 'Answer the phone, will ya?'"

"Do I say will ya?"

"You do."

She ran a finger from his neck down his spine. The current from her touch sprang straight into his cock. She arched up and he moved between her legs. The next thing he knew, he was inside her again, living for her surrounding heat and their endless pleasure.

"Damn it!" Joe jumped to his feet, or would have, if he hadn't gotten tangled in the sleeping bag. He ended up rolling into one of his tent mates.

"Animal grace isn't your strong point," Dee murmured sleepily as he scrambled away from her.

"What the hell did you give me?" he demanded.

"The truth." She yawned. "Get out of here before you wake us all up."

Joe managed to step over her to the entrance without causing any more trouble. Once outside, he looked up at the smoke-obscured stars and took long, deep breaths. He managed to get his arousal under control after a few minutes, mastering the ache in his body. But the one in his heart was still killing him.

Why on earth had he thought he *wanted* to remember?

Because—

"We can't go on like this," Sid said as he came up behind her on the balcony.

Moonlight lit her pale hair and took his breath away. Joe's arms went around her waist and he leaned his cheek into the soft strands. "I know," he answered. She'd come out to the balcony while he'd been on the phone. "The folks back at the office are not happy about our taking an unscheduled Baja holiday."

She chuckled, then sighed. "How long have we been neglecting home, hearth, and duties?"

"We've been humping like bunnies for three days."

She stiffened, then turned in his arms to look at him in wide-eyed alarm.

"Don't worry," Joe said. "I didn't tell them what we've been up to."

The Bleythin detective agency was a family-run business. The last thing he and his partner needed was to return to teasing from his brothers back at the office.

"Good. Good." She gave a relieved little laugh. "We can't let anyone know about this. I can't even let anyone suspect."

That sounded far more serious than being afraid of teasing.

"Uh, hon—" he started.

Her fingertips settled on his temples. It gave him the odd image of exotic butterflies lighting on him. "This won't hurt you a bit," she said. "Forget."

Joe threw back his head and howled at the smoke-obscured stars. He was a werewolf, nobody in the camp thought this odd. He did get yelled at for disturbing peoples' rest, and a boot came sailing out of the night to hit him on the shoulder. But nobody asked what was wrong.

He couldn't have told them anyway. His insides burned with humiliation, and his heart ached too much for him to speak. He could barely form thoughts. For a long time, his only thought was, *I hate you, Sidonie Wolf.*

Chapter Six

December 14

"Thanks for helping me move my stuff back home," Sid said as she closed her town house door.

"No problem," Tony Crowe answered. "It's not like you had that much to bring back."

"True." She set down her suitcase and laptop and looked around the living room. "I've missed my place. I don't know why I let Lady Juanita talk me into being a guest at the Citadel for so long."

To protect your son. He said cheerfully, "Well, you're home now. For a couple of hours anyway."

He followed Sid into the kitchen, where she

rummaged in the freezer and brought out a bag of coffee.

"Want some?" she asked.

"Yes, please."

Tony watched her carefully for any sign of doubt, any sign of trouble.

She turned back to him when the scent of brewing coffee filled the air. "Are you sure you don't want to go firefighting with us?"

Tony shook his head. "That's not my sort of thing, sweetheart."

"You're a Clan Prime," she reminded him. She ticked off his accomplishments on her fingers. "You've been a soldier, a cop, and you now run security for every supernatural-run business in Los Angeles."

He nodded. "Yes, all very brave and heroic, but you will notice that I'm a city Prime. Fighting forest fires is so . . . rural."

"Being a soldier during World War Two wasn't?"

He chuckled. "Honey, I got to Paris as soon as I could and stayed there." More or less. Most of the time.

"Except for a cold winter trip into Belgium," she reminded him.

He stiffened "I don't want to talk about that."

"I know." She poured two cups of coffee, then they carried them outside to the tiled patio.

Painted pots of cactus circled the perimeter of the tiny fenced-in yard. Instead of grass, the yard itself was covered in a layer of decorative stones. Tony approved of the décor, and not just because it was suited to the desert environment. Anyone coming in over the fence would have to deal first with the cactus spines, then with the crunch of stones underfoot. Their kind had to think about security before beauty every time.

"It's December," Sidonie said after they sat in silence for a while.

Tony gave her a suspicious look. "Are you making a Christmas list?"

"I celebrate the Solstice, Dad," she reminded him. "You're the one who takes an interest in Christmas. The anniversary's coming up."

Tony almost groaned in frustration. His daughter might not like to think of herself as a typical vampire female, but she had matchmaking in her blood.

He sipped his coffee. "I'm not rising to your bait, sweetheart."

She was undaunted. "I was thinking that maybe you should come up to the fire line with us—to keep your mind off of it."

"My mind would not be on *it* if you weren't bringing it up."

"Bullshit."

He sighed and sat back in his chair. "Yeah, you're right. December always makes me nostalgic."

"It breaks your heart, you mean."

"There's nothing I can do about that."

Sid nodded. "The family tendency to stoicism sucks, doesn't it?" she asked bitterly.

His tone was equally so when he answered, "We serve our Clans."

She turned her chair toward his, leaned forward, and asked eagerly, "Why should you put up with it any longer? Why not dump all this Clan Prime obedience, since the Corvus Clan Matri who made that stupid decision died decades ago? Why not fly free, Crowe?"

So spoke the trapped Wolf. He didn't blame Sidonie for chafing at the bonds of duty and custom and biology, but he didn't like her urging him to do what she could not.

"Am I feeding your rebellious spirit?" she asked.

He got up and walked around the tiny yard, his footsteps crunching on the stones. "It doesn't need feeding," he said when he came back to her.

The conversation was interrupted by the sound of the doorbell. Sid went to answer it and returned with Eden and Laurent. Tony stood to greet Eden and as usual gave Laurent Wolf a long, assessing look. And as usual, Laurent smiled knowingly in response. He was nothing if not irrepressible.

After several years of knowing Laurent, Tony still reserved judgment on Sidonie's older half brother. When he'd first met him, Laurent had been firmly in the camp of the bad guys. Born and raised a Tribe Prime, he served his evil Tribe sire. Laurent had changed his ways after falling for mortal Eden and surviving some tricky machinations Sid instigated to get him away from the Dark Side.

He wasn't the first Tribe Prime to change his ways, but such Primes were usually taken in by the Families, which had lower standards of behavior than the Clans. Laurent had been accepted as a Wolf Prime by his mother Antonia's Clan. Tony liked him—it was hard not to—but trust a reformed Tribe Prime?

"You still perceive a whiff of brimstone around me, don't you, Tony?" Laurent asked him.

"Shouldn't I?" Tony asked.

"He's never going to be an angel," Eden spoke up. She put her arm around Laurent's waist. "And we wouldn't want him any other way. I've got a question for all of you," the mortal woman went on. "In what truly stupid way are mortals and immortals alike?" She didn't give them time to guess. "Because we're as likely to run toward a raging inferno as we are to run away from it. Are we all ready to go risk our lives up in the mountains?" she added.

"Not me," Tony said. He looked steadily at his daughter and responded to the hope in her eyes. "I have to go see about a girl."

Chapter Seven

December 15

"What are you thinking?" Eden asked Sid as the old bus rattled its way up the winding dirt road. The acrid smell and haze grew stronger with every upward turn.

Sid looked up and saw her sister-in-law gazing at her intently over the back of the seat in front of her. She didn't appreciate the total attention she'd been getting from everyone she encountered today.

"I'm thinking that I wish I hadn't had so much coffee before we left," she answered.

Eden nodded sympathetically. "Let's hope there are porta-potties up at the staging area."

Beside her Laurent snorted. He looked around as well. "Ah, the glamorous vampire life."

"And werefolk," Jimmy Dyami said from the seat behind her. "I don't know why I didn't fly here instead of getting my teeth rattled out on this bus."

"Because we decided to save our energy for when it's needed," his mate Alise said.

"And the usual precautions," he added with a sigh.

They were of the raptor folk, the rarest form of shape-shifter. Jimmy and Alise could turn into eagles. In human form they were short and slender, with Native American features, but they turned into the biggest damn bald eagles any mortal had ever seen. They and their other raptor kin took special care not to be sighted by mortal eyes.

Sid was surprised and proud that this rare, secretive pair was among the volunteers. Maybe it was another sign of the changes going on among the werefolk.

Stop that, she warned herself sternly. *I will not think about changes in werefolk culture. What's going on with the shape-shifters has nothing to do with me, or with vampire culture.*

There was no hope for her, and she knew it. After all this time she ought to have been used to it. She shouldn't even have been thinking about it anymore. She stared down at her clasped hands and let herself be miserable for a few minutes.

When she took a bracing breath and looked up again, she saw Laurent and Eden watching her carefully. "Stop it," she demanded. They dutifully faced forward and didn't bother her for the rest of the ride.

". . . and I'd barely gotten my clothes back on before this television reporter stumbled into the woods and asked me if I'd seen a giant bird flying in the area," Jimmy told them as they got off the bus.

"And you said?" Laurent asked.

"I told her that the reason I was in the woods was that I was a cryptozoologist researcher who had been tracing the Thunderbird legend for years."

"She bought it," Alise said.

Jimmy grinned. "She interviewed me as an expert witness. I said that sadly, I'd never found any traces of the giant birds people claimed to have sighted in the area." The were-eagle sounded both disappointed and naïve, drawing a laugh from the volunteer group.

"I'm not sure if that's just mean, or absolutely brilliant," Eden said.

"Brilliant," Sid, and every other immortal within earshot, answered the mortal among them.

"Just expressing one point of view," Eden said as she stepped off the bus.

Sid pointed. "The johns are over there."

She and Eden crossed the parking area, leaving Laurent to unload their gear from the bus.

"What are you two up to?" Sid asked. "And don't try to look innocent."

"Laurent and I are frequently up to something," Eden replied. "Could you be more specific?"

"You're both treating me like I'm really fragile, and it's getting on my nerves."

"Ah, well . . ."

They'd reached the portable toilets, and Eden ducked inside. Sid looked at the closed door in annoyance, then entered the little green outhouse next door.

Eden was halfway back to the bus when Sid came back outside, but she caught up with her sister-in-law in a moment.

"Well, what?" Sid demanded.

Yet Sid knew, even as she asked the question. How could she be so close to Joe Bleythin and not know? She was aware of his vital masculine energy even before she saw the tall, black-haired figure standing by the bus. Her first impulse was to find somewhere to hide, or to run back down the mountain.

But anger took over and she turned on Eden, barely able to control the longing to spout fangs and claws and rip the mortal to shreds. "You *knew* he was here. You knew and you didn't tell me?"

Anger flashed briefly in Eden's dark eyes, and she looked like she was going to argue. "I di—" She shook her head. "Ours is a small world, Sid. You have to face him sometime."

"No, I don't! I'm a vampire, he's a werewolf. He's—"

Eden put herself between Sid and the sight of Joe. She came very close and whispered fiercely, "You made your choice. Deal with it. Right now."

Sid backed up a step. Her heart twisted and she wanted to cry, but the mortal woman stared her down. "Damn it, Eden. You are such a hard-ass."

Eden put her hand comfortingly on Sid's shoulder. "Somebody in this family of noble Wolf Clan wusses has to be."

Sid carefully uncurled her fists, then deliberately relaxed her tense shoulders. She ignored the anger, the regret, the fear of impending humiliation. She lifted her chin proudly. She couldn't hide behind the alpha male "I am Prime" crap, but she could wear the haughty "I am a vampire female; worship the ground I tread on, puny male" attitude. It was probably the best armor for this situation anyway.

"You're right," she told Eden. "I hate you, but you are right. It looks like our guide up to the base camp has arrived. Let's get back to our group, shall we?"

Chapter Eight

Despite the roaring fire in the distance and the organized chaos of the crowded volunteer station, Joe knew Sidonie Wolf was there. All of his senses burned with awareness of her. He was on fire, but he refused to turn around, to look for her.

Every released memory of their lovemaking raced through him and he had to work hard to remind himself that the ecstasy she'd brought him hadn't happened last night, but years ago.

Ecstasy she'd stolen from him.

"When are you coming home for a visit?" Laurent asked him.

Joe got the impression that this wasn't the first time the vampire had spoken to him.

"When are you coming back to work?" Laurent added.

Clearly, nobody at Bleythin Investigations still knew his reasons for leaving. Joe was grateful to Sid for that, for a split second at least. "That's not happening," he told Laurent.

Laurent frowned. "From your cold tone, I take it that I should back off and ask about the weather or something."

Joe nodded. "Yeah, that would work. The weather, by the way, is hot and smoky."

He barely got the words out before Sid's entrancing scent cut through his senses. She was coming closer.

The realization nearly dragged him to his knees, nearly pulled him around with the longing to see her.

Joe forcibly reminded himself of what she'd done and managed to stay perfectly still as she passed by. She didn't acknowledge him but moved to stand at the back of the volunteer group. He managed not to sneer at her or to snarl that he was surprised the Clan had allowed their princess out of the tower.

Eden gave him a nod as she came up to join Laurent. As the Prime put his arm around his wife's shoulder, their closeness tore at Joe. There were other mated pairs among this group, and he hated the reminder that he was packless. For a moment he hated them all.

Except he wasn't alone. He was a Dark Angel. He was one of the Crew, and that was enough. He couldn't walk away from this group even if Sid *was* here. He had orders from Tobias.

He gestured for the group to follow him farther away from any mortal ears, waiting to speak until they were completely alone.

"Listen up, persons of the furred, fanged, and feathered persuasion," he called.

Laughter rose, but he noticed that Sid wasn't among the ones who looked amused.

"You volunteered to help fight the fire, but that's not the real reason you are here. There are plenty of mortals for that job."

People exchanged questioning looks.

"You are here to help the Dark Angels do the work that's necessary for our survival."

"We get to kick some ass?" Rayhan, a Wolf Clan Prime, asked.

"You wish," Joe answered. "We may get to do that eventually, but first we are going to find, analyze, and then destroy any evidence that the fires were set by rogue immortals."

"Rogue?" someone asked.

"The Angels suspect *us* of arson?" someone else asked angrily. "That's ridiculous!"

"That's a typical Clan reaction," Laurent put in. "You people don't know how to think like the bad guys."

"Because we weren't born Tribe," Rayhan sneered at him.

"Tobias Strahan of Family Singan was born Tribe," Joe pointed out to the vampires. "We Angels follow him without question."

"So there," Eden said teasingly, and stuck out her tongue.

The mortal woman's sarcasm cut the tension between the Primes. Living among the discipline and camaraderie of the Crew, Joe had almost forgotten how touchy relations between various types of immortals could be.

"No one suspects *you* of anything," Joe went on. "But there have been problems in the last few years—"

"Tribe vampires selling knock-off daylight drugs that we haven't been able to trace to the source," Eden interjected. "Neo-Nazi werewolves, with a huge budget we also haven't been able to trace, trying to start a revolution against the immortal councils. Mortals doing scientific experiments on kidnapped vampires to find the secrets of eternal youth. Fanatical vampire hunters claiming they have scientists working on ways to destroy immortals. We don't know if any of it is linked, or if there's more going on behind the plots we managed to stop—but paranoia doesn't hurt when you want to live a quiet life."

Joe was almost relieved that Eden had brought all this up. Everyone was aware that she'd been born into the Faveau family of vampire hunters, a group of mortals who now worked with vampires to keep bad guys from exploiting both sides of the mortal/immortal world. Eden *knew* stuff. She was trusted.

Joe said, "In your day jobs, some of you are cops and detectives and forensic scientists. We need that expertise, along with your psychic senses, to find the cause of this devastation before the mortals have time to investigate."

"That sounds like a good idea," Rayhan Wolf conceded. "We do have talents you military muscle types don't have."

Joe let it go. "That's why you are going to be divided up to work with three Dark Angels teams to do a grid search of the fire area."

Joe paused a moment for dramatic effect, then added, "Everyone except you, Sidonie. You can't possibly be exposed to danger."

He expected an explosion and relished the thought of her furious and thwarted. Her eyes blazed red for a moment, and he awaited the lecture about how she was as strong and as fast and as capable as any male vampire in the bunch.

Instead her expression went cold. She looked at him like he was a bug and he thought his blood was going to freeze.

She asked, "What am I supposed to do?"

The last thing he'd expected was cooperation. It took Joe a moment to answer, "You can make sure everyone's packs get transported up to the Angels camp. I'll assign a couple of my people to help you."

"Fine." Sid turned away from him.

He was dismissed, forgotten.

Feeling like he was recovering from a body blow, Joe began to issue commands to the rest of the group.

Chapter Nine

"You can't possibly be exposed to danger," Sid mocked. "He said oh so solicitously. Oooh, Joe thinks he's so clever. When I think of the danger we used to get into together, I could just—oohhh!"

She tossed a backpack into the supply tent and turned around as Eden tossed her another one from the trailer hitched to the ATV. She'd been seething the whole way up the canyon to the campsite but had waited until she and her friend were alone before saying anything.

"I thought you handled it very well," Eden answered. "Your response was very mature, if a bit bitchy."

"Bitchy? *Joe's* the one who—"

"Abused his power back there? Yes, he did." Eden jumped down off the trailer and gave Sid a hard look. "But now that you've both counted coup, you are both going to act in a mature, civilized manner for the duration of the emergency. Aren't you?"

Sid gritted her teeth, and her fangs bit into her lower lip. "You didn't come along to help with the luggage," she accused the mortal. "You came along to give me that lecture."

"Yep. And I'll slap Joe upside the head the first chance I get, too."

Sidonie began to laugh. The pain in her heart and her gut wasn't any better, but her head cleared somewhat.

"You're right about my having to live with what I did, and without Joe. But damn it, how do you expect me to defend myself from how I feel?"

"Find a nice vampire boy to fall in love with."

"Do you think I haven't tried?"

"Not hard enough."

Eden's practicality made Sid want to throw things. "How does my brother put up with you?"

"He likes 'em mean and bossy."

Laurent had all the dominant alpha tendencies of any Prime, along with having survived to adulthood in Tribe Manticore. Sid had had a small taste of how rough life in the Tribes could be and knew her brother was anything but soft.

"He likes *you* mean and bossy," Sid said.

"That's good—because it's too late for me to change now."

Sid knew that she was the one who needed to change. She'd been trying unsuccessfully since the day she realized she was much too attracted to Joe Bleythin.

She sighed. "Maybe looking for a nice vampire boy to fall in love with has been the wrong strategy. Maybe I need somebody tough and hard and ruthless to get me interested in Primes."

"Maybe you do."

"But where do I look, when just about every Prime in the Clans has tried their hand at courting me?"

"Um . . ." Eden was looking past Sid's shoulder, her eyes wide. She pointed. "How about him?"

Sid turned to look at the Prime standing in front of a tent on the other side of the camp. "Oh, my goddess . . ." she whispered.

"If I wasn't already happily married . . ." Eden said.

"Is that the legendary Tobias?" Sid asked.

"He wouldn't dare be anybody else."

The object of their attention was broad shouldered, six foot six, with thick auburn hair, sharp cheekbones, a square chin, and huge brown eyes. There had to be the body of a god underneath the loose-fitting camos he was wearing.

"Well, isn't he just the Prime's Prime," Eden said, returning to her less-than-impressed-with-the-whole-vampire-mystique, sarcastic self.

Sid dragged her gaze away from him. "Yes, indeed," she said with a smile.

"Go. Introduce yourself. Have your way with him. Let me know all the details."

Sid snorted. "You know that's not how it works. The Prime always approaches the female."

"Why?" Eden put her hands on her hips. "Because it's always been done that way? I thought you were all about changing female roles in vampire culture."

"I am. Eventually. When I can."

"You've already done more than any other vampgirl to win your freedom."

But at what cost? More than Sid could bear to think about most of the time. "I have to be careful."

"You've spent the last two years being a bit too careful, haven't you? Of course you've had Charles to look after, but—" Eden looked at her worriedly. "You are okay about Charles, aren't you?"

Her son was in perfectly good hands. He was

where he needed to be. The Clan was doing what was best for him to grow up into a proper, socialized Prime.

"Of course I am," she answered her sister-in-law. "I'm actually looking forward to having time for myself again."

"Good." Eden jerked her head toward the big Prime across the way. "Then I say go for it."

Sid looked back at the legendary Tobias. He was talking to a red-haired mortal woman. Sid wasn't going to disturb him while he was busy.

"He's not bonded, is he?" Eden asked after watching the pair for a few moments. Eden was very smart and incredibly observant, but Sid knew she didn't have a molecule of psychic talent. On the other hand, Sid was extremely psychically gifted.

She closed her eyes and concentrated to get a feel for the energy around her. Sharp pain shot through her head, followed by a split second of nausea. She opened her eyes to discover that she was sitting on the ground with Eden standing worriedly over her.

"What happened?" Sid asked, dazed.

"I was going to ask *you*."

"It felt like I hit a mental wall." Sid took deep breaths.

"Do you think the Dark Angels have some kind of mental barrier up?"

"Probably, but we're inside the perimeter. I think mommy duty has put me out of practice for dealing with the grown-ups."

Eden gave a thoughtful nod. "Yeah. That's probably it."

Sid rubbed her temples. "I feel bruised. Let me try again."

She closed her eyes once more. This time she ignored the pain, and it soon settled down to a faint headache she had no trouble ignoring as she studied the local flow of energy.

"I don't detect bond energy from anybody but you," Sid told Eden when she opened her eyes.

"So the big boy's not taken."

"But there are a lot of people with crushes on him," Sid added. "The hero worship permeating this place is nauseating."

"You're just trying to find an excuse not to like him, like you do with every Prime you meet. Go."

Sid got to her feet. "I am getting tired of this need you have to be honest with me today."

Eden crossed her arms. "You know how to make me back off."

Sid held her hands up in surrender. "I'm going, I'm going."

She turned around and walked over to introduce herself to the glorious man-mountain that was Tobias Strahan.

"Welcome, Lady Sidonie," he said as she came near. He had a deep, delicious voice. "You're the one that I want."

Before she could respond, he put his arm around her shoulders and led her into his tent.

Chapter Ten

Joe felt like he was going to smell of smoke for the rest of his life. He gratefully took the bucket of water Dee offered him and poured it over his head. Soot and sweat sluiced off him as the water poured through his hair and down his bare chest.

"Thanks. That felt good," he said as he handed the bucket back.

Dee looked him over. "Looks good, too. Too bad your girlfriend's not around to get a look at your water-slicked six-pack," she added.

"Where is Sid?" The words came out before he could stop them. He glared at Dee. "Stop pulling witchy stuff on me."

"Think what you like," she said.

"You didn't answer my question," he called after her.

She turned a mischievous grin on him. "She's with Tobias. They've been in his tent for hours." She took her bucket and walked away, hooting with laughter.

As Joe stared after the witch, Laurent came up and put his hand on his shoulder. "Did I overhear something about Sid?"

Joe ground his teeth together to keep from snapping. "Sid, Sid, Sid," he muttered. "It's a stupid name for a woman anyway."

"She's not a woman," Laurent reminded him. "She's a vampire female. You have to admit that Sidonie the vampire sounds much classier than Chuck the vampire."

Joe turned an angry look on Laurent. "Who the hell is Chuck?"

"Her kid."

The news hit Joe hard in the gut. He spun around to face Tobias's tent. "She had a . . ."

"I thought you knew she had a baby." Laurent stepped back and gave Joe an odd look. "Don't you special ops types get e-mail from home? Or didn't your brothers mention all the changes back at the office since you left?"

"Sid had a baby? She's bonded?" Joe's throat tightened on the word. His heart raced.

"Who said anything about her having a bondmate? She did her duty by the Clan, and then gave my nephew the dullest, most weenie name any Prime is ever going to have to live down. I'm surprised Sid didn't tell you about Chuck, since she's always claimed you're her best friend. Are you okay, Joe? You look a little green."

She had a child. Maybe she wasn't bonded, but she'd had a relationship with someone. With another vampire, of course, with one of her own kind. He'd never meant anything more to her than a fling, a few days of slumming with a lesser species.

"Friend?" Joe laughed. "We were a little bit more than friends."

"Right, you were partners, but you're the one who left to join up with this macho bunch." Laurent looked around almost furtively. "Have you noticed that even the girls around here are macho?"

"You have to be tough to be in the Crew."

Laurent gave a mock shudder. "Eden loves it here. I hope she doesn't try to get me to join up. I've come to love the comforts of home and hearth."

"You're chattering," Joe told Laurent. "You do that when you're trying to cover up something."

Laurent glanced toward Tobias's tent. "I'll admit it, I'm worried about my sister. Funny thing is, a few years ago I didn't want anything to do with family. Now I worry about them all the time—my wife, my kid, my nephew, my mom, especially my sister."

Despite not wanting anything to do with Sid, Joe couldn't stop the question. "Why your sister?"

"Because—Well, what have we here?" Laurent asked as Sid and Tobias came out of the tent. Tobias's arm was snugly around her shoulder.

"Maybe they've been bonding," Joe said.

"You sound jealous," Laurent responded. "Don't tell me you're interested in my sister. Is that why you left?"

"It's none of your business."

That didn't deter Laurent. "If you're in love with her it's a good thing you left, because I can't think of a quicker way for you to get yourself killed."

"I am not impressed by your brotherly concern."

"That's not—"

Before Laurent could finish, two trucks came rumbling to a halt just below the campsite. Six uniformed men got out and headed uphill.

"Mortals," Joe and Laurent said together.

Everyone else in the camp noticed as well, and most people began to head toward the intruders.

Tobias lifted a hand and called, "Stand down."

The Crew waited, and made sure their guests did as well, while Tobias went down the hill to greet the military. He took Sid with him.

Joe waited with equal parts surprise and annoyance while the two vampires talked to the intruders. The newcomers were tense and not at all friendly. At one point, Sid moved away from Tobias. She reached out to gently touch the commander on the arm. In a moment she had the mortal's complete attention.

Joe's breath hissed out as he took a step forward. Laurent put an arm out to hold him back, and fury flashed through Joe at himself for reacting after Tobias had given the command to stay put, and for having to be reminded of it by an outsider.

"She's good," Laurent murmured.

The mortal commander was looking into Sid's eyes, his expression blank. It was easy to see that Sidonie was pulling her mind-muddling telepathic trick on the unsuspecting mortal. She was no doubt telling him that Tobias's group was an official part of the firefighting contingent, telling him that he had more important things to do than interfere with the work of people who had every right and good reason to be there.

When mortals had stopped by before, Tobias had made them believe this, and Joe had been as amused as every other member of the Crew. Now that Tobias had put Sid to work doing what she did best—lying to people and making them believe it—Joe didn't see any humor in it at all.

Chapter Eleven

Sid waited with the Dark Angel commander as he watched the National Guard contingent get back in their trucks and drive away. She felt the psychic weight of every eye on her from the camp behind them. The attention didn't help her headache any, and it certainly didn't help the feeling of being disgusted with herself.

If she didn't know Joe was watching, she might have been basking in smug satisfaction at a job well done. Allaying mortal suspicions about the supernatural world was necessary at times. You didn't alter peoples' thoughts for fun, but for the safety of everyone involved.

Joe knew that.

But that wasn't what he was thinking right now, was it? She knew Joseph Bleythin. He was somehow remembering what she'd done to him and hating her more by the second for it.

Maybe he was right, too.

"Screw him anyway," she muttered.

Tobias cocked one finely arched brow at her, then walked back to the camp.

As Sid followed, Eden gestured for her to come into the supply tent.

"What did Tobias want?" Eden asked as soon as they were alone. "Did he try to seduce you or recruit you?"

Sid laughed. "Since when would a Prime even think about letting a vampire female join a club like the Dark Angels?"

"Things have to change sometime."

"I doubt if it'll be in this lifetime."

She couldn't share the mortal's attitude, not from where she stood inside the luxurious cage of a female vampire's life. She hoped to have daughters and to work to get them the freedom she'd never fully have herself.

"So he wanted to seduce you."

Sid laughed again. "Primes try to do that automatically."

Eden grinned. "Is he as talented as he is lovely?"

Sid shrugged. "I wouldn't know. We had a nice flirt, but what he really wanted was to talk. Speaking of talking," she went on before Eden asked any more questions, "did you get your chance to smack Joe upside the head? Have we both promised to behave now?"

"I sent Laurent to talk to him," Eden answered. "The hope is that a talk between guys would work better than my nagging him."

"You nagged me."

"Males have more delicate sensibilities." Eden was not to be diverted. "What did Tobias want to talk about?"

"Nothing significant. He takes a morbid interest in the time I spent with Tribe Manticore. I told him that I was locked in a room the whole time I was their prisoner. I have no information about Dawn production or distribution routes or secret labs. You probably know more than I do."

"Nah," Eden answered. "The Dawn junkies I interrogated didn't know or care where the stuff came from. And the Dark Angels have access to the report I put together."

"Tobias mentioned that."

Just then, Dee stuck her head into the tent. "Outside, you two. Tobias has called dinner, with a meeting after."

"Lordy, but they do love to jump to his tune,"

Eden said when Dee was gone. She lifted the tent flap and gestured Sid out. "Shall we?"

"At least we get a meal to go along with tonight's scheduled lecture," Laurent whispered in Sid's ear as she took a seat beside him. "I was scared we'd have to live off the land. Not that I couldn't kill a bear to feed my woman," he added staunchly, with a glance toward Eden.

Eden looked up from her seat opposite Laurent at the long mess table. "I'm sure you could kill a bear, dear. Of course, then you'd wait for a gourmet chef to come along and do something with it while you studied the wine list."

"Of course I would. Darling. I started life as a monster, not as a barbarian."

Sid smiled as she watched Laurent flutter his impossibly long eyelashes at his bondmate. Eden covered her mouth to hide a giggle.

The other volunteers were scattered among the serious ranks of the Dark Angels, and silence was the order of the day as they quickly ate their dinner. Sid couldn't detect much telepathic activity, either. After all, Tobias had called a meeting; they had to get through the mundane stuff quickly so they could give their complete attention to the boss.

Sid noticed that Joe had sat as far away from her as he could get. After one glance, she deliberately didn't look his way. She told herself she imagined feeling his gaze on her.

"You two better behave," she whispered to Eden and Laurent. "Or you'll end up doing five thousand push-ups for enjoying yourself."

Eden composed her features and said seriously, "I admire the strength of character required to lead a disciplined life like this. Special Ops teams are necessary. That doesn't mean I want us to sign up," she added to Laurent before he had the chance to look horrified.

Laurent looked to the opposite end of the table. "I wouldn't have thought this would be Joe's sort of lifestyle."

"He used to be in the air force," Sid said. "He always talked about going back to the military when things at work got hairy."

She closed her lips tightly, surprised at how she'd automatically jumped to Joe's defense. Well, why not? She didn't really have any reason to be angry at him. At least, she didn't have any right to be.

"He was a werewolf working with werewolves," Laurent pointed out. "Things were always hairy."

He shouldn't have left his pack, Sid thought.

He probably just wanted another way to make me feel guilty.

Good goddess, she was pouting again! She didn't understand why being near Joe was making her emotions as volatile and angsty as a teenage mortal's. Hormones, maybe? Every fiber of her being currently burned with lust, but none of the virile Primes among the Angels and volunteers did anything for her.

Sid couldn't stop a second glance toward Joe. And this time their gazes met.

"I've never seen eyes as blue as yours."

"I probably have some husky in my background," Joe answered.

Sid couldn't laugh. She couldn't even smile. All she could do was to continue to stare deep into Joe's eyes as he stared into hers. Their souls met. And their flesh—

His fingers slid over her bare skin as softly as the tropical moonlight that poured down onto the balcony. The tang of sea salt met her already heightened senses when she licked her lips. Her fingers traced across his body, reveled in the feel of well-defined, hard muscles. The air heated between them and—

"Contrary to popular belief, vampires really do need oxygen." Eden's voice assaulted Sid's ears.

There was no salt in the air, no moonlight.

Only the faint tang of smoke when she took in a sharp breath.

From then on, she concentrated on finishing her meal.

She wasn't going to look at Joe again. She wasn't, she wasn't, she wasn't.

Chapter Twelve

"All right, people, here's what we've got so far," Tobias said.

The dishes were cleared away, and Tobias stood at the head of the table for the briefing. Joe still fought off the arousal contact with Sid had stirred in him a half hour before. He tried to keep his attention on his commander, but visions of Sid's naked body danced through his head and straight to his groin.

Sitting beside him, Dee brushed her thigh against his and said, "Just take deep breaths."

"Stop it," Joe growled. "You're not helping."

"I am," she whispered.

He finally realized that her touch was relaxing, not arousing. "Thanks."

Tobias gave him a stern look that blew away every last shred of Joe's distraction before returning his attention to the general populace.

"Our search has come up with eight separate arson sites. Eight, people. This was a vicious, systematic, and well-planned attack. Somebody was attempting to burn down California, and we've determined that that somebody swims in our side of the genetic pool."

Tobias put his hands on his hips and waited.

Surprisingly, none of the volunteers made any knee-jerk protests about the harmless intentions of the supernatural community. Joe figured they were either too intimidated by Tobias, or they'd found the evidence that the Crew had left for them to stumble on to too compelling to ignore.

The point of this exercise *was* to send them home to rally support for the coming war. The evidence was real. And these witnesses were credible, respected members of their kinds, not as easy for the elders to dismiss as a bunch of gung-ho militaristic hotheads.

Tobias continued, "It was an attack on the mortals' environment, it was an attack on the mortals' economy, and there have been five reported deaths, as well as many injuries. While I personally don't care much about mortals, we do have to live secretly among them.

"The Dark Angels have always taken on renegades, but the danger is different now. The evidence found here shows a wider conspiracy. We have found the scents of vampires, mortals, and werefolk around the eight buildings where the fires were set. Six of those buildings have left traces that tell us they were used as drug manufacturing facilities."

"Dawn labs?" Eden asked.

Tobias nodded. "Dawn was manufactured in one of the buildings. The other chemical traces we've found are still unknown. Some buildings were used for storage and as barracks. And there's a possibility that prisoners were kept in one of the buildings. The remains of a burned body were found in what might have been a cell, but that requires further investigation."

Laurent spoke up. "The layout reminded me of the werewolf base we busted a while back. Only a lot bigger."

"That lot wasn't manufacturing drugs," Rayhan Wolf said. "But Laurent's right about the similarities."

"I've seen the werewolf camp you took out in the northwest," Tobias said. "It looks like the same people financed this operation. But this time the bad guys weren't just werefolk, and they weren't busted. They finished whatever they were doing here. When they moved their operation, they set the fires to destroy evidence. The fire did its job: not even our best noses can pick up a trail among all that devastation."

"What do we do now?" Jimmy asked.

At a nod from Tobias, Dee stood up and faced the gathering. "Even we can't disguise the evidence of arson from mortal investigators. What we have to do is find out as much as we can before we turn the sites over to mortals. We'll take away our evidence, then plant evidence to direct their attention into conclusions that make sense to them.

"Methamphetamine is dangerous to produce, as well as highly illegal. We need to make it look like the fires were started by the accidental explosion of a meth lab, and that the drug-dealing mortals covered their tracks by starting all the other fires."

"None of this is too far from the truth," Tobias said. "I see nothing wrong with blackening the reputations of mortal drug traffickers while we deal with the immortal ones."

"How do we deal with them when we can't trace them?" Rayhan wanted to know.

"There are leads we're working on." Tobias

gave a brisk nod. "Divide them up into specialist teams, Dee," he told the witch.

"Yes, sir."

"Bleythin."

Joe jumped to attention. "Sir."

"Come with me."

Joe's surprise turned to dread when Tobias added, "Please come with me as well, Lady Sidonie."

Chapter Thirteen

Oh, crap, now what? Sid thought angrily.

What was she supposed to do now? The Prime had made a perfectly reasonable request and she couldn't just scream like a girl and run away because Joe was involved. He wasn't going to like this any more than she was, which was no consolation.

She gave her brother and Eden a desperate look, but their attention was concentrated on each other.

"True love sucks," Sid muttered, and forced her body into motion.

Joe walked ahead of her toward Tobias's tent,

and she found herself falling back into an old pattern: appreciating the way his long, lean body moved, the way he looked, the way he *was,* while he wasn't looking. The years she'd spent not acting on her attraction to the werewolf had honed her secret-admiration skills to a fine art—which she apparently hadn't forgotten.

It occurred to her that despite their time apart, despite her protestations to the contrary, she really hadn't tried to change.

She *couldn't* go inside the tent with Joe. The space was too small! The—

Sid took a deep breath. Panic did not become her. She lifted her chin and walked proudly past Joe when he held the tent flap open for her. Though she was careful not to brush against him, awareness of his body heat sent a damnable shiver through her.

Once inside, she went to the seat across from Tobias where she'd spent much of the afternoon, and put her attention firmly on the Dark Angels' leader. Joe remained by the entrance, and she wondered if he wanted to bolt as much as she did.

Tobias sat behind his small worktable and folded his hands on top of his closed laptop. "Lady Sidonie—"

"Sid," she corrected him, not for the first time.

"I don't require formality from a fellow vampire."

Tobias's beautiful lips thinned in irritation. He obviously wasn't used to being interrupted, or corrected. "Lady Sidonie," he went on as if she'd never spoken.

Sid was too aware of Joe's disapproving gaze on her not to let it go this time. She needed to get this over with and get out of there. She forced a polite smile and attentive attitude.

Once Tobias had her attention, he ignored her and looked at Joe. "This afternoon, Lady Sidonie and I had a discussion about her involvement with Tribe Manticore."

"Hey!" she protested. "Leave him out of this. He wasn't involved in what you want to know about."

"You were present during Lady Sidonie's extraction from the Manticore lair." Tobias continued to Joe.

"Lair?" Sid questioned.

"I was in on the rescue, yeah," Joe told his boss.

Sid sighed. She did not want to go over this again. The Manticores were not a favorite subject for any member of her immediate family.

"I remember it well. It was a very dramatic evening," she said "With lots of heroics. I've already briefed you on everything that occurred at the time. You don't need me here for Bleythin to tell you about his part in the action."

The memory of a magnificent black wolf bursting through the window of the Manticores' lair flashed across Sid's mind and she could barely stop herself from turning a dreamy smile on Joe.

"Bleythin's part in the action isn't relevant."

"It was relevant to me," she snapped. "He helped save my ass. And Eden's. And my brother's."

The faintest of smiles played around Tobias's lips. "All right. Let's say that the action that resulted in your release from the Manticores is not relevant to our current needs."

Joe stepped forward. "Current needs, sir?"

"We've gone round and round on this already," Sid told Tobias.

"But not to my satisfaction."

Frustration drove her to her feet. She accidentally bumped into Joe, and he automatically reached out to steady her.

The universe froze, if for no more than an instant.

Joe swore and backed away from her.

Sid was shaken to the core and she turned her fiery reaction on Tobias. "Your satisfaction is not my problem! We've been over and over this and I've cooperated as much as I'm going to. I don't care if you don't believe me. I'm done here."

She turned to leave, but Joe blocked the entrance. His face was hard, his body set for a fight. "What aren't you telling Tobias?" he demanded.

"Go ahead, take his side," she complained.

And good, goddess, why was she acting like a pouting teenager around Joe? It seemed like nothing in this situation with him brought out the best in her.

She suffered letting Joe take her by the shoulders and turning her to face Tobias. "Tell him what he wants to know."

Sid shivered when his breath brushed across her ear. "I don't know anything more than I've already told him—you," she added to Tobias.

The big Prime looked at her steadily, unblinking, still as stone. Michelangelo would have been proud to have done the carving. "I believe you" he finally said. "As far as it goes."

"What does that mean?" She asked Tobias.

She really wished Joe would take his hands off her. Not really. But she *needed* Joe to stop touching her before she went up in flames.

"I mean that you do not consciously remember everything you witnessed while a captive of the Manticores."

"Yes, I do."

He gave the faintest shake of his head. "There must have been conversations involving Dawn trafficking in distant rooms. There must have been stray thoughts from your captors that you didn't notice seeping into your mind. Your senses are sharp and highly concentrated, whether you're consciously using them or not. During your captivity, you were focused on staying alive and on finding a way out of a bad situation. Your senses were on full alert whether you realized it or not."

"Don't tell me what I was or wasn't doing. You weren't there."

"As I have pointed out to you before." He stood. "I need information you don't know you have."

"You're crazy." She glanced over her shoulder at Joe. "He's crazy, you know. I don't know why you follow him."

"But he does follow me, Lady Sidonie. Despite the tension between the two of you he will do as I tell him now."

She supposed the strain was evident whether or not Joe had mentioned anything about their past to his comrades.

"Just what do you want Joe to do?" she demanded.

Tobias didn't speak to her, but to Joe. "Take

her back to the places where it happened. Help her remember. Stay with her until she does."

"Hell, no!" Sid shouted.

"Yes, sir," Joe said.

Sid jerked away from Joe's hands and rounded on him. She opened her mouth to yell at him, but decided arguing wasn't going to accomplish anything. "Get out of my way," she said instead.

Joe waited, looking past her shoulder, not stepping aside until Tobias must have given a nod of permission.

Sid managed not to say *good boy* to Joe as she passed him on the way out, but she was afraid the thought escaped into the silence anyway.

Chapter Fourteen

It was actually a lovely night for a walk, Sid decided. The devastation underfoot might bring up the reek of ash with every footstep, but the burned-out undergrowth made it easier to move down the mountainside. Every now and then she'd feel heat from a still warm patch of charred ground beneath the thick soles of her athletic shoes. Maybe she should have worn hiking boots. Maybe she should have waited until morning before leaving the Dark Angels' camp, but she'd been too restless, too furious, all right—too scared—to stay.

It was a long walk home, but better that than putting up with Tobias Strahan's stupid ideas and

Joe Bleythin's accusing vibes. And the temptation he still posed for her. It was better for him that she was gone.

Maybe he's seeing that witch chick. No, probably not. He never really approved of his brother Harry marrying a mortal. Well, I'm sure there are female werefolk among the ranks of the immortal commandoes.

Sid ground her teeth, not sure whether she was more jealous of a female werewolf living a full, dangerous, active life, or of said theoretical female mating with *her* Joe.

"Both," she muttered, and kept on walking.

The crunching of the burned ground underfoot didn't disguise the sound of a vehicle coming up from behind her a few minutes later.

She should have known it wasn't going to be that easy to get away. No one had tried to stop her when she'd picked up her pack and walked away from the campsite. She'd wondered about that, but since the guard merely nodded when she saw her, Sid had kept going.

As the sound got closer and awareness kicked in from all her senses, Sid briefly considered sprinting off at an angle from the rutted dirt road to avoid a confrontation. She resisted the urge and waited with her arms crossed for the vehicle to pull to a stop beside her.

"Joseph Bleythin, I do not need or want your company," she said when he leaned out the window.

"Nor do I want yours," Joe answered.

She managed a fierce smile. "Then we agree on something."

"Get in."

The total lack of expression in his voice was really irritating. She almost asked him if the Dark Angels had stolen his soul. But she knew he would answer that *she* was the only one who'd stolen anything from him, and their descent into petty bickering would just be stupid.

"I'm going home," she said.

"You shouldn't be out here alone."

She laughed. "I'm a vampire."

"I have my orders. *Lady* Sidonie."

At least a half dozen snide remarks flashed through Sid's mind.

"You're biting your tongue," Joe said. "I can smell the blood."

Sid went around to the passenger side and got in, settling her pack on the floor beside her.

"Fasten your seat belt," Joe said, and waited until she complied before he continued the slow, bumpy ride.

"It would have been easier to walk," Sid commented after a while.

"It's a good thing you don't get car sick,"

Joe answered. "Damn!" he growled under his breath.

"It's all right," she assured him when she realized he was annoyed with himself for responding to a normal conversational comment with a normal reply. "We've spent a lot of time together. Old habits are easy to fall into. I'll take it as a given that you hate my guts, and ignore your talking to me if you'd like."

"Don't patronize me."

"I can do that, too."

She reached into her pack and pulled out her small e-reader. The backlit screen of the digital device was nice but not necessary for her vision, so she kept it on the dimmest setting. She loved the storage capacity of the little device and took it with her everywhere.

"Drive on, Jeeves," she told him. "I have something else I can do."

It didn't take long before he said exactly what she knew he would. "Whatcha reading?"

She'd always brought books on stakeouts. They'd spent many an evening sitting in the dark with her reading a paperback, frequently reading out loud to stave off boredom if Joe was interested. When they'd needed to keep quiet, she'd read to him telepathically. It had been something they'd both enjoyed.

"A vampire novel," she replied.

Sid couldn't keep from smiling as she waited for an indignant response, though it was several minutes coming. He turned the truck from the bumpy track onto a gravel road before he finally spoke.

"Why would *you* want to read a vampire novel?" Joe demanded.

"Because it was written by a vampire."

"You're kidding."

"Not at all. The general consensus is that the anonymous author is from our culture, as the hero is a Prime. It's available from an electronic publisher, for a select readership," she added. "We're calling it the Vampire Book Club."

"I bet you're also trying to keep the Matri from finding out about a book with Primes in it. They wouldn't allow anything real to get out where mortals could find it."

Sid regretted telling Joe anything about the Vampire Book Club. It was too easy to share the secret rebellions of the younger Clan females with him. That habit could prove dangerous now that he was with the Dark Angels, militant protectors of the immortal world. They might as easily go after a harmless form of entertainment as a cadre of vampire terrorists, all in the name of keeping immortals safe.

"There's nothing really real in this book," she assured Joe. "It takes place in a space empire hundreds of years in the future."

Joe showed no more interest, so Sid settled down to read while he drove from rugged mountainside to suburban foothills and on toward the city. She didn't pay attention to the outside world until she could sense more sea salt in the air than smoke.

"It's good to be home," she said.

"You haven't been gone very long," Joe said. He glanced her way. "Missing little Chuckie?"

It took her a moment to realize who he meant. "You've been talking to my brother, haven't you? My son is named Charles."

"And you're anxious to get home to your baby boy."

"Of course I—"

Sid stared straight ahead and the lights of oncoming traffic swirled and blurred around her while her mind went totally blank.

"Sid? Are you all right?"

"How odd," she murmured.

"What's wrong?"

All the blank neutrality had left his voice. He sounded like her Joe again. That was nice.

"Sidonie?"

"Charles is old enough to be in the Clan crèche now. He's safe there. I'll see him when the time is right." She smiled as the words cleared the fog from her mind. She recognized the streets now. "We're almost home."

Chapter Fifteen

"Well, good night. Thanks for the lift. Have a nice drive back." Sid got out of the truck and closed the door with a solid thump.

Joe shut off the engine and did the same.

She glared at him across the wide hood of the truck. "Ta-ta, toodleoo. Go away."

"Not happening." Joe glanced toward her front door. "We might as well go inside."

"You are not coming in my house."

"I promise not to shed on the furniture."

"I've heard that before, Joseph Bleythin."

"I wasn't feeling well that time."

"You're not well now. You've been brainwashed—by this Tobias person, not me, so don't start."

He looked around. "It's late at night in a quiet neighborhood. You don't want to start a scene."

She closed her eyes. She looked weary, and for a moment he felt sorry for her. He still wasn't leaving, though.

"I don't want to be here any more than you want me here, but we both have to live with it."

Sid shook her head and patted the hood. "This is a nice truck. I hope you enjoy sleeping in it."

Then she moved to her front door at vampire speed. She had the door open, closed, and locked behind her before Joe could take more than a few steps. He considered banging on the door or even breaking a window, but that would only cause a stir. A quiet life was a safe life. He backed away from her town house.

It wasn't as if he didn't know another way inside.

Sid barely had time to drop her pack, pour iced tea, and go out to the patio before the supernatural stirring began on the other side of the back fence. Familiar energy swirled around her and brought a fond smile, even while she wished Joe wasn't so bloody predictable.

A pack came over the top and landed on the rocks beyond the patio. A magnificent huge black wolf sprang after the pack a second later.

Sid crossed her legs. "Darn, I was hoping you'd land in the cactus. They've grown quite a bit since the last time you were here."

The wolf snatched up the pack and disappeared into the deepest shadows at the corner of the yard. Sid allowed Joe his modesty and looked at her shoes while he transformed and put his clothes back on. The temptation to look was strong, but she didn't look up until she heard the crunch of footsteps coming toward her.

Joe walked to the edge of the patio. "I figured the growth rate of your plants into my jump calculations."

"You were lucky, you mean." Sid gestured toward the second chair and the other glass of iced tea on the table.

Joe took the seat and a long gulp of the cold liquid. "You could have just let me in."

"I said I didn't want you in the house, but I knew you weren't going to give up. We're not in the house," she pointed out. "A small victory for my team."

"We aren't on different teams. Stop being difficult. Tobias wouldn't want the information if it wasn't important."

Sid didn't want to fight with Joe. The man deserved for her to leave him in peace. But what Tobias wanted was impossible to give, making clashing with her ex-partner—ex-lover—inevitable.

"Not everyone believes so implicitly in Strahan's theory." She kept her tone mild, reasonable.

Joe snorted. "You're talking about the Clan Primes who claim that he's crazy. They claim that the Clan boys are all that's needed to stand against evil. They just don't like Tobias letting the werefolk play superhero, too."

"There are Primes in the Dark Angels."

"Mostly from the vampire Families. And there are plenty of werefolk who don't like Tobias dragging their children into harm's way. I can't see *you* going along with all the arguments against the multiethnic makeup of the Dark Angels."

"Until the day comes when female vampires are asked to join, I'll have issues with your so-called open door policy. But I agree that the Primes you're talking about are arrogant jerks, and every species has jerks," she responded. "The Clans might be the most vocal in opposing your group, but it's true that there are Family vampires who don't like the Angels, either."

"The real objections, the fears, are because we make too much noise. We ask too many questions. We get results," Joe added. "We've stopped a lot of bad things from happening, and the Matri have quietly turned to us for hard solutions. Where do you think we get most of our funding?"

"I don't disagree that your group has done some good, or that the world is more dangerous than it's ever been—for mortal and supernatural people alike. I just don't think that mortals and immortals have formed any kind of conspiracy to bring down civilization."

"You haven't seen much of the evidence."

"I know that Strahan's been convinced of increasing interspecies evil ever since he walked away from that commercial airline bombing years ago. What *I* think happened is that he fell out of the sky and landed on his head."

"There's more than one conspiracy," Joe said, "whether you believe or not. People from every species are working together right now: some out of simple greed, some for political and ideological reasons." He gestured toward the burned-out mountains. "You saw the evidence."

Sid laughed softly. "Yes. You made sure we saw it."

Joe cleared his throat. "You noticed that, did you?"

"Scheming is something I'm very good at, so of course I noticed. I'm sure Eden did, too. But since we both believe Tobias's drug-dealing vampire conspiracy scenario, we're happy to help the Angels with that one."

Confusion warred with annoyance on Joe's features. "If you agree, why are you fighting us?"

She shook her head. "How many times do I have to say that I didn't pick up any information from the Manticores? I would have mentioned it back then if I did, when the Wolf Clan was following up on that incident."

"I see. You're being more loyal to your Clan than you are to the truth."

"How do you assume that from what I said?"

"Because I was there when the Manticores were brought down. I was part of the initial action."

"I know. I was there, too."

"Afterward I was told to mind my own business, and the Wolf Primes took responsibility for driving the rest of the Dawn dealers out of town. Laurent and Eden and I took down the Manticores—"

"Mom and I helped a little."

"And Cathy," he added. "It was our show. Then the great and mighty Wolf Clan stepped in. I remember that you disappeared for a couple of weeks following your rescue."

"That had nothing to do with the Primes hunting drug dealers. Mom and I were working on getting Laurent acknowledged as a member of the Clan. My only interest in the whole Dawn affair was to get my brother away from his lousy, stinking, disgusting Manticore sire's influence. You know this."

"What I know is that the Wolf Clan didn't go far enough in rooting out the evil. They stopped the drug trade in their own territory, but keeping Dawn out of San Diego didn't stop its manufacture. This arson shows that the Clan boys didn't finish the job."

"I'm not arguing with that. I'm sure Matri Juanita won't argue with it, either. Maybe some of the Clan Primes have gotten a little out of touch with the modern world."

"Those who haven't are joining the Angels."

Sid was finding the whole discussion circular and increasingly annoying. "Could we talk about something else? Or go back to not talking at all?" She stood up. "Even better, I'm going to bed. And in the morning you're going to be gone," she added.

Once again, she slipped inside faster than Joe could follow and locked the patio door firmly behind her. And shut the curtains to block the angry look on his face as he glared through the window at her.

She might have been going to bed, but she was sure she wasn't going to get any sleep.

Chapter Sixteen

December 16

Of course he'd broken in, and he knew that Sid knew it, but her bedroom door remained closed. After he swept up the glass from the small hole he'd made in the sliding door, Joe went into the living room.

He stopped in the doorway, perturbed. All of her living room furniture was different, and all the pieces were arranged differently. It was like he'd walked into a stranger's house, and it sent a chill through him.

What had she done that for? Not that changes in her life were any of his business.

He walked across the room and settled down on the new couch. Some of the lingering scents on the upholstery were familiar. He recognized members of his own family, Eden, Laurent, Lady Antonia, Tony Crowe. Other people had been here that he didn't know. One was obviously Sid's baby. There was the scent of a vampire Prime as well.

The male's identity was none of his business, Joe reminded himself.

He lay down and turned on his side. He'd already decided that the new furniture couldn't be as comfortable as the couch he remembered, but he was tired and was asleep in seconds.

He woke up to full daylight and no Sid stirring. A glance at his watch showed him that it wasn't that early. The couch had proved far more comfortable than his bedroll and he'd slept in. He stood up and roamed the room like a caged wolf while he waited for Sidonie.

He was fully aware that he was intruding on her privacy as he inspected everything within sight, smell, and sound, but maybe he'd find some important information that she wasn't consciously aware of. It was a pretty lame excuse, and he knew it. Never mind his righteous fury at her—being in her house made him seek familiar things to ease his homesickness.

Once, anywhere Sid was was home. It was almost a pity that the pain of her betrayal overwhelmed the pain of missing her.

Eventually Joe found himself standing before the shelf of framed photos. Her family; his family. Most of the pictures were new to him. Time had so obviously moved on for Sid, and the knowledge ground against his pain.

He wasn't represented anywhere in the picture collection. But there was one of the new male in her life.

"So you're Chuck," he said, picking up the picture.

Charles was a cute baby, but he didn't look much like a Wolf Clan cub. His hair was dark and curly, not wavy gold like Sid's or straight silver like Laurent's and Lady Antonia's. His eyes were dark, too. But he had Sid's smile and little baby Sid dimples.

Joe discovered he was smiling fondly at this stranger's son and put the photo down with a sudden frown.

When Sid's bedroom door opened, he turned to face her. The tousled hair framing her face and the outline of her body beneath a clinging red silk robe sent desire throbbing through him.

"I had hoped you wouldn't be here," she said.

"Who's the sire?" he sneered.

It was none of his business; he had no right to ask. But the jealousy that ate at him demanded to know.

Sid stared at him in open-mouthed shock. The hurt in her eyes bruised him and brought him back to his senses. If she'd chosen to rip his throat out he wouldn't blame her.

"I'm sorry," he said. "That was way out of line."

She closed her eyes for a moment, her expression an anguished mask. Joe couldn't help but take a step toward her, pulled by the urge to comfort as well as possess.

When she opened her eyes, they blazed with fury. When she spoke, her voice was low, but the tone was deadly. "I've stayed out of your life. Get out of mine."

Joe backed away with his hands held up before him. "I—"

Sid's bedroom door slammed, leaving the empty room echoing with all that wasn't spoken.

Joe was beginning to doubt Tobias's wisdom in giving him this assignment.

Sid sensed the moment Joe left the house, but her awareness of him was just as acute as if he was still there. How could it not be?

The mirror above her dresser revealed eyes full of bitterness and accusation. Damn, she hated feeling sorry for herself.

"It was an accident!" she reminded herself.

It was mindless lust, her conscience responded.

"It was love!"

That, too. It was still stupid. Dangerous.

But, oh, how lovely those few moments of abandon had been.

A rush of heated pleasure went through Sid as she watched Joe stretch. He stood naked in a shaft of sunlight with his back to her. She watched the play of the muscles of his arms and back, buttocks and thighs, and the sight took her breath away. Need grew in her, making her breasts heavy and her insides turn to flame.

But watching Joe brought out more than lust. Being with him brought her pure joy. He was so warm and real and alive! The sight of him heated her blood; his virile scent made her dizzy.

He glanced over his shoulder at her, and his bright eyes and come-hither look sent laughter bubbling through her.

"Why are you giggling, woman?"

"Because you're like champagne."

"Hmmph." Joe turned to face her and held out his arms. "Wouldn't you rather have good, red meat?"

Spoken from a werewolf to a vampire, this was terribly romantic. She came into his arms.

The hunger took her as skin touched skin. She

wanted—needed—so much more than his body. The hot blood pulsing through his veins called to her. The hunger as old as her species demanded what only Joe could give her.

Her fangs slid between her lips. The sensitive tips touched yielding flesh. She—

"Bit him," she said, trying to wipe the sensual haze away from the memory of the selfish, blasphemous act. Even though it had been the most orgasmic moment of her life.

Vampire females did *not* go around biting just anybody. Tasting anyone but a Prime was unthinkable. It was a breach of all that stood between survival and extinction of the species.

Sex with Joe had been one thing. But what she had done—

Sid shook her head. "I have done evil." Her reflection grinned back at her. "Okay, it didn't feel like it at the time. But I was very, very bad."

And she lived with the consequence, even if she'd never regret the action.

Chapter Seventeen

December 17, 8:00 AM

A battered old truck pulled into her driveway, deliberately blocking the carport, as Sid came out of the house. Joe had been gone for twenty-four hours, but here he was, back like a bad penny the moment she decided to leave the shelter of her home.

"Oh, come on!" she complained when she saw him sitting behind the wheel. Never mind that her heart flip-flopped at the sight of him, or that her body tingled with instant desire. "This has got to stop."

Joe got out of the truck and came up to her, presenting her with a tall paper cup of coffee. It smelled fresh and wonderful. "I was out of line yesterday," he said to her. "And I'm sorry."

She took a sip from his peace offering. "Where's the donuts?" she asked.

"In the truck." He tilted his head sideways. "Come on, I'll give you a ride to work."

Sid eyed his vehicle. "I don't know. I'm not sure I want to be seen in that thing in the daylight."

He canted an eyebrow at her. "Donuts," he coaxed. "And a cinnamon scone."

She laughed. "You know me too well."

His friendly expression didn't change a bit when he said, "I suspect I don't know you at all, but let's not go there right now."

Not knowing what to make of that, she got into the passenger seat without any more comment. She ate a donut and her scone and drank coffee while Joe drove. At least being a vampire meant she could indulge her sweet tooth without worrying about her figure.

She wasn't surprised when his route didn't take them anywhere near the Bleythin office. "I know very well that you aren't lost."

"We're just taking a short detour."

"I see."

He was wasting his time, but she decided not to waste her breath since he obviously wouldn't listen to anything she said. She watched the play of light and shadows through the palm trees lining the residential streets, pretending this was the old days—that they really were on their way to work or following a lead on a missing person. She knew it was stupid; she already missed those days too much. But it was better than thinking about where they were going.

Her imagination deserted her as she began to recognize the neighborhood, and she was tense when he pulled to a stop, knowing what she would see. She stared straight ahead.

There was a considerable silence before Joe said, "Where'd the house go?"

The house sitting on the lot was completely different than the one where she'd been held captive by the Manticore Tribe. The landscaping was also completely different.

A feral smile stretched her lips. "The old house burned down a couple of years ago."

It had been destroyed in a carefully controlled burn set by a professional arsonist. Her brother had some very interesting friends. The building was Laurent's, after all, to do with as he saw fit. Who was she to argue with how he chose to get rid of the bad memories the building represented? She'd brought the marshmallows.

"You might have mentioned this," he complained.

"You didn't tell me where we were going."

"You knew very well—"

She stuck the remaining donut in his mouth. "Shut up and eat. Of *course* no one mentioned it to you, in an e-mail or a voicemail or a text message or put some info on Facebook or wrote an old-fashioned letter which you'd never answer anyway," she added. "No one would talk to you about something when it might make you think of me. Everyone's been minding your bruised feelings for the last three years. You should thank them." She wagged a finger at him. "And send your family Christmas cards this year. They miss you. *I'm* the one who hurt you, stop taking it out on everybody else."

Joe stared ahead with his jaw clenched and his arms crossed over his chest. "You're right," he finally said. "I know it."

She hadn't expected this. "Really?"

"Hey, I may be *only* a werewolf, but I'm not completely stupid."

"What do you mean *only* a werewolf?"

It was hard work for Joe to hide a smile at Sid's indignant reply. She didn't hate him. She didn't disparage him. But his rejoicing still hit a painfully hard wall. Why the hell had she dumped him?

Not the time to go there.

He'd gotten enough information from her for now. Not from anything she'd said or done, but from the hormonal changes his delicate nose picked up scents that clearly spelled out her emotional turmoil.

Sidonie didn't like it here, and she most definitely didn't intend to talk about anything that had happened during her captivity. Ugly, dark emotions swirled around her; bad thoughts plagued her.

Why hadn't he noticed her agitation over the incident before? Years before?

Come to think of it, she'd never given more than the sketchiest of details of her time trapped among the Manticores. Sid was strong and smart and self-sufficient. It had never occurred to Joe that she'd suffered any trauma at the time.

Or maybe she'd wiped that from his memory, too. But he was aware of trouble now, and it was his duty to sniff it out.

"You can't lie to a nose," he warned her.

"What?" she asked.

Maybe it was more than duty. Maybe she needed help. Maybe he *wanted* to help her.

Damn it! He shouldn't be thinking like that.

"Nothing," Joe snapped. He put the truck in gear. "I'll take you to the office now."

Chapter Eighteen

"What do you call this color, dirty pink?" Joe asked as he stood in the center of the office and looked at the walls.

"Terra-cotta." Sid knew he wasn't going to like the changes to the agency office space, so why did it bother her?

He made a disgusted face. "Why are people always painting things?"

"To cover the bloodstains." She grinned when he gave her a sharp look. "Nah. I'm joking about that—this time."

The big room was full of desks, but they were the only people there.

"Where is everybody?" Joe asked.

"You know where Laurent and Eden are. Harry's on a case in Arizona. Cathy and Mike are off doing things with her werewolf/Romany relations. You remember them, yes?"

Joe nodded. "The Hunyara. Tobias is looking into recruiting among the ones Cathy is training."

"Do you know that our scientists are doing tests to figure out the basis of the Hunyara family's genetics? Maybe they can use the information to find more *cures* for the problems that plague us immortal types. Isn't science wonderful?"

Joe ignored her question as he walked up to the desk next to her own. "Who's using my desk?"

Sid bit her tongue on the answer that it hadn't been his desk for three years. "Dan."

He turned to her in surprise. "You're actually letting that flake work here? Officially?"

Sid put her hands on her hips. "That flake is my cousin."

Dan was the child of a Prime father and mortal mother, and was blessed, or more likely cursed, with the psychic ability to see the past.

"I don't have anything against Dan Corbett," Joe said. "He's my friend, but he's still a little . . . odd."

"Said the werewolf to the vampire. He's in much better control of his visions these days, and we've learned that his ability comes in handy when looking for lost things rather than lost people. At the moment, he's obsessed with the hunt for a scarlet egg."

Joe looked skeptical. "Dan's on an Easter egg hunt?"

She laughed. "Yes, actually. This egg was made as an Easter present. It's a gold and ruby Fabergé egg, presented to the last Russian czar in the early twentieth century. It went missing from an exhibit being set up by a private museum, and the curator approached us to quietly track it down before the exhibit opens."

"Dan's a historian. That's the sort of thing he would be good at finding."

Sid nodded. "He took off on his Easter egg hunt a week ago."

And a good thing, too, since her mortal cousin had been in a snapping, foul mood before the case came up. It was a relief to have him gone, especially with Joe now here to bug her. Of course, maybe she could have gotten Joe and Dan to go at each other while she snuck out the back.

Sid sat at her desk, ignoring Joe, while she read through several days' worth of e-mail.

She glanced his way when he pulled a chair up beside her. "Are you still here?" He plucked a framed photo of Charles off her desk.

"Hey!" she complained.

"He really is a fine-looking kid." Joe put the picture down. "I'm sorry I was rude about his sire. A werewolf has no business being jealous about who a vampire sleeps with."

His words were true, and they twisted like a knife in her gut. She kept her cool, suspicious that he was deliberately trying to upset her to get the information he really wanted.

"I have no idea who Charles's sire is." Which was true. "The Matri held an orgy. Everyone was invited." Which was not.

"Interesting lie," he observed.

"Damn it!" She sat back in her chair and glared at him. "Now I remember what you meant about the nose doesn't lie."

"You work with werewolves all the time."

"Yeah—but I forgot about *you.*" *I try not to think about you. I—* "Damn."

He folded his hands across his fine, flat stomach. "We could argue about us, but that won't get us anywhere." He leaned forward until their noses were almost touching and gazed into her eyes. "Tell me what the Manticores did to you."

Sid bumped her forehead against his as she sprang to her feet. "That is none of your—"

Her cellular phone began to play its "Tempting Fate" ringtone, and she gratefully flipped it open. "Hi, Dad. What's up?"

"She's gone!" Tony Crowe's frantic voice answered. "Rose is gone."

Sid's agitation was immediately replaced with sympathy for his loss. "I'm so sorry. But she was eighty—"

"No! I mean she's *gone*. Completely disappeared."

Okay—that didn't make any sense. "Explain to me exactly what you mean. What happened?"

Chapter Nineteen

December 16, 8:00 PM
Los Angeles, CA

"More roses have arrived for you, madam."

The enthusiasm in Gregor's Russian-accented voice made Rose Cameron smile. She didn't find smiling easy these days, not with the pain getting worse.

She put down her hairbrush and looked at Gregor's reflection in the mirror as he set the vase of red roses beside one full of white blooms. He had the grace of a cat, even with several dozen flowers in his arms. Gregor was movie-star handsome, and she knew movie stars. He was a fine, conscientious nurse—but this being Hollywood, he also had acting ambitions.

She thought that he'd have a great screen

presence with his strong features, black hair, and expressive green eyes, if this were the silent film era. When he'd first come to work at the nursing home a year ago, she'd worked with him to try to help him tone down his Russian accent before he went out on auditions.

"I heard the stories about your Christmas roses," he said.

The handsome young man turned slowly around to take in all the bright, fragrant blooms on every surface: red, white, yellow, pink, peach, even some faint green and pale lavender. The air was full of the heady scent; it almost masked the medicinal smells of the room she hadn't been able to leave for years.

"I didn't believe what I heard about Rose Cameron's Christmas," he went on. "I thought, *An anonymous admirer sends my favorite resident flowers every year, how sweet.* But I never expected he really sent enough to fill the whole room. You deserve them," he added as he faced her again.

She enjoyed his old-world style of flattery and didn't try to deny his assertion. She'd take all the compliments she could in the time she had left.

"Thank you, dear."

"And you really don't know who sends the roses? I wonder why your secret admirer isn't a

Hollywood legend, like the woman in black who leaves flowers at Valentino's grave."

Rose moved slowly toward her chair, and Gregor rushed to help her before she'd taken more than a step. She waited until she was settled in the comfortable wingback seat by the window before she answered.

"Legends grow up when people don't keep their private life private. Of course Valentino can't be blamed if a woman makes a spectacle of herself at his grave. She *wants* to be seen. I've always liked a quiet life."

"But wouldn't your secret admirer be thought of as a stalker in this day and age?"

"Maybe, but I've never had to worry about that sort of thing."

"Ah, of course. You were protected by the studio system."

Rose shook her head and cursed her failing body when the slight movement hurt. "There was someone on the L.A. police force who always looked after me."

Even surrounded by the gift of flowers, she didn't sigh romantically. Not only was she a fair actress, she'd had years of practice at keeping things to herself.

She turned a critical look on her handsome young nurse. "You didn't come here just to smell the roses, Gregor." She saw the needle he carried as he came closer. "No," she said. "No injection tonight."

"You know you need this," he said. "It will help you."

She knew there was no getting out of it, but that was no reason not to put up a fight. "I don't want the help. No one needs to live forever, Gregor. That's what you young people don't understand. You feel entitled to immortality—I know better."

"This is a very interesting philosophy, Madam Cameron, but it has nothing to do with your taking your medicine."

Talking made her tired. Everything was tiring. Still, pride and stubbornness made her give it one more try.

"I have the right to refuse a medical procedure if I wish."

"You should have that right," Gregor agreed. "But I'm afraid I can't let you. You need tonight's injection."

"Why? I don't want it."

"But I don't want you to die. Please take it for me, Madam Rose. You know how much I would miss you."

Rose was embarrassed at the way his charm worked on her. She always felt so much worse after the evening injection. She'd hoped to have this one night free of the blood-burning pain on top of the regular pain of having lived too long.

"My doctors are sadistic bastards."

"As doctors have been throughout the ages," he agreed. "May I give you the injection now?"

Oh, well, she'd put up with it for this long, she could take it a while longer.

"All right, Gregor." She presented her arm for the hated shot.

"Thank you, Rose."

He'd never called her by only her first name before and a wave of affection went through her. His touch was gentle as well as efficient as he administered the medication. She didn't feel the needle go in, but the fiery effect began instantly. Pain sliced through her, and everything around her went dark.

The scent of the flowers drew her back. When she opened her eyes Gregor was gone, and she breathed a sigh of relief at finally being alone. Rose smiled victoriously despite the pain. She was surrounded by flowers, it was December sixteenth, and she was determined to set her plan in motion. Now all she had to do was summon enough strength to get up and walk to the closet.

In 1956 she'd played Mary, Queen of Scots—in

a movie musical, of all things—with three broken ribs and pneumonia. It had not been her best performance, but she'd stubbornly gotten through the day-to-day hell of that shoot. Then there'd been the twisted ankle she'd limped on for miles in the Ardennes . . .

If you're going to commit suicide, get on with it before someone shows up to stop you, Rose chastised herself.

A great many kind people had worked hard not to let her go, so she was going to have to take care of it herself. As the pain had grown over the last year, she'd become more determined to find her way out.

Timing is everything, and you have to know when to make your exit. Now's the time.

She managed to rise to her feet and make her way across the room with slow, agonized steps.

It had taken her months of occasionally complaining of headaches to amass the supply of pills. She was certain that the medication she'd hidden in her fur coat's pockets was safe, since no one in Hollywood would dream of wearing chinchilla in this day and age.

She managed to get as far as turning the handle of the closet door when a man behind her said, "Going somewhere, sweetheart?"

At first, Rose told herself that she'd imagined it. Then she told herself that she didn't recognize his voice.

Finally, she turned slowly around and said, "Anthony Crowe, where have you been for the last sixty years?"

Chapter Twenty

Tony had been rehearsing for this moment for hours, for decades, for over half a century. But when he was finally standing face-to-face with Rose Cameron, all he could say was, "You look terrible."

Her famous indigo blue eyes were faded and they were surrounded by a sea of wrinkles, but they were still full of sharp intelligence and flashing with anger. This was not an auspicious start to their conversation.

"Of course I look terrible, you old fool." She looked him over critically. "Some of us do not have your . . . genetic advantages."

He held his hands out before him. "No—I

mean—when I was here last year, you still seemed pretty spry."

"I've been sick— What do you mean, *last year?*"

Her thin voice was raspy with pain, but the indignation came through loud and clear. Tony wanted to rush forward and take her in his arms, but she looked so fragile he feared the slightest touch would crush her.

He went to her and picked her up. She weighed nothing in his arms, but then, she never had. He carried her to the bed. Tall as she was for a woman of her era, she'd always been a skinny thing.

"You better not have anything romantic in mind," she told him.

He smiled. "You know I've never been much of a gentleman." He carefully set her on the bed and took a step back. "I have a lot of explaining to do."

Her anger didn't waver for a moment. "Start with telling me about last year. And the year before, and the year before that."

Tony perched beside her and took her hand in his. "Since you've been living here, I wait until you're asleep before I make my annual visit."

Rose breathed a quiet sigh. "So you have been watching me all these years. I didn't think I imagined it—that feeling of being protected, the occasional glimpse of movement out of the corner of my eye. You were there all along." She looked at him sternly. "But you weren't with me."

"I stayed away those years you were married. I didn't want to interfere with you having a normal life."

"Normal?" She laughed. "Thad Pearson was my best friend, but we never lived as man and wife. He was in a deeply committed relationship with another man. I was celibate. Neither condition was considered normal for movie stars and the press would have eaten us alive, so we covered for each other. We were happy sharing a house, but it wasn't a marriage."

"Oh." He winced with pain for her but couldn't help a certain amount of Primal pride when he asked, "You were really celibate?" She nodded. "That was stupid."

"I take it you weren't?"

He ducked his head, then looked up with a shameless grin. "Uh, no. It's not possible for my kind unless we're fully bonded. You *are* the love of my life," he added. "Were you really celibate?"

"I found the man I wanted when I was seventeen. Why settle for anyone less?"

"Stubborn female."

"Stop looking so pleased with your own prowess, Anthony Crowe. Don't think that it had all that much to do with you. I've never been a promiscuous person."

"Is that a hint of reproach I hear in your voice, old woman?"

"It's pain, older-but-still-gorgeous man." She touched his cheek. "I made my choice, but I never expected you not to take lovers." She stroked his cheek. "I'm glad you got rid of the goatee you grew after you retired. It didn't suit you at all."

"I guess I looked a bit too saturnine in—wait a moment. Retirement? Goatee?" He peered at her suspiciously. "What do you know about—"

"Private detective." She chuckled. "It wasn't as easy for me to keep track of your life as you did mine, but I managed. For the first few years, when you didn't keep your promise, I believed that you'd been killed in the war. Then I found the first newspaper article that mentioned your name."

"What newspaper—"

"Look in the top drawer, Anthony."

He left her side and returned carrying a shoe box. Rose watched him while he looked inside and found a small stack of newspaper clippings. In each article there was a mention of Officer Crowe, Detective Crowe, Detective III Crowe, or Detective Chief Crowe—his entire Los Angeles police career was boiled down to a few sentences in yellowed newsprint. There were a dozen photos as well, the earliest a faded Polaroid, the latest a digital print. Several of the older photographs showed him aging; the latest ones showed him as he actually looked, without the gray hair dye and makeup he'd worn during his last decade on the force.

He looked up in shock. "You've been keeping tabs on me!"

She laughed at his indignation. "Fair's fair, Anthony."

"How did you—"

"You told me you were moving to Los Angeles when we met, remember? And how if things worked out with the medicine, you'd like to join the police force after the war. My private investigator was very discreet. He said it wasn't hard to track your kind. He said he meant the romantic sort who sent anonymous bouquets from the same florist every year. But the way he said it made me suspect that he was a werewolf. Remember the ones we met in the forest?"

"I do. But—"

"You don't have to be concerned about your people's safety from me. There was never any discussion of anything supernatural between the detective and myself. What I know I will take to my grave. Take the box with you when you leave."

He put the box on the floor and took her hands

in his. "I'm not going anywhere." He kissed the palm of each hand. "I never wanted to leave you."

"You don't owe me any explanations."

"Which means you think that I certainly do, but you're being too polite to ask."

She tried to tug her hands from his, but he wouldn't let her go. "If I don't try to be polite, I'm going to start yelling and throwing things. Which will cause me to stroke out, which would send you into decades of despair and guilt—that might be fun for you, but I loathe melodrama."

He was acutely aware of the fury burning through her frail body, but he couldn't keep from teasing. "Come on, you know you'd love a great death scene."

"That's different. I intend to go gracefully, not croaking in the middle of a tantrum."

"You're not going anywhere, my darling. You are going to lie back and look lovely—"

He waited through her snort of derision.

"—and listen to what I have to say."

"It's past my bedtime."

"Stubborn wench."

They both smiled at the memories evoked by those words. Some of her tenseness relaxed and the expression in her eyes softened. She leaned against the pile of pillows at her back.

"All right, Anthony, I'll let you tell me a bedtime story."

The soul-deep happiness he felt being near Rose hadn't changed one iota. He'd known from the moment he'd found a frightened young woman hiding in a snow-covered thicket that she was the one he'd been meant to love. Their time had been stolen from them.

Not stolen—deliberately forbidden. *For the sake of the Clan.*

He sighed. "There is so much about my people that you don't know. Not that the opportunity to explain vampire culture presented itself while we were dodging Tiger tanks and German infantry. When I said good-bye to you in Paris, I didn't plan on it being for forever. I thought I'd find you after the war and tell you everything then."

"How romantic," she murmured. "Oh, don't look hurt, Anthony. I believe you, but—what on earth happened?"

"The simplest answer is that my Matri wouldn't let me have you. A Matri," he went on, "is the vampire female who rules each vampire Clan with total authority. We're a matriarchal society. I am Prime of the Corvis Clan. The Matri's word is law; her decisions are literally life and death ones."

"You got caught in some sort of political infighting, didn't you?"

"How perceptive of you, my darling."

"Making movies is a political process. Anything with a power structure involves politics, especially in uncertain times. After the war we had to deal with the death of the studio system, McCarthy, television. What did vampires have to deal with?"

"When I came home from the war there was a lot going on within the Clans; modern ideas were starting to undermine ancient traditions. I'd helped start some of that undermining and wasn't exactly in favor at home."

"The medicine you were taking to try to stay outside in the daylight got you in trouble?" she asked.

He nodded. "Good guess. If you'll recall, it didn't work all that well once the fog and clouds cleared up. But it did help some, and it was the beginning of a new way of life for our people. We'd spent thousands of years living in the dark, and not everybody was in favor of living any other way. My Clan Matri was—"

Tony bit his tongue on the many unpleasant things he thought about the last Corvis Matri. She'd had good reasons for every hurtful decision, from her generation's point of view. He still hated her, but he'd had sixty years to come to understand her.

He settled on saying, "Conservative. She probably felt the world was turning upside down—her daughter was living with a mortal male, the Primes were clamoring for her to invest in medical research, and I'd run off to fight with the American army when Primes weren't supposed to do that sort of thing."

"You told me that vampires had always defended mortals."

"Yes, but until the use of daylight drugs, we'd fulfilled our vows by helping people on a one-to-one basis. Once the drugs that let us dwell in daylight became practical, the Primes began to join the military, and they began taking sides in mortal affairs."

"They became American citizens? They served country instead of Clan?"

"Something like that. Some of the Matris were certainly scared of losing our loyalty—and of conflicts with Primes in other countries who were loyal to their own causes. It didn't work out like that; diplomacy prevailed. But there was tension at the time."

"And you started it?"

"Let's say that my Matri didn't think I'd set a good example when I defied ancient tradition by playing a grunt in khaki instead of an elite knight in shining armor."

Rose smiled. "That's true. The tank we stole wasn't very shiny."

"So when I announced that the mortal I'd found to be my bondmate was a movie star, my Matri used your fame as a reason not to allow me to complete the bond."

"What?" Rose sat up straight, although the movement obviously brought her pain. "She forbade us from being together because she decided the publicity associated with my life would 'out' all vampires?"

"That is the exact reasoning she used."

"And you went along with this?"

It broke his heart to answer. "I had no choice."

"Oh, really?"

Rose reached for the bowl of roses on the bedside table and hurled them at his head.

Chapter Twenty-one

Anthony caught the vase in a blur of speed that made Rose dizzy. He set the roses back on the table without even a drop of water spilled.

"Show-off," she complained.

He pressed a finger to her lips. "Someone might hear a crash. We don't want to make a ruckus, do we, darling?"

"Shhh . . ." He waited a moment before taking his hand away from her mouth. "If you make a ruckus, we might be heard."

Rose turned to look at her protector. Face-to-face, close together, she reveled in the warmth of his body and the virile masculine scent beneath the dirt that covered them both. There was also the unmistakable scent of blood.

"If I was screaming, it was because you were shot," she said.

"No, I wasn't."

Oh yes, he had been. She'd seen how he'd jerked as the bullets stitched a line across his body. When he'd gone down, she'd believed he'd never get up again. The loss had sliced through her. She hadn't known she was screaming until his hand covered her mouth. His rough touch sent joy leaping through her.

There was a certain feral gleam in his eyes as he studied her face. He looked hungry. It was hard to breathe with him looking at her like that. It was freezing in the ruined farmhouse, but the temperature around them rose significantly.

"I thought they'd killed you," she went on.

"I was just dodging bullets."

"You were bleeding." She touched one of the spots where gunfire had left holes in his dark jacket. Her fingers came away smeared in red. "See?"

He put his hands on her shoulders. "It's nothing. Don't worry about it."

He glanced toward the dead German blocking the doorway, then led her out of the ruined *kitchen, into a roofless area that had once been a bedroom. Snow fluttered down from the night sky overhead and swirled around this abandoned place.*

Anthony went absolutely still, listening. "There's no once else out there. We're safe for now."

She felt safe being with him, but maybe she was kidding herself. "You are what I think you are, aren't you?"

He turned his gaze on her, and his eyes glittered in the night. His voice was a dangerous whisper. "What do you think I am?"

Rose wouldn't turn away, no matter how dominating his stare. Tension stretched between them. She could no longer feel the cold. The snowflakes that occasionally touched her skin might as well have been burning ash.

"I don't want to say what I think—what I know—you are."

He stepped so close to her that their steamy breath mingled. "What am I, Rose?"

"Hungry."

The word itself granted him permission. His mouth touched hers in one swift kiss and then moved down to her throat. Her scarf and coat and shirt were all pushed aside. Cold touched her exposed skin for a moment. Only a small spot of skin was uncovered, but she'd never been more naked. Longing blended with intense pleasure when his lips touched her throat.

She needed more. Her hand came around the back of his head, pressing him closer. "Anthony . . ."

There was a second of sharp pain, then—

Her bones melted. They turned to molten gold.

Her blood burned. Pleasure sang in every vein and artery.

Her flesh was on fire. Rapture danced through the flames.

The world shattered; she became whole.

He was there with her and they were whole together. One.

His need consumed her. Her giving gave her everything.

Just before the ecstasy became unbearable she thought, So this is what an orgasm is like.

Sweetheart, you haven't felt anything yet, *Anthony's thought answered her.*

"Oh, my," she said. She was breathing heavily.

Rose tried to open her eyes and realized that they weren't closed. The darkness filling her vision came from the depths of Anthony's eyes. She blinked and the rest of his beloved face came into focus.

Rose fanned her face with her hand. She was warm in several unexpected ways. "Anthony, I'm not sure it's appropriate for a woman my age to feel like this."

"I'm older than you," he reminded her. "And I like how I feel just fine." He grinned. "And accomplished without the need for Viagra."

"That was . . . nice," she said. "Possibly a bit icky, if I think about it too closely, but nice."

"It's our memory to share."

She brushed her hand across his cheek, too aware of its wrinkled crone shape against the smoothness of his skin. "A lovely memory. Thank you for it—but don't think it excuses you in any way."

"Excuses me from what?"

"From abandoning me, you damned fool. Look at you. Look at me. Don't you dare tell me that you're here now, because your sudden appearance does nothing to make up for the years in between."

"Darling, if I had claimed you against my Matri's command, there wouldn't have been any years in between. Those who break the rules pay with their lives—my people are vampires, you know."

"We could have arranged an accident, made it look like we were killed."

"I considered it, believe me, but the chances

of our being discovered were too high. I wasn't going to put your life at risk. My death sentence would have been your death sentence as well. I didn't drag you out of the Battle of the Bulge just to get you killed because I was too selfish to live without you." He stroked her hair and bent to kiss her cheek. "But I'm too selfish to live without you anymore."

Rose was too aware that her hair was silver and thin, that her cheek was a wrinkled ruin. She didn't know if Anthony saw her as she was or as he remembered her, but she was under no illusions. It made her heart sing that to him she would always be beautiful, but it didn't make her weak heart any healthier. Nor did it stop the pain that shot through her with such sudden violence that she couldn't stop the moan she didn't want him to hear.

"What's the matter?"

Her vision had gone out of focus but she knew that Anthony's face was close to hers. "What do you think's the matter? I'm dying, you idiot."

"Not on my watch, you aren't."

She managed a laugh despite the agony.

A moment later he said, "Here."

Something hard was thrust against her lips. Then a hotsweetmetallic flavor was on her tongue. Familiar. Longed for.

It was too late for this! It was a waste!

But once she tasted Anthony's blood, she could no more stop herself than she could stop the pain. Or the love that had been part of her for so very long.

Rose's need was unbearable, and all she could do was drink.

Chapter Twenty-two

December 17, 1944, 12:40 AM
Ardennes Forest, Belgium

This was not a pleasant evening for a stroll in the forest. Though Tony wasn't likely to get frostbite, his body's resistance to cold didn't stop him from hating it. The wind whipped snow against his face with burning force; his eyelids felt frozen open. It was just not a nice time to be outdoors.

It wasn't only the foul weather Tony found irritating; there were also all those enemy soldiers sharing the woods with him. Sometimes they shot at him, but it was the overwhelming noise of gun and mortar and cannon fire that really annoyed him.

As he moved cautiously through the invasion, observing and memorizing all he saw, counting heartbeats and drinking in the scent of blood, he couldn't help but recall the almost casual order that had brought him on this scouting expedition.

"Go up to the Belgian Front and have a look around for me, Crowe. See if there's anything to the rumors of a German buildup on the other side of the Ardennes Forest," the general had said, puffing on a cigar. "It won't take long; there's nothing really going on, just some exaggerated reports from the green troops training up there who think they hear ghosts in the woods. You'll be back in Paris long before Christmas."

The general's nothing *had turned out to be a hell of a lot of something.*

As Tony was about to turn around and head back to the jeep he'd left in a village many miles to the rear, a girl's voice stopped him between the shelter of one tree and the next.

Hide over here. It's safer.

As bullets whizzed past his head, Tony dove to the ground and peered over the dubious shelter of a tree stump to look around.

Where's here? *he thought back.*

Straight ahead. Close your eyes and you'll see me.

He understood exactly what she meant and did as she said. When he blocked out all the hubbub around them he immediately sensed her heartbeat, the warmth of her flesh, the aroma of her blood. And what a lovely aroma it was!

Even more delicious was the aura of a frightened, strong, stubborn, and very sharp mind.

She was also very young.

He opened his eyes and crawled to a clump of bushes only a few feet away.

When he reached the mortal girl curled up in the middle of the thicket, he asked, How long have you known you were a telepath?

A what?

Ah. So she didn't know what she was doing. Crisis sometimes brought out latent talents.

When she looked at him, he saw that she was surprised to see him. He saw fear in her huge eyes, but not fear of him. Her instant trust caught at his heart.

"Who are you?" he whispered. "What are you doing here?"

"Rose Cameron. I'm with the USO."

Of course she was. There were several troupes of entertainers up here, in what was supposed to be a safe area, giving shows to help the boys celebrate Christmas.

He looked her over carefully, seeing her clearly in the darkness. "What are you doing in the USO? Do you have a note from your mother to be in this war? How old are you? Fifteen?"

"I'm twenty!" Her voice never rose above a faint whisper, but she put a shout's worth of indignation into it. He cocked an eyebrow and stared her down. "Seventeen," she admitted, but she was still indignant.

He took her hand. "We're between waves of soldiers for the moment. Let's get out of here."

She shook her head. "I can't."

"Don't worry, I'll—"

"My ankle," she interrupted. "I don't know if it's broken or just twisted, but I can't walk any farther. You go. I'll be okay."

They were surrounded by an invading army. It was a bitter cold night during the worst winter of the century. She was not going to be okay, and they both knew it.

When she tried to tug her hand from his, he didn't let her go.

He pulled her from hiding and picked her up. "Don't worry, Rose. You won't slow me down."

"Hey," she complained as he held her close. "I don't snuggle up to total strangers."

"My name's Anthony Crowe," he told her. "And I'm going to take care of you."

His heart told him that he'd been waiting to take care of her all his life.

Chapter Twenty-three

December 17, 1:20 AM
Present Day
Los Angeles, CA

"Feeling better?" Anthony asked. His voice sounded as though it came from a great distance, perhaps at the other end of a long, lighted tunnel.

"Yes," Rose said.

In a way, she was feeling better, emotionally. Physically—the pain hadn't gone away, but it was different, bearable. She felt more alive.

She found that she was no longer propped up by pillows but tucked in the crook of Anthony's arm. Her head rested on his chest. Like a young girl snuggled up with her lover.

"This feels good," she admitted. "I haven't been warm in a long time." After a while, she said,

"I'd forgotten about using telepathy when we met. Are you sure I really shared thoughts with you?"

"I'm sure."

"It's never happened with anyone else."

"I should hope not—it was meant for me."

"Arrogant man."

"I am. Besides, you channeled your psychic talent into your acting."

It took Rose some restraint not to point out that she might have preferred to channel her talent into making babies and a home with him. There was no use crying over spilled milk; she was content with what she had right now. But she was also exhausted.

"I think you should leave now, Anthony," she said.

"I'm comfortable." His voice sounded drowsy. He yawned. "I think I'll stay right here."

"Nonsense. You'd shock the nurse when she brings my three AM meds."

"What? Do they wake you up to give you sleeping pills?"

"Something like that. You really should go now." She didn't want him to go, but she didn't want him to stay.

"Have it your way, my love." He rose to his feet, as lithe and lively as a young man should be. "Where shall we go?"

She slapped at him when he reached down to pick her up. "*We* aren't going anywhere. Just go."

It finally began to dawn on him that she meant it. He looked like a hurt little boy, which made her want to hug him and tell him that everything was all right. But putting her arms around him would break her, physically and mentally. She'd never let him go, or she'd never stop crying if she did. Neither was acceptable at this point.

Anthony crossed his arms and cocked his head to one side. "You're playing hard to get. That's not your style."

She decided to go along with this game. "I never was easy, Anthony. If you think you can donate a little blood and then just move in, you're mistaken. It'll take more than a pint to win me over after all this time."

"What about all the roses?"

"They're a lovely romantic gesture. But still not enough."

"Is it a courtship you want?"

"I think I deserve one."

"Shall I bring chocolate next time? Champagne?"

"I'm not averse to diamonds."

He kissed her hand. "The hard stuff it is, then."

He gave her a puppy dog look designed to make her relent. She smiled and shook her head.

"Good night, then, my winter Rose."

She managed not to snicker at this blatant ploy. "Good night, Anthony."

She only hoped she still had the strength to make it to the closet and the hidden pills once he was gone.

Chapter Twenty-four

December 17, 11:00 AM

From the outside, Ocean View Retirement Center was a very pleasant place. It was a large hacienda-style building set in beautifully landscaped gardens and surrounded by a low wall. There really was an ocean view, although a freeway cut across the grounds and the cliff overlooking the water. The place offered lovely rooms, a large professional staff, and excellent care for the elderly. Ocean View was a perfectly pleasant environment in which to wait for death.

Tony knew that Rose received the best possible care there, yet he hated this prison for her aging body with his heart and soul.

I should have taken her out of there last night,

he thought. *I should never have fallen for her "I want a courtship" ploy.*

He shook his head, irritated with himself and a little bit with Rose, and a wave of love for her washed over him. *She hasn't changed a bit,* he thought fondly. He knew she'd been more worried for him than she was for herself. She'd always been that way; quick to notice his problems and quick to try to fix them.

"We're going to have to stop soon," the girl in his arms said.

He smiled despite the pain, amused because he was carrying a Rose. "I'm fine," he told her.

"You're not," she answered. "You're flinching more with every step."

"I'm fine. You don't weigh anything."

"It's not me. You've been in pain since the sun came up."

"What sun?" he asked. The snow had stopped, but clouds and fog obscured the shadows of the deep woods even further.

"What little light there is hurts you. You need to get under cover."

He wore a helmet, gloves, and boots, a scarf covered most of his face, and his body was protected by a uniform and a heavy coat, but he was suffering from hell's own sunburn. He didn't know if what was happening to his eyes was called snow blindness or sun blindness, but pretty soon he wasn't going to be able to see a thing.

"You're hurting, Anthony."

How could she know? It must be another example of the telepathy she wasn't aware of.

He'd been using his extra senses to avoid the enemy, swerving in long zigs and zags to avoid any German patrol he heard. There'd been plenty of gunfire, but he managed to keep them away from numerous firefights in the woods and villages around them. The result was that they'd spent a dangerous amount of time out in daylight. But heading in a straight line would have been more dangerous to her. He'd cope with the damage, but at some point his growing thirst was going to send him into a frenzy.

"I'm going to get you to safety," he told her.

"Of course you are," she said. "But wouldn't it be best to hide out until nightfall?"

"It'll be too cold for you to travel at night."

She laughed. "I'm from a ranch in northern Montana. I could teach you a thing or two about surviving in the cold."

Sometimes he forgot that mortals weren't as fragile as they seemed. "All right. Let's find somewhere to hide."

It wasn't long before they came across an abandoned shed. Tony ducked through the doorway and set her down. Rose closed the rickety door behind them, completely blocking out the dim daylight. Tony sighed in relief and sank to his knees.

His vision cleared quickly and the first thing he saw was her worried expression and her steady, assessing gaze. Goddess, but she was beautiful! She was a skinny kid with frizzy copper hair and freckles, but she had great bone structure and huge dark eyes.

"They're actually blue. Your eyes look black, but they're dark blue. Amazing."

"You see in the dark. That's even more amazing."

He didn't try to explain away this ability. He reached into an inner coat pocket and brought out the bottle of precious pills. The daily dosage was supposed to be two; he popped down three. The burns were already healing in the darkness; he hoped the medicine would make the blood thirst more bearable. Frankly, he wasn't sure if the stuff did any good at all. His fangs ached every time he looked at the girl.

"We'll rest here for a while. I'll keep watch. Get some sleep, Rose."

She limped away from the door and settled

down beside him. He was pleasantly surprised when her arms came around him. "We'll share body heat for a while first," she said. "You're freezing."

"Naturally low body temperature." He put his arms around her waist and pulled her closer. "Your warmth feels wonderful."

"Will the pills help you? What's a sick man doing out here anyway?"

"Until yesterday, this was supposed to be the safest area in the war," he reminded her. "Weren't you here to entertain the wounded?"

"Yes, but what are you doing here?"

"Gathering intel," he said. "I was supposed to have a quick look around and get out."

"I'm sorry your quick look turned into a rescue mission."

He pulled her even closer. "I'm not. I'm going to get you out, Rose. We'll be fine."

I'm going to get you out now, too, Tony thought as the memory faded. He chuckled and patted the pocket holding the diamond ring as he walked toward the gate of the Ocean View Retirement Center. He'd never pulled off an escape from an old folks' home before.

Chapter Twenty-five

The smell of fresh paint wasn't unpleasant but it was unexpected, especially as it grew stronger with each step closer to Rose's room. Tony expected the scent of roses, but there was no hint of the abundance of bouquets in the air. A heavy dread came over him, the anxiety so strong it muffled all his other senses. The hallway was long and wide, lit by recessed lighting and tall windows at either end, painted pastel blue and hung with cheerful landscape prints. It was also utterly empty, and although he knew his footsteps were silent he could hear them echoing in his head.

"Rose?" he whispered as he reached her door.

The door was open and the smell of paint wafted from inside, almost nauseating him as it hit him in the face. The room was empty. No furniture. No bed. No rugs on the floor. No pictures on the clean white walls. No curtains on the windows. No roses.

No Rose.

Tony took a bewildered step inside.

Where was Rose?

Confusion swirled around him, causing genuine dizziness, not a sensation he was used to. The square of sunlight coming in the bare window had moved slightly by the time his head cleared enough to realize someone was speaking to him.

"Sir?" a woman asked. "Sir, are you all right?"

Tony turned to the doorway, where a young woman in one of those ridiculously cheerful print tunics was looking at him in concern.

Where's Rose Cameron? he demanded, sending the words straight into the mortal's mind.

"Who?"

She thought the word as well as spoke it, her confusion completely genuine.

Damn!

His anger caused her pain, and for a moment he didn't care. Then Tony took a step back, took a deep breath, and resumed the civilized façade he normally used when dealing with mortals. "I'm

Doctor Crowe," he told her as he looked into her eyes. "I'm looking for one of my patients, but I seem to have been directed to the wrong room. I need to look at your files."

"Of course." She smiled pleasantly and led him to a nurses' station located in the circular atrium where all the halls met.

Along the way, Tony sent out telepathic feelers to every mortal within reach. He asked them all, *Where's Rose?* The answers he received concerned bushes, plants, gardens, and floral arrangements. There was nothing to do with longtime resident Rose Cameron in any of their heads.

This is crazy!

The terror racing through him made it hard to think. It made it even harder to control his temper. His impulse was to tear the place apart with his bare claws until he found the woman he loved.

Instead he asked to look through the nursing home's files when he got to the central desk, and looked through the computer records and filing cabinets with the same results he'd found in the mortals' minds.

Nothing.

If she'd ever existed, there was no record of it here.

If she'd never existed, why had his heart been twisted with pain for all these years? If she'd never existed, why had no lover but her ever given him the completion his soul craved?

He became aware of the people gathered in the atrium watching him. Not with hostility or wariness or guilt; not a single negative emotion was directed at him. There was curiosity, brief relief from everyday work boredom, even some female appreciation for his looks. But nothing in their awareness had anything to do with Rose.

He looked back at them with total hostility. He wanted to rip into them and spill their blood. He wanted to shred their minds to tatters and flay them alive. He wanted answers. He wanted Rose.

He wanted to kill in reaction to the pain and the panic. It was a Prime's right to have what he wanted!

He reminded himself that he was not a child. What use were all the years spent in the Clan crèche learning to control his instincts if he broke now when Rose needed him most?

He rose slowly to his feet, made his clenched fists relax.

"Thank you," he said to the watching staff.

Tony walked out of the Ocean View Retirement Center, fear and rage rising with every step. By the time he reached the street, he was seeing everything around him in shades of blood. When he stepped from shade into sunlight, his skin flared with pain and the world went completely red.

It was the mundane ringing of the cellular telephone in his coat pocket that brought Tony back to the mortal world. He became aware that he was standing at the corner of a busy street, but he had no idea where he was. He must have walked here. He glanced up at the street sign and got his bearings. The phone kept ringing.

He had no interest in talking to anyone but answered it for the sake of silence. "What?"

"There's a situation at the clinic," Dr. Casmerek answered. "I need you here right now."

The mortal doctor was usually a very cool customer. He was used to caring for vampires suffering from everything from splinters to drug-induced psychoses, so he needed to be calm and authoritative. Casmerek didn't sound like either of those things at the moment.

"I'm busy," Tony told him brusquely, but duty made him add, "What's the problem?"

"Busy?" Casmerek shouted. "You are head of clinic security and you are needed here. Now!"

Tony hated the pull of responsibility nagging at him. He had his own problems, damn it!

"I asked what was wrong."

"Bomb threat to the clinic," Casmerek answered. "It was called in to the Los Angeles police; now I've got a swarm of *mortal* police combing through a *vampire* clinic."

A roar filled the speaker, and Tony pulled the phone away from his head.

"Oh, my God! It wasn't a threat!" Casmerek shouted. "Tony!"

Tony closed his eyes for a moment as helplessness and hopelessness washed through him. "On my way."

Why was he always forced to choose between Rose and his people? This was a real emergency and he couldn't abandon them. And he wasn't going to abandon her.

But there were no rules that said he couldn't ask for help.

He dialed Sidonie's work number. He had a missing person, and his daughter was a missing persons investigator.

Chapter Twenty-six

December 17, 2:00 PM
San Diego, CA

"You can't just leave!" Joe insisted.

Sid pretended not to notice that he'd followed her into her room, though it was hard to ignore a werewolf pacing around her bed as she tried to pack.

Her first mistake had been to let him drive her home after Tony's call. Somehow he'd willfully and stubbornly gotten the false impression that she'd left the office for the day, not that she intended to leave the city. Even after she'd told him she was going to Los Angeles.

"You are *not* going to Los Angeles," he said. Again.

Sid stopped stuffing underwear into a suitcase

pocket and looked at him. "I am a missing persons detective. I have a client who happens to be my sire, who has reported a missing little old lady to me. To me. I'm going to help him find Rose Cameron."

"Rose Cameron? The movie star from the forties and fifties? How could she be missing? I didn't know she was still alive. I remember that you once made me sit through a marathon showing of all of her old films. You never mentioned she had any connection to your sire."

Sid remembered that evening very well, and very fondly, as she did all the times they'd been comfortable in each other's company. They'd curled up next to each other on the couch with all the lights out and gone through an entire boxed set of classic DVDs. It was how they'd unwound from a hard case that hadn't turned out well.

"What Tony told me in private stayed private, but I wanted to see what she was like when I rented those three films. At the time, you said watching her movies was fun. And those were only her most famous ones."

"I enjoyed the wine and the popcorn," he admitted. "She was certainly a beautiful woman in her time. The musical sucked."

"A lot of those 1950s Technicolor extravaganzas haven't aged well, but that's not the point.

The point is that to Tony, she's the woman who should have been his bondmate. And he wants her back safe and sound."

"Back from where?"

"I don't know that yet."

"But—I don't understand. If they aren't bonded, how could—"

"Sometimes you can't be with who you want to be with, all right? People don't always get to live happily ever after. Life can be complicated—even for a vampire!"

She knew from the look on his face that her vehemence had told him too much.

She picked up her travel case. "My father needs me."

He blocked the door. "Tobias needs your memories."

"Tobias can go to hell." She looked the werewolf up and down. He was tall and whipcord lean but with wide shoulders. He was strong and fast in his human form, and deadly fierce in wolf shape. "You know I could toss you aside like a rag doll," she told him.

He nodded. "But you're not the impulsive, violent type. You're sneaky, but you're not mean."

"I'll take that as a compliment, but you still better get out of my way."

Joe's stern expression relaxed. He actually

smiled as he held out his hand. "Why don't you let me carry the luggage?"

His smile twisted her heart, and the temptation to kiss those smiling lips nearly overwhelmed her. He had such a beautiful mouth. Damn him!

All she meant to do was hand him the bag. But their hands touched and their eyes met, and the air sizzled between them. The bag dropped on the floor.

Joe kicked it aside, then reached for her—and she couldn't turn away.

"Oh, hell," Sid said as she came into his arms.

His body was stiff with reluctance, pride fighting desire, but his mouth came down on hers, hard and demanding.

Sid's response was just as demanding, even more desperate. Too many years of missing him, needing him, made her reckless and greedy. He was the only one who could fill the emptiness in her soul, who could make her body come alive.

She was alive now, so alive it hurt. Being alive hurt. So what? It was wonderful! She welcomed that pain, along with every other denied sensation.

I've missed you, wanted your touch. It's been so long . . .

She'd dreamed about making love to Joe, fantasized about it, survived on memories. This very real kiss took her by storm.

He reacted just as wildly, picking her up and tossing her beneath him on the bed. For a moment she almost panicked when his weight came down on her, but she remembered that this was Joe. *Her* Joe. No silver manacles bound her. Her hands were free to roam over him, to help him pull his shirt off, to press her skin to his. She was free to kiss his face, the hollow of his throat, his chest.

She concentrated on everything she could see and touch, used her fascination with his body to ignore the heated roar of his blood and the drumming of his heart. She could have only so much of him, and no more. She would not be a vampire with him. Never again.

Her clothes came off as quickly as his. His wide-eyed shock at the sight of her flesh brought a smile to her lips.

"What the devil have you done to your arms?" Joe demanded.

He referred to the sharply angled sepia tattoos that wound like bracelets around her toned biceps.

"Sexy, aren't they?" she asked.

"Uh"—Joe stroked the marked skin with his thumbs—"yeah."

She chuckled throatily and turned onto her stomach. Joe gasped at the markings that emphasized the length of her back and the curves of her lower body.

"Sweet mother . . ." he murmured in a voice almost strangled with lust.

"Touch them," she urged.

He did just that, and she loved the way he breathed her in while he stroked and kissed the geometric swirls on her arms and back and hips. He explored the fresh tattoos, and the rest of her, with a thoroughness that was maddeningly pleasurable.

Sid arched against him, opened herself to him. She kept her lips firmly shut over aching fangs. Tasting him was one desire she would fight off. Heat rose between them, flowed through her, and she gave herself to the sensation.

Explosive pleasure took her when he entered her, but need began to curl toward a fresh orgasm instantly. It had been so long, and he was—

"Joe."

It was all she could say, though it meant so much more than a name.

"Bitch," he answered.

She loved hearing that word from his lips. From his kind it was not an insult; the harshly spoken word held all the possessiveness she longed for. She was his. At least for this moment, and it was all she wanted.

As he claimed her with hard, demanding strokes. She was surprised at how much she reveled in the roughness of their wild coupling, in the way they marked each other, scratch for scratch, bruise for bruise. She loved the way the orgasms mixed with the pain.

She'd longed for this—the way she shrieked and he roared when he exploded inside her, and how they were one, together, for that long, delirious moment.

Chapter Twenty-seven

Joe slowly came back to himself, up out of a dark well of total bliss. He sat up and swung his legs over the side of the bed, then wiped the sweat-dampened hair from his face while he stared bleakly at the floor. His body sang with life and satisfaction. His soul was shell-shocked.

"What the hell was I thinking?"

"What does that mean?"

"You're the last person in the world I want to make love to."

"Then pretend I'm somebody else," she answered.

He knew what she meant. She certainly looked

different, at least with her clothes off. "Maybe I will," he said.

Sid's emotions brought swift changes in body chemistry that came to him as the scent of hurt, quickly followed by anger. "Then just think of it as good rough sex with a stranger. Or think of it as part of your mission."

It was his turn to ask, "What does that mean?"

"That you were thinking of your duty while we did the deed," she answered. "It was the Dark Angels version of lying back and thinking of England. In the active, aggressive way of your unit."

The stinging sarcasm in Sid's voice made him turn to look at her. The sight of her naked body sent renewed desire through him. Anger at his own lack of control made him lash out at her, even while a part of him recognized that her sarcasm was trying to cover pain. "What are you talking about?"

"Everything we've been doing"—she glanced at the bedside clock—"for the last hour was to distract me, delay me. You set a trap to keep me from leaving, and I walked right into it."

Joe shot to his feet to glare down at her. That she was a beautiful naked female exuding the intoxicating aromas of sex served to make his anger hotter. Fury kept his mind off what his body wanted to start all over again.

How could she *dare* think he'd try to use her? How could she believe he'd use sex as a weapon?

"I don't play that kind of game, Sidonie. Not even for the sake of an assignment."

"Oh, yes," she sneered. She sat up and wrapped her arms around her knees as she looked over his naked form. "You always play fair."

"I'm not you."

She didn't flinch at this nasty jab. She got up on the opposite side of the bed, stretched, and rolled the stiffness from her shoulders.

He saw that he'd left her with bruises that were already healing. He felt the scratches she'd left on his back while she clutched and clawed through her orgasms.

"Where are you going?" he asked when she started from the bedroom.

She glanced back over her shoulder. "To Los Angeles. But I'm going to get cleaned up first."

He followed her into the bathroom and into the shower.

"What the hell are you doing?" she demanded.

"Saving time and hot water." Joe turned on the tap and tossed her the shampoo. He squirted shower gel into his cupped palm. To prove that he really hadn't been trying to distract her, he added, "We'll make up the time already lost on the drive."

"Fine," she grumbled. She spread lather onto his chest. "It's too late to argue now."

He looked at her glistening wet skin. It was none of his business, but he couldn't stop the questions. "Why the ink? When did you—"

"Don't worry, it won't last," she told him. "I needed a certain trashy, edgy look for an undercover job, so I opted for a lot of ink. Eden went with me for moral support when I had them done last month and ended up getting a tattoo on her hip."

"A volcano?" he guessed. "To surprise Laurent?"

She smiled and nodded. "Our lava-loving Eden went for a tasteful tattoo of Mount Fuji."

"How'd the op go?"

She gave a fierce grin. "Not only did we find the kidnapped teenager we were looking for, we brought down the cult that took her." She traced a finger around the design circling one arm. "It's mortal ink and will fade in a few months."

He was delighted the tats weren't permanent. Even though it was none of his business, he preferred Sid's naked body clean and unmarked and—

All he had meant to do was share some of the soap with her, but his hand slipped when he touched Sid's chest, and the next thing he knew his palm was covering her breast. She arched against him, her nipple going hard against his palm. He went stiff as well, his erection pressing against her thigh. Her hand came around his penis. Joe had a momentary rush of terror, but instead of causing him agony, Sid stroked a groan of pleasure from him.

"Goddess," he muttered. "Here we go again."

Sid's face was pressed against his shoulder, her voice muffled over the rush of water. "What is the matter with us?"

"I really do want to keep my hands off you," he told her. But he couldn't stop touching her, tracing the sensual lines of ink that marked her body, roaming over her breasts, her ass, between her wet thighs.

"My sire needs me," she protested weakly.

"We'll make it quick," he promised.

Sid lifted her head to look into his eyes. "You still hate me, right?"

"Completely."

"Good."

"You still think I'm trying to stall you?" he asked.

"Doing a good job of it, too."

"Nothing's changed." They said it together.

He wanted to believe that he could make love—at least have sex—with Sid and not feel anything but hatred for her. He knew he was lying. Maybe she was, too. It didn't matter. He had to have her or die.

She hooked a leg around his hip, and guided him into her. "Don't worry," she whispered in his ear. "I'd never let you die."

Chapter Twenty-eight

Sid insisted they take her car, but at least she let him drive. It was an SUV, the sort of thing a mother would drive, instead of the flashy car she'd owned when he'd left town, but at least it was a Mercedes. Not that the big engine was doing them any good at the moment.

"This traffic is ridiculous," Joe commented after they'd been on the crowded freeway for a while.

Sid looked up from her digital reader. "The wildfire's caused a lot of roads to be closed. We're stuck with all the rerouted traffic."

Joe was disoriented for a moment, having forgotten that he'd been up in the mountains fighting that fire not long ago.

Sid gave him a quizzical look. "Don't tell me you—"

"Read to me," he cut her off. "We're moving at a snail's pace and I'm bored."

"I'd have to go back to the beginning of the book," she complained.

"My heart bleeds."

"I could arrange that."

He lifted an eyebrow in response. "I'm not afraid, and don't tell me that can be arranged, too."

Sid smiled, and then sighed. "I suppose anything's better than gloomy silence or angry conversation." She backed up the screen, took a deep breath, and read.

> "Not again," Zoe muttered as the ship shook from a direct hit once more.
>
> This had been going on far longer than usual, and it was getting worse by the moment. Though her quarters were deep within the center of the command ship's many hulls, she could still feel the energy blows against heavy shielding, and how that shielding was fading. The communications stem in her ear let her know that the whole task force was in trouble and on the run.

* * *

While Joe listened to the story and kept his gaze on the road, a part of his mind roamed, assembling actions, thoughts, scents, psychic impressions, and bits of conversation between Sidonie and himself over the last several days.

"Just how did little Charles come into the world?" he asked after a while.

Sid stopped reading and replied, "Headfirst, like most babies. It was a very easy delivery."

"It wasn't a virgin birth by any chance?"

"I know you know me better than that."

"But you haven't wanted to have sex with anybody in a long time," he said. "Anyone but me, apparently."

"Don't look smug, Bleythin."

"But I'm not a vampire," he went on. "Why am I, lowly werewolf, acceptable, but not one of your own species?"

"Will you stop dissing your own species?" Sid demanded.

"The puzzle is, why are you disrespecting your own species? I have the answer to that," he added.

He didn't want to say it aloud. He wanted to turn the car around and return to San Diego to hunt down and kill any damned Manticore Tribe Prime that had survived the raid on their hideout five years before.

"Some of them took the pledge," she answered

at his emotional reaction. She didn't try to disguise her own bitterness. "They are now learning to be good little vampires under the protection of the Families."

"How can you sound so calm?" His anger was fresh, the pain deep, both for her.

"I've had a few years to practice."

Her emotions roiled, but her tone was cool, her body language and expression almost relaxed. They might as well have been talking about the traffic. Years of practice. Yeah, he could see that.

"You never told me." He hated that he sounded like a hurt little boy. "Or did you, and then made me forget?"

"I never told anyone. I can't tell anyone. I'll never tell anyone. All right?"

"Why?"

"Oh, for goddess's sake, Joe! Think about it! I'm a vampire female," she reminded him. "My mother was a Tribe captive for a long time. Look how she's been treated since she was rescued. I will not allow that to happen to me."

Joe considered, fondly remembered Sid's mom, Lady Antonia Wolf. "She's respected," Joe said. "Beloved. Revered."

"She's treated like she's made out of glass, like a poor little fragile thing that has to be kept in a padded box surrounded by armed guards." Sid laughed. "My esteemed clanfolk ignore the truth about glass, how much heat it can stand, how pliable it can be." She shook her head. "Never mind. What I'm trying to say is that I will not give anyone the chance to treat me like, like—"

"A girl?" he suggested.

"Precisely," she snapped. "Worse than a girl—a *lady.*" After an angry silence, she took a deep breath and went on. "You know how hard I've had to fight for what independence I have. Many Clan and Family females think I'm crazy to want a life outside the luxurious confines of the Citadel—they like ruling their own little world and being constantly courted by the Primes."

"That never was your thing," he agreed.

"So, yeah, I got raped," she admitted. "I deliberately put myself in the way of the Manticore Tribe, and I accept what happened."

"It wasn't your fault!"

"Of course not."

She put a hand on his arm. He was surprised at the sexual heat that passed between them, considering the conversation. "Are you really all right?" he asked her.

"No," she answered honestly. "But I am much improved. I will not let having a bad thing happen to me be used to keep me confined and protected. Understood?"

His answer was quick and automatic. "Understood."

He had to remind himself of how badly she'd betrayed him to fight off his own protective urges. He kept his gaze on the crowded highway and his mouth shut.

After a while, she went back to reading to him.

Chapter Twenty-nine

December 18, 2:00 AM
Los Angeles, CA

"Well, here we are. Sort of," Joe said as he parked on a street several blocks away from their destination.

The houses on both sides of the road were dark, their residents peacefully sleeping. Streetlights didn't give much illumination between corners. It was late enough for there to be very little street traffic.

"Sort of," Sid agreed.

A call from Tony along the way had brought them here, instead of their original rendezvous point, his house. Sid got out and stretched as she stood on the sidewalk.

"I wonder what Rose Cameron's disappearance has to do with Dr. Casmerek's clinic?" she asked as Joe came to stand beside her.

"Maybe nothing," Tony Crowe said, stepping from the shadows. "Maybe everything." He glanced between them. "Are you two back together?"

"No," they answered in unison.

"In fact, Joe's going back to his DA buddies now that he's dropped me off," Sid said firmly to Joe.

He shook his head. "No can do, Sidonie.

"Oh, for the love of—!"

"This isn't just to bug you," Joe interrupted the beginning of her irritated tirade. "You said you didn't remember anything, but on the way here you told me that there are reformed Manticore Primes now living among the Families. That's a detail I didn't know, and I was in on the bust. Tobias doesn't know that detail either, does he?"

It was Tony who answered. "When a Tribe Prime leaves his own kind, he becomes a marked man among them. They'll kill him if they can. And reformed bad guys aren't too popular with the Clans or Families until they prove they really, really mean it. So we have our own version of the witness protection program. Hiding rehabilitated Primes is not something anyone among the werefolk would know about."

"Wait a minute, what about Laurent?" Joe asked. "He's a reformed Tribe Prime."

"Laurent's a special case, since he had Mom and me to vouch for him when he came over from the Dark Side," Sid said. "And what about Tobias?" she countered. "Didn't he start out as a Tribe member?"

Joe nodded. "Yeah, but I think he was still a kid when his whole Tribe took the pledge. I'm certain he's not aware that there are Manticores alive he can question. That's a lead you gave us, Sid. There's bound to be more details floating around in your subconscious. I'm staying until you remember everything."

Sid wanted Joe gone—mostly because she wanted him to stay. She was frightened of hurting him even more than she already had. And she was frightened of somehow getting her heart more broken than it already was.

Her sire picked up on her ambiguous reactions. "Life's a bitch, kid," he told her. "No offense," he added to Joe.

"None taken."

"Let the wolf stay," Tony went on. "We can use his nose."

"He isn't here to help with the case," Sid protested.

"I'd be happy to help you find your lady," Joe told Tony.

Sid shot him a stern look. "Are you really in on this case, Bleythin? Or are you just going to get in my way with your Tobias obsession?"

His hand landed on her shoulder, but his firm gaze was on Tony. "I'm in."

How sweet . . . he wanted to help a worried man find his missing loved one. Sid pushed aside her unexpected bitterness but couldn't stop the growl deep in her throat. It was more a werewolf way of expressing frustration than a vampire one, but it perfectly suited her feelings.

Since there was no getting rid of Joe, she concentrated on business. "Why are we meeting here?" she asked Tony.

"Something's happened at the clinic," Joe said. He touched his nose at her annoyed look. "I smell smoke—and explosives."

Fear shot through Sid. "Someone blew up the clinic?"

"Only one room was damaged," Tony said. "I figure it was done as a diversion to keep me from looking for Rose. Everyone else thinks it was an attack from the Purists."

Purists were fanatical remnants of the mortal vampire hunters who loathed the truce between human hunters and their supernatural enemies. Sid hated the very word. *They* were somehow Pure, while she and her kind were somehow *Abominations*.

"Load of crap," she muttered, then got back to business. "The Purists have tried to attack the clinic before, haven't they?"

Tony nodded. "A few years back. We thought we ran them all out of town after that." His eyes went flat and cold. "I still think we did. I think this is something else."

"Something to do with Rose?" Joe asked.

"That's *my* take on it. I think they think that Primes can't multitask."

"Or ask for help when they need it?" Sid added.

Tony gave a humorless laugh. "After all those years on the police force, I know when to form a task force. Rose needs to be found, and my Prime's ego isn't going to be bruised if I don't do all the work myself."

"As long as you're the one who does the actual rescuing," Joe said.

"You've spent too much time around vampires, Lobo," Tony said, but he nodded. "Yeah. You're the detectives. She's the rescuee, I'm the rescuer," he said, defining their roles.

"Unless it works out the other way around," Sid murmured.

Tony gave her a stern look. "Enough talk. I have to get back to the clinic. You know where she was?" he asked.

"Ocean View Retirement Center." She repeated the information he'd given her earlier. "Location already programmed on my GPS."

"I love modern technology." Tony waved them toward her SUV. "What are you waiting for? Go hunt her." Then he was gone.

Joe looked after the Prime with a sour expression. "If he tossed out a stick, would he expect me to fetch it?"

"I think he was ordering *me* around," Sid answered.

She was actually quite pleased at the trust Anthony Crowe was putting in her to accomplish a Prime's work. Most Primes still believed with their whole hearts and testosterone-laden souls that female vampires' roles were limited to child-bearing and ruling empires. Derring-do and ass-kicking were only for the male of the species.

"Except when the Furies are set loose," she added softly.

"The what?"

She repressed a shudder. "You don't want to know." She was going to make certain he *never* knew.

He let it go. "I'm going to ask the question

that needs asking now," he told her. "Keep it professional and don't get all defensive about your sire."

Sid bristled but waited.

"We know that Rose Cameron was a real person."

"Yes?" She drew out the word to several syllables.

"Are you absolutely certain that she is still alive? Are you certain that Tony isn't imagining a relationship with an old movie star?"

"That was two questions," she growled.

Joe nodded and kept looking at her steadily. "And your answers are?"

Sid noticed that her fangs were pressed against her lower lip. It took her a moment, but she managed to sheath her anger and her fangs. She took a deep breath before saying reluctantly, "You're right about that needing to be brought up."

"In an investigation, you have to ask *all* the questions," he reminded her. "You can't take anything—even information from family and friends—at face value."

She nodded and gave another careful moment's thought, going through every remembered conversation. "I've never met Rose, but I've never questioned anything Tony's told me about their relationship. The details certainly seemed realistic. I do not believe that my father is delusional."

"All right, then." Joe sniffed the air. "There's certainly something up around the place Tony guards with his life." He gestured toward the vehicle. "Let's see what we can find out at Rose's last known address."

Chapter Thirty

Joe sat up from being slouched in the passenger seat. Sid glanced his way. He'd been taking a nap until the moment before. His head swiveled slowly from side to side.

"I do not like this," he said.

"L.A. traffic?" Sid wondered. Despite the darkness, the morning rush hour was already under way, or maybe it had never stopped. "Traffic hasn't let up since we left home."

Joe shot her an angry look. "Use all of your senses, Prima," he ordered.

She was tired. It had been a long day. Tony's problem, combined with being near Joe, put her on edge. But none of that was any excuse for falling into the pretense of being mortal. Joe was right and she didn't resent the reminder. She smiled. "Prima?" she asked.

"Concentrate."

"I like the sound of that."

"Then earn it," he growled. He started to unbutton his shirt.

Sid opened her senses, partially to take her mind off the gorgeous body of the werewolf beside her. "Fire on the horizon," she said after a moment.

"How close are we to the nursing home?"

"Exit is coming up."

"Thought it might be." Joe began to take off his trousers.

Sid knew that he was preparing to shape-shift and she had other things to think about, but that didn't stop her from wanting to be distracted. "There's a little old lady in danger," she said.

"Park," Joe said as soon as they were off the exit ramp.

Sid didn't question him, but pulled into the first open space she found, aware of the official mortal hubbub in the distance. Civilians would be blocked from getting anywhere near the emergency area. Better to go in quick and quiet and as their true selves.

The moment she stopped the car, Joe leapt out his side window. Sid watched for a moment as the huge black wolf that was the male she loved raced silently away. She smiled fondly at the shadow moving in the shadows.

What are you waiting for? His thought was flung back at her.

Show-off, she replied, and raced after him. She only had two feet, but she was just as fast and agile as the werewolf.

Joe enjoyed running with Sid, he always had. It was too easy to forget what she'd done to him and fall into their old routine. He made himself a promise to get back to angry later. Right now there was the job, and the excitement of getting past everyone in their way.

The closer they got the more crowded it got. The blaze of the burning building wasn't the only thing lighting the sky, or the only roar of sound. Media helicopters circled overhead, beaming down searchlights. There were news vans parked beyond the cop cars. Fire trucks and EMT vans took up the front row of this circus. Joe was mostly aware of the many mortals on the scene as he wove through pairs of legs. There were hoses and cables to jump over, and, finally, a wall. He knew Sid would make her own silent, swift way through the mess.

Once inside the grounds, Joe waited in the shadow of the wall for his partner to join him. She soon crouched beside him. Her hand touched the back of his neck, fingers stroking through thick fur.

Just like old times.

They watched the building burn and the firefighters work. Sparks flew up on a hot wind and the garish flickering light made all the shadows sharp and weird.

"There's nothing alive in there," Sid said. The relief in her voice was soon replaced by annoyance. "Nothing except maybe evidence we need."

Joe nodded his hairy head. *I have no more doubts about your daddy's sanity,* he thought. He rose from his haunches. *I'll have a sniff around anyway.*

And I'll sit here and open my mind to the universe around me.

Have fun with that.

You, too.

Again, it was their usual routine. He made a mental note to add an image of Sid as a telepathic black widow sorting through a web of stolen thoughts and feelings to his catalogue of her evilness. Not that her mental gifts weren't incredibly useful and appreciated on the job.

Chapter Thirty-one

Sid went looking for a witness among the crowd—or even better, the arsonist, here to make sure of his handiwork.

She was initially hit with a wall of mental white noise, the thoughts of all the highly trained professionals going about their jobs. Expecting this, she let herself drift among the consciousnesses of firemen and cops and EMTs. She discovered relief along with puzzlement that there didn't seem to be anyone to rescue inside. *Where are the patients and staff?* she wondered along with the mortals.

As soon as mortal thoughts became the ambient background, she became aware of the vampire. The energy from one of her own kind was a bolt of lightning, a sizzle shot across a blank sky. Sid ignored her natural impulse to contact this other bright awareness. Who was it? What was it doing here? What did it know? She needed a gentle subtle touch here. She began to investigate.

Or she would have, if heavy footsteps hadn't come clumping up to stop beside her. Sid looked up, a long way up, to the sweaty face of a hulking young fireman who was looking worriedly down at her.

Sid groaned at the interruption and rose to her feet.

"May I be of assistance, my lady?" the young Prime asked.

She put a hand on her forehead. "Kiril, isn't it?" she asked.

He grinned at her like a slightly feral puppy. He was one of her own Clan. She hadn't seen him since he'd moved to Los Angeles to become a fireman.

She sighed, but she didn't suspect him of the atrocity blazing behind him. "Kiril Wolfgang."

He put his hand on her elbow, as if she needed support. "I'll get you out of here."

"Ahem," Joe said from behind the shelter of a tree. "The *lady* is already taken care of."

He stepped out in all his naked magnificence.

At least he looked magnificent to Sid; she didn't care what the young Prime's attitude was. Except that he didn't look impressed.

"A werewolf bodyguard is hardly enough protection during such a dangerous time," Kiril told her.

She knew that Joe had meant that she could take care of herself, but she let the Prime's assumptions go.

"What do you mean, *such a dangerous time*?" she demanded. "I know about the attack on the clinic." She gestured toward the fire. "This has something to do with us."

The young Prime nodded his agreement. "I think I felt something supernatural hanging around the perimeter," he said. "Then I spotted you and came for a look."

"There're more than two vampires in the vicinity," Joe said. "At least there were."

"Can you pick up a trail?" Sid asked.

"I want to hear what else our friend has to say," he answered. "There's a lot going on."

Kiril nodded. "The bar downtown took a hit earlier, made to look like a drive-by. A car bomb went off outside Shaggy Harker's bike shop. A supposed stalker tried to attack the movie star who's really a Prime."

"Werefolk as well as vampires are being targeted?" Sid asked. Shaggy was alpha of the local werewolf pack.

"There's a vampire movie star?" Joe asked.

They glanced at each other and smiled at the way they'd asked each other's natural question.

Kiril nodded to both questions. "It's not safe for you to be out here, Lady Sidonie. I have to get you back to the Shagal Citadel right now."

Despite the various Clan and Family members who dwelled in the area, Los Angeles was the home territory of the Shagal Clan—the Jackals. Lady Serisa Shagal was Matri of this Clan, and her word was law here, the way Lady Juanita Wolf's was among all vampires in San Diego. Kiril naturally assumed that any female vampire would be a guest at the Shagal Citadel, as it was the safest place in the city and the girls had to be kept safe.

Sid didn't argue with him. "Joe and I will make our own way back to the Citadel," she told the Wolf Prime, using a commanding tone and attitude that reminded the kid that he was a Wolf and not a Jackal. "You have your own work to do here."

It got him off her case. "Watch her closely," he commanded the werewolf.

"Oh, I will," Joe drawled.

"Irony is lost on our young Kiril," Sid said

as she watched him head back to his firefighting duties. She was surprised when Kiril turned back and gave her a sheepish look.

"I'm sorry I couldn't make it home for your Severing ceremony," he said. "I know how important that is, especially the first time. Belated congratulations on your son's beginning his journey, Lady Sidonie."

For a moment all Sid could do was stare blankly, then she forced a smile. "Thank you."

He grinned and was off.

So was Joe.

"Where are you going?" she asked Joe when he shifted back to wolf form and headed away from the disaster area. She followed him all the way back to the SUV; he was in human shape by the time she reached him. He was sitting inside the vehicle but he wasn't pulling on his clothes. Instead he was talking on his cellular phone. Sid got behind the wheel and shamelessly listened in on Joe's conversation.

"They aren't going to like that," she said when he flipped the phone shut.

"Do I care?" he asked. "Do you?"

She shook her head. "My pride's not on the line. Anything that doesn't specifically affect finding Rose Cameron isn't on my agenda."

"I didn't think you'd mind."

She glanced at the glow in the sky and worried about an old lady. "Where to now?"

Joe patted her ever-so-gently on the shoulder. "I'm under orders to get you safely to the Citadel."

She flashed fangs at him but trusted that he had a reason and started the engine.

Chapter Thirty-two

December 18, 5:00 AM

"You're doing a recon," Sid realized as Joe accompanied her into the thoroughly modern mansion that was the Shagal Citadel.

He gave her a conspiratorial smile and put his finger over his lips.

It's not like you're going into hostile territory, she thought to him.

Yet, he replied.

After that, they observed mental silence while they were led to the Citadel's windowless central room. Rather, she was politely led and Joe came along in her wake, pretty much unnoticed by the vampires around them. Just the way he wanted it.

It took an effort for Sid to hide her amusement at the arrogance of her own kind.

She'd expected to find a crowd of worried vampires holding a conference in the meeting room and was surprised to find the only occupant was a female with a wireless e-reader perched on her lap.

The female vampire looked up irritably at the interruption, then a slow smile spread across her face. She was looking at Joe.

Sid barely managed not to snarl or possessively step in front of Joe to block the female's view. "Hello, Flare," she said to Francesca "Flare" Reynard. "What are you doing in town?" she added suspiciously. "I thought you'd moved back to Idaho."

"I did." Flare languidly rose to her feet out of a deeply cushioned leather chair.

All vampires were attractive, but black-haired and vividly pale Flare Reynard made other vampire females look like warty frogs in comparison. Despite her haughtiness, her temper, and her goddess looks, Sid liked her. She and Flare had shared an apartment in college, living a few years completely among mortals. They also shared a lot of the same dissatisfaction with their lot in life, but they reacted differently. Whereas Sid was sneaky and diplomatic and tried to stay under the radar to do what she wanted, Flare raged and ranted and rebelled. She still ended up obeying her Matri, under protest, in matters regarding the survival of the Fox Clan.

"Why are you in Los Angeles?" Sid asked Flare.

"I've got an appointment to get pregnant. You've started a trend, girlfriend." She gave a sharp laugh. "What does it say about our species, when the males prefer mortals and the females prefer a turkey baster?"

"It doesn't say anything," Sid answered. "Except that you need to take love where you find it, and that a couple of us are trying to preserve our species using modern science. Were you at the clinic when it was bombed?" she asked, suddenly worried about Flare's future offspring.

Flare nodded. "I'd just finished having some tests when the little bitty boom went off. Now I'm going to wait for an all-clear to sound before I can get knocked up.

"I wanted to stay at the clinic and help, but here I am. After all, it wasn't much of a bomb."

"It was enough to get the mortals' attention," a deep male voice said from the doorway.

"That was the point, I suppose," Flare added as they all turned to the Shagal Elder, Barak. "Now I'm stuck here for the duration."

"For your own safety, Lady Francesca," Barak said patiently, ignoring her ungracious attitude. "Welcome, Lady Sidonie, young werewolf," he added with a nod to her and Joe.

Sid couldn't help but smile appreciatively. The tall, dark-skinned Prime had a beautiful deep voice, and the gray in his black hair only added to his charm. He and Matri Serisa had been bonded for at least a hundred years. *Lucky woman,* Sid thought.

She introduced Joe, who said, "It's an honor to meet you, sir."

After the introductions, Barak went on. "I am told you are the finest telepath of your Clan, Lady Sidonie."

Sid couldn't look at Joe, knowing this reminded him of her betrayal. "Thank you," she managed.

"We could use your help dealing with too much mortal attention," Barak went on. "It seems that today's attacks were deliberately staged to reveal our existence, and now we're fighting to stay in hiding. We'd appreciate your adding your telepathic skills to rearrange mortal perceptions."

"I can help with that," Flare said.

Barak looked her over gravely. "That would not be wise, Lady Francesca. Your Matri would not wish it."

Flare flounced back to her chair, picked up her reader, and pretended they weren't there.

Though Sid was on a missing person case, she could continue that hunt while rearranging mortal minds. She'd been settling into a telepathic hunt when Kiril interrupted her, and there might be mortal perps involved in today's crime scenes. Those perps might lead them to Rose Cameron.

"I'd be happy to help," she told Barak. "Excuse me a moment," she added, and took Joe aside. "What'll you be up to while I'm messing with minds?" she asked her partner.

I'll finish the recon of the Citadel first," he said. "Then I'll go back to the remains of the nursing home and sniff around."

"Think you'll find anything?"

"No. But lack of evidence might also tell us something."

She didn't know what he meant but trusted his instincts. "Good hunting."

She resisted the impulse to give him a quick kiss.

Chapter Thirty-three

Joe certainly couldn't fault the vampires' security setup. Everything—cameras, motion detectors, alarm systems, panic room—was state of the art. And there were plenty of Prime guards on the grounds and in the house, unobtrusive but on full alert. No one was going to cause trouble at the Shagal Citadel. The bad guys had known not to bother trying, at least not until they were able to drain more defenders away from the place. Joe still noted every detail of the inside setup and automatically filed it away.

But as hard as he tried, he couldn't keep his mind completely on business.

Damn it, Sid, what is going on? With you? With me? Us?

With Charles?

He'd found out from Sid and Flare's conversation that Charles had been conceived by artificial means. That didn't sound like vampires. Vampires were the randiest creatures on the planet. Locker room talk had it that the females were even more sexually active than the Primes. Back in the day, didn't the females used to keep whole harems of satisfied Primes? It would be easier to understand if Sid's baby was the result of an orgy. Vampires were supposed to do that sort of thing. It was normal, healthy activity for their species.

What was Sid up to? What did she want?

Did it have anything to do with him?

Why would it?

What was he missing? And why did he care?

The confusion and questions clawed at him. It took an effort to keep his thoughts and emotions shielded. He didn't want to add to the psychic static the vampire telepaths were already working through. And he sure as hell didn't want to draw Sid's finely honed telepathic attention to his questions. To his—all right to his anguish. The melodrama was embarrassing, but his pain was real.

Damn the woman, anyway.

Not a woman. A vampire female. Too high above me or anybody bloody else to—

"But you said . . ." Joe stopped and closed his eyes.

Five Years Ago

"I love you, but I can't recall anyone ever kissing my knee before. It tickles," Sid said.

"I love this knee," he said between kisses. "I could write poetry to this knee."

" 'An Ode to a Joint'?" She laughed. "Sounds like drug humor."

Joe looked up the length of Sid's naked body and fully appreciated the way her bare breasts moved with her laughter. " 'A Poem to a Patella' " he said. "And a sonnet to your thighs," he added as he moved farther up the inside of her legs.

Her laughter turned into a breathy, needy whimper. She raised her hips; fingers tangled in his hair. "Joseph, if you stop short of where I want you to go, I'll die."

"I won't allow that," he told her. Their gazes met on his promise. "I'll never allow that."

"And I'll do the same for you."

The whole universe became suddenly . . . quiet.

Heavy. Waiting. He knew with his whole being that this moment was important. There was no one but them, and being together meant everything.

"I love you," he said.

"I love you," she answered.

The universe began to spin again, and it was filled with brightness and joy. She smiled and held her arms out to him. Her smile was everything. Holding her was everything. Making love with her was more than everything.

"Be with me forever," he said.

But Sid didn't answer.

Present Day

Joe ran a hand over his head and absently noted that he'd spent enough time in wolf form for the buzz cut to have grown out, a residual effect of the transformation. It was hard for a werewolf to wear short hair. Their natural tendency was toward long, heavy locks, the sort females liked to run their fingers through.

Sid certainly liked playing with his hair.

He smiled bitterly. Maybe that was the reason she'd spent a long weekend using him as her boy toy. Maybe Primes were too neat and tidy for her taste.

What are you doing, standing here feeling sorry for yourself, Bleythin? Your community is under attack, and there's a fragile mortal who's missing. Get on with the hunt!

The hunt for Rose Cameron would take all his attention. The hunt would keep him sane.

Besides, he'd told his partner he was returning to the burned out building and when it came to business, they trusted each other to do what they said.

Chapter Thirty-four

December 18, 1944, 7:00 PM
Ardennes Forest, Belgium

The reek of congealing blood bothered Tony more than the sight of the two bodies he'd pulled out of the foxhole. The GIs had gone to their maker. He'd make sure at least two of the enemy died to avenge them, but there was nothing he could do for the corpses. What the smell of their blood was doing to him, on the other hand, was—

"Are you going to be sick?" Rose asked.

He was, but not in any way he could explain. What he did was move closer to her and breathe in the sweet awareness of her life. Her heartbeat, her blood flowed, her thoughts were bright points of light. He reveled in her warmth when her hand unexpectedly touched his cheek.

"Because if you're going to be sick," Rose went on, "I'll join you. Not that I think of vomiting as a communal sort of activity . . . but in wartime . . ."

"It's not really possible to lighten the mood in the middle of a battlefield." He put his hand over hers. "But thanks for trying."

"I'm with the USO. It's my duty to improve morale," she reminded him.

"Your very existence improves my morale." He helped her into the shallow protection of the foxhole before kneeling up to peer around the dark woods. It was snowing again. "It's quiet."

"Too quiet?" she whispered. When he gave her a sardonic look, she added, "You're a scout. You need to find out about enemy troop movements, don't you?"

His conscience pained him, torn between his assignment and Rose's safety. "I—"

"Go do your job," she ordered. "I'll wait here. I'll be fine."

"All right," he said after a moment. "Don't you dare go anywhere."

* * *

December 18, 1:00 PM
Present Day
Los Angeles, CA

Of course, Rose hadn't been where he'd left her when he returned back then, either, Tony recalled.

"Can't you ever stay put?" he complained to his missing love as he parked several blocks up the street from the burned-out ruin of Rose's last known whereabouts. The place he had thought so safe for her was now a smoking ruin. His only comfort was in knowing that she hadn't been there when the place was destroyed.

And the other residents? his mortal-protecting conscience questioned. That was one of the things he was here to check.

The acrid scent of smoke lingered in the air, heavy enough to make Tony's throat ache. He approached carefully, moving with the silent speed that to mortal eyes seemed like a passing cloud's shadow or a moment's dizziness.

Stealth was required, as the place was far from deserted. Forensic techs and arson investigators moved through the soaked, charred ruins and smashed garden. He knew from experience that firemen intent on putting out blazes necessarily ran roughshod over any potential crime scene evidence. This always frustrated him when he was a police detective, but it wasn't his problem this time. It was supernatural evidence he needed now. To find it, he went searching for a large black wolf.

"Well?" he asked Joe when he came across the werewolf, who had his nose to the ground at the back wall of the property.

The wolf rounded on him with a snarl, then blinked very unwolflike blue eyes in recognition. Joe moved behind an undamaged hibiscus bush and morphed into his human shape.

"Why do vampires always have to make an entrance?" he asked when Tony joined him.

Tony rubbed the back of his neck. "Personally, I blame Bram Stoker. Well?" he repeated.

"I need to talk to Tobias," Joe answered.

Tony quivered with leashed fury. "You're working for *me* today."

"Your situation is only part of the problem."

It took far more effort than normal not to rip the youngster to shreds. If Joe hadn't been the love of his daughter's life, he might have killed him then and there. Then again, disposing of Joe might be the best thing he could do for her . . .

Tony moved closer to the werewolf.

He saw that Joe recognized the danger, but

he didn't back down. He locked gazes with Tony and they looked at each other steadily until Tony calmed down.

Eventually, Tony nodded. "What can you tell me?"

Joe gestured toward the ruins. "There weren't any mortals in there and hadn't been for at least four hours before the fire was set. There are dozens of mortal scent trails leading away from the place. I need to plot out a map and check them all out."

"Only mortal scent trails?"

Joe shrugged. "Werefolk can cover their scent tracks these days. And you know how vampire telepathy makes it hard for us to track you."

Tony nodded. "Anything else?"

"Roses," Joe answered. "An overpowering scent of roses."

The image summoned by those words twisted Tony's heart and his gut. Color and scent and memory overwhelmed him.

"That's my doing," he croaked through the constricting pain in his throat. "I send dozens of them to her every year. I called her my 'Rose in winter,' and—"

He turned away for a moment, overcome by the worry and fear that choked him.

"Don't blame yourself," Joe said.

Tony turned back to the youngster. "I most certainly do *not* blame myself. Not for all the years we should have been together, or for her disappearance. I do blame myself for leaving her alone. I shouldn't have done that."

"Her kidnapping wasn't something you could have seen coming." Joe gestured at the charred rubble. "You couldn't have expected that."

"I will kill the bastard that's responsible, whether Rose is harmed or not." And Anthony Crowe always kept his vows.

"Good for you. But the roses—"

"The roses I'd sent her were gone yesterday. Her room was completely empty."

His pain eased at Joe's sudden grin. "Maybe they took the roses with her. I can follow the roses."

Tony was eager to let him. But duty called. "Will the scent last for a few more hours?"

"Certainly, but—"

"You're wanted back at the Citadel. Put on some fur and let's go."

Chapter Thirty-five

Tony sat with every appearance of patience behind the wheel while Joe finished putting on the jeans and shirt he'd found folded on the passenger seat. Joe was amazed at what a fine actor the Prime was, because he could sense that Tony was not nearly as calm and collected as he appeared. Oh, Tony's psychic senses were well shielded, but being this close, the werewolf was very aware of chemical signs of agitation that were impossible for anyone to mask. Except—

There was this wonderful perfume Sid always wore . . .

Joe bit back a curse, and forced his thoughts away from Sidonie Wolf.

"Am I in trouble with the powers that be?" Joe asked.

"The powers that be wouldn't tell me if you were."

Joe knew very well that Tony Crowe was a trusted senior Prime of this territory, even if he wasn't officially a member of the Shagal Clan. Joe guessed the reason that Tony didn't live among his own Corvus Clan had something to do with Rose Cameron.

Joe had always thought he knew about vampires, but he guessed you had to be whelped and raised in a culture to completely understand it. It was clear that Tony had secrets, and issues with his own kind. As did Sidonie—who he was trying not to think about.

"Why did Sid have Charles the way she did?" he asked.

This got him a blistering look from Sidonie's sire. "And where has my daughter's best friend been the last three years?" he questioned in turn.

Joe worked hard to hold on to his temper. "You do know that she screwed me over, don't you?"

"I do."

"Do you know why?"

"Not my story to tell, even if I do."

This reminded Joe of how Sid kept her sire's

secrets. Joe admired both vampires for their loyalty to each other, but . . .

"She's no angel, that daughter of yours."

Tony gave an ironic smile. "I should say not."

Joe hated that he agreed with Tony's jovial tone. Then again, why not accept Sidonie for who she was, even if he didn't completely know her?

Unable to let his curiosity go, Joe tried for politeness this time. "Can I ask another question about Sid and Charles?"

"No."

"What's a Severing ceremony?" he asked anyway.

Tony gave him a sharp look. "How do you know about that?"

"Sid's reacting strangely whenever her son is mentioned, and I'm beginning to suspect I know why."

"You don't need to know. It's not important."

Joe took a long, deep breath. "The change in your scent says it is. Give me a break and let her partner in on this," he appealed to the retired cop. "She isn't at a hundred percent, and I think I need to know why."

"I don't see why you need to know secret vampire stuff."

"If I'm kept in the dark, I might say something

ignorant at the wrong time that could jeopardize Sid, me, and our client."

"Your client being my Rose?"

"Precisely."

Tony frowned as he drove in silence for a few minutes. Joe waited, so anxious to discover what was wrong with Sid that he ached. He shouldn't be aching with worry for her, but . . .

"There was a time when our females never left the safety of the Clan citadels. They kept harems, but they lived in purdah," Tony eventually said.

Joe knew some of the history of vampire feminism from Sid, but he kept quiet, wanting to find out what Tony was building up to.

"We thought we were keeping them safe, but when vampire hunters made a concentrated effort to attack the citadels, we almost lost our females. No females, no vampires. The females decided that they were in just as much danger whether they lived in seclusion or not, and they've gradually been coming out into the world. This is all very well and good for them on a personal level, but there is the slight problem of maternal instinct that needs to be addressed if they are going to have their freedom." Tony glanced at Joe. "Are you following this, wereboy?"

Joe shook his head. "We raise our young in the pack. It takes a pack to raise a cub."

It was an old but true saying. Even with the camaraderie of the DA, Joe deeply missed contact with his own people. And whose fault was that? Could he really blame Sid for his choices?

"I wish vampires could do it that way. Maybe we did once upon a time, when we lived in the mythical hidden cities and didn't spend so much of our time among mortals. Since we don't live in the past, we have to adjust to survive. Our females wanted—and needed—more freedom," he added reluctantly. "But one of the costs of this freedom was having to tone down the strongest maternal instinct of any species on the planet. Our female children don't give us any problems until they reach puberty. Much like teenage girls everywhere," he added with a chuckle. "But around two, our little boys quite literally turn into animals and need constant supervision."

"I know about the crèches . . . but . . . I take it they aren't exclusive private schools for young Primes, as we're led to believe?"

Tony snorted. "The crèches are where we protect, civilize, and educate our boys. To save our species we have to channel the boys' aggression, but our females don't take well to being separated from their babies."

"So you have a Severing ceremony when the kids are old enough to be separated from their mothers?"

"Precisely."

Tony seemed to think this was explanation enough, and silence ensued for a few minutes.

"And?" Joe finally prodded.

"And . . ." He sighed "We telepathically mess with the mamas' heads so that they don't go completely insane when their babies are taken away. It's for the best."

Joe noted that Tony didn't seem completely convinced of that, and he was dumbfounded himself. Werewolf parents would *never* be separated from their babies.

"Vampire females voluntarily allow their memories to be subverted?" he questioned.

"Of course not!" Tony answered. "They're the best mothers in the world, the most fiercely protective. They instinctively cannot be separated from their children. The Severing was a compromise the Matri Council came up with to bring their daughters into the nineteenth century, and it still works for the Clans. Without the Severing our females would have to return to living in purdah, but it's better to live in the modern world. So, we block the pain."

"It's barbaric!"

Tony seemed almost amused by Joe's outrage. "We're vampires."

"Have you heard of the concept of free will?"

Tony nodded. "I have. And it's all very well for mortals, but we don't always have the luxury of doing exactly as we please. Survival of the species has to take precedence over individual rights sometimes. As it is, Sidonie will be separated from her son for a few years, but the killing pain of the separation will be blunted. It was done for her own good, and you will keep your mouth shut about it. Won't you?"

The question was asked in such an unmistakably dangerous tone that Joe had no doubt his life was being threatened.

Joe wouldn't let himself be intimidated, but he now had too much to think about to push it any further. "I'll keep it to myself."

At least for now.

Chapter Thirty-six

The blue-eyed black wolf ran through her thoughts, but there was nothing unusual in that. Even with years of practice, it wasn't easy for Sid to block the awareness of Joe. It didn't help that he was nearby. Or that his thoughts kept turning to her. Or that they'd been together and made love—

Had sex.

Call it what she would, the visceral memory of their bodies moving together got in the way of her mental control. Joe pressed against her consciousness, made it hard to send her thoughts anywhere but toward him.

I was able to do this last night, Sid reminded

herself. *What did I do to—oh, yes, I was too worried about Rose to dwell on my own stupid problems. Rose it is, then.*

Rose? Where are you? You don't know me, but I am a friend. Tony told me that you are telepathic, that you could at least communicate with him. You can talk to me. I'm a friend. I'm his friend. Don't be frightened.

An analytical part of Sid's awareness separated from the psychic search. Of course Rose was afraid—or had she just sensed fear?

Do you know where you are, Rose? Show me what you see.

Sid cleared her mind of every thought, every image. She floated in darkness, alone. After a while there was no floating, no self. Only darkness.

Pink.

A thin pink ribbon swirled in the blackness. Sid stretched out to meet the color.

Yellow wound around the pink. Small explosions of white and scarlet lit the blackness. Crystal carved, cold as ice. Green.

Everything settled onto a painless bed of green.

"I hate to disturb you."

Weight returned. Heartbeat. Breathing. Sid opened her eyes to blotches of white, black, and emerald green. After a moment, she recognized that the blotches made up a pattern. That the pattern was a face. The green spots were eyes. The eyes looked worriedly into hers.

"Flare Reynard."

"You don't sound very sure of that," Flare said. Her bright laughter was as sharp as the crystal. She touched a fingertip to Sid's cheek. "Cold as ice. How deep in were you?"

It took a while for these words to sink in, longer for them to make sense. "How deep? Into someone else's head." She took a shaky breath. "I'm not sure where I was or what was going on. I sensed colors, and maybe . . ." Sid shook her head. "Whatever I was picking up was totally useless."

She became aware that she was seated in a brocade-upholstered chair in one of the Shagal Citadel's guest bedrooms.

Sid looked blankly at Flare. "How long have I been out?"

"You said you wanted to meditate before trying to reach out and touch any witnesses," Flare said to fill her in. "That was four hours ago."

All that time and psychic energy expended with so little to show for it? Sid was disgusted. So much for being the best telepath of her Clan. She could only hope that she'd picked up some details that she wasn't consciously aware of. She knew better than to try to force anything to the surface.

Something to do with Rose would pop up, or it wouldn't.

It finally occurred to her to wonder why Flare had interrupted her. "This isn't a social call, is it?"

"Oh, no," Flare answered with a sly smile. There was a glint of excitement in her emerald eyes. "There's finally a bit of excitement going on around here."

Sid wondered at Flare's definition of excitement. "Something more exciting than every supernatural enclave in town being attacked?"

"All right, let's say something I find more interesting is going on."

Flare went to a small table across the room and came back to Sid with a small cup cradled in her palms. Sid sat up straight, catching the warm scent as Flare approached.

Flare made a formal bow as she handed Sid the cup. "With Lady Serisa's compliments."

Sid stood to accept the gift. The lotus-shaped cup was of alabaster, so finely carved it was translucent. It held no more than a thimbleful of fresh mortal blood. Sid held it cupped in her hands as Flare had done, absorbing the warmth through her palms. She breathed in the aroma, savored the rich scarlet color. Her heart raced and the tang of anticipation filled her mouth and throat.

"Matri Serisa does me great honor." The words were ritual but completely heartfelt. She lifted the cup to her lips.

One drop on her tongue sent all her senses into overdrive. Sid had to sit down quickly, careful not to spill any of the precious liquid.

"Forgot the rush, didn't you?" Flare asked.

Sid looked up at her friend over the edge of the cup. "It has been a long time." She took another drop on her tongue.

The world was a sharper, more vivid place, and she was the most alive thing in it.

"Stop looking so orgasmic, girl—you're making me jealous."

"That's not orgasmic, that's just invigorated. I hadn't realized how tired I was."

Flare nodded. "Sometimes we forget that this is our natural nourishment."

Sid took a deeper sip. She could taste the ancient mixture of herbs blended into the blood that helped keep the substance from becoming a consuming addiction. She didn't know who had discovered the herbal recipe thousands of years before, but the mixture had been the vampires' first step toward civilization. It had been the first step toward living with mortals as kindred, instead of using other sentient beings as cattle. These days, almost any properly processed mammalian blood could be used for sustenance. The blood of mortals was taken as an erotic sharing with willing mortal lovers. Or, like now, a ritual tasting offered from an anonymous volunteer.

But Sid was long past the point where she could appreciate more than a few bracing sips of mortal blood.

She handed the still-warm cup back to Flare. "With my compliments."

Flare's perfect brows arched in surprise. "Are you sure you don't want this?"

"I prefer werewolf." Sid clapped a hand over her mouth, but the words were already out. The blood must have made her drunk to loosen her tongue so easily. "Oh, crap!"

Flare's eyes sparkled with interest. "I'm in love with a mortal, and you're involved with a werewolf? I think you and I have a lot of catching up to do." She tossed down the rest of the blood. "But right now, we're wanted at the meeting."

Sid was so grateful for the distraction that she followed Flare without asking any questions. A crowd of vampires, werefolk, and mortals filled the huge central room. Hostility was thick in the air, most of it aimed at the big Prime standing boldly in the center of the meeting space. Tobias

Strahan was the sort who naturally drew attention to himself, but Sid's gaze went instantly to the werewolf standing beside Tobias.

The sight of him made her heart ache and sing, but she never got tired of looking at her Joe.

Chapter Thirty-seven

December 1944
Belgium

"When was the last time you slept?" Rose asked Anthony.

He ran a hand over his unshaven face. "I don't need a lot of sleep."

"You look terrible."

Artillery fire interrupted their conversation and they flattened themselves at the bottom of the foxhole. The trees behind them and the snow piled up in front would be inadequate protection if firing was turned their way. Somehow, though, Rose felt safe with Anthony's arms around her. He was the only warm thing in this frigid hell. The darkness was lit with explosions; the noise was deafening.

"It makes me want to scream," Rose whispered in Anthony's ear.

"Nah, you're not the panicking type," he whispered back.

Or were *they whispering? When she spoke like this, she wasn't aware of her lips moving.*

"If we get out of this I intend to have a good, long panic."

"We're close to the crossroads town I told you about. Once we get there, you'll be safe."

He rose on his knees to take a look around.

"Crossroads town?" she asked when he ducked back down.

"Bastogne," he reminded her, and helped her to her feet.

Present Day

Well, wasn't that just jumping from the frying pan into the fire? An hour after we got to Bastogne, the town was surrounded by the Germans.

Wait—aren't I supposed to be dead? Then why am I dreaming? And thinking?

"She looks so peaceful."

"I've always thought she was lovely."

And hearing.

Two voices, one familiar. Her Russian nurse, Gregor, had just said she was lovely. Rose had no idea who'd said she looked peaceful. Her undertaker? No. She wasn't dead. She couldn't move, but she was aware that she was breathing, and not in any ragged, soon-to-be-her-last-breath way, either. Damn.

Rose remembered getting up to get the stash of pills, but after that—

"Once I let one of my females take my blood. It was much more fun than this."

Rose wondered what Gregor meant by that.

"Are you planning on draining me dry?" he demanded.

The edge in his voice frightened her, but the other man responded coolly, "You told me to take as much as I needed. Since you insist on leaving, I'm taking as much as I safely can. We have a bargain, if you recall."

"We've donated to you for years."

"Ours has been a symbiotic relationship with a parasitic life form. Your blood in exchange for our perfecting the Dawn drug for you has been a far more enlightened policy than our ancestors' attempts at killing one another."

"You've been behaving in a civilized manner because you discovered that we're easier to capture than we are to keep."

"That was an unfortunate scenario. It almost ruined the whole project."

"It almost destroyed everything," Gregor said. "Now my sponsors think you've experimented enough. They see the current results as the success they promised you."

"Your sponsors are wrong. The experiment is still at a very delicate stage."

"I agree. Which is why I am going to explain this to them in person."

The other man chuckled. "Heads will literally roll, I trust?"

"That would be pleasant," Gregor answered.

"How long will this take?" The other man seemed worried. "Your presence will be required if the results prove unstable."

"You don't need *me* specifically," Gregor countered. "I am making arrangements for a replacement."

"Ah, good. There. I'm finished. Would you care for a drink?"

There was something unpleasant about the question, and Gregor's answering laugh made Rose's skin crawl. It made her want to cover her ears and run away.

But she wasn't sure she even had ears. She certainly couldn't run. She was floating in a gray limbo, disembodied—frightened.

Where was Anthony? She'd gotten used to living her life alone, but she couldn't stand it anymore. Where was he when she needed him?

The same place he always was—in her dreams. All she could do was pray for the dreams to rise up out of the darkness and rescue her.

All she got was the darkness.

Chapter Thirty-eight

Music brought Rose up out of the darkness. Not music playing on a radio somewhere, though. It took a while for her to realize that the song was playing in her head. One she didn't know but must have heard somewhere. It was about bitterness and forgiveness and taking responsibility in a relationship and—it was by that Irish band, wasn't it?

Or maybe it was about religion, because the line about raising the dead kept repeating over and over, and her annoyance with it finally brought her fully awake.

Rose was afraid to open her eyes. She'd thought she'd stopped being afraid of anything a long time ago, but she knew that there was something so wrong that she couldn't bear to face it.

Coward.

She thought for a moment that the voice in her head might be Anthony's, but when the moment passed, she was all too aware that she was completely alone and talking to herself.

Coward.

And what's wrong with being a coward occasionally?

It would seem that coherent thought had returned. Rose sighed, becoming aware of her breathing and that there was something different about it. What was it?

She concentrated on the simple action of air entering and exiting her lungs. It happened far too easily. The contours of her body against the mattress felt different as well. The constant numb coldness was also absent from her hands and feet. Her body felt solid and real, but—wrong.

The wrongness frightened her, and the fear permeated her, body, mind, and soul.

Are you going to let a little thing like utter terror get you down?

Rose took a deep breath, a far deeper breath than she'd managed in years, and resolutely opened her eyes.

She saw—her room? She hadn't expected that.

And she was still surrounded by roses. She had been breathing in their scent, and maybe that was what had kept her from total, screaming panic. Was being scared spitless better than total panic? She wished that Anthony was present for her to consult on the subject.

She frowned at her own neediness.

Maybe it would have been better if he hadn't come back into her life if it meant she was going to go all soft and girlish after a lifetime of taking care of herself.

And was it possible to be girlish with varicose veins, osteoporosis, and all the other indignities life visited upon one?

It was possible to be foolish at any age, Rose decided, but all pretension to girlishness had gone long ago.

"And good riddance."

Stop stalling. There's something wrong. Find out what.

Why? She demanded of that practical, curious, braver side of herself. *Maybe I'll just ring for an aide to bring me a cup of tea.*

That will only be pretending that nothing is wrong. It'll only forestall the inevitable. Why bother?

All right. Fine.

Rose sat up, then stared straight ahead and

tried to figure out why sitting up was such a strange experience.

There were pictures on the wall opposite her: a small van Gogh that was *not* a reproduction, and three framed photographs of people dear to her. She could see each picture quite clearly. And wasn't the wall a brighter shade of beige than yesterday, with more pink in the creamy tone than she had ever noticed before?

What on earth was the matter with her eyes?

Not a thing.

She knew that was the answer, but it didn't make any sense. And the reason that sitting up had felt wrong was because she hadn't felt anything.

"No—"

She clapped a hand over her mouth, afraid that saying it would make it true. Or only prove that she was insane. Maybe she was crazy. Or maybe she was dead. Either state would make more sense than what she was feeling. Which was nothing.

"No pain. There is no pain."

Even after she made herself speak this blatant falsehood aloud it remained true. And she could see better because—her vision was clear. Cataract surgery a few years ago hadn't been able to completely restore her age-dimmed sight, but the clarity was there now.

She knew what was wrong: she felt great! She felt—no, she wasn't going to think the word.

Rose looked at her hands. She recognized them all right, but as a distant memory, not the thin, age-spotted claws Anthony had held so tenderly on his visit. She threw back the covers and slid her legs over the side of the bed. With no difficulty.

"Betty Grable, eat your heart out," Rose murmured when she got a look at her gams.

Though she supposed Uma Thurman would be the closest comparison among modern actresses. If that young woman were a tall, skinny, freckled redhead who happened to have the right bone structure to be loved by the camera.

She stood. She meant to do it slowly, and carefully, but it was easier to spring out of the bed. Instinct seemed to have taken over from the awareness that quick movement could break fragile bones. She flexed her bare toes, reveling in the sensual feel of the thick pile of the Persian rug beneath her feet. How was it that everything felt so wonderful, so new?

Rose tentatively ran her hands up and down the length of her body, then looked down the neck of her nightgown.

"Good Lord almighty."

There was a full-length mirror on the closet

door. It was the hardest thing Rose had ever done to turn around and look at herself. Even harder than walking away from Anthony. But . . .

The young woman in the mirror looked just like that young woman in Paris in 1944.

"That is the most ridiculous thing I have ever seen." Although she was in deep shock, her voice was calm. And it was a young woman's voice.

"You are beautiful."

She turned to face Gregor, who was standing in the doorway. "I am an abomination," she told him. "And *you* are a vampire."

Chapter Thirty-nine

"You're very observant, Rose."

"Then why haven't I noticed before?"

"You've noticed several times in the last year," he said as he shut the door behind him. "Before today, I've always had to make you forget."

For a moment Rose's reaction was relief that she hadn't gone completely senile, then anger exploded through her. "You've been messing with my mind?"

"Among other things."

It was the sort of smug answer a stupid question like that deserved, and Rose calmed down. She was still shaking with shock and fear, but now she was determined not to let any emotion get the better of her.

"You might want to sit down," Gregor suggested. "You look like you're about to fall."

Rose sneered. "Ever the helpful nurse, aren't you?"

He tsked. "You were such a sweet little old lady." Gregor picked her up by the waist and deposited her in the nearest chair, then took a seat on the bed. After he glanced at his watch he said, "I have some time to kill and you're dying of curiosity. Ask me anything you like."

"What happened to your Russian accent?"

"It's still there," he answered, "but I practice speaking American when I have to deal with the outside world. Which I must leave to do in a few minutes, so let us have a meaningful conversation in the time we have left, dear Rose."

That he called her *dear* grated, but she let it go. "What's a Tribe vampire doing out in the daylight?"

Gregor smiled affectionately. "You noticed that I am sitting in the patch of sunlight from your window. Of course, if you look outside you will notice that your view has changed significantly. We kept the room the same to help you remain calm while still in the test environment."

"Anything to keep the lab rat happy?"

"Precisely."

"Tribe bastard."

"And you infer that I am Tribe because—"

"No Clan or Family Prime would kidnap someone and do this to them!"

He laughed. "Do what? Make a dying crone young and beautiful again? How is that a crime? But you guess correctly; I am Tribe." He leaned forward and touched the tip of her nose. Rose managed not to flinch, but just barely. "Your Anthony told you far too much about vampires."

"Knowledge I was perfectly willing to take to my grave."

"Oh, you still will." His tone was cheerful, but the look in his green eyes was chilling.

"You were such a sweet nurse," she said. "I don't suppose you actually are a nurse, are you?"

"Tribe Primes do not pursue humanitarian careers. I did not participate in this rejuvenation experiment out of the goodness of my heart." He looked her over in a thorough, intimate way that made Rose blush. "Mortals are commodities. Some make good pets for a time, some prove inconvenient, but all are disposable animals." He smiled, showing quite a bit of fang, and she didn't recognize him at all. He added, "And you are all delicious."

She flexed her young fingers, rubbed the firm flesh of her arms, touched the soft red curls framing her flawless face. "If mortals are disposable animals, why perform an experiment to make a mortal more like a vampire? What do you get out of it?"

His smile this time was one of genuine delight. "Those are excellent questions. Thank you, Rose Cameron, for realizing that what we have done to you was for the good of the Tribes. The average mortal thinks the universe revolves around their own species." He sneered. "The mortal scientists we've worked with on this project are totally fixated on the goal of extending the lives of their own kind."

"So intent that they don't realize that they've made a devil's bargain with you?" she guessed.

"So intent that they don't care," he corrected. "Shall I tell you the whole story? Shall I shatter the beautiful illusions your Anthony fed you about his oh-so-noble Clans?"

Now that she knew how Anthony's own Matri had been the one to keep them apart, Rose doubted she would be disillusioned by any Tribe Prime's opinion of the vampire good guys.

"Tell me anything you'd like," she said. "I've got plenty of time. Apparently."

"The Clans are mad," he said. "The Families aren't much saner. Both deny their own natures. They are like wolves who've been bred into sheepdogs—a sick parody of what they should be, guarding their natural prey. Mating with their natural prey—"

"Don't tell me that the Tribes don't like mortal girls," she interrupted.

"Of course we do. But we would never breed with our female slaves. Clan Primes take mortal women as permanent mates and treat their offspring as beloved children. What they've created are half-breed mortal monsters and enemies within their midst."

"Why enemies?"

"These *children* of the Clans can never be like their sires. They are mules. They are mortal. They serve their Clan without truly being part of it. In the last century the mules' resentment has taken shape, festered, grown. The Tribes have helped stir the creatures toward rebellion."

"Tribes plural?" Rose questioned. "My understanding is that the Tribes fight with one another instead of cooperating."

"Times change: We have a loosely allied consortium these days. The Clans are the real enemy. The Families are not our friends. Once these other vampires are dealt with, I'm sure we'll fight among ourselves until one Tribe rules all the others. Until then, we are all the best of friends."

"But the Clans don't know this?"

"The Clans spend too much time protecting

mortals to watch their own backs. They are too noble to suspect traitors within their own ranks. Which brings us back to how you and I have come to this conversation. You see, many of the Clans' mortal offspring have made careers as scientists, working for the benefit of the Clans."

"They developed the drugs vampires use to live in the daylight," Rose guessed.

He nodded. "Those drugs help the sires of the mortal mules, but what's in it for them?"

"I suspect they're paid rather exorbitant salaries."

"What good is money when they're denied the longevity of their sires and bonded mortal mothers?"

"What's wrong with a normal mortal lifespan?" Rose countered.

"I wouldn't know; I don't have one. What I do know is that humans have always wanted immortality. I don't blame mortals for wanting to live as long as vampires. And I don't mind using their greed for longer life to help my Tribe acquire what we need."

"The daylight drugs," she said once again. "Anthony told me that if the drugs ever became useful, the Clans would do everything in their power to keep them out of the hands of the Tribes."

"They did become useful, and the Clans have

denied us access to them. They think we'd be more dangerous in the daylight."

"I'm sure they're right about that."

"Indeed they are. There is one way they'll allow a Tribe Prime access to their precious drugs—if we grovel and beg and humiliate ourselves by renouncing our history, our culture, and everything we believe in. If a Tribe Prime renounces his soul—"

"You have souls?"

"Deep souls," he responded. "Dark souls. Predator souls."

"Charming."

"Not at all." He gave her that dangerous smile again. "But I am comfortable with who I am, far more so than your Anthony will ever be."

"I don't think it's either your place or mine to discuss Anthony's soul. We can only speak for ourselves."

"You are quite correct. As females go, I have always found you interesting to talk to."

"You sound like some of the studio executives I used to deal with."

He looked offended at the comparison, and this almost amused her. But scoring points wasn't her goal, gathering information, was.

Rose returned to the subject. "So, the Tribes are working with the Clan traitors—"

"Among others," he added. "There are rogue werefolk involved. There are mortals looking to profit from the medical research. There are even some of the more fanatical vampire hunters in our conspiracy. We are a consortium of very strange bedfellows. We each have our own goals, but we are in complete agreement about one thing: the Clans, the Families, and the werefolk Council stand in our way, and we are going to destroy them."

"That's a rather . . . *ambitious* goal." She wanted to say *crazy* but didn't want to lead the conversation off on another tangent.

"World domination is the actual goal, and that is truly ambitious. We are proceeding one step at a time. You are one of those steps. Or rather, the longevity project is."

"I'm the guinea pig, not the reason for what you did," she said, and he nodded. "Why'd you pick on me? How did you do it?"

And what price do I have to pay? She wondered, but she was damned if she was going to ask.

"The why is because you were old, you were unattached, and we knew that you had once shared blood with a Prime. We also believed that Tony would one day share blood with you again. An infusion of vampire blood was the necessary catalyst to activate the longevity drugs already in your system. It took him long enough to see you again. The night he finally showed up, I was getting ready to give you the infusion myself."

Infusion? Drugs *already* in her system? "How long has this been going on?"

"You have been receiving the treatment for over a year. The slow increase in the dosage has caused your body to change gradually until you were ripe for picking. There's been some discomfort," he added.

His ironic tone infuriated Rose. Now she understood the horrible, inescapable, growing pain that had driven her to the point of suicide. The pain had been caused by the drugs. It had been deliberate and evil.

"You've been torturing a little old lady!"

"Yes." He gestured toward the mirror. "But look at the results. Millions would kill for this treatment—hmmm, perhaps the promise of renewed youth would help recruit a mortal army. But for now, the plan is to reserve the process for a select few who can afford our price. Revolutions need financing."

Rose gaped at Gregor as he stood. He gently cupped her face in his hands and ran his thumbs across her cheeks and forehead. She flinched when he bent forward to brush his lips across hers.

"You are so lovely," he said, stepping away from her. "I hope it lasts."

Her mind reeled in horror. “Hope it l-lasts?”

Gregor walked to the door before turning to answer her. “One of the projected scenarios of the experiment is that the anti-aging effects can’t be sustained without regular infusions of Prime blood. Since my presence is required elsewhere, I really do hope the donor I’ve arranged for you arrives in time,” He shrugged. “If not—well, perhaps the scientists are wrong and you’ll survive for a while. You’ll be euthanized and dissected eventually anyway. Good-bye, my dear Rose. It has been a pleasure knowing you.”

Rose stared at the closed door for a long time after he was gone, his chilling words ringing in her mind.

Chapter Forty

December 18, 4:00 PM
Shagal Citadel
Los Angeles, CA

Sid wondered if every vampire in Los Angeles was in the meeting room. As she took a seat and looked around, it became apparent that there were also werefolk representatives present. She found it curious, and a bit ominous, that there were no mortals present. If this was a meeting of everyone under Clan Shagal protection, where was Dr. Casmerek? And there were at least two mortal women bonded to local Primes; where were they?

"Where are Domini and Mia?" she asked.

"They are not here," Matri Serisa answered.

The Matri's cool tone told Sid that her question was not welcome. She also noticed from the glowering expressions of Alec Reynard and Colin Foxe that they weren't happy about their bondmates' absence.

Alec was Flare's brother. "Shouldn't you be protecting your bondmate?" she asked him.

"I most certainly should be," the Reynard Prime answered. He was glaring angrily at Tobias Strahan.

There was a lot of hostility in the room, most of it aimed at Tobias. For his part, Tobias stood in the center of the Council room like a great granite sea cliff unconcerned at the storm about to wash over it.

Who invited him here, anyway? She overheard Colin Foxe's thought.

She wasn't the only one who heard it; Joe held up his hand. "That would be me."

Sid hid a smile at Joe's cheeky response and saw by the quick flick of his gaze that he noticed it.

"What right does a werewolf have inviting a Prime into our territory?" a Shagal Prime demanded.

"He has the same right as any of the supernatural folk to protect our kind," Shaggy Harker, the alpha werewolf, said.

Sid thought the Shagal Prime looked like he was about to have a heart attack. This vampire had obviously never thought that not one, but two of the werefolk would ever talk back to him.

"We're in trouble. Tobias has brought his Angels to help," Shaggy continued.

"Help we don't need and didn't ask for," said a Prime with a rich Irish accent.

Sid looked at him with a start of surprise, discovering that Kiril had been correct about there being a vampire movie star. Sid figured he must be a Family Prime, as no Clan Matri would ever let one of her people lead such a public life.

"Thank you for your opinion, Jarrett," Elder Barak said to the actor. Jarrett certainly wasn't his stage name.

Jarrett turned proudly to Barak. "I realize I am a guest in Shagal territory, Elder, but I feel it is my duty to defend the place I call home."

"We all do," Colin Foxe said. "The last thing we need right now is outside interference."

"Are you going to keep snarling like pups or let Tobias have his say?" Shaggy nodded respectfully toward Lady Serisa. "Matri?"

The Matri folded her hands in her lap as everyone's attention focused on her. She was seated on a bench in front of the fireplace; Barak stood at her side, and her daughter, Cassie, sat beside her. Barak and Cassie were respected advisers, but all the power radiated from the small woman between them.

She turned that authority on Tobias Strahan. “Did I extend an invitation to you and your rabble that I don’t recall? Why did you demand this meeting? And put restrictions on who could attend?”

So, Joe’s phone call hadn’t only brought his team leader to Los Angeles; Tobias had brought all of the Dark Angels. Now Sid understood why the locals were not happy.

“Thank you for agreeing to see me on such short notice, and for agreeing to my requests, Matri,” Tobias answered.

“Your sudden appearance didn’t really give me any choice, Tobias. We already have one emergency to deal with. My Primes do not have time for challenges and combat over etiquette issues at the moment.”

“I agree. It is because of the attacks that I’ve brought in the Dark Angels.”

Every other Prime in the room bristled. Fury, indignation, and hatred roiled through the psychically sensitive crowd.

Serisa held up a hand.

No one moved, and silence reigned. The riot subsided before it got the chance to begin.

“This is going to be boring if only dirty looks are thrown,” Flare whispered to Sid.

Sid fought hard not to giggle and exchanged

an amused look with Joe. She looked away instantly, grateful that the focus was on Tobias.

She couldn't risk anyone noticing how comfortably her emotions resonated with the werewolf's. But what could she do? Other than stay away from him? She'd tried that and would have to try again. Her being half alive was better than Joe being all dead.

Chapter Forty-one

Those two are bound for trouble, Tony thought as he noted Sid and Bleythin's quick exchange. He made a note to have a stern talk with both of them, but his worries about Rose were paramount in his mind.

"Get on with it," he growled at the outsider whose appearance had just made things more complicated.

Tobias turned from the Matri to face him. "I've come to help." The sympathy in his eyes made Tony wonder just how much of his situation the other Prime knew. "I know that my belief that there is a war brewing among immortals isn't popular with everyone," he said, addressing his words to Matri Serisa once more. "But we found evidence that vampires and werefolk set the recent fires near San Diego. It was no coincidence that there have been fires set as part of the attacks on our kind here. The same people are involved. In San Diego, the intent was to cover their activities. In Los Angeles, the intent was to draw mortal attention to the immortals living among them. This was a different type of diversion, one meant to focus the vampire and werefolks' attention inward while they once more moved their base of operations."

Tony nodded in agreement. *He* was certainly diverted. Why had they picked on Rose? What did they want with her? Where had they taken her?

"Who are they?" he asked.

Kiril Wolf spoke up. "Purists. I'm sorry to contradict you, Prime Tobias, but your explanations are far too complicated. If there is a conspiracy, it is one organized by the fanatical branch of the vampire hunters."

The faintest of smiles played briefly across Tobias's features. "That's what they want you to think." He glanced toward Sid. "Lady Sidonie, what is your opinion of the evidence found at the wildfires?"

Nice move, Tony thought. The word of a

female always carried extra weight with Clan Primes. He saw by the amused lift of Sid's eyebrow, before she stood to address the room, that she was well aware of Tobias's maneuver.

"I think that there are still Tribe vampires involved in manufacturing knock-off versions of daylight drugs, and that they set the San Diego fires when they moved on. I think these same Tribe members have something to do with the nursing home fire and a missing mortal woman. I think that the nursing home was being used by bad guys, and it was time for them to move on again—so, another diversion. I think that Tobias Strahan is on to something, but I don't know what. I will speculate that the Purists are unknowingly being used by Tribe Primes to attack us. From the amount of media coverage, I'd say the attack was successful." She nodded toward Tobias and sat down.

"Media coverage," Tobias repeated. He looked around the room, catching one gaze after another. "Is that what you want?"

"We're working on covering our tracks," Shaggy Harker replied.

"How well can you hide your true existence when you're spending your time hunting Purists?" Tobias asked. "When you're guarding your homes and females instead of living your lives?"

"Werefolk females take care of themselves," Shaggy reminded the Prime.

"We could, too, if you'd let us," Flare added. And was ignored.

Tobias went on. "How can you hide in plain sight when each and every one of you deserts his daily life to protect our secret world? Don't you think mortals will notice? Don't you think that the Purists will turn media attention on your conspicuous absence?"

He pointed at Kiril. "Don't you have fires to fight?" At Alec Reynard. "You're a bodyguard: who's protecting your mortal clients right now?" At Colin Foxe. "Can you just walk away from SWAT team duty?" At Jarrett Baird. "Aren't you supposed to be on a movie set right now?" He addressed each Prime in turn, reminding them of the prominent roles they played in the outside world.

"You don't live in the dark anymore," he concluded. "But my team and I do. Let the Dark Angels deal with this matter." He gave Serisa a formal bow. "Give me permission to hunt freely in your territory, Matri."

"Great idea," Tony said before Serisa could respond.

The Matri glared at his enthusiasm. His rudeness was compounded a moment later when the phone in his jacket pocket rang.

Tony winced and pulled out the cell phone to turn it off. He caught his breath when he saw the number of the incoming calls.

"I've got to take this," he said.

"Anthony Crowe," Serisa called angrily as he turned to go.

He left the room without explanation or permission.

Chapter Forty-two

Joe was tempted to add his own comments to Shaggy and the vampire woman's defense of women's independence, but a look from Tobias kept him quiet on the subject. He supposed the reason he'd been called to this meeting was to receive a scolding from the Matri. But since he was here, his job was to back up Tobias.

"Consider the advantage that the Tribes have over the Clans and Families," Joe said. "They're using that advantage against you right now."

Once again, Matri Serisa held up her hand to quell protests. "What advantage could there be?" she asked skeptically.

"They are much better at hiding than you are,"

Joe answered. "That makes it easier for them to expose the good guy vampires to the world, while they stay safe in the shadows. But if you go about your daily lives while the Dark Angels handle the attacks, there's much less chance of the mortals finding out about your private lives."

"We already know what happens when mortals find out about our kind," Serisa agreed. "There have been bloodbaths in the past."

"Yes, but it was mostly mortal blood that was shed," Barak contributed.

"That is so," she replied to her bondmate. "I regret every drop of mortal blood shed as much as I do the deaths of our own kinds. We've vowed to avoid violence in our current contacts with mortals."

"What have the Dark Angels vowed to do about mortal contacts?" Alec Reynard asked Tobias. "If the local Primes step aside and let you handle this problem, do you promise to avoid violence?"

"Not completely," Tobias answered honestly. "I've never had any compunction about terminating the Purists."

"Awright!" Colin Foxe said. "Maybe I should join you guys. Sorry, Matri," he added at Serisa's stern look.

"I agree that violence is to be used as a last

resort against mortals," Tobias went on. "But I won't rule out its use."

Serisa sighed. "I find that . . . acceptable."

"But, Matri, you aren't going to go along with these mercenaries' crazy idea—"

"Serisa has spoken." Barak cut Kiril Wolfgang off.

Joe waited for Tobias to protest about the Angels being called mercenaries, but when his commander ignored it, Joe managed to keep his own bristling anger under control. Tobias had what he'd come for: permission to let his hounds loose on the local bad guys. What mattered now was getting the job done.

Joe could barely keep from rubbing his hands together in anticipation. Then he looked at Sid, and Tobias's agenda suddenly wasn't so important to him.

As the room began to clear Joe made his way over to Sidonie. He cupped his palm under her elbow as she looked his way. The contact was disturbing as their skin touched and their gazes met.

"Let's talk."

She nodded, but they stood staring at each other, communicating, but without either words or telepathy. There was nothing in the world but them until a hand landed heavily on his shoulder.

"Are you being bothered, Lady Sidonie?" Kiril Wolfgang asked.

Joe turned on the young Prime with a snarl.

"You know Joseph and I are old friends," Sid answered Kiril.

"Friends, yes, but—"

"Go away, Kiril."

Her tone was soft. She was faintly smiling. And about as dangerous looking as Joe had ever seen her. Kiril went.

"How did you do that?" Joe asked her.

"We take lessons in Prime management from a young age. What was it you wanted to talk about?"

He couldn't remember why he'd approached her initially, though there were many things he needed to talk to her about. But his body wasn't interested in verbal communication, just scent, touch, taste—mating.

"Why am I half-crazed to have you when I hated your guts yesterday?"

Joe hadn't meant to say the words aloud, but when he looked around he saw that they were the only ones left in the room.

"You still hate my guts," she said. "The other stuff is just biology and chemistry. And proximity." She sounded very certain, but her gaze shifted away from him as she spoke.

"No, it isn't." Yes, it was. But . . . "It's more than that, and you know it."

"Please go back to being pissed off at me, Joe. It's better that way."

She managed to piss him off, all right. "Stop telling me what to do all the time. Do you ever stop giving orders? Do you ever stop making other people's decisions for them?"

"No."

Her simple answer turned his anger to curiosity. It still simmered beneath the surface, but the need for information took over.

"Why?"

"Why what?"

Her confusion made him smile. "Why do you have to *rule* everybody around you?"

Now Sid was getting angry. "I don't know. Why do you have to howl at the full moon?"

"I don't have to; I just like to. Maybe you just like being the boss all the time."

Or maybe she just didn't know any different.

"Of course I do. I'm a female. The Primes are aggressive. We females are—"

"Pack alphas." He supplied his own kind's term for her kind's behavior.

Sid nodded. "I guess that comes close enough."

"Actually, there's a huge difference between how vampire and werewolf females think and act. And the difference makes werewolves better."

Sid crossed her arms and lifted her chin belligerently. "Oh, yeah? How so?"

"No alpha female arbitrarily decides the fate of any other adult pack members."

"Werewolves act for the good of the pack," she reminded him.

"Always, but the process is a bit more democratic."

"But just a bit."

"And we treat one another like adults. We can make our own decisions about our private lives."

"Lucky you," she said. Her defensive posture relaxed a little. She put a hand up. "All right, I admit that taking your memories away without asking was wrong. It was high-handed and unethical. But it was for your own good, damn it!"

"You should have asked first!" he shouted back. "But that isn't how vampire females do it, is it? You just decide what's for the best, and never mind what anyone else thinks."

"Joe—I—"

"You should have explained *why* you needed to seal yourself from me, Sidonie! You should have treated me like an adult!"

Chapter Forty-three

Sid stumbled backward into a chair and covered her face with her hands, fighting down the sob that threatened to escape her throat. She refused to shed the tears burning her eyes.

Afraid that all the emotional turmoil between her and Joe would bring the other psychics in the house to see what was wrong, she fought for calm. The thought of a squad of protective Primes showing up terrified her. She wasn't going to let her years of protecting Joe go to waste now because her own wounds were open and bleeding.

"Stop making me want to cry," she mumbled behind her hands. "Stop making this so hard."

"Why shouldn't it be hard for both of us?"

Sid put her hands down and looked up at Joe, expecting the stony expression he'd turned on her when they'd first met again. That wasn't what she saw at all. There was pain in his eyes, but sympathy and compassion as well.

She gazed back warily. "What are you looking at me like that for?"

"I can't tell you."

Sid wasn't sure whether she was amused or furious. She was on the verge of complete, exhausted defeat. She gave a faint laugh. "Playing vampire games, are you? I suppose I deserve it."

"I can't tell you because I'm not sure how I'm looking at you."

She let him lie to her. It was only fair.

"I have been a fool," she said. "A complete and utter fool."

"You followed your instincts."

"Don't you go defending me, Joseph Bleythin."

"At least you responded in the way you were raised to handle trouble," he went on. "There *is* some sort of trouble involved, isn't there?"

"I reacted; I didn't think. I can't change anything now."

"Have you considered that maybe *we* could change this thing, whatever it is?"

She shook her head and watched the angry tension fill him again.

"Then at least tell me why, Sidonie. Make me understand. Did you sleep with a werewolf to try to forget being raped by your own kind?"

"Would that make what I did forgivable? Would it let me off the hook?"

"It would make it understandable."

She wished she could tell him that was the reason, that their problems stemmed from what the Tribe bastards had done to her. But she'd only been able to deceive him once.

"Your timing's off, Joe. Our affair was before my run-in with the Manticore Tribe."

"Then—"

She stood quickly and put her fingers over his lips. "This isn't the time or place for the explanation you deserve."

She shivered when he kissed her fingers. His lips were warm and soft, the kiss maddeningly gentle. She wanted so much more than a kiss . . .

"Damn it, Joe—"

He grabbed her shoulders and pulled her close. He knew too well what she—what they both—needed. Her mouth opened hungrily beneath his. Their tongues twined and teased.

They both heard a door open and were apart in an instant, but Sid didn't think it was quick enough. Her body still buzzed with desire as she turned to face the door.

Lady Serisa stood there for a moment, her expression completely blank, before she stepped back and closed the door.

"Think she saw us?" Joe asked. "Think she cared? Should she have cared?"

Sid was gripped by too much fear to answer him. Dear, conservative cousin Kiril must have ratted them out.

Chapter Forty-four

"Stupid, stupid, stupid," she said at last. "I am *so* stupid."

Joe gaped at her. "What are you talking about?"

The expression in her eyes was suddenly wild. "Run! Hide. Get away from me!"

He'd never seen her like this before. "Are you hysterical?" he asked.

"Pretty close," Sid answered.

"Why?"

"A female vampire getting caught kissing a werewolf by a Matri—you figure it out."

"I didn't mean to embarrass you. But aren't unbonded females encouraged to make love to whoever they want?"

She waved her hands in front of her. "Never mind that. We have more important things to do right now. Tobias needs you, and I have to find Rose."

She turned around and walked away. Joe's head spun as he watched her go. For a second he was consumed by a stab of hunger as he took in the sway of her hips and the shapely length of her legs. He realized that his response to her wasn't just recovered memory; she was getting sexier all the time. Every moment he was with her made him want her all the more.

Even worse, he admired her. She'd betrayed him, and yet . . . She wouldn't let him give her excuses for her actions. She was determined to find the missing woman.

And she was protecting him, wasn't she?

It hadn't been embarrassment that radiated from Sidonie when the Matri saw them together. He should have noticed it instantly, but lust must have dulled his senses. He was aware now of the lingering scent of terror in the room.

"Idiot," he muttered at himself.

He remembered something Laurent had said back at the camp. *"If you're in love with her, it's a good thing you left, because I can't think of a quicker way for you to get yourself killed."*

At the time, he'd thought the words were a brotherly warning not to hurt Sid. Now he suspected that the Wolf Clan Prime had been speaking literally.

What dark secrets were the vampires hiding?

Did she somehow, some way, believe that what she'd done when she took his memories was protecting his life? How did that make sense to her? If that *was* the reason. Or was he trying to give himself another reason to forgive her?

He had to know.

"Lucy, you got some 'splainin' to do," he murmured, and hurried after her.

But when he caught up to Sid in front of the Citadel, the wide brick courtyard was crawling with vampires. The thought gave him a horror movie image, when in fact nobody was crawling and there were five Primes in sight doing their jobs: two guards at the entrance, another pair by the front gates, and the fifth on patrol around the intersection of the house, the front garden, and the multicar garage. Sid was standing in the center of the courtyard, circled by the males of her kind. The Primes were all going about their duties, but Joe could tell that they were all also intensely interested in the female's presence.

Sid's eyes were closed, her attention focused inward. Joe cautiously approached her. She swore as he reached her side and took her cell phone out of its belt clip.

"When telepathy doesn't work . . ." she grumbled.

"Try technology," he finished for her. "Who are you calling?"

"Tony. He's not in the house. No one's seen him since he left the meeting. Can you . . ." She waved a hand through the air.

"Sniff him out?" Joe shook his head. "You know what being around a bunch of vamps does to our noses."

"His car's gone." She shut the phone with an annoyed snap. "He's not answering the phone, and his psychic shields are buttoned up tight."

"Which means he doesn't want to be contacted."

She nodded. "But why? Something to do with Rose, I bet." She put her hands on her hips. "No doubt he's off trying the usual Clan boy heroics. He's going to need my help. He brought me in on this op, and I'm in until he tells me different."

"But you need to find him first." Joe thought through his options, then went with his gut—and his heart. "Tobias hasn't pulled me off working with you, and I told you I'd help find Ms. Cameron. I think I have a way of tracking her down."

"Then that's what we have to do."

He was pleased that she didn't argue about his

help. They had fallen easily into their old partnership. Maybe she'd missed it as much as he had. He wondered if she'd told herself that she didn't miss it as often as he had.

"How do you plan to track her?" Sid asked curiously.

"Roses." Joe smiled at her confusion and led the way toward the garage where her SUV was parked.

Chapter Forty-five

Sid followed his directions and didn't ask Joe any questions on the drive. She was too consumed with trying to convince herself that nothing had happened with that kiss that they needed to be concerned about.

He told her to stop the car in front of the burned hulk of the nursing home.

"What are we doing back here?" she asked.

"Hunting for roses." He got out of the car.

Sid frowned and followed. "Is there more than one Rose we're looking for?" she asked. "I think Tony collected a single Rose and not a bouquet of them."

Joe just smiled in reply. He moved across the grass toward what was left of the building.

The grounds were completely dark, the garden in trampled ruins and still soaked from the water used to fight the fire. Sid took a careful look around, watching her partner's back as she always did. Only when she was satisfied that the ruins were as deserted as they seemed did she join him.

Though he was still in human shape, she could tell that he was concentrating with his werewolf senses.

"What are you hunting?"

He frowned at the distraction, but explained. "For some reason they took everything in the room when they took her, including the several dozen roses Tony sent her for their anniversary."

"He sent her roses?" Sid was as indignant as she was incredulous. "No one's ever sent me roses."

Joe shrugged. "The older generation's more romantic, I guess."

"You think the roses and Rose are still together, and you're hunting for their scent?"

"I picked the smell up earlier. I think it must still be here."

Sid gestured. "Then do your thing."

He nodded and returned to walking around the ruins taking slow, deep breaths.

Standing back to keep her vampire energy out of his nose's way, she recalled, "When I telepathically searched for her, I saw colors: pink and yellow and . . . rose colors. I think I was seeing where she's being held."

He flashed Sid a toe-curling smile. "Coming at the same thing from different angles, as usual."

"As usual," She repeated.

They smiled at each other, but the moment of joyous communication passed instantly. They stared into each other's eyes. Joe's expression hardened, and all his tension and anger came roaring back with a force that rocked Sid down to her soul.

"I had to!" The words burst out of her in a helpless wail of anguish. "I couldn't—"

She turned away from him as she bit off the words. His hands were on her shoulders instantly, and there was no gentleness in his touch.

His breath was hot on the back of her neck. His voice was a low, dangerous rasp. "You couldn't what?"

Sid closed her eyes as the terror she'd lived with for so long washed through her.

"You couldn't what?" he repeated. "I smell the fear, Sidonie. Vampires can't hide every emotion from us. That fear isn't *of* me."

Sid tried to fake a semblance of calm. She shook off his touch and stepped away, trying to make her movements seem casual. She turned to haughtily face Joe. "Of course I'm not afraid of a werewolf," she told him.

"You're a bad actress, Sidonie."

"And you're—nosy!" she threw back at him.

To her surprise they both laughed, but not an iota of tension was eased between them.

"You told me I deserved an explanation," he told her.

"Yes, but—" She gestured, a quick, nervous jerk of her hands. "We need to find—"

"I'm not waiting for a time and place of your choosing." His harsh voice crackled between them. "Right now. Right here. Talk to me."

He stepped close again, put his hands on her again. The pressure of his nearness, his touch, was both threatening and comforting. She couldn't run away any longer.

"Female vampires bond with Primes," she answered. "*Only* with Primes. Do you understand?"

The sounds of freeway traffic roared in the distance, with the murmur of the ocean beyond sounding in the night, but silence reigned for a long time between them. Sid waited, shaking a little, sometimes remembering that even vampires need to breathe.

"No," he finally answered.

She let out her breath in an exasperated rush. "How can a member of a psychic species be so dense?"

"We're from different psychic species," he answered. "I only know how werefolk bond."

"See? You do get it!"

"What? That you can't bond with anyone but another vampire?"

"No! I'm not *allowed* to bond with anyone but a Prime. There's a big difference between what's possible and what—"

"Are you saying that we could be bonded if we wanted—"

"What either of us *want* hasn't got a damn thing to do with it. Joseph, if they discover what I've done, the Furies will be let loose for sure. Or the Primes will act on their own."

As she spoke, she could almost feel eyes on them in the dark. She looked around, all her senses alert for the presence of hunters surrounding them.

"We're alone." His tone was assured, but not reassuring.

She knew he was right, but the fear of the hunt weighed on her.

"What have you done?" he asked.

"Fallen in love with you." But that wasn't the sin. It brought her pain, but it wasn't what put his life in danger. "I tasted you," she confessed. "I took your blood more than once during those days we spent in Cabo."

"You bit me." He nodded. "I remember. Now."

"I made you forget to save your life," she told him. "If it is ever discovered that I'd begun to bond with someone other than a vampire—"

"Wait a minute," he cut her off. "Primes bond with mortal women all the time."

"But I'm not a Prime! The rules are different for females."

"You've always broken those rules."

"No, I haven't. I've skirted around the edges, but there's only so far even I could go. Until I fell in love with you," she added. "I crossed the line then, and I've tried very hard to protect you from the danger I put you in. I acted selfishly, stupidly. The crime is mine, but you'll pay with your life if they ever find out."

"I still don't understand. I remember what you did. I remember what you told me in the garden three years ago. In my dreams I can hear the fountain in background, smell the flowers, feel the moonlight. They aren't dreams, they're nightmares. But it really happened, and the humiliation of what you said sticks to me like cold sweat."

"Joe, I—"

"Do you remember any of that, Sidonie?"

Chapter Forty-six

Three Years Ago
San Diego, CA
Clan Wolf Citadel

"Lucy, you got some 'splainin' to do."

Joe was furious. He tried to cover it with curiosity, he tried to cover it with humor, but he felt the anger growing into a raging fire. Just how badly had she betrayed him? Made a fool of him?

Suspicion gnawed at him as he confronted Sid.

"Explaining?" She tried to smile, but her expression was tense. She couldn't look him in the eye for more than a moment. "I don't—"

"You told me that vampires and werewolves couldn't possibly be attracted to each other. You've had me convinced for years that all we

could ever be was good friends. I've been going along thinking—believing—that the partnership was enough."

"We are best friends," she said. "The best of partners. Why—"

"I just found out that our friend Cathy and her Hunyara cousin are the descendants of a mating between Primes and werewolves. So don't try to tell me that we can't be more than friends."

"I didn't know anything more about the Hunyaras than you did!" she protested.

He could believe that, but he knew as sure as life that there were other lies she was hiding. "You've done something to me—messed with me."

"Why would you think that?"

He touched the side of her nose. "You don't have any sex scent to me. I should be able to sense your gender and every nuance of arousal—from vague interest in a passing stranger to complete turn-off—from you even if we were just friends. You read neutral to me. You took that part of yourself away from me. What are you hiding from me, Sidonie?"

"Damn!" She turned her back on him.

He pulled her back around. "Are you angry at yourself because you did too good a job messing with my head?"

"You know me too well, Joseph."

At least she wasn't denying it. "What happened?"

She lifted her head, and this time she held his gaze. "We had an affair."

His senses reeled. "We what?"

"You heard me."

"I don't love you," he said.

"Yes, you do. You just don't remember."

"What are you talking about?"

"We've been lovers, Joe. I made you forget. It was just a fling," she went on coldly. "It shouldn't have happened. I didn't want to mess up our partnership with any trivial baggage—so I made you forget."

December 19, 12:03 AM, Present Day
Los Angeles, CA

"You even lied about the lie!" Joe accused. "You told me it was just a fling that you made me forget. And you made me believe it!"

"Well—yeah," Sid answered. "And now you remember what really happened. But knowing what we really shared doesn't make you feel any better, does it?"

"You sent me away hating you."

"I didn't send you anywhere. You ran off to join the foreign legion on your own." She took a deep breath that sounded almost like a sob. "I was glad you went, though. I tried to be strong for you, but being near you was a constant temptation. I had to protect you from me."

"Oh, please—"

"I'm not joking! I'm a vampire, damn it! I crave blood—your blood and only yours. You're all I want in every way a female can want a male, and if my people find out, you will die." She put her hands on his shoulders and shook him. "Do you understand *now* why I did what was necessary to save your life? I put you at risk. I'll suffer the consequences of my own selfish lust, but I'll be damned if I let them kill the man I love! Find yourself a werewolf girl and forget about me."

He pulled her close. "I don't want a werewolf girl."

Sid twisted out of his arms and backed away, her hands covering her mouth. Her eyes glowed red, and she closed them until she got herself under control. When she looked at him they were blue once more. She put her hands down when she no longer had to hide her fangs. He knew that she was barely under control, but her reactions amazed him.

She loved him.

She'd acted for his own good. He wished she'd explained sooner, given him a choice, but that was a vampire for you—especially the females. When Sid decided to save you, she didn't go halfway. He recalled the tattoos currently marking her body. The hours spent getting the work done must have been excruciatingly painful, but she'd done it to save a girl who needed her help.

"Can we please go save Rose now?" She interrupted his thoughts.

Joe ran his hands through his hair. This was one more person she was committed to helping, and he'd promised to partner with her in the search for the little old lady.

"Yeah. I guess we should."

Chapter Forty-seven

Minds didn't change with age, bodies just got harder to deal with. Rose had known that for a very long time. She was brand new, but she was still herself. And her self was hungry. She was also nervous and restless and bored, and so angry she could spit nails as the hours passed and her captors left her alone.

She sat on the bed with her chin on her propped up knees and blushed when she finally put a name to the other thing she was feeling. It was also a kind of hunger.

"Well, isn't that just . . . typical," she complained, and slid off the bed to stand barefoot on the cool hardwood floor.

She wiggled her toes. Yep, that felt good.

She stretched, then twirled around and tried a karate kick like she'd seen in movies. That landed her on her butt, but she let out a joyous laugh just the same. If she'd tried that a few days ago, she'd have broken a hip for sure. Not that she would have tried anything so silly then.

"Now I know why it's called *hard*wood," she muttered as she got easily to her feet. She tried a few of the dance steps she'd learned so very long ago. "A product of the studio system learns many useful skills."

For example, she could fence and ride and dance and sing (though not well), walk like a model, talk like a duchess.

The studio had not taught her how to pick locks. That was a skill that might have been useful, had there been anything but a smooth surface to the door when she went to check it. That was one way in which this cell was different from her room at Ocean View.

She walked around the room, checking everything, noting the differences along with the similarities. She refused to look in the mirror and refused to think about the fear, but she wanted to scream. She went into the bathroom and took a shower, but the feel of the warm water, the smooth, fragrant lather, and her own hands on her young skin nearly drove her mad.

"Bad idea," she muttered.

She dried off briskly, avoided looking into the bathroom mirror, tied on a very plush terry robe, and went back to exploring her surroundings. The soft cloth against her damp, naked skin was disconcerting.

The roses were beginning to fade. Which was no comfort at all considering the irony that she was brand new while the flowers were dying. She and Anthony would have laughed about it together, if he'd been there. She buried her face in a bouquet and took deep breaths, glad that the fragrance was still delightful. How she'd counted on the annual arrival of Anthony's Christmas gift every year! She appreciated the way they reminded her of him still, no matter how odd the circumstances.

But being reminded of him only made things worse.

Her fists were clenched tightly at her sides when she finally went to look out the window. She didn't know why she'd put it off for so long. Maybe it was that every change in her environment, even the littlest ones, frightened her. Seeing the view from her prison cell was certainly not a small change; it showed conclusively how different her world now was.

Not a prison, she reminded herself. *I'm a lab rat.*

She had been for a long time. She didn't yet know if being aware of the experimentation made it worse.

Instead of the yellow hibiscus bush outside her window, she saw daylight fading and mountains that were green from winter rain and full of gathering shadows. Acres of pastureland and a distant line of trees separated the house from the hills. She caught a glimpse of a gated fence and a dirt driveway through the barred window. The room was at least three stories off the ground. If there were guards she didn't spot them. She could hear traffic, but in the far distance. She was on a ranch, she decided. How far from Los Angeles? She'd been an invalid for the last six years, first living with a nurse in her home before moving to Ocean View. She didn't get out much, and the city changed and grew constantly. She thought they'd brought her somewhere isolated, yet not far from the city, but that was only a guess.

Oh, Anthony! Rose thought, picturing him in her mind, hoping the telepathic link he claimed they shared would work.

She closed her eyes and mentally pictured herself jumping up and down and waving. *I'm here, dear. Please come get me.*

No answering thought came back to her through the ether. But all her senses were alive and sensitized with the thought of him. She felt the weight of her young breasts and growing heat between her legs.

"Oh, dear."

She hugged herself around the waist and turned from the window.

As much as she would have liked to deny it, she was feeling . . . frisky.

Was there something about being in hopeless danger that stirred the sexual part of her? Experience would say that there was.

December 22, 1944
Bastogne, Belgium

Anthony's excuse for making her hide in the attic of the abandoned house was that it was better not to disturb the commander of the American forces defending the town with the knowledge that there was a female civilian in their midst. As if there weren't plenty of other female civilians to worry about; not all the natives had been able to flee the fighting. The people who'd tried to peacefully live here were as trapped as the Ameri-

can troops surrounded by German Panzer units.

"As if General McAuliffe didn't have more to worry about than one lost USO hoofer," she complained as she lay on her back and stared at the ceiling. Dust sifted down from above as a shell exploded nearby. The old building shook a little, then shook again as another shell hit closer still.

Rose shivered. She'd lived in California for a year, so she knew what earthquakes felt like. They were scary enough, but the random shaking of the earth wasn't anywhere near as frightening as the continuous barrage of huge guns from the enemy Tiger tanks. Earthquakes weren't deliberately trying to kill you.

Fear coiled inside her, and she wanted to cover her ears and scream in terror. Instead, she concentrated on her annoyance with her traveling companion.

She was certain Anthony Crowe had her hiding in this dark, freezing cell because he *was the one who wasn't supposed to be here. He was a vampire. He lived by night, and he lived in secret. His habit was to hide. Stashing her away while he skulked around in the dark was just his way of operating.*

He got to be heroic. She had to wait here like a lady in a tower, when she could have been helping at the field hospital. She hated *waiting.*

And why was she doing what he told her to?

Rose stood, preparing to leave, but the little trapdoor in the floor opened before she could move. Anthony crawled into the attic and closed the opening after him.

He grinned, white teeth flashing in the dim light. "Guess what just happened?"

How could she possibly know anything that was going on? "We surrendered?" she asked sarcastically.

"The Germans sent a note asking us to. Do you know what General McAuliffe said to that?"

Rose had to bend over in the cramped space to step up to Anthony. "How would I know anything?" she snarled.

He was so amused he didn't notice her anger. "He said 'Nuts.' That was his official answer to the German commander—'Nuts.'"

Terror flashed through Rose while Anthony chuckled at the general's bravado.

Nuts. A flat-out refusal to surrender to the overwhelming force that completely surrounded the town. There was too much cloud cover for air support to help the trapped Americans. God knew when or if reinforcements could get to them.

"We're going to die," Rose said. "I'm going to die."

Anthony's arms came around her. "Don't be afraid."

She held him close, too aware of his hard male body, "I'm not afraid to die." She looked him in the eye. "But I'll be damned if I'm going to die a virgin."

Chapter Forty-eight

Anthony held her out at arm's length. "What are you talking about?"

"You know exactly what I'm talking about." She grabbed him by the front of his coat. She tried pulling him back to her, but he wouldn't budge. "I want you to make love to me, Anthony!"

"That's not going to happen, young lady."

"I'm not a lady, I'm an actress."

"You're still too young."

A loud explosion shook the house and he pulled her close again. She dug her fingers nervously into his shoulders.

"I'm not going to get much older if this keeps

up," Rose pointed out. "You've already drunk my blood. That's pretty intimate, isn't it?"

"Very." A wicked smile played around his lips. She very much wanted those lips kissing her.

"Then how much different is making love?"

"They're closely related," he admitted. He glanced around the small, dim attic. They were standing hunched over to keep their heads from bumping the low ceiling. "Hardly a romantic setting."

She nodded. "And it's freezing cold in here, too. I don't care. Make love to me, Anthony."

"What if the building gets hit while we're performing the act? Do you want to die bare naked in a compromising position?"

Rose giggled. "We don't have to be bare naked. If I understand the mechanics, only the lower parts need to be exposed. It's too cold to take our clothes off, anyway."

He kissed the top of her head. "Practical creature." She pushed aside his coat and began to unbutton the shirt beneath, just far enough to kiss his exposed throat. He gave a gasp of pleasure, and she fumbled to unfasten his belt.

"Young lady, I take it that you intend to have your way with me, no matter how much I protest." He didn't try to stop her.

"Help me," she said.

In response, his hands slid up under her layered shirts to cup her breasts. His mouth came down on hers, drinking in her moan of pleasure.

Present Day

"And things just went on from there," Rose murmured, sitting on the bed, staring at her feet. Her toes were tightly curled against the pale wood floor. A lifetime's worth of pent-up desire coursed through her.

She realized she'd been shaken out of the erotic memory by the sound of the door opening, and stood. A knot of fear twisted her insides, but she managed a mask of bravado as she faced the doorway.

"Please tell me you've finally brought food— Well, it's about time you got here," she said as Anthony Crowe was shoved roughly into the room.

"I knew you wouldn't want to start the party without me." His voice was slurred and his eyes were dull, but he managed to smile at her.

"You're naked." She rushed to him as the door slammed shut behind him.

"You've never minded before," he said as he collapsed into her arms.

Rose managed to swing him around onto the bed before his weight dragged them both to the floor. Not only was he naked and groggy, but his hands were cuffed behind his back. He continued to smile at her. Somehow it eased her terror.

"I don't mind now," she told him. She settled beside him and ran her fingers through his thick black hair. "But you look awful. How did you find me? How did you get captured?"

"Didn't. Someone called to tell me where you were at. Got a call from your cell phone," he tried to clarify. "I saw your phone last year and found out your number."

"What?" Rose jumped to her feet. "You deliberately walked into a trap? I don't know why I let Gregor convince me I needed a cell phone at my age—Gregor!" she spat out angrily.

"Gregor," Anthony confirmed. "Told me to come alone if I wanted you to live. Very melodramatic fellow. Looking forward to killing him." His voice became slower and fainter with each word.

Rose patted Anthony's bare shoulder. "I'm looking forward to your killing him, too."

"Give you his head for a present." His eyes slowly closed.

"Thank you, dear. That would be nice."

She was aware of the instant Anthony became

unconscious. His vulnerability sent cold dread through her.

"Idiot. How could you put yourself in danger like this?" But she loved him desperately and deeply for his putting his life on the line for her and wanted nothing more than to protect him.

All she could try to do was make him comfortable, which he certainly couldn't be with his hands fastened behind him. She rolled him onto his side and propped a pillow behind his back. When that didn't do any good, she squeezed herself onto the narrow bed beside him. It took some time before she managed to wriggle and heave them into a position where she could hold him in her arms, his head resting on her shoulder. His body was warm and heavy and wonderfully solid against the length of hers, and his steady breathing subconsciously calmed her.

She sighed and held him close. After a while, she felt safe enough to follow him into sleep.

Chapter Forty-nine

"This is another fine mess you've gotten me into." Tony meant the words as a joke, but the rasp of pain in his voice made him fear Rose might take him seriously.

"I think you got yourself into it," she answered calmly. "I do appreciate the sentiment, but turning yourself in to the bad guys was stupid."

"It was a romantic gesture."

"Less romance in the future, more practical solutions, please."

He grunted in reply. Rose's fingers stroked through his hair. He couldn't bear to let her know how much the slightest touch hurt—not when he loved her to touch him, no matter what.

Tony ignored the agony filling his head and attempted to get his bearings. He couldn't quite bring himself to open his eyes yet. He decided that his head rested on her shoulder. Lovely. He felt her stretched out beside him, the softness and warmth of her skin connected to his along the length of their bodies. Nice.

The pain kept him from any psychic awareness of Rose, but he was instinctively aware of the call of her life-giving blood. The girl always had made his fangs ache.

"I vant to dreenk your blood."

She patted his head. "You go right ahead, dear."

"When I'm sober," Tony added reluctantly. "I don't know what was in the shot they gave me, but I'm not up to much just yet." He let out a moan when Rose gently eased away from him, instantly missing her warmth and softness. "Aw, honey!"

"Try sitting up," was her cruel response. She took him by the shoulders and helped him.

Once his feet were flat on the floor and the rest of him was stable enough that, with effort, he wasn't going to fall over, Tony forced himself to open his eyes. This brought a fresh shot of pain, but the sunburst brightness soon faded to blobs and shadows.

At least he could now remember who he was

and how he got there; he hadn't been able to for a while after he first came awake. He hoped the effects of the shot would soon be completely out of his system. He'd gotten the impression from his gleeful captors that they thought one dose would keep him helpless for several days. Unfortunately, being drug-free wouldn't help the headache or the psychic disruption from the subsonic screech of the zapper they used to shield the hideout, but one thing at a time.

"You are far from all right," Rose said.

His gaze followed the sound of her voice and eventually, the blob right in front of him resolved into Rose's form. She was wearing a short, pale pink bathrobe. It showed off her glorious gams, and the top gaped loose enough to give him a nice view of her bosom.

The sight brought a smile to his lips, and a shot of desire warmed his blood. If his hands weren't fastened by silver handcuffs, he'd have tugged off the belt that kept the robe precariously closed.

Rose passed her hand in front of his face. "What are you smiling about?" She gasped as her gaze moved to his groin. "Anthony Crowe, are you lusting at a time like this?"

"Do I hear indignation from the woman who practically raped me during the Battle of the Bulge?"

"Funny you should mention that, because—" She caught herself and looked at him with narrow-eyed suspicion. She turned around slowly and asked when she faced him again, "Have you by any chance noticed anything . . . *different* about me since the last time we met?"

Tony gave Rose a thorough looking over, from the tips of her pretty pink toes to the top of her coppery red head.

He tilted his head sideways. "Are you wearing your hair differently?" he asked in puzzlement.

She was not amused. He could tell by the way her big eyes narrowed and her lush lips thinned and how her fine skin went alabaster pale. She took a deep breath.

"Sometimes when you get really angry, I think your freckles are going to explode," he added.

The air rushed out of her in a laugh instead of a furious yell. "You are impossible," she told him, but her gaze had softened.

"You are the most beautiful woman in the world."

"Maybe in 1944—no, I was still a skinny teenager then. In 1952 I was incredibly gorgeous, and I would have accepted the compliment then. But we've moved into a new millennium, darling, and I should be dead, not"—she ran a hand down her sleek, elegantly curved body—"new."

"You've never looked any different to me."

"This is not the time for charming lies, Anthony."

"I am a psychic who fell in love with your mind and spirit and soul. Do you think I have ever given a damn about your appearance?"

"Yes."

It was his turn to laugh. "All right, you've got me there. Of course I lust after your luscious body. But I love *you.*"

"Luscious! I haven't been—oh, never mind, we went through this discussion days ago. What day is it, anyway?"

He glanced toward the room's one window. "It's night." He looked at her again. "And you're about to tell me that's the most sensible thing I've said since I woke up. And—" Tony swiveled his head to follow her as she rushed around to the other side of the bed. "Where are you going?"

She pulled open a drawer in the bedside table. She rummaged around and after a few moments gave a deliciously wicked, triumphant laugh. "Idiots! I don't know why the fools brought all my stuff with me, but it's their own fault." She held up a small red leather case and waved it triumphantly. "My husband left me this."

Tony grimaced at the reference to the late Thad

Pearson, even though he now knew Pearson's relationship with Rose had been platonic.

He craned his head as Rose knelt on the floor beside the bed and unzipped the case. "What is it?"

"A manicure set, among other things." She slid a nail along a section on the inside of the case and flipped open a panel beneath the grooming instruments. Rose grinned up at him.

"Are those lockpicks?"

"Thad claimed he was a stage magician before he got into movies, but I think he might have been a cat burglar. He taught me a few things."

"At least not in bed," Tony grumbled.

She chortled at his jealousy. "Stretch your hands back, and hold still." She tugged on the cuffs and he winced. "Are these things silver? Of course they are; you wouldn't still be wearing them if they were anything else. Damn those bastards! There are burn marks on your wrists."

"There won't be for long when you get them off."

"Be patient. I'm out of practice. With everything," she added with a deep sigh.

But soon he heard a grunt of triumph, a sharp click, and then came the sweet, instant cessation of the burning pain as the silver fell away from his wrists.

With his hands finally free, he grabbed Rose

and pulled her onto the bed. "You're getting plenty of practice from now on," he promised.

His hands shook as he ripped the belt from the robe to get to her naked flesh. He breathed in her scent, ran his tongue over the inside curves of her breasts. The reality of Rose was better than even the most vivid memories.

His voice was rough with the desire he'd had to deny all these years. "And now we're going to practice every way a man and woman can bring each other pleasure."

Chapter Fifty

She wanted Anthony's hands on her.

"Not dreams." He spoke her thought.

"Not memories." She spoke his.

"Now and forever," he told her.

He pressed her back against the bed, his weight hard and real. Her fingers played over his skin, finding nothing soft about him. He was all hard muscle and pent-up tension.

Rose closed her eyes as a lifetime of loneliness and longing flowed away. Sensation took the place of thought.

"Heaven," she whispered. "I've died and gone to heaven."

"Better than heaven," he said.

The sharp prick of pain when he bit her breast sent a burning rush of ecstasy through her. Rose's fingers clamped onto Anthony's shoulders as she tried to hang on for dear life.

What are you holding on to? his seductive thought whispered in her mind.

Sanity, she thought back. *The world.*

Let yourself go. I'm with you.

His touch, his thoughts, his solid, virile presence were all she needed, all she wanted. Anthony brought her back to life and—

Rose screamed.

She couldn't stop. The sound went on and on, even though a small part of her mind tried to make it stop. Even though Anthony held her close, held her still when she clawed at him.

"By the Lady of the Moon, woman, do you know how much of a headache I already have."

These were the first words that made any sense to Rose, although she thought he'd been speaking to her the whole time the panic ran its course.

"Get away from me," she said. "Don't touch me."

He let her go and backed away, leaving her sitting alone on the bed. Her fingers dug into the side of the mattress. Her throat ached. Her face was wet, and there was the taste of salt in her mouth.

"My vision's blurred," she rasped. "I can barely see you. I'm getting old again."

Anthony disappeared and she heard the sound of running water. He came back and handed her a warm, damp washcloth. "You've been crying, that's all," he told her. "Wash your face and you'll feel better."

She responded to the tone of gentle command and did as he said. Though her eyes burned, her vision did clear as soon as she wiped away the tears. She'd been breathing in wild, ragged pants, but the painful racing of her heart was calming down.

"What was that all about?" she asked.

"You're the one who had the fit, darling—you tell me." He rubbed his temples. "You could have made a fortune as a scream queen in horror movies."

"I am in a horror movie. Only it's real."

"Hey, just because your boyfriend's a vampire—"

"I'm the monster!" She was on her feet shouting, and she couldn't stop. "I'm not real! I'm this horrible construction! Frankenstein's monster! I'm the result of a horrible experiment! I'm an abomination!"

"No, you're *not*!"

Anthony's shout was a roar of fury that shook

her into silence. Rose stared as he grabbed her by the shoulders.

"What did those bastards tell you? What kind of nonsense did this Tribeson Gregor feed you? Whatever he said was a lie." He put his fingers under her chin and forced her to look him in the eyes. "You and I are of one blood. Whatever it is that flows in me that keeps me young, flows in you."

Rose jerked her head away from his touch. "That's what he said—that your blood was the catalyst that made the experiment work."

"You *did* need my blood, but that was the only truth he told you. Everything else must have been a con game he was running on these mortal scientists to get something he wanted from them." Tony shook his head. "No one made you a monster. I claimed you as my bondmate. The rejuvenation worked a lot faster than I thought it would—and I wasn't even sure it would work at all—but it's our connection that brings us to where we are right now."

She tilted her head sideways. "Are you sure?"

"Your skepticism wounds me."

"I think you're trying to make me feel better so you can get into my pants."

"You're not wearing any," he reminded her. His eyes glittered mischievously. "Do you feel better?"

She sighed. "I feel exhausted."

"Hysteria will do that to you."

She reached out and brushed a wave of black hair back from his forehead. "And you have a headache."

"The bastards have a zapper going. But I'm not using it as an excuse to say 'Not tonight, dear.'"

"And a zapper is . . . ?"

"A device the vampire hunters came up with to mess with our heads. We've developed some immunity to it, and massive amounts of painkillers can block the effects too, but—"

"I can give you massive amounts of painkillers," Rose interrupted. "If they brought my fur coat, she added, looking toward the closet door.

Tony let her go. "Please say you have something stronger than aspirin—"

"I've got a stash of Vicodin."

"Well, aren't you the modern movie star? Is an entourage going to show up any moment now?"

"I'd rather somebody showed up with a meal. I'm starving."

Rose didn't explain that she'd been saving the hidden medication for a suicide attempt. She didn't want to upset him. She laughed with relief when she found that the coat and all her other clothes was in this closet. She prayed that nobody had searched the pockets, and whooped with joy when her hand closed around her hidden treasure.

Tony was standing right behind her with his hands cupped when she turned around. *This is too good to be true!* he thought as he gulped down the Vicodin.

My thought, exactly, she responded.

Who cares? He added.

He swung her up into his arms and headed toward the bed. "I'm going to make love to you now," he told her firmly. "And this time we will *not* be interrupted."

Rose pressed her head to his chest and kissed the place over his heart. She put her arms around his neck and held on tight, breathing him in, never wanting to let him go. "I promise the only screaming I'll do this time will be with pleasure."

"Then you're going to be screaming a lot," he promised.

Chapter Fifty-one

December 19, 3:00 AM
Outside Los Angeles, CA

Have you ever seen werewolf CAT scans or MRI images? Sid asked Joe telepathically.

No, the black wolf loping beside her across the barren field answered. *Shh.*

Sid backed away a few feet and kept her telepathic shields tightly closed while Joe worked.

He stopped, lifted his head to taste the air, and shifted their course slightly when he padded forward again.

They'd left her SUV on the side of a gravel road a few miles back to cut across country on foot and paw. Joe'd shed his clothes for wolf form, and she'd brought a small shoulder bag stuffed with useful supplies. The night was clear, the moon was bright, but they had no trouble moving silently from shadow to shadow. The game was afoot, so to speak, and their partnership was working as smoothly as ever. Sid was almost giddy with the pleasure of being with Joe like this. Maybe nothing was settled between them, but she had this time with him to treasure.

Have you? he asked after they'd walked in silence for a while. *Seen them?* he prompted.

It took her a moment to recall the thread of the conversation. *I have indeed seen images of werewolf and other werefolk skulls.*

Why would you want to?

I was hanging out at the clinic when I was pregnant with Charles. I got bored between tests and wandered into one of the research labs, and I ran into a researcher dying to talk to somebody about her work.

And this research proved conclusively that werewolves are sexier and more glamorous than vampires.

I already knew that. Her interest was in your sense of smell. She had images of werewolf heads in human and transformed states. Guess what?

You tell me.

Werewolves in human form have the same olfactory organs as mortals. Considering that you have a superior sense of smell when you're in hu-

man shape, she believes that what you think of as scent is actually your way of defining a psychic sense.

Well, duh . . .

Apparently werewolves already know that about themselves.

Of course we do, but scientific proof is always a good thing. As long as the information stays where it should.

Anthony Crowe is head of the clinic's security, Sid defended her sire. *He's vetted everyone who works there. Nothing gets past him.*

Except small explosive devices, and missing little old ladies.

Joseph—

What else have Dr. C.'s mortal researchers come up with recently? DNA studies? New super-drugs? What sort of experiments are your mortals doing on our people?

A great deal of suspicion flowed from Joe with the thoughts, and she hated the implications. *Your boy Tobias suspects that our mortal cousins are traitors.*

They're not my cousins, my vampire darling.

He'd called her *darling,* which didn't stop her from arguing with him. She welcomed communication with Joe no matter what they were talking about. The last thing she wanted was for him to return to the angry silence of a few days before, now that she'd told him the whole truth.

You can't possibly suspect everyone, can you? Sid asked.

Guilty until proven innocent is the best policy with mortals. You vampires have created this security risk, you know, by reproducing with mortals like werebunnies.

There is no such thing as werebunnies.

You take the daylight drugs; they make you more like mortals; that makes it easier for you to have kids with them.

Laurent wasn't taking daylight drugs when he got Eden knocked up, and they weren't even bonded then. Hell, they weren't even friends! Having Toni was a happy accident. Babies just—happen.

Charles didn't.

For a moment, the ache to hold her baby stopped her in her tracks.

Charles is fine, she thought. *Everything is fine.*

The voice in her mind was hers, but it seemed to come from a distance.

Are you all right, Sid?

Everything's all right.

Joe stopped at a thick tree trunk and turned into human shape. "Your turn," he told her.

Sid was glad of the chance to do something for

the case. She closed her eyes, cleared her mind, and thought of Rose. Dear, sweet, gentle, elderly Rose Cam—

Sid's entire being turned to flame, and the rush of lust drove her to her knees. Everything was fire. Everything was need. There was nothing but desire, and she reached for the naked man beside her.

Chapter Fifty-two

Joe was barely able to keep from shouting in surprise when Sid pulled him down beside her. The scent of damp earth and old pine needles did nothing to mask the powerful aroma of arousal boiling around Sidonie.

"What are you—"

Her roving hands soon showed him exactly what she intended. She knew how every part of him responded to every touch. Her caresses weren't gentle, but they were perfect. His body responded with quick arousal.

The woman could have made him come in a few moments, if he didn't fight the rising sensation.

"Honey, sweetheart, we can't—"

She seemed to have suddenly gone mad with desire. Under other circumstances he would have been happy to go along for the ride.

Her mouth covered his, her tongue twisted with his, and for a moment he matched her hunger for hunger. It took more than superhuman effort to pull away, to hold her back. He wanted to devour and be devoured, but he held on to sanity instead.

"Sid, sweetheart, stop."

She slipped out of his grasp and pressed her body to his. A strand of her hair brushed across his chest, and this simple touch sent more heat through him than anything else she'd done. He didn't want her to stop. His hands roamed over her back; and he discovered that he'd pulled up her shirt so that his palms were pressed against warm skin.

"We can do this later. Somewhere with a bed and—"

He gasped at the pressure of sharp teeth just above his left nipple.

Words obviously meant nothing to her, but he kept trying.

"We're close to the enemy. This isn't the time, and Rose—"

"Rose!"

The word came out as a gasp of hunger, and she was on him again. Joe ended up on his back, with Sid on top of him.

This time when she kissed him, Joe couldn't stop kissing back. Even as his hands moved over her without conscious will, his mind made the effort to touch her thoughts, to calm—

Big mistake.

Their minds touched, blended. There was a moment of utter clarity, sharing, understanding. A moment that lasted no more than a nanosecond, before Joe, too, went up in flames.

They tumbled around on the soft pine needles in a frantic, straining heap. He was already naked and hard. Sid's clothing took him only a moment to push aside. Joe entered her in a deep, brutal thrust. She responded with a fierce growl deep in her throat that brought an answering snarl from him. Her thighs wrapped around his hips, rising to meet his thrusts, drawing his hardness deeper into her sweet heat as he claimed his mate.

His world exploded in total completion when her teeth sank into his shoulder. His mate had claimed him.

Sid lay on her back, stared at the stars through the tree branches, and remembered how to breathe.

She was aware of who they were, and that she was utterly, happily, complete, but everything else was a blur. Joe was collapsed on top of her, keeping her warm in the cool darkness. For a long time she combed her fingers through his hair, drawing deep pleasure from this simple gesture.

"What the hell was that all about?" she finally asked.

"Uh . . . ," came Joe's muffled reply. "Shouldn't I be asking you?"

"I have no memory of anything but great sex."

"Try."

Sid watched the moon and searched her mind. "I recall your asking me to look for Rose. I let down my shields, trying to find the rose colors that reached me before . . . but what I got was . . ."

"Turned on," he supplied.

"*Somebody* was, and I don't think it was me—not initially. I think I tapped in to somebody's libido." She realized that she also had a fading headache. She found her bag on the ground by her head and rummaged around for the container of painkillers to dull the distant security device's effects.

"And?" Joe prompted.

"I reached through a zapper into a couple of very active libidos—*oh!*" She sat up, pushing Joe off of her. "Oh, dear."

"What's wrong?"

"I've never been so embarrassed in my life. That was Rose and my—no, I'm not going to even think about it." She got to her feet and pulled her partner up after her. "My apologies for attacking you like that."

He grinned and rubbed his shoulder. "No problem."

Sid looked closely at his shoulder. "Damn! I bit you again! I am so sorry—I shouldn't—"

"I liked it."

"Of course you did! But it was wrong. I had no self-control and—"

"Get over it," Joe said. "Suck it up and get it together. We're not far from our objective."

She was half tempted to salute at his brisk tone. Instead, she nodded and rearranged her bunched clothing.

Then she took Joe's hand. "We'll find Rose," she said. "But first you're going to tell me what you know about Charles."

Chapter Fifty-three

Uh-oh.

"Charles? What about Charles?"

"You couldn't sound innocent to save your life, Joseph Bleythin."

She was right; he was no good at lying and never had been. A gift for prevarication was one of the things she brought to the team.

"How does your son come into this?" he asked, genuinely puzzled. Then he recalled. "You were in my head!"

"Not on purpose and you know it, so don't sound so accusing. I didn't mean to pick up your concern about Charles. Only the concern wasn't about him, was it? What do you know about my son—about me—that I don't?"

"I've got lots of information in my head; lots of trivia, lots of classified stuff. Why'd you pick up on that bit about your kid? Oh, right, because we'd been discussing children earlier." Joe rubbed his jaw with his free hand. Sid's grip on his other wrist was like iron, a not at all subtle way of reminding him which species was on top of the food chain. "You've got me in a wolf trap, darling, and I know it. But there are some things I can't tell you."

She released his wrist and turned her back to him. "I know what I did to you was wrong. Wanting revenge is fine, but keep my son out of—"

"I don't want revenge." A couple of days ago, yes. But now: "I promised Tony not to tell you." He took Sid's shoulders and turned her gently to face him. Her assumption that he wanted to hurt her stung him, but he understood it.

"I'll relish your pain some other time, okay? But I wouldn't use Charles to hurt you. All you picked up on was some info Tony gave me."

He couldn't help but smile faintly at the puzzled look she gave him. "What's Tony got to do with Charles?"

"What specifically did you pick up from my thoughts?"

He waited patiently while she got her own thoughts in order.

"I sensed something that you didn't like—something about the way Charles is being raised. Something secret from me . . ."

Joe nodded. "I promised not to tell you, and I was assured that it's for your own good. But you're right, I don't like it."

He tried to keep his opinions to himself, tried to find a way to skirt the issue—but, damn it, he *hated* what the vampires had done to one of their own!

"I know your kind has to raise your sons differently than our wolf packs do, but this Severing custom sucks."

"Why? It's just a party before we send a two-year-old away to the Clan crèche."

Joe shook his head. "It's a telepathic severing of a mother from her son," he told her bluntly. "Your thoughts and memories were altered by your loving Clan to keep you from missing Charles. I was told that it was done so that you can live in the outside world without going crazy from an instinctive need to care for your child. It was done for your own good."

Bitterness at what she'd done to him *for his own good* crept into his voice, but anger for her burned away his lingering resentment. He hated what had been done to Sid even more than having his own memories stripped by her. Vampires spent altogether too much time making high-handed decisions about what other people should do, feel, want, think, and believe—even if it was all done with the best of intentions.

"You can't miss Charles because they've used mind control on you." She was looking very thoughtful. "Do you understand?"

"Charles is safe in the crèche," she answered. "That's what's most important."

She didn't sound like an automaton; she sounded perfectly reasonable and sincere. And that worried him. "What are you up to?" he asked.

"It's true," she said.

"Maybe it is, but I know you're up to something. I can smell it."

She stroked his cheek. "You knsow me too well, Joe." She glanced past his shoulder. "There's a place over the next hill where bad guys are holding Rose Cameron and Tony prisoner. They need rescuing, and that's what we're going to do right now."

"One thing at a time," he agreed.

Sid set off at vampire speed. Joe changed back to wolf form and loped after her.

Chapter Fifty-four

We're upwind and I've got a vampire with me, so I think we're safe from mental and physical detection. At least until sunrise, when they can see us moving across the open field.

"We'll get it done before then," Sid answered Joe's thoughts.

He'd returned to where she waited in the trees after making a quick recon of the bad guys' property. Rose was being held in a big four-story house surrounded by open ground.

Heardfelt anything else from the prisoners? Joe asked.

No. Thank goodness. The last thing she wanted was another blast of over-the-top lust.

Business now, pleasure later. *What's the layout? Disposition of guards?*

You ought to come to work for the Dark Angels.

Sid had a moment's fantasy of running off with Joe to live and love in secret while fighting the good fight with his special forces team.

"Yeah, right," she said.

I counted two mortals with guns and three ferals patrolling the grounds. Lots of activity—stuff being brought out and loaded into vans. I get the impression that this is a temporary safe house and they're planning on leaving real soon.

Then it's a good thing we didn't arrive late for the party. "How do you want to do this?" Sid asked.

Joe's lips pulled back, showing a muzzle full of razor-sharp teeth. He growled low in his throat.

"You really hate feral werewolves, don't you?"

Somehow the werewolf managed to laugh evilly.

"I'll take the mortals, then. You take the bit boys." She couldn't resist ruffling the fur on his head before setting off. This brought another growl, but no matter how fierce Joe Bleythin could be, he never intimidated her.

"Have fun storming the castle, darling," she told him.

Don't get dead, he thought back.

One of the many things they shared was a love of movies, and they were always quoting them to each other. Saving a movie star really was the perfect job for them.

"Well, that was certainly—"

"Invigorating?" Tony suggested as he ran a finger slowly from the base of Rose's throat all the way down to her belly button. She was lying on her back, her head propped up on pillows. He was stretched out on his side next to her. Her eyes were heavy lidded, her skin still flushed and glowing with a faint sheen of sex sweat. "You look incredibly decadent," he told her.

"I was about to say that what we've been up to was certainly distracting."

"Distracting?" he asked in mock outrage. "Young lady, do you think that I would stoop to making love to you as mere distraction?"

Her hand came up to stroke his cheek. "Oh, no," she answered with an exaggerated flutter of eyelashes. "You'd never try to get a scared woman's mind off of impending doom and disaster in such an ungentlemanly fashion."

He wiggled his eyebrows. "It worked, didn't it? You want to do it again?"

"Oh, yes. But not just yet."

"Aw . . ."

"I also noticed that we shared quite a bit of blood along with other bodily fluids. It was . . . beyond amazing."

He gave a one-shoulder shrug. "It's the vampire way."

"It was wonderful." Rose wriggled away from him and got out of bed. "Can I ask you something?" she asked after she'd pulled a nightgown on over her head.

"Can I stop you from asking?" He sat up and watched as she picked up a brush and began working tangles out of her coppery hair. He noticed that she didn't turn toward any mirrors to help with the job. He held out his hand. "Come here and let me do that for you."

Rose sat beside him and gave him the heavy ivory brush. "That's nice," she said as he stroked the soft bristles gently through her hair.

She was silent for a while, and Tony hoped he'd escaped a coming inquisition. But he'd only delayed her curiosity for a while.

"You were lying about my restored youth being your doing, weren't you?" She shifted on the bed to face him. The fear was back in her eyes, but her jaw was set stubbornly.

He couldn't lie to her this time. "It was a strong supposition on my part. Blood sharing in a bond causes mortals' bodies to stay young. Bondmates age together, slowly."

"But sharing blood doesn't make old bondmates young again, does it?"

"I don't know," he admitted. "I hope so. Why not? I don't think it's ever been tried before." He grinned. "We can be the first."

"You are an impractical romantic and always have been." She smiled. "And I love you for it." But the fear hadn't left her eyes.

He took her hands and kissed them. "You want to go somewhere and get a bite to eat?"

"I'd love to," she said. She tilted her head toward the door. "I think we have a slight problem, though."

"Why use a door when a window will do?" He stood and urged her to her feet.

"But—there are bars on the window. And guards outside."

Even with her youth restored, Rose's mortal hearing was no match for his. A pity, because she was missing a minor, if muffled, riot in the distance. "We don't have to worry about the guards. My daughter's finally joined the party." He led her toward the window.

Rose balked. "You have a daughter?"

He nodded. "And she brought her werewolf boyfriend."

"You have a daughter," Rose repeated. She looked toward the window. "And she's come to rescue us?"

"Hell, no," he replied with a wild grin. "I'm the rescuer. Sid and Joe are creating a diversion."

With that, he wrapped her bathrobe around his hands, broke the window glass, and quickly studied the last barrier blocking the way out. What Rose had referred to as bars was actually a less conspicuous heavy mesh barrier.

"This chicken wire is silver—nice touch on their part." His skin warmed at the touch of silver even through the cloth. Normally the daylight drugs in his system would have combated the silver allergy, but he guessed whatever antivamp potion the mad scientists had pumped into him still had a lingering effect.

"Be careful," she said.

"It won't burn through before I'm done," he told her as he twisted and worked at the metal.

Silver was harder for a vampire to bend than steel, but Tony didn't let a little thing like that stop him, not with the woman he loved watching him. It was his duty to be her hero. It took him a while, and every muscle in his body ached by the time the silver mesh dropped to the ground.

"Time to go, sweetheart." He turned back to Rose and held out his hand.

To his shock, she was standing with her back against the door, her palms pressed flat against it. She stared at the opening he'd made for her to the outside world, her indigo eyes huge with terror.

"I can't go out there," she said. "I can't."

Chapter Fifty-five

"For crying out loud, woman! Now what is your problem?"

Anthony's anger brought Rose somewhat out of the paralyzing terror. "Well, excuse me for having a few issues, Mr. Perfect Hero! I haven't been outside of this room—or one just like it—in years. Years!"

"Don't tell me that you're scared of the outside world."

"Precisely."

"This from the woman who faced down a German tank?"

"That was 1944. I belonged in that time . . .

but now . . . Anthony, I'm a dinosaur. I barely know what the Internet is. I—"

He stalked across the room to lean his palms flat against the door on either side of her head. His long, naked length pressed against her as he brought his face close to hers. "You've been given the chance to live again. I don't believe that you're too much of a coward not to grab on to that chance and discover a new life. But you're the only one who can make the decision to step out into the world." He gave her his most charming smile. "What's it going to be: me and happily ever after? Or are you going to take your chances with a bunch of mad scientists?"

She sighed. She wanted to be with him more than anything—even if it meant stepping out into a strange world where the only thing she had to rely on was his love. And that, come to think of it, was quite a lot for her to hold on to.

"Are you going to pick me up and jump out the window if I decide to go with the scientists?"

"You bet I am."

Rose put her arms around Anthony's neck. She'd been afraid plenty of times in her life, and the only way to handle it was to do what had to be done.

"All right, we're going out the window. But not until you put some clothes on."

* * *

Sid's head hurt and she didn't like the smell of fresh blood, but she fought off the temptation to inform Joe that killing wasn't always the answer, no matter how much pleasure it might give him.

Werewolves fought each other to the death; it was not her place as a vampire to complain or condemn. She was careful not to watch the business Joe was about behind her as she silently moved toward the mortals that were her targets.

She could smell the men at the back of the house because they wore the bulbs of garlic that the most fanatical Purists still used as an antivampire talisman. It must be an almost religious custom, because the vampire hunters knew very well that most vampires took drugs that made them immune to the old curses.

"It's a waste of a perfectly good member of the onion family if you ask me," she muttered as she approached her first target.

He heard her and whirled around, bringing up a rifle as he moved.

"Make pasta sauce, not war," Sid said as she ripped the weapon from his hands.

He was unconscious before he had a chance to make any noise, and she secured his wrists and ankles with a flex cuff from her pack. She made equally quick work of the second mortal, then paused on one knee to examine one of the weapons she'd confiscated. She wasn't pleased to find that the rifle had been modified to fire bullets containing substances toxic to her kind—silver, garlic, and hawthorn wood.

"Bastards," she muttered.

Purists really did make it hard to believe that most mortals were perfectly nice people. As she started to stand, her attention was caught by movement at the top floor, and she smiled. A male figure dropped to the ground, took a few steps back, and held up his arms. A few seconds later, a figure in a white nightgown leapt from the fourth-floor window to be caught in the waiting male's arms.

"Rescue accomplished," Sid said.

She began to stand once more, only to crash flat onto her face when the werewolf she hadn't noticed pounced on her back. Fangs sank deeply into the back of her neck before she could throw the creature off.

Sid reared back in a moment of hideous pain, which instantly filled her veins with sexual fire. Her fingers scrabbled at the grass and she bit down hard on her tongue to stifle the scream.

Of ecstasy.

Damn it, Joseph! What do you think you're doing?

Turnabout's fair play, darling, her werewolf lover thought back.

It had been a long time since she'd known the sexual release of anyone tasting her blood. An orgasm paled in comparison with the completion calling to her now. Sid's body shook with arousal and her mind begged to give in to this pleasure like no other.

Not now, darling! Please, not now! Her mind shouted the words while her body begged for more.

"I hate it when you're right," Joe said.

Sid didn't know when he'd switched into his human shape, but at the sound of his voice she became far too aware of his naked body pressing against her.

"Please move," she said.

He shifted position and Sid rolled onto her back. His blue eyes glittered with an expression that was at once amused, aroused, and possessive. She liked the way he looked at her. She grinned up at him while she got her breathing and the rest of her responses under control.

"We have things to discuss," he said.

Sid got to her feet as she nodded. She gave Joe a hand up, making herself ignore the shiver of desire at the contact. By the time they'd turned to face the building, the two escaped prisoners had reached them, holding hands.

Sid stared at the strangely familiar young woman, then at her sire. "Tony, why are you wearing a pink bathrobe?"

Chapter Fifty-six

"Because Rose insisted that people don't run around outdoors naked."

Rose was all too aware of her beloved Anthony's sarcasm as she tried not to stare at the nude male standing beside the young blond woman. She, at least, was clothed. Rose breathed in the fresh night air and remembered that not only was she a fair actress, but that once upon a time she'd enjoyed interacting with other people. Time to renew old habits.

"Thank you for your assistance," she said to the woman. Curiosity got the better of her. "Anthony called you his daughter . . . ?"

"This is Sidonie Wolf." Anthony's glance moved

suspiciously between the other couple for a few moments, his eyes narrowed. "And this is her—bondmate?—Joe Bleythin." He did not sound the least bit pleased at what he'd said.

"Uh—" naked Joe began.

"You *are* Rose Cameron! Aren't you?" Sidonie said.

Rose nodded. Fear that the young woman would respond with revulsion knotted her stomach.

"Wow," said Joe. There was nothing but awed appreciation in his tone. "You're a movie star."

"And he's a werewolf," Anthony said. "Who's somehow attached to my daughter," he added grumpily.

The vampire female reached out to touch her but stopped at Rose's automatic flinch. Sidonie turned her attention to Anthony. "How—"

"Long story," he cut her off. He jerked a thumb over his shoulder at the building. "No one's noticed our absence yet, and it's time to go."

"I couldn't agree more. Anthony, what are you doing?" Rose asked as he swung her up in his arms.

"We'll travel faster if I carry you."

Good Lord, it was the Ardennes all over again! "My ankle's fine and I have no intention of living in the past. Put me down, Anthony Crowe." He responded so quickly that he almost dropped her, but at least she was on her feet. "You have a car waiting somewhere, I take it?" she asked when she was standing upright. "Please tell me that you didn't bring a tank this time."

He chuckled. "Well, it is a Hummer. I left it parked half a mile from here."

"You two get going," Joe said. "Sid and I will cover your withdrawal." He tapped his forehead. "I've already called in reinforcements from the Dark Angels."

"When did you do that?" Sidonie asked.

"I reported back just before we ran into zapper interference."

It all sounded terribly military and interesting to Rose, but before she could ask for any explanations, Anthony put his arm around her waist and said, "Come on—we're getting out of here."

After Tony and his hot teenage girlfriend were gone, Sid turned to Joe with her arms crossed and anger in every line of her body. "And just why do you think we need help from your precious Dark Angels?"

"I'm following standard procedure. What are you annoyed about?"

"I do not need any help in securing this objective—or whatever military term you want to use."

The reason for her attitude began to dawn on

Joe. She thought he was treating her like a *girl,* the way the males of her own kind would. As if he ever would—although the thought of treating her like an incredibly sexy woman whenever the opportunity arose was appealing.

"Of course you don't need help," he told her. "I'm not disputing that you're the big bad vampire and can rip everyone in that house to shreds with a dirty look. But I thought your only objective was to rescue Rose Cameron. The Angels' assignment is to take down the whole conspiracy her kidnapping was part of, so I called them in."

The explanation mollified her somewhat. "That's lame," she said. "But I'll let it go because we have something far more important to talk about. You're biting me was wonderful, but the complications are—"

"Shouldn't we kick some ass before we get into that?" he interrupted.

Sid frowned but went along with the distraction. "Don't you think that's interfering with your Dark Angels assignment?"

He shrugged. "Yeah, but it'll be fun."

They started toward the house. "Don't kill anyone you don't have to," Sid advised.

* * *

Once the house was secured, they waited on the front porch. Sid had moved the guards she'd cuffed earlier in to join the two mortals they'd left secured in the cell on the fourth floor. There'd been no supernatural bad guys inside. After shutting off the zapper, they'd made a thorough search of the house and grounds. Nobody and nothing else was found. Sid had considered questioning the prisoners, but Joe wanted to wait for the Dark Angels to show up.

She'd shrugged and said, "Sure. My work here is done anyway."

He'd gone back to her SUV to retrieve his clothes, which she found mildly disappointing, but he'd declared he was cold just sitting around. So now they waited, seated side by side on the porch steps while dawn lightened the sky. The rising sun brought a little warmth into the frigid air.

After a long silence, Joe yawned and stretched. "Is it Christmas yet?"

It really wasn't a holiday Sid paid much attention to. "Not for a few days, I think."

"It was a rhetorical question."

She sighed. "Sorry. I think I'm too tired for rhetoric." She sighed again. "We need to talk, though."

Joe put his arm around her shoulders and she relaxed against his long, lean form. "Yeah."

Silence stretched out between them for a long time after this acknowledgment.

Finally, Joe said, "I can still taste you—feel you—inside of me."

Sid waited, holding her breath.

"And I like it," he told her reluctantly. "I guess I never understood before what sharing blood really meant to you. I still don't understand, but I feel it. As a hunter, I thought I understood the taste of blood. I've taken prey in wolf form—rabbits, deer, wild boar—I've known the chase and the kill and the feeding. I've tasted the death of the werewolves I've brought down. But this give and take, this sharing and becoming one, that's the essence of . . ."

"Bonding," Sid said when it seemed that Joe couldn't form that word.

"I bit you because you've bitten me." He squeezed her shoulder. "I realize now how stupid and childish and dangerous and wonderful it was. Especially wonderful. I've tasted you once; I want to do it again. The werewolf part of me doesn't understand this need at all."

"I'm sorry," Sid told him. "Maybe it'll wear off."

"Do you want it to wear off?"

"Hell no. I just don't want to get you in trouble. And what do you mean, *the werewolf part* of you? What part of you isn't werewolf?"

"I know I'm not defining it correctly. Maybe there's a part of me now that's vampire."

Sid grunted. "Not likely. Do you think that your biting me will turn me into a werewolf?"

"I doubt vampires can be turned." He ran his hand through her hair. "You'd make a cute golden werewolf, though."

A large black SUV turned into the long driveway then, so they put the conversation aside and stood to await the arrival of the Dark Angels. But when the vehicle stopped, three Primes got out; it was Sid's cousin Kiril and a pair of Shagal vampires. They all wore grim expressions as they approached her and Joe.

Kiril made a formal bow to her. "Lady Sidonie: for you, from Lady Juanita." He handed her a small red velvet bag.

Sid felt the weight of the object inside the bag and knew exactly what it was. "Damn," she muttered.

She spilled the bag's contents into her palm, and sure enough, it was a ruby ring, the symbol of Lady Juanita's authority as the Matri of Clan Wolf. It meant that the Matri wanted to see Sidonie *right now.* There was no ignoring this summons.

Sid squeezed the ring in her fist. "Of course," she said to Kiril. "I want to discuss a matter of importance with her anyway. I'll leave for San Diego immediately."

"She's not in San Diego," Kiril answered. "She's at the Shagal Citadel." He gestured toward the SUV. "Please come with us."

"The werewolf comes as well," one of the Shagal Primes said.

Oh, goddess, she'd been afraid of this! "That won't be necessary. He's waiting to report to the Dark Angel commander."

"Lady Serisa commands that the werewolf accompany you," the Prime answered.

"But—" Kiril began.

"Of course I'm coming," Joe announced. His arm went around her shoulders again and he looked calmly at the trio of glaring Primes. "Let's get this over with, shall we?"

Sid didn't want to get it over with; she was terrified that at the end of the upcoming meeting, Joe Bleythin would be dead—punished for her crime.

She was so sorry. So very sorry. But he insisted on being brave and there was nothing she could do but love him for it.

Chapter Fifty-seven

December 19, 10:00 AM
Vampire Medical Clinic
Los Angeles, CA

Rose frowned at the Band-Aid covering the inside crook of her elbow and flexed her arm. The needle hadn't hurt going in, but she hated Anthony and his doctor friends' insistence on yet more medical testing. They'd taken three tubes of blood before she'd pointed out that a vampire's girlfriend really didn't have that much to spare, and the tech had agreed to leave her alone for a while.

"I spent at least a year as a guinea pig," she'd complained.

"We're going to make absolutely certain you're not being used as one now," the mortal in charge—Dr. Casmerek—insisted. He had a kind smile to go along with a no-nonsense demeanor. "We're going to make sure you stay as young and healthy as you are now."

He was very sincere, and he talked a good game. Besides, Anthony trusted him. So Rose held out her arm and let them take her blood. She knew they had a whole battery of other procedures planned as well, but not right now. She was determined about that.

"I want strong black coffee," she said as the examination room door opened and Anthony walked in. "And all the cholesterol I can get—although knowing the way people eat in this town, finding fried, greasy food might prove a hardship."

Anthony smiled lovingly at her. "You know I'll provide you with anything you want."

She didn't know if she wanted this *Your wish is my command* business to last. That was no way to run a relationship, but she decided to go along with it for now.

"You look gorgeous," she told him.

He posed for her, holding out his arms and turning around slowly. He'd shed her pink robe for an ensemble of black, black, and more black—shirt, slacks, jacket, tie, shoes. The clothes fit the way only expensive tailoring could.

"Armani?" Rose asked.

"The designer of choice for well-dressed vampires," Anthony acknowledged. "Since I run security here, I have a room and a well-stocked closet on the premises." He set a large bag from an upscale department store down beside her. "To provide your wardrobe, I had to go out shopping."

Rose almost squealed with delight as she snatched up the bag. "Merry Christmas to me!" She spilled the contents out on the examining table, then picked up the pieces one by one. "Underwear! Thank God, you brought me a bra!" She exclaimed over every piece of clothing as she found it, and when she was done looking she let Anthony help her put it on.

"Everything fits," she said when she was dressed in a linen skirt and silk knit tunic. She wiggled her toes in the black leather sandals. "Even the shoes."

"I guessed at your sizes from memory." He ran his hands over her from shoulders to hips. "Tactile memory," he added, then took her arm. "Let me show you our garden, Rose."

"I'm delighted to get out of any place that contains medical equipment," she answered.

Outside, Rose turned her face up to the sky and breathed in air rich with—

"Bacon! And coffee!" She gave Anthony a look of surprised delight. "You're wonderful!"

"So I am. So is the staff here at the clinic. Right this way, young lady." Anthony led her to a small wooden table set for two and pulled out a chair for her. "I thought you might like breakfast alfresco."

Rose's stomach rumbled. She kissed his cheek before he went to sit opposite her. "I'll take breakfast any way I can get it."

Anthony poured coffee for her into a china cup, then whisked the cover off a plate full of all the bad-for-her food she could possibly want. Rose dug in with the gusto of—well, of a teenager.

"You do know that Dr. Casmerek thinks you're robbing the cradle with me," Rose said between bites of toast she'd covered with scrambled egg.

"He's just jealous." Anthony sipped coffee. "Tell me about Gregor," he said after she was half-done with her meal.

By then, Rose was ready to slow down enough to savor the flavors and textures of her food while they talked.

She gazed at Anthony, so perfectly groomed, so handsome, so seemingly relaxed. So very angry beneath the polished exterior. Rose sighed romantically. "How I do love a dangerous man."

He frowned. "Gregor?"

She laughed at his jealousy. "No, you." She sat

back, coffee cup in one hand, a triangle of toast in the other. "Give me a moment to get my memories in order."

She'd been used to memorizing scripts for film and stage, and she hadn't lost a bit of her mental acuity over the years. It didn't take her long before she was able to repeat almost verbatim her conversation with Gregor while she was being held prisoner.

"I assume he wanted all of that information conveyed to somebody, or he wouldn't have told me all the plans of the Tribe vampires," she concluded. "I don't think real-life villains really spill their evil plans while gloating over their prisoners."

"You think he isn't a villain?"

"I've been in pain for a long time because of him. I think he's a sadistic bastard." A vision of the handsome Tribe Prime formed in her mind, and she wanted to spit into that perfect face. "But I also think he arranged our escape for some reason and provided information he wants you to know about."

Anthony nodded. "I concur." He rubbed his jaw. "No doubt he was sowing lies and working plans within plans. It will all be checked out and—"

"Tony! Tony, I'm so glad I found you!"

Anthony stood and Rose turned to look as a frantic young man hurried toward them. He was big and blond and very handsome. Rose figured he was another Prime. Dr. Casmerek followed after him.

"What's wrong now, Kiril?" Anthony asked.

The Prime stopped in front of him. "It's Lady Sidonie. She's in a lot of trouble—and it's all my fault!"

Chapter Fifty-eight

Shagal Citadel

Sid protested when she and Joe were separated upon entering the Citadel, but no one listened to her. She wasn't used to being ignored by Primes, but Joe looked back and said, "Let it go, Sidonie," as he was led away. His warning to keep her cool kept her from having a screaming tantrum. Tantrums were not normally her way, but fear for Joe's safety drove her to the brink.

She kept reminding herself that they'd shared enough blood and their souls were entwined enough that if anything happened to him she would know it. This didn't keep her from pacing the room they'd put her in, her arms wrapped around herself in fear, but she managed not to break anything or try to escape.

The Matri demanded my presence. I have no choice but to await the Matri's pleasure.

Sid repeated the mantra constantly. It didn't help that they'd also taken her cell phone from her, and that there were too many telepathic shields guarding the Shagal Citadel for her to call out in a psychic way.

She was stuck in another Clan's territory without a clue and feeling helpless.

"Which is just what they want," she muttered after an endless amount of pacing. "They're trying to break me."

The door opened and a Shagal Prime looked at her. With no expression on his face or in his voice, he said, "You will come with me."

"Fine."

Sid didn't follow him, but led the way to the Citadel's windowless central meeting room. She waited for the Prime to enter first and announce, "Sidonie Wolf as you commanded, my ladies."

Sid tightened her mental shields and schooled her features to absolute blankness as she stepped inside, only to have her barriers explode in surprise when she saw how many Matris were waiting for her.

There was Lady Serisa Shagal, of course, mistress of the Citadel. Lady Juanita occupied a deep leather chair beside Serisa. Seated on a couch were Lady Angelica Reynard and Lady Cassandra Crowe. Sid also recognized the Matris of the Snake and Wolverine Clans, though she didn't know those women.

Why were they all here? Why were they staring at her? This was a gathering of the Furies, wasn't it? Oh, Lady, this was going to be bad.

Sid acted as if there was no one else in the room but her own Clan Matri. She put the Matri's ruby ring into Juanita's outstretched hand before she stepped back, planted herself in front of Lady Juanita's chair, and said, "I want my baby back."

"We are not gathered to discuss Charles," Juanita replied.

"I am. My son is my only concern. You know my rights, Lady Juanita. I have provided my Clan with a child. I am head of House Sidonie. My child is *mine*."

Cassandra Crowe responded, "Nicely played, Sid, going on the offensive to throw us off track, but we aren't going to discuss a child who's safely in your Clan crèche."

"It is your illicit relationship with the werewolf that's the problem," Lady Serisa said.

"What problem?" Joe asked.

Sid had known when he came in the door behind her, but she'd kept her attention on Juanita. Now she turned to him and said, "Yeah, what problem?"

His warm smile told her everything she needed to know about how he felt about her, about his forgiveness, about their love and partnership.

"I don't see any problem," they said together.

Vampire Medical Clinic

The sunny garden seemed to fill with shadows around Anthony. "What's happened?"

"The werewolf," Kiril answered.

"I knew Joe was going to get her into trouble."

Rose stepped to Anthony's side, and he took her hand. "Isn't Joe the naked young man who helped to rescue us?"

"Lady Juanita sent for Sidonie because of the werewolf," Kiril explained. "It is right and proper for the Matri to discourage such involvement. But the Shagal Primes made the werewolf go to the Citadel with them as well, and it wasn't a friendly request." The young man looked devastated. "I didn't mean to put their lives in danger when I reported seeing them together. They've convened a meeting of Matris to judge them—to condemn him."

"This is bad." Dr. Casmerek twisted his hands together. "I hate it when vampire biology overcomes civilized behavior."

"How bad?" Rose asked, only to be ignored.

"I'd hoped it wouldn't go this far." Anthony shook his head. "Poor Sidonie. She's going to take losing him very hard. And poor Joe Bleythin. That boy's likely to be a spot of bloody fur by the time this is done."

Fear shot through Rose and she squeezed Anthony's hand as hard as she could. "Talk to me!" she demanded. "What is going on? Why would you say something so awful about Joe?"

"Vampire females aren't allowed to bond with anyone but Primes," he explained. "It is forbidden by ancient custom and law."

"Why?" Rose asked.

"Because—"

"Did obeying ancient custom and law do you any good?" she asked. "Or me? Us? I saw those two together—they're in love. What's wrong with that?"

"The Matris rule and—"

"Joe was there to help us. You can't stand aside and let him be killed for no good reason."

"Executed," Anthony corrected. "It's not the

same thing as a simple killing. There's no way—"

"Is Sid your daughter?"

"I'm her sire, but there's nothing I can do to—"

"Do you love her?"

Anthony looked stricken by her questions. She watched intently while his warring emotions flashed across his face.

She finally twisted the knife. "Are you going to let anyone hurt your little girl?" She knew very well that he was aware of the unspoken end of her sentence: *the way you hurt me.*

"You fight dirty, love of my life."

Rose nodded. She also didn't have to add that her wish was his command. "Help Sid," she said. "You won't forgive yourself if you don't try."

Anthony ran a hand through his hair, and his stricken expression turned thoughtful. "There is someone who can help. Maybe. Come on," he told Kiril.

"Where to?" the other Prime asked.

"To find Tobias Strahan. He's not going to let anything happen to one of his Dark Angels."

"No man left behind?" Kiril asked. "Would the Angels rebel against the Matris over one life?"

"We can hope so," Anthony said.

"By the goddess, what have I started?" the worried young Prime asked.

"Vampire bonding with werewolf," Dr. Casmerek said thoughtfully. He nodded as if he'd come to some important decision. "I'm coming with you as well."

"Thanks, doc, but a mortal shouldn't put himself in harm's way like that."

"Braving a den of Matris? I agree, but I can help. I am coming."

"Me too!" Rose piped up. Now that she had her life back, she wasn't going to spend it sitting on her hands.

Anthony grinned at her. "Of course you are. You're never leaving my side again."

Chapter Fifty-nine

Shagal Citadel

"I love you," Sid said to Joe.

"I love you," he answered. They stood face-to-face, gazes only on each other.

"You two are not making this any easier on yourselves," Lady Juanita said. "Stop showing your defiance."

Joe turned to face the Wolf Matri. "You know that I and my pack respect your Clan," he told her. "But I'm not going to deny what I feel for Sidonie. She's tried to deny what she feels for me for years, and it's done nothing but cause her pain. Your females are precious to you—why do you want one of them in pain?"

"Because I'm nothing more than a breeding

machine to them," Sid said. All the bitterness she'd hidden for years was in her voice, and in the sneer she turned on the seated women.

"Don't be ridiculous," Serisa said, radiating disapproval.

"She's not far from being right," Lady Cassandra said. There were shocked gasps from some of the other Matri, but Cassandra spoke to Sid. "But there are many other considerations besides your breeding uses that weigh into the rules against a female bonding with anyone but a Prime."

"Such as?" Joe asked. He didn't flinch from all the glares turned his way. "You're going to kill me no matter what I say," he told the women. "I don't know why you're bothering with this trial—or whatever it is."

"Yeah, Mom," Cassie Shagal said from the doorway. "What are you trying to accomplish here?"

Everyone's attention now turned to the heir of Clan Shagal. She walked into the council room, but she didn't come alone. Several other vampire females came in with her. Joe recognized Flare Reynard, and, of course—

"Mom," Sid said to Lady Antonia Wolf. "What are you doing here?"

"Flare said you were in trouble when she called," Antonia answered, serenely smiling at

Sid. She turned that smile on the Matris. "And she mentioned something about starting the revolution. I knew I had to be in on that."

"You don't want to go in," Barak said, his tall, wide body blocking the Citadel entrance. "You really don't want to go in there."

Tony glanced from where Barak stood, at the center of a line of guardian Primes on the steps of the mansion, to the crowd he'd brought with him on the brick-paved drive.

"If my daughter isn't sent out, I'm going in." Rose tugged on his hand. "My daughter and Joseph Bleythin," he added.

"Are you holding a pack member prisoner?" Shaggy Harker asked the Prime Elder. "Do you want a war with werefolk as well as the Purists?" the Los Angeles werewolf leader demanded.

Shaggy had been with the Dark Angel leader when they'd caught up with him. Once Shaggy discovered what the problem was, he'd insisted on coming along to add his voice to the cause. Tony was aware that the situation was now way too complicated, but there was no backing off.

"If I may." Tobias Strahan stepped to the front of the crowd and looked at the opposing Primes. "I see males from more than the Shagal

Clan here. May I ask why?" His tone was mild, but he had an air of command that even Barak responded to.

"A group of Matris is holding a council inside," Barak answered. "Their Primes are here to protect them."

Tobias rubbed his jaw. "I see. You realize that this puts Lady Serisa in violation of her agreement with the Dark Angels. I'll be withdrawing my troops—although I doubt even your force of Primes can get the Matris out of this trap."

Like everyone else, Barak wasn't used to the implication that a Matri could do any wrong. "What are you talking about?"

"This territory is already under attack from the Purists," Tobias reminded Barak. "Purists who have excellent intel about vampires' current movements. They know the Matris are here. And you know what Purists do to our females."

Tony, Barak, and all the other Primes exchanged uncomfortable looks.

"I hadn't thought of that," Tony muttered.

Apparently Barak hadn't, either. "You should speak to Matri Serisa," he said to Tobias. "I'll take you to her."

"I have important information for the Matri as well," Dr. Casmerek said when Barak tried to stop him from going into the house.

"I'm head of security for the territory outside the Citadel," Tony reminded Barak.

"I speak for the werefolk," Shaggy said.

"I'm with the band?" Rose piped up.

"All right, all of you come with me," Barak said. "With the crowd already gathered in there, who's going to notice a few extra people?"

Chapter Sixty

"Revolution?" Lady Juanita asked, slowly rising to her feet.

Her attention was on Antonia, and Sid resisted the urge to move protectively to her mother's side.

"What sort of revolution do you have in mind?" Cassandra Crowe asked. This Matri's attention was on the younger females who had come to stand near Sid. "Are you showing a united front against your elders?"

"We're making a stand for our rights," Flare Reynard said.

"Rights? Oh, please!" Anjelica Reynard scoffed. She pointed at her daughter. "You're a spoiled-rotten disgrace to your Clan."

"As you have pointed out many times before." Flare put her hand on her abdomen. "I'm going to give my Clan a vampire child." She gestured at Sid. "She gave her Clan a vampire child. We're as dutiful as we can be, considering when and where we live."

"When and where?" Serisa asked. "What has that to do—"

"Twenty-first-century America," Cassie Shagal said. "It makes a big difference to our lives. We're suffocating."

"You have more freedom than we had," Cassandra pointed out.

Sid looked at Joe. "Do you think we could sneak out while this is going on?" she whispered to him.

"I heard that," Lady Juanita told her.

Sid shrugged at the Matri's stern tone. Was she supposed to apologize for bringing a little levity to her own execution?

"I want our daughters to have a freer life than I've had," Antonia said.

This turned Juanita's attention back to Sid's mother. "After the years you spent as a prisoner of the Tribes, that is understandable."

"I'm speaking of the years after I was returned to the loving, stifling bosom of my Clan," Antonia said. "I've been treated like a fragile piece of porcelain. If there's one thing being with the Tribes taught me, it is that I'm as tough as nails. I can survive anything. I want my daughter to have the freedom to find out how strong she is."

Juanita gestured at Sid. "Your daughter has had too much freedom. Look at what she's done."

"She's bonded with a werewolf," Serisa said.

"I fell in love with a mortal in my youth," Cassandra Crowe said. "I loved that man, and I love him still, but I didn't bond with him."

"A bond is a psychic link that's meant to be," Flare said. "That's what we're told all our lives. Is that just romantic drivel you feed to the Primes? Or is it the truth? Is the joining of two souls, spirits, and bodies the core of what we are?"

"Of course the bond is the most important thing to us," Serisa said.

"Then where is my crime?" Sid asked. "What have Joe and I done wrong?"

"He's a werewolf!" Serisa told her.

"The fact that they were even able to bond proves that it was meant to be," Flare argued.

"Stop and think about how prejudiced you're being, Mother," Cassie said to Serisa.

The door opened again. "My apologies for this interruption, my love," Elder Barak said as he ushered in yet another group of people, including Tony, Tobias, Shaggy, and a couple of mortals. "I am convinced that what these people have to say is important."

Serisa folded her arms and glared at the newcomers. "It had better be." Her fangs flashed as she spoke.

Tony recalled that there was a saying among vampires: *When a Matri shows fangs, bare your throat and die like a Prime.*

Either Tobias Strahan hadn't heard this saying, or he didn't care. "Matri Serisa, you are the last person on Earth I took for a fool." He made a sweeping gesture, taking in all the females in the room. "In fact, I didn't expect any *one* of you to be rash enough to walk into a war zone."

"They didn't walk, they came in limos," Flare Reynard muttered.

"If you recall," Tobias continued to Serisa, "you authorized me to put this city on lockdown. It is not our custom to call Convocations in the middle of an emergency."

Serisa stared at the Prime in shock. After a few moments of absorbing his words, she closed her eyes. "By the Lady of the Moon, I am an idiot."

Tony watched the Matris carefully, aware that they were holding a swift telepathic communication. Energy in the room buzzed and crackled, and he got the impression that the younger females were having a confab of their own.

Tobias didn't wait for the Matris to return their attention to their subjects but said loudly, "The Purists are going to find a gathering of females irresistible. Their current strategy is to try for public attacks. How do you hide this Citadel from the world when media helicopters will be flying over the place, showing the battle on news shows with live feeds?"

"Maybe this will convince them that we're living in a new age and that we have to change to cope with modern reality," Cassie said to Tobias.

"I am Prime," he answered. "My duty is to protect vampires. Creating policy is for you females."

"Oh, that's a nice one," Tony heard Sid whisper to Joe.

She was reading nuances and power plays into the situation even while she and her boyfriend were in danger, and he smiled, proud of his smart kid.

"We will close this Convocation," Lady Juanita announced.

"But what do we do about the werewolf?" Serisa demanded.

"We will reconvene after the emergency. The werewolf will be kept prisoner until—"

"The hell you say!" Shaggy shouted.

"You cannot hold one of my men, Lady Juanita," Tobias interjected. "While I and all other Primes in the Dark Angels would obey your commands, the Angels are made up of every type of supernatural being. Our policy is to protect our own. I would not order werefolk and witches and elves to stand down from storming the Citadel to rescue one of our own. They might not obey me if I did."

Tony almost looked forward to the hubbub this was going to cause as soon as the stunned Matris got their voices back.

But instead of a riot ensuing, Dr. Casmerek took the opportunity to jump in. "Ladies, Primes, werefolk," he said loudly. "There's no need for this dispute at all. No crime against either of your subspecies has been committed."

Chapter Sixty-one

"What the hell are you talking about?" Shaggy Harker asked.

The scientist had everyone's attention, and this was the first time Tony had ever seen the mortal brave enough to give Primes shots look nervous.

"What's up?" Tony asked the doctor.

Casmerek kept his attention on the Matris. "I have research findings that I've been putting off sharing with you for some time. I told myself it wasn't relevant, but I used that as an excuse because I knew you weren't going to like it."

"What is *it*?" Serisa demanded. "Cut to the chase: no scientific gobbledygook."

The mortal took a deep breath, "Okay." He pointed at Sid and Joe. "DNA testing shows that vampire/werewolf mating that resulted in the psychic talents of the Hunyara Romany tribe could only have been the genetic product of a female vampire having offspring with a male werewolf."

"What?" Serisa shouted.

"How is that possible?" Juanita asked.

"That is a perversion of everything we believe," Angelica said.

"Maybe history lies," Cassandra put in.

"Could this be true?" Serisa demanded.

"I knew you weren't going to like it," Casmerek said. "But scientific facts and history frequently don't get along. Please remember that modern vampires accept science and use it even when it contradicts folklore."

"This has happened before? We aren't the first?" Joe asked. "A werewolf and vampire bonding? Cool."

"What do you mean *cool*?" Shaggy asked. "That's—"

"Scientific fact," Casmerek put in. He took a flash drive out of his coat pocket. "I have all the data here for you to study."

Tony put his hands on Sid and Joe's shoulders. "So, no harm, no foul," he said cheerfully to the gathering. "Can we all go now?"

"We have already closed this Convocation," Juanita said. "While we still have much to discuss and decide—"

"We aren't done," Sid said. "What about Charles? I told you that I want my baby back."

"Not *now,*" Tony whispered in his daughter's ear.

"You don't miss him, do you?" Tobias said to Sid. "You agree that the crèche is the safest place for a child in wartime?"

"I see your point, but—"

"The Rite of Severing was performed? The telepathic block still holds?"

"Yes!" Sid answered him angrily. "What's it to you?"

Tobias looked at the younger females before he spoke to Sid. "I need your telepathic talents. I want you to join the Dark Angels."

"Yes!" Cassie and Flare shouted, and high-fived each other.

"Do it!" Antonia urged.

Sid and Joe looked at each other for a long time, while everyone else in the crowd seemed to hold their breath and the tension between the generations grew.

"Your people need you to do this," Tobias urged quietly.

" 'Come live with me and be my love . . . ' "

Joe quoted poetry to Sid. "And we'll kick butt together."

Sid sighed deeply and gave a small nod. Then she looked to the younger females, who gave her thumbs up and grins, and a friendly but jealous glare from Flare.

Finally Sid looked at Lady Juanita. "Matri, have I your blessing?"

"Blessing?" the Wolf Clan Matri answered. "No, you do not have my blessing." She looked first at her fellow Matri, then at the younger females before returning to Sid. "You *do* have my permission."

While Sid and Joe shared a fierce hug and the younger females shouted their approval, Juanita looked at Tony. "I agree with you that everyone can go home now."

Good, Rose whispered in his mind. *All's well that ends well . . . and I really want to have sex again soon.*

Sid took a grateful breath of air when she and Joe finally stepped out into the daylight. She ignored the smells of car engines and the people moving purposefully to obey Tobias and Barak's orders to get the Matris and females out of town. She wasn't going anywhere but to a post with the Dark Angels.

Joe put his arm around her waist and pulled her close. "You look relaxed, but your scent's still scared."

She rubbed her head against his shoulder, loving his solid presence. "It'll take me a while to stop rerunning what I thought was going to happen in there," she admitted to him. She didn't mind letting him know she was scared. She was never going to lie about her emotions to him again. She didn't have to. Besides, their blood flowed as one; they *were* one. She'd almost lost this chance for completion.

"What did you think was going to happen?" he asked cautiously. "I know they wanted to kill me, but . . ."

"Kill you, yes—while I watched. Your death would have driven me mad, or killed me, too. And what happened to me would have been used as an example to keep other females from following in my wicked footsteps."

He stiffened with protective anger. "Nasty."

"We are vampires," she reminded him. "Predators use harsh measures when they have to. You know that, werewolf. And the Matris were thinking of the good of all the Clans—they would have grieved our passing. Fortunately, the Clans seem ready to change whether the Matris like it or not. The struggle's just started but . . . And there's the

Prime responsible for setting this whole mess in motion," she added as Tobias came out of the Citadel.

"How is Tobias responsible?" Joe asked as the Prime gave them a nod and walked past.

Sid stuck her tongue out at her new boss's back and explained to her bondmate. "It has occurred to me that when he assigned you to find out what I knew about the Tribes, he had more than one motive for sending you."

Joe looked after his leader. "Clever."

Sid knocked her head against his shoulder. "Clever? You ought to be outraged! Somehow he unblocked your shielded memories, so that you and I would interact the way we did, and he stood back to see how far it would go. He could have gotten you killed."

"You're angry at him for my sake? That's so sweet. Tobias *is* a Prime—and if there's one thing I've learned about vampires, it's that you all do what you think is right, even if you don't ask permission."

"He should have let you in on what he intended."

"The Dark Angels work on a need-to-know basis. All I needed to know was what you and I had been to each other."

"I see. It's all right for big, bad Tobias Strahan

to use you, but you get pissed off when I try to protect you," Sid sniffed.

Joe smiled at her. "I don't want you to protect me. I just want you to love me."

"I do. But you're making me angry enough to bite you, and you won't enjoy it."

He pulled her into his arms. "I missed you in every way possible. I love you in every way possible." He kissed her in a way that filled her being with fire. When they were done, Joe added, "And if you ever want to get your memories of Charles unblocked, I know a witch who makes a mean cup of coffee."

Epilogue

December 20
New York, NY

"He will see you." The low-status Prime who spoke didn't try to hide his envy.

Gregor nodded. The idiot had tried to send him away because he had no appointment. Slamming the worm's head onto the top of his desk a few times had convinced the secretary that he should consult his master. He'd just returned with a bloody cut healing on his cheek.

Gregor waited for the cur to open the door to the inner office, then looked around inside while he waited for the door to close. The large room was of the glass-walled-corner-office type that executives were supposed to covet. It was sparsely and expensively furnished. A laptop sat on the glass-topped desk. Only the heavy curtains that covered the windows gave any clue that a vampire occupied the premises.

The Prime studying the computer screen did not look up.

Gregor came forward and placed the small black memory stick on the desk. "The research is complete," he reported. "It's all here. The treatment clinic is set up. You may start the treatments whenever you wish."

The Master Prime finally looked at him. "You perform to expectations."

Gregor nodded in gratitude but waited for the stick after the carrot.

"I hear that you allowed the test animal to escape. I hear that the mortal scientists were captured. I gave no orders for the project to be terminated by you."

"It seemed the right time to dispose of the mortals involved in the drug development," Gregor answered. "We have their data. Our own people are trained. We have a large supply of the Dawn drugs. The Clan morons are easily duped into believing that only the mortal Purists are involved. I made sure that the mortal prisoners they will interrogate also believe that they were the only ones involved. My actions leave the Tribe freedom to maneuver."

"For a while," the Master said after he studied Gregor.

Gregor nodded. "The Clans and the Families still pose a threat to our plans. We will be there to counter whatever they do. I will be there."

"You have done well—even if you do think for yourself too much." The Master gestured toward the door. "You have your life. Get out of my sight."

mjf

MICROBE

Are We Ready for the Next Plague?

Alan P. Zelicoff, M. D.

·

Michael Bellomo

MJF BOOKS
NEW YORK

This publication is designed to provide accurate and authoritative information in regard to the subject matter covered. It is sold with the understanding that neither AMACOM nor Fine Creative Media, Inc., is engaged in rendering legal, accounting, or other professional service. If legal advice or other expert assistance is required the services of a competent professional should be sought.

Published by MJF Books
Fine Communications
322 Eighth Avenue
New York, NY 10001

Microbe
LC Control Number 2006930953
ISBN-13: 978-1-56731-824-1
ISBN-10: 1-56731-824-X

This edition published by MJF Books in arrangement with AMACOM, a division of American Management Association.

Printed in the United States of America.

VB 10 9 8 7 6 5 4 3 2 1

I would like to thank and bless my partner in life, Mary Frederick, for putting up with long nights and even longer headaches as we put this book together.

—DR. ALAN ZELICOFF

No book can be written without the selfless support of loved ones. I would like to thank my parents, Paul and Thu, for the gifts of education, persistence, inspiration, and artistic sensibility to create this work.

—MICHAEL BELLOMO

Finally, we dedicate this book to the thousands of public health officials who deal with uncertainty, tight budgets, and scientifically bereaved bureaucrats every day as they try to anticipate and forestall the next pandemic. Among them are a special few who are creatively trying to change from within a system that is long on history but short on creativity. They are the purveyors of new knowledge, novel approaches, and personal sacrifice in service to the public that we all unknowingly depend on for our present and future safety.

—MICHAEL BELLOMO AND DR. ALAN ZELICOFF

CONTENTS

FOREWORD by David R. Franz, Chief Biological Scientist, Midwest Research Institute and Former Commander, U.S. Army Medical Research Institute of Infectious Diseases vii

ACKNOWLEDGMENTS xi

CHAPTER 1 The Birds That Fell from the Sky—*West Nile Virus* 1
CHAPTER 2 Corona of Death—*SARS* 21
CHAPTER 3 Arroyo Muerte—*Sin Nombre Hantavirus* 37
CHAPTER 4 Outbreaks, Reservoirs, and Dead End Hosts 57
CHAPTER 5 Shards of Glass in the Brain—*Bovine Spongiform Encephalopathy (Mad Cow)* 69
CHAPTER 6 Out of the Shadows—*Legionella Pneumophila (Legionnaire's Disease)* 83
CHAPTER 7 An Ill Wind—*Smallpox* 96
CHAPTER 8 Natural Born Killers—Why Some Germs Stay Bad 115
CHAPTER 9 Something in the Water—*Cholera, Cryptosporidiosis* 124
CHAPTER 10 When Hours Count—but Days Don't Matter—*Anthrax* 137
CHAPTER 11 Healer, Heal Thyself: Curing What Ails the Public Health System 161
CHAPTER 12 Project BIOWATCH—*Plague Vials Vanish in Texas* 172
CHAPTER 13 A New Weapon in the Fight 189
CHAPTER 14 DNA-Based Vaccines 204
CHAPTER 15 Three Ounces of Prevention—*Scenarios Involving Avian Bird Flu, Bioterrorism Using Smallpox* 218
CHAPTER 16 Into a Crystal Ball, Darkly—A Look at the Future 237
APPENDIX Letter by E-mail to Lev Sandakchiev 247

Glossary 250

Index 263

FOREWORD

David R. Franz

Chief Biological Scientist, Midwest Research Institute
Former Commander, U.S. Army Medical Research Institute of Infectious Diseases

What is the likelihood that a natural pandemic could kill a million people in the United States . . . or that a bioterrorist attack could kill tens of thousands? We lose more than 30,000 Americans to influenza in a typical year, 80,000 to automobile accidents, 320,000 to obesity, and 440,000 to smoking-related illness. But it's difficult to find any but a few activists—and some ordinary people who have experienced personal loss—who maintain interest in these problems for more than a few minutes after the end of the nightly news. We haven't had a true large-scale public health disaster—a "pandemic" that wasn't caused directly by human behavior—for nearly a century. We're a resilient people, but we may be taking disease too lightly in this new, smaller, and very changed world.

In 1992, Nobel laureate Joshua Lederberg and Professor Robert Shope, in a National Academies of Science Report entitled *Emerging Infections: Microbial Threats to Health in the United States,* made an impressive case for improving our preparedness to deal with emerging infectious disease. There was little response from government to the well-thought-out plan to enhance our public health system. (Public health is, by its very nature, a function of government, although each of us can and should practice preventive medicine). Eight years later, Pulitzer Prize–winning author Laurie Garrett, in her book *Betrayal of Trust: The Collapse of Global Public Health,* told us of the woeful state of the United States' and the world's public health systems. Again, there was little response.

Then in 2001, when, in the wake of the World Trade Center attacks and the contaminated letters that followed, five Americans died of inhalational anthrax, our government responded with a $6 billion per year program to prevent and respond to intentional attacks with bacteria, viruses, or toxins. This unprecedented health-related response, in the context of our much greater but "expected" human losses to naturally occurring infectious and behavioral disease, should tell us something about ourselves: (1) We're willing to die of preventable causes if it takes a long time and we feel we have some control . . . and we enjoy the behavior that puts us at risk, for example, smoking. (2) We're willing to let tens of thousands of our neighbors die as long as it's of natural causes and they are the elderly or the immunocompromised, for example, seasonal epidemic influenza. (3) We are not, however, willing to accept deaths at the hand of someone else, especially if it's with an invisible weapon like biologicals. In short, we accept the consequences of well-known risks if there are beneficial tradeoffs, but we deeply fear the unknown because we perceive it to be completely beyond our control. If our society is to arrive at a balanced solution to the problem of recognizing and managing new infectious diseases, while at the same time avoiding overreaction that might threaten individual privacy and confidentiality, we must each become a bit better educated about managing risks in order to overcome the fear of the unknown.

What is it going to take to convince us that we should take seriously the next natural pandemic—let alone a biological weapons attack? It's an especially difficult sell, since we skillfully dodged the SARS bullet in 2003. But it's been estimated that the next influenza pandemic—and we're watching some pretty bad strains that have recently jumped from Chinese birds and pigs to man—could sicken 50 to 100 million Americans and kill more than 200,000 before we could stop it. It has happened in the lifetimes of some of us; 20 million people worldwide died of a hot strain of flu when my 95 year-old mother was in elementary school . . . and the majority of those were not infants or the elderly, but strong, healthy, young adults.

That's where this book comes in. I've known Dr. Alan Zelicoff for ten years or so, and I'm stimulated intellectually every time we talk. I've never seen him not question what's going on around him or not try to make things better for his fellow humans. He's always rational, always probing, always pushing the margins—one of a kind. We in America haven't traditionally integrated biology and the physical sciences very well, but in *Microbe,* Al, both a physician and a physicist, with his crisp, analytical mind, moves us in that direction, just as he has done on numerous occasions throughout his impressive career. His intellectual courage, confidence, and willingness to challenge common wisdom, just what we need most at this critical juncture, are well demonstrated in this worthy contribution to the literature. I respect him greatly.

And owing also to Michael Bellomo's intrepid research and detailed, commonsense explanations of sometimes difficult biological concepts, *Microbe* is the kind of wakeup call we need in this country today. As a society, we tend to just "believe" that everything will always be alright. Only dramatically tragic events such as Pearl Harbor and 9/11 really stir us out of our complacency. Of course, our confidence is not entirely unreasonable. Large oceans, friendly borders, a position of military strength, sound technologies and food processing practices, and modern health policy have protected us for years. Unfortunately, the world and its threats have changed. First, there are some very dangerous pathogens out there in nature. Second, we no longer need go to them; this smaller world now brings them to us. Finally, we know there are people who would harm us with biology if they could . . . and we know advances in biotechnology are making that easier every day. It is possible that we can't change fast enough to protect ourselves from these emerging dangers. But we can't not try.

Naturally occurring microbes are becoming increasingly deadly. Many can outdo even the most capable biowarrior. Just look at the natural evolution of the bird flu threat over the past six to seven years. In 1997, it was a danger only to poultry flocks. Two or three years later it became lethal to mammals, and by 2003 it was killing humans. By 2004 the virus infected forty-four people and killed 73 percent of them. Those are Ebola-like mortality rates!

We now have more tools than ever before for the fight—both electronic and biomedical—but do we have the will to integrate the sciences and modify the way we live and work together to win this war? *Microbe* shines the light of reason on what are probably the two most important keys to winning this battle with the bugs, whether presented to our species naturally or by humans seeking us harm.

First, we've got to break into the disease cycle as close to the index case as possible. Prevention is always less costly than treatment, and early identification of disease in a population gives us the luxury of using prevention for the many. We learned after the 2001 foot-and-mouth disease epidemic in the United Kingdom that more rapid identification of infected farms, followed by isolation and culling of animals, all of which were technically feasible at the time, could have reduced losses by more than 60 percent. Making the hard call at the front end of an outbreak requires information. Information includes awareness among health care providers for both humans and animals. Most of us will not be good enough to say, when the index case walks into our clinic, "Oh, that's Lassa fever; I remember it from the ten minutes devoted to it in medical school." No, for the rare or exotic, the ones we really worry about, it will more likely be "quantitative," not "qualitative" diagnostics that trigger our response. However, someone must connect the dots of likely very disparate data and sound the alarm so many can do what must be done to prevent the spread of disease. If we had done that in three days rather than three months when West Nile hit New York City, we might have had a shot at snuffing out a disease that is now here to stay in North America. We've made progress with awareness tools, but we're not there yet. We have mechanical sensors in more than thirty American cities, sniffing the air in a few places, collecting samples to be analyzed every twenty-four hours . . . but those tools are for terrorist attacks with pathogen clouds. They're unlikely to do anything for us when Rift Valley fever or another exotic arbovirus (a virus spread by insects) is blown in on some errant mosquito. We have medical surveillance programs in a few regions, but most are still pretty complex and disconnected. We've shown that data collection, where the doctor meets the patient, must be simple or it won't be done at all. Zelicoff and Bellomo make the critical importance of this issue crystal clear.

Second, public health and medical professionals must accept the fact that we're all in this together: the humans, the animals, and the bugs. The authors introduce the concept of "one medicine" and know it can save hours when hours really count. *Microbe* shows what happens in real-world outbreaks—West Nile, SARS, Hantavirus, food-borne illness, Legionella, smallpox, and cryptosporidiosis. It exposes a pattern of poor communication and people making hard decisions with less information than they need. Despite these challenges, we can win this war. But to win it, the "field commanders" and the "troops" of public health must have the right bits of information in hours, not days, and the decision-makers in Washington must understand the importance of our all working together against a common enemy. The world's human and animal populations—and the microbes circulating within them—now just move too fast. No longer do we have the luxury of letting a new zoonotic disease firmly establish itself in our domestic or wild animal populations before we respond. We can't have veterinarians treating pox lesions on animals and physicians treating similar lesions on humans with neither connecting the dots. We can't have a zoo veterinarian reporting something very strange and new in exotic animals while part of the public health community ignores the relationships with human disease and another epidemic spreads across America. We can't afford not to have an integrated system of health surveillance and awareness that is species neutral. The potential for harm, even just from nature, is significant. As Nobel laureate Josh Lederberg stated, "Pandemics are not acts of God, but are built into the ecological relations between viruses, animal species, and human species. There will be more surprises, because our fertile imagination does not begin to match all the tricks that nature can play. The survival of humanity is not preordained. The single biggest threat to man's continued dominance is the virus."

Finally, this book isn't just for medical professionals. It's for everyone interested in understanding how changes in our world in the last ten to fifteen years are bringing new microbes to our cities, farms, homes, and bodies, microbes like those that the less privileged world has lived with for centuries.

ACKNOWLEDGMENTS

Little did we know when we began our journey how much we would depend on many hardworking experts who struggle with limited resources, competing needs, turf-battles and just manage—somehow—to keep the US public safe from infectious disease threats.

Leading among them is Ms. Tigi Ward, RN of the Lubbock Department of Health. No one has taught us more about the absolute need for a robust, doctor-, nurse- and veterinarian-friendly electronic surveillance system. The people of Lubbock have much to be grateful for—as do we—from her tireless efforts and wise counsel. She is a Texas treasure.

Dr. Robert Kadlec, a USAF Colonel, practicing physician and true master of public health works on the National Security Council. He has served the past four administrations as a high-level bioterrorism advisor, inventor, and creator of much of the civilian biodefense architecture now in operation in the US. It was Bob who led us out of the darkness.

Dr. David Franz and Dr. Tracey McNamara of Midwest Research Institute gave us the benefit of many decades of hands-on experience in dealing with infectious disease emergencies and the valuable process of long-term public health planning. Dr. Franz led numerous teams into Iraq to uncover what we know about Saddam Hussein's biological weapons program—which was much closer to fruition than the vast majority of newspaper accounts have the patience or column-inches to make clear—and he did the same in the much more dicey inquiry into the former Soviet Union's biological weapons program.

Dr. McNamara spoke out—loudly and often enough to lose her job as chief pathologist at the Bronx zoo—when she realized that Federal officials were ignoring the clearest possible evidence that West Nile Fever had entered the US. The disease is now with us permanently, and thousands of people and animals will contract the illness every year. This probably could have been avoided if Dr. McNamara's wisdom had been heeded.

In the annals of post World War II medical practice, there are probably no greater heroes than Dr. Bruce Tempest of the Indian Health Service in Gallup, New Mexico and Dr. Gary Simpson of the New Mexico Department of Health. Against all odds, these two physicians uncovered the initial cases of Hantavirus during the outbreak of 1993, identified the scope of the illness, and with the serendipitous but nonetheless invaluable knowledge of rodent experts Drs. Terry Yates and Robert Parmenter of the University of New Mexico Department of Biology put a rapid end to an epidemic that could have undermined the personal and economic health of the citizens of Arizona, New Mexico and Utah for years.

Dr. Wendy Orent, a cultural anthropologist by training but a biologist in all-but-name-only, provided us with a clear understanding of evolutionary biology and at the same time guided us in selecting meaningful, accurate illustrations of the threats we humans are likely to face from the tiny microbes—most as yet unidentified—that surround us.

We would also like to thank the people who helped with the mechanics of bringing this book to fruition: Our tirelessly patient editor Jacquie Flynn, literary agent Carole McClendon, and Jo Ann of Jo Ann's Secretarial Service. And of course, we would like to acknowledge the many people at ARES Corporation who have played a critical part in our recent and ongoing work, especially Kathryn Naassan, Dr. Richard J. Stuart, and Daniel J. Weinacht, Ph.D.

Finally, we'd like to acknowledge Richard Preston, perhaps the most famous of all modern American writers on disease and biological weapons. He knows how to do much more than spin a good yarn; he has a gift for clarity that explains his success and popularity among the well-read. We thank him for slashing our sloppiest prose, untangling our tortured technical explanations, and for seeing to it that we describe the real-world actors in our book as the thoughtful and occasionally fallible people that they are. The latter applies especially to us, and we take full responsibility for any errors—technical, factual or historical—in the text.

CHAPTER 1

THE BIRDS THAT FELL FROM THE SKY

West Nile Virus

It had been brutally hot in New York City during the summer of 1999. Since the end of spring, the humidity had been hovering at levels that would plaster a freshly ironed shirt to one's back in a matter of minutes. For that reason, the die-hard fitness addicts who did their jogging along the riverfront walkways or in the parks did so perhaps a little earlier than usual so as to burn off calories without risking heatstroke.

At the northern end of Queens, where the Civil War–era Fort Totten juts out into Little Neck Bay on a compact knob of land, it was probably these early-morning risers who began making grisly little discoveries in late June. All over the north side of Queens, residents began reporting unusual numbers of dead crows scattered throughout parks and open lots where the birds would commonly roost. The sanitation agencies that handle animal control would likely have been annoyed by the pickup in business, but would have not sounded any alarm bells to the public health agencies. Certainly, an uptick in the number of deaths in a common bird species that was noisy and not particularly liked would hardly merit a second glance.

Crows are the best-known members of the Corvid family of birds. The family includes magpies, jackdaws, rooks, and Edgar Allan Poe's favorite bird, the raven. Corvids have extremely large, well-developed brains for their size. They understand the linkage of cause and effect better than many similar species: They have been observed dropping walnuts in front of passing cars so the vehicles will crack the nuts open for them, and they have even demonstrated a tool-using capability comparable to Paleolithic man. Given the bird's evident intelligence, it would have been especially shocking to discover crows with no visible wounds hobbling around in a daze, unable to fly. The June reports made by local Queens residents described the birds as disoriented and dying.

A MYSTERY IN THE BOROUGHS

Eleven miles to the north across the Long Island Sound, dead crows began showing up in the Bronx. As the summer dragged on, the increased number of dead birds had begun to spread to other parts of the city. The die-off started to attract media attention, as if New York was slowly awakening to find that something strange and deadly was stalking the parks and waterways of the city. The interest was tempered only by the fact that human beings were not its target, at least not yet.

The New York Times devoted an entire article to the situation when it highlighted a report completed by Department of Environmental Conservation in August. The department had concluded that the increase in the number of dead crows was most likely linked to the regional drought that summer. It was noted that the birds most affected were ones that lived near waterways (see Figure 1-1), such as the common American crow and the fish crow.

As the ground dried up in the arid conditions, the crows would be more pressed than usual when foraging. Therefore, it was supposed that they could be probing deeper into the ground for food such as seeds, worms, and insects. This in turn would increase the exposure of the birds to old toxins in the soil. What these toxins could be was pure speculation, but events quickly began to overtake the theory that the birds had begun dying simply from redoubled efforts to find food.

In late August, Flushing Hospital in Queens admitted two elderly patients who were suffering from what looked like, for all intents and purposes, a neurological illness. The symptoms included high fever, weakness, and severe mental confusion. Dr. Deborah Asnis, the infectious disease specialist who treated these patients, made a tentative diagnosis of encephalitis.

Encephalitis is an inflammation of the brain that almost always has some infectious cause. Unlike a stroke, which is typically caused by the obstruction of an artery and thus produces severe damage to a portion of

FIGURE 1-1

CDC chart showing number and location of crow deaths reported through the summer of 1999.

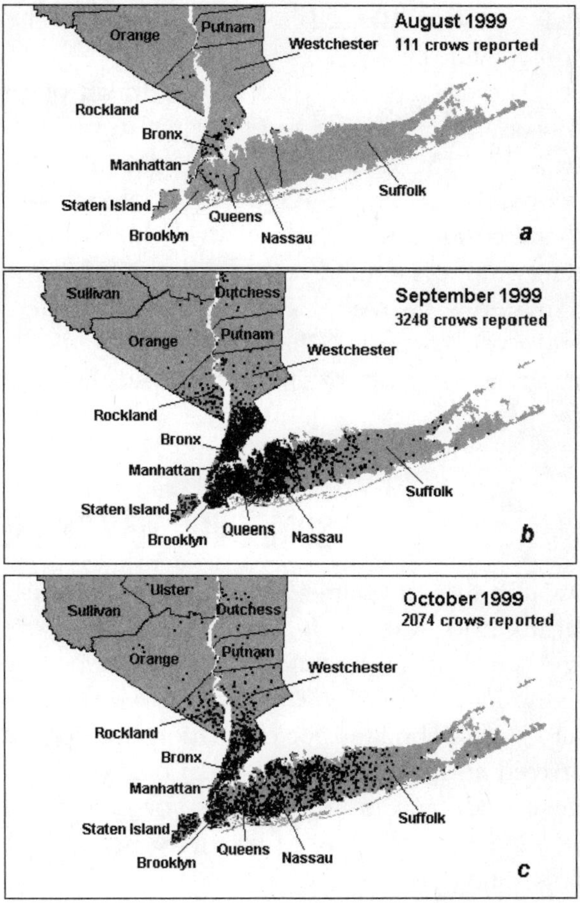

the brain, encephalitis involves virtually the entirety of the brain matter substance, producing an infiltration of white cells throughout. This is a serious problem for the victim because, in the body's efforts to get rid of the infection, the powerful chemicals manufactured by the white blood cells end up destroying many healthy cells, similar to the way an innocent bystander might be injured during a shootout between police and a bank robber. Thus, all functions controlled by brain cells damaged by the body's cellular defense mechanism—judgment, reasoning, memory, movement, and sensation—were affected in these patients.

Dr. Asnis called the New York City Department of Health with the news and sent samples of her patients' blood and spinal fluid to the New York State Department of Health and the Centers for Disease Control and Prevention (CDC) in Atlanta. With any luck, the scientists at these centers would be able to identify the pathogen that had emerged not from the fringe of a rain forest in Africa, but in the middle of the most populous city in the United States.

The city's branch of the Department of Health was both efficient and thorough. In the course of its investigation, a new, disturbing discovery came to light. A cluster of a half-dozen elderly people suffering from encephalitis was found in Queens. The only constant between the cases was that the individuals were relatively healthy older people who spent a lot of time outdoors in the evening. The cause and origin of the disease remained a mystery, however. Encephalitis can be trigged by a wide variety of viruses and even bacteria. Which pathogen starts the inflammation often determines the severity of the disease and the possibility of its spread to other people.

SOMETHING NEW ON THE WIND

Around the same time, Dr. Tracey McNamara, the head pathologist at the Bronx Zoo, was dealing with the same puzzle: What was causing the increased deaths in the local bird population? As Dr. McNamara later related to the *Journal of Homeland Security,* by mid-August several hundred crows had been submitted for evaluation but no conclusive diagnosis had been arrived at, nor was there a great deal of pressure to find one. Crows play no economic role in agriculture or industry, and since they are not kept domestically, there were no angry pet owners demanding to know what was killing their birds.

Still, Dr. McNamara was very interested in what was happening to the crows that summer for two reasons. First, she was the head of the department of pathology at the Wildlife Conservation Society. As free-ranging, nondomestic animals, wild crows fell squarely into the wildlife category.

Second, several of the birds were dying on the grounds of the zoo itself, where they could have spread disease to the zoo's collection of exotic and endangered species. For this reason, zoos continually perform active disease surveillance to identify and neutralize potential bacterial and viral threats. According to Dr. McNamara, who gave a detailed interview to the authors of this book after the incident, "It was our routine policy that any indigenous wildlife found on our grounds that could be a source of transmission or a disease will routinely be necropsied. Dogs can introduce disease to zoo animals. Skunks. Migratory birds. We always looked at those things because we were always looking for the first indication that there might be a problem in our collection."

The heat of the summer had been followed by torrential rains, which in turn resulted in clouds of mosquitoes. Dr. McNamara recalled, "We had a spike in our avian malaria incidents. That's something we see when the mosquito population really explodes . . . so we knew we had mosquito problems, and the zoo was already trying to address them because of that [malaria] issue." The mosquito problem, cropping up at the same time as the spike in bird deaths, was especially troubling to her. She continued, "It was unusual for crows to be dying, and in the history of the zoo, no one could remember similar die-off. Literally, [wild crows] would just fall into an exhibit and then drop dead."

Dr. McNamara had been sending the dead crows to the headquarters of the New York State Department of Environmental Conservation in Albany for examination. But in the absence of a diagnosis, she conducted her own dissections and meticulous evaluations of tissues under the microscope. Given the high risk of unknown disease to the zoo animals, she wanted to pull out all the stops on establishing a cause for why the crows in the area were dying in droves.

Aside from the wild crows found on the grounds, the zoo had lost an Asian pheasant, a bald eagle, a pair of Chilean flamingos, and a cormorant, an exotic water bird. The necropsies themselves presented a challenge since a virus can react differently depending on the species of its host. Some of the birds had intestinal lesions, others did not. A few of the birds did not have gross symptoms of encephalitis, but others did, particularly the ones that showed bleeding from the brain and badly damaged hearts.

"When I looked at the dead crows," said Dr. McNamara, "as a pathologist, the first thing I had to think of was: What are the differential diagnoses I need to consider? Well, the top two would be exotic Newcastle disease and highly pathogenic avian influenza, both of which could threaten our poultry industry." A "differential diagnosis" is medical jargon for a list of most likely causes of the symptoms. Yet there were facts that didn't square up with either of the two diseases that were suspected.

The main argument against Newcastle or avian influenza was the simple fact that the Bronx Zoo had a healthy flock of common chickens and turkeys. These birds were kept in the children's petting zoo, which was an outside area. Far from being isolated, these birds could conceivably be exposed to more pathogens on a daily basis than most of the animals in the zoo, because they interacted directly with the public. Furthermore, domestic chickens and turkeys are highly susceptible to exotic Newcastle disease and avian influenza. Either disease is what epidemiologists call a "slate wiper" when it gets into the bird population, killing vast numbers of the animals.

A third suspect pathogen, Eastern equine encephalitis (EEE), was also ruled out. Dr. McNamara was familiar with the appearance and pathology of EEE in emus, a large, shaggy species of flightless bird similar in some ways to an ostrich. As with the chickens and turkeys, emus are kept outside—in fact, the species is the second-largest living bird, after the ostrich, making it difficult to keep emus isolated inside a cage.

Dr. McNamara knew that Eastern equine encephalitis virus, if it were indeed the one circulating, is virulent for emus and kills them very quickly. Yet the zoo's emus were in good shape. It was at that point that the worrisome thought crossed her mind: *I think this is something new, and I think it's really bad.*

SCOURGE

On September 3, 1999, the CDC completed tests on the samples sent by Dr. Asnis to its labs in Atlanta. The CDC had tested the samples for antibodies the human body would produce if exposed to six relatively common viruses transmitted by insects such as mosquitoes. There had been a hit for St. Louis encephalitis, or SLE.

Viruses are typically named after the place they are first discovered, even if the pathogen is not native to the area. SLE was first recognized in St. Louis in 1933 and is the most common variety of viral encephalitis in the United States. Most people who are infected never show any outward symptoms, but those who do show the flu-like symptoms are at serious risk and need to be hospitalized immediately.

The last outbreak of St. Louis encephalitis in the New York area had taken place over twenty-five years ago; however, viruses endemic to a geographic area can slumber unnoticed for years or decades, then announce themselves in a burst of new cases. The CDC announced such an outbreak in September, and the prevailing thought was that the summer drought, followed by the heavy rain, was to blame. After all, such conditions did in fact create a perfect breeding environment for the mosquitoes that could carry the virus.

New York City Mayor Rudolph Giuliani announced a $6 million campaign to wipe out the city's mosquitoes using chemicals. A public health campaign was kicked off to promote awareness about the threat posed by disease-carrying mosquitoes. Thousands of samples of insect repellent were passed out free. Helicopters sprayed clouds of a powerful insecticide called Scourge across the city.

There is no doubt that these measures did a certain amount of good, but the evidence continued to mount that SLE was not the real culprit. Continued testing of the samples from the elderly patients in Queens turned up negative for St. Louis encephalitis, as well as for other viruses endemic to the United States that were known to cause similar symptoms. Additionally, Dr. McNamara was continuing to build her own case to determine the real agent behind the outbreak. By Labor Day, she knew the illness wasn't bacterial because none of her routine cultures tested positive for bacterial pathogens. She had also been able to rule out unusual chemical exposure, thereby shutting down the theory that toxins had been responsible for the crow die-off around the New York waterways.

Despite the insecticides which had blanketed portions of the city, that week two more flamingos died, and they were quickly dissected for examination. Dr. McNamara said, "I almost fell off my chair when I saw the first slides. The amount of inflammation in the brain of the flamingos that died the day after Labor Day was startling. . . . I was worried." She knew that experts said a bird-human link was impossible, but the facts spoke for themselves. The human encephalitis patients were beginning to die, she had barrelfuls of birds that were also dead from encephalitis, clouds of mosquitoes were plaguing the city, and none of her tests were coming up positive for the usual suspect pathogens.

She had spent Labor Day weekend rereading all of the textbooks in the zoo library. She went through not only the veterinary textbooks, but the medical texts that talked about *flaviviruses,* one of the many families of virus that carry but a single strand of RNA.

Viruses are classified in part by the type of genetic material they contain. They may possess double-stranded DNA, much like the gene in a typical mammalian cell. Or they may contain single-stranded DNA, which is one half of the distinctive double-helix shape that is shown in most textbook pictures of DNA. Finally, viruses may possess RNA, which are special nucleic acids that are associated with the control of a cell's chemical processes.

Flaviviruses and other RNA-containing viruses are distinct from *retroviruses,* which were first described in the 1980s. Retroviruses have the peculiar ability to convert their RNA into DNA, which can then integrate into the host's genomic structure. This means that they can permanently place themselves inside the hosts' own genes.

The best-known human disease caused by a single-stranded RNA virus is hepatitis C, which is transmitted by blood transfusions, contaminated needles, and sexual intercourse. However, other deadly diseases caused by flaviviruses are often transmitted by insects: yellow fever, Japanese encephalitis, and dengue fever. On September 9, Dr. McNamara called the CDC in

Atlanta to report her suspicions about a link between the bird deaths and the sick human patients.

Her conversation with the agency was decidedly mixed. Since work on animals was not part of its mission/charter, the CDC had, at best, a very limited number of veterinary pathologists on staff. It was unlikely that CDC scientists would be as receptive to Dr. McNamara's findings as she had hoped. They refused to accept samples of the inflamed bird tissue she offered to send them, in the hopes that they could identify the pathogen; instead, they pointed out that SLE and related human encephalitis viruses do not normally kill birds.

Dr. McNamara next called the National Veterinary Services Laboratories (NVSL) in Ames, Iowa, and insisted that they take the samples of bird tissue and culture them as soon as possible. When she ran into resistance from the lab, she flat out demanded that NVSL rule out the usual diseases and find out what the pathogen was. They finally agreed to her requests, perhaps only because of her absolute certainty that there was a novel killer bug on the loose. As she had put it at the time, "I'll eat my veterinary license if this isn't something new."

THE LAB ON PLUM ISLAND

Dr. McNamara was accustomed to running samples down to the Albert Einstein Medical School, which was just a few blocks away from her New York office. The Einstein school had an electron microscope (EM) laboratory, and given its easy availability, she liked to use electron microscopy as a routine diagnostic tool. As it happened, the person who was in charge of the EM lab was on vacation, and the pathologist Dr. McNamara routinely worked with was in China.

In retrospect, not having the necessary people available at just the right moment at Einstein was a perfect example of how much chance plays into the discovery and treatment of deadly disease. For example, the EM lab at Einstein would have easily discovered that the structure of the virus in question was the classical geometric pattern of a flavivirus. Had Dr. McNamara been able to get her samples to Einstein and have them tested that same day, it's likely that the virus would have been spotted a lot sooner, and Einstein's researchers would have been able to take credit for being the first to identify the pathogen.

On the other hand, luck was working against the virus as well as for it. First, it just so happened that New York City had a major metropolitan zoo. Second, it was one of only seven zoos in the United States that actually had a full-time pathologist on staff who could do in-house pathology, process the slides, and perform all of the necessary tests.

It was also sheer luck that, as the zoo's pathologist, Dr. McNamara had received training at Plum Island. This triangular-shaped piece of land located between Long Island and the U.S. submarine base at Groton, Connecticut, is home to the Foreign Animal Disease Diagnostic Lab (FADDL), a full-service diagnostic laboratory. Because of the nature of the work done there and its location, Plum Island is only accessible by government ferryboat.

FADDL is one of the few labs in the New York area that can (and does) receive samples of zoonotic diseases from around the world for testing and identification. Zoonotic diseases refer to pathogens that can be passed to humans from either wild or domesticated animals. The best-known outbreak of zoonotic disease in history is the appearance of bubonic plague in medieval Europe, which ended up killing at least a third of the continent's population.

Plum Island was designated as a Biosafety 4 facility, qualifying it as a location where work with dangerous and exotic agents that pose a high individual risk of life-threatening disease could be performed. The Level 4 status enabled Plum Island scientists to study and research diseases, and vaccines for diseases, that would not be allowed in the continental United States. The critical factor allowing for this designation was its island status. In theory, Plum Island could work with anthrax, plague, or Ebola virus. However, given its emphasis on animal treatment, the facility is used when testing for suspect foreign animal diseases such as foot-and-mouth, rinderpest, hog cholera, and African horse sickness.[1]

"I had to fight [Bronx Zoo management] for that training," said Dr. McNamara. "At the time, before West Nile [virus] appeared in New York, I was just a resident [pathologist] and they usually only trained department heads." She vociferously argued her case, at one point telling the directors of the Bronx Zoo, "Let me get this straight. *I'm* the one dealing with birds for quarantine in New York City from overseas, and you don't want me to have this training?" Faced with that logic, they found space in the course to admit her.

During her training at the lab, Dr. McNamara was able to actually view cases of encephalitis that had been intentionally induced in experimental birds. She had also seen what highly pathogenic avian influenza looked like in a necropsy of a dead bird at Plum Island. There are very few scientists in the United States who have this experience. Because of this training, she had immediately realized that there were simply too many differences between what she was seeing in the crows and zoo birds in the lab and the initial diagnosis for St. Louis encephalitis. Had it not been for her specialized training and experience, the public health officials might have ignored her warnings and gone on believing that the waves of bird and human deaths were the result of SLE.

NARROWING DOWN THE SUSPECTS

Because Einstein's EM lab was unavailable, Dr. McNamara had to take her bird tissue samples elsewhere for testing. It wasn't until September 15 that the National Veterinary Services Laboratories used electron microscopy to determine that the particles of viral pathogen were a mere 40 nanometers (40 billionths of a meter) in diameter. Even in the infinitesimal realms of microbiology, that is an impressively small measurement.

For example, the smallest known bacteria are relative giants at over 200 nanometers. Viruses are smaller than bacteria. The common cold virus is typically about 75 nanometers. In comparison, the diameter of the DNA helix itself is only 2 nanometers, while the thickness of a typical cell wall is 10 nanometers.

The incredibly small size of the organism was indicative of its likely identification. This is because size is one of the ways that viruses are classified. Other ways to categorize viruses are by shape, type of genetic material, host range, and whether the organism can be transmitted by a vector.

Since the viral particle in question was barely half that size, had a hexagonal shape, and was surrounded by a thin membrane, it put the disease in the category of a flavivirus. The NVSL contacted the CDC with its findings. Once sent, the findings were disputed and debated over. But someone at the CDC must have begun to become alarmed. Four days later, the CDC requested avian tissue samples from McNamara to study and come to their own conclusions.

Frustrated with the lack of timely response from the CDC, Dr. McNamara had had enough. She recalled, "It was like a eureka moment at two o' clock in the morning. A lightbulb went off in my head." She reasoned that while the NVSL had established that what they were dealing with was indeed a flavivirus, at that point no veterinary lab could pursue it further, because flaviviruses were predominantly human pathogens. She realized that this particular pathogen had never been a veterinary problem. Therefore, it was unlikely that any *veterinary* lab had the equipment necessary to further characterize this virus.

The next morning, she got in touch with the U.S. Army Medical Research Institute in Infectious Diseases (USAMRIID) in Fort Detrick, Maryland. Within two days, she established a scientific collaboration with USAMRIID scientists. Alarmed, they urged her to send them samples immediately. Within twenty-four hours, they were able to confirm that the size and shape of the virus placed it in the flavivirus family.

In the third week of September 1999, both the CDC and USAMRIID were closing the net over what the pathogen could be. They were doing so, in part, by conclusively determining what it wasn't. Though it sounds odd when taken out of context, the accumulation of negative data is essential in almost all cases when trying to determine the identity of a pathogen.

The process can be likened to being able to eliminate suspects in a police lineup. Even if the killer isn't picked out immediately, at least less energy will be spent chasing down false leads. As in a serial murder mystery, the clock continued to tick. By now, there had been nine deaths due to mysterious encephalitis in New York, and nine more cases had shown up and were feeding the public's anxiousness over the new disease.

USAMRIID reported that the bird samples sent from the Bronx Zoo all tested weakly positive for SLE based on antibody studies. Antibodies usually bind tightly and specifically to their "target" pathogen, but in this case the antibody binding was not very strong. This told the scientists that while the pathogen wasn't SLE, at least it was distantly related to it. Later, the CDC called Dr. McNamara to request more tissue samples. They began to test for a wider range of diseases, including West Nile, Japanese encephalitis, dengue, yellow fever, and a tick-borne virus that caused Powassan encephalitis. Finally, working independently on the West Coast, a University of California researcher narrowed down the viruses in samples of human brain tissue to one of two known flaviviruses: Junin or West Nile.

To make sure that their conclusions were correct before going public, the scientists involved in the investigation of the mysterious organism performed genome sequencing on the pathogen. Following that final step, the CDC, USAMRIID, and the researcher in California all came to the same conclusion. At a press conference held on the evening of September 24, the pathogen on the loose was identified as the West Nile virus. It had taken almost three months from the time Dr. McNamara first voiced her strong suspicion that something odd was going on to finally make the diagnosis.

FROM UGANDA TO UPSTATE NEW YORK

As with many diseases, we will probably never know when the West Nile species of flavivirus made the jump from an unknown avian species into a human being. It's possible that hundreds or thousands of years ago, the virus was passed along through an open wound caused by the bite of a wild—or even domesticated—bird. What we do know is that the first recorded case of West Nile to be brought to medical attention took place in Africa during the winter of 1937.

A woman in Omogo, the West Nile district of the northern province of Uganda, contracted the specific form of encephalitis. It is not recorded whether she had come into contact with birds, been bitten by or eaten an infected animal, or even whether she survived her experience with West Nile. Like many details of index cases from long ago, the details are blurred or lost as they recede from us in time and space.

The virus was isolated and studied using samples from patients, birds, and mosquitoes in Egypt in the early 1950s. Surprisingly, it turned out to be rather widespread throughout Africa and Eurasia. Like many of the other viruses that cause encephalitis, the primary mode of transmission was via mosquitoes that took blood meals from birds and then bit human beings.

More recently, West Nile virus had cropped up in sporadic outbreaks, noticeable for producing cases of human and equine illness in Europe. Outbreaks of West Nile have been noted in Israel in early 1950s and southern France and Russia in 1962. It made scattered appearances in Belarus and the Ukraine in the 1970s and 1980s, Romania in 1996, the Czech Republic in 1997, and Italy in 1998. Of these, the most deadly outbreak was the one in Romania, where 500 people fell ill and fifty died.

Luckily, the fatality rate in Romania, which was one in ten, proved to be the exception to the rule. It is possible that an exceptionally deadly strain of West Nile arose in Romania and then died out. It could be that Romania in 1996 lacked adequate medical care for its West Nile patients. And, of course, it could have been sheer bad luck that a larger number of the victims in Romania were elderly or infirm.[2]

By and large, West Nile appears to be among the less lethal of the flaviviruses. This explains in part why it hasn't been well known around the world, at least compared with measles or smallpox. West Nile is a killer to the elderly and those with less than healthy immune systems. These people are also called the "immunosuppressed" in medical terminology. However, since healthy people survive, when West Nile sweeps through a country, it does not leave depopulated cities and piles of human corpses in its wake.

What troubles epidemiologists, who are the scientists who study the incidence, distribution, and control of disease in a population, is the fact that West Nile made the journey across the Atlantic at all. In today's world of mass cargo transport, West Nile underscores the troubling fact that any virus is only a jet ride away from any of the major modern cities around the world.

A pathogen from, say, the African savanna can infect an unknowing person and be transported to Nairobi, Kenya by jeep in six hours. From there, it is only a four-hour plane ride to Cairo. A change in planes could take it across the Mediterranean to Athens in three hours. Five hours to Rome. Seven to London. Eleven to New York.

At present, it is unknown why large bird die-offs did not occur prior to the outbreaks in Europe, Israel, and Russia. It is possible that the virus emerged only gradually into the avian population so that large numbers were not all killed at once. It's also possible that the majority of bird deaths simply went unnoticed. Eight hundred crows dying in the rural Ukrainian countryside are far less likely to be noticed than 800 birds dying in the middle of New York City, which is one of the most densely populated urban areas on the planet.

It could be that the bird deaths were noticed but not reported as a significant finding. Consider, for example, how difficult it was for Dr. McNamara to get the CDC to even take a look at the bird tissue samples she had collected while West Nile continued to spread in New York. And, of course, perhaps the same deadly strain that hit Romania was the one that happened to resurface in Queens.

The specter of intentional infection—a bioterrorism event—was also briefly considered and dismissed. When organisms are altered, traces are still left, like fingerprints at a crime scene. With this in mind, the CDC did a detailed genomic sequencing of the virus, looking at each strand of its genetic code.

The CDC determined that no one had bioengineered this strain of West Nile. Furthermore, the genetic code was nearly identical to a strain of the virus that had broken out in Israel in 1998. A test called reverse transcription-polymerase chain reaction showed that the genomic sequence in viral samples from a dead goose from Israel was 99.8 percent similar to the samples taken from the New York outbreak. For a virus that inherently mutates frequently due to its RNA structure, this is considered to be a perfect match.

Dr. McNamara noted that "Israel is a real crossing point of all these migratory paths for birds. It really wouldn't be surprising if [West Nile] would show up first in a place where you have large congregations of migratory birds." From there, it is possible that an infected human or animal could have arrived via the John F. Kennedy International Airport. This busy airport lies at the south end of Queens, a scant dozen miles from the Fort Totten area where the first reports of dead crows surfaced.

Philip Tierno, the director of clinical microbiology and immunology at New York University Medical Center, takes a different viewpoint in his work, *The Secret Life of Germs.* He notes that wherever West Nile has been found, so has a species of Asian mosquito called *Aedes japonicus. Aedes* is not native to North America, but is today found throughout the Northeastern United States. After West Nile broke out in New York City, the U.S. Army determined that *Aedes* is a much more effective transmitter of the virus than the common American mosquito. According to Tierno, this suggests that bites resulting from this species of mosquito led to the most severe cases of West Nile, although we now know that a least *eight different species* of mosquito can transmit the virus with varying degrees of efficiency.

This knowledge, in turn, begs three more questions. First, how did *Aedes* become endemic to the United States? Second, how did an insect native to Japan, Korea, China, and the Ryukyu Archipelago to the southeast of Japan (whose best known island, at least to Americans, is Okinawa) come into contact with a virus from East Africa? Third, how did this insect become a carrier for the virus?

We simply do not know, and perhaps we never will. It's perhaps the oddest aspect of the field of epidemiology that only some answers come into razor-sharp focus. Yet other details become so badly blurred that one must grope for answers and rely on logical guesses or intuition. For example, through a combination of old-fashioned detective work and our advances in both epidemiological and forensic science, we can pinpoint many things: the final cause of death, the exact time it occurred, and even the position of the body at the time of death. Yet we can't tell every detail of where the person went in the last three weeks, or whether they had been bitten by an insect or come into contact with substances that they normally would never be exposed to.

BLOOD MEALS

By October, the virus had been detected in more than fifty bird species from eight states. The virus proved to be quite the survivor when throughout the remainder of 1999, it was discovered in horses, bats, raccoons, and the eastern chipmunk. Perhaps confirming the CDC's worst fears, by 2001 scientists learned that fifty-eight different species of animals were found to be carrying the virus.

This didn't mean that every single mosquito carried West Nile, or that a single bite meant that a resident of the Northeast would be infected. But it did raise the level of concern. For example, it may not sound alarming if only two or three percent of a given population of mosquitoes carries West Nile—until one realizes that mosquito populations easily run into the millions and tens of millions.

Furthermore, the interaction of bird and mosquito expanded the range of the virus much more quickly than if it had spread by insects alone. Mosquitoes rarely fly more than a few miles from where they hatch and pupate. Birds, on the other hand, easily migrate hundreds or thousands of miles. In the first week of October 1999, the virus cropped up in birds across the Hudson River in New Jersey. Two weeks later, West Nile was found in a dead crow in North Carolina, more than 500 miles to the south.

A year later, there were more than sixty confirmed cases of encephalitis due to West Nile in Long Island, the Bronx, and upstate New York. Seven more deaths were reported. Estimates on how many people were infected with West Nile but never developed symptoms range widely. But it is safe to say that at least two thousand New Yorkers acquired the virus and likely passed off their symptoms as a mild summer cold or "flu." The cases in the next year followed the pattern of spread beyond the boundaries of New York City (see Figure 1-2), especially to the south and west as infected insects and birds continued on their separate ways.[3]

As many wild bird species that could sustain the insects' need for a blood meal were eradicated, causing the infected mosquitoes to look for new hosts, owners of domestic animals also began to worry about the health of their animals. Dr. McNamara's exotic birds in the Bronx Zoo were already on the danger list, but any bird that humans kept as house pets—parrots, canaries, and cockatiels—were also susceptible to the virus. Worse, outside-dwelling domestic animals such as horses were also affected by the pathogen. While no exact numbers are available for domesticated animals, the veterinary community had observed that quite a few animals died as a result of the introduction of West Nile.

FIGURE 1-2

Locations of 1999 versus 2000 reported human cases of West Nile virus.

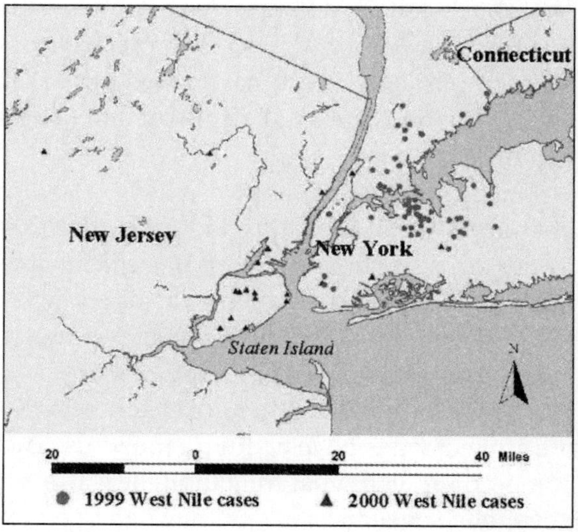

At the end of 1999, the CDC allocated $2.5 million to detect and prevent West Nile outbreaks in the following year. There was some question as to whether enough of the infected mosquitoes and birds in the area would survive the winter to continue the spread of the virus. To be on the safe side, come early spring, several anti-mosquito measures were implemented.

New York began to stock *Gambusia affinis,* otherwise known as the mosquito fish, in the open areas of the city's wastewater treatment plants. *Gambusia* is hardy enough to survive the dirty water at the waste treatment centers, and it has a ravenous appetite for mosquito larvae. A two-pronged campaign to destroy mosquito larvae was also implemented. The approach was to combine a bacterium that directly attacks the water-dwelling larva with a growth-stunting chemical regulator to prevent adult insects from pupating. This mixture was dumped into thousands of drains and catch basins in all five boroughs of New York City.

While it was hoped that controlling mosquitoes would stop the spread of the virus, disturbing signs continued to appear throughout the remainder of 1999. A laboratory experiment performed by the National Wildlife Health Center of the U.S. Geological Survey (USGS) demonstrated that West Nile could be passed from one bird to another, even without an insect vector. Healthy crows were infected by crows carrying West Nile when living in an enclosure where they shared food, water, and perches. Although it is unlikely that this is a significant source of the outbreak's spread, it did show that the organism continued to baffle and surprise its researchers.

Despite the anti-larva measures and a relatively frigid winter throughout the Northeast, it turned out that the virus's hosts survived in great enough numbers to continue the pathogen's spread. By June 2000, dead crows and other birds collected in upstate New York were necropsied and tested positive for West Nile. With each successive year, the virus, spread by the dual route of bird and insect, has moved out in all directions across the United States, adding virtually all of the country to its list of endemic regions (see Figure 1-3).

As of this writing, approximately 10,000 cases of West Nile fever have been reported to the CDC, and more than 200 deaths have been attributed to the virus. It should be remembered that the 10,000 cases reported are likely only where the patient was ill enough to seek medical help outside the home, and the attending nurse or physician was astute enough to look for and report the findings to the CDC.

Outside of this number, it is likely that 50,000 to 100,000 people across the United States have acquired the virus. Though a few of them may have come down with what they thought was a severe cold, many more would never have even known that they had been infected, since they likely never

FIGURE 1-3

The current worldwide range of the West Nile virus.

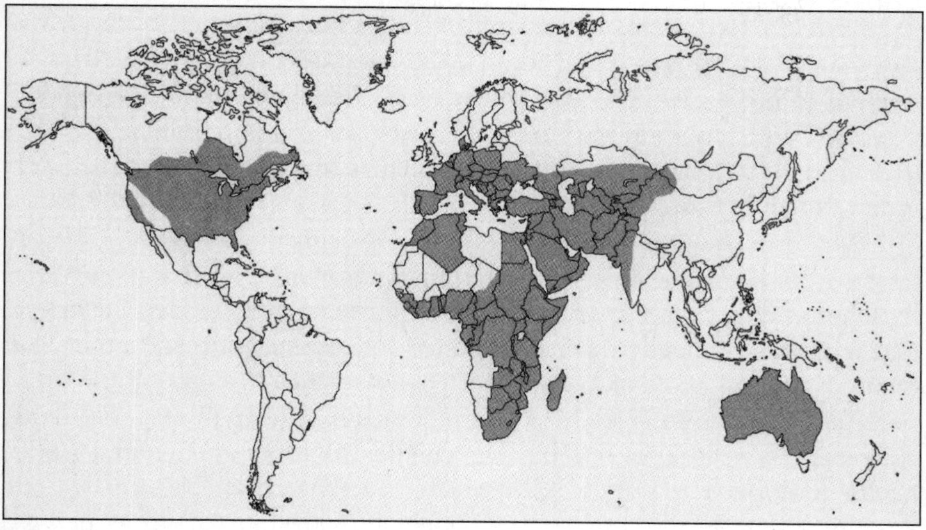

showed a single symptom. At present, there is no known cure or vaccine for the virus—though the people who were infected and successfully fought off the virus now carry their own antibodies against the virus and will remain immune for the rest of their lives.

VETERINARIANS IN THE VANGUARD

Could West Nile have been stopped before it had a chance to become an ongoing threat throughout the United States? What if there had been better communication and a sharing of findings between Dr. Tracey McNamara at the Bronx Zoo, the CDC, and Dr. Deborah Asnis at the Flushing Hospital in Queens? This is yet another epidemiological question that can never be fully answered. But it does call into question whether public health agencies are prepared for—and quick enough to respond to—the next killer microbe that shows up in the United States.

The appearance of West Nile also highlighted that when it comes to detecting outbreaks of new disease, we are ignoring an important fact: that many of these pathogens are zoonotic. Lyme disease, which comes from deer ticks, is a familiar zoonotic disease. Rabies, which one can pick up from dogs or horses, is still another well-known example. Bats are also known to carry rabies, and they are the prime suspect in Ebola, which is the latest in a long line of terrifying hemorrhagic fevers from Africa. Even the domestic house cat may carry organisms for plague, anthrax, cowpox, toxoplasmosis (a parasite), as well as a myriad of bacterial infections.

There are two points that need to be kept in mind about zoonotic diseases such as West Nile. First, because the organisms do not normally need humans to propagate, they can be extremely deadly if contracted. Second, if a disease has to jump into the human species from an animal, it makes logical sense to keep some sort of surveillance trained on the animal communities that live around us.

"Veterinarians are the vanguard," Dr. McNamara concurred. "We are on the front line of defense. . . . Veterinary pathologists were the ones who took the lead on figuring out where this virus went, what tissues it attacked, and what tissues needed to be submitted for testing." She and other like-minded medical professionals in the veterinary field are pushing hard to bring about some kind of reform in veterinary education and improving their communication and reporting abilities to local and federal public health authorities.

She also cites the training she fought for on Plum Island as being a decisive factor. Although veterinarians are taught about Newcastle disease or avian influenza in school, she's deeply skeptical that many of her colleagues have seen either in the real world. Currently, all veterinarians take an exam to be accredited in the ability to recognize foreign animal diseases, but she notes that there are no continuing education requirements to stay fresh and up-to-date in that area. Even for diseases as potentially devastating as foot-and-mouth disease (FMD) in animals, it is doubtful that a community veterinarian would recognize the disease, simply because he has never seen a case before. Yet FMD can be carried miles, via the wind, from one animal herd to another, infecting hundreds of thousands of animals in enormous feedlots in the course of a day or two.

Dr. McNamara notes that because technology has advanced so fast—today, for example, it's routine to do MRIs for cancer in house cats—it has compressed the amount of information that should be covered in veterinary school. Furthermore, it has shifted the coursework toward "small animal medicine," meaning more work on the few species that humans keep as household pets.

The problem that Dr. McNamara has with this approach is that the portion of the curriculum that deals with foreign animal disease recognition has gotten short shrift. "As far as I'm concerned," she said, "if you're a veterinarian, you have taken a vow to recognize disease in all species, not just poodles. If you just want to deal with one species, be an M.D., not a vet."

WHERE THE LIGHT IS BETTER

In 2001, almost two years after West Nile began knocking crows out of the trees in north Queens, Dr. McNamara attended a CDC-funded conference to discuss how to create working relationships between zoo pathologists and their public health counterparts across the country. A great deal of progress was made on many fronts to build these relationships; it is a first step in the direction of actively watching for zoonotic threats.

Yet there's still a way to go before the gap between public health and veterinary science is bridged. At the time of this conference, a great number of dead birds were being reported in spots around the nation. The suspect could have been a different flavivirus or a new form of avian influenza. Both viruses are zoonotic in nature. When Dr. McNamara asked the public health officials in attendance what their labs had found in the birds that were negative for West Nile, she got a blank look. The findings, to them, were self-evident: It wasn't West Nile, so the case was closed.

Dr. McNamara disagreed with this limited approach. Most of the birds that had been collected were found dead in the field, so there was no clinical history. There was no way to tell if they might have shown neurologic symptoms, pointing to West Nile or some other, yet unknown zoonotic virus. When she asked if the birds had been tested for anything else, the answer was, "No."

She was amazed. In her opinion, this went right to a fundamental flaw with existing human and veterinary medicine: the "one disease" mentality and approach. In essence, medical professionals look for what is already known. Looking for something that is unknown falls outside of their day-to-day responsibilities. Dr. McNamara had gone out of her way to impress upon her students to expect the unexpected. "I would train my residents to rule out all known diseases in domestic species," she added, "because that's where the majority of work has been done for hundreds of years. They should always be prepared for the fact that they might be seeing something entirely new."

The answer she had received at the conference was highly ironic. In her estimation, the money that the CDC poured into the West Nile surveillance program probably resulted in the single largest wildlife disease control program that had been undertaken to date in the United States over a three-year period. Hundreds of thousands of dollars had been spent for people to collect the birds, get them to a lab, and sample the tissues.

Having done all of that work, it is unfortunate that once the tissues made it to a lab they were only analyzed for one—and only one—pathogen. After all, public health was, for the moment, only concerned about one disease: West Nile. Because they were only looking for one pathogen, it wasn't in their scope to look for anything else that might have caused the mysterious bird deaths.

There is an old joke about a drunk who is searching for his car keys under a streetlamp. A policeman comes along and asks the drunk where he last saw the keys. The drunk points toward a shadowy alley down the block. "Then why aren't you looking over there?" asks the policeman. The drunk replies, "Because the light is better over here."

To the public health agencies participating in the CDC's program, this logic is sound. The spotlight was certainly a good deal brighter when it was trained on the West Nile virus. It didn't really pay to wander beyond the range of the light—even if the correct answer was somewhere out in the dark.

NOTES

1. Currently, Plum Island uses Biosafety Level 4 measures and does not handle more pathogenic organisms that demand a higher level of biocontainment. The measures it employs include negatively pressurizing labs to prevent pathogens from escaping the designated research area.
2. A second report on the 1996 Romanian outbreak of West Nile virus gives vastly different numbers: 90,000 confirmed cases and seventeen deaths. If this figure is correct, then the virus is even less lethal than suspected—but much easier to catch.
3. The reason that mosquitoes are able to transmit West Nile and not the HIV virus is twofold: First, in feeding, a mosquito picks up fewer HIV particles from an infected human than is required for transmission. Second, HIV remains inert in the mosquito's stomach, where it is digested and rendered inert.

CHAPTER 2

CORONA OF DEATH

SARS

The Metropole, one of the many high-rise hotels in Hong Kong, looks like a stately rectangle of white marble sitting at the end of the city's touristy entertainment district. The hotel is definitely upscale, boasting panoramic city views from many rooms. The rooftop has been converted into a swimming pool and health club, and the in-house restaurant boasts several award-winning chefs.

It's worthwhile to mention how glamorous and well run the hotel is, because it illustrates how many people mistakenly feel that if they are in a sanitary environment, they are safe from infectious diseases. Certainly, in a luxurious, Western-style hotel where one can order cocktails at the Sip-Sip Bar and enjoy the lights of the city, there's no chance of meeting a killer pathogen, particularly one that may have gotten its start among village chicken farmers and small-time salesmen peddling dried shrimp.

And yet, the events that took place at the Metropole turned an outbreak of severe acute respiratory syndrome (SARS) into a disease that has killed at least 800 people in places as separate as Vietnam and Canada. SARS was, in a way, the modern world's first test in tracking and corralling the outbreak of a novel disease that was both highly pathogenic and contagious. The results have been decidedly mixed.

Information was suppressed by government officials from the start. This interference nearly crippled the valiant efforts of the World Health Organization and medical professionals called in to fight the disease. And in the end, what saved the world from a suffering a devastating pandemic may have been the very nature of the pathogen's limited ability to spread itself.

THE CITY OF FLOWERS

The disease that causes the SARS syndrome probably first appeared in the autumn of 2002 in one of the southeastern provinces of the Chinese mainland called Guangdong. We say "probably" because while we can make guesses as to when, where, and how the disease entered, we will never truly know.

It's not unusual to have problems finding the first, or "index," case where a virus jumped into the human species. Typically, this is because the index case can happen in some remote environment where it is particularly difficult to collect data. But in the case of SARS, there were plenty of opportunities to collect data. What obscured the ability of the international health organizations to find the point where SARS jumped into humans was a decision made by the Chinese government to suppress information about the initial outbreak.

Consider newly emerging diseases such as Ebola and HIV. We do not know the index case of either virus, nor do we know the original reservoir hosts with any degree of certainty. In large part, that's because both viruses originated in the African equatorial rain forest. The sheer density and exotic nature of animals, plants, or insects that could be the reservoir threaten to overwhelm any hunt for an original source. Also, given the sporadic density of the population in this climate zone—and even more spotty access to any medical care—it's easy for a newly emerging disease to go unnoticed for quite some time.

Mainland China is about as far removed from that reality as possible. What makes the case of the SARS virus different from the beginning were state-sponsored efforts to block and obscure vital information on what allowed the virus to adapt to the human species and spread like a wildfire in dry grass.

The most reliable stories place the first reported case of SARS along the Pearl River in Southeast China, near the city of Foshan, in November 2002. This early case, in a forty-year-old man whose name has never been determined, came down with a high fever and dry, rapid cough. He eventually recovered, but not before infecting four nurses at the local hospital where he was admitted. This case was reported as pneumonia, but only months later was determined to be caused by the SARS virus.

Reports continue to be sketchy even after this point. It's reported that an unnamed shrimp salesman infected in Foshan likely carried the disease to Guangzhou, a city of over six million. Guangzhou is a thoroughly modern city, capital of the province and home to the best universities and medical centers in the area. It is known by a pleasing moniker: the City of Flowers.

The city's tranquility was shattered as the outbreak took hold between November and February the following year. In that time period, at least 300 people became sick from SARS in Guangdong and five died. The medical community in the city was baffled by what was causing the strange sickness as laboratory analyses for influenza all came back negative.

As always happens when any outbreak begins to spread, panic began to bloom under the surface of the well-ordered society. Rumors of hundreds of people falling dead with the mysterious coughing sickness spread throughout Guangdong province. That these rumors were quickly disproved did little to calm the populace. Antibiotics flew off shelves and pharmacies quickly reported shortages. A thriving black market developed for such commonplace items as white vinegar, which people were using to disinfect their homes as a way to stave off the pathogen.

Despite all of these frightening events, the Chinese government kept the outbreak a secret for at least three months. The first inkling that the World Health Organization (WHO) had of the severity of the situation didn't come until February, when the virus had at least ninety days to establish and amplify itself among the population of Guangdong.

TINDER AND MATCH

On February 10, 2003, the WHO office in Beijing received an e-mail describing a "strange contagious disease" that had killed several people and sickened over a hundred in the Guangdong province within a single week. According to later reports, the message described a panic where people were emptying pharmaceutical stocks of any medicine thought to ward off the mysterious ailment. This tallied frighteningly well with the whispers that the WHO had heard about the outbreak through the winter. But by international law, the organization could not assist unless a request was made.

The following day, the Guangdong provincial government stated that 300 people had contracted a form of atypical pneumonia since November. This statement marked the first public announcement by the Chinese authorities about the outbreak. Finally, the Chinese Ministry of Health asked for help from the World Health Organization of the United Nations. The next day, the WHO issued an alert, but it was already too late. The virus had already jumped beyond the province and into the heart of one of the busiest commercial centers in the world—Hong Kong—thanks to the unwitting help of a modern-day Typhoid Mary.

One of the doctors involved in the existing outbreak in Guangdong became further ensnared in the story of the virus. Dr. Liu Jianlun, a sixty-four-year-old professor of medicine with a specialization in respiratory diseases, had helped treat several of the SARS patients in Guangdong's Sun Yat-Sen Memorial Hospital. In an odd turn of events, during the height of the outbreak in Guangzhou, he left the city to attend a relative's wedding in Hong Kong.

It is unclear whether a formal quarantine was put in place around the city or the province. If so, it was clearly not observed. The physicians attending the SARS cases did not understand the nature of the disease until it spread beyond their control—and that included Dr. Liu. It turned out that SARS hit the health care professionals quite hard, as one in three people infected in China was either a nurse or doctor for the SARS patients. Only later would it become clear that intimate contact with patients—and handling equipment contaminated with respiratory secretions or performing procedures on patients—was the single strongest "risk factor" for acquiring SARS.

Dr. Liu leads us back to the Metropole in Hong Kong, where he and his wife had booked a room on the ninth floor before meeting up with his soon-to-be brother-in-law. It appears that he wasn't feeling particularly under the weather, though he had a slight cough and occasional sneezing attacks. He and his family spent the day sightseeing and enjoying the tourist attractions of the nearby Kowloon district, mingling freely with the hundreds of people out shopping and enjoying the day.

By the following morning, Dr. Liu's cough had become extremely heavy, and he was suffering from severe chills, as if he were beginning a bad case of influenza. He knew better than that. It probably frightened him that he was now in close proximity to his family and had been circulating in several crowded environments for the last two days.

He went directly to the hospital and explained to the doctors treating him that he had been working with patients stricken with the mysterious disease in Guangzhou. It is recorded that he specifically warned the medical staff that he was probably highly contagious. Yet from the reports, his warnings were either ignored or not taken seriously.

As surprising as it seems in retrospect, few of the doctors or nurses giving him treatment wore gowns or masks to protect themselves. Shockingly, precautions weren't taken, despite the fact that by then, the WHO had issued two health alerts. In addition, at about the same time, newspaper stories of the outbreak in Southeast China were commonplace, as the seal that the government had put in place to stop the flow of information was beginning to leak.

Three days after Dr. Liu admitted himself to the hospital, his brother-in-law came down with similar symptoms and joined him at the hospital. It is known that during his stay at the Metropole, Dr. Liu infected at least a dozen other people, four of them from Canada.

At the time, it was thought that he could have coughed or sneezed in their presence, perhaps while they took the elevator to the ninth floor. Two of the people who became extremely ill also stayed on the ninth floor in rooms close to Dr. Liu's. Unfortunately, there was no way for them to know that the virus had checked in along with a fellow hotel guest.

THE BREATH THIEF

SARS victims developed a serious respiratory ailment characterized by widespread fluid in the lungs and in the tiny little air sacs known as alveoli. The presence of the fluid is also known as *diffuse infiltrate.* The production of fluid wasn't localized to a single lobe of the lung as is typical with most forms of bacterial pneumonia. Instead, it was spread throughout each of the lobes in both the right and left lungs. More frighteningly, the presence of the fluid was associated with difficulty in oxygenating the blood.

The fluid, which is a thin mucous-like secretion produced by the body in reaction to the virus, acted as a block between the airway and the blood in the lungs for diffusion of oxygen. People with SARS died because they were unable to diffuse oxygen through the alveoli, the tiny little air tracts in the lung that are physically close to a little tangle of blood vessels that absorb oxygen and dump out carbon dioxide (CO_2). In essence, SARS killed people by stealing the body's ability to get oxygen into their bloodstream through the fluid—as if the virus's victims were drowning on dry land.

When the first SARS deaths were reported to the World Health Organization, they were mostly ignored. But by this time, information was starting to leak out of China through scattered news reports. It was certainly not a voluntary choice on the part of the Chinese government to release any news of this sort, nor did the government have a history of forthcoming behavior in release of public health information. The lack of correct information caused by the almost paranoid need for secrecy in the Chinese government led to people simply putting face masks on, thinking that this might be a new form of influenza.

Ultimately, the World Health Organization, in collaboration with the Centers for Disease Control (CDC) in the United States, initiated two important actions by early March 2003. First, they established a *case definition* for SARS. A case definition refers to the specific signs, symptoms, and demographics of the individuals who are affected. The definition can also include age, travel history, and whether someone has had preexisting illness.

The definition for SARS was the essence of elegant simplicity: A bad respiratory illness, often fatal, was being spotted in otherwise healthy adults who had recently traveled to Southeast Asia, or who may have been in close contact with people who had recently been in Southeast Asia. What made the illness's case definition stand out was that it specified people who had some travel connection to Southeast Asia, but who were otherwise healthy, with no good reason for the sudden onset of dramatic breathing difficulties.

Second, once that case definition was established, the WHO (in collaboration with the CDC) set up a Web site where medical professionals around the world could report cases that were consistent with the symptoms of SARS. Individual physicians and national/regional-level public health departments could report in. Historically, when travelers returned home, physicians in most countries—Canada included—did not take the time or effort to report single cases of respiratory disease to international or even national-level public health entities. Rather, the physician would report the suspicious case to their local public health department, which might be a tiny office employing one part-time person on a municipal level. The public health department would slowly gather up the total number of cases, check to make sure that they met the case definition, and then send it on to the CDC or the World Health Organization, perhaps weekly.

But now, for the first time in history, public health officials began to use real-time, Internet-based communication for data gathering, analysis, and dissemination of information—and they *were* reporting individual cases directly to a single dataset operated collaboratively by the CDC and WHO. This, in and of itself, was a huge advance over routine practice. So, compared to other epidemics, there was a very small delay in the reporting process—literally a few hours instead of many days.

SIGNS AND PORTENTS

A syndrome definition is a combination of signs and symptoms. In its simplest form, signs are what a doctor finds upon examining the patient. Symptoms are what the patient complains about. When this information is combined with the patient's travel and health history, a lot can be determined about a disease in a short time. Cases can be tallied up on a daily basis, allowing the WHO to put out a daily bulletin on a given outbreak. Typically, a WHO daily bulletin states: "Here are the number of cases that meet this case definition, and here's where we're finding them." The bulletin is typically broken out on a country-by-country basis.

In spring 2003, alarm bells starting going off at the WHO once the bulletin started showing cases in multiple countries. Immediately, the reaction from the world press was fear—the fear that a pandemic was being caused by a new, unknown organism. A pandemic, which is usually defined as a disease that appears more or less simultaneously on multiple continents, could indicate an easy person-to-person transmission, probably by an aerosol (e.g., sneezing or coughing).

It would take an aerosol to infect so many people quickly. A single infected individual could infect dozens more, and when multiplied out ten or twenty times, it is easy to see how many millions of people could become ill. There is virtually no other way for a true pandemic to take hold.

The WHO researchers first thought that SARS could be an outbreak of an old organism, perhaps one in a slightly mutated form. They began to culture the organism from the fluids of the infected individuals. In due course, the researchers stained the respiratory secretions from affected people with fluorescent antibodies against every known organism. This was an amazingly wide test by any standard. The antibodies had been collected from people who were afflicted by all types of influenza, all types of pneumonia, and all types of infectious diseases reported over the past twenty-five to thirty years.

Antibodies are protein molecules manufactured by the immune system. They are exquisitely sensitive for attaching to a foreign pathogen, and they are extremely specific. This is why when you recover from one of the hundreds of rhinoviruses that cause the common cold, you are not immune to any other variation of rhinovirus—because the antibodies in your bloodstream simply are not keyed to react to anything except the same strain of virus.

When looking for an existing form of organism, scientists can put a molecule of a fluorescing material called "fluorescence" into the stain. Fluorescence chemically binds to an antibody and allows it to give off an infinitesimal bit of light, which allows a scientist to see which cells or viruses the antibodies bind to under an ultraviolet (UV) microscope.

The SARS researchers would have taken a patient's nasal secretions as well as secretions from the trachea, which is usually obtained by passing a pipette down the respirator tube. The secretions are smeared on a slide, and an antibody fluorescence tag is drizzled onto it. The researcher washes off the slide with a little bit of saline, and if the antibody binds to the pathogen, the antibody will not wash off.

The researchers investigating SARS at the World Health Organization and the CDC performed this test against their bank of thousands of antibodies for all known organisms. What they saw under the fluorescent microscope startled them—or more precisely, what startled them was what they did not see. The tests turned up nothing. Not a single cell infected with the pathogen glowed green from the fluorescent dye. Every antibody test had turned up negative. Whatever else SARS was, it was a killer that was new to the scene.

SAVING LIVES IN REAL TIME

Even though the pathogen was unknown, the assumption was that it was a new form of virus as opposed to bacteria. This was a solid guess, because as a general rule of thumb, viral disease causes a diffuse collection of fluid in the lung. In cases of bacterial pneumonia, the disease tends to cause localized or so-called low bar pneumonia, where fluid fills up only one lobe of a lung.

By now, SARS patients had been hospitalized throughout Southeast Asia, China, and in Canada. The physicians treating the infected individuals had very little to work with as far as treating the disease, so they focused on the symptoms of the patient in order to keep them from smothering from the inability to oxygenate their blood.

Two related treatments were used to get around the diffuse fluid barrier. The first was to intubate the patient and put a high percentage of oxygen into the lung through the respirator tube. This was a necessary but dangerous step, because high levels of oxygen are toxic to the human lung.

The second treatment was to blow oxygen into the lung under high pressure, both during inhalation and exhalation. The trick is to keep the pressure high during the exhalation using a technique called *positive end-expiratory pressure,* or PEEP. PEEP enhances the diffusion of oxygen molecules across the unnatural barrier of fluid in the lung caused by SARS partially by forcing oxygen through the fluid barrier at higher-than-normal pressures. It also literally squeezes the fluid out of the lungs like a sponge. The problems with PEEP are that it decreases cardiac output and increases oxygen toxicity if the oxygen is already at a high percentage.

In addition, doctors treating SARS patients had to artificially support their blood pressure. Blood pressure can sink like a stone if a patient cannot oxygenate well. The pressure can be sustained with drugs that are called pressors. Pressors are good to a point. The problem is that they increase the workload on the heart, which in turn increases the oxygen demand to the heart.

Used incorrectly, a physician can turn this effect into a vicious cycle where the oxygen demand of the heart goes up. However, if there's not enough oxygen to deliver, the heart starts to fail. It's similar to a gasoline-powered engine that begins to stall if deprived of air for ventilation. Without adequate oxygen, the heart muscle cannot contract vigorously enough to push the blood through the aorta and out to the body.

The key point to make about the different techniques used to combat the worst symptoms of SARS is that modern communications technology allowed physicians to accelerate the learning curve in dealing with the organism. SARS was the first outbreak where a central Web site, initiated and maintained by the WHO and CDC, existed to allow doctors to enter, store, and retrieve information. Since almost all of the cases could be reported and tracked, therapeutic protocols for this syndrome were established very early on.

In other words, in virtually real time, a syndrome definition began to form so that doctors didn't have to wait for weeks or months until they had a confirmed laboratory diagnosis. Based on the syndrome definition alone, individual medical centers began treating patients effectively, right in the midst of the beginning of the epidemic.

The physicians who were watching the CDC Web site learned that corticosteroids didn't help against SARS. At the end of two weeks, the same numbers of people were dead whether they got or didn't get corticosteroids. The miracle of the Internet allowed the rapid institution of therapeutic trials, the first time this has ever happened in history.

Therapeutic trials usually are done after the organism is identified, and after the first wave of people have come down with a disease and recovered or died. The SARS therapeutic trials were done in real time. While they did not necessarily stop the syndrome, the rapid dissemination of information about symptomatic treatment undoubtedly contributed to saving lives and finding out the nature of the pathogen.

A remarkable thing then took place. Two laboratories, one in Germany and one at the CDC in Atlanta, Georgia, got the same sputum samples from the same patients. They began attempting to isolate the organism using a variety of techniques at the same time. They were thus able to validate each other's work in real time.

This allowed the researchers to avoid problems such as inadvertent contamination of one laboratory versus another. It helped eliminate mistakes that could have led to either false positives or false negatives at one laboratory or another. Not only was there a real-time therapeutic trial going on, there was a real-time collaborative—even somewhat competitive—effort between the two labs to identify the organism.

The labs used all kinds of techniques to try to identify the organism. They put it on various cell cultures to see what it could and could not infect. They even tried to isolate its DNA and amplify it using a technique called polymerase chain reaction, or PCR for short. In developing and perfecting the PCR technique, scientists have essentially duplicated what happens naturally inside of a cell when DNA replicates shortly before a cell divides. However, they have also been able to greatly speed up the process.

Once the DNA has been amplified in this manner enough times, a researcher can isolate the DNA on a gel slide and study it by subjecting it to a series of specific biochemical tests that produce a "fingerprint" of the genetic material of essentially all known organisms. If the fingerprint is absent, then so by definition is the organism.

THE GRAND TOUR

As the worldwide epidemic continued to spread, the World Health Organization sent a team of laboratory officials to visit Beijing. However, epidemic or not, the need of the Chinese state to control the flow of information remained the top priority. When current CDC director Julie Gerberding and her team from the WHO went to Beijing, they were given far less than the whole story.

Today, we know that a political decision had been made to hide a significant number of the patients from outside investigatory teams. When the WHO team showed up, medical or government officials—to this day we're not sure which—moved SARS patients onto ambulances and took the patients out of the hospital. A macabre shell game was played as the ambulances were driven around the city for the entire day, avoiding the WHO team at all costs.

Essentially, what the government did was to move people around with an infectious disease for at least twelve and possibly eighteen hours. It's doubtful that precautions were taken in trying to keep the air inside the ambulance from getting outside. A mobile ambulance is not a contained Level 4 biolab, by any means. This was a very dangerous game for the Chinese government to play, given that no one at that time—not even the Chinese scientists and leadership—knew how communicable SARS was from person to person.[1] If it were possible that it was spread via an aerosol, SARS was getting a free tour of the entire city of Beijing.

The decision was probably made for the usual reasons that countries make decisions about infectious disease. It is possible that the Chinese Communist party did not want to undermine the belief that it was fully in control of the health and welfare of the Chinese people. It is also likely that they perceived, rightly or wrongly, that the outside world's perception would have been so negative that it would have derailed the explosive economic growth in Chinese commerce and trade. In other words, taking their sick citizens and possibly exposing thousands—or millions—of people to an unknown virus could have been a decision made in purely economically selfish terms.

By April 2003, a cumulative total of 2,671 cases and over a hundred deaths were reported from SARS, spread over seventeen countries around the globe. Dr. Liu had passed away from his infection three weeks earlier, as did several of the people who had also stayed on the ninth floor of the Metropole in Hong Kong. But against the growing alarm and economic disruption, progress was being made in the lab where the organism had finally been successfully grown on a culture medium.

When viewed under the electron microscope, it appeared to have the morphology (i.e., microscopic appearance) and structure of a coronavirus. On April 16, the WHO announced conclusive identification of the SARS causative agent: an entirely new coronavirus, unlike any other human or animal member of the coronavirus family. The scientific name given to the organism was coronavirus urbani pneumonitis.

A coronavirus is the class of virus that includes many of the viruses that cause mild respiratory disease in animals. It is called a coronavirus because when looked at under the electron microscope, the area around the virus takes on a ghostly, whitish shade. At the right angle, it looks like a light halo, or corona.

Once the coronavirus identification had been made, the WHO and the CDC could do two things. First, they could narrow the field of medications to ones that could specifically treat coronaviruses. Second, they could immediately develop an antibody test. Samples of the SARS coronavirus would be taken and injected into guinea pigs. The guinea pigs would in turn generate antibodies against it. The antibodies produced could then be linked to fluorescence molecules, which can be used as the diagnostic test for the disease.

The discovery that the agent was a coronavirus was disturbing. In humans, coronaviruses had never been known to cause anything other than a syndrome that is the same as the common cold. That sparked serious concern. Why would a relatively benign organism suddenly start to cause a fatal disease?

In addition, since coronaviruses were also known to circulate among animals, there was a strong indication that the disease was zoonotic. That is, the virus somehow jumped species from animals to humans. Zoonotic diseases, by definition, circulate in animals, and every once in a while, for reasons still not understood, a virus gets transferred into the human population.

Because the organism depends not at all on the human species for its continued procreation, it has a tendency to multiply wildly and to kill the human host. While it is not always the case that zoonotic diseases result in the death of incidental human victims, as a rule of thumb, zoonotic infections are among the most deadly of human diseases. Ebola, anthrax, plague, and virtually all hemorrhagic fever illnesses are zoonoses.

SAFETY IN STRAIGHT LINES

By late February 2003, a lot was going right in the intensive hunt to identify SARS, but much effort was still being devoted to the old-fashioned way: culturing the organism first. Meanwhile, SARS was continuing to spread. There was great fear that the "epidemic curve" that plotted the number of cases of the disease (much as the police detective puts pins on a map to chart a pattern of murders) would begin to show that the disease was getting out of control and spreading wildly like a new form of influenza.

But as gruesome as the statistics for SARS were—more than 2,000 cases in less than six months—they weren't nearly as bad as they could have been. If SARS had been as contagious as influenza, the number of cases would have been exponentially greater. The *initial* suspicion, once the WHO and the CDC began their work, was that SARS was indeed spread via aerosol—a particle mist (usually generated by a sneeze or a cough) so fine that infection-laden droplets would travel many hundreds of feet on tiny currents of air before either striking a surface or finally settling to the ground and sticking. Patients were thus quarantined in isolation rooms in hospitals with HEPA-filtered air. The researchers were successfully ruling out what the disease wasn't. They were significantly less successful in determining what it was.

In early March 2003, author Alan Zelicoff, a medical doctor and senior scientist at Sandia National Laboratories, began plotting the WHO data on a graph. At issue was whether a syndrome surveillance program could predict the dynamics of SARS as it spread worldwide early on in the epidemic. In other words, based on the very earliest number of cases per day and the symptoms alone (without even knowing what organism was involved), could one arrive at a statistically valid approximation of the future behavior of the epidemic?

The question was of utmost importance. Would it become a pandemic? Would it die out on its own? Or would it be something in between? It was a tremendous challenge, given the lack of data on the newly identified virus.

No one really knew what the pathogen was in any detail. It was classified as a coronavirus, but clearly it was not a garden-variety one. No one knew exactly how it spread. The origin of the virus was sketchy at best and was to remain so for a long time. As of March 2003, the World Health Organization was having problems getting the Chinese to let them visit the province where the virus supposedly originated, so conclusions couldn't be drawn for months.

A syndrome surveillance program, even with the relative lack of data, could at least predict how bad SARS could truly be. What every epidemiologist or statistician does first is create a graph of the total number of SARS cases and plot it against the time elapsed. The results were astounding.

The graph that came up was a straight line. It was a *perfectly* straight line, a result so startling and unexpected that Zelicoff began publishing a thrice-weekly unofficial summary of the accumulating data that made the conclusion more and more solid: SARS was not spreading like influenza. Typically, straight lines of real-life events show a great deal of variation, but the SARS line did not; as more data came in each day, each new point fell on the same straight line. It conclusively pointed out one important fact: Whatever the coronavirus was, it was not primarily transmitted as an aerosol. It was unlikely that someone could catch the SARS coronavirus from an infected person who was sneezing or coughing nearby, otherwise a rapidly upwardly tilting curve would have been found, and would have been a cause for great concern.

One exception to this rule of transmission took place in a Hong Kong high-rise apartment building. In high-rises, you often need high pressure for the waste material from a toilet to get into the sewage system. It turned out there was a break in a pipe and the high-pressure flushing caused the coronavirus to be dispersed as an aerosol. Thus, one or two people who were sick with coronavirus managed to infect many people with whom they never came into direct contact. As a result of a plumbing defect, the organism did in fact get dispersed as an aerosol in one episode of the SARS story.

So, a straight line graph shows a gradual increase in the number of cases over time in SARS. More to the point, it suggests that one person infects at most one or two other people. If you had a highly contagious organism with a reproductive rate of ten or twenty, it would look like an exponential curve.

Zelicoff's work was later picked up in the prestigious magazine *Science,* but only after the SARS epidemic had long passed. Unfortunately, it was also long after policies had been put into effect to limit travel and trade to Southeast Asia for fear that SARS was a disease just like influenza—lethal and easy to spread. Billions of dollars in trade were lost, and the economic impact was felt throughout East Asia for many months. This was the cost of ignoring what syndrome surveillance was telling researchers early on in the epidemic: SARS was plenty lethal if you happened to catch it, but catching it was really quite hard to do.

REPRODUCTIVE RATE

An organism's reproductive rate simply means the number of people that one infected person goes on to infect. Obviously, it depends on several things. It depends on how mobile that individual is once he falls ill or becomes contagious. Once an infected individual becomes sick enough to want to stay in bed or at least at home, the reproductive rate of the organism tends to fall. In our highly mobile society, organisms that were otherwise of low reproductive ratio would tend to have their reproductive ratio substantially increased.

The reproductive rate also depends on how the organism is shed into the environment. Does it then communicate to other people through an untreated water supply? Does it shed as a result of coughing or sneezing where there is sufficient energy to aerosolize it? An aerosol requires a certain amount of energy to be expended by a host.

So, in a disease that has a reproductive ratio of greater than one, the curve climbs more quickly than linearly. If the reproductive ratio is exactly one, the curve would be precisely linear, meaning one person goes on to infect one more person. Therefore, if an organism with a "1" for its ratio creates ten cases in one day, there will be twenty cases the next day, thirty cases on the third day, and so on.

Now, among the diseases whose reproductive ratios we think we know, the most infectious are likely measles or influenza. These diseases are thought to have a rate on the order of thirty or forty. One person with the flu can typically infect up to forty others, which is why flu regularly sweeps through our world every year.

This is also why it's relatively easy to control diseases, such as pertussis (also known as whooping cough), that have a low reproductive ratio. By contrast, it's very hard to wipe out diseases, such as measles, that have a high reproductive ratio. In fact, even though it's believed that humans are the only natural reservoir for measles, we still haven't wiped out measles despite intensive vaccination campaigns around the world, because it spreads so easily between people.

STATISTICS AND SARS

Plotting the line of SARS cases over time showed that the disease's reproductive ratio was less than two. The graph indicated that, while serious, SARS was not going to be a major pandemic health hazard that would change life as we know it. Zelicoff's analysis was distributed to the public health organizations, the CDC, people in government, and a biostatistician—Dr. John Pezzullo of Georgetown University—to check the math.

The responses were mixed. While some agreed with the conclusions, others aggressively discounted the findings. Without originating from a researcher with a formal degree in biostatistics, some scientists felt they could disregard Zelicoff's work.

In the end, the mathematical model of the disease's behavior was proven correct. The death rate, predicted to be approximately five percent, was off by only a tenth of a percentage point after all the numbers were in. The analysis further predicted that SARS would turn out to be a non-aerosol-transmitted disease, which meant that the reproductive ratio had to remain between one and two.

Though it may have been cold comfort to those infected with SARS, as long as you received proper health care to remain oxygenated, your chances of dying were limited to about one in twenty, which is roughly the same as the death rate with community-acquired pneumonia of any kind. Most of the people who succumb to a disease of this level of lethality are elderly or immunosuppressed.

Several important lessons were learned from the SARS outbreak. One was that it is all too easy to overreact to a health crisis. A second, more important lesson is that syndrome modeling and surveillance is a useful tool when trying to sort out the confusing (and often emotionally charged) information that explodes on the scene at the beginning of an epidemic. It *was* and *is* possible to extrapolate from the data in what appears to be nonspecific syndrome surveillance, and get a very good picture of how the disease is progressing—and if it is truly a threat. At the very least, it can help formulate guidelines for travel and trade that affect tens of millions of people and hundreds of billions of dollars of commerce.

We can hope that this recent lesson regarding surveillance will guide us in responding to the next inevitable infectious disease challenge. By its case definition, SARS is a bad respiratory illness, and to get it you either travel to East Asia or come into contact with somebody who did. That's certainly simple enough to implement quickly and widely without confusion or mind-numbing definitions.

Finally, syndrome surveillance provides one last advantage in cases such as SARS: Because it is *not* a specific disease, it carries little political baggage (as opposed to a specific diagnosis of "plague" or "Ebola"). This may make it possible to bypass the heavily politicized reporting approval processes in government-run public health agencies, getting the reports directly into the hands of medical and health professionals.

Today, there is still a certain amount of controversy over various aspects of the SARS coronavirus. The primary mode of transmission is still being debated. A more contentious issue is what the organism's natural reservoir or animal host could be. For example, a coronavirus that almost exactly resembles the one that causes SARS in humans has been found in civet cats, raccoon dogs, and even a ferret badger in an animal market in Guangzhou. The source of the species "jump" could have occurred in a butcher shop or restaurant kitchen in that same market, as civet cats are a gastronomic delicacy in the Guangdong province. Thus, we don't know if SARS will reappear in substantial numbers. As of this writing, only a small handful of new cases have been reported in China.

Are there other animals that may harbor the organism? We just don't know. We can only say two things for sure. First, the SARS coronavirus that can smother a person's lungs in a film of fluid is still lurking out in the Chinese countryside, perhaps looking for a way to cause more havoc. Second, had SARS truly been as deadly and as easily transmitted as influenza, we would be living in a much less crowded world today.

NOTES

1. In retrospect, some Chinese biologists have published papers indicating that they believed SARS to be much less infectious than influenza. It is difficult to know when they came to this conclusion, because much of the experimental work that was done at the time has still not been released in open publication for study by other scientists around the world.

CHAPTER 3

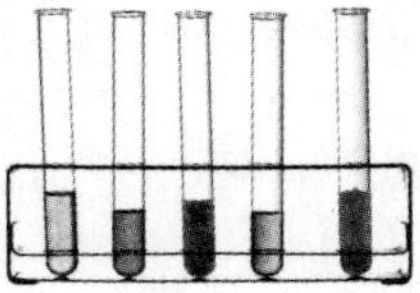

ARROYO MUERTE

Sin Nombre Hantavirus

With its rugged southwest terrain and open azure sky, the Four Corners area of northwestern New Mexico is achingly beautiful. It is called the Four Corners because it is the only place in the United States where the borders of four states touch—Arizona, New Mexico, Colorado, and Utah. At the Four Corners monument, a stone plaza marks the exact spot where the borders come together.

Perhaps the most popular picture taken by visitors to the site is one where they lie down in the plaza's center, then stretch out their arms and legs so that their bodies reach across four different states. Yet, on the whole, the Four Corners region is a quiet place. It's off the beaten path, so it doesn't bring in hordes of tourists. In the spring and summer of 1993, it also held a dark secret: Something was killing young, healthy people amidst the land's almost surreal splendor.

AN INTERRUPTED WEDDING

Contrary to what many people envision when they think about New Mexico, the state does not look like the postcard-perfect arid canyons of Monument Valley or the sandy forests of giant saguaro cacti near Tucson, Arizona. New Mexico actually gets a surprising amount of rain, and dustings of snow in the state capital of Santa Fe are not an uncommon occurrence. Even so,

1993 had been an exceptionally wet and stormy winter, from the southern border near El Paso to the opposite end of the state in the Four Corners.

The extra moisture would have been a boon to the state's nut-bearing tree, the piñon pine, and the prairie-like grasses that grow wild throughout the area. The Navajo Indian Reservation, which encompasses much of this beautiful region north of Gallup and west of Shiprock, would have been exceptionally green from all the rain. As the weather began to warm and clear up from the blustery winter, a young Navajo couple living in the area began their final preparations to be married.

Merrill Bahe, a track star at the Institute of American Indian Arts in Santa Fe, was recently engaged to his girlfriend, and they were busy putting together the plans for the wedding. In the first week of May, his fiancée (whose name has never been released) suddenly came down with a high fever, muscle aches, coughing, and a severe shortness of breath. She probably shrugged off the symptoms as merely a bad cold brought on by the stress of organizing the wedding details.

We don't know all of the details, but it's likely that she only reluctantly put aside the tasks of orchestrating her wedding day and allowed friends or family to carry on while she rested. She was no more than twenty years old and typically in good health; surely she must have thought that whatever she had acquired, her body could fight off. But the marriage ceremony never took place. Instead, her condition worsened over the next four days, and she died on the ninth day of the month.

The history of killer diseases is riddled with cruel ironies such as this. Within a week's time, the young man was preparing for a funeral instead of a wedding. And the twist of fate does not end at that point. While en route to the funeral for his bride-to-be, Merrill also began to feel seriously ill. Some reports indicate that he had collapsed suddenly just as he was to leave for the ceremony.

A few days before he began his journey he had developed flu-like symptoms disturbingly similar to his fiancée's. Again, he likely thought that his illness was a cold brought on by the terrible stress caused by the recent events in his life. But by May 14, it was clear that his sickness was no ordinary kind of cold virus or influenza. His condition had worsened to the point where his relatives brought him over to the Gallup Indian Medical Center in western New Mexico, the U.S. Public Health Service's largest tertiary referral hospital serving the Navajo Reservation.

The young man was struggling to breathe and was on the edge of going into cardiac arrest. It is likely that he was hooked up to a heart-lung machine to pump oxygen into his blood. The hospital staff struggled valiantly to save him, but he died of acute respiratory failure within hours of his arrival.

The hospital personnel involved were baffled. With the exception of occasional cases of plague—which is present in local wildlife and crosses over to humans a few times each year—they had never seen anything like the unknown agent that could kill an otherwise healthy patient. But this illness didn't behave like the plague; the symptoms were different and the rate of progression was frighteningly rapid. Upon reviewing the results of Bahe's case and interviewing the relatives and friends who brought him to the medical center, they found out about his fiancée's death. This immediately moved them from confusion to serious concern.

That a cohabitating couple had both died within a very short time span, suffering identical symptoms, meant something serious was going on. It implied that the same pathogen was responsible for both cases. And it indicated that whatever the pathogen was, it was contagious and deadly enough to take down two healthy, athletic people within a week's time.

The New Mexico Office of the Medical Investigator, known locally as OMI, immediately launched an inquiry. Its first priority was to find out whether this incident was truly isolated or a horrible sign of things to come. The goal was to comb the Four Corners region for any signs that others were ill with this mysterious sickness, or to find records of others who had died under similar mysterious circumstances.

The main reason the OMI wanted to find out about past and present illnesses of this sort was the fact that the pathogen had announced itself in a rather spectacular fashion. The events that took place in Gallup could point to a new and deadly mutation in an existing virus or bacteria that had recently emerged. On the other hand, it was possible that prior cases had taken place unnoticed, hidden in the background by statistical noise or the rural nature of northwestern New Mexico.

Dr. Bruce Tempest was one of the doctors who had worked on Bahe's case at the Gallup Indian Medical Center. A consultant in internal medicine and the recognized expert in the unique infectious diseases of New Mexico, he had been present when the young man died. Dr. Tempest immediately noted the frothy fluid that had filled the young man's lungs and caused his heart to fail.

Not satisfied to merely mark the deaths of two patients, Dr. Tempest went the extra step that few physicians even think to take: He began making phone calls that weekend all over the area between the towns of Gallup and Shiprock. He was startled to find that there had been three other deaths in the area that had strikingly similar case histories.

The indications were frightening. He immediately noted that one of the common characteristics of the victims was that they were all young, healthy people. Merrill Bahe had been a nationally recognized track star, a rising talent in his field. His cardiovascular system had been in optimal shape. And yet his heart had given out on him, deprived of oxygen by acute respiratory failure. The symptoms that the patients had suffered were almost identical—fever, muscle aches or cramps, coughing, and above all, a difficulty in breathing that led to death. This was a microbe that killed swiftly and painfully.

On May 17, Dr. Tempest alerted the New Mexico Department of Health about the five deaths in the Four Corners area. Dr. Tempest is something of a legend in his field. He is known for his almost photographic memory, which allows him to cite the page and column of entries in the 3000-page long medical text, *Pathological Basis of Disease.* Tall and sandy haired, even after nearly thirty-five years as a physician in Gallup, he still took his turn in the nightly call rotation, working every bit as long as the interns serving under him. He is dismissive and humble of the role he has played in the past to save many lives and prevent outbreaks of deadly disease.

Tempest was, and remains, "the physicians' physician" on the Navajo Reservation, with an encyclopedic knowledge of infectious disease, cardiology, and gastroenterology. He is also imbued with a deep respect for the mores of the subtle Navajo culture. New Mexico is home to several dangerous organisms—for example, it is one of only four places on earth that harbor the plague organism—so Dr. Tempest was, by good fortune, precisely the right doctor at the right time when the mysterious disease took hold. That May, his message to the health department was a clarion call to action. When Dr. Tempest warned of something unknown and dangerous on the horizon, people tended to listen carefully and move promptly.

THE TIPPING POINT

One of the people that Dr. Tempest called that Monday was Gary Simpson. Dr. Simpson is the director for infectious diseases at the New Mexico Department of Health. Like Tempest, he is surprisingly young looking, with the hint of the outdoorsman about him. Above all else, he is a man with a quiet voice and a calm demeanor that is extremely difficult to shake. Yet Dr. Tempest's call made him pay attention immediately.

As Dr. Simpson put it later in an interview for this book, "Bruce said he thought something strange was going on, and that was not something he did lightly." The fact that Dr. Tempest had identified three other people who had died mysteriously with similar case histories was key. "That was the tipping point. We knew we had serious problem. It was enough information to think: *epidemic,*" said Dr. Simpson, who in turn contacted the office of epidemiology to see if any of the patients had been autopsied.

The autopsy was a critical point in the investigation, and it almost didn't take place at all. The process was complicated by the fact that the index case, Mr. Bahe and his fiancée, had been Navajo.[1] The Navajo Nation was understandably wary of the medical investigation because of the newspaper and television news headlines about the mysterious illness that were already beginning to appear in the national media, sometimes verging on the cataclysmic. The last thing they wanted to happen was for reporters to falsely claim that the disease was specific to their tribe.

In fact, the young couple's deaths might have never been reported in the first place had they not been taken to the Gallup Medical Center. The Navajo Nation retains the right of self-government and is not required to report deaths on their land to the Office of the Medical Investigator. Therefore, the situation was already a sensitive one when an OMI investigator stepped forward and took the amazing step of interrupting the tribal funeral that had been prepared for Merrill Bahe and his bride.

The investigator, whose name has not been released, had concluded that the disease involved in the couple's deaths was a significant and imminent threat to public health. Given the microbes endemic to the Western United States, it had to be assumed that it was an outbreak of deadly pneumonic plague until proven otherwise. Plague can be transmitted person-to-person, and if the couple had had a common source exposure, it would be a threat to the rest of the tribe as well as to the public at large. As such, he assumed OMI "responsibility and authority" over the bodies even as they were being prepared for burial at the gravesite.

The OMI office for all of New Mexico is located in the pathology department at the University of New Mexico School of Medicine in Albuquerque, and this single office performs more than 90 percent of all autopsies in the state year in and year out. Therefore, although forensic pathologists in most states don't normally have a significant or timely public health role in alerting officials to statistically meaningful trends in unexpected deaths, in New Mexico they played a much more active role than elsewhere in the country, simply because forensic pathology is done in, for all intents and purposes, by one office in New Mexico.

In addition, the New Mexico OMI processes more than 6,000 autopsies a year, with review by a team of pathologists with comprehensive subspecialty training in highly focused fields of the discipline.[2] There is probably no finer repository of pathological expertise, resources, and archived knowledge anywhere else in the United States. This proved to be extremely helpful in the next stage of the investigation.

The bodies were flown by helicopter to the OMI office on Friday night, and autopsies were performed immediately. It just so happened that one of the foremost microbiologist-plague technicians in the country was working at OMI at the time. She was able to definitively say that whatever had killed the two young people, it hadn't been the plague organism.

A battery of standard tests was ordered to try to culture whatever the organism was. By early on Saturday morning it was known the pathogen wasn't plague, anthrax, or tularemia. Bolstering these results was a third autopsy that had been conducted separately by a different pathologist on one of the additional three cases that Dr. Tempest had identified. A microscopic inspection of the lung tissues had also been undertaken in all three autopsies.

The results in each autopsy ruled out an invasive form of *Streptococcus* bacteria and all of the common bacterial pneumonia species. Although the results had been completely negative, the information that was provided was important in narrowing down the field of likely candidates. It was now likely that what the physicians and examiners were seeing was not a well-known bug, nor a mutation of an existing bacteria or virus. It was probably something entirely new to the area, or at least a new category of previously unrecognized infectious disease.

On May 24, the team of doctors and epidemiologists working on the case alerted the medical community that a new disease might be in the process of emerging from the Four Corners region of the state. The Navajo Reservation was beginning to attract reporters from all over the United States who caused great annoyance by entering sacred sites and asking prying questions of the people who lived in the vicinity.

What the news reports failed to reflect was that although a disproportionate number of patients continued to be Navajo, non-Navajo patients were being seen as well. To shut down press reports that might ignorantly tie the Navajo name to the disease, officials temporarily assigned the term adult respiratory distress syndrome, or ARDS, to describe the condition.

FIRST REPORT

Serendipitously, Dr. Simpson had written a chapter for an emergency medicine text on the topic of high-risk pathogens. The main point of the chapter was to try and answer the question: How can a physician identify one of several of the world's most lethal pathogens if the physician has never seen a case of the disease before? Dr. Simpson had just completed a review of the world's literature on the subject of deadly bacteria and viruses. His work was designed to give an emergency room physician a summary of what those pathogens could be, what their symptoms were, and how long their incubation periods lasted.

He was drawn in particular to the breakdown of four virus families:

- ***Filoviruses,*** which include Ebola and Marburg. These two viruses cause catastrophic hemorrhagic fevers that cause anywhere from 40 percent to 90 percent of their victims to bleed to death.
- ***Bunyaviruses,*** which list nairovirus, hantavirus, and tospovirus as members. Each of these viruses can also cause catastrophic hemorrhagic fevers in patients.
- ***Arenaviruses,*** such as Lassa and Machupo, which are hemorrhagic fever viruses from West Africa and Bolivia, respectively.
- ***Flaviviruses,*** which cause yellow fever and West Nile encephalitis and even some forms of hepatitis.

Each of the diseases caused by these pathogens could cause severe respiratory system distress. What didn't quite fit the pattern was that the deaths from ARDS were from heart failure. Still, the classical symptoms—enlarged heart, fluid in the lungs, poor contraction of the heart muscle itself—were close enough so that Dr. Gary Simpson could ask the question of whether a person suffering from ARDS might have an unknown variation of the viruses that caused any one of the many hemorrhagic fever syndromes, since the viruses causing this syndrome frequently depress the heart's ability to function, contributing to the rapid demise of patients.[3]

Daily conference calls were organized to share data gathered by the different researchers working on the outbreak. The attendees included Dr. Simpson and Dr. Tempest, the Department of Health, OMI, and state health lab researchers and clinicians. Dr. Simpson particularly remembers that for the first week, "It was just a blur of phone calls among clinicians and hospitals . . . it was a constant effort to acquire information." The conference attendees were collecting ongoing laboratory findings, further research on whether any other cases had been reported in the past, and updates on surveillance for "suspect cases"—any one patient who turned up with suspiciously similar symptoms.

To expand the ring of surveillance, the Department of Health notified every one of the thirty-eight hospitals in the state of New Mexico. It also notified all of the hospitals in the Four Corner states located in cities close to the border to be on the lookout for suspect cases. Finally, the Centers for Disease Control (CDC) in Atlanta was also notified about what was going on so that it could prepare to move a team in to investigate further.

The conferences were frequently tinged with fear—a fear that perhaps the disease would break out in a new area or direction and cause a cluster of fatalities. The fear was justified—at least two to three suspect cases were being reported every day. "We tried to refer as many patients to hospital at the University of New Mexico [UNM] in Albuquerque," said Dr. Simpson. "We had to proceed under the assumption that whatever was causing ARDS was a communicable disease, from person to person. Intensive care units—ICUs—in most hospitals do not have an isolation room. UNM was the best place to bring patients because [the facility had] isolation units with laminar flow."

That means that air will flow into, but not out of, the isolation area until it passes through extremely fine filters, reducing the chance that an airborne pathogen could escape and wreak havoc throughout a hospital or even the surrounding community.

Dr. Simpson noted that one of the ARDS victims had also had a gastric hemorrhage, or bleeding in the stomach. During one of the conference calls, Simpson discussed the subject with one of the pathologists. It turned out to be the only case of stomach bleeding among the ARDS patients, but it did spark more speculation in the group as to what the pathogen could be. Simpson was worried that the organism could be a variation on the virus that caused Lassa fever, because gastric hemorrhage is a classical complication resulting from Lassa fever. The group agreed that although there wasn't an exact match between the patient's symptoms and those of the well-described hemorrhagic fever illnesses, they would keep the possibility open that they were dealing with a new, unknown member in the family of hemorrhagic fever viruses. It is highly unusual for any given patient to have the full range of symptoms of any given disease.

As Dr. Simpson later said, "I was pleasantly surprised how open-minded the participants were to the idea. Often times, people in the medical profession are trained to be reductionists, to seek out a single, known answer to a problem." He added, "It's true that an uncommon presentation of common illnesses is more common than common presentation of uncommon illnesses. But there was a general agreement in the group that the common illnesses had all been eliminated."

The CDC completed its tests, which concurred with the findings from the New Mexico OMI office: Every serological test had come up negative. In serologic testing, antibodies from victims of disease are taken from the blood and placed on slides containing every known pathogen in the CDC collection. If the antibodies bind to the pathogens—easy to recognize under the microscope—a diagnosis is most assuredly in hand. But every CDC office and microbiologist at the University of New Mexico involved had failed to find a known disease among the victims, making it certain that this was a pathogen that had never been seen before. The CDC Special Pathogens Branch began a joint investigation with the state health departments and the Navajo Nation by sending a team out to investigate the trailer home where Merrill Bahe and his fiancée had lived.

The team's findings, which kept everyone in suspense for the better part of a day, were anticlimactic. They looked for toxins everywhere, including in the food that was left in the couple's refrigerator. Samples were sent out to the CDC's laboratories in Fort Collins, Colorado. The initial report didn't show anything specific or suspicious, though it was noted that there were rodent droppings in portions of the home.

The first press conference was held jointly by the CDC and the Department of Health that evening only days after the medical community had been alerted. It was—to the undoubted annoyance of the reporters looking for a front-page scoop—fairly low key. The attendees at the daily conferences were still concerned, but they were slowly eliminating the organisms of greatest concern (for example, those that transmit easily between people, such as Lassa fever), which gave them slightly more confidence that they were beginning to get a handle on the situation, since "ruling out" known diseases is a key process in guiding the investigation in any outbreak.

BREAKOUT

Then a disturbing call came in on the first full weekend after the outbreak had been announced. The brother of Merrill Bahe's fiancée had become ill with fever and severe muscle pain. He had moved into his sister's trailer after she had left to live with Bahe. He was transferred to Albuquerque as soon as possible and immediately placed in the isolation unit. His fever spiked at 104 degrees, he had trouble breathing, and he looked as if he might go into respiratory or cardiac arrest at any time.

The patient's wife had arrived with him. The public health officials started asking her questions about everything they could think of regarding where her husband had been and what he had been doing over the last week. It was especially important to find as much out as they could because her husband's case didn't quite fit in with the idea that the pathogen could have been local to Bahe's trailer. He hadn't interacted with his sister much before the wedding, nor had he visited Bahe's trailer. Had the disease been transmitted by touch, Bahe's bride would have given it to many more people than her brother.

It was at that point that events started to frighten the team of CDC and public health officials. The patient's wife started to come down with a severe fever at the hospital. She was intubated by that evening. Close on the heels of that event was an explosion of new suspect cases.

The child of the original young couple had suddenly broken with fever. Two of the nurses who had cared for Bahe and his bride were also admitted with fever to the hospital in Gallup. Finally, one of the autopsy assistants who had worked on the case came down with fever and had to be admitted. There was a new undercurrent to the investigation now: the feeling that things were starting to spin out of control. "There is almost a rhythm to these events," said Dr. Simpson. "You really sense when things are becoming more intense. We began to wonder: *Just how bad could this turn out to be?*'

The case investigators decided that a formal request would be made to the CDC for increased assistance. Acceptance of the request would mean that the CDC would assume authority over a significant number of patients, as many were Navajo living on federal land. Yet bringing in the CDC to assume blanket control was also risky. Given the broad reach of the CDC's mandate, it did not have any local agents on the ground to know where to look and who to ask for information. The CDC officials would also be unfamiliar with Navajo culture and its inherent modesty, and might not show respect for the sanctity of the individual and religious sensitivities.

Before they made their request, a special meeting was convened on Thursday night at Dr. Simpson's house. As Simpson recalled, "The focus of the discussion was: What is it—precisely and exactly—that we need from the CDC? The answer: experienced people who could do more interviewing and contact tracing [that is, identifying all individuals who came in contact with known victims of the new syndrome and assessing their daily routine, possible exposures, and determining if they too were becoming ill]. . . . We also identified who else we wanted to have at the meeting to present the epidemiology, the path, [and] the summary of the lab work and the radiology." These last specific requests were especially important, because the flow of specimens had become so enormous that the local UNM laboratory resources were simply overwhelmed.

On Friday, the request was made during a long telephone discussion with the CDC. It was agreed that the agency would send three Epidemic Intelligence Service (EIS) officers and a supervisor to assist. Sending an EIS supervisor was a previously unheard of move by the CDC. More typically, the young EIS officers alone take over any disease investigation once the

CDC is invited in. This move obviously indicated that the agency was worried that this outbreak was a very serious matter. By that point, there had been ten suspect deaths in the state, and the number of suspect cases continued to increase.

That same evening, a middle school graduation program took place near Red Rock, New Mexico. Red Rock is a tiny town about a two-hour drive from the nearest city, Las Cruces. It was also more than 300 miles to the south of the Four Corners region. A thirteen-year-old Navajo girl was dancing at the party after the graduation when she fell over and went into arrest. An emergency medical services person at the dance gave her mouth-to-mouth resuscitation, then intubated her to provide oxygen directly into her lungs.

The young girl was placed in a medevac helicopter and flown to the isolation ward at the UNM hospital. It was to no avail. On Saturday morning, the girl arrested again and died. This latest death shook Dr. Simpson more than the others. He had been asked to come and see the girl on Saturday because he is the chief infectious disease consultant for the New Mexico Department of Health. He routinely makes rounds on all patients with diseases that are suspected to be infectious. He had seen the girl on Saturday during his rounds, before she went into cardiac arrest, and she had reminded him of his own daughters. Although still "early" in the outbreak, there was no evidence that anyone who had been hospitalized was starting to recover—an especially worrisome finding.

WITCHCRAFT

The first big meeting with the CDC took place on that same Saturday morning at the Office of the Medical Investigator in Albuquerque. Simpson felt that this meeting was a major organizational turning point because for the first time the group had a lot of information with which to rule out false leads that would sidetrack the investigation. "We invited the group to identify any agent that could account for even some of the findings and put them on a flip chart," said Dr. Simpson, "We ended up with fifty infectious agents and some toxic agents. We then went over each possibility in detail to see if we could eliminate a certain agent or not."

The meeting ended up with three possibilities that could not be discounted. First, the organism was some kind of viral hemorrhagic fever. Second, it could be some kind of influenza virus. Finally, it could be an entirely novel agent.

In response to the meeting's conclusions, the CDC Viral Special Pathogens Branch began to test fluid samples from each of the suspect patients against the agency's enormous panel of substances and antibodies to identify the agent. According to Dr. Simpson, this testing was especially helpful. The Department of Health was worried that the mystery agent might be a Biosafety Level 4 pathogen. They had inoculated chickens and mice and sent specimens to a dozen labs, but if the pathogen were truly contagious and dangerous, they needed someone with a more secure facility to work with the organism. The CDC's laboratories fit the bill.

In the meantime, the casework had to continue. Agents at the Department of Health went out to talk with the family of the girl from Red Rock. It was a difficult task. The girl's family members were very traditional, and some suspected malign magic, or witchcraft. Again, the victim in question was a healthy young person. The team found it slightly off-putting when they had to ask the bereaved parents intrusive questions about drugs and sex.

In the meantime, the media scrutiny had gotten even worse. Word had leaked out about the case in Red Rock, so now the pundits on the news programs fueled the fire by theorizing that the agent that caused ARDS had "escaped" from the Four Corners region. The eager reporters became a serious nuisance to the researchers.

In one instance, a news team parked down the street from the university hospital in Albuquerque where the ambulances would admit patients to the emergency room, using a telephoto lens to take pictures of whoever was admitted. News reporters assumed that any patient coming out of an ambulance wearing an oxygen mask was a victim of the outbreak. This was a grotesquely incorrect view, as just about every patient with cardiac or respiratory disease that ends up transported by ambulance is placed on oxygen as a precaution.

The harassment also intensified on the Navajo Reservation. The residents of one village, fed up with the constant stream of attention, simply abandoned their dwellings en masse and moved somewhere else beyond the range of the cameras. (Dr. Simpson believes that we were lucky that the organism that caused ARDS wasn't spread via touch. Given all of the reporters tramping through the Navajo land, and the fact that an entire village had to move, the media coverage could have been the perfect way to spread the pathogen far beyond the Four Corners area.)

The following Friday, information arrived from the CDC. It had identified the agent as a member of the bunyavirus family. The group's first guess—that they were dealing with a new form of virus—had been correct. They suspected the pathogen was a form of hantavirus (see Figure 3-1). Hantaviruses are round, lipid-enveloped structures, 90 nanometers to 100

FIGURE 3-1

The new hantavirus strain isolated in the Four Corners region of New Mexico.

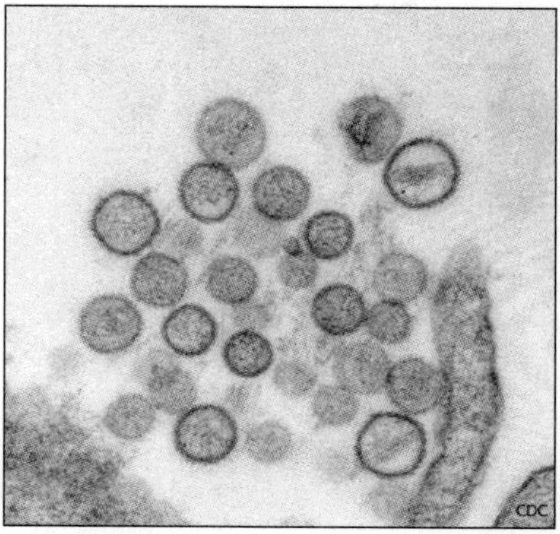

nanometers in diameter, that contain only a single strange of ribonucleic acid (RNA).

LETHAL PESTS

Viruses are named after their place of discovery, and hantavirus was no different. The first member of the hantavirus family was discovered during the Korean War in the Hantaan River Valley in South Korea. The existence of the virus had to be deduced before it was ever found—all that was known about it for a long time was that it caused a serious condition, hemorrhagic fever with renal syndrome, or HFRS.

HFRS was very different from what was being seen in New Mexico. In the Korean cases, soldiers died not of respiratory disease but of kidney failure. There were no such cases in the ongoing New Mexico outbreak.

Twenty years later, the agent for HFRS was finally isolated in a lab and classified. It quickly became a family of viruses when it was determined that different variations of the organism were found throughout the Far East, Asiatic Russia, the Balkans, and in Scandinavia. What set hantaviruses apart from other organisms in the bunyavirus group was that it was not spread by an insect vector, like malaria or West Nile virus are.

Instead, all of the known hantaviruses at the time had a rodent as the reservoir host. Each variant of hanta was adapted to a single host rodent species. For example, the "original" hantavirus from South Korea normally resided quite peacefully inside the striped field mouse. Only if the droppings were kicked up into dust—aerosolized, to use the medical term—and inhaled could the virus enter the human body and begin its lethal infestation. This was why soldiers who often came in contact with mice while camping out in the wilderness or in trenches came down with the Korean variety of hanta. The researchers quickly put two and two together. The seemingly minor detail in the investigative report when the team went into Merrill Bahe's trailer home was that there had been rodent droppings in the house. The evidence was gone through again, this time with an eye for the new details. Bahe and several of the other suspect cases were uniformly in the lower-income bracket. They had all either lived in a trailer or a traditional Navajo Indian dwelling called a hogan.

Hogans are dome-shaped structures built out of wood and earth. There is typically little or no furniture in a hogan, and the floor is simply fine dirt or sand. Manufactured housing such as trailers are made of more advanced materials, but there is a premium on how quickly they can be assembled. Because of this, there are many large holes in the walls for pipes and wires—a perfect opportunity for ingress of a wide variety of rodents and other creatures.

Mouse-proofing either structure is especially difficult given that the dominant rodent of the area, the common deer mouse, *Peromyscus maniculatus,* is able to pass through a hole the size of a nickel. The researchers also discovered two more facts that gave them pause. First, the deer mouse has the greatest propensity of all rodents to come indoors when it is cold, as it had been that winter. Second, due to the wet spring and the incredibly lush growth of foxtail and bear grass, there had been an abundance of seeds for the mice to eat and the rodent population had gone through the roof.

The CDC Special Pathogens Branch had seen enough reactivity in its antibody tests that it could definitively state that the organism was in the hantavirus family. But the agency wanted to do more testing before any of the investigators made a statement to the press. In particular, they wanted to try to culture the virus before going public.

Dr. Simpson was frustrated. He felt that at that point, there was no other credible explanation for the nature of the organism, which he had predicted much earlier. Rightly or wrongly, he felt that the CDC didn't want the announcement to be made because the CDC wanted to be the one to make the conclusive statement to the media. He told them, in essence, "We understand, but this is our community. We can and will make it clear to the press that the findings are preliminary." After all, many more lives were potentially at risk, and Dr. Simpson realized that getting the message out for people to avoid rodents and their nests or droppings could prevent more deaths.

Dr. Simpson also wanted to make the announcement so that he could take two potentially controversial actions. First, he wanted to use the finding to acquire and justify giving the hantavirus patients ribavirin, a potent antiviral drug. Second, he needed grounds for halting the impending "cleansing" ceremony on the Navajo Reservation.

The elders of the Navajo Nation had decreed that all traditional Navajos would perform a cleansing ceremony. The elders had laid out the cause for the illness that had struck down the members of the tribe, which was that the community had fallen out of harmony with nature. The cleansing ceremony was a simple one, but to Dr. Simpson's alarm it included sweeping out the hogans and the areas around the dwelling.

He knew that the sweeping of the area would be the perfect way to create dust aerosols that would include desiccated mouse droppings and infect even more people with hanta. Yet the last thing that he wanted to do was disturb the Navajo Nation's ceremony without a very good reason. The Navajo had already shown tremendous restraint and tolerance, given the interrupting of a burial ceremony and the incredible disruption caused by story-hungry reporters and photographers. A public announcement would give the credibility needed to stop even more people from coming down with hantavirus.

THE KILLER WITH NO NAME

The CDC finally agreed to the demand, and New Mexico's secretary of health at the time, Mike Burkhart, started off the press conference that day with the announcement that the investigators had new information. "As soon as the announcement was made, you could feel the whole thing just deflate, because at least now there was an answer," said Dr. Simpson. "Also, we knew some fundamental things: The host was probably a rodent—we didn't know which one yet—so we could tell people to stay away from rodents. We knew it was transmitted by inhaling urine or feces by aerosols, so we would suggest not sweeping up mouse nests."

Among the other announcements made that day, people were told to use bleach or Lysol when cleaning up mouse droppings, and to double-bag dead rodents while wearing a mask and gloves. Physicians were told that if they had patients with hantavirus symptoms, they were to call a special number to have their patient transferred to UNM for treatment. As for the people who lived in hogans and trailers, they were told to keep the dwelling free of mice and, if possible, to simply not sleep on the floor, so as to avoid being exposed to tiny mice that frequently foraged for food indoors at night.

Dr. Simpson's insistence on not waiting for the virus to be cultured before a public announcement was made turned out to be a wise move. The virus was actually not grown in a lab culture until October 1995, over two years later. Much as with the original hantavirus that was discovered in Korea, the American version of hanta also turned out to be a difficult organism to grow or detect in a lab.

Just a few weeks before the 1993 outbreak of hanta, Dr. Simpson had received a call from C. J. Peters, M.D., the head of the Special Pathogens Branch at the CDC. Dr. Peters was concerned about a sick friend of his named Terry Yates. Dr. Peters had been in the South American country of Bolivia with Yates, trapping mice in order to search for Bolivian hemorrhagic fever (BHF), and he was worried that Yates had come down with the very bug he'd been chasing, so he asked if Dr. Simpson could examine him. It was one of those "small world" meetings, as Terry Yates turned out to be one of Dr. Simpson's neighbors. Luckily, it turned out Yates did not have BHF, but because of the incident, Dr. Simpson knew exactly who to call to find out exactly which rodent the OMI had to be worried about.

It also turned out that Yates was a world-renowned expert of rodents and their growth. He knew that the rodent population in New Mexico in May and June 1993 had a density of ten times more than usual due to the mild, wet winter. The Sunday after first calling the CDC, the UNM biology department was trapping mice in Gallup and elsewhere. They subjected their samples to a battery of tests and confirmed within a week that what they were seeing was a previously unknown strain of hantavirus, and that it was indeed carried by about one-third of the deer mice (see Figure 3-2) in the state.

The naming of the new hantavirus strain generated a surprising amount of controversy. Politics weighs in heavily, even during a dangerous disease outbreak. According to the traditional nomenclature, the new pathogen was going to be called Four Corners virus. Of course, this not only offended the Navajo Nation, who lived nearby, but the tourism boards from Utah, Arizona, New Mexico, and Colorado. A second proposal was made to name it after a nearby waterway, appropriately called (due to some unknown tragedy in the distant past) Arroyo Muerte—the Stream of Death. This proposal was also rejected.

FIGURE 3-2

The common deer mouse, carrier of the newly discovered hantavirus.

In the end, the virus was named after the Sin Nombre Valley. This choice satisfied everyone because it was impossible for anybody to take offense. *Sin nombre* means, literally, "No name." Thus, the American version of the hantavirus is the only killer pathogen in the world that does not, strictly speaking, have a name at all.

RED HERRINGS AND NEW DISCOVERIES

By late June 1993, physicians and public health specialists confirmed that thirteen of the suspect deaths from ARDS had been caused by the Sin Nombre hantavirus. As suspected, many of the cases during the outbreak turned out to have been ill from different causes, unrelated to hanta. For example, it was later determined that the young girl from Red Rock did not have hanta and so was not part of the outbreak at all. Influenza was the likely culprit.

Sin Nombre played no part in the admittance of several other people to the hospitals in Albuquerque or in Gallup. Neither did it have a role in the illnesses affecting the two nurses or the medical examiner's assistant, who had all worked with the index patients that had been found or treated by Dr. Bruce Tempest. They simply had the unfortunate timing of falling sick with other, common diseases during an outbreak of a new and frightening disease. In a mystery or suspense novel, they would be considered red herrings that had nothing to do with the main plot.

Yet for all the false leads and scary twists to the story, the ending was one that vindicated the work done by the public health agencies in New Mexico and the CDC. Once it was determined that the pathogen was a virus that could only be acquired with difficulty, the fear factor rapidly diminished. Contact with mouse excreta was a lot less likely to happen to most people on a daily basis than, say, sitting next to a coughing person on the bus or at the office.

Once the guidelines had gone out to the public, the outbreak essentially came to a halt. Only sporadic cases would continue to come in over the next few years.

It turned out that Sin Nombre virus is found in deer mouse populations throughout much of the Western United States, but by 2004, the number of cases of hanta nationwide, both current and historical, was still under 300 (see Figure 3-3). Warnings about how to go about dealing with wild rodents went a long way toward keeping the case total low. And although a cure or vaccine has not been found, hospitals today know how to treat hanta patients and vastly improve their chance of survival.

FIGURE 3-3

Map of hantavirus cases in the United States.

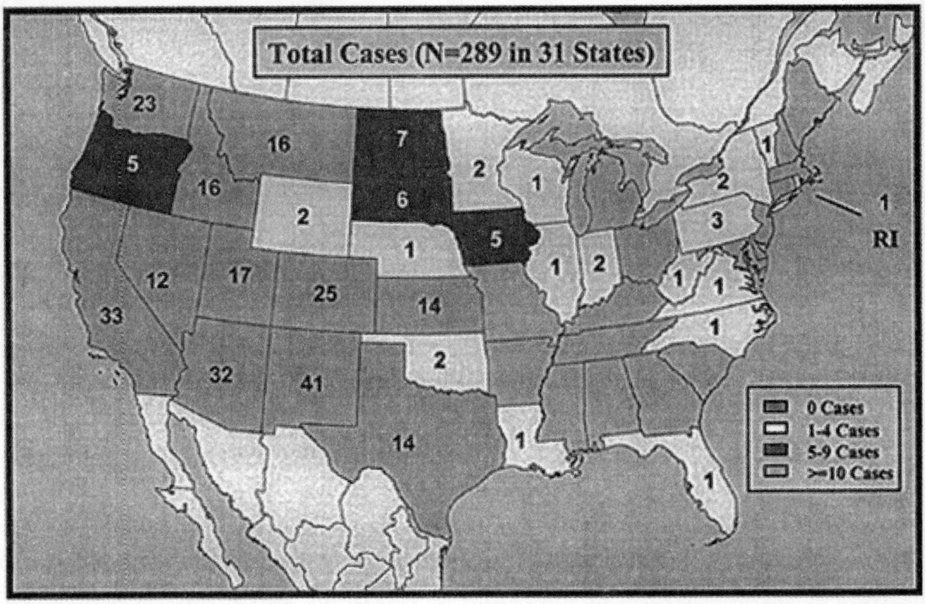

As Dr. Simpson would later attest, the outcome provided many lessons, and the strength of the entire process reflected the serendipity and multidisciplinary nature of the people involved. Indeed, the Sin Nombre hantavirus episode serves as an all-too-rare example of how disease surveillance and containment should actually function when public health agencies work together. Even during the worst of the crisis points, Dr. Simpson pointed out, none of the New Mexico agencies ever got into a paralyzing turf war with the federal agency—the CDC. "By stating specifically what we needed from the CDC, we never lost control of the situation," said Dr. Simpson. "And by keeping our daily conferences on productive topics, we managed to pool and disseminate critical information."

This information was not limited to plotting out the numbers of new cases and deaths. It also included what worked—and what did not—in treating the patients who had come down with hanta. This extra edge in sharing information prevented doctors from having to guess what to do across each hospital, and this policy doubtless saved many lives.

THE ROCK WITH WINGS

The Navajo land in the Four Corners region contains a spectacular plume of volcanic rock that rises 1,700 feet above the surrounding high desert. It is called "Shiprock" in English, but the feature is sacred to the Navajos, who call it *Tse Bi dahi,* or the Rock with Wings. Indeed, when the rock is viewed from a certain angle, one can easily imagine a celestial being emerging from its sleeping place from within the red stone.

It is also the mystical, sacred nature of the Navajo culture that may have provided scientists the reason for the virus's episodic forays into the human species. To begin with, it's likely that Sin Nombre has been circulating within its rodent hosts for a very long time, doing the deer mice no appreciable harm. The virus is clearly adapted to the mouse in a way that would have taken hundreds or thousands of years. Human beings, whether Native American or European in origin, have been extremely recent arrivals on the scene, in evolutionary terms.

The virus has certainly come into contact with humans before the 1993 outbreak caught everyone's attention. Dr. Simpson notes that for years after the events in the Four Corners region, cowboys, rangers, or ranchers would say, "I thought I had the worse case of flu in my life several years ago—I bet it was hanta."[4] Later still, upon reexamining stored serum from patients who had died from unknown respiratory disease dating back to the 1960s, it appeared that sporadic cases of hantavirus pulmonary disease had probably been occurring in the United States for many decades. It turned out that the earliest known fatal case of Sin Nombre took place in 1958, when a Utah resident succumbed to the virus.

The Navajo elders had certainly seen the effects of hanta, even if they did not know its cause. Twice before in the last hundred years—specifically, in 1918 and 1933—the Navajo had observed a connection between a mild, wet winter, a bountiful growth of the wild grasses in the area, an increase in the number of mice, and a number of inexplicable deaths among their healthy young people.

Similarly, there is evidence that the Navajo had encountered hanta before the Spanish or American settlers arrived in New Mexico. There are references in Navajo folklore to the effects of Sin Nombre. In one parable, it's said that if you let mice into your dwelling, they'll "take away the breath" of your children.

Today, it is theorized that the Sin Nombre outbreaks are tied somehow to the El Niño weather phenomenon. El Niño leads to drought in some places in the world and heavy rainfall in others—among them, the Four Corners region of the southwest United States. Yet the pattern, while it correlates, does not exactly match the historical frequency of El Niño. It appears that some years lead to outbreaks while others do not.

Like much of the science surrounding the outbreaks of killer microbes, studies of Sin Nombre virus are a work in progress. In the meantime, the Four Corners region knows beyond the shadow of a doubt that at certain times of the year, following a rainy winter, that a murderer walks the land. In 1993, that murderer was identified—and ultimately stopped—by the alert observation of Dr. Bruce Tempest, who saw no other way to explain the deaths of two healthy young Navajo. Let us all hope that a Dr. Tempest exists at the scene of humanity's next encounter with an emerging killer.

NOTES

1. An index case is typically the earliest documented case of a disease that is included in an epidemiological study. Although at least three other people had been identified by Dr. Tempest as having died before the young couple, none of the three were sufficiently documented. Therefore, even if the couple wasn't the first to contract the pathogen, they are properly considered to be the index case for the investigation.
2. As in just about all medical disciplines, there are "subspecialists" within the field of pathology. There are surgical pathologists who examine tissues removed during operation and render a diagnosis of the disease they may observe under the microscope; laboratory pathologists, who run and certify the chemical and microbiological tests that are done within a large clinical laboratory; and forensic pathologists, whose main role is to determine the precise, final causes of death in any patient who has succumbed to disease or trauma.
3. Hemorrhagic illnesses are usually viral infections that cause fevers and gastrointestinal symptoms, followed by capillary hemorrhage. In the most severe kinds of illnesses of this sort, the patient literally bleeds to death from the inside out.
4. In fact, during the Sin Nombre outbreak, Dr. Gary Simpson received a call from an old Army veteran, who described barely surviving a disease with the exact same symptoms when he was fighting the North Koreans in the 1950s. The veteran turned out to be closer to the truth than just about anyone who was studying the pathogen up that point.

CHAPTER 4

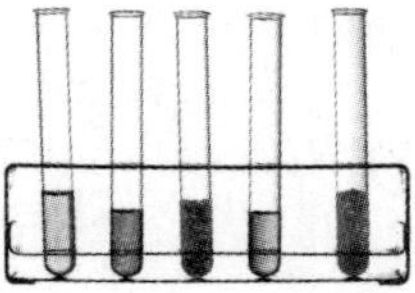

OUTBREAKS, RESERVOIRS, AND DEAD-END HOSTS

There is no exact number that defines an *outbreak*. Public health officials treat the word with extreme caution the vast majority of the time. It's an extremely politically charged word, laden with the possibility of unnecessarily terrorizing the public, and one that is difficult to withdraw once used. It carries far higher power than almost any other word besides *epidemic*. Consider these two headlines:

CENTRAL CITY SHOWS A POSITIVE TREND IN PLAGUE CASES
or
OUTBREAK OF PLAGUE SPOTTED IN CENTRAL CITY

Which one carries the greater potential for economic, social, and political disruption?

Disruptive power isn't always negative; it often serves a greater purpose when a public health official is demanding quarantines or asking for more resources to combat a disease. There is no question that judicious use of the term *outbreak* is appropriate for a great variety of human and animal diseases.

For example, the foot-and-mouth disease (FMD) crisis in the United Kingdom in 2001 was a true emergency. Action within even a few hours after the first cases were verified might have eradicated the disease more quickly and saved billions of dollars in agricultural trade. Yet use of the word *outbreak* undoubtedly motivated ranchers and the general public to do whatever they could—including giving up their national pastime of hiking across private rural land—to stop the spread of the disease. As awful as it was for the ranchers and those who had to witness the euthanization of mass numbers of animals, the FMD outbreak in the United Kingdom could have been much, much worse. Slower action could have led to the loss of international status as an FMD-free country for years or even decades.

The FMD example further demonstrated that the number of cases of a particular disease that need to be reported in order to confirm an outbreak depends on two factors: its *acute fatality* rate and the *severity of the disease.*

The acute fatality rate is simply the number of people (or animals in the case of veterinary diseases) who die divided by the number of people ill. Smallpox, for example, historically has killed one out of three people who come down with it (although there have been outbreaks of particularly virulent strains where the fatality rate was over nine in ten). Therefore, the acute fatality rate of smallpox is accepted as 30 percent on average.

A less severe, though potentially deadly disease is influenza, which holds the dubious distinction of being the most common human infectious disease. The flu has an acute fatality rate of a fraction of one percent except among the very old, the very young, or those who have poorly functioning immune systems. In these latter groups, fatality rates can easily reach one in five or higher. And the recently arrived West Nile fever in the United States kills very few of its victims, though it can certainly cause severe symptoms in 10 percent of infected individuals.[1]

Determining a disease's "severity" is more an art than science. No exact definition exists, but the dividing lines that determine how severe an illness is usually include the patient's:

- Ability to continue to work
- Need to recover at home
- Need for hospitalization
- Need for hospitalization in the ICU

Say that in a major metropolitan area, one or two elderly people show up at the same health clinic with a cough and a high fever. It could be an organism called *Streptococcus pneumoniae*—a typical cause of community-acquired pneumonia[2], or it could be many other things.

Although the result may be severe in the two patients, there is no reason to think that there is a general health hazard. This is because we have enough experience with the problem of pneumonia in elderly people to know that a few cases are, generally speaking, not a warning of a serious infectious disease threat in the community. Elderly people are, by virtue of advanced age and other concurrent conditions (e.g., diabetes or cancer or even lack of proper nutrition), *immunocompromised,* meaning that their immune systems no longer function optimally to protect them.

Replay that scenario with, say, a dozen young and otherwise healthy people showing up at clinics or doctor's offices around a city with the same symptoms. This is much more frightening to health professionals for two reasons. First, it means the organism could be in wide circulation. The fact that it is attacking healthy people who are not normally immunocompromised is another red flag. Organisms that are pathogenic enough to make healthy people ill can produce a catastrophic death rate among the immunocompromised: the elderly, people suffering from AIDS, and those receiving chemotherapy or radiation treatment.

However, the numbers are never hard and fast. Just a single case of measles, for example, would immediately be called an outbreak. This is because the measles organism spreads very quickly. In rare cases, measles can have devastating consequences, including pneumonia or encephalitis. Both conditions may be fatal and, in the case of encephalitis, may also lead to chronic, irreversible brain damage in those who survive the acute infection.

It is currently estimated that one person (a child, usually) with measles infects, on average, about *forty* other people. There have even been situations where hundreds of people have been infected from one person (the so-called index case in the outbreak). So, a single case of a very bad illness can be identified by public health officials as an outbreak. And, in the case of measles in particular, because of the illness is able to spread rapidly, public health officials have precious little time to initiate vaccination campaigns before cases begin to appear in widely dispersed geographic areas.

More famously, an outbreak of hantavirus pulmonary syndrome in 1993 in New Mexico was defined when two cases were identified by one doctor (as described in Chapter 3). Were these two cases enough to label the disease with yet another charged word—an *epidemic*? Not at that point.

An epidemic, according to Webster's dictionary, is a phenomenon "affecting or tending to affect a disproportionately large number of individuals within a population, community, or region at the same time." Epidemics require a judgment of not only severity or acute fatality, but one of geographic dispersal as well. Hantavirus did in fact become an epidemic—but only when cases started showing up at various spots around New Mexico.

Finally, it's worth noting that the term *pandemic* never came into play with hantavirus. Pandemics, as one can divine from their name, refer to diseases that have a global dispersal. With the exception of a severe, related variety of hantavirus-induced illness that was reported during the Korean War, hanta has never really been reported in anything more than scattered cases outside the Four Corners region of Arizona, Utah, Colorado, and New Mexico. Therefore, it has never qualified for the distinction of a pandemic disease. Outbreaks that grew to pandemic levels include the infamous influenza pandemic of 1918; the 1996 outbreak of cholera, which spread across the Pacific from Asia to Peru via the bilge water of oceangoing ships; and the relatively recent arrival of SARS into the United States and Canada from China.

In a curious way, epidemics and pandemics are slightly less charged words than "outbreak" to an epidemiologist. This is simply because they can describe pathogens that do not have a high fatality rate, though they may affect a large number of people. A pandemic of common cold viruses (which sweep the world every year) does not keep the people at the Centers for Disease Control up late at night. Outbreaks of Ebola or hantavirus do.

FUEL FOR THE FIRE

Once a disease has been spotted in a new outbreak, or is being watched as an epidemic/pandemic, it is accepted that the pathogen has entered into a population of hosts. When doctors are trying to stop or slow the spread of the organism, the *extinction rate of the infection* is what is used to shadow the pathogen the way a hunter will track a large predatory cat, looking for clues about its quarry.

The extinction rate of the infection is a concept for determining:

- The speed at which it spreads through a population
- The rate at which it induces immunity
- The rate at which it makes its own environment unsatisfactory for its continued proliferation

The first concept is widely known in popular culture and in the media by the frightening—and somewhat inaccurate—term "burn rate." True, just as flames burn wood in a fireplace, a disease can consume its population of hosts. Just as there are factors that would cause a fire to flare up more quickly (e.g., dry wood, wind conditions, ambient temperature), there are factors—not as widely known outside medical circles—that can determine an organism's spread. They include the method of transmission and the number of people—both healthy and with compromised immune systems—who have been exposed to the infectious agent.

To continue with the fireplace analogy, as the flames burn through the wood, they change the material by rapid oxidization to crumbly black ash. Once the wood has been completely converted to ash, the fire dies. In other words, the fire's mere act of burning in one spot when no more fuel is added makes its own environment unsatisfactory for its continued existence.

Similarly, without a continuous supply of hosts, any pathogen will sooner or later make its own environment unsatisfactory for its continued proliferation by "using up" its hosts. It does this either by granting enough of its hosts immunity or, in the more macabre cases, by killing off the population of available hosts.

In addition, some biologists would point to the environmental hardiness of an organism—that is, its ability to remain infectious as it resides on a nonliving surface (e.g., a tabletop, in clothing, or even in the soil and water)—as another factor that determines the likelihood of extinction of an epidemic. If an organism can survive on an inanimate object, it may be inadvertently acquired when a human (or animal) comes in contact with the contaminated object. As but one example, the smallpox virus (called variola) can remain infectious for weeks or months if it falls onto a dry surface that is not exposed to sunlight. The bedclothes of smallpox victims can expose many others to the virus, thus making the elimination of a particular outbreak even more problematic.

For most communicable infectious diseases to maintain their own existence, there has to be a certain number of available hosts where a certain percentage remains susceptible to organism. This notion, which has long been discussed in epidemiology circles, has been talked about in a very nonquantified way. This is because physicians traditionally have not been very well trained in mathematics.

More specifically, they are not good at using math to create models that can help predict the likely course of a disease by taking into account, in a quantitative way, the likelihood of spread of an infectious agent, its "lifetime" outside of host, the development of immunity (either as a result of vaccination or exposure to the organism), and the complicated movement of people, especially in our modern era of mass transportation.

CRITICAL MASS

The problem of estimating the percentage of a population that is likely to become infected by a given disease remained untouched for most of the twentieth century. Then, in the 1970s and 1980s, with the arrival of a little bit of math in medicine, a mathematical model of this very problem was brought to the epidemiology community. The model went by the acronym of SEIR, which stands for "susceptible-exposed-infectives-recovered." The SEIR model served as a way to measure the number of people who could get a disease, versus those who would get it, be infected, and recover—or die.

A great deal of mathematics comes into play, something that is rarely employed by physicians or even most public health officials, despite the requirement to pass a calculus course before admission into medical school. Four complex equations (called "differential equations" for the mathematically minded reader) are employed to describe the "behavior" of a particular organism in time and space. The calculated behavior is based on its mechanism of spread (e.g., as an aerosol mist from a sneeze or from direct contact with a victim of an illness), its incubation period, the time a given victim is infectious for others, and the rate of development of immunity.

Anyone who suffered through math class can probably figure out that you need more than a pencil and piece of paper to work through the equations. In fact, they normally can only be simulated on a computer. Even then, the computer can only approximate the conclusions, as the results tend to be startlingly different depending on the "initial conditions" of how many people are infected at the start, how much they move, and the uncertainties of spread of the organism from one person to another.

The answers produced are not precise numbers. Instead, the answers help identify patterns of the progression of an infectious disease as it burns through a community. In short, what you get is similar to a grainy photograph taken with an old box camera: a more or less recognizable image of the process taking place, but with many of the fine details missing.

The SEIR model makes some assumptions that are simple enough that it actually makes it possible to write the equations down. This was a big breakthrough when the equations were first derived. Even so, the model makes some crude estimates about each of the key variables—such as the amount of movement between individuals among the population. In order to model how one of the hosts has been exposed and become infectious to other people (the "I" in SEIR), you must first estimate how much someone who is infected will move around. Is the probability of moving five miles equal to the probability of moving five meters? SEIR assumes that it is—which is not be too far-fetched in the modern world, where it may take as much time (and less effort) to hop on a transatlantic jet than to walk five miles across town.

You cannot have sustainable outbreaks of smallpox, for example, given how rapidly it moves from person to person, unless there is a population of at least 200,000 people (something discussed in more detail further on in this chapter). This is precisely what was observed before vaccination against smallpox was begun in earnest in the mid-1800s: Smallpox was largely a disease of children. Few adults ever came down with smallpox because those that survived to adulthood had already been exposed as a child and were permanently immune.

FORTY DAYS AND FORTY NIGHTS

A disease's burn rate, which describes how quickly people are infected, also provides a logical reason for isolation of infected patients. (A disease's burn rate is distinguished from its extinction rate, which describes how soon an epidemic comes to a halt.) We can even isolate an entire population that is sick and wait until the pathogen has burned its way through the isolated group. Assuming that precautions are taken so that the disease cannot spread another way, such as through contaminated water or clothing, then people can be reintroduced back into the main population without risk. This is the underlying rationale for the quarantine.

We often think of the use of a quarantine as a means of controlling infection. Many of us grew up in towns or cities where patients with tuberculosis were forced to remain in their homes or in an isolation room of a hospital to prevent others from getting the disease. But one frequently overlooked aspect in a discussion about quarantines is that public health officials are not limited to only quarantining people because they are infectious. They can also quarantine people if they are *susceptible* to coming down with the disease. This type of quarantine is sometimes called "isolation," to distinguish it from the act of separating those *known* to be infected.

For example, young children or hospital patients undergoing chemotherapy could be quarantined from infected people. In the case of pathogens dangerous to the public at large, health professionals can quarantine adults who have not yet gotten ill and who don't want to get sick. With certain diseases like Ebola, isolation was the traditional way the African villages stopped the disease, and it actually worked. Every settlement in the Congo simply imposed self-isolation by barricading itself and not letting outsiders in. This strategy worked particularly well with Ebola, because transmission of the disease requires human-to-human contact.

The Oxford English dictionary's definition of the term *quarantine* is revealing in itself as it shows how the dimension of time as well as space plays out in disease control. The earliest root of the word comes from the term "forty" in Latin: *quaranta*. Indeed, a quarantine was originally forty days, during which people thought to be contagious were isolated from the rest of the community. As travelers were most suspected, ships or caravans were required to wait outside the harbor or city gates for the quarantine period before they were allowed to enter.

The first recorded, systematic use of the quarantine in the Americas is noted in a traveler's diary in 1663. The diary referred to a law on the books in the colony of Connecticut that made all ships arriving in port from New Amsterdam (later New York City) perform a thirty-day quarantine before unloading goods. Although undoubtedly from a much older time, the quarantine has quite literally passed the test of time in preventing or reducing the risk of transmitting disease.

Quarantine is really the extreme limit of identifying potential disease spreaders. When thinking about using quarantine procedures, the epidemiologist starts with the question: Who is either carrying the disease or susceptible to it? In the case of the 1918 flu epidemic, it wasn't obvious at first that the vast majority of people who were getting sick and dying were young. It was thought to be a much more general disease, because there was no way to gather accurate statistics.

In 1918, public health officials advised people not go outside their houses any more than they had to, and individuals who had a cough would be restricted in their movement. It wasn't recognized that there were old people who had coughs but didn't have influenza—they probably had something else, such as the common cold virus. Because anyone who coughed was feared to be carrying influenza, quarantine was a broadly applied strategy. Unfortunately, the strategy led to a great deal of resentment in the end. Indeed, many of the bad memories of the 1918 quarantine procedures account for people's general reluctance to consider it as a disease-management strategy even today.

This historical, overaggressive application should not be used to rule out the use of quarantine at all times. It would have been reasonable, for example, to quarantine all of the people who came into contact with SARS patients.

In order to limit the inappropriate use of quarantine while working against a rapidly spreading novel pathogen, public health officials have to make quick decisions. They try to identify specific "risk factors" for the acquisition or the propensity to spread a particular disease as quickly as possible. Examples of risk factors may be any of the following:

- Demographic (e.g., males age 40 to age 65)
- Behavioral (e.g., regular users of intravenous drugs)
- Medical (e.g., people undergoing chemotherapy)

There is little question that when based on sound science and clear understanding of disease dynamics, quarantine is an effective tool in halting an epidemic. But for better or worse, it is typically a weapon of last resort because it is perceived as a bludgeon for dealing with a situation that might respond equally well to a more finessed approach.

NATURAL RESERVOIRS

Another kind of disease, one that can slip by the barrier of a quarantine, is one that has a natural reservoir. A natural reservoir is any host or habitat in which an infectious agent normally lives, including humans, animals, or something in the environment. Diseases that operate in this manner can recur at any time.

Plague is a disease of this sort, since the natural reservoir is a rodent (usually a rat, ground squirrel, marmot, or prairie dog), with the disease transmitted by fleas that feed on these animals. The flea is called the vector, or source responsible for transmitting the disease. A more modern example would be the birds across the United States that now carry the West Nile virus, and mosquitoes of several types are the vectors for spreading the disease among birds and from birds to other species: horses, humans, and even exotic zoo animals such as the rhinoceros.

In the case of West Nile, there are a huge number of susceptible people in the target group—essentially, everyone in the United States that hasn't acquired the virus yet. However, West Nile does not spread directly from person to person. Instead, it is communicable through the insect vector. So an infected person is bitten by a mosquito that in turn bites another person, giving the virus to the second person. This is probably a minor contributor to the incidence of West Nile; bird-to-human transmission via mosquito is undoubtedly the major route of spread. There are some exceptions to human-to-human spread (for example, blood transfusions and possibly dialysis), but these are isolated cases that are extremely unlikely to blossom into an epidemic.

For now, birds are the natural reservoir. Humans could become a primary vector if enough humans are carrying the virus in their bloodstream during mosquito season. However, for now at least, humans are dead-end hosts for West Nile. A dead-end host is, by definition, a victim whose presence is not required for the continued propagation of the organism.

The term *dead-end host* has been used rather thoughtlessly by people who have not sat down to try to quantify its meaning. You could argue that people with smallpox who are isolated before they can spread the disease are dead-end hosts. This isn't because they are dead, but because the organism ends its life cycle with a particular person by either killing him or rendering him immune. In fact, the whole strategy of immunizing people around the infected person is to explicitly turn them into dead-end hosts so that the virus cannot jump into any new hosts and continue the cycle of infection.

In the case of smallpox, it also assumes that all of the clothing of the victims is burned and their homes disinfected. It turns out that smallpox has a half-life in water of up to thirty days (meaning about half of the population of variola viruses will survive and be able to propagate in host cells after being stored in plain water for a month), and water is a very reactive substance. The smallpox virus can live practically indefinitely on dry, non-UV-radiated surfaces that remain reasonably temperate. This is why deliberately passing on blankets infected with smallpox to Native Americans worked so efficiently to spread the disease and wipe out their populations during the French and Indian Wars in the 1700s.

The classical dead-end host is one in which the host is of a different species than the host for which continued propagation of the organism is required. So, for example, plague fleas are the hosts that propagate the disease and humans are dead-end hosts. If you managed to remove all humans from the four places on earth where plague occurs (Central Asia, Madagascar, Mongolia, and the Western United States), the plague organism would still be circulating happily in the environment. If humans are introduced again at a later time and they come into contact with, say, a plague-carrying prairie dog or marmot, the outbreak cycle begins anew.

For a disease to burn itself out in a given population, first there must be no natural reservoir that is not human in the area. Second, everybody must be exposed and either die or develop immunities before new people are born into the population. Finally, of course, there must be no intentional reintroduction of the disease, such as with a bioterrorism event.

Interestingly, we now know that newborns acquire a transient immunity for up to six or eight months against most diseases if the mother has been exposed. Maternal antibodies do cross the placenta. This is why smallpox in newborns has been rare, even in places such as India, where smallpox was endemic and more or less continuously present. Smallpox was seen in infants as young as one year old. By then, presumably their antibody base protection against the disease had waned, because the antibodies acquired from the mother have a limited lifetime of several months and begin to fall apart in the bloodstream.

At present, we believe that a high enough concentration of antibodies, as opposed to having to have certain white cells that are primed to kill the virus some other way, is indeed protective against smallpox. This is not the case all of the time—there are some diseases for which having the antibodies is not protective against the disease. For example, as of this writing, unfortunately there is no antibody protection against HIV.

In fact, the way we make the diagnosis of active HIV is to detect the presence of a specific antibody that the body produces to fight the virus. It used to be that if you had the antibody to a given virus, by definition you were immune. With HIV, that turns out not to be the case. Another disease that falls into this unfortunate category is hepatitis C. You might have the antibody against hepatitis C and be in a fully recovered state. Alternatively, you can have chronic infection of hepatitis C even though you have the antibodies. Hepatitis C is a good example of how certain diseases will never truly burn themselves out.

From a new pathogen's point of view, there will always be fresh wood for the fire. For these reasons, we need to keep even the old weapons of isolation and quarantine available. More important, as the computer models tell us, we live in an age where disease can run rampant and even lethal ones can sustain themselves on our high-density populations. The public health agencies we charge with our well-being need to remain vigilant, even if they have to use a socially and politically charged word like *outbreak.*

NOTES

1. Infectious disease experts continue to assume that West Nile fever is an "acute" disease in humans, meaning that once the episode of infection is over there are no progressive effects on the brain. There is now some evidence—mostly from animals but from a few humans as well—that West Nile fever may induce a slowly progressive degeneration of nerves in the brain and spinal cord, resulting in a disease that has symptoms similar to Parkinson's disease. If this turns out to be the case, then we may be looking at an enormous burden of chronic neurologic disease among humans who have been infected with West Nile fever. Only time will tell, but this problem illustrates the limitations of focusing only on the acute impact (i.e., fatality or hospitalization because of severe symptoms) of any disease.

2. Interestingly, the "reservoir" or source of many of the organisms that cause pneumonia in both young and elderly humans is often unknown, particularly for bacterial illnesses. As we will see later in Chapter 6, the

environmental "niche" of a few bacteria, such as the bacteria that causes Legionnaire's disease, are well known. It may well be that we all harbor organisms in our mouths and throats that from time to time change from a benign state to one that causes serious disease. This is thought to be what happens in the case of the most common community-acquired pneumonias (i.e., lung infections that start not in the hospital or some other special setting, but rather in the places where we live, shop, and work), but no one yet knows for sure. Fortunately, there are an ever-increasing array of vaccines that can prevent the most common community-acquired pneumonias. Furthermore, the rate of introduction of new vaccines will accelerate due to tremendous advances in exploiting technologies that are able to isolate and then use the DNA of bacteria and viruses as the actual source material for vaccines.

CHAPTER 5

SHARDS OF GLASS IN THE BRAIN

Bovine Spongiform Encephalopathy (Mad Cow)

Food-borne illness is part and parcel of human history. Early attempts to preserve food from the microbial growth that causes decay and disease led to developments as varied as the grain silo (to keep stored wheat dry) and the pepper trade (the application of pepper helped people ignore the offensive taste of half-rotten meat). Up until the nineteenth century, the methods developed to preserve food were still limited to smoking, drying, and salting. Remarkably, it was a warmongering European emperor who jumpstarted modern-day food preservation.

The millions of men who made up Napoléon Bonaparte's armies around 1800 depended on nourishment primarily from salt-preserved meats. These cured foods provided only incomplete nutrition. Both the army and navy endured frequent outbreaks of scurvy due to the complete absence of vitamin C in the men's diets. To counteract the debilitating diseases caused by malnutrition and to better feed his armies on the march, Napoléon put out a contract offering 12,000 francs to the person who devised a safe and dependable food-preservation process for his forces.

The winner was a Parisian bottle-washer, confectioner, and restaurateur turned chemist named Nicolas Appert. Though Appert didn't really understand why, he had observed that food heated in sealed containers was preserved as long as the container remained unopened and the seal did not leak. Since Appert was familiar with the bottling process, he chose champagne bottles in which to store food. Champagne bottles were ideal because they were cheap, strong for glassware, and the corking process was effective in creating an airtight seal.

Once the bottle was filled and sealed, bathing the bottles in steam completed the process, and fresh vegetables could be kept in the field or aboard a ship for months at a time. Eventually, the same idea was picked up by a French-English metalworking firm that decided to make the containers more durable by building them out of tin. These first tins are the ancestors of the cans of corn, Boston baked beans, or Spam sitting in your kitchen pantry today.

Fifty years after Appert won his 12,000 francs from Napoléon, there was a second breakthrough. Another Frenchman, named Louis Pasteur, determined that there was a direct relationship between the presence of microorganisms and food spoilage. The process by which we heat foodstuffs today to kill bacteria, named *pasteurization* in his honor, has vastly increased the dependability of the food-preservation process.

With these advances in our knowledge about food-borne illness, for the past century we have felt more or less safe from deadly organisms in our food. But in the age of mass farming and industrialized meatpacking, that sense of safety could quickly be coming to an end. It turns out that, as a completely unanticipated result of our animal husbandry and food-processing practices, we have created an opening for a totally new, infectious organism.

It is not alive like a virus, and it would be difficult even to classify it as a life-form. Yet it holds the potential to wreak havoc on our food supply. It is a proteinaceous infectious material and is called by its abbreviation: *prion.*

YOU EAT IT, THEN IT EATS YOU

By far the best-known example of a prion-based disease is mad cow disease, more properly known as bovine spongiform encephalopathy, or BSE. The story of the prion that causes BSE in cattle and a variation of Creutzfeldt-Jakob disease (CJD) in humans—now referred to as "new variant CJD," or nvCJD in the medical literature—is strange because it is shocking in its ramifications, but ponderously slow in its development. Rather than emerging in a bloom of new cases and causing the media to turns its eye on the country or town that disease is burning through, these prion-based diseases have emerged slowly over time. CJD provided only a steady drip of cases until a critical mass of evidence emerged.

In 1986, an epidemic of BSE ravaged the British cattle industry. It was discovered that some 178,000 cows had come down with the disease, which was first reported by a farmer who said that his cows were "dancing." Given the strange way that cattle were behaving, it was perhaps inevitable that the press would dub the affliction "mad cow" disease.

It appears now that that the epidemic was caused by a protein supplement in the cattle feed that contained parts of slaughtered animals that people didn't want to consume—such as intestines and brain matter from cattle as well as sheep. This animal material-cum-animal feed contained prions, perhaps from sheep, who had long been known to have a prion disease all of their own. Though the 1986 epidemic dealt a bitter blow to the cattle industry, there had never before been a case of BSE-like disease jumping species (including, by the way, from sheep to cattle). In fact, the exact cause of the cattle's neurological breakdown wasn't even understood. In the absence of further evidence, the meat supply was considered safe for human consumption.

A decade later—and originally not associated with BSE—more than a hundred people across Europe, primarily in England, had come down with a new variant of a disease that had been known for over seventy years: Creutzfeldt-Jakob disease. CJD is a strange affliction because it does not "act" like a disease. That is, it does not cause a fever or other symptoms commonly associated with a bacteria or virus. Instead, people with CJD experience the slow development of profound insomnia, depression, unusual "prickling" sensations on the skin, and hyperexcitability. Even a modest stimulus, such as someone clapping their hands together, can startle the patient enough to cause a seizure. As the illness progresses over the course of a year, mental impairment increases in variation and severity. Patients may experience problems with muscular coordination and short-term memory loss, and they even undergo a personality change. Blindness sometimes follows, and then patients lose the ability to move or speak. In the final stages, severe dementia sets in and brain function deteriorates to such a severe extent that automatic functions—such as coughing or even breathing—simply cease.

Some symptoms of CJD can be similar to symptoms of other progressive neurological disorders, such as Alzheimer's disease. Much like Alzheimer's, CJD could properly be said to destroy the "who" of the person before destroying her body. Horrifyingly, CJD causes unique changes in brain tissue, riddling it with small holes and giving the brain a unique appearance that can be seen under the microscope (see Figure 5-1).

FIGURE 5-1

A picture of the damage done by prions in a CJD patient.

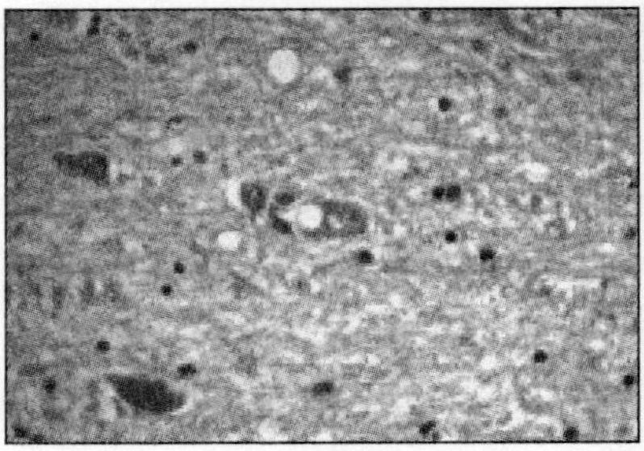

In 1996, a suspicion that BSE had been transmitted to humans from beef or beef by-products caused a scientific and economic furor. Then British health secretary, Stephen Dorrell, like numerous other government representatives, had been reassuring the public that the beef used in their hamburgers, kidney pies, and sausages was perfectly safe. However, by March that year, he had to recant his words when he reported to the British House of Commons that a government advisory committee had concluded that mad cow disease was indeed the "most likely" cause of the CJD cases.

The results were dramatic. The European Union imposed a three-year ban on the export of British beef, causing a slump in the British economy. The U.S. Department of Agriculture banned the import of cattle and many cattle by-products from most European nations because of BSE. Consumers and markets alike simply dumped or burned the beef stocks on hand because no one would risk eating the meat. The tabloids had a field day; given the grisly nature of the disease, their headlines ranged from parody—"Never in the field of human conflict has so much beef been banned from so many by so few"—to the utterly sensationalist "You Eat It: Then It Eats You!"

For many years cattle ranchers had been feeding "protein supplements" to their animals to speed up the animals' growth and shorten the time to market. This supplement was made in part from the remnants of cattle carcasses after processing at slaughterhouses. The material—containing animal organs (called "offal"), bone marrow, and ground bone—was fed to growing cattle along with corn and plant-based feed.

One reason for refeeding animal carcass waste to other animals was that the enormous mass of animal intestines, bone, skin, and brain created a disposal problem. "Recycling" it as part of animal feed thus solved several problems at the same time.

Since some the animals with BSE were known by the 1990s to have microscopic abnormalities in their brains (see Figure 5-2), it was hypothesized that an infectious agent of some sort was involved. But, despite the

FIGURE 5-2

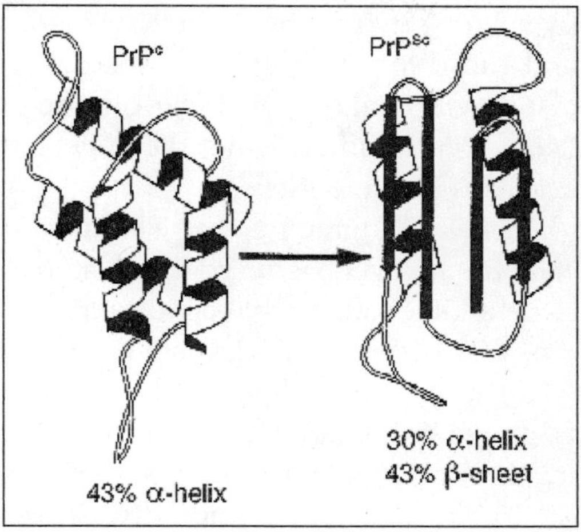

boiling of offal and bone meal before packaging and shipment to cattle feedlots, the agent somehow survived to reinfect additional animals.

At some point in this grisly process, prions that could attack bovine brain matter emerged in the feed. To this day, no one is sure when, where, and exactly how this happened. It may have occurred as a result of a mutation of the sheep prion. It may have happened because of the way sheep offal was rendered with heat and lye to make it more palatable to cattle. It is likely that we will never know the exact cause and time of the occurrence.

Today, even though cattle feed processes have been updated to break the chain of transmission (offal and bone meal are forbidden in the cattle food supply), there are lingering repercussions. Reports of possible sightings of BSE in the beef supply keep consumers skittish on both sides of the Atlantic. It is not yet known exactly how BSE is passed from animals to humans, where it manifests itself as CJD. What is known is that there is no effective treatment for any prion disease.

Once the infectious agent enters the human brain, it can lie dormant for as long as ten to fifteen years before causing even subtle clinical symptoms. When activated, the agent kills brain cells, leaving large areas of spongy holes. Large clumps of abnormal prion proteins known as plaques are found in brain cells. The disease runs its course in less than one year in most victims, and to date it has left no survivors.

REPRODUCTION WITHOUT A BLUEPRINT

Twenty years ago, if a PhD student had considered doing a doctoral thesis on a theoretical particle like the prion, the idea would have been rejected by an adviser. The idea is ludicrous—a particle that manages to reproduce and cause infection in other species yet possesses none of the types of genetic material that we believe to be essential for life (namely, DNA and RNA). Yet the prion is not theoretical; its existence is now unequivocally accepted by biologists.

What is stunning is that it *is* an *infectious* organism that is capable of *reproduction* yet has *no* genetic material—at least as far as we've been able to determine today with very detailed experiments reproduced hundreds of times. The infectious organism has no DNA, no RNA, and no genetic code whatsoever. Yet somehow it is able to infect, reproduce, and then spread from one host to another. Thus the "prion" receives its name from shortening this descriptive phrase: "*pro*teinaceous *in*fectious" agent.

The classic human prion disease we know of—though it was one that we did not even recognize as being caused by prions until recently—was a malady specific to cannibals living in the hills of New Guinea. The tribes called it the "laughing sickness," or *kuru*. Kuru was described in the 1950s and had a very peculiar epidemiology in that it seemed to mostly affect only women.

Kuru manifested itself slowly, as a progressive neurological disease characterized by ataxia, which is the inability to walk without listing or stumbling from side to side. We associate this gait from someone who has imbibed a little too much alcohol. A person afflicted with kuru then progresses to dementia. Ultimately, the disease leads to a complete failure of the nervous system and death.

It was a disease that would take years to progress. As it ran its deadly course, the victims of kuru would also be prone to sudden mood swings and outbursts of laughter. The last few months—even years—of life were absolutely miserable. Not only were the victims robbed of all normal mental faculties that we associate with being human, but they were also subject to an extremely strange phenomenon. Even the slightest stimulus—turning on a light, opening a door, a sudden sound—would make patients literally have a seizure.

Kuru remained an epidemiological enigma, although after careful observation over many years it was noted that the people who tended to get kuru had two commonalities. First, they were members of New Guinea tribes who engaged in ritual cannibalism. Second, they were active participants who dined specifically on either the brain or parts of the central nervous system of whoever was to be consumed. Kuru was thus quite similar to CJD. But unlike kuru, CJD was observed in Europeans, whose cultures tend to frown upon ritual human consumption, to put it mildly.

The theories about the causes of kuru or CJD remained completely obscure until 1981,when the idea of disease-causing protein particles was first postulated by Stanley B. Prusiner, the neurologist who coined the term "prion." It was an incredibly controversial thesis, right up until he received the Nobel Prize in 1997 for describing the prion. What is still difficult for the medical world to accept is how a prion can meet the criteria of "life" for a microorganism.

How could infection, reproduction, and spread of a disease take place without having any genetic material whatsoever? No DNA, no adenine, no thiamine, no guanine, no base pairs, no double helix at all. Watson and Crick, the scientists who discovered the DNA molecule and coined the term "molecule of life," would have been left scratching their heads at this new development.

Viruses do not conclusively meet the basic requirements of a living organism because they cannot reproduce on their own. However, they can at least be classified as a life-form because at least they had the same basic genetic structure as all other forms of life. Viruses contain DNA or RNA, and they use processes for reproducing their DNA and RNA so that they can, in fact, spread from cell to cell and then from host to host. Prions have none of these characteristics. They contain not a single gene, nor a single base pair of nucleotides that are the building blocks of DNA and RNA.

LIKE SO MUCH SWISS CHEESE

Prion diseases are causing great worry among scientists who are concerned that once they are established in the human species, their spread will no longer be primarily through consumption of infected meat. It has been discovered that a few hundred patients who received cornea transplants from patients who died from Creutzfeldt-Jakob disease had a high likelihood of going on to develop CJD.

Then patients who had received growth hormones from the pituitary glands of someone who had Creutzfeldt-Jakob disease started to come down with CJD. Patients who were having brain tumors removed were at risk as well. During brain tumor removal, the surgeon has to cut through the dura mater—the tough lining over the brain. To repair the dura mater damaged during surgery, transplanted pieces of dura from a donor (typically a cadaver) can be used. This practice could now put the patient at severe risk if the donor had CJD, even in its early, presymptomatic states.

If you are thinking that these situations only apply to a few people and that the answer is simply to stop donations from people infected with CJD, that is an understandable mistake. The prion story soon took a turn toward the bizarre. It was observed that the use of the same *instruments* that had been used in surgery on someone with CJD could spread the disease, despite the thorough cleaning and antimicrobial treatment of these instruments after each and every use. Just as the discovery that prions had no genetic material surprised the medical field, the idea that some disease-causing substance could survive decontamination was a tremendous shock.

CJD was spread from surgical tools that had been properly sterilized under an autoclave device that uses superheated steam under high pressure. Until the prion, autoclave treatment was able to kill every organism known, including all viruses and the hardiest of bacteria. In fact, an autoclave inevitably blunts the instruments themselves because it's such a chemically and physically reactive environment.

But even when instruments were autoclaved, if they had been used on somebody with Creutzfeldt-Jakob disease, then there was a high likelihood that the person who was on the receiving end of those instruments anytime down the line, even years later, would have a high risk of developing CJD. Sterilization fails to destroy the prion. Even bleach under high pressure was found to be insufficient for decontamination of the Creutzfeldt-Jakob agent.

What exactly was this agent? What we learned in the 1980s and 1990s was that it was clearly infectious because you could, in fact, transmit it from animal to animal. It was clearly associated with certain specific abnormalities of the brain tissue of animals or humans who had it. It came to be called spongiform encephalitis because the brain tissue was filled with tiny holes reminiscent of a sponge. On a microscopic level, a slice of tissue would look like so much Swiss cheese.

Because the material was clearly infectious and caused a reproducible pathology, it met the threshold for being a disease as defined by what scientists call Koch's postulates. According to Robert Koch (a famous nineteenth-century pathologist and microbiologist), before an agent can be classified as a disease, you must be able to identify the disease and make sure it has some unique characteristics. You must also show that the disease can be transmitted from one host to another and that when observed in the recipient, the disease is identical to the disease in the donor, so that you can once again isolate the causative organism. Koch's postulates are for the vast majority of scientists a useful set of definitions for primitive "life." Thus, prions could no longer be dismissed. They were infectious—and lethal—life-forms, consistent with Koch's postulates, albeit ones devoid of genetic material as had been thought necessary for any and all life-forms.

TRACKING DOWN AN INDESTRUCTIBLE KILLER

The final requirement under Koch's postulates, that you isolate the organism, proved to be the hardest part. It took until the 1980s for prions to fulfill this requirement. When scientists began trying to isolate CJD, the first thing they did was to take brain material from a lab animal such as a monkey or a rat that had spongiform encephalopathy. They would inject it with an enzyme called DNase or RNase. These enzymes are extremely pathogenic to genetic material and mangle the single or double strands that made up the RNA or DNA. At a molecular level, the enzyme literally chops up the long DNA strains into hundreds of thousands of base pairs. The upshot is that one can be certain that if you subject a traditional infectious agent such as a virus or bacteria to a DNase or an RNase, you are in fact getting rid of any genetic material. The prions shook off the chemical manipulation of these enzymes: They remained highly infectious. Thus, scientists at least were sure that the infectious agent had no genetic material.

The next thing that scientists were able to demonstrate was the incredible tenacity of the prion particle. It was discovered that if you subjected infected brain tissue to autoclave temperatures, strong bleach solutions, formalin, and formaldehyde, the brain tissue *still* remained infectious. Scientists were only able to destroy the prion when the tissue that contained it was heated to 400 degrees. Of course, brains exposed to that level of temperature either completely disintegrated or caught on fire.

By any standards, under the usual conditions that we have available to us in the microbiology lab or in the hospital decontamination unit, this infectious material was unnaturally resistant. Essentially, once surgical equipment had been used on somebody with this disease, the equipment had to be thrown away. It was forever contaminated unless the metal that made up the material was melted down.

The final test they subjected the prion to was exposing it to huge doses of radiation. Tests were carried out by exposing the infectious material to neutron particle radiation, electron radiation, ultraviolet (UV) radiation, and X-ray radiation. The doses were enormous, well into the hundreds of thousands of rads. A rad is a measure of the amount of energy deposited per gram of material. In a human, the typical dose of radiation that is lethal within a few hours is around 30,000 rads. As it happened, doses that high and even higher did not render prions noninfectious in the brains of new hosts. Amazingly, the prions still remained as infectious and lethal as ever.[1]

This was a second pointer to the fact that there was no genetic material in a prion. If there had been, the material would have been smashed to bits by the high doses of radiation. The end conclusion was that the mysterious prion was an unusual protein. A protein is nothing more than a series of amino acids that are linked together in a long chain. Amino acids aren't really exotic—you can buy amino acids like tryptophan or tyrosine at the health food store. Amino acids are also a building block of regular muscle protein, so eating a piece of animal flesh such as a hamburger or sirloin steak means that you are ingesting long chains of amino acids.

When you eat a hamburger, your stomach acid breaks the hamburger down into individual amino acids or compounds called bipeptides or tripeptides. Bipeptides are pairs of amino acids; tripeptides, logically enough, are bundles of three amino acids. These amino acids are what gets absorbed in the intestine and then gets used as a building block for the proteins that make up our own body flesh and the enzymes that power our cells. Some proteins were already known that resisted destruction by radiation and even autoclaving. Thus, it was not unreasonable to postulate that the prion was nothing more (and nothing less) than a peculiar protein that happened to do damage to normal nerve tissue.

THE ROGUE PROTEIN

At this point in the research, the prion protein postulated by Stanley Prusiner was the last remaining candidate for the infectious agent. No one could theorize anything else. But the remaining hurdle was an especially troubling one: that proteins aren't supposed to be able to reproduce. They can be part of a chain of chemical events. They can be enzymes, for example, that assist in reproduction of DNA, but in and of themselves they cannot reproduce on their own.

The unexpected breakthrough came when it was discovered that some animals were, in fact, completely resistant to the effects of prions. Scientists were, at this point in the story, obviously interested in whether prions from one animal that died of encephalopathy could be spread to any random species of animal by direct injection into their brains. In general, this would not happen. A prion isolated from a human who died from CJD would not make a rat or a cow ill (but on occasion, it might cause neurological disease in a primate). Thus, prions seemed to be more or less specific to one species. Therefore, if you had a cow that had spongiform encephalopathy, that material could successfully be used to infect other cows or closely related ruminants like sheep. But it was extremely difficult to transfer the infection to a mouse or a monkey.

The theory had therefore changed so that not only did the infectious agent lack genetic material, but it somehow managed to be more or less species-specific. This meant it wasn't just any ordinary protein. It was a protein that varied from species to species. What researchers did next was to look for a protein of some sort that was in the central nervous tissue of various mammals that varied from species to species. Ultimately, their search was successful.

The culprit was a protein that is *normally* present on the surface of neurons, the nerve cells that transmit impulses throughout the body. In each and every mammal tested, there was a more-or-less similar, long chain of amino acids that was anchored in the membrane of the cell. To date, the function of the prion protein in normal nerve cells is unknown. Indeed, some animals have been genetically modified so that they do not have any normal prion protein at all, and they seem to suffer no ill effects.

But if the prion protein was a *normal* constituent of brain cells, how could it also cause disease? The answer turned out to be surprisingly simple. The normal prion protein—which looks like a long, loose string of beads—could adopt one of two specific three-dimensional twists and turns, called a "conformation" by biologists.

One conformation was the normal prion protein that seems to happily sit on the cell surface doing very little if anything. But another confirmation of the prion protein turned out to be able to do two things: damage the nerve cell and, strangely enough, induce the "normal" conformation prion proteins to reorient into the abnormal conformation. How the prion actually damages the nerve cell is, as of this writing, unknown, but it has been repeatedly demonstrated in numerous experiments.

It turned out that this process occurred slowly but relentlessly. The abnormal prion protein (abbreviated PrP-Sc in honor of the first discovered prion protein of sheep that caused scrapie) binds to the normal prion protein. It then changes its three-dimensional structure. Once again, the details of the process have yet to be worked out, but it is clear that it occurs in the test tube as well as in nerve cells.

When sufficient numbers of normal prion proteins are transformed into the abnormal shape, they are engulfed by the nerve cell. This sets into motion an extraordinarily complex series of chemical reactions that lead to the death of the cell. The neuron degenerates, leaving a microscopic hole in the brain. As more and more of these holes appear, the net of neurons in the brain becomes tattered like a worn-out rug, which is the reason for the sponge-like appearance of brains infected and damaged by prions.

An equally unanswerable question is, "How did the first prion come to be?" The normal prion protein is enormous. It's tens of thousands of amino acids long. Because of this fact, a prion forms in areas that are sort of curled in a coil and other portions of the protein that are relatively flat, or simply folded over itself like a blanket on a bed. It turned out that the prion protein has a much flatter shape than a normal protein's configuration.

The story gets even more bizarre. All cells in the body continually absorb proteins to degrade and replace them. It is part of the normal cellular processes, similar in some ways to recycling. However, once an abnormal prion protein is absorbed, the cell will attempt to degrade it, but cannot.

Eventually, the abnormal prion material builds up in the cell to such a high concentration that it ultimately kills the cell. It is still a matter of speculation whether the abnormal protein itself is pathogenic for the cell or whether the presence of the prion causes an immune response that ends up killing the cell.

Whichever theory is correct, the result creates the sponge-like holes in the brain, and it forms what are called *plaques*. These aren't things that can be seen with the naked eye, and they are very different from the plaque on your teeth. These items are called plaques because of their appearance under the microscope. They look like deposits of glass shards embedded within the brain and may represent accumulation of abnormal prion proteins along with debris from dead neurons.

A NEW FORM OF LIFE ARISES

The prion story isn't over by any means. There still is contention within the medical and microbiology world over the connection of the prion to CJD. There are factions that believe that prions just cannot be the cause and that there has got to be some other component of the infectious agent beyond just a protein. To date, no one has ever been able to definitively prove otherwise.

Scientists can purify prion protein to a very high level, meaning that there is nothing else in a given sample besides prion protein. The sample would contain no DNA, no RNA, no chemicals, and no toxins. And it has been proven that this sample of pure protein is all that is required to infect a susceptible species. So, Prusiner's hypothesis seems to have been borne out, unique and iconoclastic as it was in the early 1990s.

One last story about prions in our modern world may offer a theory into how abnormal prions come to be. In the 1990s, a new disease called chronic wasting disease began ravaging herds of elk in the Rocky Mountains portion of the United States—Colorado, Wyoming, and northern New Mexico. How this disease started, we don't know. It was determined to be a prion disease, and it is only transmitted from one elk to another, and perhaps to a closely related species of deer.

The disease does not appear to have occurred as a result of elk coming in contact with or grazing alongside cows infected with mad cow disease.

It is difficult to make the argument that it was a species crossover from cow to elk, although the case can be made. After all, cows on ranches in these areas are often left to graze up in the mountains, in the same pastures that elk frequent.

The epidemic is spreading particularly fast among farmed elk, which would suggest that the density of the population has something to do with the likelihood of a susceptible elk coming down with the disease. However, it's not the only explanation, because there are clearly elk out in the wild that also have chronic wasting disease of elk.

There is one explanation that might also explain the origin of kuru and mad cow disease. The theory is that one day a normal prion protein gets hit by a gamma ray or some energy particle, which flips the protein from one shape into another. The injection of extra energy changes the protein from the normal confirmation into the abnormal confirmation, denoted by PrP-Sc (prion protein, scrapie form) rather than PrP-n, a shorter way for biochemists to describe prion protein "normal."

There is also a theory behind why the abnormal prion protein doesn't appear to come about in birds, reptiles, fish, or cockroaches. Mammals are thought to be the most highly evolved of all of the animal species. As such, mammals tend to have more complex protein structures in their building blocks.

These complex proteins are very large, at least compared to other structures on the cellular level. Because of their size, there is a higher likelihood that a stray particle of radiation could hit them. For example, our skin cells absorb radiation all the time when we go outdoors—one response of the body to protect us from cellular mutations leading to skin cancer is to produce melanin, which gives us our suntan.

A protein particle that takes a hit from radiation could possibly flip around into the pathogenic version of their three-dimensional confirmation. Interestingly enough, the function of the "normal" prion protein is unknown; there are strains of mice that have been genetically altered so that they produce no prion protein at all, yet they seem to show no behavioral or other ill effects.

The lesson is that even when we apply our best science to protect us from pathogens in our food, nothing can truly be considered foolproof. Simply by our decision to turn cows into cannibals in order to boost the amount of protein they received, a niche was formed where a new form of life arose. This form of life could today be circulating, unnoticed and deadly, hidden in our food supply.

NOTES

1. Radiation—a stream of particles that may or may not also carry electrical charge—does its damage to DNA and other genetic material by breaking chemical bonds in the material. When chemical bonds are broken they often reform, though not usually between the same atoms that previously shared the bond. Thus, the actual chemical structure of the material is altered. In the case of DNA (or RNA), radiation in sufficient doses makes it impossible for enzymes inside of every cell to read or interpret the genetic code in the DNA. The alteration in the DNA is, by definition, a "mutation" and radiation is one of many "mutagens" that can alter DNA, leading to a cascade of disastrous events for the cell or infectious particle carrying DNA. From years of experimentation, the dose of radiation required to damage DNA has been well established, yet despite exposing prions (or prion-carrying cellular matter) to many orders of magnitude greater levels of radiation, the prion remained infectious—providing the strongest evidence of all that it did not depend on DNA in order to reproduce inside a susceptible cell.

CHAPTER 6

OUT OF THE SHADOWS

Legionella Pneumophila (Legionnaire's Disease)

Legionella arrived on the public scene with a dramatic appearance in a Philadelphia hotel the summer of 1976. The hotel was hosting the American Legion Convention, a veteran's organization that boasted more than 4,000 attendees at its gathering. More than 200 of the elderly attendees at the convention began coming down with mild coughs and low fevers.

Soon after the convention, many of the afflicted developed a rapidly progressive pneumonia, muscle aches, and an incredibly high fever spiking up to 105 degrees. Thirty-four of the attendees passed into a coma and died because of exposure to Legionella. The public's fears about the unknown, deadly pathogen weren't answered until the following year. In 1977, the bacterium *Legionella pneumophila* was identified by the Centers for Disease Control and Prevention (CDC) and named after the first unfortunate victims.

VISION IN SILVER

Legionella pneumophila turned out to be one species in the large family of Legionella bacteria (see Figure 6-1). While, to date, all major outbreaks of Legionnaire's disease were determined as being caused by *L. pneumophila,* sporadic cases have been caused by the other subspecies. It was determined that although exposure to Legionella was unlikely to result in infection, the mortality rate is startlingly high. As many as one out of eight people

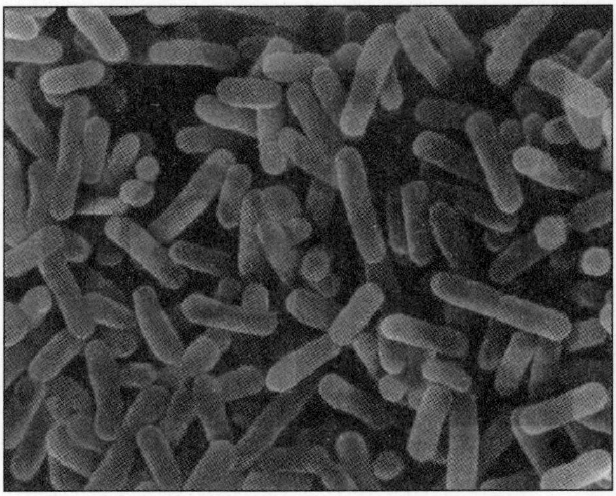

FIGURE 6-1

A culture of Legionella bacteria.

who come down with Legionnaire's disease will die, and the rate jumps to four in five among the elderly or with immunosuppressed patients.

The appearance of Legionella created great unease in the medical community for more reasons than the fact that it could cause fatal pulmonary illness. Once the CDC identified the bacterium, the scientists realized that it had caused a number of pneumonia outbreaks prior to 1976. Indeed, it is likely that Legionella has been causing serious human pneumonia cases for many, many years.[1]

In 1957, several dozen employees at a meatpacking plant in Minnesota were hospitalized with an acute pulmonary illness and at least two died. Their symptoms were identical to the outbreak in Philadelphia. Seven years later, dozens of patients at the St. Elizabeth Medical Center in Washington, D.C. came down with an unknown pulmonary illness that killed seventeen and then vanished without a trace. In both cases, the infectious agent demonstrated the exact same characteristic that alarmed health officials about the outbreak in Philadelphia: It did not respond to antibiotics, the wonder drugs that had come of age during World War II.

But the real importance of Legionella's emergence is that it is now recognized as the classic *human-induced environmental disease.* In other words, we created an environment that we like to live in—one that is moderately well humidified, unchanging in temperature, associated with the ability to take hot showers whenever we wish. Unfortunately, this environment has turned out to be the perfect breeding grounds for Legionella, which is an otherwise obscure soil organism that rarely, if ever, comes in contact with human beings.

Its limited contact with humans was only one of four reasons why Legionella's family of bacteria went unnoticed by science until 1977. The second reason was that Legionella is a very picky eater. Specifically, they require trace minerals such as iron and amino acids like cysteine; but calcium—which is a common constituent in just about every culture media preparation—may inhibit its growth. Because of this behavioral quirk, they simply would not grow in usual lab cultures. It took time to identify, by trial and error, the right combination of nutrients that would permit Legionella to grow in the laboratory (which, after all, is not its "natural" environment).

Third, the natural reproductive cycle of Legionella simply did not involve human beings; rather, Legionella inhabits the soil and, in fact, inhabits *other organisms,* particularly amoeba-like organisms in soil and certain bodies of water. It was only when humans actually brought the Legionella's favorite environments closer to concentrated populations that it infected humans. Thus, the organism never became a recognized pathogen until 1977.

And finally, in addition to being hard to culture in usual laboratory growth solutions, Legionella also resists most of the typical, widely employed laboratory staining techniques used to make otherwise nearly transparent bacteria visible. Consequently, it is often extremely hard to see under the microscope. Until recently, only layers of silver-containing stains could outline the bacteria's cell wall, allowing a shadowy image to be seen.[2]

A DEADLY NICHE

The Legionella organism has a peculiar tendency to cause severe vascular inflammation in the lungs, much more so than just about any other organism known to cause pneumonia in humans. This inflammation would cause fluid to leak out of the blood vessels and accumulate in the alveoli of the lungs. The alveoli are small sections of the lung where oxygen is infused into the bloodstream and carbon dioxide is released. If a patient's body cannot exchange these two gases, they suffocate and die.

Whenever a new pathogen is discovered, scientists recognize that it is not truly "new" but only "newly recognized." Researchers want to know why they hadn't been aware of the pathogen previously. In the case of Legionella, two puzzles vexed scientists studying the organism: One was the *source* of the pathogen. The other was whether it could be *transmitted from person to person.* Over the course of several months, after the outbreak in Philadelphia in 1976, the organism was isolated and antibodies were found in patients who recovered from Legionella. These antibodies bind very specifically to Legionella, which meant medicine now had a probe to look for Legionella.

A slew of samples were taken from all over the hotel and in the convention meeting areas, as scientists theorized that there was probably some environmental source for the organism. The samples were tested for the presence of Legionella bacteria. Much to everyone's surprise, the organism's source turned out to be the water supply in the cooling tower that was part of the building's air-conditioning system.

Although it turned out that Legionella was not spread person to person through coughing or sneezing, the transmission route did involve the air. The water supply in the hotel's cooling tower was kept in open troughs. Since the water was open to the air and sunlight, the algae and microbial growth in the troughs provided a tremendous bounty of food for the bacterium. Almost all bacteria require an external energy source since they cannot generate energy from sun. Therefore, the artificially created niche allowed the Legionella and the amoeba to multiply into a population concentration not normally found in nature.

Cooling towers are an integral part of modern air-conditioning systems and serve to keep the machinery of the air conditioner from overheating. Water is pumped up to the roof where it evaporates or radiates heat out into the atmosphere to cool the water. Because warm water is constantly being pumped into the cooling towers, they tend to remain at or around 80 degrees Fahrenheit. This turns out to be a perfect environment for Legionella to grow.

This water, which was now infested with the bacteria, naturally evaporated under the high temperatures and sunlight. The evaporate was, in turn, aerosolized by the nearby ventilation fans and blown through the vent systems throughout the hotel. The hotel's interior was showered with microscopic droplets of vapor containing billions of Legionella bacteria, which the poor conventioneers inhaled throughout the entire event.

WHEN THE EARTH WAS YOUNG

Legionella loves heat, so it is what microbiologists classify as a *thermophile*. In fact, the organism does quite well at temperatures up to 150 degrees Fahrenheit, a temperature that is close enough to boiling to kill almost all other forms of microscopic life. It is also the temperature used to pasteurize soup or milk for safety from food-borne pathogens.

This ability to survive high temperature is very rare in nature. But then, the chemical constituents that make up Legionella's membrane are very unusual. Most organisms have a membrane made up of a mixture of proteins and certain fats, which are technically referred to as fatty acids. Legionella's fatty acids are unique in the bacterial world in that they branch out like trees or fans. They act as an insulator against temperature and other environmental extremes, which include the hostile environment inside the amoeba where Legionella typically live. This complex membrane structure has also led some scientists to speculate that Legionella is related to the early archaebacteria that were the primary form of life on earth around three billion years ago. If so, the Legionella family of organisms is old indeed.

Legionella's strange characteristics are not limited to its resistance to heat and its unusual structure. In fact, the bacteria are some of the most versatile pathogens around. To start, Legionella has the ability to swim by developing flagella—whip-like tails that rotate at blinding speed, like a gelatinous propeller, moving the organism forward. Then when Legionella enters a drier environment, the microbe can reabsorb the flagella and grow a microscopic anchor to keep it attached to a surface.

These actions appear to be adaptive responses to whatever the local environmental conditions are. For example, if Legionella finds itself in a nutrient-poor environment, such as highly pure water in a fresh mountain stream, it can develop flagella to swim over to an area where nutrients are more abundant, then anchor itself to stay attached to that area.

Legionella is also odd in that the bacteria require residence inside of a protozoan (a single-celled organism like an amoeba) for their reproduction. This is probably because Legionella makes use of some of the protozoa's own reproductive machinery, making organisms like freshwater amoeba the "reservoir host" for the disease. Open troughs in the water-coolant system were tested for organisms known to grow in the warm water of a cooling tower. Even in the 1970s, there were rather stringent environmental checks made of cooling towers because it was known that open water will attract birds that fly in to drink, bathe, or relieve themselves in the water.

Today, the problem of Legionella and the protozoa that harbor them are a manageable threat. Rooftop air-conditioning systems are now designed to use closed water troughs. Service buildings such as hotels and hospitals are required by law to check periodically for Legionella contamination. If the microbe is found, the systems are purged with superheated water that will kill even thermophilic bacteria.

It turned out, however, that decontaminating water-cooling systems was not enough. Specifically, it was discovered that Legionella lived quite happily in the slime that lines water pipes, also known as *biofilm* or *bioslime.*

SLIME WITH A PEDIGREE

Biofilms are mysterious, extremely complex constructs of nature that scientists have only just begun to study in the laboratory (see Figure 6-2). And, as odd as it may seem, they pose a baffling array of problems to our efforts in public sanitation and public health. They are, indeed, much more environmentally complicated and potentially dangerous than the algae growth seen in ponds or the slime molds on forest leaf litter.

Biofilms are comprised of complex molecules that act as a *community* of bacteria that secrete thick, protein-rich ("proteinaceous") compounds that serve as a novel, safe environment where organisms can survive despite a wide variety of change in the surrounding level of humidity or temperature. The "slime" itself includes special signaling molecules originating—like all constituents of the slime—from the resident organisms that can transmit information to the bacteria in the slime. For example, one organism in the bioslime community sends a chemical message to the other members that indicates if there is a change in the salinity of the environment, a dearth of basic food sources such as glucose, or even the presence of toxins like chlorine.

A bioslime community is almost like an ant colony. Surprisingly, each of the thousands or millions of single-cell organisms in the bioslime is capable of very rapid signaling, allowing it to respond to changing environmental conditions with amazing speed. If a portion of the colony comes under chemical attack—for example, when a homeowner pours a cleanser like liquid detergent down the sink and down the water pipe—the organism would release chemical signals to the rest of the biofilm colony to prepare for the attack. Even if some of the Legionella organisms die, their internal contents would still be able to send a message into the biofilm and stimulate the remaining organisms to secrete more bioslime to protect the rest of the community.

FIGURE 6-2

Schematic of a biofilm.

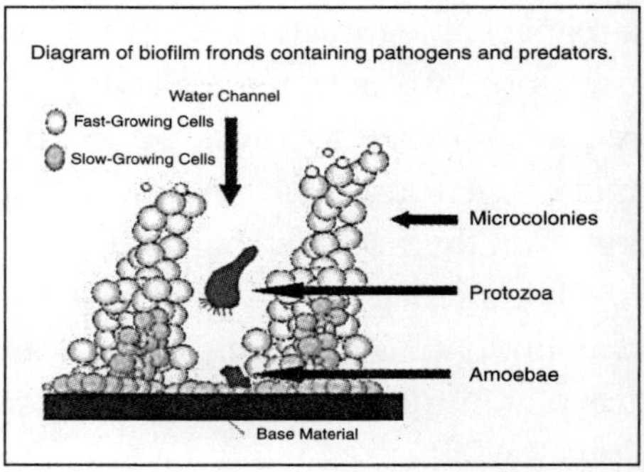

Probably more than any other single organism, Legionella has generated interest and therefore research into the general problem of biofilms or bioslime. These bacterial communities were once a wholly unrecognized phenomenon, even though they've been sitting in front of our faces for centuries. Anybody who has cleaned a toilet knows that there is goopy slime that has to be scrubbed off once a week or so. This film is just teeming with organisms—Legionella among them.

In certain situations, engineers and chemists have had to reformulate our decontamination solutions and plumbing because of the emergence of the bioslime community. It's highly likely that in the future, other dangerous organisms are going to find their way into the bioslime and ultimately become dangerous to humans. And just like Legionella, the organisms will likely cause considerable illness[3] because humans are dead-end hosts. As we discussed in Chapter 4, "dead end" hosts are not required for continued existence of the bacteria.

Ironically, Legionella and biofilm communities excite scientists because they're an excellent example of evolutionary biology at work. It shows us how organisms can adapt to a niche—in this case, modern plumbing—that never existed before.

SELECTIVE ENVIRONMENTS

Biofilms are surprisingly hardy, protecting the Legionella bacterium and allowing it to come into contact with our species much more often than has been suspected in the past. For example, though chlorine kills Legionella at current recommended doses, it only works if it comes in direct contact with the organism. The slimy, sticky residue of a biofilm is a good barrier against chlorine.

At its most basic level, this is why you still have to manually clean your toilet bowl with a scrubbing brush, even if you have a harsh chemical mixture to kill the organisms. Chlorine supplements for the toilet tank, which are marketed as "automatic toilet bowl cleaners," usually claim that they'll last for a thousand or a couple thousand flushes. But even at the end of their lifetime of use, you may notice that you still have to scrub every once in a while. This is because biofilms form even in this rather nasty chemical environment. Therefore, it is necessary to mechanically disrupt the protective biofilm to get rid of the organisms that attach tenaciously even to porcelain.

On an even more eerie note, our teeth are covered with biofilm. It's commonly called plaque. Technically, since plaque contains a whole host of organisms, it's a biofilm community.[4] This is why tooth decay occurs, why flossing is needed to disturb the development and reformation of the biofilm between teeth, and why when one person bites another, a nasty infection is often the result. The maintenance of good oral health requires a daily or twice daily scrub simply to remove—albeit temporarily—the bioslime that anchors countless organisms to teeth and gum tissue.

It is now well known that dental equipment can become contaminated with Legionella. The bacteria develop their flagella and can swim against the flow of water in the tube used to suction the mouth during a routine dental exam. Today, to prevent biofilm formation, dental equipment is usually rinsed before work and between each patient. Flushing water through the equipment for two minutes in the morning and for twenty to thirty seconds between patients is considered the norm for dental surgery procedures, and longer flushing is suggested after weekends.

Surprisingly, though, when their blood is tested, dentists or dental hygienists don't have a higher prevalence of antibodies against Legionnaire's disease, which means they have not been exposed to the bacteria. It is theorized that the barrier methods the dental offices use are very effective in deterring Legionella. Where once only a cloth mask was used, many dental hygienists are virtually donning upper-body space suits when they clean your teeth. Of course, this precaution was initially adopted to protect against HIV. But it may be that the barrier methods are what are saving them from Legionnaire's disease, because the organism hasn't figured a way around. At least not yet.

DISTURBING PUZZLES

In early September 2004, a nurse working in the inpatient wards at the hospital at the University of New Mexico came down with a serious case of pneumonia. Given her work at the hospital, which potentially placed her near immunocompromised patients, she was immediately examined by the New Mexico Department of Health. Legionnaire's disease was suspected, so a Legionella-specific test was performed to make the diagnosis.

Because of the difficulty in culturing and staining samples to see the microbe, a new test, called *direct fluorescent antibody,* has been developed to stain samples of respiratory secretions (also called sputum) with specific anti-Legionnaire's disease antibodies.[5] What is "direct" about this test is that it contains an antibody that binds exclusively to Legionnaire's disease. The antibody has a fluorescent molecule or two attached to it. Once the antibody is introduced to the sample, a doctor can view the sputum sample under a microscope that has an ultraviolet light source. The sample will grow orange or green when and if—and only if—Legionella bacteria are present. As it happened, the nurse's sample did glow, confirming that she had contracted the first case of Legionnaire's disease spotted in New Mexico in a very long time, other than cases imported from other states.

Because she was a nurse, she not only had contact with many patients, but she also had contact with lots of equipment where Legionella may have adapted to a new environment. For example, she may have worked with respirators. Since respirators are used for extremely injured, sick, or weak individuals who cannot breathe on their own, air in the respirator tube is kept very wet so as not to dry out the lungs. The air is also kept very warm, close to body temperature, so as not to cool off the patient.

Could Legionella have taken up residence somewhere deep in the mechanism of the average hospital respirator? The hospital has looked into this possibility and claims to have found no evidence of such a contamination. Could Legionella have contaminated the tube that shuttles oxygen to the patient, and the nurse picked up the microbe when changing the tube? Interestingly enough, a very thorough survey of the all the hospital's air-conditioning, heating, and air-handling equipment revealed no trace of Legionella.

The possibility of transmission of Legionella from a mechanical respirator to nursing staff cannot be ruled out. As was learned during the SARS outbreak, hospital personnel in Hong Kong contracted SARS when they had difficulty intubating a panicking, dying patient. Indeed, it is par for the course: Intubating a scared or resistant patient is very difficult, since it involves inserting a tube into the patient's throat to assist breathing—a terrifying experience to children or adults who are not fully coherent. The patient had SARS and was coughing and writhing around. It took a half-dozen doctors in the emergency room to subdue the patient. Somehow, perhaps through the aerosolization of the virus caused by the patient's spitting, coughing, and thrashing, every doctor assisting the patient came down with SARS. Perhaps the same thing could have happened in this Legionella case in New Mexico. For the moment, though, how the nurse got Legionella is a mystery.

It appears, then, that synthetic materials used in hospitals become the unexpected new environment where the Legionella organism has learned to survive. Doubtless, there is a biofilm inside of every respirator tube. It's warm, wet, and harbors a community of organisms. It doesn't get any better than that for Legionella. And yet, as of this writing, there is no provable conclusion for how the nurse in New Mexico contracted Legionella. Documented cases of Legionella are rare in any case in the generally dry climate of the Southwest, and most of the cases that *have* been diagnosed in New

Mexico over the past twenty years involved tourists visiting from other parts of the country. As with many pathogenic organisms and puzzling outbreaks, we are left with a tenuous handful of facts that we can only test by hypothesis and then attempt to deduce an answer.

A CHOICE OF EVILS

Bioslime communities and the Legionella bacteria they can harbor have created a more difficult problem for public health because residential hot water systems, unlike cooling towers, are everywhere. Many people today use water-saving nozzles. When you turn them up all the way, trying to get some water pressure, they aerosolize Legionella if it is present in the water so that it can be breathed in. For people with compromised immune systems, such as people with AIDS or those undergoing chemotherapy, the home itself presents a series of hazardous risks as organisms find their way into the very infrastructure that improves comfort for most people.

Now, the overwhelming majority of people who breathe in Legionella this way end up, in effect, getting vaccinated against Legionella—simply from intermittent exposure to small numbers of the organism—and they don't get disease. There are actually somewhere between one and three cases per million people of Legionella pneumonia a year in large cities, where the individuals get sick from residential hot water systems. The reason these cases don't get much press coverage is that the outbreaks are normally very mild. Most of the identified cases are just severe enough that the body creates an immune response, thus immunizing the person from future Legionella-induced pneumonia. Yet, despite the relative rarity of the disease, it appears to be on the increase (at least in immunocompromised patients). This teaches us that organisms can find their way into places that we have long assumed would remain bacteria- and virus-free.

To solve the problem of Legionella for the immunocompromised, one recommendation has been to clean out internal water systems—an exceedingly expensive procedure that would have to be repeated at some regular interval that has yet to be clearly identified. This solution may also be impractical because while the protozoa exist in surface water, most places around the world get their water from underground supplies.

Unfortunately, cleaning out the water pipes in a typical residence is very difficult. Also, few people want to completely replace the piping in their house because it's even more expensive. So the recommendation was to raise the water temperature in water tanks high enough so that it would effectively kill Legionella bacteria and the protozoa that harbor them. The required temperature is about 160 degrees.

But raising the water temperature to 160 degrees led to other problems, not the least of which was the scalding of children. So, when looked at clinically, Legionella led to a bizarre chain of events: A previously harmless organism adapted to a new, artificially created environment—pipes and cooling towers—and thrived. Attempts to mitigate its harm actually turned into a problem of its own—children and adults scalding themselves with hot water directly from the household tap.

THE LAW OF UNINTENDED CONSEQUENCES

The problem of Legionella pneumonia forces us to look at the goal of controlling or eliminating a public health concern as a matter of social utility. It means making some calculations and asking some questions. For example, "What is the cost of the extra energy to heat water to 160 degrees?" It should be taken into account that this water will then be diluted by cold water when it comes out of the showerhead because people can't expose themselves to 160-degree water without receiving a first-degree burn.

It needs to be asked, "What is the actual energy cost for 100 million residences around the United States and apartment buildings with a central hot water supply? What benefit do you get?" Well, the benefit is that we can, in fact, prevent one to three cases per million of community-acquired Legionella among the non-immunocompromised population.

The cost, it turns out (depending on the actual cost of the energy needed to heat the hot water), is between $1 million and $3 million per case of Legionella prevented. But, remember, most cases of Legionella are nasty but not fatal. So, as a matter of public policy, do we want to devote that level of resources, a million dollars per case prevented, that might be better used, for example, for purchasing influenza vaccine? Would the money be better spent developing other techniques for decontaminating water supplies of Legionella? We've only begun to tackle this issue in the United States, and as of this writing, there is no consensus on what direction should be taken.

The Legionella story is an excellent story of the law of unintended consequences. We humans created the environmental niche for Legionella and protozoa to grow. Today, we face a solution that could divert money away from things that make much more sense in terms of public health. This is not to argue that it's a good thing that anybody gets Legionella, particularly those who are HIV-positive. But it needs to be asked whether there are better things we could be doing with $300 million or $400 million a year than heating up our hot water tanks and scalding our children.

Despite the efforts already put into protecting cooling systems by using strong chemicals to kill protozoa and by heating up hot water tanks to ridiculously high levels, we still have intermittent outbreaks of Legionella. We still don't understand the organism or its place in biofilm communities very well. It may come from exposure to particularly high concentrations of the organism in soil, for example, when buildings are leveled or excavation takes place.

The organism has found its way into human environments, and typically in urban settings, almost exclusively as a result of human activities. It is unsettlingly different from diseases that crop up in individuals when humans enter into places where humans were probably never designed to go, like deep into the rain forests of Central Africa. Indeed, it's our urban lifestyle and our demand for centralized heating and cooling of air that has created a new disease, and it's a disturbing model for what could happen in the future.

NOTES

1. These determinations are also known as *retrospective studies.* These studies can help to pinpoint the pathogen that caused a death many years ago. For example, a retrospective study of the "sweating sickness" that plagued Europe in the 1600s bolstered the theory that it was caused by a variant of the Sin Nombre hantavirus that broke out in New Mexico in 1993. However, the study could only offer clues and likely guesses, not unequivocal answers.

2. Silver is rarely used in any staining technique for bacteria, although it has been used for looking at mammalian cells.

3. On a related note, Dial soap and Palmolive products use an antibacterial agent called triclosan. The vast majority of skin organisms have become resistant to it. Although consumers purchase soaps with this substance in it, the agent does virtually no good. It's another example of how our attempts to clean the environment unintentionally end up breeding better germs. We have to ask if we really want to have this agent out in the community, or if we want to reserve its use for places where we really do worry about transmitting bacteria like staphylococcosis from person to person, such as inside a hospital.

4. Antonie van Leeuwenhoek, the discoverer of bacteria, was once quoted in 1864 as saying, "The number of animalcules in the scurf of a man's teeth are so many, that I believe they exceed the number of men in a kingdom." He was slightly off in his guess: The number of microbes in the human mouth is closer to 10^{11} (ten to the eleventh power), or 100,000,000,000.

5. Antibodies are usually incredibly specific. If you get a flu shot for H1N1 influenza type A and you come into contact with a strain of H1N1 influenza A virus from downtown Beijing as opposed to the suburbs of Beijing, you still may get sick. That's how specific antibodies can be.

CHAPTER 7

AN ILL WIND

Smallpox

The half dry, half dead Aral Sea lies in the heart of Central Asia like a shattered blue marble on a tattered brown mattress. Until the mid-twentieth century, the Aral Sea was the fifth largest inland body of water in the world, supporting vast numbers of birds, fish, and small mammals and the industry and recreation that went along with these flourishing resources. Yet after only three decades of intensive cotton farming, the shoreline has receded by several miles and the use of pesticides have turned the sea into today's drainage pool of salt and toxic chemicals.

After the Second World War, the central planners in the Soviet government made the decision to make the country self-sufficient in cotton production. Cotton is a very water-intensive crop, so massive irrigation projects were undertaken to divert millions of gallons of water from the Amu and Syr Dar'ya rivers that fed into the Aral Sea and created the improbably lush lake in the middle of the dry Asian steppe. But, by the late 1960s, it was recognized that the Aral Sea was dying. Far too much water had been diverted from the two rivers. The price for the increased cotton yields was the literal drying up of over half the sea.

HOT ZONES IN THE COLD WAR

If that wasn't bad enough, in addition to being one of the worst environmental disasters the world has yet seen, the Aral Sea was also host to the

"Aralsk event." Aralsk is the name of the northern-most town on the Aral seacoast, though it is a cruel jest to call it a port any longer. Due to the recession of the sea's water, it is now about sixty miles away from what is left of the shoreline.

Aralsk was the site of the largest smallpox outbreak in the world that has never been officially reported by the responsible government to the World Health Organization. The circumstances were so mysterious that it appeared as if smallpox had materialized out of thin air in Central Asia, struck like lightning, and vanished without a trace. And ironically, one of the two factors that triggered the outbreak was the very fact that by the 1970s, the Aral Sea had begun its slow death spiral.

The second factor that led to the Aralsk event was the shadowy politics that prevailed between the Soviet bloc and the Western world in the post–World War II period. Back in 1971, the Cold War was more or less at its height. Glasnost wasn't even a twinkle in the eye of Mikhail Gorbachev—as a matter of fact, it might very well have been illegal to even say the word. Leonid Brezhnev was soon to be in power, and the "nyet" policy of Foreign Minister Andrei Gromyko was the official line of the Soviet Union.

And yet, in what was a startling departure from the closed-door mentality of the Soviet state, in the late 1960s the Russians proposed a breathtaking project of international cooperation: the eradication of smallpox. This was not a charge led by any Western democratic state such as Holland, France, or the United States. The secrecy-obsessed, totalitarian Soviet government led the charge, proposing the project and, with considerable diplomatic power, nearly railroaded it through the World Health Organization (WHO).

The Soviet assistance was substantial. The Soviets helped provide adequate amounts of the vaccine for distribution in places as far afield as India and Africa. Given their de facto control over the countries inside the Iron Curtain and their close relationship with central and northern African governments at the time, the Soviets also held the key to making it politically possible to enter Eastern European countries to make sure they were smallpox-free.

The political stance of the Soviet Union is very intriguing, especially in light of what later happened on the shores of the Aral Sea. Was it possible that the Soviet Union proposed and carried out the WHO's smallpox eradication campaign while it was also perfecting smallpox as the deadliest biological weapon the world has yet seen?

Although we in the West didn't know it at the time, the Soviet Union envisioned using smallpox in several post-nuclear war scenarios. The people that nuclear bombs did not kill during a massive war would be especially susceptible to biological weapons. Those "lucky" enough to avoid immolation by the initial fireball and blast effects would certainly be in no shape to fight off a killer bug.

The survivors' immune systems would certainly be severely suppressed by the bombardment of nuclear radiation, which destroys or cripples every cellular system in the body. Those not suffering from radiation emitted by the warhead explosion or the fallout of toxic materials would almost surely be weakened by starvation caused by the disruption or destruction of the transportation system. Finally, since smallpox spreads easily from person to person, a few hundred pounds of variola—the virus organism that causes smallpox—lobbed over the skies of the United States in a few dozen missiles would surely finish off those few people that missed being incinerated by the first round of nuclear warheads.

MARK OF THE RING

The person who first proposed the global eradication of smallpox to the WHO was a man named Victor Zhdanov. Zhdanov was the minister of health in the Soviet Union, which was as Orwellian a name as could ever have been devised for an organization. Throughout the 1970s, the Ministry of Health was infamously associated with the Soviet biological weapons program. It may well still be the case today; many Central Intelligence Agency reports associate the Russian Ministry of Health with clandestine, illegal, unauthorized, and unacknowledged Russian biological weapons programs.

Zhdanov set out a vision for eradicating a disease completely. There was tremendous skepticism in the world's medical community at the time as to whether this feat were truly possible. Today, in retrospect, we know that there are several reasons smallpox could in fact be eradicated, even with the limitations of 1950s or 1960s technology and despite the political hurdles (which turned out to be the bigger obstacles).

First, and most important, it was determined that smallpox was a human-only disease. No other animal could serve as a host to the virus and provide a reservoir by which the disease could slip out of a vaccinated area like a thief in the night. Second, due in part to the Soviet contribution to the project, an extraordinarily effective vaccine was available for mass distribution around the world.

Third, the disease itself caused a rash that was so horrifying and unforgettable that it was possible to make the diagnosis without any diagnostic tests at all. The so-called "centripetal rash" raises red blisters filled with whitish, opalescent pus with the consistency of curdled cream. The blisters cluster most thickly at the body's extremities. Just by looking at the rash, even an untrained civilian could spot and report an outbreak.

Finally, a curious fact about smallpox that makes its eradication easier is that a lasting mark is created on the body of anybody who has been vaccinated against smallpox. The site of the injection turns into a single hard blister that oozes clear pus, then seals itself and leaves a small, whitish weal. There are similar marks by the dozen left on people who have had smallpox and survived, and the marks are slow to fade.

So it was easy to check if someone was immune either because they had been vaccinated or survived the disease, because the marks were more or less permanent. Once vaccinated against smallpox, someone would more or less be immune, at least to serious disease. A person could still contract smallpox, but the vaccine prevented you from dying. It also decreased the person's ability to shed it and infect other people. Any individual who had in fact been infected with smallpox was permanently protected from reinfection or from carrying the organism to infect others.

Whenever smallpox was spotted doing its deadly work in a person, then doctors could stop the disease from burning through a community. The technique would be to isolate the individuals, then vaccinate everybody around them. This is the basis of the so-called *ring containment vaccination.* It is akin to sweeping kindling away from a fire, so the fire can consume its final source of fuel and die out. Similarly, ring containment effectively bars the virus from jumping into a new area, using a wall of vaccinated bodies to snuff it out.

Amusingly enough, the key to the success of the ring containment concept—and the salvation of the world from smallpox—was, arguably, a lack of cheap, available asphalt and discount airline tickets. The fact was that people didn't travel over long distances very often, at least in places where smallpox was still endemic in the 1970s. At the time, Central Africa and South Asia had not developed year-round road systems, to say nothing of access to intercontinental jet travel. Therefore, it was likely that someone who did have smallpox would be unable to infect many people simply because most travel was limited to walking distance.

To be sure that smallpox had been successfully eradicated in an area, there had to be complete reporting of *anything* that looked like the disease. If the WHO didn't know there was an outbreak, then it couldn't go in and vaccinate. That in turn would mean that susceptible humans would continue to carry the disease, perhaps beyond the containment rings that were so painstakingly set up to snare the virus.

Implicit to Zhdanov's proposal was the need to report every single case where smallpox was even suspected. The way the World Health Organization ultimately dealt with the problem of getting adequate reporting was both simple and brilliant. The WHO's case workers would simply take pictures of smallpox victims into villages and pay people to identify anybody who had a rash that was compatible with what they saw.

In essence, the WHO paid people to be reporters in the interest of public health. The results for giving people a substantial monetary incentive to report outbreaks were dramatic. On occasion, there were false alarms when chicken pox was spotted and reported rather than smallpox. Luckily, false reports were of little consequence because repeatedly vaccinating someone, even by mistake, carries very little risk. Without the open, complete reporting of outbreaks, the entire campaign would have failed.

The man who took the lead in the campaign and made it a personal crusade was D. A. Henderson. Through force of will and a lot of dedicated medical personnel, he ran the World Health Organization's smallpox eradication campaign and carried it through to completion. The last "wild" case of smallpox was identified and eradicated in Somalia in 1977. In 1980, after waiting a period of about two and a half years, smallpox was declared eliminated. The WHO published an official document stating this fact, amid great celebration. In epidemiological circles, this was as great a feat as the moon landings, and perhaps the single greatest triumph in the history of public health.

But it turned out to be a lie, at least in part. Smallpox may have been eliminated in the wild as a naturally occurring disease (it was, after all, a human-only disease believed to have no natural reservoir), but the threat that the smallpox could reemerge remained very real—and only the government of the Soviet Union knew it. What makes this lie particularly galling was that the falsehood was perpetrated by the very same government that led the charge to eradicate smallpox. It would probably never have been known except for what happened in Aralsk in 1971.

THE EXPEDITION OF THE *LEV BERG*

The story of the 1971 Aralsk outbreak begins with Bayan Bisenova, a twenty-one-year-old who had just graduated from school as a ichthyologist (an expert on animal sea life). As a recent graduate, she was likely very lucky to be assigned right out of school to an expedition on the Aral Sea. At that time, the sea hadn't yet reached a critical level of degradation. At slightly over 400 kilometers long and 300 kilometers wide, it was still a very large body of fresh water. The name of the ship Bisenova would be traveling and working on was the *Lev Berg*.

The *Lev Berg,* named after a famous Russian biologist, was a research ship assigned to survey and collect fish, plankton, and plants. The expedition was to run for two months. The *Lev Berg*'s mission was to generally assess the state of health of the Aral Sea to see just how bad the situation was. This was a matter of serious concern to the Soviets because the Aral Sea was not only a rich fishery for human purposes, it was also a veritable oasis in the desert for birds and other wildlife. Even in the 1970s, people recognized that three decades of river diversion was already depleting the ecology of the area.

According to an official, top-secret Soviet report from 1971 describing the Aralsk incident—obtained for the first time in the United States in 2002—the *Lev Berg* was in a town called Uyalu on the eastern side of the Aral Sea on July 29, 1971 and was berthed for an overnight stay. The official report goes on to say that the crew got off the ship and went into town on shore leave. It's likely that the crew of Russian fishermen and scientists did a little shopping, both to resupply the ship and to send souvenirs and mail back home.

Although Uyalu is really nothing more than a small, out-of-the-way town with no known attractions, the crew probably decided to play tourists for a day. Uyalu is located in what is now the culturally Turkic country of Kazakstan, and the crew probably shopped in the town bazaar and enjoyed a meal cooked at a Kazak restaurant rather than on the gas stove in the ship's cramped galley.

Two days later, the *Lev Berg* had continued on and traversed the width of the Aral Sea. Its next port of call was in what is presently Uzbekistan in a town called Komsomolsk-on-Ustyurt. It was another backwater town on the isolated lake, and another chance for the crew to stretch their legs. This time, though, it appears that only a few people went ashore. On July 31, the *Lev Berg* left Komsomolsk-on-Ustyurt and on or about August 4, went down to the southern-most port on the Aral Sea and a town called Muynak. The ship then spent about six days traversing the longitudinal breadth of the Aral Sea (see Figure 7-1) before going back to its home port of Aralsk in the north.

The ship arrived, according to the official report, on or about August 11 at the home port of Aralsk, and everyone disembarked. The expedition had been completed, plenty of samples had been gathered for the institutes in and around Moscow, and the entire trip had gone without incident. Or so it seemed at the time.

One crew member apparently had a biological time bomb ticking inside of her. Shortly after the *Lev Berg* returned to Aralsk, again according to the official report, Bayan Bisenova came down with a strange skin rash. The

FIGURE 7-1

The map of the Aral Sea and the route of the Lev Berg.

family called in a physician, who stopped by their house and examined Bayan's skin, which had turned a bright, raw red color with numerous blisters.

Perhaps because the symptoms were so general in nature—many things cause rashes, from allergic reactions to insect bites—the doctor made a nonspecific diagnosis. He said to Bayan, "It's probably a viral illness." He gave her some antiviral medication, her condition noticeably improved, and the family thought the worst had passed.

THE ARALSK EVENT

A few days later, Bayan's nine-year-old brother, Sakijan, came down with what looked like the same rash that had afflicted his big sister. On August 31, Sakijan was visited by a pediatrician, a different physician than the one who had visited Bayan. He looked at the eruptions on the boy's skin and diagnosed the boy with hives. The doctor treated Sakijan by giving him a couple of aspirin pills, probably similar to the children's aspirin that we still use today, and a dose of tetracycline, neither of which was the right medicine to give to someone who has hives. And even if they were, they are absolutely useless against smallpox.

The reason that the date of August 31, 1971 is noteworthy during the Aralsk event is because it was the day before school began in the Soviet Union. Sakijan's parents were deeply worried that he would miss the opening day of school. Sakijan was worried about the same thing, since he would have wanted to rejoin his friends at the end of their summer vacation.

Because of their concern, Sakijan's fourth-grade teacher came to visit the boy and his parents at his home in late August. It's likely that the teacher discussed the various options with the family if Sakijan started late and assured them that their son would be able to rejoin class without much trouble in a week or so.

Ten days later, the teacher came down with the same rash as Bayan and Sakijan. She was admitted to the single hospital in the town of Aralsk at about the same time that a second adult in Aralsk came in, suffering an identical red, blotchy rash. According to the official report, an unnamed physician noticed that there were two adults in the hospital at the same time with the same symptoms: a reddish rash that was rapidly breaking into waves of angry scarlet pimples.

This physician made the unthinkable diagnosis: He had two cases of classical smallpox in his hospital. It was "unthinkable" because, aside from imported cases, there hadn't been a single incidence of smallpox reported in the Soviet Union since 1938. By the 1930s, the most totalitarian government the world had yet seen was able to go out and vaccinate mass numbers of people—whether they wanted to take their shots or not.

The Soviet medical system was also pretty good at checking visitors who came into the country to make sure that they had smallpox vaccinations recorded. The few imported cases occurred when students arrived from India carrying variola with them. (At the time, India and the Soviet Union had a very cozy relationship, and students would frequently spend four years in Moscow getting in their political education as well as their degree.)

On the basis of this physician's astute diagnosis, Aralsk was immediately quarantined. Already a remote region, it was completely cut off from the outside world. Trains were instructed to pass through Aralsk and not stop. No one was allowed to leave the city, and the only people allowed in were physicians from Moscow. According to the official report, approximately 200 people who were suspected as having contracted the virus were removed from the town and placed in a field hospital in a tent on the outskirts of town.

No one in Aralsk was permitted to leave home. The town would have been completely silent, shops shuttered, and the streets as empty and quiet as if the town had been hit by a neutron bomb. Food was brought to people at their homes to reduce the amount of movement and interpersonal contact that could spread the disease.

More than 50,000 people were vaccinated in less than three weeks—an astounding achievement, especially given the tools available to the medical community in 1971. Authorities had enforced a classic ring vaccination strategy on a very large scale (although that term wasn't used at the time). It was helped immeasurably by the fact that Aralsk was geographically isolated from any other major population centers.

The authorities made sure to give booster shots even to people who had been vaccinated before. Although it is not known exactly why, the effect of a smallpox vaccination begins to slowly wear off after five to six years. Therefore, the doctors made sure that they gave the vaccine to everybody. And, according to the official Soviet report, that was how the epidemic was stopped in its tracks.

The official report concludes by saying that the disease spread to half a dozen other people. A total of ten people living in Aralsk came down with the virus. Three of these people died, which is the average statistical lethality rate for smallpox. One of the people who died was Sakijan's teacher, who, surprisingly enough, was one of the very few people the Soviet government had never vaccinated.

The two other deaths were infants, and they had not been vaccinated because it's thought to be too dangerous to give an infant a live virus vaccine. Given an infant's undeveloped immune system, horrific complications could occur. Therefore, smallpox vaccinations are usually given after the age of one year.

The only other important point to be addressed by the chroniclers of this event was how the epidemic started in the first place. The conclusion that the official report arrived at was that someone in the town of Uyalu had apparently been carrying smallpox and gave it to Bayan Bisenova. That conclusion was reached because everybody got off the boat to go shopping in Uyalu on July 29. However, Soviet authorities were unable to find any evidence of smallpox in Uyalu.

The officials putting the report together also looked in Muynak and in Komsomolsk-on-Ustyurt. They were unable to find any cases of smallpox whatsoever. Since Bayan had gotten off the boat during the stopover in Uyalu, they concluded that she had to have picked up smallpox when she went shopping in the bazaar at Uyalu on July 29, 1971.

And that's as far as the report went. It was just assumed somebody had drifted into that portion of Kazakstan, perhaps from Afghanistan or some other non–Soviet Union central Asian country where smallpox was still endemic. It was perhaps a trader selling carpets or spices in the bazaar who simply went undiscovered.

Yet the conclusions did not add up. The area around the Aral Sea was a thinly populated area in a part of the world that hadn't been a major trade center since the days of the Silk Road back in Marco Polo's time. It wasn't exactly a crossroads of commerce. Given the security-conscious nature of the government officials, the remoteness of the area, and the lack of wealthy customers, it certainly wasn't a place where foreigner traders from nearby countries were likely to end up on a business trip.

DEATH ON THE CLOCK

Other puzzles remained in the case. Because smallpox was a human-only disease, no animal or insect reservoir could have existed nearby to harbor the virus, although it is distantly possible that some inanimate object such as a blanket or clothing could have harbored a decades-old virus if it had been protected from water and sunlight. But if the supposed trader who arrived in Uyalu had been carrying the virus, either on his person or a piece of contaminated merchandise, why hadn't there been an outbreak in Uyalu to match the one in Aralsk? An infected person couldn't manage to slip into a town and slip out and only infect a single person. And yet, that singularity of what happened to Bayan Bisenova—and no other crew member—made it seem as if she had spontaneously contracted smallpox out of thin air.

In addition, anybody who has smallpox isn't very mobile—simply because they just don't feel like moving. After the skin rash initially boils up, it turns into an ocean of hard pustules that often merge into gelatinous sheets of fluid under the skin, making any movement extremely painful. In short, anyone in this state is unlikely to have been out in the bazaar doing active trading. On top of that, the rash is so characteristic and so extreme, even a layperson who came in contact with an individual with smallpox would have recognized that there was something wrong.

Still more holes appeared in the story. The official report brazenly states that Bayan got sick several days after *Lev Berg* arrived in Aralsk on August 11. When they say "sick," that means that she broke out with the initial rash of smallpox blisters. This is a critical bit of evidence, because smallpox is one of those diseases with a very narrow incubation period. The period is about thirteen days, and it doesn't vary a lot from human to human. In that way, smallpox is the biological equivalent of a finely tuned Swiss watch. It operates on its deadly timetable almost like clockwork. So, to assert that she was exposed on July 29 and became ill on August 15 is just not consistent with smallpox.

Finally, in 2001, Bayan Bisenova, the woman who survived her mysterious encounter with smallpox, granted an interview to one of the authors of this book on the Aralsk incident. She currently lives in the former Soviet republic of Kazakhstan. Although she was well aware of the outbreak that she had started, she had never heard of the official report or its finding. When the official report was read to her, one of her first comments was: "Well, there are several things that are just completely incorrect there."

"First of all," Bayan said, "I was already sick the day we came back [to home port in Aralsk]. Second, I didn't get off the boat in Uyalu, because as anybody from the time will tell you, it was forbidden for Russian women to get off the boat in a port that was a non-Russian port. This was because the Kazaks hated the Russians, and their women. It was simply too dangerous."

Having suffered under the various heads of the Russian and Soviet state, Kazak people disliked ethnic Russians. That much was true and is still true today, which is why many Kazak citizens of Russian descent have voluntarily uprooted themselves and crossed the northern border of Kazakhstan. Since she was the only woman onboard, recalled Bayan, "[I was] particularly vulnerable to being raped and beaten." She added, "I didn't go shopping; that would have been foolish.

"Furthermore," she continued, "Nobody on the boat was sick at any time. The only way for me to have contracted smallpox would have been for somebody on the boat to have contracted smallpox and been ill, and nobody was ill." She said, "That's the first problem. The second problem was Sakijan got sick exactly two weeks after I came home, precisely."

When asked how she could remember the timing of events that were three decades past, Bayan replied, "You must understand. I was getting married. I was scheduled to be married on August 30, [1971] and I was worried I was going to miss my marriage date. So, I remember everything that happened day by day while I was recovering from smallpox.

"And the third thing wrong with the official report," Bayan added, "was it said I had a mild rash and a fever. I was covered with lesions, and even though I had, in fact, been vaccinated against smallpox, I got very, very ill and came damn close to dying."

This firsthand information, then, reopened the question, "When did Bayan Bisenova get sick?" If you clock the course of the *Lev Berg* based on the ship's records, what you find is that on July 29 or 30, about thirteen days before Bayan Bisenova got ill, the ship was immediately south of Vozrozhdeniye Island. Vozrozhdeniye Island was known then to the local population, and known to the United States several years later, as the major Soviet outdoor biological weapons testing center.

Why was it chosen? Because Vozrozhdeniye is in the northwest corner of the Aral Sea, and the wind almost exclusively blows from north to south. The researchers on Vozrozhdeniye Island knew that there were hundreds of miles of open water between whatever they were doing and the nearest human nose. They could carry out their outdoor experiments without worrying about infecting the local population, because few microbes can survive hundreds of miles of dissemination across open waters.

In fact, the Soviet researchers were so confident about the way the wind blew, they actually built residences for the families of the scientists who worked on Vozrozhdeniye Island on the northern part of the island (see Figure 7-2). Of course, the testing part was on the southern part of the island. Since the wind was always blowing in one direction, no one living on the northern part of the island ever became ill as a result of experiments or accidents taking place in the laboratory on the southern shore of the island.

If Bayan Bisenova didn't get off the boat, nobody on the boat was ill, and the incubation period of smallpox is almost precisely thirteen days, then there is only one viable conclusion. The only way she could have gotten smallpox was because of something that happened on Vozrozhdeniye Island. In fact, the ship was directly south of the island, and the wind always blows from the north to the south.

FIGURE 7-2

The bioweapon test facilities on Vozrozhdeniye Island.

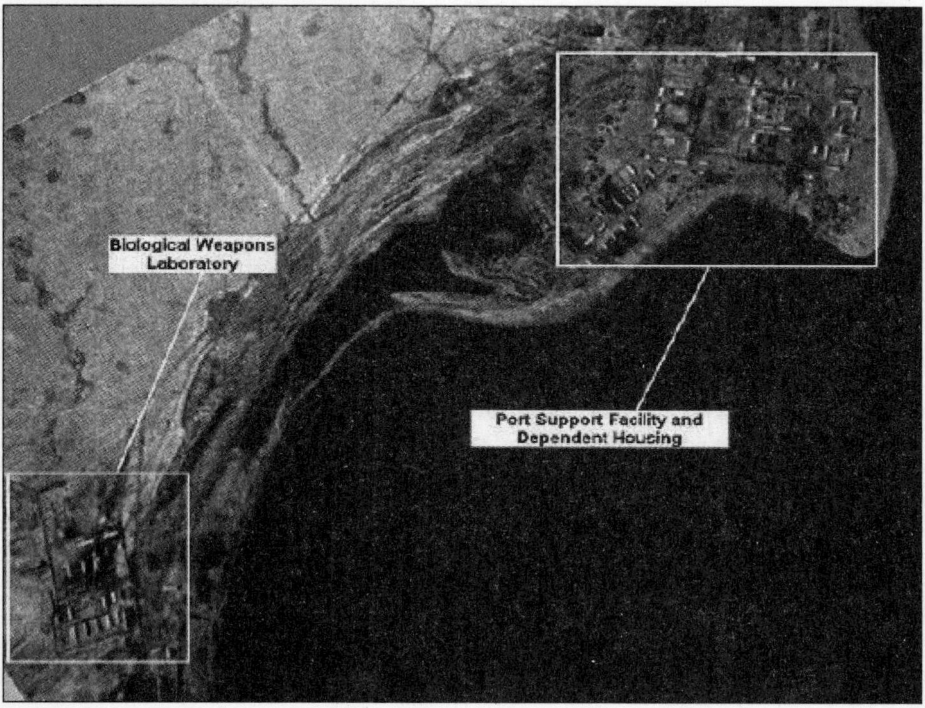

The conclusion also fit the time frame of when she got ill. It explained when Sakijan got ill, which was thirteen days later, and then when the teacher got ill, which was thirteen days after Sakijan. It all fit with an exposure to smallpox while she was on the boat when the boat was directly south of Vozrozhdeniye Island.

Why Bayan? Why nobody else on the *Lev Berg*? The answer came from Bayan's interview in 2001. She said, "Well, I was the youngest member of the crew, and I was the one who had to get up several times in the middle of the night to pull up the nets and to drop more nets for doing our sampling. Everybody else below was drunk or asleep." The bottom portion of the small ship was at or below sea level. So there was not a lot of free airflow. Obviously, on the deck there was. And that explained why Bayan and nobody else fell sick.

VIRAL SMOKE

Bayan may have inhaled as few as five or six particles of variola when she was up on deck late at night, hauling in the heavy nets. It's unclear how many particles have to be inhaled in order to contract smallpox, but it is thought to be a very small amount. What is startling is that Bayan Bisenova got smallpox when the ship was many kilometers away from the source of the virus. We don't know exactly how far away the ship was from the island, but from the charted course of the *Lev Berg,* it was certainly more than ten or fifteen kilometers.

This is the distance across a fair-size city, which underscores an ominous fact: that back in the 1970s, the Soviets had made two key advances in biowarfare. First, they knew how to grow smallpox in large quantities. Second, and more important, they knew how to aerosolize it. This second feat was something that the experts in the United States said could never be done.

Smallpox in nature does not aerosolize; that is, it does not travel in the air in nature. The smallpox particle can be found in the skin, the scabs that fall off a victim, and in most body secretions. Patients experience some coughing with smallpox, and a sort of spitting and the clearing of the throat. But when the smallpox falls off the skin or dribbles out of the mouth, there is insufficient energy to create an aerosol. Making an aerosol requires a large amount of energy.

The smallpox virus can also be found in *fomites,* which means matter other than the virus that the virus is occupying, such as clothing or blankets. Heavy particles of virus or other biological material (in excess of twenty microns in size) fall to the ground within a few meters of wherever object they are released from—the mucous lining of the throat in an individual with smallpox who is coughing, for example. In reported cases of smallpox, the largest distances over which smallpox were measured are tens of meters, not hundreds of meters. The one exception was an outbreak in a German hospital in 1969, where the ventilation system in the hospital served as a conduit for infection. The air-handling system moved the virus around on air currents like smoke coming off of a blown-out candle.

Because the movement of the smallpox virus over any real distance does not occur in nature, what happened at Aralsk had to have been a man-made event. This story about what really happened during the Aralsk incident was first presented to the National Academy of Sciences (NAS) in early June 2002, when the academy was reconsidering a new vaccination policy for smallpox in the United States. At the very least, NAS members planned to make recommendations for restarting vaccinations for some groups of people—such as emergency response and National Guard personnel—because of the concerns that had been raised post-September 11 about biological warfare and the need to protect the homeland.

D. A. Henderson, who once headed the WHO smallpox vaccination program and had been dean of the John Hopkins School of Public Health in the United States, objected to the interpretation of the findings at Aralsk. "First, this didn't happen," he said at the NAS meeting. "Second, it's not possible to aerosolize smallpox because the humidity over the Aral Sea was such that even if you had figured out how to make an aerosol, just the water in the air would cause smallpox particles to glom together and then fall toward the ground or sea.

"Third," he argued, "the pathology of the people who died—two infants, one adult—was inconsistent." That pathology showed hemorrhage in multiple organs and essentially bleeding out into the skin and into the intestinal cavities. What people died from, the final event of death, was internal bleeding.

There the story stood until someone turned up an interview with a fellow by the name of Burgasov who, in the 1970s, held the "chief sanitary position of the Soviet Union." In reality, he was a major leader in the Soviet biological weapons program. Burgasov was the same man who fooled Matthew Meselson, the Harvard professor who had performed an investigation into the alleged 1979 outbreak of anthrax in the city of Sverdlovsk (now known as Yekaterinburg, as it was in pre-Soviet times). In that incident, Burgasov had said that the anthrax outbreak was caused by bad meat.

Meselson bought the story and then went about trying to convince the Reagan administration that the anthrax outbreak was a naturally occurring event, rather than the then postulated—and now proven—theory that the Sverdlovsk epidemic was caused by the leak of a small amount of anthrax from a biological weapons facility. Burgasov was the man who lied about it, then went around the world and lied about it again. Meselson later discovered Burgasov had lied, but never himself apologized for misleading the U.S. government and perhaps setting back international efforts to ban the development and ownership of biological weapons.

In 2001, in his extreme old age, Burgasov was interviewed by an obscure publication called the *Moscow News* about the Sverdlovsk anthrax outbreak. And, as seems to happen frequently with former Russian biological weapons scientists, he decided to come clean in his old age. Burgasov said, "Well, I can sit here and talk to you about anthrax, but that's not a real biological weapon. You want to know about a real biological weapon? Smallpox. In 1971, we tested a weapon, 400 grams of smallpox, and it just so happened that there was a boat that was in unauthorized water fifteen to twenty kilometers downwind, and a person on the boat got sick and started an epidemic." Thus, Burgasov precisely confirmed the epidemiology that was dictated by the incubation period of smallpox defined by looking at when Bayan Bisenova got sick, when her brother got sick, and when the other index cases got sick.

Indeed, it was the case that Burgasov, in his November 2001 interview with the *Moscow News,* said that there was a test or an accident involving smallpox on Vozrozhdeniye Island that started an epidemic as the result of one person on one boat inhaling the organism. He went on to say the organism they had selected was a very special strain—a strain selected to be highly pathogenic for people who had not been vaccinated with smallpox. He also said that many people died, more than cited in the official report. Bayan and her brother Sakijan agree with what Burgasov says. They independently say that there were many more people than the ten cited in the official report who came down with smallpox. It fit perfectly with Burgasov's story.

VEKTOR

Today, we know the following things as a result of the Aralsk outbreak. First, there was an illegal biological weapons program in the Soviet Union working with smallpox (among other deadly agents) in the 1970s. Second, the Soviets were able to brew up smallpox in large quantities. Third, they did something that the experts in the United States said could never be done: They *aerosolized* smallpox in such a way that it could drift downwind many miles and still remain viable—that is, capable of causing infection. U.S. experts had long contended that this scenario was simply impossible.

Finally, the Soviet scientists managed, even with the limited technology of the time, to isolate a specific strain of smallpox that was not the routine smallpox we're used to seeing in pictures, which typically has a mortality rate of one in three. Instead, the virus seemed to cause hemorrhagic smallpox in the unvaccinated individuals. So, the Soviets had selected by far the worst kind of smallpox. In hemorrhagic smallpox, the victim's skin can detach from the underlying surface, forming a bag that the patient bleeds into until death. The mortality rate is, for all intents and purposes, 100 percent. There are few, if any, documented cases of anyone ever surviving a case of hemorrhagic smallpox.

What, exactly, is this exceptionally deadly strain of smallpox? Where did the Soviets get it? To this day, the answer is, "We don't know." In 1984, the World Health Organization, having declared the world free of smallpox several years earlier, requested that all laboratories that had samples of smallpox either destroy them or send them to one of two repositories The repositories were the Centers for Disease Control (CDC) in Atlanta and the Institute for Viral Preparations in Moscow. (Obviously, there had to be *two* places for political reasons. You couldn't send all the smallpox to just the United States or the Soviet Union, given the political climate of the Cold War.)

Sometime around 1989, the smallpox strains at the Institute for Viral Preparations (IVP) were moved to NPO VEKTOR, a research laboratory just outside of Novosibirsk. The reason given was that the political situation in Moscow at the time was unstable with the Soviet government in collapse. It was thought to be unsafe to have smallpox in the freezers in the IVP in Moscow as the Soviet government went through its final death struggles.

There was also trouble in the Eastern Europe Soviet satellite bloc, and trouble on the southern front with the Muslim central Asian countries. So the government moved its stores, but it did not inform the World Health Organization as required by the government's agreement in providing one of the internationally sanctioned repositories for the organism. In fact, the movement of the smallpox strains didn't come out until years later, when the director of VEKTOR, a man named Lev Sandakhchiev, revealed this fact at a meeting of the orthopox committee of the World Health Organization. (Orthopox refers to the family of viruses of which smallpox is a member. Monkeypox, cowpox, and even the vaccinia virus used as the live smallpox vaccine are also members of the same virus family.)

In 1999, the committee was debating whether to recommend one more time to the World Health Organization to destroy the official remaining stocks of smallpox. It was a noble goal—to rid the world of smallpox for all time. Then, at this meeting, the Soviet Union revealed that it had illegally moved the smallpox strain, without first informing the World Health Organization, from the IVP to VEKTOR in Novosibirsk.

Yet the WHO executive committee wanted to go forward with destruction of the remaining official stores of the virus. The attitude toward the revelation was surprisingly dismissive; even though the Soviets had "cheated" by not reporting when they moved their viral stocks, the WHO believed that they actually moved all of the samples to Novosibirsk. Therefore, the spirit of the law, if not the letter, was intact.

But a World Health Organization official had gone to VEKTOR to do a review of the bill of lading and to look in the freezers to see if all of the strains had, in fact, been moved from the IVP to VEKTOR. Again there was a shock: Three samples of a specific strain of the virus were missing. More telling, the missing samples were those from each of the three people who died in the Aralsk event of 1971.

Thus, the question before the WHO committee in 1999 was: What was the origin of Aralsk strain? Where—if anywhere—did the Aralsk strain samples reside? Were they destroyed (as the Russian government now claims)? To this day, we still don't know.

At the meeting of the National Academy of Sciences in June 2002, the testimony of Burgasov and the conclusions about the origin of the Aralsk event began to roil the present-day community of epidemiologists. Scientists—including Joshua Lederberg, a Nobel Prize winner; Tom Monath, former commander of the U.S. Army Medical Research Institute in Infectious Diseases (USAMRIID); and world-famous vaccinologist Peter Jahrling—coauthored a letter to Lev Sandakhchiev, the director of VEKTOR.

FIGURE 7-3

Lev Sandakhchiev of VEKTOR.

The letter stated that the scientific community was deeply worried about the reports of the Aralsk incident. (The full text of the letter is reproduced in Appendix B.) And it demanded to know what happened to those samples of smallpox that vanished from the VEKTOR labs. Lev Sandakhchiev replied, in essence: "The Aralsk event never happened. We don't know what you're talking about." It's telling that even today, years after the fall of the Soviet Union, the director of the official WHO repository for smallpox in Koltsovo, Russia, refuses to acknowledge that the Aralsk event took place.

When Dr. Alan Zelicoff, senior research scientist at Sandia Laboratories, stated his opinion in an interview with *Science* magazine that the Russians were lying about the existence of a bioweapons program at Aralsk—a view largely shared by many members of the U.S. biological weapons defense community—it soon became apparent that the "nyet" policy was still in place. Since 2002, the Russians have refused to discuss the Aralsk event with anyone. Sandakhchiev and the rest of the senior VEKTOR leadership appear to believe that the Cold War is still on.

STOCKPILES AND SECRETS

It is not known where the smallpox strain that caused the Aralsk event is kept. Suspicion is that the samples are in a military biological laboratory controlled not by the civilian sector but by the Ministry of Defense (MOD). If so, the samples are in a town called Sergeev Posad, which is located about sixty kilometers north of Moscow, in the MOD Institute of Virology. It is highly likely that the matter has been discussed between the U.S. vice president and his Russian counterpart.

What does this mean in a practical sense? At least a couple of important concerns are immediately clear. Independent of whether or not the Russians still have smallpox, they proved that it could be aerosolized. They selected a strain that has a high likelihood of causing hemorrhagic smallpox. It's unlikely that the Russians have large stockpiles of smallpox when measured in grams. However, they certainly have a large number of different samples from multiple outbreaks that took place around the world in the 1940s through the 1970s. The reason that large stockpiles probably do not exist is that there is no need for them. If the Russians ever felt the need to go to war using smallpox, they can brew up what they need a few weeks.

But some apologists for the new Russian government ask: "What are the odds that there is another stock of smallpox outside of the official, internationally monitored repositories in Russia and the United States?" Perhaps it's best to turn the question around and ask, "What are the odds that there isn't another stock of smallpox to worry about?" Smallpox was an organism that was ubiquitous around the world. It was unique in the disease that it caused. And its genome is so large that it contains instructions to create proteins that do all sorts of strange things to the human immune system.

In fact, many people would argue that the smallpox genome is a mirror of the human immune system. For any phenomenon in the human immune system that you can characterize, there is almost certainly a protein or two created by the smallpox virus that can interfere with it. It is uniquely adapted to humanity, tied in its existence to our species like a malevolent twin.

If not by intent, then smallpox is likely to be in several countries by accident, kept in freezers in hundreds of places around the world. During the WHO global smallpox eradication program, medical professionals from many different countries both vaccinated and treated thousands of people for smallpox. And it is a fact that biologists and physicians tend to keep samples of everything, out of habit if nothing else.

When these folks die, they don't exactly leave a will and testament that says, "Please destroy my smallpox samples." A medical center may go for years before getting around to cleaning out samples collected by long-dead physicians and tucked away in a basement freezer. Therefore, it's quite probable that there are collections, compiled intentionally or otherwise, of smallpox in places outside of the two official repositories in the United States and in Russia.

One final point should be made. The North Koreans are the only people on earth who continue to vaccinate their troops against smallpox to this day. Is it possible that they're vaccinating their troops against smallpox because they think we're going to use smallpox against them? Or is it possible that they vaccinate their troops because they have a stock of smallpox that they're going to use as a biological weapon, and they don't want their own troops to get sick?

Whichever theory you believe probably stems from how cynical you are about human nature.

CHAPTER 8

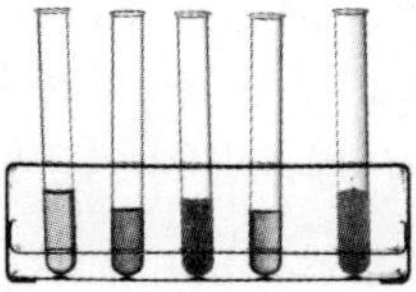

NATURAL BORN KILLERS—WHY SOME GERMS STAY BAD

In high school biology classes, we routinely teach the concept of Darwinian evolution, or what is often called "survival of the fittest." Darwinian principles apply to all life forms—from the lowliest of bacteria to complex multi-cellular mammals. But for many years, the principles have often been misapplied, even by experts. An understanding of these concepts is necessary in order to appreciate the highly dynamic nature of evolution in microorganisms. Their ability to rapidly multiply allow them to adapt to new hosts—and develop resistance to medicines—with frightening speed.

It is helpful to begin with a misnomer, one that we are all taught in school. It goes like this: Bacteria and viruses become more and more benign the longer they are in contact with their host populations. In other words, organisms adapt toward a symbiotic (i.e., cooperative) relationship with their hosts. This, we were told, explains why serious infectious diseases were on the wane in many places in the world.

It is the also the explanation for why, in certain settings like refugee camps, there would inevitably be a sudden explosion in cases of diarrhea that would slowly dissipate as the organism "learned to adapt" to its hosts—because by killing its hosts the organism was depriving itself of new victims.

It seemed to make sense, and we happily regurgitated this knowledge on examinations.

Until recently, the same paradigm was taught in medical schools and schools of public health: Organisms evolved toward causing milder and milder diseases so as to guarantee that they could pass back and forth among hosts and continue their own existence.

But all of this is quite wrong.

REVOLUTIONARY BIOLOGY

In the 1970s and 1980s, a group of young biologists—academic experts who thought about and experimented with organisms in the laboratory—came up with quite a different view of infectious disease. This view was almost completely at odds with the simplistic, standard teaching of Darwinian principles that says organisms evolve toward less lethal organisms. The biologists noticed that there were many situations in which the "tendency toward benign-ness" was simply incorrect.

For example, despite careful documentation of massive smallpox outbreaks over the past three centuries, there wasn't the slightest shred of evidence that smallpox (an *exclusively* human disease) was treating its hosts any more kindly in 1950 than it did in 1650. Furthermore, among the most common of all diseases—influenza, malaria, and mosquito-borne viral diseases that cause brain inflammation—there was, if anything, an *increase* in the mortality rate from these diseases. What was going on? Was Darwin wrong?

The answer became clear—and it also became clear that Darwin was *not* wrong—when the young biologists took the next step. They applied the principles of Darwinism when looking not just at the organisms themselves, but *how they transmitted from host to host* and *how well they survived (if at all) outside of their natural hosts.* In so doing, they invented a new field now called evolutionary biology. But the insights of these scientists could really be called "revolutionary biology" because they completely transformed our way of looking at the development of organisms around the world.

Consider the smallpox virus, which is also called variola. It is the largest of all known viruses and appears like a well-wrapped brick underneath the electron microscope. Patients whose bodies were being ravaged by smallpox were almost always severely ill. They could usually be found huddled up in a corner, covered with blankets and shivering away as their disease raged. They weren't up and about shopping, walking, or having much contact with people. Frequently they died.

Yet smallpox outbreaks raged on and on, sometimes for many months in large cities before finally killing so many people (or rendering those who survived immune) that the epidemic stopped. Then, inevitably, smallpox outbreaks would return four, five, or ten years later. How did this happen?

It turns out that smallpox is an extremely hardy organism. The virus can sit on a tabletop, in blankets or clothing, or in the dust in the corner for many months or years and still remain infectious for susceptible humans, just as long as it is protected from moisture and the sterilizing effects of ultraviolet radiation from the sun. In short, for its own continued survival, smallpox did *not* require direct human-to-human contact from one infected individual to a susceptible one.

Rather, as long as the smallpox organism was protected from water and light, eventually it would come into contact with a not-previously-infected human. That's why, during the French and Indian War, combatants attempted to spread smallpox to the enemy by sending blankets, handkerchiefs, and clothing from dead smallpox victims to other side. And it worked all too well.

At the other end of the spectrum of environmental hardiness is the influenza virus. Once it is sneezed into the air, it rapidly starts to dry out. Within a few minutes or hours, it is no longer infectious. The virus is so weak that it doesn't last on doorknobs or other inanimate surfaces for very long, either. How, then, does influenza manage to survive year after year if it is so fragile?

The answer is that when the organism induces its host to cough or sneeze, the host produces an *aerosol* of billions of the viral particles. An aerosol is a collection of particles so tiny that they remain buoyant in the air indefinitely or until they come into contact with a surface like a desktop or computer keyboard. Once they come to rest, they slowly dry out and die.

Inside large rooms, the aerosol moves along with the air currents. Imagine, for example, a single person with influenza sneezing inside the main entrance hall of Grand Central Station in New York. The virus will travel hundreds of feet before it perishes from dryness. Within that few hundred feet, there may be a thousand people at any moment, a few of whom are surely susceptible (i.e., nonimmune) to the disease. And so it takes hold in the new host and continues its vicious cycle.

How does one stop influenza? With simple barriers to aerosols—like covering your mouth when you cough or using a handkerchief. When that habit becomes widely spread—as we've all been taught as children to do—

the organism has a much harder time spreading effectively. Indeed, it can only spread by other means that bring people in much more intimate contact, and for *that* to happen, people have to be up and about and not ill in bed. If they are isolated, the organism can't be spread at all.

In any given person with influenza, there are probably several variants of the virus that differ in very subtle ways at the genetic level. Some variants multiply very quickly, overwhelm the host, and kill him. As long as there is a susceptible individual nearby (within sneezing or coughing range), that virulent or disease-causing organism will continue to proliferate. But if there is *not* a susceptible person nearby, the organism will die along with the host.

At the same time, there are less virulent types that are mutations of the original virus. These viral types produce much less severe disease in their hosts, who are able to be up and around, perhaps not even sneezing or coughing. So, the hosts of more benign influenza virus spread the organism by direct contact—shaking hands, kissing, or sharing drinking glasses or utensils with other humans they meet during the course of their mild illness. One could even argue that the influenza organism has "adapted" to our practices to prevent transmission through coughing and sneezing and the introduction of the cloth handkerchief or the Kleenex tissue!

Our growing understanding of evolutionary pressures shows that we did precisely the *wrong* thing during the influenza pandemic of 1918. The severity of this pandemic is hard to overestimate because it killed as many as 50 million people—or one in twenty of the world's population at the time. Then, the medical response for people with influenza, particularly in the military, was to place them all together in one large open ward, just a few feet apart. This procedure *guaranteed* that the most rapidly multiplying variants of influenza (which were inevitably the most virulent because they destroyed the most host cells in their wild procreation) would be transmitted to someone else because there was always a susceptible host nearby.

This explains why the pandemic raged and why the disease was so severe. The organisms that could multiply the fastest—and thus cause the worst disease—survived. If victims and susceptible hosts had been kept further apart or isolated, the victims would have had to have been more mobile (i.e., less sick) in order to spread the virus, which would then naturally select for the flu viruses that would cause less severe disease. This is the scientific basis behind the principle of quarantine and isolation of suspect cases.

VECTORS

By contrast, *vector-borne* diseases—such as malaria, dengue fever, or West Nile—that are spread by mosquitoes or other insects require only three things in order to survive indefinitely. First, they must be present in a host's bloodstream in high concentration. Second, a vector (e.g., mosquito, tick, or flea) must come along and bite the host while the organism is in the host's blood in high concentration. Third, the vector must survive long enough to bite a new, susceptible host and transmit the organism.

Mosquito-borne diseases do not benefit from causing less severe disease in the host. That's because, to spread to another victim, they do not depend on the mobility of humans, or people who are not so sick that they can't move about. That is why, in general, malaria is every bit as severe a disease today as it was hundreds of years ago.

But what happens when people start to use mosquito netting at night when the mosquitoes are active? Then mosquitoes carrying malaria can't transmit their dangerous viral cargo, nor can they get to patients who have malaria to pick up a new load of the organism. When mosquito netting is used routinely, not only do the *number* of cases of malaria drop, but the *severity* of cases tends to drop as well, because it is only patients with "mild" forms of malaria who are up out of bed providing mosquitoes opportunity to acquire the parasite from the host. If patients have severe malaria, they are not likely to be mobile, but rather confined to bed and covered with mosquito netting.

Thus, it is now easy to see why zoonotic diseases—infectious diseases that typically affect animals but get into the human population from insect transmission—are often so severe in humans. Humans are not the usual hosts, so when the organism is introduced into a human it often multiplies wildly, killing the host. But since animals are the natural reservoir (continuously maintaining a form of the organism that keeps the animal alive but permits transmission to other animal hosts), knocking off a few humans along the way is irrelevant to the long-term survival of the bug.

The lessons of evolutionary biology have helped our understanding of brand-new (i.e., previously unrecognized) diseases as well. For example, when the Ebola organism somehow gets into a human, it almost always kills its human host. In addition, it is an extremely fragile virus, losing its ability to infect another host quickly as it dries out. Yet, in Central Africa, where the Ebola virus is found, the religious ritual is for the entire family to wash the body of the relative who has died.

In the ritual, the Ebola organism is kept moist. Worse, the process of washing aerosolizes the bloody foam that oozes from the dead victim's body—even through the pores of the skin—practically guaranteeing spread to others. Each and every Ebola outbreak to date has been halted simply by stopping the religious ritual of washing the dead body. No vaccine, no medication, no germicides—just removal of the vector: the aerosolizing of the Ebola-laden blood by washing.

Thus, for many diseases that are untreatable—ranging from smallpox to the hospital-acquired infections that kill thousands of inpatients every year—the "cure" is a simple one. Stop the chain of transmission by stopping the vector. Something as simple as forcing physicians and nurses to wash their hands in between *each and every* visit to a patient's room or when going from one examining room to another in a doctor's office may be all that's necessary. If we don't appreciate the link between virulence and vector, we all but guarantee the continued proliferation of the most dangerous strains of any organism.

CHOLERA IN PERU

One of the most public examples of the link between virulence and vector was the cholera outbreak in Peru in 1991. Cholera is a disease that is transmitted by the fecal-oral route. That is, fecal material that contains the cholera organism gets into the water supply and then affects people who drink the contaminated or untreated water.

Although it is not known for certain how the outbreak started, the leading theory is that there was a massive contamination of seawater along the coast of Peru. The organism was jettisoned—or leaked—from the bilge of a ship arriving from Asia and carrying people infected with cholera. The cholera found its way into the water treatment system of Lima, the capital of Peru and its largest coastal city.

An explosion of cholera in the city's residents followed, peaking at 45,000 cases per week during the first few weeks. Thousands of people came down with abdominal pains, vomiting, and severe diarrhea, which transmitted the organism back into the local water supply. During the first year of the epidemic, almost 300,000 cases were reported.

The organism got into the local water supply because the source of the water supply was contaminated by the bilge. Because the water treatment in Peru was not very effective, the vast majority of people drinking the city water came down with cholera. Cholera is not a mild illness, in general. When people come down with cholera, they get very, very sick. They tend to lie on the ground or lie in their beds with uncontrollable diarrhea.

The proper treatment for cholera is not, in fact, directed against the organism, because if you live long enough your immune system will kill the organism, and drugs don't help much in that fight. The treatment for cholera consists of replenishing the depleted body with fluids. It is dehydration resulting from the diarrhea, rather than systemic infection from the organism, that kills people.

This is why the World Health Organization's solution is to use an oral hydration compound for the treatment of the horrific cholera outbreaks that occur all too often in filthy refugee camps. No antibiotics needed—just salt, potassium, and some electrolytes in an oral solution while the victim's immune system is given sufficient time to destroy the pathogen. It's simple, inexpensive, easy to administer, and most important, it works.

The epidemic in Peru continued because the poor water treatment system couldn't handle the contaminated human waste. People infected and sick were literally pouring out gallons of biologically hot material every day, which ultimately found its way into the water system. The organism didn't need its victims to survive or be mobile in order to survive. The water supply did the trick.

SEWAGE SYSTEMS AND NATURAL SELECTION

Later that summer of 1991, the organism spread into the neighboring country of Chile. This probably happened because some people who were infected with cholera traveled to Chile and introduced the protozoan into the local water supply. However, something interesting happened: The cholera outbreak that resulted was much milder. The symptoms limited themselves to a very mild case of diarrhea. Like a fire stoked with damp logs instead of dry kindling, the epidemic burned out. What accounted for the stark difference between the two outbreaks?

Surprisingly, the answer lies not in the organism itself, but the water treatment facilities in each country. The water treatment system in Chile is much more extensive and better equipped to purify the water than in Peru. The most pathogenic of the cholera organisms—the ones that multiplied most rapidly within individuals and made those individuals very sick—were killed by the Chilean treatment system.

In this way, one of the two evolutionary pressures put on the organism was the Chilean water treatment system. For reasons we don't completely understand, the more pathogenic the strain of cholera, the more susceptible it is to water treatment. This is probably because the most rapidly reproducing strains of cholera are vulnerable to any highly reactive chemical like chlorine. When the "worst" of the organisms are killed or filtered out through water treatment, the remaining varieties of cholera that can get into humans cause a far less serious illness.

What remained were organisms that not only survived the water treatment, but organisms that resulted in a slightly different version of the disease. Because of the better filtration system in Chile, people had to be well enough to move around to transmit the germ. Now, did the organism sit down and reason this out? Of course not. Organisms don't do that.

In strictly evolutionary terms, the organism that triumphs is the one that multiplies the most. If a strain of cholera is pathogenic enough that it makes people so sick that they become immobile, it can only spread if there is a nonhuman means of getting into another human. In Peru, the sewage system was a readily available transmission route for the cholera bacteria. In Chile, that route was not a good bet for survival.

The need to find a different way to get into other hosts is the second of the two evolutionary selectors. Certain strains of cholera survived because they didn't immobilize people. Since they only made people mildly ill, the person could walk around and pass the organism to another person by direct contact, say, with a handshake. Ultimately, the outbreak was completely stopped just by having people wash their hands, which put a chokehold on the only other channel that the organism could use to spread itself.

The point is that for a while, the cholera organism literally became dependent on the mobility of humans for its survival. Because of this need, in a matter of weeks to months—not years—the cholera epidemic went from being a disastrous illness in Peru to a much milder illness in Chile. Yet, it is not the fact that change occurred that interests us. It is the *speed* at which the change took place.

The cholera epidemic in South America was an excellent example of how fast evolutionary change can take effect in an organism. It happens at such an accelerated rate in bacteria or viruses because there are literally tens of billions of organisms in any infected person's body, many of which are mutating all the time. Most of these mutations don't survive. In the case of cholera, what survived was the organism that multiplied fastest—but not in such a way that it made its victim so sick they couldn't move.

FALSE BELIEFS IN EPIDEMIOLOGY

It's a false belief—one that is almost akin to a bad urban legend—that a disease will tend to become less lethal over time. They don't necessarily have to. It's bad science, bad logic, and it's not an idea that Charles Darwin would have even entertained.

For example, suppose that a strain of a virus evolved that, for whatever reason, benefited by reproducing twice as fast—thus killing humans within six hours instead of twelve. Naturally, the more lethal organism would be selected or favored in evolutionary terms. A good example of that paradigm in the real world is anthrax, at least in mammals other than humans. Anthrax is virtually 100 percent fatal in every cow it infects. How can that possibly be good for the anthrax?

The answer is that it happens to be one of the few organisms that forms a spore to protect itself. In every practical sense, the spore is indestructible. If the organism kills the cow but, in the process, reproduces hundreds of trillions of spores that then lie in the ground and wait for more cows to come along and ingest the organism when they eat the grass, then it does perfectly well.

This is why highly lethal organisms tend to have one of two characteristics: Either they have some vector associated with the organism, such as a water supply, or alternatively, they are environmentally stable. That is, they are not adversely affected by usual environmental conditions such as extremes of temperature or humidity, ultraviolet radiation, or even the ubiquitous plant, insect, and bacterial enzymes that permeate soil and water.

This is precisely why you see cholera outbreaks in refugee camps in most of the world. There is severe crowding and poor sanitation of the water. The cholera cases are severe enough to immobilize the victims, but that is fine by the cholera organism. As long as the immobilized individuals excrete gallons of liquid near the limited, untreated water supply that someone else is drinking, the survival of that strain of cholera is assured.

There is absolutely no evidence to indicate that as the organism continues to ravage refugee camps that it somehow becomes a more mild disease. Instead, exactly the opposite takes place: It becomes a more deadly disease.

CHAPTER 9

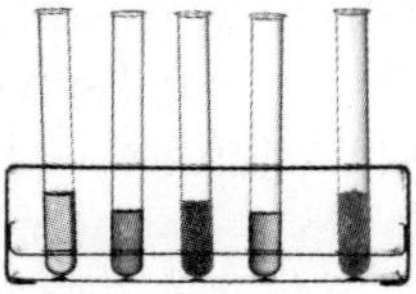

SOMETHING IN THE WATER

Cholera, Cryptosporidiosis

When cholera began to kill hundreds of London residents in the summer of 1854, one doctor put forth a very controversial theory: that a germ was responsible for the killer disease. Dr. John Snow, a London medical practitioner from an extremely modest background, felt that the still-controversial "germ theory" was the best one for explaining the outbreak. Of course, he faced a certain amount of ridicule—the tiny "animalcules" that had been observed under a microscope were certainly fascinating, but there was no hard evidence that they did anything to the human body.

The prevailing theory of the day was that disease was caused by bad air entering the lungs. The odor that supposedly caused illness went under two names at the time, the first being *miasma.* The second, more descriptive term came from the Italian phrase for bad air, *mala aria,* which translated into English as one word: malaria.

Despite the scorn of more learned scientists of his time, John Snow attained lasting fame as the person who could arguably be called the first formal epidemiologist in history. His achievements saved many lives and are all the more remarkable for the simplistic nature of the tools he had available to him at the time. Like a medical Sherlock Holmes, he investigated and identified the likely cause of the London cholera outbreak using nothing more than city maps, pencils, and string.

A WELL OF SICKNESS

Cholera was a disease that first truly began to plague Europe with the rise of the first cities. As with many organisms that become a public health concern, cholera thrived in the dirty, crowded conditions of cities with their inadequately sanitized water and sewage systems. In fact, cholera was so often prevalent in city water that drinking from the tap during an outbreak was considered a fairly reliable way to die. Russian composer Pyotr Ilich Tchaikovsky, best known for his "1812 Overture," is said to have committed suicide simply by intentionally drinking a glass of contaminated water from the city supply in Saint Petersburg.

The London outbreak began in late August 1854, with more than 500 deaths and hundreds more falling ill and spreading the disease back into the local water table. The outbreak took place in the Soho region of London, in and around the area of Broad Street (see Figure 9-1). Dr. Snow was quite familiar with the area, having lived there as a student when he attended the University of London's medical school in 1844.

As he later wrote:

> The most terrible outbreak of cholera which ever occurred in this kingdom is probably that which took place in Broad Street, Golden Square, and the adjoining streets. . . . Within two hundred and fifty yards of the spot where Cambridge Street joins Broad Street, there were upwards of five hundred fatal attacks of cholera in ten days.

From his days living in the area, Snow also noted that when the homes of cholera victims were plotted on a map—a brilliantly simple technique still used in public health offices today—most of the cases of cholera

FIGURE 9-1

Map of London's Soho neighborhood and the Broad Street water pump: the cholera outbreak epicenter.

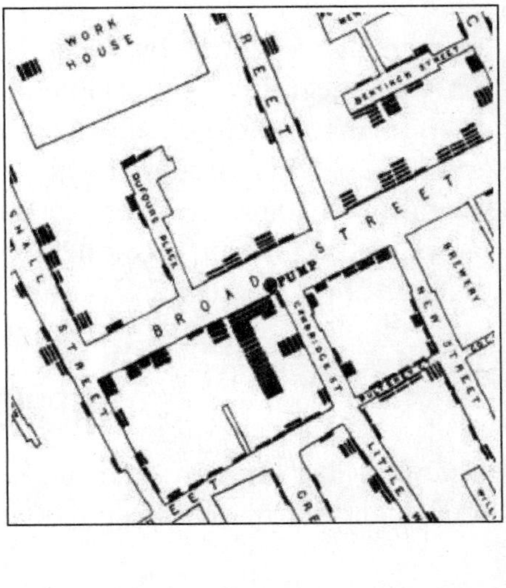

seemed to have an epicenter: a water pump located on the busy thoroughfare of Broad Street.

As he began plotting more and more cases from the outbreak, he noticed two interesting items that seemed to be anomalies at first. First, there were cases outside the Soho area, which seemed to draw attention away from a single source of contamination. However, he soon leaned that those who fell ill elsewhere all crossed paths at one point in the city: the Broad Street pump, where they had stopped to get a drink.

The second anomaly was that extremely few cases of cholera were reported from a large neighborhood workhouse next to the pump and a local brewery in the nearby area. Snow's investigation found out two more facts that strengthened his suspicions. The workhouse apparently had its own water supply on the premises, so few bothered to drink at the well down the street. As for the brewery, the employees simply preferred to take advantage of a job perk and drink some of the excess beer they were producing.

Again, all signs pointed to the same source—a single contaminated well. Dr. Snow spoke to the Board of Guardians, the age's equivalent to our local health department today, and they agreed with his findings. On September 8, 1854, they authorized Snow to remove the handle on the Broad Street pump, and the outbreak stopped almost overnight.

Snow's simple—but novel—statistical technique represented the first major triumph of epidemiology over disease. Snow showed that through disease monitoring—including the collection of important geographic information and establishment of the time of onset of disease—public health officials could not only divine the source of a disease but suggest an immediate intervention to *stop* it. Remove the source of the scourge and the epidemic comes to an end.

Thus, even before the germ theory of disease was defined, described, and finally accepted by most of the medical community in the late-nineteenth century, Snow showed that simple statistics (literally clusters of cases on map) could identify a causal relationship between certain practices and disease, even though the actual "cause" of cholera—the *Vibrio* cholera organism—had not yet been isolated and identified in any textbook or laboratory of the time. It was a most amazing triumph upon which the entire practice of public health was built and promulgated.

THE HIDDEN SPORE

A second, less known waterborne disease is caused by cryptosporidium, a single-cell protozoan whose name means "hidden spore." It's an apt name since the parasite is extremely difficult to detect in random water samples. More specifically, the cryptosporidium organism (see Figure 9-2) resides in the gastrointestinal tract of many species of ruminants, primarily cows. Deer and other wild animals carry it as well, but only cattle are found in mass herds as part of the industrialized farming system.

When removed from its natural environment in the intestines of many common farm animals, the cryptosporidium parasite will form what's called an oocyte, a globular structure that is like a spore. Think of it as an impenetrable shield against all assaults from the outside world. Though the spore is much larger than the one created by the anthrax organism, like the anthrax spore, it is environmentally almost indestructible. So, even if cryptosporidium is deprived of food—say in freshwater with low concentrations of any processible organic material or the warm, dark surroundings of the intestinal tract—it can survive for years in its inert state as an oocyte spore.

When you have herds of cattle upstream of a watershed (the area where rainwater or underground springs soak the ground and then drain to reservoirs used for human drinking-water storage), you run the risk of finding extremely large quantities of manure near a major water supply. The vast majority of cities in the United States primarily get their water from rivers. The likelihood of the cryptosporidium protozoa getting into the water that ultimately becomes a city's drinking supply is essentially 100 percent.

The only way to get rid of the protozoa is by filtration and a process called *flocculation.* With flocculation, you put in a material that forms a sort of cloud in the water and grabs particulate matter. The tiny particles grabbed by the filter can then be filtered out.

In 1993, that process of flocculation and filtration somehow failed in the Milwaukee municipal water system and led to the single largest outbreak of infectious disease in U.S. history that took place in under a single month.

FIGURE 9-2

The cryptosporidium organism.

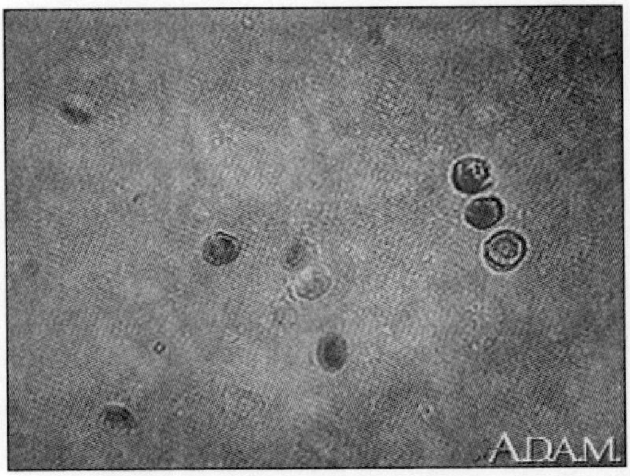

Even the influenza pandemic of 1918, which it took months to sweep across the globe, wasn't quite as dramatic as this outbreak.

NEVER A MENACE BEFORE NOW

Although cryptosporidium was known about since 1976, it was never considered a public health menace until the Milwaukee outbreak because of the effectiveness of filtration and flocculation. In 1993, due to an unseasonably heavy rainfall, huge volumes of water overwhelmed the filtration and flocculation processes. The rising water level flooded over the holding ponds where filtration took place and thus the organism passed into the city's water supply.

It took almost four weeks after the first cases were identified to determine that what was sickening tens of thousands of people every day was the untreated water. Not a single case was diagnosed as the outbreak was taking place, so the public health officials were completely blindsided by the fact that 400,000 people in the city were moderately to severely ill. The only reason they realized something was wrong was when a pharmacist in one of the large pharmacy chains reported that there was (no pun intended) a "run on the diarrheal medicine."

It was only after that initial report that public health officials began to query hospitals and physicians' offices. They determined that the vast majority of people in the Milwaukee area who were suffering from severe gastrointestinal symptoms—vomiting, diarrhea, dehydration, and fever—were in fact infected with cryptosporidium.

As is the case with many other diseases, immunocompromised people run the risk of becoming extremely sick and even dying. Cryptosporidiosis is particularly nasty in that there is no effective drug treatment for the disease. However, if the patient can be kept hydrated, the body will develop an immune response against the organism that gets rid of the infection, giving the patient something like 60 percent to 80 percent protection against a reinfection.

Strikingly, after reviewing the records in local hospitals, it is now known that there have been multiple episodes of cryptosporidiosis in Milwaukee. These episodes took place at least five or six years before the first major outbreak. However, not one of those diagnoses was made until the massive outbreak hit in 1993. In any case, all of these episodes were strong indicators that routine public health surveillance had failed—multiple times over the years—ultimately resulting in significant economic losses and, worse, unnecessary deaths.

MEDICAL MYOPIA

How could nobody in the medical community notice when almost half a million people in a medium-size city were sick enough to visit the drugstore and physicians' clinics for relief? With the benefit of hindsight, at least three reasons become apparent. First, the overwhelming majority of physicians had never even heard of the word *cryptosporidium*. They didn't even suspect it was a cause of the symptoms showing up in their patients. Therefore, they didn't order the diagnostic test for it.

Second, the diagnostic test, which is a careful examination of stool samples, is only about 25 percent to 50 percent sensitive on any given sample. There is a relatively high chance that a physician or laboratory technician could miss the telltale parasites of cryptosporidium in any given stool sample submitted to a laboratory. Unlike many organisms, cryptosporidium can't be cultured on a petri dish. A knowledgeable physician or laboratory technician has to look for it with special staining of stool samples viewed under the microscope; the process is time-consuming and thus expensive. And even when done properly, one could miss it two out of four times.

The third, and probably the most important, reason is that the public health community has done an extremely poor job at alerting physicians to even look for the organism in the first place. This goes to the notion that is well established and even well accepted among practitioner physicians, which is: "If you don't know about it, you don't suspect it." It remains a sort of blind spot among otherwise knowledgeable doctors.

Interestingly enough, in a large outbreak like the one in Milwaukee, it isn't necessary to perform a test for cryptosporidiosis on every patient with symptoms consistent with the disease. Once the diagnosis has been made in a few people, and more importantly, *if* the extent of the symptoms are known, it is sufficient to treat based on the suspicion of cryptosporidiosis. It becomes the "leading" diagnosis—in fact, a virtual certainty—and thus repetitious diagnostic testing is not necessary unless patients manifest unusual signs and symptoms inconsistent with the disease.

This is the power of public health surveillance from the physician's perspective: It provides physicians with adequate information to make a diagnosis without having to resort to voluminous, expensive testing. And, from the standpoint of the community as a whole, the value of a properly run public health department is the early detection of disease and identification of its source so that preventive measures—such as boiling drinking water until the filtration process is back "online" at the municipal water treatment plant—can be put into place.

But the public health system failed in both regards in Milwaukee. Even though it's likely that every single primary care physician in the city saw at least one case of moderately severe diarrhea during the outbreak between early March and early April of 1993, few of them were mentally prepared for the possibility that it was anything other than viral gastroenteritis. An immense public health disaster—and one whose scope could have been easily limited with simple instructions, such as drinking bottled water or boiling tap water—was what occurred.

Because of glib dismissiveness or programmed ignorance, the total costs incurred in the outbreak have been estimated to be nearly $100 million, of which about one-third were medical costs and two-thirds were loss-of-productivity costs. Approximately 42 percent of all costs were attributable to persons with mild illness, 22 percent to persons with moderate illness, and 36 percent to persons with severe illness. The CDC's April 2003 issue of *Emerging Infectious Diseases* substantiate these figures. In addition, there were the purely human costs, including several dozen deaths from cryptosporidiosis, mostly among the immunocompromised.

TABLE 9-1 Total Dollar Cost of Illness Associated with the Cryptosporidiosis Outbreak in Milwaukee.

Costs, by severity of illness	Dollar amount
Direct medical costs	
Mild	$790,760
Moderate	2,700,000
Severe	28,200,000
Total Direct Medical	31,690,760
Lost productivity	
Mild illness	$40,200,000
Moderate illness	18,200,000
Severe illness	6,200,000
Total Lost Productivity	64,600,000
TOTAL COSTS	$96,290,760

INDEX OF SUSPICION

How did cryptosporidium slip through the filtration system in the first place? The answer was that the Milwaukee water department didn't do a simple test for water turbidity. Turbidity is a measure of how much light traveling through a given water sample is blocked—thus indicating the number of light-scattering (or absorbing) particles contaminating the water. When the department eventually did find increased turbidity, it didn't inform the local public health department as would usually be the case. Perhaps officials were overwhelmed with other administrative duties, or perhaps the reporting process was slow and cumbersome because it was not electronic or Internet-based.

The communication breakdown between the departments was almost absolute. When the public health department wasn't informed, it didn't suspect the possibility of contamination of the water supply. The health department therefore did not alert physicians to the possibility of an unspecified waterborne illness, let alone cryptosporidiosis.

So the system broke down, partially from complacency. After all, there hadn't been an outbreak of a serious waterborne disease anywhere in the United States for many years. Arguably, it was also because a simple turbidity test wasn't done (or was done improperly). It would not be an overstatement to claim that the public health monitoring system broke down at all levels. The water department did not adequately survey the water for evidence of contamination with what was effectively simple dirt, which includes manure, which in turn includes cryptosporidium. Then it didn't inform the public health officials.

The public health officials had no way to rapidly communicate with doctors even if they did know about it (newspapers and radio were then, as they remain now, the primary source of "public health information" for physicians). Furthermore, the historical information about previous, much smaller but very real cryptosporidiosis outbreaks in Milwaukee never percolated from the public health system to the local clinical community. Given all of these factors, it was logical that the doctors had a low "index of suspicion" for the protozoa—meaning that there was a low probability that a physician would even think to look for a disease like cryptosporidiosis.

Since there was no communication, physicians who hadn't ever seen a case of cryptosporidiosis were exquisitely poised to fail to diagnose it and provide feedback up the chain in the timely way so that the water department could isolate the specific source of the cryptosporidium. In this case, it turned out that one of the large water-processing facilities that was getting a direct feed from Lake Michigan was the culprit, piping millions of gallons of water contaminated with cryptosporidium directly into the city.

A MAGNITUDE WORSE THAN ANTHRAX

The outbreak could easily have been identified much earlier with a surveillance system that would have made a difference. We can say that with certainty, because there is a very simple solution to dealing with water that is contaminated with cryptosporidiosis. You simply boil the water before you drink or cook with it, or you buy bottled water until the contaminated water is cleaned up.

But the warning was never sounded, hundreds of people died, and almost $100 million in economic losses were incurred, all unnecessarily. Arguably, this was an order of magnitude worse than the anthrax attacks in 2001. The difference here is that the only people who died were the elderly and the immunocompromised.

The public health system was asleep at the switch in 1993. Once the public health system had identified what had happened, it was too late to do anything. In this case, no one had the presence of mind to take the handle off the pump, as Dr. John Snow had done in the 1850s.

In retrospect, had just two physicians reported within the same week that they had admitted to the hospital a person with stable HIV disease who developed debilitating diarrhea and fever, and if that information were made available to a half a dozen public health officials, it would have been enough to raise suspicions. The public health agencies would have said, "Something weird is going on," and gone out to investigate and stop it. Like canaries in the coal mine, the HIV patients would have served as early indicators that something was wrong. It might have saved many lives.

It is possible that the outbreak would have raised an alarm within the medical community had healthy people—not just the chronically immunocompromised—become ill. But even then, without the ability to rapidly communicate information to busy physicians, the outbreak would have raged on until it became so obvious that there was a problem that everyone finally realized that something was amiss. By then, of course, it would be too late to do much for those who had already died or the hundreds of thousands of people who were already ill, nor was it possible to recover the economic losses.

More than a decade later, people are still writing papers about the 1993 cryptosporidiosis outbreak in Milwaukee. While medical or health education papers continue to be written, strikingly, nothing has changed of substance in the communication and surveillance practices of most public health departments around the United States. The outbreak took place years ago, yet we still do not have a surveillance system in place for any kind for diarrheal disease. There are no systems in place to watch for waterborne or food-borne pathogens that could enter the community. Someone has to suspect that something odd is going on, pick up the phone, and deal with the public health bureaucracy in order for the public health system to know about it.

It short, it is no different now than it was in 1993, except that many doctors are themselves more aware of the disease and likely to notice it now. That is a very sad statement as to how well we, as a society, learn about threats to public health. The only thing that may have changed is that the water districts have much more rigorously examined water samples.

Even this new system provides only approximate results through the turbidity test. Turbidity is a very crude measurement of contamination of the water supply. If there was another organism that, in much lower doses, could cause severe disease, it would be easy for it to pass through the water supply without being detected. Therefore, we still depend on the clinical community—the doctors, clinicians, and veterinarians—to report unusually severe illness, even if they don't know what the disease is.

SHOE-LEATHER EPIDEMIOLOGY: ONE WAY PUBLIC HEALTH IS SUPPOSED TO WORK

Our dependence on the public health community to report unusually severe illness is not completely misplaced. Where the system has fallen apart is in its refusal to adapt to the newer, deadlier threats and to take advantage of the latest technology to gather, analyze, and disseminate data. The system that was founded decades ago was quite sound for the time, given the technologies and training available. Much of the credit must go to Major Walter Reed.

Walter Reed was arguably the first great public health doctor that the United States produced. His commitment to the eradication of human suffering in the latter half of the nineteenth century is remarkable; he became justly famous because he determined that it was yellow fever that was stopping the progress of the building of the Panama Canal.

More specifically, he identified the risk factors for acquiring yellow fever, which were mosquito bites. Reed passed sentence on the mosquito when he said, "The spread of yellow fever can be most effectively controlled by measures directed to the destruction of the mosquitoes and the protection of the sick against these insects." He intervened in just such a way, killing mosquitoes so that workers could complete the Panama Canal. That was probably the single largest triumph of public health in the Americas at that time.

Reed's work was never formalized in any systematic way until Dr. Alex Langmuir came along a half century later. In the 1950s, the Korean War was being waged against communist North Korea and China, and America was becoming exceedingly tense about biowarfare. As an epidemiologist and civil servant at the newly formed Communicable Disease Center—the predecessor to today's Centers for Disease Control and Prevention (CDC)—Dr. Langmuir thought the country needed "a lot of epidemiologists responsive to a nationally coordinated surveillance system."

Langmuir and his agency offered training in the investigation and analysis of disease outbreaks—something that was completely absent from any medical curriculum up until that time. Regrettably, these subjects remain absent from most medical school curricula, even today.

Shoe-leather epidemiology, the term coined after Langmuir instituted his techniques, refers to the on-site investigation of unusual signs and symptoms in animals or humans by interviewing directly the people (or animal owners) involved. If the patients have died before they could be interviewed, their families and the environment are studied to determine two items: first, the behaviors of those families, and second, the specific kinds of behaviors that could have accounted for the acquisition of what appears to be an infectious disease. For example, if a patient died of a disease that appears to resemble a bird flu, it would be worth determining if the patient or his family worked around birds, raised them, kept one as a pet, or regularly hunted them.

Even when one doesn't know what the organism is, or doesn't have the science to isolate it, grow it, or develop an antibody test for laboratory use against it, identification is still possible. Part of the science of epidemiology is identifying risk factors on a population-size basis that gives you clues as to the origin of the organism. That's done by interviewing patients to see where they have traveled, what they have eaten, what their water source has been, or even whether they have been in contact with people who appeared, even to a layman, to be ill. The collection of this information gives an epidemiologist an idea of what steps can be taken to put a barrier

FIGURE 9-3

Dr. Alex Langmuir.

between the organism and the human host, like Dr. Snow removing that handle from the water pump.

That simple, extremely cost-effective approach is, with a few rare exceptions, not taught in a standard medical school curriculum anywhere in the country. Arguably, the ability to gather information that would assist the public health system is the kind of service that every general practitioner, internist, family physician, and physician-assistant should provide every day because they represent the "front line" of medicine. Unfortunately, this is the kind of material that physicians only learn if they also get a master's degree in public health. Although it's not exactly rocket science, it's very valuable in an age of bioterror and emerging diseases.

The bad news about Langmuir's approach is that it hasn't changed in over sixty years. The CDC is somewhat mired in shoe-leather epidemiology, becoming overly dependent on field researchers and person-to-person interviews and autopsies. Data collection seems to rely on either epidemiology cowboys or reporting based on a diagnosis from lab results, which can take days or even weeks to complete. As a result, the public health community tends to publish information in retrospect after months of investigation. This information is, of course, of much importance for advancing medicine and for publishing academic papers, but it is not useful for early intervention and prevention and for stopping an epidemic before it becomes too large to snuff out at the source. The CDC has failed to take advantage of the potential of technology, both to collect data and to disseminate it, for purposes of understanding disease spread and the likelihood of recurrence of disease.

TRAINING WITHOUT UNDERSTANDING

Where Langmuir left off was in creating methods to gather data on human behavior and environmental factors related to the acquisition of infectious disease. In short, he taught epidemiology by rote, by outlining procedures and processes that at the time were a huge advance over the disorganized, poorly structured teaching of public health. But where modern epidemiology has failed to advance is in taking that information and putting it into robust computer models—similar to those used across all of the rest of science for all kinds of other complicated phenomena that are analogous to infectious disease—then communicating the results of those predictive models to health care practitioners and even local political leaders during times of disease outbreaks.

Physicians are trained to respond based on certain clues or indicators that they find on examination or in the laboratory. They are not taught how to develop and test a hypothesis, which is what science does. In the scientific method, when you observe a new phenomenon you propose a hypothesis, then propose a means to test the hypothesis, and then you either accept or reject the hypothesis based on the means that you identified. If you fail to prove the hypothesis, you then come up with a new hypothesis and repeat the process.

But physicians don't behave as scientists, in part because they have so little time to see patients and in part because they are taught by rote memorization. Physicians respond almost programmatically to a set of signs and symptoms that leads to a diagnosis that leads to a prescribed treatment. It is no coincidence that when you ask physicians about their education, they talk about their *training* (as in "I did my surgical training at Johns Hopkins School of Medicine"). One would seldom hear a scientist speak this way. Rather, the scientist would speak of her research thesis, hypothesis testing, and the scientific method.

This is not to say that training doesn't serve medicine well. It serves medicine extraordinarily well as long as nothing *changes*. Unfortunately, in the world of infectious disease, if we've learned anything over the past twenty years it is that new diseases are cropping up that have never been identified before. The list is almost endless: SARS, Creutzfeldt-Jakob disease, Ebola, Marburg, and multidrug-resistant tuberculosis.

New diseases are cropping up and old diseases that we have forgotten about (in other words, haven't been taught about in medical school for decades) are reemerging. Plague, anthrax, tularemia, tuberculosis—all are diseases where the overwhelming majority of physicians have never seen a single case.

When scientists see something that they do not recognize, they form a hypothesis and test it. That's not what happens in medicine. What happens in medicine is a response based on what we know. When we fail, only then do we start doing hypothesis testing. When it comes to highly pathogenic and communicable diseases, it's usually too late at that point.

This attitude of training without trying to understand science leads to a group of public health practitioners who prefer to allow enough cases to pile up, so that observations become obvious, rather than take a risk by doing some unsophisticated thinking and statistical analysis. This practice manifests itself as well-written academic papers, years after an outbreak has occurred and taken many lives.

If we truly are in an environment now where old diseases are reemerging, new diseases are being discovered, and we have the treat of bioterrorism hanging over our heads like the sword of Damocles, then we don't have the luxury of that kind of reflective process any longer.

CHAPTER 10

WHEN HOURS COUNT, BUT DAYS DON'T MATTER

Anthrax

The American experience with biological warfare dates back to the battles fought during the very revolution that founded our country. At the height of the war against the British, General George Washington received reports that the British were spreading "the pox" (i.e., smallpox) among the colonial troops. The reports turned out to be true as the Continental Army began suffering manpower losses from the disease.

On January 6, 1777, Washington gave the order for the army to be variolated against smallpox. Variolation was not like vaccinations today. In fact, it was much more dangerous that anything we in the modern world would accept. Instead of receiving an injection of a weakened virus or a relatively benign cousin of smallpox known as cowpox, variolation meant inserting material from a fresh smallpox lesion into the skin or nasal lining of a healthy individual.[1]

It was a grim but necessary calculation for the Virginian general. The mortality rate from variolation is approximately one in 300. However, the death rate of troops exposed to smallpox with no prior protection was closer to one in six. The army's cohesion as a fighting force could be preserved with a casualty rate caused by variolation. To expose the army to smallpox would quite literally decimate the American forces and force Washington to surrender to the British.

That organisms too small to be seen by the naked eye can and do change the course of human history is no surprise to microbiologists or epidemiologists. This would undoubtedly have been true in the case of the Revolutionary War. At the nadir of the conflict for the Americans, the Continental Army reached what Thomas Paine called "the time that tries men's souls" at Valley Forge. With blizzard-like conditions and soldiers lacking winter clothing and proper meals, smallpox could have run through the weakened troops like wildfire.

Whether Trenton could have been taken with smallpox afflicting a fifth of Washington's men is very much an open question. But, there seems little doubt that the possibility of biological warfare was, at the time, already realized and being actively practiced. It was the beginning of the American experience with this deadly and particularly disturbing way to kill large numbers of people with a weapon that could not be seen or smelled, and for which defenses were far from perfect.

TOXINS, BUGS, AND BACTERIA: A BRIEF LOOK AT BIOLOGICAL WARFARE

Today, the U.S. Department of Defense maintains a threat list that has largely been agreed to by consensus in the world of academia and military defense; it is a list of agents that are most likely to be used in a bioterrorist attack against either civilians or troops. The selected organisms fall into three broad classifications—toxins, pathogenic bacteria, and pathogenic viruses—though each category makes for extremely grim reading. The first group, toxins, includes organisms that act in a manner similar to chemical agents.

Interestingly enough, two of the entries in Table 10-1 may be more familiar to many people than at first glance. Ricin comes from the seed of the castor bean plant, which is a woody herb sometimes grown as an ornamental plant in gardens or as a houseplant (see Figure 10-1). The flat, brown seeds are housed three to a seedpod that explodes upon ripening.

If the seed is swallowed without chewing, and there is no damage to the seed coat, it will most likely pass harmlessly through the digestive tract. If it is chewed or broken and then swallowed, the ricin toxin will be absorbed in the digestive tract with less than savory results, as just one milligram of ricin can kill an adult. It may seem ironic that castor oil, which is used for medicinal purposes, is extracted from the beans. However, commercially prepared castor oil contains none of the toxin because the toxin is soluble only in water and not in the oily component of the bean.

FIGURE 10-1

The castor bean plant: an ornamental shrub with a toxic secret.

TABLE 10-1 Toxins.

Organism	Initial Effects	Vaccine Available
Botulism	Dry mouth, blurred vision, nausea, and fatigue leading to respiratory failure	Yes
Clostridium perfringens	Intense abdominal cramps and diarrhea leading to death from dehydration	No
Ricin	Similar to Clostridium	In experimental stages
Staphylococcus enterotoxin B	High fever/chills, headache, myalgia, nonproductive cough, leading to septic shock and death	In experimental stages
Trichothecene mycotoxin	Weakness, ataxia, collapse, reduced cardiac output, shock, and death	No

Botulism is also familiar to millions of people. Tiny amounts of this toxin can be used to deaden muscle function. Therefore, this deadly toxin has become quite popular as Botox, the cosmetic treatment for people who wish to smooth out wrinkles caused mostly by contraction of tiny muscles just under the surface of the skin around the eyes and mouth and on the forehead. Botox injections have even been used to eliminate underarm sweating, because the toxin blocks the chemical transmitter that makes sweat glands produce sweat.

There are also much more important medical indications for the use of Botox, such as the treatment of painful muscle spasms of the neck (called torticollis) and uncontrolled blinking of the eyes. For these patients, Botox has erased the difference between normal life and severe disability. Indeed, before the introduction of botulism toxin as a treatment for these two conditions, patients became so desperate with their symptoms that they often committed suicide. Now, one injection of Botox into the tiny muscles around the eyes or the large muscles of the neck can relieve intractable symptoms for months at a time.

No such positive effects come from the next group of potential bioweapon organisms, which comprise some of the most pathogenic forms of bacteria currently known on earth.

TABLE 10-2 Pathogenic bacteria.

Organism	Initial Effects	Vaccine Available
Anthrax	Symptoms similar to flu, with chest discomfort that will progress to severe respiratory distress.	Yes
Cholera	Intense abdominal cramps and diarrhea leading to death from dehydration	Yes
Plague	Initially flu-like, followed by either buboes or pneumonia.	Yes
Tularemia	Slow-growing ulcer at the site where the bacteria entered the skin (e.g., through a bite or cut); if the bacteria are inhaled, pneumonia-like symptoms can occur.	Yes

Most of the diseases in Table 10-2 are, unfortunately, still well known in the public consciousness. While anthrax is a soil-borne organism, cholera is waterborne and still emerges in major outbreaks throughout the Third World where adequate water treatment systems are not available. (See Chapter 9 for more about waterborne cholera.) Tularemia, also known as rabbit fever, is one of several deadly ailments that people can contract from wild animals—rabbits, but also rodents, skunks, and raccoons as well. Plague has been permanently seared into the public consciousness since the time of the best-known epidemic in history, the Black Death, which eradicated or maimed up to half of the population of Europe in the 1300s and almost extinguished Western culture. The term "plague" is now synonymous for pestilence of any kind.

In the final group of potential bioweapon agents described by the Department of Defense are the pathogenic viruses that cause forms of encephalitis (i.e., inflammation of the brain and central nervous system tissues) and hemorrhagic fevers.

TABLE 10-3 Pathogenic viruses.

Organism	Initial Effects	Vaccine Available
Crimean-Congo hemorrhagic fever	High fevers, severe headache, general malaise, muscle aches, confusion, sore throat, chills, sweats, nonproductive cough, nausea, vomiting, diarrhea, abdominal pain, and chest pain	Yes, but restricted
Q fever	Similar to symptoms for Crimean-Congo hemorrhagic fever	Yes, but restricted
Rift Valley fever	Flu-like illness with fever, weakness, back pain, dizziness, and weight loss	Yes, but restricted
Smallpox	High fever, head and body aches, followed by rash on the extremities that progresses to raised bumps and severe blisters	Yes, but restricted
Venezuelan equine encephalitis	Fever, chills, headache, nausea, vomiting, lower back pain, and myalgia, which may progress to encephalitis	Yes, but restricted

All of the infectious agents listed in Table 10-3, with the exception of smallpox, have one thing in common: They are zoonotic diseases—that is, animal diseases that can be transmitted to humans but for which human hosts are not necessary for the survival of the organism. This is important, because not only do we know that zoonotic diseases tend to cause serious disease in humans, but they are virtually never seen by medical practitioners, especially in the United States.

The average primary care physician can go through his career without having experience in zoonotic disease. Even physicians working in the field of infectious disease may never encounter a zoonotic disease in a human. West Nile is, of course, a present-day exception. But before West Nile had been detected in New York in 1999, it had never before been seen in humans in United States and had never before been thought of as a bioterrorism agent.

The "odd man out," so to speak, would be smallpox. The significance of this disease is that, unlike the zoonotic diseases, it is directly communicable from human to human. Unfortunately, smallpox is like the other pathogenic viruses in one respect: It is highly unlikely that most physicians would recognize smallpox because they've never seen it. The last case of smallpox treated in nature (as opposed to the result of a laboratory accident among scientists working with the virus) took place in 1977—over a quarter of a century ago.

DOCTORS SEE WHAT THEY KNOW AND KNOW WHAT THEY SEE

Much of the energy spent by modern medicine in treating infectious disease is targeted at one very narrow area. The kinds of diseases most commonly treated, aside from cold viruses and influenza, tend to be opportunistic infections. These are infections that afflict immunocompromised people. To refresh your memory, immunocompromised people are either (1) sick from some other disease and its complications, such as diabetes; (2) suffering from a suppressed immune system from HIV or other viruses; or (3) afflicted with what is called a nosocomial infection, acquired while the person is in the hospital undergoing treatment (rather than acquired somewhere out in the community).

Infectious disease specialists today also focus on treating surgical infections, or infections acquired in an intensive care unit, such as while a patient is on a respirator. These so-called overgrowth infections occur when people who are ill and have been receiving broad-spectrum antibiotics for bacteria end up with a fungal infection. These are the kind of things that occupy the vast majority of treatment of infectious disease in United States.

Infectious diseases specialists are only rarely called in to see a young, relatively healthy person with a mysterious rash or fever simply because such cases are, in and of themselves, very uncommon. It would be even rarer for an internist to be called in—only an incident that would be part of a Grand Rounds would make most noninfectious disease specialists aware of unusual infectious diseases. (A Grand Rounds case is one that is so unusual that it becomes the subject of weekly teaching lectures or the main topic of discussion at medical conferences.) Therefore, it's extremely unlikely that a primary physician or infectious disease specialist will have ever seen a zoonotic disease or be able to identify it.

So, the "frontline physicians" in medicine—in primary care clinics, family practice offices, and emergency rooms—are likely to be poorly prepared to recognize even dramatic symptoms as indications of an unusual disease. The problem is compounded by the enormous pressures on doctors to see patients quickly and the heavy bureaucratic requirements (e.g., filling out forms and other paperwork), which leave doctors little time to research information on uncommon diseases and the way they initially manifest themselves in patients. Experienced clinicians sometimes put it this way:

> You see what you know, and you know what you see. And if you've never seen a case of anthrax or smallpox or even West Nile fever, then it's very unlikely that you'll ever make the diagnosis.

Tracey McNamara, the intrepid veterinary pathologist introduced earlier in Chapter 1, notes that physicians are so focused on one species—humans—that they are almost completely unaware of the infectious diseases that routinely affect animals and that, on occasion, find their way into the human population. Dr. McNamara also notes that there are essentially no professional meetings where veterinarians and physicians discuss their own clinical experiences. It is as if the two communities of health care providers don't even know that the other exists; nor do they know what a valuable resource they can be to one another when an unusual infectious disease strikes a community.

WHAT THEY DO NOT SEE, THEY DO NOT KNOW—AND THAT CAN HURT YOU

A classical example of a serious disease that can kill patients because the diagnosis is often missed is diphtheria. Today, diphtheria is largely prevented by vaccines given in childhood. It's a very serious disease caused by a bacterium, but interestingly enough, it's not the bacterium that kills you. If you don't recognize and treat diphtheria early on in its course, it secretes a toxin that is almost uniformly lethal. It is this deadly toxin created by the bacterium as it grows that leads to the neurological symptoms and heart failure that ultimately cause death.

Surprisingly, the toxic side effect of diphtheria is also the reason that the diphtheria vaccine was incredibly effective, even before the origin of mass-produced modern vaccines. In the old days of vaccinology, the creation of medications or vaccines was a purely empirical art just bordering on science. Doctors knew how to ward off diphtheria from simple empirical studies. When the researchers brewed up a batch of diphtheria in a vat, killed the organism, then took the resulting broth and injected into an experimental animal such as a horse, the animal would succumb very quickly. There were no living bacteria in the broth, so the correct conclusion was that there was something secreted by the organism that was the actual cause of death.

To create the vaccine, the process was to first grow the bacteria on a culture medium. Instead of grinding pieces of the organism up into a mixture, which is normally how you create a vaccine, they took the exotoxin (*exo* meaning "out of") that was secreted by the organism. The next step was to take the fluid that the organism was growing in and denature it—literally rendering the toxin "non-natural" so that it no longer caused symptoms. Denaturing, which turns out to be the act of altering the complex three-dimensional structure of a protein, is done by mixing in a generous dollop of formaldehyde or some related chemical that breaks certain bonds in the complex protein. Mixing in formaldehyde ends up twisting the toxin's protein around into a different shape so that it doesn't cause damage to cells. However, it remains similar enough to diphtheria that it will still elicit an immune system response. The early vaccinologists would then dilute this mixture and use it as a vaccine against the organism. This is an example of what is called a *toxoid vaccine.*

In fact, several toxoids are commonly mixed together in a vaccine given to many children—the DPT (diphtheria, pertussis, tetanus) shot that Americans may remember getting as a child.[2] Even today, a booster shot roughly every ten years or so is required to protect oneself against diphtheria, since the organism is still endemic in many places around the world. During the 1990s, epidemic diphtheria broke out in several states of the former Soviet Union, causing more than 5,000 deaths.

The DPT shot and DT boosters essentially ended diphtheria epidemics in the Western world. As a result, many practitioners have never seen a full-blown case of diphtheria or tetanus. We are really victims of our own success in regards to these diseases in that we fail to recognize them all the time. Often the diagnosis is made at autopsy, and it was only recently that pertussis was identified as a major cause of chronic cough in adults who were previously thought to be immune for life after a DPT vaccination in childhood.

In fact, just a number of years ago *The New England Journal of Medicine* published an article on a clinical pathological case in which somebody actually died of tetanus, the disease that causes lockjaw. It was an unusual circumstance, involving an intravenous drug user who was infecting himself with a dirty needle while engaging in an practice known on the street as "skin popping." The diagnosis was missed for days, even at a prestigious medical center.

Skin popping is a technique used by drug addicts who have run out of veins for injecting their substance of choice. Instead, they inject the drug into the subcutaneous level of the skin. Of course, this is extremely painful, but the rush of the substance outweighs any incidental pain. The plentiful blood supply in the subcutaneous level of the skin allows for the drug to be distributed in the body, though less efficiently than a direct injection into a vein.

When injecting into the subcutaneous layer of the skin, the addict is inserting substances and organisms into what is an oxygen-poor environment. This unfortunately puts the tetanus spore in a perfect environment, since it is an organism that grows best in an environment with little or no oxygen. In nature, tetanus spores are found in the soil, but not in the topsoil region, which, as most gardeners know, is relatively well oxygenated and encourages the growth of plant roots. Instead, tetanus cannot be found unless the soil sample is taken from at least a foot down.

This means that organisms that require oxygen for growth (so-called "aerobic" organisms) generally do not survive when forced under the skin. But organisms that do not require oxygen for growth—"anaerobic" organisms—proliferate, and since they are also not competing for space and other nutrients with their aerobic cousins, such oxygen-loathing bacteria grow even more quickly than they otherwise would. Biologists explain this complex phenomenon by saying that the oxygen-poor environment "selects out" for anaerobes, and one of the most common anaerobes is the tetanus bacterium.

Additionally, many drug addicts in the advanced stages of their addiction are by their very nature immunocompromised. So the organism not only takes its initial hold, but it multiplies unchallenged by the host's immune system. The disease lockjaw is really a general description for the symptoms caused by the toxin that the tetanus organism produces: uncontrolled contraction of large muscles (including those that clench the jaw), resulting in paralysis of the muscles involved in respiration as well. Needless to say, that's not good, because the patient can no longer move air in and out of his lungs.

In fact, one of the immune system's strategies unfortunately works in favor of tetanus gaining a foothold. Most places in the human body are actually fairly well oxygenated thanks to the ever-present hemoglobin found in red blood cells. However, it's not as well known that one of the immune responses of the body is to limit blood flow to an area infected with disease, precisely for the purpose of depriving it of oxygen. It is normally a successful strategy because the vast majority of pathogenic organisms require oxygen to grow. Once a wound is inflamed with an infection, reducing the amount of oxygen in the area can slow or stop the disease's growth, allowing the body's white blood cells to gain the upper hand.

Whereas any nineteenth-century physician during the Civil War would have been able to identify tetanus immediately, nowadays the disease makes it into the case records of the Massachusetts General Hospital in *The New England Journal of Medicine* simply to remind physicians about the symptoms of a disease they may have never seen before. Our training as physicians in infectious disease is largely directed at the treatment of complications of medical care. Nosocomial infections, surgical infections, and infections that result from the treatment of cancer and other immunosuppressive conditions are the main focus of today's doctors. Very few physicians have seen diphtheria or tetanus, let alone the zoonotic diseases on the Centers for Disease Control's list of potential bioweapons.

More chillingly, almost no physician practicing today has seen a case of smallpox, a disease that has likely killed more human beings than any other pathogen in history. The first new cases of this disease will go undetected by physicians without advanced knowledge.

CLASSICAL RULES OF DIAGNOSIS

Given that background, we need to approach the question of how effective a bioterrorist strike in the United States may truly be. When the first case appears, just like the first case of anthrax in Florida in 2001, it will almost certainly be missed. The diagnosis will not be made until the cause is so blatantly obvious that a medical practitioner or pathologist would have to try hard to miss it.

In the case of the Florida anthrax attacks in 2001, the diagnosis was really made when the initial patient became comatose and the puzzled doctors undertook a lumbar puncture to look for bacterial meningitis. During a lumbar puncture, more commonly known as a spinal tap, doctors insert a needle into the small of the back to withdraw fluid within the spinal canal. Examining this fluid under the microscope, the doctors saw a long, thin, rod-shaped bacteria that stained bright purple. It was like viewing pictures out of the medical textbook for anthrax—but first nobody believed it.

By then, of course, it was too late for the patient in question. Once anthrax has made its way into the fluids of the central nervous system, there's nothing that anyone can do for the patient; the survival rate is zero because the organism erodes through blood vessels causing massive bleeding into the brain. Given the very limited terrorism experience that doctors in the United States have had with biological weapons agents such as anthrax, one prediction of the experts has actually been borne out: No one will make this diagnosis promptly.

West Nile virus is another example that proves the point. The delay in identifying the organism was a prime factor in allowing it to become endemic in the United States. As discussed in Chapter 1, it was several weeks before people even stopped to think that there could be a novel encephalitis virus that was killing both birds and people in the outer boroughs of New York City. Dependence on physicians to make a timely diagnosis when they have never seen certain types of disease is foolhardy and naïve. Doctors who use the classical approach to treating disease and reporting disease are doomed to fail in the setting of a biological weapons attack.

There is also no guarantee that physicians operating under classical rules will be much better off should bioterrorists choose to use an organism with which doctors are familiar, such as a deadly strain of influenza. Why would even this be missed? It is true that the flu may be easily diagnosed by physicians—but there would be no way for them to tell that this strain, released specifically to kill or sicken thousands, would be any different from one of the more common strains that are typically deadly only to elderly patients.

Smallpox is again the exception to this rule. Even today, it's likely that the horrific symptoms of the centripetal rash and pustules would be spotted and identified, especially after the bioterrorism fears raised in this country post 9/11, where physicians and laypeople alike have become slightly more educated as to what to look for. Had the question "What is the classical rash of smallpox—centripetal or central on the trunk?" been on the medical boards exam in 1990, fully half of the physicians would have gotten it wrong—because it would have been a pure guess on their part.

All of the bioterrorism diseases have one more thing that they share: Nearly all are inherently untreatable once they start to cause symptoms. However, they are not all uniformly lethal. Tularemia, for example, causes severe cases of pneumonia, but only has a lethality rate of around 5 percent.

Should you be unlucky enough to contract tularemia, as long as you receive proper medical care in the hospital, your odds are nineteen out of twenty that you will survive.

By comparison, once patients begin to show symptoms of anthrax, the lethality rate is a great deal higher. It is not automatically lethal, as contended by many in the mass media at the time of the attacks, but it certainly creates long odds for the patient. Symptomatic patients in the 2001 anthrax outbreaks suffered a mortality rate of slightly less than nine in ten.

Remember also that in the case of anthrax, there was one special condition—that after the first few cases were reported to the media, we were poised to look for it. In a large-scale bioterrorism attack involving thousands of victims, the mortality rate would likely climb to near 100 percent, simply because the intensive care needed for each and every patient will not be available. There are just too few intensive care beds and trained nursing staff to care for large numbers of anthrax victims.

Once anthrax was identified, anyone who was in the risk factor group—in this case, postal workers in Washington, D.C. who came down with a fever—immediately got attention and treatment with antibiotics such as ciprofloxacin. Many, if not all, of the cases were brought to the intensive care unit, where they received an abundance of attention. The people who survived the anthrax outbreaks survived by virtue of the fact that they had access to the most intensive medicine available. This resource would certainly be rapidly exhausted in a large-scale anthrax outbreak or attack.

There are relatively few intensive care unit (ICU) beds in any hospital. If there were a large release of anthrax that produced more patients than could conceivably be cared for with such a high level of attention, it would completely overwhelm the medical system. For example, in the entire city of Albuquerque, which has a population of approximately 600,000, there are no more than fifty to a hundred ICU beds. Even counting additional beds that conceivably could be converted into ICU beds, such as those in cardiac units, it's unlikely to do more than double that small initial number. Certainly, it would be nowhere close to the number needed to handle, say, a thousand patients who could be infected with several million particles of aerosolized anthrax.

The upshot is that we cannot depend on physicians to make the right diagnosis when an unusual infectious agent or toxin is involved. It is unlikely that we can depend on physicians to have even the *suspicion* that they are dealing with a deadly organism so that they order specific laboratory tests that are not part of the typical suite of diagnostic tests. Missing the diagnosis will mean that many people who could otherwise be saved will, in fact, not be saved, all because of medicine's blind spot.

WHY HOURS MATTER AND DAYS DO NOT

Let's consider the bioterrorism scenario of a truck equipped with a delivery device that pumps out a finely powdered culture of anthrax in an aerosol that can settle up to 500 yards away. The terrorists drive down Massachusetts Avenue in Washington, D.C. on a Monday morning and spray around two-and-a-half pounds (about one kilogram) of anthrax spores over its route of approximately five miles. This amount, which would weigh no more than a single ream of copy paper, ends up contaminating the entire area.

The incident directly exposes tens of thousands of people on their morning commute to anthrax: people who are on the street, coming off the subway, driving by in their cars with their windows down or the car's air intake open. Contrary to what you might have seen in the latest Hollywood thriller, nothing will happen immediately. People will go about their daily lives for hours without the slightest hint of anything having gone wrong. This is entirely unlike an attack on the American public using chemicals, explosives, or nuclear material.

Twenty-four hours pass. Depending on the dose of anthrax inhaled and the condition of the individual's immune system, only nine or ten of the 20,000 people exposed will come down with symptoms serious enough that they go to their doctor. They will have come down with what they may think is the flu—a high fever, accompanied perhaps by some difficulty breathing.

Only these isolated individuals will be the ones seeking attention. What are the odds of these nine or ten people seeking treatment from the same doctor, on the same day, in a metropolitan area the size of Washington, D.C.? Obviously, the odds are so low that for all practical purposes it is zero. That means that the patients see nine different doctors, and no one has the information to realize that nine people have just come down with the same symptoms in the same area at the same time.

Keep in mind that even post 9/11, it's still possible for something as deadly as anthrax to be misdiagnosed. After all, the symptoms of early-stage anthrax are extremely nonspecific. There are literally two or three dozen other, less serious diseases that could cause similar symptoms. It is not hard to imagine that a physician might advise a patient that it is simply an early case of pneumonia, and to say, "Take antibiotics and you'll be better in a few days."

If only half of those people get a chest x-ray, the readings will show that they have a diffuse pneumonia—which shows up on an x-ray as fluid in many portions of the lung, not just localized to one lobe or section of the lung tissue, combined with a swelling of the lymph nodes in the center of their chest. If even one of those cases were reported to public health officials, it would unquestionably garner some attention because severe pneumonia along with swelling of the central chest lymph nodes is most unusual in any given day or even month. If two of these cases were reported in the same day, then alarm bells would start going off for the local public health officials.

What might the response be? If the public health officials got this information in a central place and contacted the doctors who reported these worrisome findings, they would discover that these two patients were actually doing worse, and that both worked in a specific, common location: downtown Washington, D.C. They would probably do the following things immediately:

- They would begin sampling the ground and the air for the presence of anthrax spores, since few organisms other than anthrax cause diffuse pneumonia and lymph node enlargement. Since anthrax occurs naturally in the environment, they would be bound to find some spores, but an aerosolized release of anthrax will provide a spike of readings. If someone had spread two-and-a-half pounds of anthrax down Massachusetts Avenue, there would be a significant amount of anthrax left to recover, even a day later, on street surfaces, windows, and perhaps even on the leaves of trees or blades of grass.
- They would ask emergency rooms that are seeing patients who are febrile with a respiratory syndrome to do a blood culture, which is a procedure that is not typically done in those cases. Culturing the blood means to "plate it out" by smearing the blood on petri dishes and growing the organism so that it can be identified. The anthrax organism grows very quickly in the petri dish. In as little as twelve hours, sufficient reproduction has occurred that a tentative diagnosis can be made just by looking at the organism under the microscope and observing the swirling pattern of growth on the culture medium.
- They would call veterinarians to see if any animals were coming in sick. Given the depth of the intentional exposure, it is certain that domestic animals would also come down extremely ill within anthrax's incubation period. This is because anthrax is not in the least specific to any species; to the anthrax bacteria, any and all mammalian tissue is a medium it can use to convert as much of the animal—or human—into a pile of anthrax particles.

About eighteen hours after the first blood culture has been taken, diagnosis will be certain. Anthrax grows so fast and is so distinctive looking under the microscope, with its long, thin, rod-like shape, that physicians cannot help but recognize it for what it is. Physicians will know instantly that they have a crisis on their hands. No more than forty-eight hours after the release of anthrax into the Washington metropolitan area, the diagnosis of anthrax would be made and confirmed.

Believe it or not, what is described here is an "ideal" scenario. The way events would usually take place, one or two people initially infected with anthrax would die. An autopsy would be performed a day or two after that. Laboratory tests would be requested at this point to confirm the cause of death. Diagnosis of the mass anthrax attacks would occur sometime on the *fifth* day.

All of which leads us to ask: What is the difference in outcome when the difference in time is a mere seventy-two hours? Three days might not seem like a great deal of time. In fact, it makes all the difference in the world. As the graph in Figure 10-2 shows, the number of fatalities are extremely low at the three-day mark while they are close to peaking by the fifth day.

When anthrax is identified and diagnosed within seventy-two hours, then those thousands of people who were exposed to the anthrax bacteria are still mostly asymptomatic. They are all treatable with appropriate antibiotics, such as ciprofloxacin. Public health officials can identify the contaminated area and encourage people to get treatment if they were there. Everyone exposed to anthrax will have to be watched carefully, but the diagnosis of anthrax is not a death sentence.

FIGURE 10-2

The number of people infected (in this case with anthrax) versus the number of fatalities over the stated time period.

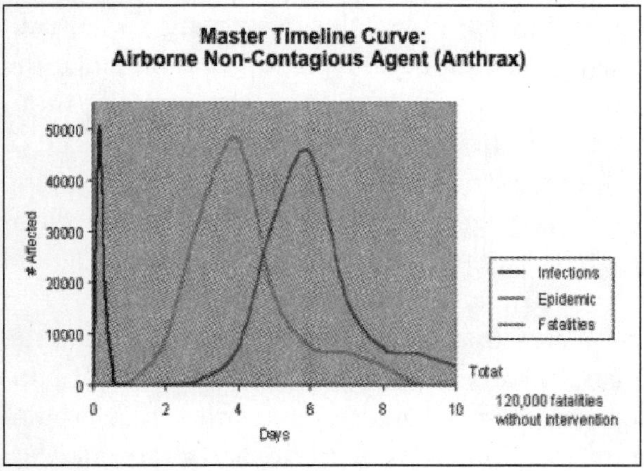

However, if anthrax isn't diagnosed until day five, many more of the people who have been exposed are now symptomatic. They will be seriously ill with high fevers, a persistent cough, weakness throughout the body, and swollen lymph nodes. If 20,000 people were exposed, at least 5,000 will be completely untreatable on that fifth day, even in an adequately supplied intensive care unit. Another 5,000 or 6,000 are probably also going to die of the anthrax exposure, even with immediate administration of antibiotics.

All of this presupposes that our medical system doesn't simply buckle under the strain of the terrorist event. After all, 10,000 to 12,000 seriously ill people is a burden that would overwhelm any regional medical facilities. The best that can be hoped for medically is that the patients can be airlifted by helicopter to every single regional hospital in the mid-Atlantic area, at least as far away as Pittsburgh or Cleveland. In trying to reduce the strain on the local facilities, the ripple effect is felt far, far beyond the initial anthrax release area. But even worse would be simultaneous attacks in several places at nearly the same time.

THE RELOAD PHENOMENON

The reload phenomenon has been written about extensively by Richard Danzig, the former Secretary of the Navy during the Clinton administration. Danzig was the only senior administration official who took the biological weapons problem seriously, in part because U.S. Navy ships are especially vulnerable to biological weapons attacks. It would be especially easy to make 5,000 people staffing an aircraft carrier ill, given the relatively confined environment they work in.

Operating a modern warship is impossible if 20 percent to 30 percent of the crew is incapacitated by illness. Physically destroying the aircraft carrier and its attack planes becomes unnecessary at that point, since the vessel cannot safely launch planes or keep up with maintaining the thousands of mission-critical systems on the ship. Attacking the centerpiece of American naval power in this way brings the added benefit of bypassing the rings of defense that the U.S. Navy has spent millions of dollars developing to protect its warships, such as state-of-the-art antiship, antiaircraft, and antimissile technologies.

The reload phenomenon states that we currently operate under the naïve assumption that terrorists will attack once and wait to see what happens. However, there is little or no reason that terrorists cannot attack multiple times, either in a different location or even the exact same one. For example, terrorists intent on disrupting economic activity in a given location may seek to perform multiple releases of an organism at set intervals of time, leading first to temporary—and then permanent—displacement of people and economic activity.

Another possibility is that the goal of the operation could be to systematically overwhelm the nation's medical response system. For example, the only way that the metropolitan Washington area can deal with a hypothetical anthrax attack is to shuttle patients outside the immediate region. This ripple effect can be exacerbated with a second and third release in the immediately adjoining areas of Baltimore, Richmond, or Philadelphia.

There is also no assurance that terrorists could not attack again with a completely different biological agent. Using different biological warfare agents is especially troublesome, since many of these agents have nonspecific symptoms. Again, there are several dozen diseases, both lethal and nonlethal, that can produce flu-like symptoms at the onset. If day zero is the day of the anthrax attack and on day three the same terrorist organization decides to release plague, then on day six there will be the potential for a massive misdiagnosis.

Given the difference in the incubation periods of each disease, the huge number of patients with late-term anthrax will coincide with the newly arriving people infected with plague who have similar symptoms. It's not likely that overtaxed medical professionals, who have been seeing case after case of anthrax, will be able to identify the new pathogen as plague. The treatment for plague is completely different from the treatment for anthrax. But the presumption will be made that the newly arriving patients are sickly new cases of anthrax.

The bad news is that not only is the treatment different, but that depending on the strain of plague used in the attack, the disease could be communicable from person to person. Yet public health organizations have already been giving people completely different advice about anthrax: If you come into contact with someone who has a fever and a cough, and if they have anthrax, you should not be too concerned for your own safety—because anthrax, while deadly, is not communicable from person to person.

This is exactly the *wrong* advice to give in the case of an outbreak of plague. The contradictory and life-threatening advice would lead not only to a loss of confidence in the medical organizations, but also in the government's ability to handle the situation.

DIFFERENT STRAINS, DIFFERENT DISEASE

There is a reason to explicitly mention plague when discussing the subject of misleading symptoms and mass-scale misdiagnosis. It used to be thought that plague made a very poor biological weapon because it could not be aerosolized and survive. We now know from the work of a man named Igor Domaradskij,[3] the former deputy director at the Institute for Applied Microbiology in Obolensk, Russia, that the Soviets solved that problem in either the seventies or eighties. Not only did they come up with a way of preserving the organism so that it would survive aerosol dispersal, they were actually smart enough to realize that distantly related strains of plague around the world *cause different types of disease.*

In the United States, the Centers for Disease Control (CDC) maintains most of its expertise on plague along with large laboratory resources devoted to the disease in Fort Collins, Colorado. Traditionally among both animal and human victims, plague in North America has caused the "bubonic" form of the disease. Rarely does "pneumonic" plague occur in the United States, except as the end stage of bubonic plague, where the organism has spread throughout the dying victim's body. Furthermore, it is believed (and taught to U.S. medical students) that the mechanism of transmission of plague—in this case, biting fleas—determines the clinical picture. Primary pneumonic plague can only occur, it is said, if a victim inhales the organism directly.

But this supposition is probably incorrect. Recent revelations from scientists who worked in the Soviet Union's biological weapons program indicate that the strain of plague that infects Central Asian ground animals, such as marmots, causes a form of plague that is a totally different beast from the flea-borne form of plague that is endemic in the Plains States of North America. So, some strains of plague are peculiarly adapted to spread via an airborne route when one infected marmot comes in contact with a susceptible and not-yet-infected marmot.

The swiftness by which the Russian pneumonic plague organism can spread, and its degree of communicability from person to person, turn out to be strain-specific. Unfortunately, this is the very strain that has been effectively weaponized by the Soviet government and could today be in the hands of different governments or organizations that would not object to using it on us. This remains an issue of contention with many scientists who study plague at the CDC, and it is their belief that the strain of plague has little (if anything) to do with the disease and that only the mechanism of transmission is important. However, they are generally not aware of the work done by the Soviets in this area.

So, going back to our imaginary example, terrorists might not only use a second biological agent in a second attack, but they would choose to use a strain of plague because it so confuses people. It would cause a respiratory disease that, for all the world, would look like anthrax but then appear to spread from person to person, such as the strain of plague from Central Asia does.

As a matter of fact, as of late 2004 there was plague outbreak in Turkmenistan, one of the Central Asian republics that have risen up from the shattered remains of the old Soviet empire. The Turkmenbashi, the title of the current ruler of Turkmenistan, has been so frustrated by the ineffective attempts to control this outbreak that he has declared plague *illegal* in the country. The mere mention of the disease has been outlawed, and contracting plague is a serious crime. Whether the spread of plague bacteria can be stopped by the use of Soviet-style state edicts is an open question, and not one that favors the Turkmenbashi.

Thus, there are many problems in identifying outbreaks—and communicating timely information to health care providers and political decision makers—rooted in common misbelief and national pride. As we have seen with the SARS experience in China, the mere mention of the name of a disease may result in a political decision to stonewall release of information.

Waiting for a lab to identify an organism after an autopsy is never going to be a good solution to stopping an outbreak. The results will simply arrive too late. And the solution is not even in waiting for public health officials to come out with pronouncements about the safety of coming into contact with somebody who is infected, because they may be wrong. Instead, we must utilize physicians, veterinarians, and other people who observe animals and humans—school nurses, clinical operators, and wildlife rehabilitators, to name a few—to simply report what they are seeing. This is because the people who work at this level know when they're seeing something unusual as measured in either severity of symptoms, uniqueness of symptoms, or simply the number of cases. They may not be able to identify what it is, but they will know what is unusual and what is not.

In some ways, knowing when something is outside the norm, then sharing that knowledge quickly, is more valuable than the identification process itself. When you can disseminate information quickly so that enough trained eyes can see it, then the overall situational awareness is raised and we can arrive at the diagnosis much more quickly than we otherwise would have, effectively cutting the waiting time from days back down to hours.

THE PRINCIPLE OF DIAGNOSTIC PARSIMONY

To summarize where we've been: Zoonotic disease and smallpox are generally not seen (or have never been seen) by doctors, so diagnoses are missed and disease identification would not be made until people start dying and someone does an autopsy. Then laboratory tests allow doctors to positively identify the cause of death. By this time, the number of patients presenting with symptoms of the disease is skyrocketing.

In addition to our inability to effectively diagnose an outbreak quickly, we have made assumptions about any potential terrorist attack that are, frankly, unreasonable. We assume that terrorists will:

- Attack only one time
- Use the same organism if they attack twice
- Use an organism that we know about and can diagnose

There is no reason to believe any of these assumptions will be true. And, when you are talking about people who are intent on causing massive social, economic, and political disruption, it would be better if we were prepared for the worst they can do.

WHY HAVEN'T WE FACED THIS PROBLEM YET?

Let's take a moment and look at the feasibility of a terrorist attack using the reload phenomenon. Building on the hypothetical scenario we already discussed, let's imagine that a terrorist group decides to hit the United States with a one-two punch of a release of anthrax spores, followed a few days later by plague. The initial goal will be to sow panic; the secondary goal is to destroy trust in both the public health service and the government. For the second attack, the group decides to use a follow-up disease, the initial symptoms of which mimic anthrax, but which is transmissible from person to person. So, could this really happen?

Both anthrax and plague are organisms that are fairly easy to obtain. Anthrax is an organism that can be found in the soil, while plague is endemic to small mammal populations in several places around the world. We also know that once you can make one, you can make the other. If you have a scientist who understands how to make anthrax and has all the equipment needed to grow it, then he can grow plague at no additional charge.

There is one significant barrier to using plague in the same way as anthrax. The plague organism does not come in hardy spores as anthrax does. Instead, the relatively fragile cellular structure of the plague bacterium can come apart when pressured through an aerosol-dispersion device.

However, we also know the Soviet Union solved the "fragility" problem, according to accounts of former weapons scientists who have since emigrated to the West. These accounts have been confirmed by aging biological researchers still living in Russia. The Soviets devised a way to preserve and protect the plague organism so that it could be dispersed as an aerosol.

This technology is probably not available in the West. In the 1960s, the United States gave up on development of this technique with plague. Therefore, one can conclude that developing plague in a way that could be delivered as a bioweapon would be extremely difficult if done from scratch. However, the knowledge can be purchased outside of the Western world.

This brings us to a final question that is well worth asking: If the means and the knowledge can be purchased, why is it that we have not yet seen a massive bioterrorism attack in the United States? To date, the anthrax attacks in 2001 remain the one true instance of bioterrorism causing large-scale disruption, though luckily a relatively low loss of life. The only other known instance of the use of a biological agent to cause disruption in the United States was fairly low key, comparatively speaking.

In 1984, members of the Rajneesh religious sect intentionally contaminated salad bars with salmonella in Dallas, Oregon, in an attempt to influence the outcome of local elections that could have brought unwanted political pressure on their organization. Nearly 750 people fell ill with mild food poisoning, but none died or required hospitalization.

One answer to our question, then, is that although it's possible to prepare a bioterrorism attack, it is not simple to execute. It is relatively difficult to get hold of most deadly organisms, handle them safely, grow them in sufficient quantity, and create an efficient dispersal device. Yet we've also learned that a relatively small attack can spread fear at an extraordinary level.

The other important reason why we probably have not seen a massive attack is that conventional explosive devices and firearms are a more reliable means of sowing terror. The sniper attacks in the Washington, D.C. area in 2002 showed how just two riflemen could potentially disrupt an entire region. And of course, September 11, 2001 showed us all how machines that were not designed with the intent of destroying buildings or people could be turned to that end.

Compare those incidents with the investment of knowledge and equipment that would be required to successfully complete a biological weapons attack and it becomes clear that conventional methods are just that much easier and less expensive. Only once conventional methods have been exhausted—or are fully anticipated—does the biological alternative look to be a superior option.

RELEASING THE DEMON

Let's consider one final scenario that could be much worse than the anthrax attacks of 2001. Assuming that a terrorist group could get hold of smallpox, it would take no more than a few ounces of the substance to kill upwards of 50,000 people—if it could be properly dispersed. A major sporting event that takes place indoors or under a partially covered dome would be the ideal opportunity because it would expose a large number of people who will then depart for various locations within a short period of time.

What happens next in this scenario is almost too horrifying to consider. Throughout history, classical smallpox infections have spread either through person-to-person contact or by contact with a contaminated item such as clothing. When smallpox is contracted in this manner, the "infectee" receives the deadly dose of several hundred particles of smallpox—all that is necessary to overwhelm the immune system and cause death in about 30 percent to 40 percent of cases. Because the particles are relatively large in size—around ten microns in diameter—they will very rarely get down into the lungs. Instead, the particles will settle in the back of the throat, causing lesions, disseminating through the lymph nodes, and culminating in the classical smallpox rash within a week to twelve days.

With an efficient dispersal device, which could be hidden in something as small as a backpack and placed in the front row of a large audience, each exposed person at our hypothetical sporting event would be inhaling several *million* particles of smallpox before halftime. Aerosolized particles of smallpox will be much smaller than ten microns in diameter. Instead of sticking to the mucus membranes of the mouth and throat, they will travel all the way down into the air sacs at the base of the lungs. This means of acquisition of smallpox—by breathing in millions of organisms deep into the lungs—would almost surely cause death in all victims.

Smallpox has virtually never been reported as pneumonia in humans—only in experimental exposures of animal test subjects. Smallpox-originated pneumonia would turn into the most highly infectious form of smallpox yet seen. Since smallpox will be resident in the lungs of the victims, each cough would throw thousands or millions of particles back into the air, creating an infection rate the likes that we have never seen in history.

Even though the people exposed in this hypothetical attack would come down with severe chest congestion three to four days later, they would not show the classical stigmata of smallpox, making it that much more difficult for doctors to diagnose the outbreak and stop the epidemic. More likely than not, a diagnosis would only be made once the first victims began to die and autopsies were performed.

The pathologists would do a double-take as soon as they saw this virus on microscope samples. Smallpox is distinctive in its appearance, most notably for its dark, dumbbell-shaped core. And of course, smallpox is never seen anymore in humans. Scientists would work speedily trying to isolate the organism and gathering data on where the victim had been, but it would probably take twelve hours or more to correlate all of the information before sending it off for confirmation at the CDC.

Given the frequency with which people travel, there would be multiple outbreak centers in the hundred largest cities in the world. And just like the mythical opening of Pandora's box, the results of releasing this demon would be devastating to humanity. This most ancient disease that was eradicated in the wild would again become endemic and take years—even decades—to bring under control.

NOTES

1. It is not known why the *intentional* introduction of smallpox virus into the skin or nose so rarely results in full-blown smallpox or death. Because smallpox was eradicated as a naturally occurring disease years before the tools of modern molecular biology became available, there is only speculation as to how the process of variolation works without being detrimental to most patients. Current thinking suggests that the smallpox organism can be introduced in limited quantity, along with the antibodies that are inevitably found in the lesions of actual smallpox victims, such that the recipient's immune system can fight off the virus quickly, before it spreads systemically and causes typical smallpox symptoms and widespread rash. Nonetheless, variolation is a dangerous practice. Many thousands of people died in the past when variolation was the only known method of inducing protection against the most extreme manifestations of smallpox.

2. The DPT vaccine—containing diphtheria toxoid, pertussis toxoid, and tetanus toxoid—is given only once in Western countries. Booster shots for tetanus and diphtheria contain only these two toxoids and not the pertussis component, since it is thought to be unsafe to give the pertussis shot more than once. Work is currently under way for a new adult pertussis vaccine because it is now known that immunity to pertussis (also known as whooping cough) wears off after a few decades. While pertussis can cause a chronic cough in adults lasting three weeks or more, it is rarely fatal. However, adults are the major reservoir of infec-

tion for children. And in young children whose respiratory system can easily become swollen and plugged with mucus due to pertussis, the disease remains a cause of fatalities even in 2005.

3. For a fascinating insight into one portion of the massive Soviet biological weapons program, see Igor V. Domaradskij and Wendy Orent, *Biowarrior: Inside the Soviet/Russian Biological War Machine* (Amherst, New York: Prometheus Books, 2003).

CHAPTER 11

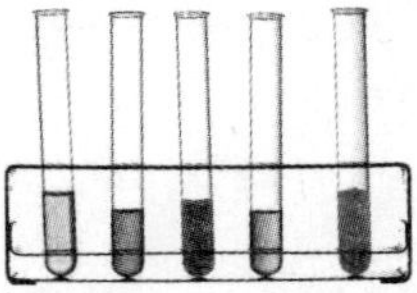

HEALER, HEAL THYSELF: CURING WHAT AILS THE PUBLIC HEALTH SYSTEM

We have already seen how quickly infectious disease can spread through a population, and the particular rapidity of spread that is likely during a large-scale bioterrorism attack. Unfortunately for the public at large, physicians receive lackluster training during their education when it comes to the management of epidemic disease. In fact, they are generally taught very little about diseases of public health importance, such as whooping cough, measles, and even influenza, let alone the more exotic organisms that might be used in a terror attack such as smallpox, anthrax, or plague. These are diseases that, once they attain a foothold in a dense human population, such as a medium-size to large city, can wreak havoc in both economic and human costs.

Physicians in medical school are also rarely exposed to the way the public health system operates. It is even less likely that they've taken a course that recognizes public health as a critical component in our modern medical system. The value of public health in *preventing* or *intervening* to stop epidemic disease from taking place has never been emphasized. Broadly speaking, physicians today only learn about public health if they decide to pursue a position in the field as part of their post-graduate training for medical school.

Put another way, in the busy medical school curriculum, far more time is devoted to obscure anatomical discussions than to discussions about how to keep the public—the readers of this book—healthy and protected against deadly disease.

PUBLIC HEALTH—WHO NEEDS IT?

Why should physicians be studying public health in the first place? Some might argue that the subject is better suited for discussions among graduate-level political science majors. Among academic physicians who design medical curricula, there has been a long-standing feeling—probably based on the mistaken belief that infectious disease would be wiped out in the late 1970s[1]—that it is inappropriate or at least unimportant to train medical practitioners in public health issues unless they plan to get into the field of setting public health policy.

This is demonstrably not the case. In fact, to this very day, we still owe a great deal of thanks to the early successes of public health, which include water quality monitoring, government-sponsored vaccine programs, and fluoridation. It's because the processes for protecting our family's health seem so mundane that we've become inured to their ability to prevent infectious disease from spreading through our local neighborhood. But it seems that public health has largely been resting on its laurels, depending on old techniques for detection and intervention while the infectious disease "background" and the possibility of bioterrorism have dramatically changed the nature and potential time-course of the threat. When our public health control system fails, as it did, for example, in the Milwaukee cryptosporidiosis outbreak in 1993 (see Chapter 9), we are shocked and outraged that such things actually can take place in this modern age.

In theory, all doctors carry around two responsibilities—one to the individual patient they are treating and one for the well-being of the general public.[2] These aren't separate aspects of medical practice; they are closely related, indeed. The stronger emphasis is placed on the individual over the public. But it is not possible to truly treat the individual and to care for the individual (or even care about the individual) unless there is some appreciation for the importance of public health. Physicians have to understand that they hold a direct responsibility to report to public health officials (PHOs) when they see a disease—or even symptoms that are indicative of a dangerous, communicable disease.

Today, the vast majority of physicians don't even know the name of their local public health officer. Just as politically apathetic people cannot be counted on to know the name of their local congressional representative, it's naïve to expect a physician who is apathetic about public health to know this information. Few physicians have ever contacted a public health officer—in fact, it's likely that only a small minority even have the phone number of the local public health office handy.[3] Most physicians would tell you that the primary responsibility of the public health office is monitoring the water supply and treating people for sexually transmitted diseases.[4]

While the public health office does in fact do those things, it is, most importantly, our first line of defense against epidemics. In a properly structured public health system—one that includes close collaboration with physicians, veterinarians, school nurses, wildlife rehabilitators, and infectious disease specialists—the system would try to detect the earliest manifestations of disease. It should also be operated with the goal of effectively intervening before a single case spins out of control and becomes a full-fledged epidemic. Clearly, this ideal is far from our current reality.[5]

To illustrate, there were several significant failures of the public health system worldwide in just the past two decades, not the least of which included the SARS epidemic in Asia and, in the United States, the cryptosporidiosis outbreak and West Nile virus, which became endemic to North America for the first time.

In each of these cases, there was a near-complete absence of communication among physicians, veterinarians, and public health officials until the diseases became entrenched in the population and affected many thousands of people. The SARS outbreak is an example of the public health system *overreacting* while the cryptosporidiosis outbreak is an example of the public health system *underreacting*. In fact, during the outbreak of cryptosporidiosis in Milwaukee, the system was completely oblivious to what was going on.

Then, amazingly, in the case of West Nile several years later, though the critical information about the outbreak was reported to public health officials, the information was dismissed because it came from a mere *veterinarian* rather than a *physician*. In each of the three events, the opportunity for early warning and intervention to prevent the spread of disease was squandered. The case of West Nile resulted in the permanent establishment of a new disease from Africa and the Near East in the continental United States. Had West Nile been as pathogenic as, say, yellow fever, then we would be living in a much different world today.

INVESTIGATING THE INVESTIGATORS

What distinguishes public health officials from physicians? To begin with, while many public health officials attend medical school like physicians (or veterinary school like veterinarians), after graduation they go on to receive specific training that involves the study of the way disease is spread through populations. They also learn several things that ordinary physicians would never encounter in their normal coursework or practice. For example, they learn:

- How to use simple statistics for detecting the outbreak of disease
- How to use these statistics to model how a disease might spread in a given population
- How to use this model, in turn, to decide how to effectively marshal limited resources in response to an outbreak or epidemic and also to determine the optimal data-gathering requirements to carry out detection

Public health officials are potentially very important people in protecting and providing health care to humans and animals. They can assert themselves using police powers anytime there is suspicion of either a disease outbreak or a threat to a population that could result in a large number of casualties. For example, on mere suspicion alone, public health officials can exhume bodies for autopsy. They can insist that patients who have died unexpectedly be subjected to autopsy. The New Mexico official who halted the Navajo funeral during the hantavirus outbreak in 1993 (see Chapter 3) did just this, and while the family was terribly upset, the official was well within his legal power. On rare occasions, PHOs actually have the authority to institute isolation or even a full quarantine.

So, public health officials, if they are medically trained, know how to make effective use of population biology computer models and statistics for detecting and understanding the spread of disease. It immediately makes them foreigners to the rest of the medical community because they simply speak a different language.

On the negative side, very few public health officials have even practiced clinical medicine, and if they have, their exposure to patients during their few years in medical school was probably limited. A few may have done a yearlong internship in a hospital and had rotating responsibilities in the surgical or care unit service. By and large, however, public health officials are not clinicians. In fact, a large cadre of public health officials, sometimes called *medical investigators,* are often not medically trained at all. They may, for example, be retired policemen or detectives.

Someone who performs an autopsy is a trained pathologist who has a medical degree and has done a residency to study of the basic mechanisms of disease and death. The individual may have even done a subspecialty residency in forensic pathology to learn how to diagnose the means of death in a murder.

Forensic pathology is a relatively glamorous subspecialty in medicine that has been highlighted on television series such as *CSI.* But there are many other people who work as medical investigators whose role is strictly to identify a suspicious death or set of suspicious deaths. They then notify authorities who are medically trained to make a judgment about whether autopsies and specialized testing should be performed. Perhaps not so glamorous as you might think, but certainly important.

DISEASES THAT ARE COMPLETELY UNTREATABLE . . .

Public health is also very concerned with untreatable illnesses. Once the disease strikes it's going to run its course regardless of what the physician does or does not do. If you come down with a case of tularemia, which is actually a relatively mild infectious disease, you are going to recover more or less independently of what a doctor does. The same is true for most cases of anthrax, dengue, West Nile virus, and a whole host of other zoonotic diseases. In the relatively few cases of these diseases that have been treated in modern times, intensive care unit (ICU) technology has resulted in only a very modest improvement in outcomes at enormous costs.

Doctors can offer what is called "supportive care." They can make patients more comfortable or pull them through an event that could kill a borderline patient. For example, if a disease is causing the lungs to fill with fluid, then a patient can be given oxygen so that she does not suffocate. But the actual event—the process by which the lungs are filling up as a response to the organism in the patient's body—cannot be remedied in the slightest.

The best single example, of course, is what happened with the anthrax outbreak in Washington, D.C. in 2001. In that case, many of the people who fell ill with anthrax went on to die, despite the treatments available in advanced intensive care units, including the ability to perform dialysis if the kidneys failed, to give medications to raise the blood pressure if somebody went into shock, and to put people on respirators if they could not breathe.

Despite the availability of all those things, the mortality rate was very, very high—about 80 percent, and of those who survived, few have returned to their pre-anthrax level of health. Only one of the eleven postal workers who contracted anthrax has returned to work. The rest are either dead or disabled—and most of the workers were young. If someone were to deliver anthrax not in a letter, but rather as an aerosol, ICU resources in the entire region where the event took place would rapidly be overwhelmed. For example, in the United States in the early 1990s, there were about 30,000 ICU beds across the entire country. There are substantially fewer today due to economics.

Hospital systems have been forced to cut back wherever they can to achieve economies, and unoccupied ICU beds are very expensive things to maintain. In addition, the amount of time that people spend in hospitals, even if they go into intensive care, has shrunk in recent years because ICU treatment has undoubtedly gotten better. Indeed, hospital stays are significantly shorter for problems ranging from infectious diseases to heart disease, even though patients are often admitted "sicker" or chronically ill more often now than a decade ago. We've been more efficient in getting people in and out of the ICU—and that has enabled hospital administrators to save resources by cutting back intensive care unit beds.

The end result, then, because of both cost-cutting measures and shorter stays in the ICU, is fewer beds. If there was a large-scale use of an agent like anthrax in a city the size of Pittsburgh and 100,000 people got ill, that number alone would be three times larger than the total number of ICU beds available in the entire United States. Even if medical centers were set up out in the field, rather like the mobile army hospitals from the 1970s series *M*A*S*H,* it's difficult to imagine a scenario where we'd have sufficient numbers of beds to take care of all of these patients.

It's even more difficult to imagine a scenario where you would have a sufficient number of trained personnel to handle the thousands and thousands of sick and dying patients. Intensive care nursing, for example, generally is one-on-one nursing, where one nurse is occupied with the care of just one patient (thus the meaning of "intensive care").

There's a lot going on in intensive care units. The medical staff is managing respirators and managing medication either to keep the patient's blood pressure high enough or to keep it from getting too high. People in ICUs are there because they could die at any given time. And that is the condition that most people arriving in the hospital after an anthrax exposure would be in (or soon would be). For example, *everybody* who actually came down with anthrax disease in the 2001 letter-bomb attack had to be placed in an intensive care unit. There were no exceptions.

Fortunately, there were only about a dozen or so cases in 2001. What if there had been just a hundred times that number? If 1,000 people came in, all needing intensive health care treatment at the same time, it would overwhelm all of the hospitals in the largest of our metropolitan areas.

There are also going to be equipment inadequacies. Most people exposed to anthrax end up on respirators. Generally speaking, their lungs become waterlogged with fluid or end up stiff with inflammation from the battle that is going on between the bacteria and the immune system in the lungs. People often end up incapable of breathing on their own. To save their lives, they have to be put on a ventilator. Roughly speaking, there are approximately the same number of ventilators as there are ICU beds. Once this number is exceeded, how will the medical personnel at the hospital decide who gets the ventilators?

One could argue, "Well, we could scare up the staff that we need by calling in everyone who is off-duty, part-time, or even recently retired." But you can't scare up equipment that you don't have. For most diseases of public health importance—ones that include, but are not limited to, the bioterrorism diseases—you're talking about people who need respirators.

For example, with Legionnaire's disease, almost every person coming down with the disease inevitably ends up on a respirator. It's also the rule with hantavirus patients. Just about everyone who has come down with hantavirus pulmonary syndrome (HPS) has ended up on a respirator in an intensive care unit.

So, these diseases are, generally speaking, untreatable—there is no *specific* therapy or drug regimen to direct at them. Our effort in medicine is to keep them alive long enough so that the body's immune system and natural healing processes enable the patient to recover, giving the patient time to fight off the offending organism or toxin. No matter how confident your physician may sound, should you be unlucky enough to come down with one of these diseases, there is really nothing else that anyone wearing a white coat and stethoscope can do for you.

. . . AND DISEASES THAT ARE READILY DEFEATABLE

There is one final item that characterizes all of the diseases of concern to public health. That is, they are easily prevented. We can defend against them quite easily if we know that an outbreak has taken place.

To use a mundane example within the veterinary community, let's look at foot-and-mouth disease. Let's say that a single case of foot-and-mouth disease is reported on an isolated farm in the United States. If the local vet recognizes and reports it within six or ten hours of the appearance of the characteristic lesions on the animal, the farm is quickly quarantined. The animal can either be housed for treatment or, if necessary, euthanized so that there's no risk of disseminating the foot-and-mouth virus downwind to the next ranch.

However, if people move in and out of this ranch, say, when trucks are delivering hay from one ranch to another, they will transport the organism around the countryside very efficiently, sometimes even if the ranch is quarantined for animal movement. Because visitors can pick up the foot-and-mouth virus on their clothing or even on the tires of vehicles, it is often necessary to ban *all* interactions of *any* kind between the farm and the outside world.

Soon, the local health department would have an enormous epidemic on its hands that could, if nothing else, create the need for the killing, burning, and then burying of tens of thousands of animal bodies. It would be an extremely challenging, stressful, and economically costly task.

In 2001, during an epidemic of foot-and-mouth disease in the United Kingdom, literally millions of animals were slaughtered and their carcasses burned. It is awful from the humanitarian standpoint of seeing so many animals sacrificed and because of the economic losses. It was also psychologically devastating to the farmers and to the people who were assigned the task of shooting and burning the thousands of animals.

If a new strain of influenza arrives that is highly pathogenic and easily communicable from person to person, the same situation will be more or less identical in operational terms. We won't be euthanizing and immolating people, of course. But if we cannot detect the earliest cases, recognize what we're dealing with, and take appropriate action to prevent people from passing on the virus, then what starts off on day one or two as a few people being ill will, by the end of the week, turn into thousands—if not tens of thousands—of people becoming ill.

Furthermore, a substantial percentage of the ill will die, as happened in the 1918 flu pandemic, where well over twenty million people perished. Among young adults between the ages of eighteen and thirty-five, as much as 12 percent of the population died.

The key to making sure such a calamity does not happen is for clinicians of all kinds to report these completely untreatable but easily defeatable diseases to public health officials. A helpful mnemonic emerges that can remind us all of the types of infectious disease that cause the most concern to experts and public health officials: CURED. It stands for Completely Untreatable, Readily Defeatable.

EXQUISITELY DESIGNED FOR FAILURE

Public health officials and clinicians, as a group, are very busy people. (How many times have you noticed doctors running "a bit behind" when it comes to seeing patients in the appropriately named waiting room?) It turns out that physicians and PHOs are not generally doing the kinds of things that they would like to be doing, such as spending time with patients. Or, in the case of PHOs, gathering and analyzing information to gauge the health of the population in local areas.

Physicians in particular have enormous administrative overhead, especially in the world of primary care. They simply do not have time to be bothered with additional responsibilities, and most physicians correctly complain that they have insufficient time to carry out their most important responsibility: listening to, examining, and caring for patients.

For physicians to take the time to report to a public health official, they have to believe at least two things. First, that reporting won't take much time. Second, that as a result of investing the time, their patient will benefit directly. Neither of these stipulations is true in the current public health reporting structure.

It takes a Herculean effort to fill out the standardized forms for reporting diseases to public health officials—generally an hour or more, with the ever-present possibility that more information will later be requested on yet more paper forms. The turnaround time for getting feedback from a public health official could be measured in weeks or even months. This simply isn't very useful to the physician's patient who may be ill or dying.

Furthermore, if the doctor has to pick up the phone and call the public health official, it may mean waiting on hold. It may mean having the public health official call back and the physician not being available. In other words, the existing process for communication is extremely inefficient.

Public health officials are very busy as well. They get lots and lots of phone calls, generally about things that they know are of little public health information value and distract them from their primary job of detecting managing disease outbreaks. This is not to say that the lay public can be expected to know what is needed information and what is not, but PHOs just don't have time to squander unless they know that the time they invest is going to make a difference in their productivity, and that means quickly identifying and preventing the spread of disease.

When judged on this basis, the current system is exquisitely designed to fail, both from the standpoint of efficiency and the initial motivation to do anything. That is why the vast majority of physicians have never reported a disease that they are *legally mandated to report* in their state.

In New Mexico, for example, there are about fifty "reportable diseases." If you, as a physician, see one of these fifty diseases, you are obligated, by law, to report it to the local public health official. There is nothing equivocal about this. Yet, even with laws on the books, reporting of deadly maladies just doesn't happen. The reason is because the process is too hard to follow.

One of the things that makes it hard is that most physicians don't know what those fifty reportable disease are. Most doctors could figure out two or three of them if you gave them a pop quiz. Tuberculosis, HIV, and plague are fairly obvious. But while most physicians know how to identify these distinctive diseases, most of them have never seen a case of brucellosis and therefore have no idea that it's a reportable disease.

Brucellosis is an animal disease that occasionally gets into humans from unpasteurized dairy products, and it causes a tuberculosis-like disease. So it's a zoonotic disease that looks like tuberculosis, but the diagnosis is often missed simply because physicians have never seen it. Obviously, if they haven't seen it, they aren't about to test for it or report it.

If you started off with a clean sheet of paper and were asked come up with a system that was more exquisitely poised to fail when you need it most, you couldn't create anything worse than the system we currently have. But the solution to this problem is simple, and it has two objectives. First, we have to make medical and veterinary practice part of public health. Second, we have to make public health part of medical and veterinary practice.

NOTES

1. Dr. William Stewart, the U.S. Surgeon General and head of the U.S. Public Health Service in 1967, was famously quoted as stating that it would soon be time to "close the door on infectious disease" because of the progress in developing antibiotics and vaccines. While there were doubtless some reasons for this optimism, no one foresaw the arrival of antibiotic-resistant bacteria, a huge number of new viral diseases that spread from the animal population to humans, and, of course, the presence of HIV, SARS, and new strains of influenza. Even today, many deans and department heads of medical schools believe that infectious disease will play an ever *smaller* role in the total disease burden suffered by mankind, believing that degenerative diseases, heart disease, and stroke will dominate the health care needs of people around the world. Ironically, there is now some evidence that even this latter group of diseases has an infectious basis, although the data is still too slim to draw firm conclusions.

2. The oath of Maimonides, often cited as a more comprehensive statement of the role of physicians than the Hippocratic oath, notes the responsibility that physicians have for the well-being of the population at

large: "The eternal providence has appointed me to watch over the life and health of Thy creatures. May the love for my art actuate me at all time; may neither avarice nor miserliness, nor thirst for glory or for a great reputation engage my mind; for the enemies of truth and philanthropy could easily deceive me and make me forgetful of my lofty aim of doing good to Thy children."

3. Physician compliance with most *legally mandated* disease reporting requirements is less than 10 percent nationwide (see *American Journal of Epidemiology* Vol. 155 (No. 9), May 2002, pp. 866–874). In addition, very few medical schools offer any courses or rotations in public health (see "Prevention Education and Evaluation in U.S. Medical Schools: A Status Report," *Academic Medicine* Vol. 75, July 2000 (7 Suppl), pp. S14–S21.).

4. "U.S. Medical Students' Rotations in Epidemiology and Public Health at State and Local Health Departments," *Academic Medicine* Vol. 77 No. 7, August 2002, pp. 799–809.

5. There are a few countries in Europe (primarily France and the United Kingdom) where the linkages between clinicians and public health officials are well maintained. But even in those countries, important information from the veterinary community, school nurses, and others who see patients (either animal or human) is not routinely archived and shared electronically with physicians or public health authorities.

CHAPTER 12

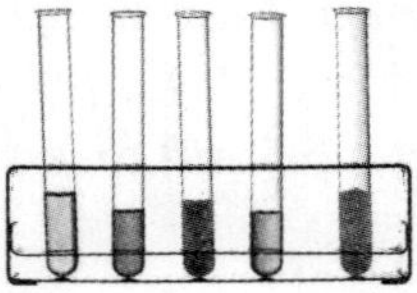

PROJECT BIOWATCH

Plague Vials Vanish in Texas

To date, we've been fortunate in the United States to have avoided a large-scale bioterrorism attack. Even though many national leaders believe that bioterrorism represents the single largest threat to the United States[1]—at least when measured in terms of casualties or economic devastation—terrorists have not yet chosen to use this kind of weapon. Perhaps they have been caught by our intelligence agencies before they could develop or use such weapons. But an alternative explanation is that terrorists tend to stick with what they know, and conventional explosives (albeit delivered by less-than-conventional means) have been enough to change our lives forever after September 11, 2001.

Most people believe that terrorists want to "send a message" more than bring down a society. If that truly is the case, then after 9/11 it was not surprising to see anthrax show up in what appears to have been a small-scale attack using an unconventional delivery system. The anthrax letters were guided missiles of paper and pathogens, sent to their targets not by Global Positioning System satellites but by the ink of a ballpoint pen scratching out the address on an envelope. These were weapons, and they were specifically designed to send a message and generate terror. The terrorists seemed to be saying: "We can get to you and your leaders with multiple weapons and through many means that you cannot possibly anticipate." (At the time of this writing, those responsible for sending the anthrax letters have yet to be identified and no arrests have been made.)

If biological weapons are going to be the next step beyond the use of conventional explosives, what has the U.S. government done to protect us from this threat? After five people were slain and nineteen sickened by the letter-borne anthrax weapons in 2001, political movers and shakers finally began to take this risk seriously. The National Security Council (NSC), the president's staff charged with both domestic and international security issues, was asked to come up with an implementable, near-real-time, cost-effective process for identifying a bioweapons attack.

The project was initiated by the thinkers and policy makers on the NSC in late 2001. It had three separate initiatives: Project BIOWATCH, Project BIOSENSE, and Project BIOSHIELD.

The first effort, BIOWATCH, consists of air-monitoring devices emplaced around the country to perform "aerosol surveillance"—essentially looking for organisms in the atmosphere, most of which would be naturally occurring, of course, but some of which might be intentionally introduced in a terrorism attack. The air-monitoring devices are designed to detect particles of organisms or toxins that have been drifting in the air over long distances, because there cannot be samplers everywhere. Thus, anything that *is* detected might have come from nearby or from miles away. This is in fact the very definition of an aerosol—something that behaves like the air, as opposed to something that falls to the ground.

Project BIOSENSE—which is still not implemented in any substantive way—includes a national disease surveillance system. And Project BIOSHIELD is an ambitious research project to identify and manufacture new antibiotics, antiviral drugs, and vaccines that would be effective against a wider range of organisms than anything we currently possess in our pharmacological armamentarium.

THE AIR-SUCKERS

One brilliant idea proposed by several members of the National Security Council was to use the Environmental Protection Agency's existing network of particulate samplers and press them into service as quickly as possible. The EPA's particulate samplers are essentially large air-sucking devices that pass the air they intake through filter paper to see what particles and organisms end up stuck to the filter, like bugs on flypaper. They also survey the quantity of the organisms and inert particles collected on the paper.

Most people are actually very familiar with this work. You can find the data taken from these filters when reading your local newspaper's weather report. Toward the bottom of the multicolored or line-diagrammed forecast maps, the levels of smog, pollen, and mold are reported if data is available. The NSC's goal was to adapt the air filters to be able to preserve either the living organism or the DNA of the organism in a way that could be tested in the laboratory.

The EPA traditionally used plain old filter paper similar to a coffee filter. This kind of paper was not adequate for biological sampling because it was designed to capture industrial and urban dust that has heavy metal content such as mercury and lead, as well as particles from fossil-fuel combustion, specifically coal. The problem with cellulose-based filter papers is that they inhibit sensitive biological studies such as the polymerase chain reaction (PCR), which is a very sensitive technique for identifying minute quantities of DNA from organisms such as anthrax or smallpox. Unfortunately, that means it's tremendously more difficult to identify genetic material that may belong to something as innocuous as ragweed pollen or something as dangerous as an anthrax spore.

To upgrade the air filters to the new task, the EPA needed a very special grade of filter paper, one made of high-purity cellulose (i.e., plant fiber) or Teflon with a minimal amount of ash content and heavy metal content.

By swapping out the type of filter paper used, the NSC was able to perform PCR tests. Generally speaking, though, because of the delay between the time that a particle might be captured and the time it was assayed in the laboratory—which could take up to seventy-two hours—there really wasn't much chance of culturing a living organism.

Few microorganisms are as a hardy as anthrax. Most microorganisms will dry out and die on the filter paper, or their DNA will have been knocked to pieces from the sun's ultraviolet radiation. However, if you could preserve the DNA and create a forgiving environment where you could do PCR analysis, then you can identify any given organism by its genetic fingerprint. The final choice of sampling filter paper remains a carefully guarded secret so as to prevent terrorists from finding ways of interfering with its function as a biological capturing device.

The planners at the NSC realized from the start that the first phase of BIOWATCH would have one major flaw. The flaw was one of simple uncertainty. They knew that all sorts of unknown organisms in the air would turn up on the filter paper, because no one had ever undertaken such a large-scale, nationwide, continuous air-sampling project. As for known pathogens, because no one had looked for them before, they would not be able to know if there was a low, high, or abnormal number of any given organism since there was no data with which to compare the readings.

UNKNOWN WORLDS AROUND US

One popular misconception that the public holds is that scientists have, by and large, discovered and categorized the vast majority of organisms that exist in the local environment. When new microbes are discovered and noted in the media, they are at most often in numbers of ones or twos. In fact, there are thousands of organisms that exist in the air, in the water, and especially in the soil that we have yet to identify, let alone name and classify.

Perhaps the best example is the ordinary-looking topsoil in your backyard. The concentration of organisms in the upper layer of soil is higher than just about anywhere else you can imagine, with the possible exception of raw sewage. Soil is also a rather uninviting medium in which to do PCR tests. There is a component of soil called humic acid; it is a naturally occurring group of chemicals that aid in the decomposition process. Humic acid interferes with the enzymes used in the PCR process, making the test ineffective.

Regardless of the difficulty in using genetic identification techniques, it is generally stated by soil ecologists that we have perhaps identified one percent of the organisms living in topsoil. Of the remaining 99 percent, most of the unidentified numbers of organisms in biology are bacteria. And, as of yet, we have no idea how many thousands or millions of species of viruses may also exist in this tiny sliver of our world.

As a result, the Project BIOWATCH managers were smart enough to know that unusual things would be identified by the highly sensitive PCR technique, leading to a high potential for false alarms. They tried mightily to combine the aerobiology test with some other kind of surveillance for human or animal health that would allow them to put their findings into a context so the data could be useful. But, as noted earlier, Project BIOSENSE has yet to be implemented.

Some preliminary work to address the "false positive" concern was done in the late 1990s by the scientists at Lawrence Livermore National Laboratory. The scientists collected the filter sheets that are part of air-handling devices for large commercial buildings in a few cities around the United States and performed PCR tests on them. They found all sorts of organisms on the sheets, including several new organisms that had never been previously identified.

Not that these organisms were necessarily pathogenic, but it made the point clear: The PCR technique was so powerful that it would identify a plethora of new bugs as well as large quantities of well-known organisms.

But it could not answer the key question: What was the *significance* of the organisms being present on, for example, filters on the air-intake manifolds for large buildings, sports stadiums, and auditoriums?

BEYOND THE THREE PHASES OF U.S. CIVILIAN BIODEFENSE

Because it was easy, fast, and relatively inexpensive, the first part of Project BIOWATCH was completed. The second part of the project, which would link public health departments together, was never completed because it was hard, expensive, and no one really knew how to make it happen. Only very recently has the federal government begun devoting effort to try to establish some sort of national disease surveillance system. It is still unclear whether it will take place at the state level and be funded by the federal government through the Department of Homeland Security.

Even if all three phases of the federal government's civilian biodefense program are ultimately implemented and maintained, another daunting problem remains: how to integrate all of the data and process it into knowledge tailored for various users, including public health officials, political decision makers, law enforcement, and others. "Standards" for such systems are hard to develop and promulgate. Indeed, there is an argument to be made that except for standards for interoperability of databases, the fewer standards the better, so as to promote as much creativity as possible to find solutions.

Since BIOWATCH has really only completed phase one, but not phase two and three, one could assume that all sorts of false positives would start to show up. Without a way to evaluate and disseminate the data, people would have a difficult time interpreting what a positive result meant. There are at least two events of this sort that have been made public to the mainstream media, and one other event in rural Texas that is not well known regarding the use of these air-sucking devices. We will review them now, as well as some of the lessons learned from the events.

ANTHRAX COMES TO NEW YORK CITY

The event that is best known took place in New York City just as phase one of Project BIOWATCH began. In winter 2002, a particulate sampler somewhere in the metropolitan New York area inhaled at least one spore of anthrax. Since the PCR test performed on the filter paper is an extraordinarily sensitive one, only a few strands of an organism's DNA (literally as few as one or two spores of anthrax) were needed to produce a positive identification.

Therefore, while it was not known exactly how much anthrax was inhaled by the air-sucking device, even one spore of anthrax would have set alarm bells ringing. When analyzed, the filter paper showed the presence of anthrax. Most disturbingly, the PCR test was able to show that it was a spore of a virulent, dangerous strain of the disease.

As is often said in science and in police forensics, "If you look hard enough, you will always find something." Whether that something is meaningful or useful is another question. In this case, the anthrax readings were worse than worthless. Once anthrax was confirmed, the local public health departments in New York City received a phone call from either the EPA or the FBI saying that anthrax had been identified on an air-sucker somewhere in Manhattan.

The exact wording of the message has never been released. However, one cannot help but wonder if it said, "We've just detected anthrax in your jurisdiction; we just thought you'd like to know that." That's because, in essence, the message delivered was the same: Traces of anthrax have been discovered, but it is up to the people at the public health department to decide what to do with the information.

Unsurprisingly, in the face of such disturbing information—coming on the heels of a national investigation and manhunt for the person or group that had already infected and killed several Americans with inhalation anthrax—the reaction was close to panic. Proving a negative—in this case that there is nothing "bad" going on—is always very difficult. It easy to tell when something of importance is going on; it is exceptionally hard to prove when something of importance is *not* happening or about to happen.

The situation was complicated even further because no one knew what the natural background level of anthrax spores in the environment should be. Because anthrax can reliably be found in the soil wherever cattle are present and it can travel several miles in the air, it's not unreasonable to assume that a spore could blow in from a farm in New Jersey.

And so the New York City Department of Health spent several million dollars and hundreds of man-hours trying chase down the anthrax "hit" on the EPA filter paper. Though the PCR had correctly identified the presence of anthrax on the filter paper, the reading in and of itself represented no threat to public health.

What the test could not do was determine whether the presence of anthrax on the filter paper was meaningful enough for any public health agency to make a firm decision on. Without additional information—for example, a report of a sudden spike in respiratory or skin disease—it was impossible to know how to interpret this hard-to-ignore single piece of information.

The entire episode was extremely expensive for the people at the Department of Health because they had to stop just about every single thing they were doing to focus on this one threat. It takes hundreds or even thousands of anthrax spores inhaled over a few minutes to hours in order to sicken a person. To top it off, health department officials never figured out where the anthrax spores came from. It's highly probable that every day in New York City an anthrax spore or two, or even ten, are blown in from somewhere outside the city.

The anthrax could have come from agricultural sites in New Jersey, upstate New York, or even from a ship that may be berthing in the harbor. But its significance from a public health standpoint is exactly zero. For the New York Department of Health, it was an expensive lesson learned: Without a clinical "context," such as knowledge of the actual symptoms in the local population, the EPA anthrax "hit" was a false-positive alarm. It was like the old story of the boy crying "wolf."

TRIPLE ALARM IN HOUSTON

Project BIOWATCH also turned in a positive result in Texas in October 2003. Three of the air impactors in the Houston metropolitan area turned up traces of tularemia, commonly known as rabbit fever.

Tularemia is dangerous enough to have made the short list of deadly pathogens categorized by the U.S. Department of Defense as a potential biological weapon. Unlike anthrax, only a few particles of viable tularemia are required to cause pneumonia in humans and animals. Adding to the alarm was the fact that the three air-suckers in question were in a straight line along the path of the prevailing wind. Although a straight-line pattern of detection is not conclusive evidence of a bioterrorist attack, it does imply a heavy downwind source of a particular pathogen. Otherwise, three rather widely spaced air samplers would not have been positive for tularemia at the same time due to dilution in the wind.

The Houston Health and Human Services Department swung into action immediately. It drastically increased environmental sampling, collection, and testing of wild rabbits and rodents. And yet, once again, the decisions had to be made within a vacuum of data. No one knew at this point what the normal background level of tularemia in the environment was, nor was there any way for local public health officials (PHOs) to get an accurate, real-time assessment of patients with significant respiratory disease. And like a shadow that is glimpsed before disappearing into the darkness, the pathogen was not found on filters tested in subsequent days.

To this day, no one has any idea where the tularemia that ended up on the filter paper came from. But it sure got the attention of the public health department in the city of Houston. And just like the case in New York City, the local PHOs spent a lot of time and money trying to chase down an ephemeral threat.

THE PLAGUE VIALS THAT VANISHED IN LUBBOCK COUNTY

Finally, an interesting example that illustrates the opposite side of the coin comes out of the syndrome surveillance work performed in Lubbock County, Texas. It shows the power of appropriate syndrome surveillance in and of itself. It also demonstrates how a surveillance system, combined with data from the BIOWATCH detection equipment, is the most effective defense we have against outbreaks.

The story begins with Dr. Thomas Butler, a professor at the medical school for the Texas Tech University Health Sciences Center in Lubbock, Texas. Lubbock, which is the seat of a county at the base of the Texas panhandle, was first settled during the cattle boom of the late 1860s. Interestingly, the town hosts a center devoted to Buddy Holly and the Crickets, and in 2002 it was also home to a renowned plague researcher, the aforementioned Dr. Butler, who had traveled the world collecting samples of his favorite organism.

A moderately tall, snowy-haired man in his sixties who engendered a certain amount of affection from his colleagues, Butler was described as "the absentminded professor." He kept his samples of plague bacteria in his laboratory in test tubes, not in a deadly aerosol form but in a somewhat safer formulation. As long as a researcher is reasonably careful, plague is not particularly dangerous. In fact, many laboratories keep the organism in this manner for diagnostic purposes.

In January 2003, Dr. Butler called the FBI to report that while he was tending to his laboratory, he noticed that thirty vials of the plague samples he kept were missing. The samples had been collected during Dr. Butler's work in Madagascar, which is one of the four places in the world where plague is endemic in local mammals. The samples were stored in test tubes small enough to fit in a jacket pocket, thermos, or fanny pack.

Upon receiving this information, the FBI called the City of Lubbock Health Department. At the time, the department consisted of one part-time secretary and one full-time public health coordinator, an extremely bright and perceptive woman named Tigi Ward. The FBI told the department that it had received a report of some plague samples falling into unauthorized hands. This time the notification had a distinctly different result from the cases in Houston and New York City. This was because Tigi Ward had three advantages over her counterparts in the other cities.

First, she was a knowledgeable and experienced "hands on" public health nurse directly responsible for monitoring local health conditions; she was not a bureaucrat. When she got the phone call, she reasoned that because it was January and students were returning to the local university after the holidays, she expected to see a spike in respiratory illness that would be unrelated to potential release of plague in Lubbock County. After all, students returning from winter break are bringing back any cold viruses that they may have picked up from immediate family and spreading them in crowded dormitory conditions to other students. Because she had been testing a syndrome surveillance system and had it in daily use by doctors in the community, she always knew exactly how many cases of serious respiratory disease there were in the community.[2]

Thus, if there was a spike in respiratory disease caused by plague, Tigi Ward would know about it.

Ward's second advantage was that as the local PHO of the area, she personally knew most of the staff and faculty at the Texas Tech medical school. Therefore, she was able to do something that very few other officials in Texas could have done. She called up her friends in the local medical community to find out more about the circumstances surrounding the disappearance of Dr. Butler's plague samples. She found that Dr. Butler might not have been exactly truthful in his reports to the FBI. It turns out he was considered to be something of a grandstander who craved public attention. Causing a modern-day outbreak of plague is certainly one way to draw attention to yourself.

Third, because she had a basic syndrome surveillance system running, she was able to put out a message to 10 percent of the doctors in the local community who were routinely using it and listing the diagnostic criteria for plague. Ten percent is a statistically valid sample of physicians to accurately reflect what is happening in the community at large. In her message, she asked doctors and nurses to be especially sensitive to any patient who came in complaining of severe respiratory illness.

What happened was *nothing*. There were no increases in the cases of respiratory disease in Lubbock County. There was no increase in the number of clinics or hospitals ordering tests to detect rare respiratory illnesses such as plague. And, most important, the very limited budget that Ward had to operate her small public health department was not squandered chasing a shadow, as had happened in New York City.

In the end, it turned out that Dr. Butler's plague cultures had never, in fact, been stolen in the first place. Why Butler called the FBI is still not clear to this day. It could very well be that he had delusions of grandeur, or was simply a publicity hound who knew exactly what, in this day and age, would draw maximum attention. Or maybe Dr. Butler was as absentminded as his nickname suggested, and he had simply destroyed his plague samples without carefully recording notes in his laboratory journals.

The investigation of Dr. Butler uncovered additional irregularities. He was accused of illegally importing plague specimens from various parts of the world into United States without a license. Ultimately, he was convicted for embezzlement of overhead money that he had received for his department and several other charges, none of which had anything to do with a biological weapon or the possibility of someone creating one using material from his lab.

WHEN DATA IS WORSE THAN WORTHLESS

It's interesting to note that, unlike New York City and Houston, which had health departments with enormous staffs and a sizable budget, the little public health department in Lubbock County, Texas did not waste precious resources looking for a threat that did not exist. There were no unnecessary diagnostic tests performed, nor was there any panic in the medical community.

In short, the situation in Lubbock was resolved with a minimum of fuss. Tigi Ward's most significant advantage over her big-city counterparts was that she was able to fit the data given to her into a *clinical* context—that is, she analyzed the possibility of a potential threat by using her real-time knowledge of the health of the local population. The syndrome surveillance system allowed her to accurately determine that a real threat did not exist.

Had two or three vials of plague actually been stolen, what could have happened? It depends on whose hands the plague samples actually fell into. Let's say the samples ended up with a disgruntled employee or a mentally disturbed individual. To make a statement, the individual decides to throw the vials into the Lubbock County reservoir. Would this have made even one person in Lubbock County ill? Absolutely not.

To get plague into people where it can do harm, it must be injected or inhaled. Even if someone is aware of this fact, the difficulty of delivery is still a tremendous obstacle. For example, let's say that instead of tossing the vials in the reservoir, they smash the vials in an air-conditioning duct to release plague bacteria into the ventilation system of a local office building. Again, would this have made even one person ill? Possibly, but it's still very unlikely. In the first place, smashing the vials is unlikely to result in bacteria becoming aerosolized so that it can enter the system. Second, the standard filters in heating and air systems would likely screen out any bacteria that make it into the system.

This doesn't mean that we can routinely dismiss an incident where vials of plague go missing. The key is whether the person who gets his hands on the vials has the knowledge and equipment to effectively grow and distribute the organism. It is a difficult process, but unfortunately, it is not beyond the reach of a well-financed bioterrorist operation.

The lesson learned from New York, Houston, and Lubbock County is this: If you don't have a background context against which you can compare your data, then a positive finding of a known infectious agent can actually do more harm than good.

Perhaps there have always been a small number of instances where spores of anthrax or particles of tularemia have drifted from farmland or prairie into nearby towns or cities, causing serious disease. After all, we still don't know exactly where the most common community-acquired pneumonia organisms are acquired by patients. These patients just seem to show up in the emergency room with pneumococcal pneumonia (the single most common bacterial pneumonia) or staphylococcal skin infections that include the famous but somewhat sensationalized "flesh eating" bacteria. So, while we don't know for sure, it's certainly possible that some of the unexplained deaths that occur around the country are the result of pathogens that we have not been screening for until recently.

For example, the case of Ottilie Lundgren, the ninety-four-year-old Connecticut woman who was the nation's fifth fatality when the anthrax letters were being sent out, is still a mystery. To this day, it's still not clear if she was slain from a spore that came from the letters or if she inhaled it from her surrounding environment. Jumping to the conclusion that her death was related to the letter attacks is foolish without knowing what the natural level of anthrax spores were in her local environment.

Part of the reason that it's possible that the woman in Connecticut may have died from inhaling a naturally occurring spore of anthrax is the isolated nature of her case compared to the distribution of anthrax in the mail.

As the news media repeatedly told viewers, the relatively porous nature of paper fibers used in the manufacture of envelopes meant that as the anthrax-laden letters moved through the mail system, other envelopes could have become contaminated with anthrax spores. However, the anthrax letters certainly did come into contact with hundreds or thousands of letters sitting in the same mail bins. Given that we did not have multiple outbreaks of anthrax throughout the country, it's more likely that if the spores were released during the mechanical processes of mail sorting, they did not stick to additional envelopes and instead remained in the mail processing center, where they made additional postal employees sick.

The underlying lesson is that we still have difficulty agreeing on what a normal background count of an organism such as tularemia or anthrax really is. And that limits our ability to attach significance to any given finding of a pathogen. We have much to learn about "usual" infectious disease spread, let alone the novel situation of a bioterrorism attack.

ACTIVE AND PASSIVE SURVEILLANCE

In order to advance our knowledge about the spread of infectious disease among humans or animals (and sometimes between them), scientists have long tried to monitor the health of populations using various disease reporting systems. It comes as a surprise to most people that their physicians do not routinely report to local public health offices the diseases they see.

The vast majority of physicians have no electronic system for recording their own medical records, let alone automatically informing PHOs about the number or type of infectious diseases they see. Unfortunately, it is only rarely the case that physicians recognize an unusual disease and take the time to fill out the massive forms that public health officials demand. More time passes as the paper moves through the mail, sits on someone's desk, and is analyzed. Feedback to physicians can take weeks or months.

For many years, physicians, veterinarians, public health officials, and even political decision makers and government authorities tolerated this situation. After all, it appeared that infectious disease was on the wane and that other illnesses, such as heart disease, diabetes, and stroke, were much more pressing and the dominant concern of physicians. There's little urgency associated with monitoring what are believed to be "lifestyle diseases" that are thought to be noninfectious and noncommunicable from person to person.

But with the arrival of HIV/AIDS in the 1980s, those views began to change. And as the number of international travelers skyrocketed in the latter part of the twentieth century, a whole new set of diseases began to emerge that were previously unrecognized. The need for routine, accurate, real-time awareness of the incidence (i.e., percentage of people ill) with a given disease became more and more imperative.

The government of France was perhaps the first to realize that it could begin to gather data quickly and easily from physicians. In the 1970s, France installed the Minitel system. Minitel was a small computer that could display text on a screen. It connected to the existing telephone system and provided a low-speed but effective means of gathering all kinds of data (for example, what movies were playing at the local cinema) that people could tap into with a phone call via the Minitel box. Soon physicians began using Minitel to report cases of various diseases—measles, chickenpox, influenza—to regional and national public health authorities.

Despite its simplicity, Minitel-based disease surveillance was a gigantic step forward in the world of epidemiology, helping to dramatically increasing the understanding of how certain diseases were introduced into a community, how they spread, and how quickly they resolved. It suddenly became possible to alert physicians to be on the lookout for certain diseases, and even laypeople could determine if serious illness was occurring among the local schoolchildren. For many years, Minitel served as the "state of the art" in disease surveillance.

But Minitel had its limitations. First, the way doctors were using the system was by definition "disease based," meaning physicians had to diagnose a specific disease first before they could report it. So new diseases might be missed or misdiagnosed and reported incorrectly. Second, there were parts of France where Minitel was not available, thus the surveillance was not truly "population based" but rather based on where Minitel was installed. And finally, some physicians simply didn't have the time to deal with the slow, purely text-based data input screens.

The arrival of the Internet and the ubiquity of computers began to change thinking about disease surveillance. Instead of asking physicians or nurses to enter data, might it be possible to look at other data sources and infer the health of the population? For example, if we knew the rate of sales of antidiarrheal drugs from the local pharmacy, could we calculate the amount of gastrointestinal virus circulating in the community? This concept is known as data mining—utilizing easily available data streams (perhaps intended for other purposes such as inventory and product shipment) for health monitoring. Because no decision making or action is required of the physician, nurse, or veterinarian, this approach also is called "passive surveillance."

Active surveillance is the use of judgment based on experience among professionals in deciding whether to report data in the first place. While it runs the risk of perhaps dismissing what could turn out to be valuable data, that's not very likely to occur. When it comes to disease, doctors and their medical staff are very good at figuring out whether somebody is sick.

So while passive surveillance might show that cough medicine was selling out at local stores, it might be because there was a mild cold virus circulating around the community rather than a severe disease of public health importance that carries with it a high risk of death or need for hospitalization. Physicians or veterinarians, on the other hand, might not be able to tell what organism they were dealing with if they had a patient with high fever, cough, shortness of breath, and evidence of fluid in the lungs; however, they are very good at immediately recognizing that they have a seriously ill person on their hands.

In other words, medical professionals tend not to be very good at determining precisely what pathogen is afflicting you during the first visit, but they are extremely good at determining the *degree* to which you are ill. Standard tests, such as the chest X-ray, urinalysis, and white blood cell count, tell doctors how sick a patient is, regardless of how the person feels at the time. This kind of clinical data gathered in the doctor's office is far more likely to be of public health relevance than the passive data about sales of drugstore products. Active surveillance depends on health care professionals of all stripes making a judgment and separating the wheat from the chaff.

By contrast, passive surveillance is the act of continuously looking through (i.e., "mining") information that is collected for signs and portents of trouble. The advantage of passive surveillance is the enormity of data streams available. Monitoring the raw number of calls placed to a health hotline is one example of how you can mine data passively. Calls to a hotline indicate the health of the population at some level. For example, if there are no calls to the health hotline run by an HMO that covers a city of 100,000 people, it's very unlikely that a substantial number of people are sick. Passive data tends to be nonspecific but easy to get; active surveillance data, which requires the judgment of a professional as to whether or not to report it, is much more specific (and thus more valuable), but perhaps harder to obtain.

It's an easy task to subdivide the data into more specific forms because hotlines can focus on different health issues, such as stomach ache versus cough versus skin rash, then further subdivide the data based on the age of the population or whether an individual has a chronic disease, such as an elderly person with diabetes. Depending on the quality of the nurses who staff the hotline, a great deal of information can, in theory, be gathered at the ground level.

Most hotlines have a protocol where they ask for information to determine over the phone whether you should see a physician. If you're dealing with an HMO, then the criteria that the nurse will use for screening to make a recommendation about whether you should see a doctor will be very stringent indeed (since HMOs want to limit the number of visits to a hospital). The line of questioning often runs along these lines: "How bad is your pain on a scale of one to ten, where ten is beating yourself on the head with a hammer? Only a seven? Well, call us back when it reaches an eight."

The main health indicator will be the raw number of calls. During flu season, you could expect the number of calls to a hotline to increase, but does it really tell public health officials anything they don't already know? Probably not. You could argue that if you did very fine measurements of the statistics, perhaps breaking the calls down by time of day, you might end up with a more selective measure of the health of the population. However, to date, no one has proved that additional selectivity improves the data in any way. Thus, while one can gather *more* data, it's not yet clear that leads to better *knowledge* about the health of the population.

The main problem with passive data mining is that it is easy to confuse correlation with causality. Just because event A takes place and then later that day event B takes place, that does not mean that event A caused event B. People frequently jump to conclusions of causality without reason to do so.

As noted previously, another area of data that can be mined passively is pharmaceutical sales. Pharmaceutical sales come in two types: prescription and over-the-counter. The Milwaukee cryptosporidiosis outbreak in 1993, which sickened more than 400,000 people and contributed to the deaths of more than a hundred, wasn't detected at first by the local public health department. Health officials only became suspicious that something odd was going on when pharmacists all over the city ran out of over-the-counter antidiarrheal medicine.

The local pharmacists, of course, thought their record sales of Lomotil were very unusual and called the public health department. That's when the public health department was alerted that there were significant levels of diarrheal disease in the community. Not because physicians called in a week earlier when the diarrhea started. Not because hospitals reported an increase in cases. It was because pharmacists ran out of Lomotil and other antidiarrheal drugs several weeks into the outbreak.

By the time the public health department received the tip from the pharmacists, the outbreak was well into its natural course and there was nothing the public health department could do to really halt this particular outbreak, beyond treating people who had already become symptomatic. The public health department was able to identify the source of the outbreak and stop future incidence, but in terms of preventing the damage from this particular outbreak, it did virtually nothing.

There may be other problems in using pharmacy sales data. Pharmacy chains generally do not like to release information about their sales. Among other things, reporting sales would make public information that their competitors could potentially use. In addition, there is a problem with the timeliness of the data.

Typically, the first place that people look for medicine is in their bathroom medicine cabinet. Usually, they only go out to the pharmacy when they've run out of the over-the-counter medication they keep on hand. Additionally, it takes some time for a well-stocked pharmacy to completely run out of a given drug.

For example, during the cryptosporidiosis outbreak, the people afflicted with the disease probably first attempted to cure themselves with the three or four tablets of Lomotil they had in the medicine cabinet from last year's camping trip. It might have been twelve to twenty-four hours before they ran out of pills. Then everyone might have gone down to the neighborhood drugstore to purchase more medication. Another twenty-four to forty-eight hours might have elapsed before the local stock of Lomotil was exhausted and the pharmacy reported to its corporate headquarters that more medicine needed to be shipped. In a case where hours matter, and days prove too late to make any difference in stopping an outbreak, this data is extremely limited in value.

Perhaps the amount of Lomotil sold could correlate with the presence of diarrhea in the population, but it could also correlate with whether the item is on clearance sale at the pharmacy that week. In mathematical terms, pharmaceutical sales are a signal with a lot of statistical "noise." Just as random static can block out the signal of the radio station you want to hear, statistical noise, or data that is not relevant to the relationship you're trying to establish, can prevent you from reaching the correct result. Formal experiments in a laboratory normally require several steps in order to reduce this noise. Applying the same expectation of low statistical noise to data gathered in the real world is more than a little unrealistic.

Two additional, commonly identified indicators of population health one might want to consider are employee or school absenteeism rates. In general, employee absenteeism is of limited value. Absenteeism can occur because of disease, but there are many more reasons that adults may choose not to show up at work on a given day. Excessive use of alcohol on the weekend, for example, is likely to blame for the statistical fact that the vast majority of employee sick days are taken on Mondays.

On the other hand, parents don't like to keep their children home from school unless they are extremely sick. A good school nurse not only keeps a record of the total number of absentees per day, but will call a subset of the homes where students are sick to find out what is going on. School nurse data is especially valuable because there is some professional judgment already involved in the process, which to date has largely been ignored. The nurse's reports are written down on paper and typically filed away until the annual report comes out. Yet even the daily report can be a valuable tool in spotting the early stages of a deadly outbreak.

And so we have seen that many professionals—pharmacists, school nurses, physicians, and many others—come in contact with patients (be they human or animal patients), and their observations and data are carefully recorded on paper and then shared with no one, with the possible exception of other people in the offices in which they work. Were we able to bring all of this valuable information together with minimal effort and in near real-time, it would likely be possible to draw conclusions about the early stages of disease outbreaks and act well before a small outbreak turned into an epidemic. In short, for public health to best serve the population at large, we must turn data into actionable knowledge. We illustrate ways of doing just that in the next chapter.

NOTES

1. In January 2005 at the annual World Economic Forum in Davos, Switzerland, U.S. Senate Majority Leader and physician Dr. Bill Frist, commenting on the subject of biowarfare, said, "We need to do something that even dwarfs the Manhattan Project," referring to the U.S. effort to build an atomic weapon during World War II. "The greatest existential threat we have in the world today is biological," Frist said. "Why? Because unlike any other threat it has the power of panic and paralysis to be global."

2. The syndrome surveillance system used by the City of Lubbock Health Department was called the Rapid Syndrome Validation Program (RSVP), and it was developed by one of the authors, Alan Zelicoff, when he was employed by Sandia National Laboratories. RSVP is no longer in use, but the results from its testing and from other, similar systems led to the redesign of a new system called the Syndrome Reporting Information System (SYRIS). SYRIS has now replaced RSVP in Lubbock and is in operation in other public health jurisdictions as well.

CHAPTER 13

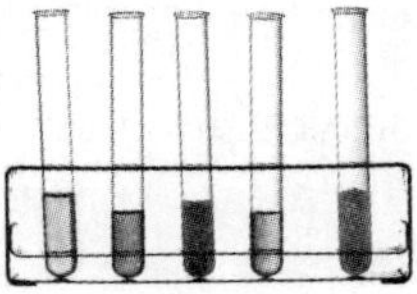

A NEW WEAPON IN THE FIGHT

Since early 1999, the City of Lubbock Department of Health (DOH) in Texas has evaluated several syndrome-based disease surveillance systems. A "syndrome" is not a diagnosis, of course, but rather a concise description of the symptoms (i.e., what the patient complains of when visiting the doctor) and signs (i.e., what the doctor finds on examination). The very thoughtful people at the City of Lubbock DOH hypothesized that by using syndrome-based surveillance instead of the traditional disease-based systems, they could cost-effectively address the major responsibilities of public health departments that have been laid out by the Centers for Disease Control and Prevention (CDC). Those responsibilities include:

- Preventing epidemics and the spread of disease
- Protecting against environmental hazards
- Preventing injuries
- Promoting and encouraging healthy behaviors and mental health
- Responding to disasters and assisting communities in recovery
- Ensuring the quality and accessibility of health services

In theory, a syndrome-based disease surveillance system (SBDSS), by virtue of its timely reporting capabilities and volume of information flows, could assist in meeting these central public health responsibilities. In practice, however, the underlying technical features, scientific approach, and ease-of-use design of each SBDSS is dramatically different across the dozens of systems currently in existence. Some of these systems have been implemented only in narrowly defined demographic settings or have other limiting features. In short, the promise is often not met in real-world use.

Every SBDSS falls into one of two basic categories:

1. Automated or "passive" surveillance systems seek to exploit existing data streams and employ various statistical algorithms to detect the presence of infectious disease. Some of the data sources that are tapped by these passive systems include:
   - Pharmacy sales (including over-the-counter medications)
   - Total volume of nurse "hotline" calls
   - Brief "chief complaint" summaries from emergency room logs
   - School and work absenteeism rates

2. Active or "clinical" surveillance system depend on *selected* reporting from physicians, veterinarians, emergency medical services (EMS), and other health care providers, based on the provider's *clinical judgment* when assessing severity of illness among patients, which can be either animal or human.

It is also important to note that the overwhelming majority of SBDSS data-gathering systems focus solely on human patients—despite the fact that in all significant outbreaks of novel diseases over the past decade or more in North America, animals were the primary source of the diseases. Each of the following disease outbreaks among humans was very large or economically significant; in the end, each disease had an animal source:

- Hantavirus pulmonary syndrome in the Four Corners region of New Mexico (1993)
- West Nile fever (1999–2000)
- Human plague in New York City in visitors from New Mexico (2001)
- Cryptosporidiosis in Milwaukee (1993) in which 400,000 people were sickened
- Monkeypox in the Midwest (2003)
- SARS (2003)
- H5N1 avian influenza in humans (1997, 1999, 2005)

Furthermore, all of the CDC's "highest risk" bioterrorism diseases, with the sole exception of smallpox, are animal diseases (sometimes also called zoonotic diseases). Thus, it is highly likely that if a large-scale bioterrorism event were ever to occur, animals will almost certainly become ill in large numbers and probably with classical syndromes recognized easily by the veterinary community.

Because public health offices are charged with wide-ranging responsibilities yet are relatively underfunded, the City of Lubbock DOH began to explore means of leveraging limited resources. The four people who constitute the entirety of Lubbock's infectious disease section began utilizing electronic SBDSS in 1999. Although these systems were advertised as easy to implement and low cost, the DOH personnel found that all of the "automated" SBDSS systems they evaluated were problematic in at least four areas:

- The vast majority of cases reported from hospitals and emergency rooms—based on chief complaints, billing codes, or simple census information—resulted in a very large amount of "noise" (i.e., data that was of no utility). The possible need to respond to "spikes" that were merely manifestations of statistical randomness created a serious liability.
- Pharmacy-sales data was inherently delayed or complicated by items being "on sale" at large pharmacy chains.
- Information is almost always reported in tabular or textual format without mapping tools for analysis.
- In all cases, since the historical background was largely unknown for any of the data streams, comparisons to identify "true positive" deviations from normal was impossible.

RSVP

At the same time as the personnel at the Lubbock DOH were reviewing the automated disease-surveillance systems that were proliferating across the United States, they identified one clinician-based or active SBDSS called the Rapid Syndrome Validation Program (RSVP). Developed by Alan Zelicoff, M.D. (then at Sandia National Laboratories and one of the authors of this book), RSVP[2] defined six common syndromes worded in the daily parlance of medicine and public health. It further provided an electronic interface that operated on virtually any computer connected to the Internet, as well as primitive but useful geographic information system (GIS) mapping tools.

Key to the RSVP design philosophy was the central notion of "clinical judgment," in which participating physicians—some 10 percent of all of the practicing physicians in Lubbock, for example—were asked to report those individuals seen in emergency rooms, clinics, and private offices where the patient was assessed as seriously ill and who fit into one of six syndromes strongly suggestive of infectious disease of public health importance:

- Fever with influenza-like illness
- Fever with skin rash
- Fever with mental status change or neurological change
- Severe diarrhea
- Hepatitis (presumed to be nonalcohol and nondrug related)
- Adult respiratory distress syndrome

Only fifteen to thirty *seconds* of a physician's time is required for reporting a case over the Internet, and all new reports are immediately reflected on maps of the local public health jurisdiction, where the data could then be further analyzed using GIS tools. RSVP's "front page" screen also allowed Lubbock public health officials to send out alerts instantaneously to physicians.

The experience with RSVP was almost uniformly positive. Physician compliance was high, contrary to the popular but incorrect belief that physicians will not take time to enter cases. The number of cases of seriously ill patients who fit into one of the syndrome categories was, on average, a case per month per physician except during large epidemics.

Furthermore, RSVP provided information of immediate clinical importance to physicians, thus increasing their cost-effectiveness in practice. Finally, on rare occasions, RSVP enabled public health officials to contact doctors within minutes of a case report when the data suggested unusually worrisome symptoms that might require immediate contact investigation. Thus, RSVP reduced the time to initiate contact investigation from days to mere minutes.

But there were criticisms of RSVP as well:

- Because it was a Web browser–based system, some operating systems would not fully accommodate the RSVP code, so some of its features were inaccessible for certain users.
- Mapping functionality, while useful, was slow and cumbersome.
- There was no ability to report key veterinary syndromes that would often presage human disease.
- Statistical analysis via RSVP was somewhat difficult because of the nature of the database where all information was stored.

- It was unclear to the developers whether RSVP complied with the National Electronic Disease Surveillance System (NEDSS) architecture described by the CDC.[3]

Despite these criticisms, the City of Lubbock had two very important public health successes with RSVP. First, the Lubbock DOH was able to manage the threat of a plague bioterrorism event in January 2002, when a local professor called the FBI to report that strains of his collection of plague organisms were stolen from his laboratory at Texas Tech University medical school during the Christmas vacation.

By monitoring respiratory disease cases on a minute-by-minute basis and providing diagnostic information via RSVP to clinicians, the Lubbock public health department prevented the near panic that occurred in New York City that same year, when small amounts of anthrax were found in air-sampling devices in Manhattan. There were no unnecessary diagnostic tests; no wasting of public health resources. Using clinician-based syndrome surveillance it was possible for the public health officials in Lubbock to predict that they were dealing with a false alarm—exactly as turned out to be the case.

Their second success was in early 2003 when they discovered, based on clinical symptoms, the need for earlier-than-usual testing for influenza. As a result, the Lubbock DOH found influenza cases in the local community approximately three weeks earlier than would otherwise have been possible, probably mitigating much morbidity in the population.

THE SYNDROME REPORTING INFORMATION SYSTEM

RSVP was a useful and highly successful "alpha" product, but it is no longer in existence. Lubbock DOH officials are currently employing a SBDSS from ARES Corporation called SYRIS—Syndrome Reporting Information System. Distinct from RSVP and all of the passive SBDSS in the marketplace, SYRIS addresses all of the critiques of past systems and offers the following improvements:

1. It is platform-independent and does not require a Web browser. Thus, it will run on virtually any Internet-connected device, including many handheld devices.

2. SYRIS is comprehensive and allows input from *all* critical health care providers, including:
   - Physicians, physician-assistants, and nurse practitioners

- School nurses (who report absenteeism and commentary)
- EMS professionals (reporting transport cases by syndrome)
- Veterinarians, who monitor nine separate syndromes covering all major domestic, agricultural, and exotic animal species
- Coroners/Offices of the Medical Investigator (who have a list of syndromes based solely on information from unexpected death reports)
- Laboratory technicians, who can report all lab tests for infectious agents in less than one minute per week
- Animal control and environmental health officials, who report on captured stray animals or wildlife and the number requiring euthanasia due to severe illness
- Wildlife rehabilitators

3. The enhanced mapping features provide for near-instantaneous map updating and queries to any region where SYRIS is in use.

4. SYRIS is in full compliance with all CDC requirements for electronic reporting systems:
   - It permits extremely rapid data entry; it takes less than fifteen seconds for physicians and veterinarians to input data.
   - It generates automated and manual alarms. Public health officials (PHOs) can be notified by digital paging and e-mail when cases that meet specifically defined criteria—at the discretion of local PHOs—are met.
   - It does easy statistical analysis of all current and historical SYRIS data.
   - It requires minimal training. SYRIS is intuitive to use, and a full manual is available online; documentation is tailored to each of the eight user communities defined previously.
   - It is a low-cost solution, costing approximately $0.07 to $0.08 per capita. So, for example, in the Lubbock area of approximately 250,000 people, SYRIS will cost in the range of $18,000.

It appears that SYRIS will solve the vast majority of our disease surveillance and response needs, including emergency response in the case of bioterrorism, with a *low* false alarm rate. It can do this while maintaining an exquisite sensitivity to identify unusual cases quickly and bring them to the attention of public health officials and, if necessary, government decision makers or even law enforcement. This kind of real-time responsiveness is absolutely required to minimize the impact of a new infectious disease. It will also prevent overreactions to disease outbreaks that are either minor or do not spread quickly through the population. The costs of "too much" response can be as great as failing to detect a major epidemic early in its course.

FROM THE SPEED OF MAIL TO THE SPEED OF LIGHT

Let's take a quick look at how SYRIS would work in a case study. For example, say that a thirty-year-old male from Albuquerque, New Mexico, comes into the office of Dr. Lynn with a serious cough, body aches, high fever, and a sore throat, but without a runny nose or inflammation of the eyes. The patient is in above-average shape, since he's an avid runner and hiker, so it's rather puzzling that he appears so ill. Flu season is long past, but the patient has just returned from a ten-day backpacking trip in the nearby mountains. He was careful to drink only boiled water and has no gastrointestinal complaints.

Upon examination, the lymph nodes are visibly swollen in his neck, and there's scattered wheezing in the chest and moderate enlargement of the spleen. A blood test shows a strangely low platelet count, but the test comes back otherwise unremarkable. The chest X-ray comes back normal. The physician judges that this patient is acutely and at least moderately ill.

Dr. Lynn is concerned about the swollen lymph nodes and low platelet count, but she does not yet have enough information to make a diagnosis. Instead of waiting an extra thirty-six to forty-eight hours, she decides that the severity—and more important, the strange novelty of the case (the physician has never seen anything like it)—warrants entry into SYRIS.

Upon logging into the system (see Figure 13-1), immediately Dr. Lynn sees from the map that a variety of human (solid colors) and animal (striped color) "syndromes" have been reported in the past thirty days in the Albuquerque area. Equally important, she reads on the right-hand side of the screen that even though influenza has been reported in the area (as expected because it happens to be winter-time when this report is made), there is much *less* influenza activity than usual. This kind of information is what physicians call pertinent *negative* data—that is, knowing what *isn't* happening can often be as useful as the positive knowledge of what is happening. The fact that this healthy man has an influenza-like illness in the background of a relatively limited number of influenza like cases encourages Dr. Lynn to report even more: Perhaps she is seeing something other than influenza that may be of public health significance.

Entering the data is quick (taking fifteen seconds) and requires clicking on a few buttons (see Figure 13-2) that identify the location of the individ-

FIGURE 13-1

SYRIS log-in screen.

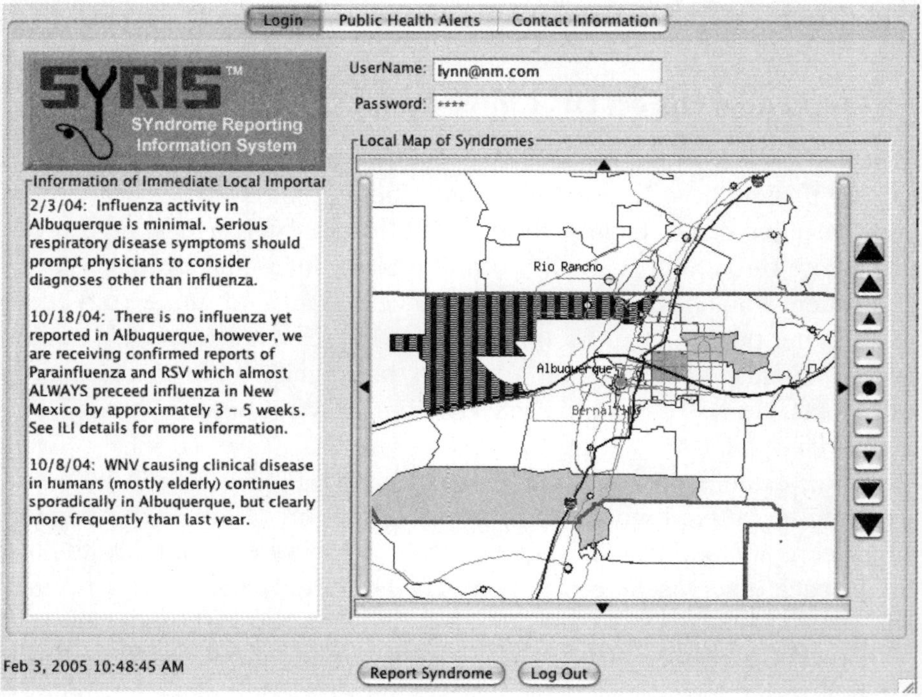

ual, confirm that he has recently traveled in the United States, and describe that he appears to have an influenza-like illness (which may, of course, not be influenza at all).

Dr. Lynn enters a few more details by clicking on the "Syndrome Information" button and gets an information screen that, in this case, is specific for the "influenza-like illness" syndrome that Dr. Lynn has picked (see Figure 13-3).

After clicking on "Submit Report," the physician (and anyone else who happens to be checking SYRIS) sees that the map has been updated, along with graphs that show the number of cases of influenza-like illness reported in the past thirty days. This updated report, shown in Figure 13-4, is generated in less than ten seconds.

On the left-hand side, Dr. Lynn can see that there have been very few cases of influenza reported (under the "Raw report count"), which she expected from first reading the front page of SYRIS. She also notes (under "Lab data") that very few lab tests on samples submitted from doctors offices have shown any evidence of influenza (the individual organisms re-

FIGURE 13-2

Screen for inputting patient information.

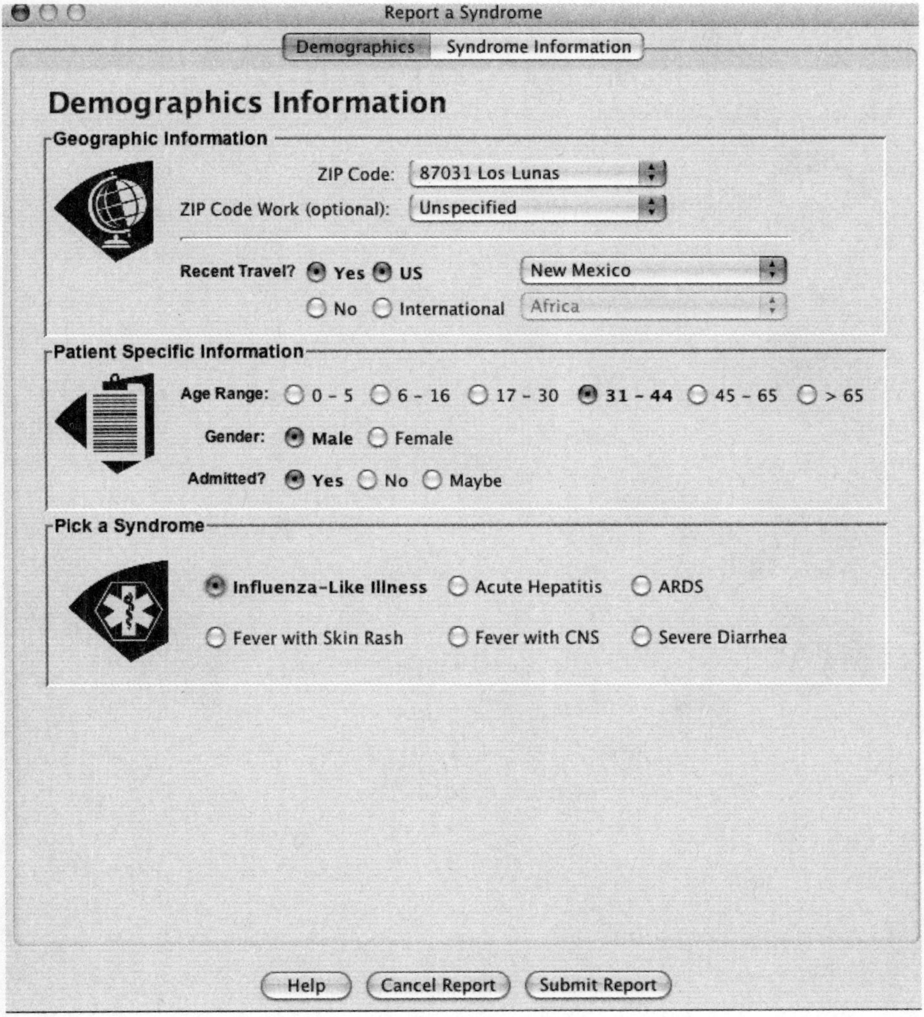

ported by the lab at any time can be identified simply by placing the computer mouse over the colors on the bar graph). In addition, the ZIP code of the mountain area where the patient was hiking is highlighted now in blue at the lower portion of the map.

It turns out that public health officials were on the alert for plague in New Mexico because it had been a very wet fall and winter, creating the appropriate environmental conditions for a dramatic increase in the ground squirrel and prairie dog population in the state—the perfect setting for more fleas to proliferate and carry the plague organism.

FIGURE 13-3

Screen for inputting details for influenza-like illness.

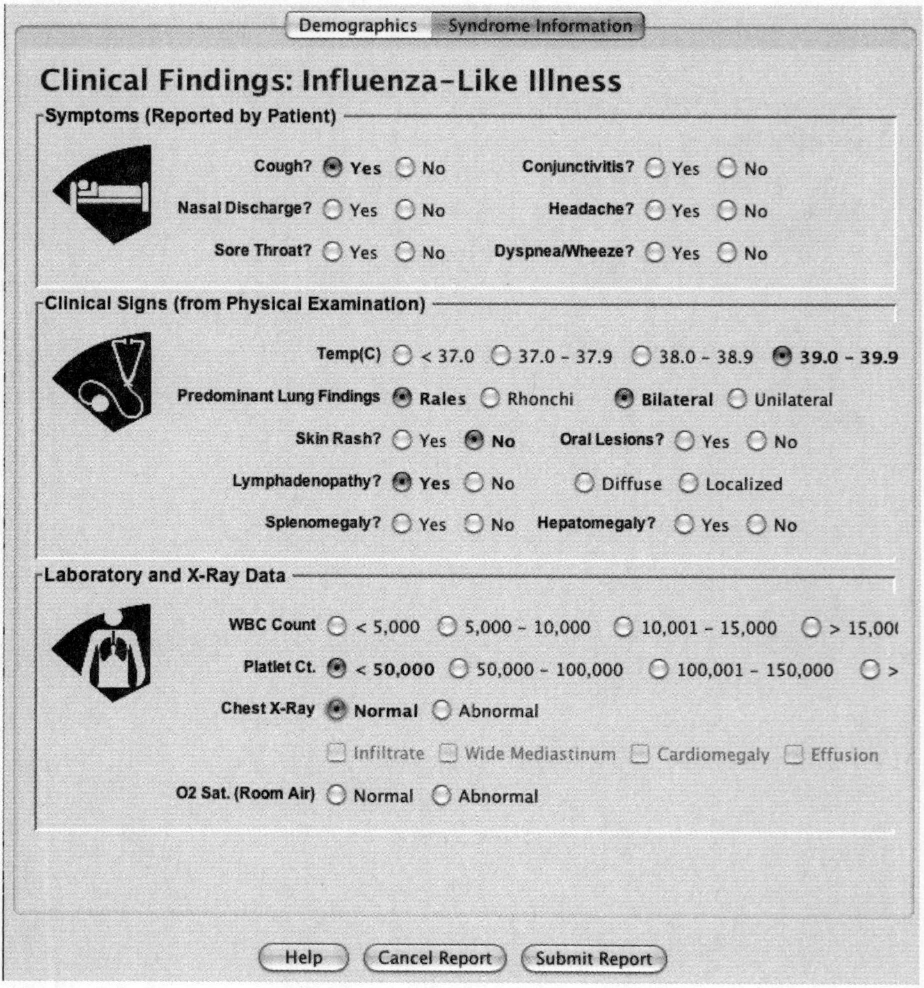

Unbeknownst to Dr. Lynn, a local public health official had used SYRIS to set an "alarm" feature such that any human or veterinary case that involved swollen lymph nodes and fever would result in SYRIS sending an instantaneous e-mail and digital page to the local public health official on call. (There is a local PHO on call virtually everywhere in the United States at all times.) Thus, the following information shows up on the digital pager of PHO Dr. Simpson:

*** SYRIS ALERT ***
Physician: Dr. Lynn

FIGURE 13-4

Updated map showing the number of cases of influenza-like illness reported.

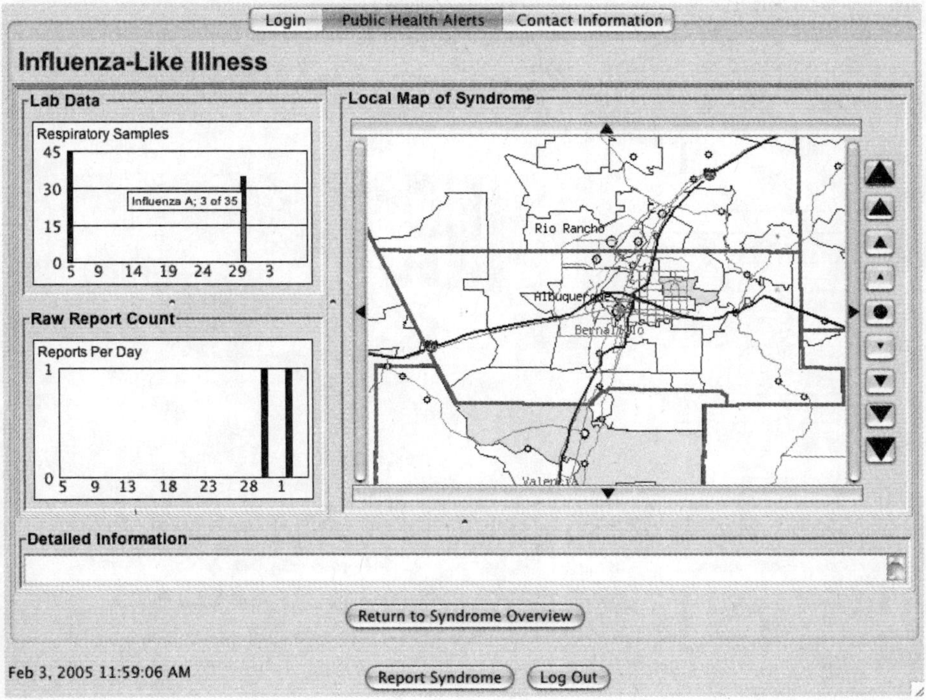

Clinic: University of New Mexico outpatient Urgent care center
Phone: 505-555-1111
Syndrome: Flu Like Illness
Symptoms and Signs: Lymphadenopathy
Recent travel in North America

Dr. Simpson logs into SYRIS as a public health official and notices the case that Dr. Lynn has just reported *and* an almost simultaneous animal syndrome report in the same general area as the human patient (see Figure 13-5).

Dr. Simpson decides to use the mapping features of SYRIS to look at two specific syndromes only, lymphadenopathy in animals and influenza-like illness in humans, by turning off all of the syndromes except the those two. This is accomplished with a few computer clicks in less than ten seconds; the new report that is generated in shown in Figure 13-6.

The "striped" area in light green indicates reports of veterinary lymphadenopathy, which is a strong indicator of plague and a few other diseases. The area is right next to the area where the human patient was hiking.

FIGURE 13-5

Map of influenza-like illness alongside animal syndrome report.

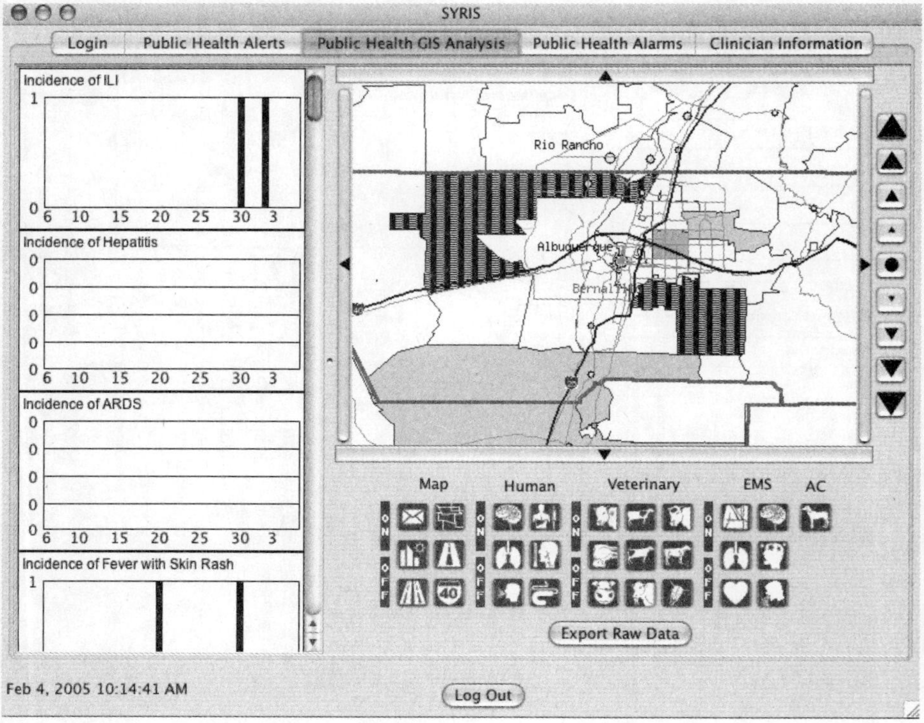

Furthermore, by looking at the graph on the left-hand side of the screen, Dr. Simpson notes that there have been five cases of animals with swollen lymph nodes reported in just the past few days.

Using SYRIS statistical tools, Dr. Simpson is able to determine that it is very likely that the human and animal cases are related. Since there are few diseases that cause lymphadenopathy in both humans and animals, *and* since swollen lymph nodes in domestic cats (which turn out to be the species reported by the veterinarians, according to a quick look into the raw data in the SYRIS database) are almost *always* due to plague, Dr. Simpson is able to make a presumptive diagnosis of plague based on this information alone.

Dr. Simpson then calls Dr. Lynn and advises that her patient probably has plague. The patient is hospitalized and antibiotics are begun immediately while laboratory tests are conducted. Three days later, blood cultures confirm the diagnosis of plague. By now the human and animal patients are recovering; without the early information generated by SYRIS, the human patient might well have died before the diagnosis was made.

FIGURE 13-6

Map of veterinary lymphadenopathy reported cases.

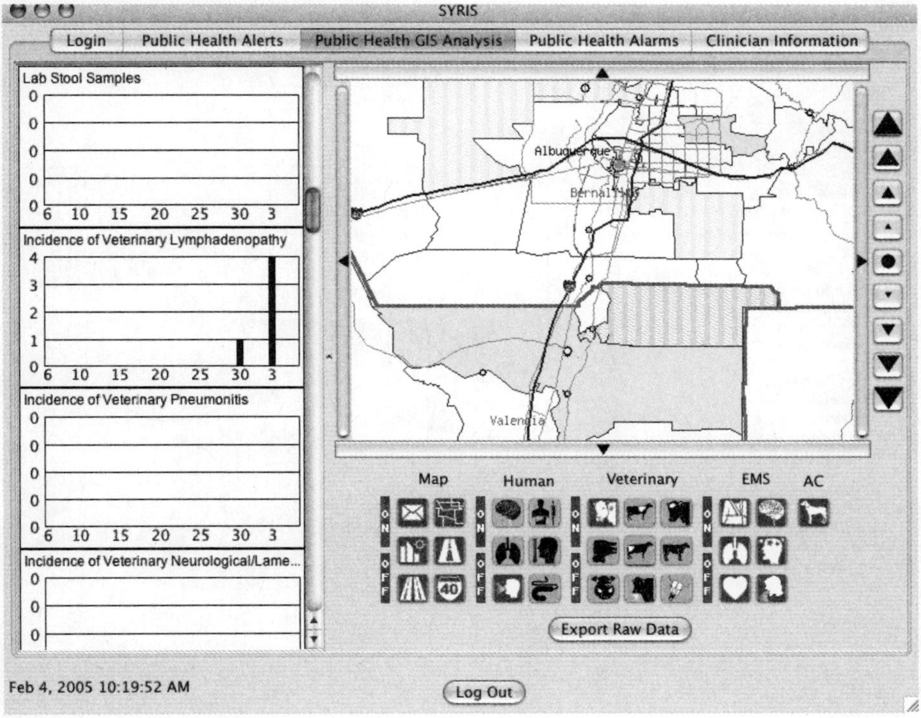

As a final action, Dr Simpson updates the front page of SYRIS (see Figure 13-7).

SUMMARY: BRINGING IT ALL TOGETHER

SYRIS is the first generation of a working syndrome-based disease reporting system that unifies the observations and reports of all of the professional communities that deal directly with human or animal health. By making information available in real-time and by "screening" that information through the professional judgment of clinicians, EMS officials, and others, public health officials can make presumptive diagnoses of unusually dangerous or novel diseases—or at least they can dramatically narrow down the possibilities and communicate them quickly to all health care providers.

In most infectious diseases of public health importance to animals or humans, hours matter. Waiting days to detect and classify an outbreak is

FIGURE 13-7

Updated SYRIS front page noting information of immediate local importance.

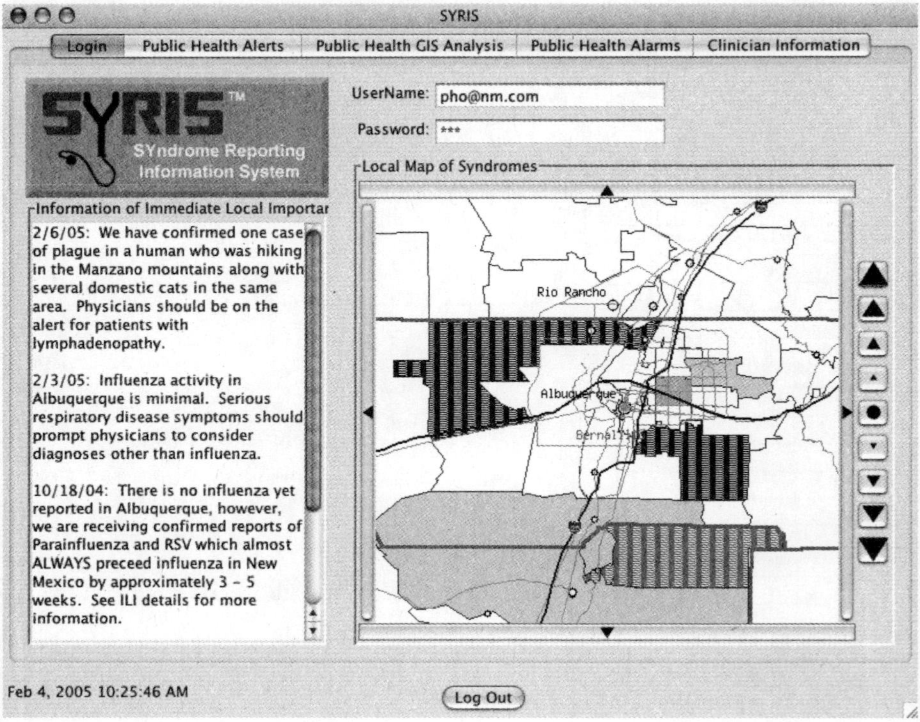

almost worthless if the goal is to intervene and limit the spread of an epidemic. As the scenario described in this chapter illustrates, rapidly exchanging information can be critical for saving the life of an individual or an entire community.

However, in addition to *speed* of communication, one must also have *accuracy*. That means the ability to find the "needle in a haystack," especially since the vast majority of humans (or animals) with, for example, a respiratory illness, are of little or no concern to public health officials. Only by combining the observations of clinical professionals—veterinarians, doctors, school nurses, physician-assistants, nurse practitioners, and environmental health experts—is it possible to avoid "false positive" alerts while at the same time maintaining sufficient awareness and sensitivity to prevent a small outbreak from becoming a massive epidemic. As of this writing, SYRIS is the only commercially available, fully tested tool that meets these exacting, life-saving requirements.

NOTES

1. Dena M. Bravata, M.D., et al. "Systematic Review: Surveillance Systems for Early Detection of Bioterrorism-Related Diseases," *Annals of Internal Medicine* Vol. 140 (June 2004), pp. 910–922.
2. A. Zelicoff, et al. *The Rapid Syndrome Validation Project (RSVP)* (Albuquerque, NM: Sandia National Laboratories, 2001).
3. The National Electronic Disease Surveillance System (NEDSS) project is a public health initiative to provide a set of guidelines for a standards-based, integrated approach to disease surveillance and to connect public health surveillance to information gathered in clinical laboratories and, eventually, clinicians' offices as well. NEDSS is *not* a reporting system per se, but rather an architecture description promulgated by the Centers for Disease Control. See http://www.cdc.gov/nedss/Archive/Stakeholder2/Appendix_B_CSTE_Guidance_Document.pdf

CHAPTER 14

DNA-BASED VACCINES

Here's how a major new influenza pandemic might unfold. Let's imagine that a wild duck on a migratory path in China passes a strain of influenza to farm chickens via the fecal-to-oral route. The ducks may land in ponds or near chickens being raised for food, defecate, and release new strains of avian influenza. The new strain enters the local environment, where previously existing strains of influenza are still being exchanged among the dense population of chickens (thousands of birds can often be found in one large egg-production operation). On these same rural farms, the chickens may be in close proximity to pigs and transmit the virus—or almost as likely, multiple viruses—to the pigs.

The pigs in turn serve as a reservoir for the viruses—literally becoming a culture medium where the multiple strains of the virus can mix their RNA with one another. Within the tens or hundreds of thousands of recombinations that take place, it takes only one or two to emerge that appear to be infectious for humans. The strains may be similar to ones that emerged only a few years ago.

Why do epidemiologists single out China when other places around the world, such as India, also have extremely high population densities? The reason is that high population density in and of itself is not enough to generate or sustain the development of new strains of influenza. China is one place in the world where humans, birds, and pigs come into close contact with each other on a more or less continuous basis and where duck migratory "overflies" are routine and well established.

This phenomenon is less likely to occur in India, since pigs are not raised en masse because of the different climate zone and cultural and religious mores. Pork is generally not part of the Indian diet. Thus, there are not a lot of pigs per person in India. But there are many pigs per capita in some Southeast Asia countries.

So, perhaps by summertime, the CDC and the World Health Organization decide which influenza strains are likely to be the ones that will emerge from China. Epidemiologists and researchers then isolate the new virus directly from human beings who have contracted this new species-jumping strain; they also carefully study every influenza virus they can isolate from pigs attempting to infect human cells in the laboratory. If the human cells take up the virus and die, officials may consider manufacturing a vaccine based on this virus, especially if there have been human cases suspected or confirmed as being caused by it.

This scenario, of course, is eminently logical. The viruses that have jumped into the human being are somehow able to bind to human cells lining the respiratory tract (from nose to lung), infect those cells by getting through the cell membrane, and multiply within the human cell (often killing it in the process). In addition, the viruses may be able to spread from one human to another. Now that scientists have identified the strains of flu that the vaccine needs to combat, they need to create the vaccines.

VIRUS SEEDS AND CHICKEN EGGS

Broadly speaking, there are three ways that vaccines are typically created. The first method, used most commonly when creating flu vaccines, begins when the researchers isolate the new strain by taking a sample of the patient's saliva or nasal discharge. The sample is then grown by placing it in a test tube or a petri dish, a process that is also known as "plating out" the sample. The mixture is impregnated with certain human cells (sometimes respiratory cells, sometimes skin "fibroblast" cells) that are exceptionally vulnerable to infection by the influenza virus.

Once placed in this mixture, the influenza virus performs its microscopic biosurgery on the cell, inserting its DNA into the cell's genetic blueprint and effectively hijacking it until it ruptures. In an astonishingly short amount of time, the mixture will have changed from a culture of human cells into a slurry of virus particles and a slimy residue of dead organic matter. This is called the virus's "seed culture." Given its artificially high concentration of pathogenic material, it is what virologists would call *radiantly hot,* and therefore extremely dangerous.

The seed culture is examined to ensure that it is reasonably pure. *Purity* refers to whether the mixture contains a single strain of virus particles, though it may seem an alien term when talking about enough virus or bacteria to make a city the size of Chicago sick. Scientists need to ensure that the seed culture isn't co-infected with additional types of virus or contaminated with bacteria or fungus. Furthermore, if there are multiple strains of virus, there is some concern that pieces of the viruses—even though incapable of causing disease—might overwhelm the immune system's ability to process all of the different types of "foreign" material, resulting in no response at all.[1]

Next, the mixture is exposed to high-frequency ultrasound, a process known as *sonication.* If you've ever taken your glasses or jewelry to be cleaned, you may be familiar with this process. High-frequency ultrasound is exceptionally effective at cleaning certain items by transmitting vibrations through a sound medium such as water or polishing fluid. As it happens, high-frequency ultrasound is also extremely good at breaking up cells.

Further separation in the mixture is achieved by placing it in a centrifuge, a machine that spins tubes of the slurry at very high speed, causing the heavy cells to accumulate at the bottom of the tube. Since the cells are much heavier than the virus particles, the centrifuge is extremely useful in separating out the two substances. When the lighter, more buoyant viral particles are removed from the centrifuge, at the top will be a fine, clear liquid that looks like white wine. It is an almost pure sample of billions or trillions of virus particles.

This liquid is skimmed off, much like skimming fat off of the top of a soup. It is then injected into literally tens of thousands of chicken eggs. Why chicken eggs? Because they're cheap and readily available. The virus then amplifies at great speed inside the eggs, killing the embryo inside and converting its cellular matter into even more virus particles. Toward the end of the process, what started out as a tiny seed culture has become literally pounds and pounds of virus. But there are at least two problems with this simple-sounding approach: On occasion the virus is so lethal to the cells in chicken eggs that it literally kills the cells before much new virus is produced. And it usually takes months to produce sufficient virus for a nationwide vaccine supply.

The vaccination "cookbook" can vary a bit at this point, depending on the technique used and the pathogen grown. Generally speaking, a chemical procedure is performed that strips two surface proteins, known as antigens, off of the virus's surface. These two proteins are simply long chains of amino acids. Though they are not the virus, they are unequivocally required for the virus to bind to specific receptors on human cells and eventually enter the cells.

An antigen is, by definition, anything that stimulates an immune response, usually resulting in the vaccine recipient's production of antibodies that will fight the virus. We think of the body as sensing a virus and then employing the immune system to fight it; however, the immune system is actually responding to these antigens on the surface of the virus. Antigens don't carry the disease, but if you can expose someone to the antigens, the body's immune response will defend itself against the disease. And, as a result, the patient is vaccinated.

One of these proteins is called neuramidase, and the other is called hemagglutinin. The hemagglutinin protein is so called because in the test tube environment, it makes red blood cells clump and stick together, a phenomenon first observed many years ago. Current research indicates that both of these proteins play a role in helping a virus to bind itself to human cells, allowing it to unload its deadly genetic cargo.

Once the chemical procedure is complete, the researchers now have pounds of these two proteins. They refine this mixture further to remove any additional proteins that might have found their way into the mix. They particularly try to remove the egg albumin, since some people are allergic to eggs. After these multiple procedures of concentration and refinement, the remaining proteins are finally freeze-dried.

The same procedure is followed for at least two more strains of influenza. The same chemical process is used to strip them of the same two proteins. The multiple samples of these proteins are then placed together in glass bottles for shipment to whichever vaccination center needs them. These freeze-dried mixtures of protein particles, which can be safely shipped worldwide and remain viable, are used in the flu shots that are offered each and every year.

Given how involved the process is, it can take up to six months—sometimes even longer—to go from identification of this year's predominant flu strains to production of the vaccination material and delivery to the doctor's shelf. And every now and then, the experts guess wrong, leading to an unfortunate loss of life among those most vulnerable to the flu virus.

The creation of the yearly influenza vaccine is a very time-consuming and involved process. It's labor-intensive, requires a great deal of capital, and is extremely vulnerable to contamination, to boot. Indeed, a large percentage of the vaccination lots produced in Europe in 2004 were contaminated with other organisms because the chicken egg is a very rich "growth medium" containing just about everything that other viruses or bacteria need to multiply, just like the influenza virus itself. Because of this cost, it's often asked why the yearly flu shot does not simply contain the vaccines for every single identified strain of influenza so that we have solved the influenza problem once and for all.

Unfortunately, the solution isn't that simple. As noted earlier, when multiple flu proteins are mixed in a vaccine, they can actually interfere with each other—in effect canceling each other out, without triggering a vigorous response from the human immune system. Whether or not that interference occurs is a matter of chance. We do not understand just how many different proteins from different strains of virus are required to actually suppress an immune system response. But it is reasonably clear that combining every single set of flu proteins in a one-size-fits-all mixture could create a vaccine with a low probability of consistently stimulating an immune response to the influenza viruses that are prevalent in any given season.

More disturbingly, on occasion an overabundance of these proteins could lead to an overwhelming immune response that could hurt the recipient of the vaccine. As everyone who has received a flu shot knows, the side effects of the shot can range from a sore arm to a mild fever to a high fever with systemic symptoms of fatigue and sometimes nausea. These side effects are, in fact, the result of the immune system's response to the foreign proteins that have been injected. (Although it is commonly believed among lay people that the side effect of a flu shot is caused by actually getting a flu infection, this is never the case.) On rare occasion, side effects can be severe and lead to dehydration, low blood pressure, and the need for hospitalization, particularly in elderly recipients of the vaccine.

The selection of how many influenza strains should be placed into the vaccine developed for the annual shot is not scientific in nature. There is no theory that tells scientists precisely how many strains one person can take at one time. However, they settle on protecting the recipient against three strains of virus because experience has shown that this approach seems to be reasonably safe.

HARNESSING *E. COLI*

A second approach to creating a vaccine is to take the genetic material of the pathogen itself and integrate it into a bacterial cell such as *Escherichia coli* (*E. coli*). With the correct manipulation of genetic material (usually DNA) that codes for the antigens of the virus, the *E. coli* bacteria begins to produce the protein in gargantuan quantities.

E. coli is found naturally in the human gut, and since it grows very easily on culture media, it's also the favorite bacteria for use in what is called "recombinant vaccines"—so called because they are recombining some other organism's DNA with the *E. coli* DNA, in this case influenza. With a little bit of biochemical cajoling, *E. coli* will happily take up other organisms' DNA—and the instructions that are on it—to make proteins in huge quantities.

Instead of using chicken eggs to grow the virus, extracting the virus from the gelatinous yolk and then purifying the proteins from it, now you have *E. coli* immediately churning out the substance of your choice—the major surface antigen to which the immune system responds when influenza virus is present.

This is precisely how the pharmaceutical industry grows hepatitis B virus antigens. This technique is also used to make many useful proteins for treatment of chronic diseases, such as human insulin for diabetics (the repertoire of the lowly *E. coli* bacterial cell is quite amazing, given a little push in the right direction). So instead of taking genetic material from an infectious organism (e.g., one of the hepatitis viruses) and using it to infect bacterial cells, we take genetic material from *humans* and in essence infect the bacteria with human DNA. Once the genetic integration is complete, a fermentation vat filled with the *E. coli* bacteria happily churns out pounds and pounds of human insulin. This is called *recombinant synthesis,* because the process recombines the DNA of one organism with another. Amazingly enough, this entire process can be accomplished in a few days.

Even with a recombination approach, you still have the problem of isolating the specific virus of interest and then growing it in sufficient quantities to get its DNA. Furthermore, it means integrating that DNA into either *E. coli* DNA or putting the whole virus into chicken eggs and waiting to get adequate amounts of protein. And the problems don't end there: When DNA is translated into the final product—a protein that has some important functional significance—that protein must be in the proper three-dimensional configuration.

Rarely is a protein a simple linear chair of individual amino acid pieces. Rather, it is more commonly a folded, complex structure with just about every conceivable geometry—from a glob-like teardrop shape to a treelike branching structure—so that it can act as a receptor, and enzyme, or a structural support component of a cell. Bacteria may not possess the same enzymes that avian cells have, which result in the final "processing" of the viral antigen, twisting it into the correct three-dimensional configuration, so one can easily end up with a functionless protein that is correct in the sequence of its fundamental components but unable to literally "fit" into its niche in the complex world of the cell.

So, any way you look at it, there is still a long development time involved in making a vaccine by creating large quantities of the viral surface proteins that engender an immune response when injected into a human or animal. Whether you are using the long-standing technique of growing a virus in chicken eggs to get the protein "antigen" that elicits an immune system response or, alternatively, forcing DNA into organisms that then make protein, the process takes time, much effort at purification, and painstaking quality control.

COLD-ADAPTED INFLUENZA

The final method that the medical community uses to create vaccines is called *attenuated live virus vaccines.* Weakened live virus is injected into the recipient in order to stimulate an immune response. These viruses become attenuated, or weakened, by passing them through nonhuman cells (hamster cells are one popular candidate) that are kept at a lower-than-optimal temperature.

For unclear reasons, such mistreated viruses adapt to their new "unnatural" environments and often become less able to cause disease in their usual hosts. Yet they still retain enough similarity to the fully virulent virus to engender an immune response when administered. They are often administered in a spray into the nose or upper portion of the throat.

Viruses growing at a lower temperature will become adapted to growing in cold conditions. Since they are cold-adapted and not warm-adapted, when you inject them into a warm human being, they will only multiply a few times before they die. These few generations will be enough to trigger the immune response, yet not enough to make the host come down with a full-blown disease.

Doctors use the cold-adapted influenza virus today, administering it as a mist through the nose. This is the product known as FluMist. It's brand-new, very effective, and above all, extremely expensive. There is also nowhere near enough FluMist available to vaccinate all of the people who need it because the marketplace hasn't been willing to pay the price for the current version of the vaccine. Although prices can vary considerably between years, a dose for a FluMist has been reported as costing up to eight times the price of a standard influenza shot. Perhaps as competing cold-adapted influenza vaccines come to market, prices will drop and production will increase to meet the increased demand. It is simply too soon to know what place FluMist (or something like it) will have in the protection of the population against influenza.

Thus, the scientists and pharmaceutical companies that are interested in producing influenza vaccines have traditionally been stuck between several less-than-ideal options. Both the recombination synthesis method and the more traditional use of chicken eggs are extremely labor-intensive and require months of advance planning. There is also the risk of selecting the wrong influenza strain to grow. That leaves the option of using attenuated live virus vaccines, such as cold-adapted viruses in a nasal spray vaccine. While this kind of vaccine requires a third less time to produce , the production expense precludes it from being a cost-effective solution for large numbers of people.

NUGGETS OF GOLD, CHAINS OF DNA

A new approach has actually been in the research phase for the past decade, and it offers a brand-new alternative. Instead of taking a living organism, or even an attenuated living organism, and injecting it into an animal or human being (i.e., a recipient), we simply take the DNA of that organism and attach it to a little pellet.

The pellet itself is microscopic. Typically, it is a tiny particle of gold no larger than five nanometers (billionths of a meter) in diameter—about a hundred-thousandth of the width of a human hair. Gold is the metal of choice because it is chemically inert and nontoxic to cells, so human cells will often engulf it and internalize it into the cellular milieu with little additional prodding.[2]

If the gold particle is injected into muscle cells, the muscle cells will take up the pellet. The cells aren't particularly interested in the gold particle. But since there is DNA stuck to the gold particle and that DNA codes for hepatitis B surface antigen protein, or the hemagglutinin protein found in influenza, the protein will be expressed in several thousand or several tens of thousands of cells—literally as a result of the cell "translating" the genetic code of the DNA into the amino acid sequence that makes up a specific protein. Therefore, not only does the immune system recognize the protein, but it recognizes it in the context of an actual infected cell. By comparison, in traditional vaccines, the protein is floating freely in the blood, and it turns out that it is much harder for immune system cells to "recognize" a foreign protein that is unanchored to another cell surface. In fact, it is usually the case that the newly synthesized foreign protein will be transferred to the surface of the muscle cell in combination with yet other specialized proteins that are designed to attract the attention of a wide variety of immune cells. This is sometimes referred to as *surface expression.*[3]

When this happens, there is a particularly potent form of immune system reaction, since both of the human immune system's responses are stimulated. One is the antibody-based response, which is secreted by a certain kind of white cell. The antibodies secreted bind to an invading virus. Once the antibodies bind to a pathogenic organism, such as an influenza virus, that organism is then identified by the immune system's cells, which then destroy it.

The second arm of the immune system involves stimulation of a direct white blood cell response, without the production of an antibody. The result is the direct destruction of the infected cell. DNA vaccines are particularly effective in initiating this direct immune system cellular response, which is sometimes called a "cell-mediated immune response" to distinguish it from an antibody response. These white blood cells are also known as T-cells, because they were first identified in the thymus gland found near the thyroid in the neck. The T-cells move into action quickly because the vaccine created a group of cells within the patient's muscle that directly recognize the presence of the infectious organism.

Therefore, a DNA-based vaccine has the following advantages:

- Because scientists can replicate DNA very quickly in the laboratory, they never have to worry about finding a suitable culture medium in which to grow the organism in large quantity.
- DNA can be made with almost 100 percent purity because chemically it is not, in and of itself, a protein. Therefore, specific chemical separation techniques can precipitate out the DNA from the myriad of proteins that are found in a cell culture medium. In short, DNA it can be separated very easily in the purification process.
- Scientists can precisely control the DNA (or portions of DNA) they want to have in the vaccine.
- When the vaccine is injected into muscle cells, there is not only an antibody response, but a T-cell or cell-mediated immune response.
- Finally, the cells that are infected with the foreign DNA are usually eliminated by the host's immune system, meaning that there is little or no danger that the foreign DNA will spread from cell to cell or cause damage elsewhere in the body. In the end, only a few hundred muscle cells are lost—an amount unnoticeable amid the billions and billions of muscle cells in the human body. Amazingly enough, the priming of a few thousand immune system cells this way is enough to protect the entire body because, once stimulated, the immune system cells multiple in vast quantity and seek out evidence of infection just about everywhere (though sometimes the central nervous system is inaccessible to certain types of immune system cells).

DNA-based vaccines are currently in human trials for several diseases such as hepatitis B. Initial results have shown immune system response even in people who have weakened immune systems, such as people who test positive for HIV. Despite optimism in the medical community, it will be a while before the Food and Drug Administration (FDA) approves this type of vaccine as completely safe.

However cautious the positive news has to be, it is still an exciting development. A responsive public health system, combined with a DNA-based vaccine that can be created and distributed within a reasonable amount of time, could very well be our best bet to stop a major outbreak or a bioterrorism event.

SOLVING THE FLU VACCINE SHORTAGE

In November 2004, the World Health Organization called an international summit on pandemic flu. It was not primarily due to the lack of flu vaccine. Instead, the summit was to address the real worry of a novel strain of avian influenza managing to make it through all of the requirements (outlined previously in the section on "The Trans-Species Jump") to infect humans.[4]

Amid this warning, the United States unexpectedly came up short in its available supply of influenza vaccine. This is a moderate-size annoyance to the public and a major headache for the public health community. Were the country suffering from an epidemic of an especially virulent and pathogenic strain of flu, annoyance would quickly escalate to a public health disaster. Therefore, it's worth examining why the vaccine industry is structured in a way that causes shortages to occur.

The primary reason, as you now know, is that the process for making flu vaccines is extraordinarily labor- and equipment-intensive. The operational system of mass-culturing the organism, isolating it, drying it out, putting it into bottles, and distributing it can barely be accomplished in time for flu season each year. This season, which runs from mid-winter to early spring, is the time when the vast majority of people who are susceptible to flu actually contract it, mostly due to the cooler weather, which leads to slightly more crowded conditions where airborne disease can spread.

Second, in the past, much of the demand that was calculated for a given flu vaccine was simply not realized. Large vats of vaccine material had to be thrown out because the CDC does not permit carrying the flu vaccine over from one year to another. The reason is, in part, because the flu organisms that are circulating may change. But the CDC also takes the hard line on keeping old vaccines around because there's risk involved—the legal risk of causing problems as a result of trying to prevent rather than cure disease. Most experts perceive the legal risks due to unexpected side effects to be worse in vaccine-science than in antibiotic research. That's because in the first instance a medication is given to healthy people in the hope of preventing illness, whereas in the second an already desperately ill patient is treated in the hope of saving his life.

As a result, companies that produce vaccines focus on:

- Vaccines with more predictable demand
- Vaccines with much lower legal risks
- Vaccines where costs are therefore much easier to calculate

An excellent example of a product that meets all of these requirements would be the pneumococcal vaccine. It is a vaccine with unquestioned efficacy, for which need is ever-increasing because of the growing elderly population. It is also a vaccine against which lawsuits have been very few and far between, unlike certain vaccines (particularly pediatric vaccines for prevention of measles, mumps, and pertussis) that have generated countless lawsuits over the years.

None of these conditions apply to manufacturing influenza vaccine because (in marketing terms) it is a "moving target." The viral composition changes every year in subtle ways, and some years it changes dramatically. When this happens, we have difficulty anticipating what should be done because we have such grossly inadequate surveillance at present. If we cannot detect what is happening early in the evolution of a new influenza strain or any novel infectious disease, the probability of reacting in time to prevent a major epidemic is seriously reduced. This is especially true if the disease is easily passed from person to person.

THRESHOLD OF COMPLACENCY

Though anticipating the arrival of new influenza strains is very difficult (as is the development and introduction of new vaccines or medications to treat them), it does not mean that the influenza problem should be ignored. Instead, it suggests that we need a new business model or paradigm to produce flu vaccines for the country. This work needs to be conducted with an eye on the same general considerations—timeliness, safety, and efficacy. But the practical evidence strongly indicates that it should be done through the use of DNA-based technology.

Let's say that scientists isolate an avian strain of influenza that appears to have completed a trans-species jump into pigs, and that some humans in the area are dying from severe respiratory illness that is presumed to be related to the new multi-species influenza. Consequently, the strain poses a serious health threat to billions of humans. Through the process described earlier in the chapter, scientists at the CDC can use the DNA of the organism with a high degree of knowledge that it is safe and effective when used to vaccinate patients. An additional bonus may well be that this kind of vaccine engenders not a yearlong or a six-month response, but perhaps a permanent response against a much wider variety of influenza organisms.

There are still serious obstacles to overcome in this vaccine creation method. Even though the theory has been well proven in other situations, it has not been proven out yet in influenza. Clinical trials promise to be expensive. A great deal of capital will be required up-front.

It is reasonable to speculate that several pharmaceutical companies are already capable of doing this kind of DNA vaccine development with influenza. But they are not proceeding with research because they are waiting for an epidemic. As cold-blooded as it sounds, a large enough epidemic would allow companies to garner the kind of seed money that they would need from investors, the federal government, or both. Only then would they engage in what would be a two- or three-year-long clinical trial for a DNA-based vaccine for influenza.

If history is any guide, a major epidemic in the United States will indeed be an effective crisis to sweep over the threshold of complacency. We have not had a serious influenza outbreak in the United States since 1968, and even that epidemic was mild compared to the 1918 flu that killed millions of people, most of them young adults, worldwide. Even when a new flu epidemic does occur, it tends to kill the elderly, the homeless, and people with chronic disease who are seriously immunosuppressed. Consequently, it garners less attention than a disease that cuts down people in their prime, such as HIV or the 1918 flu.

It is unfortunately the nature of our policies—and perhaps human nature itself—that we respond to crisis. And we have not had an infectious disease crisis of any magnitude since the 1960s, with the exception of the cryptosporidiosis outbreak in the early 1990s in Milwaukee.

We certainly have not encountered anything as deadly as the 1918 flu that took 20 million lives around the globe. And we have not encountered a version of the SARS virus that is transmissible from human to human. It short, we haven't bumped into any pathogen that has caused enough of a shock to our system to allow us to overcome our complacency.

It is only a matter of time.

NOTES

1. It is well known that by introducing too many foreign proteins into a vaccine recipient at one time, scientists can actually induce a state of "immunologic tolerance," where the immune system literally shuts down. Unfortunately, there are no models for predicting when this phenomenon occurs, so vaccine experts seek to avoid this outcome by keeping the number of virus proteins as small as possible.

2. As with many of the techniques adopted in biology, the discovery that human cells will take up tiny gold particles was a serendipitous finding that dates back to the early years of treatment of infectious disease. Then, various heavy metals—including arsenic, silver, and even mercury—were used to try to kill bacteria causing disease. Most of these attempts were dismal failures, often killing the patient. Some treatments, though, gave unexpected results. In the case of gold, which was used (unsuccessfully) to treat tuberculosis at one time, it was discovered that some TB patients who happened to also suffer from rheumatoid arthritis had miraculous improvement in their arthritis symptoms. Gold is still used today to treat rheumatoid arthritis (there is even an oral gold drug that is well absorbed into the systemic circulation) and many different types of immune system cells seem to internalize it, mitigating the postulated "overactivity" of the immune system in rheumatoid arthritis. The action of gold in treating rheumatoid arthritis has yet to be fully worked out. Nonetheless, researchers have also noted that nonimmune system cells—especially muscle cells—will internalize gold particles, and apparently without toxic effect to those cells.

3. When a cell is infected with either a virus or infected in the artificial sense with foreign DNA, the translated proteins are exported to the cell surface (e.g., on a muscle cell or the cell lining the respiratory tract) and then bound to a class of proteins called the major histocompatibility complex (MHC). These proteins were so-named in the 1970s and early 1980s when it was realized that they largely determined whether an organ transplant would be compatible with a recipient's immune system (the very definition of *histocompatibility*). But the MHC proteins—which are roughly divided into four different classes, each of which has dozens or hundreds of subtypes—are actually signaling molecules to attract antibody-producing cells or other elements of the immune system to evaluate a foreign protein to which the MHC molecules bind. The immune system cells may decide to simply ignore the protein, or they may destroy the cell displaying the protein. Indeed, this is the basis

of the symptoms that occur with influenza and other infections: The body's own immune system destroys cells expressing foreign proteins (presumed to thus be infected) and causing fever, muscle aches, and on occasion, dysfunction of an entire organ.

4. In early 2005, the WHO and CDC predicted a higher-than-average likelihood of a severe influenza season (from "usual" influenza strains) due to the lack of vaccine. As of this writing and for reasons that are unclear, 2005 has been surprisingly benign as far as flu is concerned—a strong indicator that we understand very little about the interaction of the numerous factors that result in "bad" flu seasons. Although flu has been studied intensively since the end of World War II, with the investment of tens of billions of dollars, much more modeling work needs to be done just to understand the single most common serious infectious disease in the world.

CHAPTER 15

THREE OUNCES OF PREVENTION

Scenarios Involving Avian Bird Flu, Bioterrorism Using Smallpox

Novel and not-so-novel infectious diseases can appear quickly in human or animal populations. These diseases can wreak tremendous havoc before they are recognized or diagnosed by local public health officials. Most of the recent novel diseases that have appeared in the United States (e.g., hantavirus, cryptosporidiosis, and West Nile fever) were well established months or even decades before they appeared in numbers large enough to be identified by medical doctors and their colleagues in public health.

Yet, despite the painful lessons that these actual outbreaks have taught us, little has changed in public health surveillance of the human or animal population. We remain highly vulnerable to the inadvertent introduction of a serious new disease, such as foot-and-mouth disease in animals or newly evolved strains of adapted avian influenza in humans. Worse, we remain *especially* vulnerable to an intentionally introduced disease, which is possible as a terrorist act.

To illustrate the potential scope of the problem of each type of disease appearance, this chapter provides two speculative scenarios of what *could* happen in the United States. In one scenario, we show what can happen without a continuous, near-real-time syndrome surveillance system that physicians, veterinarians, and emergency rescue teams could use to notify public health officials and others with a "need to know" about an unusual illness seen in the community. In the other example, we show how the results can be strikingly different if such a system is in place and effectively utilized.

We stress that these are fictional—but highly realistic—examples of what could happen in the next year, the next decade, or the next month. None of the people mentioned are based on any existing persons. Local communities, developments, and organizations discussed in these examples are also fictional in nature.

ON AN EARLY SEPTEMBER MORNING: A HYPOTHETICAL SCENARIO OF AVIAN BIRD FLU

Special Report from the *Southern California Weekly,* April 28

A Look Back at the Naranja Huerto Virus

At 0600 hours on Labor Day morning, the radar station at the Miramar Marine Corps Air Station north of San Diego picked up a large, low-flying object coming in from the north. The new tracking computer, installed less than a day ago, was still having teething problems, and the fact that it gave out a warning signal over this contact proved it.

The unit was designed to pick up and track missiles that were traveling above the speed of sound. Instead, the contact was meandering along at the speed of a jogging man, much too slowly for a fighter jet or a missile to even stay aloft.

The operators logged the contact, according to their protocol, and promptly ignored the signal. It is ironic that the machine's warning was cast aside. As it turned out, the contact's payload proved to be as devastating as anything ever carried by a cruise missile.

The contact was a huge flock of birds, flying in a tight V formation. They were heading southeast toward Lake Cahuilla, the only body of water in the area that could sustain their hunger and thirst. This wasn't in itself unusual; many bird species stopped along the shores of the lake on their way south to their wintering grounds in northern Mexico.

What made the event unusual was the fact that no bird-watcher in the state could have identified their strange markings. From a distance, their gray-and-black plumage blended into a cloudy sky, but up close it resolved into a bold pattern of dark stripes. They were East Asian cross-barred geese, and they were off their normal flight plan by over 6,000 miles.

The waters of Lake Cahuilla regularly teemed with millions of birds each fall, all on separate migration paths to the far corners of the country.

The lake was shallow and surprisingly salty because of the heavy use of irrigation in the surrounding area. The waters of the lake were the engine that drove the intensive farming of poultry and produce in the area. At the time, the southern Imperial Valley was providing almost a quarter of the United States' domestically grown produce, half of its lettuce, and—owing to an early frost in Florida—more than 60 percent of its orange juice.

Some of the geese in the flock were slightly underweight and more passive than normal. If the birds were startled by a threat on the shore and took flight, they would react a second or two later, lagging behind their flock. They weren't deathly ill—wild animals tend to be quite healthy, otherwise they succumb to environmental stress or predators very quickly—but they probably weren't foraging as effectively as they normally could. These birds were afflicted with a new variation on the influenza virus, one that was extremely contagious across avian species.

On the east side of the lake was a poultry farm. This farm had expanded rapidly in recent years by capitalizing on the growing popularity of free-range chickens. Contrary to what many people think, chickens generally do not roam over several acres the way cattle are known to. Like their caged predecessors, chickens tend to stay in a localized area and scratch at the dirt for food. This particular farm went out of its way to feed the chickens using open troughs in outside pens, using only organically grown corn.

The abundance of food left out in the open was probably the key reason the cross-barred geese overcame their normal reluctance to come near humans. Hungry and slightly ill, the easy pickings of the corn trough would have been an extreme temptation for at least a couple of the geese on their way south. It is not known whether one of the roosters on the farm got into a fight with one of the interloping geese or whether the virus was picked up as the chickens pecked in the dust mixed with guano (dried excrement) left behind by the migrating birds.

What is known for sure is that one week after Labor Day, the local farmhands worriedly reported to the manager that many chickens were listless and irritable. They would hiss and peck at the workers and the other birds until they simply fell over on their sides, kicked convulsively once or twice, and went still. Alarmed, the managers quickly quarantined the flocks with the affected birds—which totaled more than 600 chickens—as best they could and called the local farm veterinarian.

Migrating Pathogens

Veterinarian Martin Kimmel considered himself to be an escapee from the typical vet-tech clinic. A native of North Dakota, he decided at the age of forty to simultaneously ditch the snowy winters and the brick-faced single-story office he'd worked in for twenty years for the California sunshine and a new routine. Now, he used a beat-up red pickup truck to travel a roving circuit through the orchards, ranches, and fields in the Imperial Valley of southern California. The life suited him, and he liked the variety: One week he could be working with horses that felt under the weather, the next he'd be examining prize birds on an ostrich farm.

He never forgot the look on the faces of the workers at the farm when he arrived. When he asked where the sick birds were, no one answered. They simply took him to the holding pens where the symptomatic chickens had been quarantined.

At first, he thought that someone had whimsically plucked the birds and lay the feathers down in a brown-and-white mat along the floor of the pen. With a start, he realized that what he was looking at was a sea of dead chickens, laid out in a rough tumble of stiff, feathered bodies. Almost in shock, he grabbed the nearest animals he could to take back to his office to examine.

"I remember demanding to be told the truth," Dr. Kimmel later recalled. "I thought that the birds had died over a period of several days and the farm hadn't bothered to call me." But the owners insisted they were telling the truth—in the twenty-four-hour period since they had separated the birds and called him, the chickens had started falling over in droves. He told them to watch for any signs or symptoms in the rest of the animals, then he drove back to his lab as fast as the pickup would take the potholes in the country roads.

Dr. Kimmel had performed many autopsies on animals in his years of practice. What he saw wasn't in itself unusual. The fluid in the animal's lungs, speckles of blood, and pronounced swelling in several of the major organs all pointed to a virus, perhaps a potent strain of avian influenza, also known as bird flu. Most forms of this virus are rarely harmful to wild birds but often deadly to domesticated animals.

On rare occasions, these viruses were known to jump species into humans. But what truly concerned Dr. Kimmel was the organism's virulence. He'd never seen anything that could kill a couple hundred domestic chickens within twenty-four hours.

An interesting turn of fate crops up at this point in the story. As Dr. Kimmel was pondering whether this was indeed avian influenza, he received a call from one of the local ranchers. As luck would have it, one of the ranch hands had come across a sick goose by the lake. It had extremely strange barred markings on its wings and body. Dr. Kimmel wanted it brought to his office.

The bird died en route, and an autopsy was quickly performed. The organs were in the same state as Dr. Kimmel had observed in the domestic chickens, which fueled his concern that this goose may have been the wild animal vector carrying the virus. Kimmel kept a large collection of avian taxonomy books at his office, and he stayed up late into the evening paging through the text until he was able to identify the bird.

"It wasn't until then that I put two and two together," Dr. Kimmel said. "There had been some news reports that geese and ducks in China were suspected of having caused outbreaks of avian flu in the human population. But what this bird—and its entire species—were doing on this side of the Pacific, I had no idea."

The East Asian cross-barred goose typically migrates from its summer home near the Arctic Ocean down south to Southern China. It's unclear what caused the cross-barred geese to change their migration path. Was it because of a change in the global climate, the rapid urban development along the Chinese coast, or a subtle change in the earth's magnetic field, which the navigational part of their brains couldn't make sense of? The upshot was that a species that normally migrated up and down the Pacific Coast of China was now moving in the same pattern along the curve of the Western United States. And the birds were bringing their unique pathogens with them.

Dr. Kimmel's sense of foreboding increased as he read about the scattered outbreaks of disease related to these birds. The reports usually centered on or around agricultural areas near coastal Chinese cities. Unfortunately, lacking a better resource, he could only use the Internet to find scattered news articles that were often written by casual foreign correspondents who knew little about medicine and less about epidemiology. He called the poultry farm and asked whether anyone there had become ill. The answer was no—but given the transitory nature of the workers in the valley, they couldn't be sure. There was simply no way to know if anything unusual was taking place on other farms or ranches in the area.

Dr. Kimmel next called the local hospital, located in the valley town of Corazón about ten miles away. He asked if there had been any unusual cases of flu admitted in the last couple of days. He was put on hold and transferred between departments a number of times. Ultimately, the best answer he could get from the hospital staff was, "We don't think so."

Dr. Kimmel later recalled, "There was nothing else I could do. I had gone as far as I could with the data I had—no one else was sick, no more birds were dying. What could I do, call the county health official and tell him I was worried because some chickens had died? They had their hands full with a case of listeriosis at the local grade school."

Unfortunately, though Kimmel couldn't have known, three "strange" cases of flu had indeed cropped up. The Imperial Valley has a large number of migrant workers, and just as in the time of John Steinbeck, they still perform most of the farm labor that brings produce to our supermarket shelves. Three of the workers, whose names have not been released by their families, had all worked at the poultry farm and were now coming down ill with muscle aches, fever, and a wheezing cough.

We don't know for sure how the virus entered the system of these three men. The exact mechanism by which a virus jumps species is poorly understood at best. It's possible that they simply breathed in fecal matter left by the infected chickens and kicked up by the rest of the flock. It's possible that they were bitten or scratched by the infected birds, opening up a direct route for the virus to enter their bloodstream.

Many of the people who work the fields in the Imperial Valley are illegal immigrants—or, in the sensitive political parlance of Southern California, they are "undocumented." We don't know the status of the three men who worked at the poultry farm. But it is possible that they or their families chose to avoid going to the hospital because they didn't have a green card or other form of official documentation and didn't want to cause problems with the law.

The men showed up at a small but relatively well equipped medical clinic at the other end of town from the hospital where Dr. Kimmel had called to check for strange cases of flu. Since the clinic had no way to send or receive public health information or requests from the hospital, it did not get the veterinarian's query. The men were taken in for chest X-rays, which showed diffuse fluid infiltrates in their lungs, signifying a strong immune system reaction to either a pathogen or inhaled toxic substance. Their oxygen levels were precipitously low and dropping, with each of the patients struggling to breathe as the clinicians raced to figure out what was wrong.

The clinic managed to marginally improve their condition by fitting them with nasal tubes to pump oxygen into their lungs. Lacking better options, the clinic's doctors called ahead to the main hospital in Corazón, alerting the hospital that three critically ill patients would be arriving who were at risk of drowning as their lungs filled up with fluid. Within the hour, ambulances buzzed through early-morning traffic and shuttled the patients to the hospital's intensive care unit.

Dr. Julie Salazar was working ICU that day and got the message that the patients were on their way. When they arrived, her first impression was that one patient's lips were slightly blue, a sign of poor oxygenation. She didn't have more time to ponder this because the final patient to be wheeled into the ICU went into cardiac arrest, and all hell broke loose.

"The patient who went into cardiac arrest was a huge, muscular man," she remembered. "It took two orderlies and a pair of nurses to control him." Patients who arrest often will thrash about, much as drowning victims do, trying to escape whatever it is that is blocking their ability to breathe.

"It was a messy intubation," she said. "There was a bubbly, frothy fluid that he coughed up from his lungs. It sprayed everywhere." Dr. Salazar managed to avoid the worst of it because she was protected by a surgical mask and her eyeglasses (her only concession to age). Both of the nurses and one of the orderlies were less lucky, and the doctor remembers sending them to clean off the spittle that had landed on their faces. She immediately ordered a battery of standard bacterial and specialized viral tests from swabs of the sputum while she prescribed medications to assist the patients' breathing.

Within the next thirty-six hours, the standard test results returned as negative—the lab was unable to culture the organism. The viral test was similarly unrevealing since the standard antibody testing showed no response. Whatever the bug was, it hadn't been seen in Corazón before.

Wave of Panic

Dr. Salazar had read the results with a certain amount of foreboding, but she decided to follow up on the problem tomorrow. She had gotten the report at the end of her shift that day, and she was tired. On her drive home, her Blackberry beeped. At the next stoplight she read the text message from a coworker: *You'd better get back here.* There were ten patients in the ICU, all suffering from the same symptoms: difficulty breathing, high fever, and muscle aches and cramps.

"There were two men who had been fishing at separate points around the lake," Dr. Salazar later recalled. "Five others were migrant workers who had been picking oranges in the local orchards for a juice company. But the other three patients in the ICU were the ones that really stopped me in my tracks."

The three patients were the two nurses and the orderly who had helped her intubate the patient from two nights ago. One had already been put on oxygen. Of the other seven patients, two had gone into arrest and one was comatose. Of the original three patients, two were still fighting for their lives, and the man she had intubated went into arrest a second time later that afternoon. That time, he didn't come out of arrest.

The members of the man's family were all devoutly religious and refused an autopsy. But Dr. Salazar was sufficiently alarmed to call the county public health official and ask for a public health alert to be issued. In these extreme circumstances, the medical examiner in charge overruled the family's request and performed the procedure. The autopsy confirmed that the alveoli in the dead man's lungs had been overwhelmed by the production of mucus from an extremely aggressive pulmonary disease.

The family's objections had delayed the procedure by twelve more hours. By then, six more day-laborers and orchard workers who had shared lodgings with the prior patients arrived at the ICU complaining of chest pains and difficulty breathing. Dr. Salazar and the local public health officials had contacted the Centers for Disease Control and Prevention (CDC) and sent samples off to their lab in Atlanta, Georgia. The CDC inoculated guinea pigs and birds with cultures taken from the sputum samples from the patients in Corazón. The birds came down ill by the next day, and a cell culture came back strongly suggestive of influenza. Under the microscope, the cells appeared to be damaged in the pattern typical for influenza viruses. Distorted cell membranes, loss of small cellular structures found in normal cells, and other nearly unique "fingerprints" for influenza infection were observed.

One of the researchers at the CDC suggested that the team working on the mystery virus could identify the virus by chemically bonding fluorescent stain to the bird antibodies and using them as markers on the sputum samples. The samples sent in from California and later tested on all of the new patients arriving at the hospital in Corazón each glowed positive because the bird antibodies were binding to the fluorescence material—making the diagnosis of avian influenza passed to humans all but certain.

Small groups of reporters from local news stations from El Cajon and San Bernadino were joined by the ranks of nationally known journalists from CNN and Fox News when the announcement was made that a new strain of avian flu had jumped into the human species. The press corps set up shop outside the hospital, peppering ICU staff members leaving the hospital and patients on their way in with questions. Upon learning that many of the patients had been picking fruit in the local citrus groves, the press dubbed the pathogen the *Naranja Huerto,* or "orange orchard" influenza.

The information on the virus finally reached Dr. Kimmel that evening as he watched a CNN news roundup. He immediately called the CDC and reported what he had seen at the poultry farm. At last, the public health officials and the CDC had all of the pieces—the likely host of the virus, the jump into domestic fowl, the three known index cases, and a test to detect the presence of Naranja flu. Unfortunately, Dr. Kimmel, Dr. Salazar, the CDC, and the clinics and hospital in Corazón might as well have been working in separate countries. Without coordination or early warning, the time elapsed was more than six days from the first spotted cases at the poultry farm to the final call made by Dr. Kimmel to the CDC.

By then, both the hospital in Corazón and the local road system were overwhelmed; all intensive care unit beds were occupied, and makeshift ICUs were set up, even though staffing them proved to be impossible. Hundreds of patients had to be sent—under biocontainment "tents"—to dozens of hospitals with advanced intensive care units (so-called tertiary hospitals or referral hospitals) in the area. The hospitals' emergency rooms were packed with people who were either coughing or complaining of muscle aches and difficulty breathing. Many became belligerent when they learned that they would have to wait hours before receiving even basic medical care.

"The worst part was the paranoia," said Dr. Salazar. "Only about a quarter of the people who showed up even had Naranja. The rest were people who had a garden-variety common cold or bacterial pneumonia—but they were convinced that they were going to die unless we gave them every drug we had in the pharmacy. Some weren't even ill—their temperatures had only gone up one degree, well within the variation of body temperature throughout the day, yet they thought they needed immediate intensive care."

Unfortunately, even if one-quarter of the arriving cases had mild to severe Naranja flu, that meant more than a hundred people needed ICU treatment, and with recent cutbacks in hospital fundings, ICU beds (the most expensive to maintain and staff) had been reduced to a minimum. A wave of fear, which was much more highly contagious and potent than the influenza itself, spread through the valley's farming communities. The local roads onto Interstates 8 and 10 became jammed with pickup trucks, minivans, and SUVs as people began to flee the area.

Overheated cars and a single multivehicle accident turned an already tense situation into a highly unstable one as families abandoned their vehicles en masse and began to trek west toward San Diego and Riverside, California, and east to Arizona. From space, the weather satellites could make out the twinkling lines of abandoned cars, their batteries still running, that traced along the gridlocked freeways.

The local police were inundated with calls from property owners complaining that hundreds or thousands of people were ignoring their fences and walking through their land. When a discarded cigarette or a campfire turned into a blaze of wildfires, the state's governor finally called in the National Guard to close off the area between Yuma, Arizona and the eastern suburbs of San Diego.

Things took a turn for the worse as people started challenging the National Guard units on the freeways. In one incident, captured vividly by a local news camera crew, the guard units had to shoot the tires out from under drivers attempting to run their roadblocks. Editorials decrying the state of affairs began to run in the Los Angeles newspapers, but they were quickly wiped away by a further development from across the Pacific.

The Damage from Naranja

As California's governor went public with announcements to restore calm, the Chinese government, facing outbreaks of similar avian flu, claimed that imported American agricultural goods had spread the disease to their country. Angry congressmen and U.S. Commerce Department officials argued that this was a disingenuous move made by China to ban American goods from Asia so that Chinese merchants could dominate the market. The following month, at the Asian-Pacific Economic Consortium (APEC) meeting, China pressured countries from Japan to Indonesia to refuse to accept imports of American medium-grain rice, citrus products, and alfalfa.

The revenue generated from these products alone cost California hundreds of millions of dollars and plunged the state into recession by the end of the year. The economic ripples were felt throughout the country. Because there was no labor to pick the harvest, acres of the plants rotted in the fields, while the price of imported produce—items such as lettuce or artichokes—tripled. Orange juice became a rare commodity, selling for $20 a gallon in the upscale markets of New York City.

The CDC set up a special ward to treat Naranja patients, separated from the main hospital so as not to spread the infection to immunocompromised patients. The disease kept spreading, however. By the next month, almost a thousand cases of confirmed avian flu had been reported. Four hundred of these cases were tended to at the ward in Corazón. It turned out that the disease had a fatality rate of one in twenty, which is quite lethal—roughly the death rate of the much rarer bacterial pneumonias that are occasionally acquired outside of hospital settings (so-called community-acquired pneumonia).

The CDC had little cheer to spread as the holidays approached. It was determined that the Naranja strain of influenza grew extremely slowly when injected into chicken eggs. Since chicken eggs were the primary medium used to grow mass quantities of virus used in vaccines, the first batch of effective vaccine wouldn't be available for another six to eight weeks.

Throughout the winter, the new influenza cropped up in outbreaks throughout California, Arizona, and Nevada. Only the direct intervention of the governor prevented an even wider spread, when air traffic out of Southern California was shut down immediately after the CDC issued its first warnings.

At present, the efficient introduction of the vaccine into the Western states and its ongoing distribution across the country has allowed public health officials to blunt the worst that could have happened. Where many hundreds of thousands could have died, less than 3,000 people actually lost their lives.

While the human cost of this outbreak is immeasurable, there is also unbelievable damage to the national economy. California, the eighth largest economy in the world, has suffered losses into the billions of dollars. The blows ranged from boycotts of Californian exports to an almost complete halt of tourism into Los Angeles. For the first time, the theme parks in Hollywood and Anaheim have shut down, because it's just not economically feasible to run them at 10 percent attendance.

The medical, veterinary, and public health communities have been shaken to the core, and today they are examining what they could have done better to head off this catastrophe. Dr. Kimmel is pessimistic. Even if he'd been able to find out whether humans were coming down with Naranja flu early on, he's not sure that anyone in the medical community would have listened to a veterinarian.

Dr. Salazar disagrees. "We didn't have anything in place to help us watch, help us communicate, back when it would have made all the difference. I would have paid close attention to massive numbers of animals reported as ill, even though we physicians are taught almost nothing about veterinary diseases. We're smart enough to know that in the past ten years, many new diseases have clearly been demonstrated to pass from animals to humans." She paused to reflect for a moment, then added, "The worst part was that we could have stopped it. The virus got a six-day head start, and that was more than it needed to get out of our control. Had this been a kind of bug that killed 50 percent of its victims instead of 5 percent, we'd be living in a much different world right now."

END GAME: A HYPOTHETICAL SCENARIO OF A BIOTERRORIST ATTACK[1]

Selected Columns from *The New American Scientist,* January–April, Volumes 5–8

Always Vigilant: Slamming the Door Shut on the Bioterrorists

The Colorado high school basketball championship takes place every spring in Denver, attracting students, parents, and fans from the entire state to the city arena. The arena was a new addition to Denver's glittering downtown area and a crown jewel of the urban planner's blueprints. Newly refurbished at a cost in the low seven figures, it provided better climate control (a must in the chilly spring and snowy winter), a state-of-the-art sound system, and comfortable seating for 8,500 people.

In a marathon two-day session, eight teams, comprised of four boys and four girls each, battle for their state crowns. Some of the more dedicated viewers stay for both games on each day, while others grab seats for a select game or two. The event is covered extensively by local news organizations and is broadcast live on Denver radio and television. By all accounts, the event has become so popular that all games are sold out months in advance.

The sports arena is located in a densely populated and rebuilt residential section of "old" downtown Denver. About 50,000 people live or work within a two-mile radius of the facility. On the days of the games, the local hotels are packed and a party atmosphere pervades the entire neighborhood. It's little wonder that the mayor and local businesses look forward to each year's playoff and championship games.

On the early afternoon of Friday, April 22, basketball fans began filing into the arena for the first game. As is the case at most modern sporting venues, security was as tight as a drum. Everyone went through a metal detector and some people were "patted down" and thoroughly searched in a ritual that is now familiar to anyone who has traveled by air since 9/11. Despite the inconvenience, everyone was in high spirits, looking forward to a closely fought set of games between the equally talented teams.

A review of the security tapes after the incident showed the now infamous pictures of the Gang of Four. Sitting among the 125 most expensive seats at floor level were four young white males, each occupying a front-row seat on different sides of the court. Each also carried in his pocket an asthma medicine "inhaler," a small, pressurized container that releases a puff of aerosolized medication each time the inhaler is squeezed.

They were labeled as albuterol, a medicine used to relax the bronchial tubes that become inflamed during asthma attacks. The labels were a deliberate deception because each inhaler actually contained about three to four ounces of variola, the virus that causes smallpox. Individually, the young men had successfully—and with little effort—managed to sneak the equivalent of four biological atomic weapons into the packed stadium.

We know from later interviews with security personnel that each of the young men had placed his inhaler into a small bowl along with his keys and pocket change when he went through the venue's metal detector. All had received the items back once they were scanned as "clean." Like the other 5 percent or so of the attendees with asthma, their inhalers passed through security unchecked beyond a cursory glance at the official-looking pharmaceutical labeling. Since asthma is such a common condition, there are around 400 people with asthma inhalers in the crowd. Even some of the players have to use inhalers during the game.

A Deadly Mist

The arena itself was about the size of a football field: about a hundred meters long, a hundred meters wide, and five stories tall. Huge lights hang down from the ceiling to illuminate the court. Enormous fans move air in and out of the building to remove the heat generated by the lights, the screaming fans, and the sweating players, coaches, and referees.

At about four o' clock in the afternoon, the first game in the Final Four girls' basketball tournament began. The security cameras captured what happened next, although at the time, nothing out of the ordinary was remarked upon.

On the tapes, the fans are mostly up on their feet as the scoring is fast and furious. Players, referees, and the coaches are running up and down the length of the court. More players come off the bench, and cheerleading squads and bands fill every second of the time-outs. The players huddle to discuss strategy for keeping the pressure on their opponents.

Unnoticed during this massive celebration of classic American sport, the four young men remove their inhalers from their pockets and once every thirty minutes, they squeeze them gently as they are pointed up in the air while they cheer with the rest of the enthusiastic crowd. One of the young men actually makes a show of shaking the inhaler the first time, as if clearing it or testing it. The rest of the time, all four are simply depressing the inhalers' triggers in the middle of the crowd's largest cheers.

It's a chilling tape to watch for many reasons. Two of the young men have a glassy-eyed look, as if they are robots, almost unaware of the game going on around them. They leap up with the crowd and cheer in a mechanical way. The other two have inscrutable expressions that turn to grins only when they trigger their inhalers. With each gentle puff, an invisible mist of particles—many tens of billions of particles of variola—was released into the air. Then the variola particles floated in the complex air currents at floor level generated by jumping fans, jumping players, and the inhaling and exhaling of thousands of pairs of lungs.

During the course of the two-hour game, the four terrorists succeeded in disseminating about 200 grams (eight ounces) of variola particles into the air. They had successfully detonated a biological weapon, delivering their payload perfectly onto their target. Instead of using a multimillion-dollar

Global Positioning System and a solid-fuel rocket, they accomplished the same goal with four inhaler devices that can be bought at the corner drugstore.

The terrorists attacked again, in the exact same way, at 7 P.M. during the first boy's playoff round, on the subsequent day of the tournament. And the initial result of the exposure of some 20,000-odd fans to trillions of variola particles is chilling: nothing at all. There wasn't the slightest indication to any of the fans attending the game that they had inhaled and would carry back with them one of the oldest plagues to afflict humanity. Yet they had been turned into biological weapons, ticking time bombs of virus.

Detonation and Fallout

The following Monday, an eight-year-old girl with leukemia comes to Denver children's hospital with a fever and a skin rash. She had been at the game, thanks to the help of the local Make-a-Wish Foundation. A rash is typical with a low platelet count, and it is one of the unfortunate side effects of the child's recent chemotherapy and the leukemia itself, which is no longer in remission.

Further examination shows *petechiae*—tiny pinpoint blotches of blood on the skin and hard palate of the mouth. A chest X-ray shows a diffuse fluid infiltration. The girl is admitted to the hospital with an initial diagnosis of pneumonia. Since the fluid in the lungs is diffuse, the infection is probably viral. The girl's parents are given the bad news that she probably won't survive this infection. It is the "end stage" of her leukemia and the breakdown of her immune system after two years of chemotherapy and radiation treatments.

The admitting physician who took care of the little girl knew that her immune system had been compromised and potentially open to any new virus or bacteria that could be out in the environment. He entered his findings in the electronic surveillance system that the local department of health had encouraged the hospital to purchase to report cases like this one.

On the same day, 105 miles away in Green Valley, Colorado, a twenty-two-year-old college senior—an alumnus of the winning girls' high school basketball team who had attended the tournament in Denver—comes into the local university's student health center with a bad sore throat, joint aches, and a mild cough. A careful examination is performed because this student is known to be HIV-positive, a condition acquired when she traveled as a student missionary in central Africa four years earlier and had received an HIV-tainted blood transfusion during emergency surgery following a car accident that ruptured her spleen.

The attending physician at the university health center is concerned, but finds nothing alarming on examination. The student is taking her "AIDS cocktail" faithfully and has a normal count of white blood cells. Even though it is far from flu season, the physician makes a flu diagnosis and prescribes bed rest and aspirin.

The health center at the university recently installed software that allows examining physicians to report strange symptoms in their patients. Although hesitant at first, the physician who examined the student decides to enter the information. She realizes that should there be a new outbreak of flu or chicken pox, it's likely that an immunosuppressed patient would be the first to be infected. It is worth spending three minutes to log in and check the boxes indicating her findings.

Later that morning, several students fail to show up at school in Whitechurch, Colorado. Whitechurch is located in the opposite direction of Green Valley from Denver, in the southern part of the state. As per school procedures, the school nurse calls the students' parents and discovers that none have decided to skip class and play hooky. Instead, the parents say that they're "down with the flu," but should be up and around within a day or two.

The nurse frowned: Something did not look right to her. As she ran down the list of boys reporting in ill, she realized that the list was identical to the names on the basketball team. Each of the sick boys was a basketball player for the first-round boys' team during the weekend's championship playoffs. She'd seen most of them in her infirmary for bumps and bruises, not for colds. In other words, these were some of the most active, healthy boys at the school. And somehow, a pathogen had targeted them as specifically as if they'd been called out at gym class.

She turned the power on the old computer in her office; it was slow and cranked along on a dial-up modem like a lumbering dinosaur. Luckily, the program she needed to log the cases with the local public health officials (PHOs) ran well, even on her ancient machine. The information she entered set off alarm bells in Denver and effectively signaled the public health agencies that something strange and potentially deadly was going on.

Red Tide

The PHOs reviewing the "hits" on the map knew immediately that several of the boys who played in the tournament were ill. They knew that an HIV-positive college student who had attended the game was severely ill. Finally, they saw that a second immunocompromised patient—the young girl with leukemia—was critically ill. All the patients had similar symptoms. The patients were geographically dispersed all over the state—but their paths had crossed at one point in time and space: the Denver arena during the last weekend's games.

The public health office immediately sent out medical professionals to reexamine each of the patients and biopsy the suspicious-looking lesions in the back of their throats. Immediate access to an electron microscope at the University of Denver in Boulder—a precious resource always in great demand—was arranged on short notice.

When the slices of tissue taken from the leukemia patient and the HIV-positive student were placed under the electron microscope, what the physicians saw was enough to seriously rattle them. From the first images, large viral particles were scattered throughout the sample. The result provided them with enough information to make the presumptive diagnosis of smallpox. The team of physicians, aware of the awful consequences of the diagnosis if they are right—but keenly aware of the panic they could cause if wrong—decided to send samples by overnight courier to the CDC in Atlanta for analysis before they made any announcement.

During that evening, the eight-year-old girl with leukemia dies in her sleep. It appears that she simply went into shock—not uncommon in patients with leukemia, though a bit odd so early in the course of a viral pneumonia. Because of the disturbing reports that the hospital has seen on the surveillance system, an emergency autopsy is planned for the next day.

At three o'clock in the morning on April 27, one of the Whitechurch basketball players gets up in the middle of the night because of the sudden onset of abdominal pain and vomiting. He collapses on the way to the bathroom, and his parents are unable to bring him to consciousness. He is taken to the local hospital, found to be profoundly dehydrated, and given intravenous fluids. He is admitted to the hospital with the diagnosis of "viral gastroenteritis" and dehydration.

One physician notices a few small blister-like lesions on the back of the young man's throat and is surprised to find that his spleen is enlarged as well—something very uncommon in viral gastroenteritis. The doctor makes a note of it online, and as soon as he's logged in, he reads that multiple reports of similar events are taking place all over the map of Colorado.

At around breakfast time on the following morning, multiple incidents occur in the Denver metropolitan area. Two of the coaches, four cheerleaders, and a number of elderly fans who attended the game develop muscles aches and sore throats and decide to visit their doctors—though none of them visit the same clinic. One cheerleader has large bruises on her legs and arms—attributed to bumping against the floor when she jumped off the shoulders of another cheerleader at the game—and is found to have a platelet count well below normal. She appears very ill, though not in any specific way, and is admitted to the hospital.

The physicians in emergency rooms and hospitals electronically reported these cases of "flu-like illness," along with the occasional finding of blister-like lesions on the throat. The distinct, deadly pattern was beginning to come into focus. The reports displayed as scarlet points on a map that was rapidly becoming dotted with a rising wave of red.

Out of the Bottle

Around noon, the initial findings on the autopsy of the dead leukemia victim were recorded, then transcribed onto a paper record. The child apparently died from overwhelming pneumonia. Her lungs were filled with fluid, the blood vessels congested to the point of bursting. Nothing was seen under the microscope with routine Gram staining designed to reveal the presence of almost any known bacteria. Finally, the CDC's lab tests using an electron-microscopic examination of the tissue samples sent by the PHOs confirmed that a large number of unusually large viral particles were found.

At 3 P.M., a "preliminary" announcement was given to the Colorado governor's office and the president of the United States: The leukemia patient died from smallpox, a disease that was last seen in the United States in late 1940s. According to the data given to the governor and the president, within ten days after the initial exposure at the Denver basketball arena, there will be hundreds of thousands of people ill in Colorado, New Mexico, Utah, and Wyoming.

Dozens of people were already falling ill with smallpox-like symptoms in several major U.S. cities, and only the ones with electronic, Web-based surveillance were able to give accurate counts and reports. Public health officials asked the media to inform the public; in this case, they had accurate data and were confident that "getting the message out" was the right thing to do. The PHOs also informed physicians, since it was the only way to quickly reach a high percentage of the medical community. They immediately held a press conference early that same evening to inform the public that a probable bioterrorism event with smallpox had taken place.

The national vaccine stockpile was mobilized, and prepositioned "push packs" containing millions of doses of vaccine were sent to major cities around the country; they arrive within twelve hours. To combat panic and keep a semblance of order, the CDC, in conjunction with the U.S. Army Medical Research Institute in Infectious Diseases (USAMRIID), sets up hundreds of vaccination clinics. CDC officials knew from the start that they had a major fight on their hands, because it will be at least twenty-four hours before the first doses of vaccine are administered. In that time, many more people will become infected with the highly contagious disease.

Thanks to the diagnostic information available over the Internet, it was quickly determined that the window of opportunity was still open to stop the disease before it blazed into a worldwide pandemic. Since all who were ill were known to have been at the basketball game, the earliest date of infection would have been April 22. That meant that at the latest, the CDC and USAMRIID were coming into action on day four of the nascent outbreak.

This was an important fact, since the smallpox vaccine is known to be effective if given within four days of exposure. From the start, the CDC knew that not everyone receiving the vaccine would be protected from dying from smallpox, since some people near ground zero of the terrorist event obviously inhaled massive numbers of smallpox particles. But many of these people would survive. Perhaps more important, contacts of those individuals—the family members and coworkers who didn't go to the game but interacted with them the next day—could be vaccinated and saved.

The president gave full authority to kick off a national vaccine effort. It was, after all, a foregone conclusion in the age of rapid travel by car and airplane that the outbreaks would otherwise spread all over the country. The results are well known. Not all efforts to distribute the vaccine went exactly as planned. Due to poor logistics, several boroughs of St. Louis suffered delays in getting the vaccine, and riots broke out in several areas, preventing the Federal Emergency Management Agency from setting up effectively. Martial law had to be declared before vaccination stations, protected by National Guard and U.S. Army contingents, could be safely set up.

In addition, for unknown reasons, several public university systems in the Pacific Northwest received shipments of vaccine that were improperly manufactured. This resulted in patients receiving a "dud" vaccine. The CDC did its best to fly in additional medical assistance, but in the end hundreds of people—many of them college students—either died or had to suffer brutal scarring from the rising epidemic of smallpox.

And yet, despite the mix-ups and the draconian decisions that had to be made to get resources where they were needed, the program was remarkably successful. The economic costs for this attack ran into the hundreds of millions of dollars, and several thousand people died in those first few months. To this day, wherever scattered pockets of individuals who refused to be vaccinated live, we still hear of occasional flare-ups of the disease. Yet this gruesome toll is not even a tiny fraction of what could have been: tens of millions dead, trillions of dollars lost, and the very security of our nation compromised.

Even taking into account the incidents in the Northwest and St. Louis, over 90 percent of the vaccine distribution went off acceptably—not smoothly or efficiently perhaps, but with just enough time to get people vaccinated. It was precious time, purchased by the alert school nurse and hospital attending physicians in the Denver area who spotted the strange cases of infection and got public health officials to act once the epidemic became apparent in its earliest stages. Early detection—within a few hours of the earliest cases, rather than days or weeks—made all of the difference.

We have since learned that the key to stopping a repeat of the Denver incident is twofold. First, rapid communication is paramount. Second, a high "index of suspicion" (continuous awareness of the possibility of the unusual) among the true experts in disease outbreaks—the public health officials—needs to be built and shared. In the absence of shared information, no physician, nurse, or even pathologist would even suspect an unusual disease. But, with a few pieces of simple data, the pace of the investigation and the final outcome can change dramatically.

The Internet-based software that allowed many of these people to share their findings and sound the alarm bell before the virus turned into a global conflagration was simple to install and easy to operate. Yet this tiny software package did more to save millions of Americans than anything else. Without this basic information-sharing tool, all we would have today would be the security tapes of those four men who killed so many fellow citizens.

Much as the Al Qaeda terrorist group did at the start of the twenty-first century, the Gang of Four has changed the way we live today. Since there was insufficient vaccine to immunize the world's population, smallpox is back as a global endemic disease. All the brilliant work of the World Health Organization (WHO) in the 1960s and 1970s must be redone. Like an evil genie, smallpox is again out of the bottle. WHO estimates it will take years to eradicate smallpox in the wild again, though it has been done before and can be done again.

Children born after the Denver incident will need to get their smallpox vaccination and adults their boosters, and they'll lose a day of their lives to the flu-like symptoms caused by the vaccine. And yet, to change our lives does not mean defeat. By cheating the bioterrorists of their victory, we have proved that with the right preparation and vigilance, they simply cannot win.

NOTES

1. We are grateful to William Stanhope, PA, associate director for special projects at the Center for the Study of Bioterrorism and Emerging Infections at St. Louis University, who developed much of this scenario with coauthor Alan Zelicoff for a CDC counterterrorism exercise.

CHAPTER 16

INTO A CRYSTAL BALL, DARKLY—A LOOK AT THE FUTURE

Ever since a now-obscure U.S. Surgeon General declared that infectious diseases were soon to be relegated to the ash heap of history because of advances in medical treatment and the promise of ever more powerful antibiotics, government funding for public health and the role of public health in daily medical practice have suffered enormously. Most government officials and congressional appropriators think of public health as a nineteenth-century collection of aged practitioners inspecting restaurants and occasionally identifying exotic diseases that happen someplace other than the United States and the economically privileged countries. There has been little wisdom in this pecuniary approach and, until recently, nothing but luck has ensured that large outbreaks of disease haven't visited our shores.

Near the dawn of the twenty-first century, however, the appearance of West Nile fever, the massive outbreak of severe diarrheal disease in Milwaukee, and the ever-growing problems of mad cow disease (now also found in elk, deer, and goats) and avian influenza may finally be the crises needed to reorient our collective attention to the evident rise of unusual infectious disease among animals and humans.

Our public health surveillance system is highly balkanized, essentially a group of 5,000 or more independent offices that cover jurisdictions as populous as Manhattan and as tiny as counties of 1,500 people or less in Maine, New Hampshire, Wyoming, and elsewhere. These local public health offices communicate poorly with each other and even less well with the "consumers" of their information: physicians, veterinarians, and government decision makers who must decide if, for example, a case of meningitis warrants a massive, immediate, regionwide vaccination campaign (at great expense to the public treasury) or if the situation can be observed for a period of time. As is often the case in the United States, it may take a tragedy of massive proportions—perhaps something along the lines of a 9/11–style attack, only this time with a biological agent such as smallpox or anthrax—before we are girded into action.

But it needn't be so. This chapter explores a future that might be a bit less uncertain and frightening with regard to newly emerging disease and bioterrorism. In this future scenario, much suffering and expense can be avoided even if only the "usual" mortal infectious diseases are managed in a much more effective manner than they are today. But it requires that we improve and replace our current haphazard patchwork of a public health system where isolated officials, doctors, and nurses do their daily work largely in a vacuum, without the slightest idea of what is brewing around them and what they might have to face in the next days or even hours.

Are we overdue for the next pandemic? Well, by any comparison with history, it's been a long time since humanity's last pandemic. If you believe in luck, we've been lucky. If you take a darker view, we're "overdue."

Typically, a pandemic-level disease ripples through the human population roughly every five or six decades. It's arguable that the last real pandemic—one that resulted in the deaths of more than 20 million people worldwide—was the great influenza epidemic of 1918. Of course, many would counter with the proposition that with the emergence of West Nile, SARS, and HIV, many diseases have spread around the globe, due in no small part to an ever-increasing population density and the modern intercontinental transportation system that drives the world economy.

And yet these outbreaks have lacked the twin characteristics of pandemics. The first of these would be a high degree of transmissibility. HIV, to take one example, is extremely hard to contract compared with many viruses, since it is a fragile virus and doesn't live long outside of the human cells it infects. For this reason, it is transmitted by bodily fluids and not a handshake. The second would be a high degree of lethality or the ability to cause serious illness. HIV does pass this test, because AZT or exotic drug cocktails do no more than relegate this killer to the "chronic disease" status.

The more easily transmitted West Nile virus does not pass the tests, either. The true scourges of mankind throughout history, such as smallpox, plague, or influenza, have unfortunately passed both of these tests with flying colors, proving to be highly transmissible and highly lethal.

One can predict that an increase in the interaction among wild birds, domestic food animals, and people will also increase the chance of us seeing a new strain of flu in the upcoming decades. This flu could have the pathogenic qualities of the 1918 strain—or it could be much more lethal.

We have seen the result of people entering into areas where humans have not gone before and coming into contact with creatures that harbor deadly new plagues such as Ebola. And perhaps most disturbingly, we have altered the feeding habits of stock animals in a completely unnatural way. Until very recently, industrial farming involved feeding animal parts back into the same species, resulting in problems with new variant Creutzfeldt-Jakob disease (also known as mad cow disease) entering our food supply.

But the central roadblock to communication of infectious disease milestones such as these, and by far the biggest obstacle, is political. Few countries want to admit when they have a problem with an outbreak of disease. As result, diseases tend to enter a population and spread like wildfire when intervention could have stopped the process from getting out of hand.

China's reaction to the SARS epidemic is a classic example, but there are other ones. Consider the 1994 plague outbreak in India. The incident began with a report of plague from the city of Surat in the Gujarat province where India borders Pakistan. Instead of getting out as much information as possible on the outbreak, the Indian government responded by keeping people from moving and shutting down all information channels. The end result was mass panic and chaotic evacuation of the city led, ironically enough, by physicians who too succumbed to the rampant *rumors* of plague.

Based on the research done after the incident, the Surat outbreak may not have been much of an epidemic at all. There were probably one or two people who had plague, but the government mistakenly thought it was more extensive than it really was. It seems likely that there was another type of infectious disease circulating at the same time, such as influenza. It was almost certainly the *lack* of information that led to panic and the spontaneous mass evacuation of Surat. Dissemination of carefully chosen information would probably have helped to control the panic and minimize the disruption of the entire local economy.

Regrettably, the story of government mishandling of public health information was repeated in China with SARS. The Chinese government remained unforthcoming with information about the disease up until the last possible moment. It had hoped that suppressing the information would prevent the loss of trading income into China. Yet exactly the opposite happened. The lack of information produced high uncertainty, and China paid an enormous price in human life and commercially. In the end, the international cover-ups by the Chinese and Indian governments made things worse.

This, then, begs the question: Why do countries behave this way in the first place? Well, they don't want to be stigmatized as the infectious disease source. Viruses are typically named after the place where they are discovered (e.g., Ebola-Sudan or Venezuelan encephalitis) or where they have caused an outbreak of disease (e.g., the Marburg virus or Ebola-Reston). Hantavirus was initially called the "Four Corners virus" until vociferous complaints from the local residents of the Four Corners area of Arizona, New Mexico, Colorado, and Utah altered the name and removed the stigma that would have come along with the designation.

A way to get around that label is to have a uniform method of naming new infectious agents that does not use geographic references. Instead of labeling the outbreak as "Indian flu" or "Surat disease," as happened in the 1994 plague outbreak in Surat, India, you would have more names like SARS (severe adult respiratory syndrome). SARS is an excellent example of proper, nonstigmatized nomenclature that is much more neutral than "Shanghai pneumonia" or the "Chinese flu."

WHAT PATHOGEN WILL CAUSE THE NEXT MAJOR OUTBREAK?

Predicting exactly what the next outbreak could potentially be is, of course, pure speculation. Even with decades of tracking influenza, we don't have a viable mathematical predictive model for the most common of fatal infectious diseases in the United States. In large measure, this appalling lack of predictive ability is due to an essentially random surveillance system that is based solely on laboratory samples collected at the whim of physicians and not in any systematic fashion. Yet, as with any kind of guess, one can at least follow trends, think a bit about the natural evolutionary forces involved, and make an educated estimate. The next pathogenic organism to emerge upon the scene in a pandemic fashion is likely to have the following characteristics:

- It will be zoonotic in nature. The primary host will not be human and may very well be a domestic food animal.

- It will be highly lethal to human beings, because humans will be dead-end hosts to the organism. Thus, the organism will not depend on mobile or moderately ill humans to continue to proliferate.
- It may be transmitted by vectors such as mosquitoes or ticks, but could very well be spread by aerosol, especially in places where there are high concentrations of people.

What the Centers for Disease Control and Prevention (CDC) worries about most is the emergence of an avian strain of influenza that directly enters the human population. The worry stems from the fact that virtually every human being in Southeast Asia visits a live animal market to buy chickens. Even in relatively urbanized parts of Southeast Asia, people purchase live chickens at the market, and therefore are exposed to a full complement of parasites and pathogens. If those chickens are infected with a highly transmissible form of influenza, the probability that it can jump from the birds to humans is high.

One has to be even more cautious about making predictions about incidents of bioterrorism. However, again we can make some educated guesses based on our current knowledge. For example, bioterrorists bent on overwhelming destruction probably would not choose anthrax, because it is not communicable from person to person. To start a true pandemic you need something highly contagious, like smallpox or new strain of influenza.

HOW WORRIED SHOULD WE BE ABOUT BIOTERRORISM?

Bioterrorism is relatively hard to implement compared with more conventional methods of terror, such explosives or chemicals. However, the sheer level of societal disruption does make it an attractive option to those bent on our destruction.

Once the right technology and knowledge have been purchased, there are quite a few advantages to implementing this form of terror over conventional methods. Manufacturing bioweapons takes less space than a large tractor-trailer truck, and delivery systems can be the size of a test tube or a backpack. A simple aerosol pump, a crop-dusting plane, or the U.S. mail service can take a pathogen directly to its target.

As recently as twenty years ago, bioterrorists needed the resources of a nation-state in order to create an effective weapon. State-sponsored infrastructure was needed to synthesize DNA—one step at a time—by hand. We know now that this was successfully done in the former Soviet bioweapons program in the 1980s.

We also know that the Soviets managed to grow lethal organisms like smallpox in large quantities and were able to effectively preserve them. They were able to locate naturally occurring strains of certain organisms such as plague that happened to be much more lethal than more commonly occurring strains around the world. And finally, we know that the Soviet techniques of gene splicing, no matter how crude by today's standards, managed to enhance the strains of plague bacteria with resistance to the world's existing stockpile of antibiotics.

Today, these the techniques and tools are well known because they have become standards in the field of molecular biology and are helping scientists understand, at the cellular level, how organisms cause disease. So rather than requiring the resources of a state, many American university campuses have everything you need to brew up a bioweapon. The infrastructure and the know-how would likely cost in the tens of millions, not the hundreds or billions, of dollars.

In short, what the Soviets accomplished with a massive program in the 1980s is now part and parcel of medical school microbiology. The techniques have become ubiquitous. But the creation of a hypothetical "superbug" is not the real threat resulting from biological experimentation. The real advances and biotechnology that are of import to biological-weapons creation are *not* in the field of genetically altered organisms. The germs, in other words, are deadly enough on their own.

The advances in biotechnology that are particularly worrisome are twofold. One is our ability to grow vast quantities of organisms. In many cases, this is the same technology that has been developed by pharmaceutical companies in order to produce mass quantities of vaccines and lifesaving medicines, such as human insulin.

The other advance is our ability to make an already-dangerous organism hardier. Using gene splicing and other techniques, we can make an organism resistant to dehydration or ultraviolet (UV) radiation. This does not make a germ any more likely to kill the people it infects, but it does significantly raise the probability of a mass outbreak.

Today, scientists can consistently create particles in the five- to ten-micron range. The average human hair, by comparison, is around fifty microns in diameter. This is a triumph for medical researchers developing treatments for patients with asthma and other serious respiratory diseases. This technique, which is called *microencapsulation,* is most commonly used in allergy treatment products such as Flonase or in asthma inhalers. The same technology is being developed for inhalable forms of insulin and other hormones, in the hopes of freeing people from needle-based injections.

Unfortunately, microencapsulation technology can also be applied to dangerous pathogens to make them more environmentally stable and better able to survive dissemination as an aerosol. When particles are extremely small and this fine, they don't clump together and fall to the ground, which ensures that they are inhaled deeply into the lungs and, therefore, become much more deadly.

This technology has an added benefit as a bioweapon as well. Particles of a disease like anthrax can float on even the tiniest air currents and travel for miles before being inhaled by a human or animal. In fact, this ability to effectively spread pathogens in the air worries the CDC even more than our ability to make the pathogens themselves hardier and more dangerous.

The lesson of the Russian bioweapon program's smallpox outbreak in 1971 is one that we would do well to remember today. The conventional wisdom at that time was that the smallpox virus could not be effectively encapsulated to protect it from natural degradation when exposed to sunlight and water. Therefore, it was thought that you could not aerosolize smallpox and have it survive when traveling in the air over long distances. Conventional wisdom was proved wrong. In either a test or an accident—to this day, we are not sure which, and we may never know the truth—smallpox wafted from the facility to the outside environment like invisible smoke, and people up to ten miles away broke out with the oldest plague to afflict humanity.

This was a phenomenon that had never been seen in nature. This was smallpox with the ability to travel up to city-size distances on the wind.

CAN WE FIX OUR PUBLIC HEALTH SYSTEM?

It's often a frightening time when public health and epidemiology must cross paths. It's extremely difficult for a public health official to know what to do because so much of the knowledge available during an outbreak is negative in nature. Many times, at the onset of any outbreak—or bioterrorist event—it will be easier to determine what the organism is *not,* instead of what it is.

All that the public health official may know is that the organism that is afflicting a given area or city is not influenza, not smallpox, and not anthrax. Typically, a limited amount of negative information may narrow the field, but it hardly provides an exact course of action, especially in a time-critical situation where hundreds or thousands of people may be infected with an unknown pathogen.

To begin with, public health officials need to be able to make decisions based on whether the organism in question is something that really needs to be worried about. To know whether the unknown pathogen could become a pandemic, much like the influenza pandemic of 1918, they have to estimate the epidemic's growth rate. For example, as discussed in Chapter 2 on SARS, public health officials determined that, on average, one SARS patient could infect one other individual.

Then we need an effective public health system to respond successfully to medical emergencies. That means fixing the broken public health system by providing the funding and the support to enable health officials and other medical authorities to do a number of specific yet critical things:

1. Public health offices need to be able to detect when something "unusual" is going on that could be an indicator of infectious disease. This unusualness may be recognized in:
   - The appearance of odd symptoms
   - The appearance of symptoms across a large geographic area or specific age groups
   - A sudden increase in the number of ill animals or people that is out of the range of past experience

2. Public health officials need to be aware of what is going in the animal community as well as the human one. Many pathogens are zoonotic in nature. The anthrax spore, for example, does not see a cow as a four-legged bovine and a human as a separate, distinct sentient being. For all intents and purposes, the cow and the human are the same: They are meat. They are meat to be consumed by the bacteria, just as a predatory cat or a great white shark tears into its prey.

3. Once something strange is detected, public health officials need to be able to quickly identify the risk factors for acquiring the new pathogen. Young versus old. Black versus white. Asian versus Native American. Rich versus poor. Only then can they target populations that need intervention most quickly, based on whatever information is available.

4. Physicians and veterinarians need to be actively engaged in the public health system. There are many more practicing doctors than there are health officials, and yet, because public health officials very rarely give explicit instructions on what to do, physicians rarely have meaningful instructions to give out to patients. Veterinarians are equally important to our disease detection system, if only because *all* of the major disease outbreaks in the United States in the past thirty years have begun as animal diseases. On the off chance of a bioterrorism attack, since the disease organism(s) that will be employed will be primarily animal

pathogens (e.g., anthrax, tularemia, encephalitis viruses), there is virtual certainty that animals will get ill even before humans do.

With improvements in our public health system, once sick patients are identified, even if we do not know a single thing about the organism that is causing their illness, we at least stand a better chance of isolating it. Then we can envision using pieces of the DNA of the germ as a vaccine that is likely to be far more effective, taking effect far more quickly, than the protein-based vaccines we currently use.

WHAT LESSONS HAVE WE LEARNED?

Physicians can appropriately amplify instructions that are given to them by public health officials. Let's look at the concrete example of the hantavirus outbreak in New Mexico in 1991. On week two of the outbreak, no one knew what the organism really was. People were getting sick and dying, and there was still no clue about what the organism could be, what its reservoir might be, and how it was transmitted.

By interviewing the families of patients who were sick, doctors were able to determine the "risk factors" for acquiring the disease. In this case, the risk factors identified included being Navajo, being poor, living in a hogan (a Navajo dwelling made of logs and mud), sleeping on the floor, or disturbing the nests of field mice. So even though no one had any idea what the organism was, doctors were able to tell people that if they were Navajo, poor, and lived in a hogan, they shouldn't sleep on the floor and should avoid disturbing the nests of field mice.

It later turned out to be the case that the field mouse was, in fact, the reservoir for the organism. The virus has been living inside the mice for tens of thousands of years. The reason the virus broke out so heavily that year was because there had been a wet, El Niño winter, which caused the grass to be exceptionally abundant, leading to an explosion in the population of field mice.

Even in the absence of a complete hypothesis unifying all of the observations made by physicians, veterinarians, and other health care providers and biologists, identifying and acting upon the risk factors played a major part in slowing and stopping the spread of hanta—even when the risk factors were not causal. For example, sleeping on the floor did not cause you to be infected with hantavirus. However, sleeping on the floor put you at risk of contracting hantavirus from some unknown source. That source turned out to be a little field mouse that entered the hogan at night and sprayed its urine around the dwelling. When people were advised not to sleep on the floor and to avoid exposure to field mice, it was just enough information to hamper the virus's chain of transmission.

It wasn't a vaccine that stopped the hantavirus outbreak. Nor was it medication. There wasn't a single vaccine or medication in the world that could have treated hantavirus at that time. It wasn't a brilliant new medical invention or even a genius insight by a scientist or researcher that saved many more people from dying of respiratory distress. It was just two easy-to-follow bits of advice.

A FINAL WORD ON THE FUTURE

Hantavirus pulmonary syndrome was originally called Four Corners pulmonary syndrome. The description was a concrete application of syndrome surveillance. It stated what the area at risk was—the northwest corner of New Mexico—so epidemiologists knew they needed to focus attention on that part of the state, even when they didn't know what the organism was.

The risk factors for acquiring the bug were also quickly deduced through commonsense observation and a small amount of luck: A single physician recognized that the deaths of two young people (who turned out to be related to each other) were highly "unusual." He called other hospitals scattered across the vast Navajo Nation and found a few other cases that were similar to the patients he had just seen die. This alone was enough of a beginning to guide epidemiologists to identify risk factors and ultimately, the source of the virus—the field mouse. This story proved that much sophisticated data collection could be reduced to very specific, very basic steps that reduced the risk of the public contracting a given disease.

The only reason the hanta story had a happy ending was because this one doctor—Dr. Bruce Tempest—was observant, patient, smart, and courageous enough to say, "There is something strange going on here that needs to be checked out." There are too many people in medicine today who would not—or could not—have done those things.

Let us hope that we can do better the next time.

APPENDIX

LETTER (BY E-MAIL) TO LEV SANDAKHCHIEV

15 July 2002

Prof. Lev S. Sandakhchiev
General Director
State Research Center of Virology and Biotechnology
633159 Koltsovo, Novosibirsk region, Russia

Dearest Lev Stepanovich:

As your friends and colleagues, we are writing in an unofficial capacity to ask that you extend your personal efforts to obtain and share as much information as possible regarding the Aralsk smallpox outbreak in 1971. We know that VEKTOR could not have been involved in any way in the testing of smallpox on Vozrozhdeniye Island, but we also believe that you are the best-situated person in all of Russia to seek and find the answers to critical questions regarding the outbreak.

We believe that the Aralsk smallpox outbreak is extremely significant because it indicated that smallpox can indeed be carried as an aerosol over long distances, and this has great importance for all of us who care about defending against the possibility of terrorists using biological weapons. Also, there are other questions about the nature of the smallpox strain used in that biological weapons test, as you can understand.

As a measure of the new relationship between your Institute and ours, we ask that you:

1. Do all in your power to find out what strain was involved in the outbreak, and whether that strain resides in the VEKTOR collection today.

2. Try to determine the amount of variola used in the Vozrozhdeniye test in 1971, and what kind of preparation (growth media, special coatings, or "hardening") was used in that test.

3. Help us to find appropriate ways to transfer samples of the Aralsk strain to the CDC in Atlanta. If necessary, we will seek funding and personnel to carry out this important task, and will work with our colleagues in the U.S. Department of Commerce and Department of Transportation to create a channel for movement of the samples.

In return, we propose that all research on the Aralsk strain take place collaboratively; we will do all in our power to arrange for funding for this work. The details of the research will be negotiated of course, but, in our opinion, it is first necessary to accomplish the steps outlined above. From our informal discussions with various U.S. Government officials, it is clear that the future success of the CTR and ISTC programs may depend on finding the answers to these questions quickly.[1] We very much hope that these collaboration programs can continue. We pledge that we will try to convince these officials to maintain funding for collaborative programs, but we will surely require help from you in order to guarantee success.

Lev Stepanovich, this unfortunate outbreak occurred over 30 years ago, under the Soviet regime, and prior to the coming in force of the BWC [Biological Weapons Convention]. A new era is upon us, and we hope that information from these dangerous experiments can help us to work with you to prevent the use of smallpox as a biological weapon. We know that you share with us a passionate attachment to that goal. We have little interest in raking up the past, except where that is necessary to protect our future.

If there is evidence to suggest we are asking the wrong questions about the 1971 outbreak, we would be more than happy to get that advice.

What we have to emphasize is the importance of candor and frankness to convince high U.S. officials that support for our international collaborations is in our mutual best interest.

Respectfully Yours,

Joshua Lederberg, MD
Tom Monath, MD
Peter Jahrling, PhD
Alan Zelicoff, MD

NOTES

CTR (Cooperative Threat Reduction): This was a Department of Defense program entered into with Russia to convert weapons production infrastructure (chemical, biological nuclear) to peaceful, civilian use.

ISTC (International Science and Technology Center): A funding entity of the US and European Union that provides grants to scientists in Russia's biological and nuclear industry to keep them employed locally as opposed to providing expertise in these areas to rogue nations.

GLOSSARY

aerosol A particle (made of any material of any density) that is small enough and in the correct shape (usually round, but not necessarily so) so that it remains buoyant in the atmosphere without external energy to keep it aloft. From a functional standpoint, an aerosol particle behaves essentially "like the air itself."

In the context of disease, infectious particles that behave as aerosols (e.g., the influenza virus expelled during a cough or a sneeze) can spread long distances—many hundreds of feet or even miles—and infect other susceptible hosts. As a result, much of the research in biological weapons programs—both legal "defensive" and illegal "offensive" programs—is focused on the generation of aerosols and engineering organisms that can sustain the processes by which they can be converted into aerosols.

Some organisms (e.g., the bacteria that cause tularemia) appear to aerosolize naturally whereas others (e.g., pneumococcus) do not, at least under typical environmental conditions. As a general rule of thumb, in order for infectious particles to behave as aerosols, their size must be in the range of 2–8 microns (millionths of a meter) in diameter.

Alzheimer's disease A poorly understood degenerative disease of the human brain leading to memory loss, personality changes, and dementia, and ultimately ending in death. The cause of Alzheimer's disease is unknown, but based on the best scientific evidence to date, it is *not* due to a disease-causing protein or ***prion*** (q.v.).

amino acid The basic chemical constituent of proteins. Multiple amino acids strung together are, by definition, a protein. About 20 amino acids are found in most of the proteins that make up life on earth. Some examples of amino acids are well known to those who purchase them as dietary supplements: tryptophan, lysine, arginine, etc. A small subset of amino acids (e.g., valine, phenylalanine, tryptophan, lysine, and histidine) are called "essential" amino acids because they cannot be synthesized by humans or other mammals and must be obtained from external food sources.

antibiotic Natural or chemically synthesized materials that inhibit the growth, reproduction, and survival of organisms. "Antimicrobial" drug typically refers to an antibiotic directed against either bacteria or viruses (bacteria being the more common-use meaning of the term); "antiviral" drugs are effective only against certain viral species and not against bacteria.

Antibiotics are often characterized by their "spectrum"—that is, the range of organisms they kill. "Broad spectrum" antibiotics are effective against a large number or large group of organisms but are seldom as effective as a "narrow spectrum" antibiotic chosen to counter the effects of a specific organism. The improper use of broad-spectrum antibiotics is probably responsible for the large number of antibiotic-resistant organisms now present in the environment at large and in hospital and surgical suites in particular.

arenavirus A single-stranded, RNA-containing virus most often carried by rodent hosts and spread to humans via direct contact with the rodent or its urine or droppings.

bacteria Organisms that are single-celled and may be free living (in soil or water) or parasitic (depending on external sources of energy for their life processes). Bacteria may "cooperate" with one another by exchanging genetic material (e.g., genes for antibiotic resistance) or exuding a complex film-like material for protection against adverse environmental factors.

The overwhelming majority of bacteria are not known to cause disease in otherwise health humans or animals, but it has been recognized in recent years that certain "benign" bacteria can cause disease in immunosuppressed animals and humans. Bacteria may be motile and may also form essentially inert spores that then germinate when environmental conditions are appropriate.

The classification scheme for bacteria is extremely complex because of their ubiquity and the fact that they occupy essentially every known environmental niche (including those with extraordinarily harsh temperature extremes).

biofilm A layer of material containing microorganisms and their very complex external secretions that may be found on almost any surface given sufficient moisture and appropriate temperature. Biofilms have only recently been subjected to serious study, even though their existence (on teeth, for example) has been known for a long time.

It appears that biofilms are "communities" of organisms and that the biofilm matrix permits signaling molecules to be easily passed from organism to another, acting as a communications medium.

Biofilms may result from adverse environmental conditions and permit the continued survival of organisms; they also permit organisms to colonize medical equipment (e.g., catheters, respirators, dental equipment, etc.) and may thus serve as sources of infection in patients in the hospital or visiting a clinic.

Biosafety levels in laboratories The CDC provides the following definitions for Biosafety level laboratories in the 4th Edition of *Biosafety in Microbiological and Biomedical Laboratories* (1999):

(1) BIOSAFETY LEVEL 1 is suitable for work involving well-characterized agents not known to cause disease in healthy adult humans and of minimal potential hazard to laboratory personnel and the environment.

(2) BIOSAFETY LEVEL 2 is similar to Level 1 and is suitable for work involving agents of moderate potential hazard to personnel and the environment.

(3) BIOSAFETY LEVEL 3 is applicable to clinical, diagnostic, teaching, research, or production facilities in which work is done with indigenous or exotic agents that may cause serious or potentially lethal disease as a result of exposure by the inhalation route.

(4) BIOSAFETY LEVEL 4 is required for work with dangerous and exotic agents that pose a high individual risk of aerosol-transmitted laboratory infections and life-threatening disease.

bovine spongiform encephalopathy BSE or "mad cow" disease. A prion-caused degenerative disease of the central nervous system in cows, causing tiny holes to appear in the brain (making it look much like a sponge underneath the microscope), leading to abnormal behavior and movement disorders, and ultimately ending in death. BSE is closely related to scrapie in sheep (from which it *may* have originated, though this theory is controversial), chronic wasting disease of elk, and new variant Creutzfeldt-Jakob disease (nvCJD) in humans.

CJD occurs as a result of consuming BSE-prion contaminated animal parts, usually brain, lymph node, or intestinal tissue. Pure muscle is rarely infected with the BSE prion, but since so many meat products contain lymph nodes and nerve tissue, some contamination may be inevitable.

The number of cases of BSE exploded in England in the 1980s as a result of the practice of feeding waste animal parts and bone meal (so-called "offal") back to bovines. Once that practice was discontinued by law, the number of cases of BSE dropped dramatically. However, human cases of nvCJD started to appear several years later, probably because of the long incubation period of all prion-induced diseases.

bunyavirus A single-stranded RNA virus family, most of which are transmitted by mosquitoes. Hantavirus is a member of the bunyavirus family and is an exception to the insect-vector rule in the case of the disease hantavirus pulmonary syndrome, which is transmitted to humans from rodents via droppings or urine. Some encephalitis viruses such as La Crosse virus (named after the upper midwestern location of its original discovery) are also in this family.

coronavirus A family of single-stranded RNA viruses that, when viewed under the electron microscope, resembles a crown because of the numerous protein projections from the viral surface.

Coronaviruses have long been known to cause disease in animals and mild disease in humans, but a novel coronavirus (named coronavirus Urbani, after the World Health Organization physician) has been determined to be the cause of the severe adult respiratory syndrome (SARS) outbreak of 2002.

DNA Deoxyribonucleic acid. The helically shaped strand of ***nucleic acids*** (q.v.) that forms the basis of the ***genome*** (q.v.) of all organisms and cells. In naturally occurring DNA (also called "double-stranded DNA") the nucleic acids are found in pairs, with each pair spanning across the central axis of the helix.

These "base pairs" are the genetic code that specifies specific ***amino acids*** (q.v.) that are assembled in order to form a protein. The structure of DNA was originally described in detail by James Watson and Francis Crick in 1953. Along with Maurice Wilkins, they were awarded the Nobel Prize in Medicine in 1962 for the discovery.

Ebola A virus of the "filovirus" ("hair-like") family that can cause a fatal hemorrhagic illness in humans. Ebola disease was first recognized in the 1970s, although the cause of the illness remained unknown for many years.

The natural reservoir of virus is unknown, although primates are occasionally infected. Ebola spreads from human to human more or less exclusively by contact with the infected blood of dead or dying victims. Thus, simple barrier precautions (such as gloves and masks) are effective at preventing transmission and ending Ebola epidemics.

encephalitis A diffuse (i.e., nonlocalized) inflammation of the brain that often leads to behavioral changes, memory disturbances, and confusion.

enzyme Chemical entity with a protein structure (that is, made of amino acids) that catalyzes a specific reaction or set of reactions within cells.

Enzymes may destroy other proteins ("proteases") or nucleic acids ("endonucleases"), or they may cause smaller molecules to join together into larger ones ("synthetases").

Enzymes are ubiquitous in all forms of life, from highly evolved, multicelled mammals to viruses, bacteria, and even ***prions*** (q.v.), which are, in fact, disease-causing enzymes in and of themselves.

epidemic An outbreak of disease (not necessarily an infectious disease, but perhaps one resulting from a common source exposure to a toxin) that, in general, affects a large number of people at more or less the same time and in a geographic space that is reasonably well defined. The word "large," just like the word "epidemic" itself, is a term of art in the practice of epidemiology and is subject to the context in which the disease occurs.

epidemiology The study of patterns of disease and disease progression in a population, including the behaviors and risk factors that may contribute to the acquisition or spread of disease.

equine encephalitis A group of viral-induced, mosquito diseases that affect primarily birds and horses, though sometimes humans may be infected as "bystander" or "dead end" hosts. *Eastern* equine encephalitis has a mortality of about 50% to 60% in humans, and horse mortality is in excess of 85%, whereas *Western* equine encephalitis carries a mortality of less than 7%. Fortunately, both of these diseases are rare in humans, with fewer than 1,000 cases of each reported since 1964.

evolutionary biology The study of the descent of animals, plants, and microorganisms by modification of their genome to adapt to new (or changing) environments and permit continued survival. While this academic discipline dates back at least to the late 1930s, most universities in Europe and United States had few courses with the explicit term "evolutionary biology" in their titles until the late 1970s.

Evolutionary biology includes the complex mathematical modeling of survival strategies of organisms based on their fundamental transmission modes (e.g., vector versus host-to-host spread) and pathogenicity (i.e., ability to cause disease symptoms or disability in hosts).

flavivirus A small (50 nanometer) virus that is made up of a single strand of RNA surrounded by a protective membrane. Yellow fever, Japanese encephalitis, dengue fever, and hepatitis C are all members of the flavivirus family.

Many flaviviruses are transmitted by mosquitoes (e.g., dengue, encephalitis viruses), while others (e.g., hepatitis C) are not.

gene The portion of the genome of an organism that contains sufficient genetic material to permit the complete synthesis of an entire protein.

These proteins may be structural (e.g., components of a cell wall) or functional (e.g., an enzyme, toxin, or protective material).

genetic engineering The intentional alteration of the genome of an organism or cell in order to change any of a large number of behaviors (e.g., host range, disease severity or symptoms, environmental hardiness, antibiotic resistance) or to cause the organism to produce a product that it normally does not produce (the most widely applied type of genetic engineering).

For example, most human insulin is no longer isolated from the pancreatic glands of dead animals, but rather is produced by the common intestinal organism *E. coli,* into which the *human* gene for insulin has been inserted. This permits a high-purity, relatively inexpensive insulin to be manufactured in huge quantities that is completely identical to natural human insulin. The same approach has been successful with multiple other hormones.

genome The collection of all genes within an organism.

hantavirus pulmonary syndrome (HPS) The CDC describes HPS, commonly referred to as hantavirus disease, as "a febrile illness characterized by bilateral interstitial pulmonary infiltrates and respiratory compromise, usually requiring supplemental oxygen and clinically resembling acute respiratory disease syndrome (ARDS). The typical prodrome consists of fever, chills, myalgia, headache, and gastrointestinal symptoms."

highly pathogenic avian influenza One of several influenza viruses that results in markedly depressed activity of birds, swelling of their combs and wattles, and diarrhea and often diffuse hemorrhage (bleeding) in the feet and throat. The disease is usually fatal within 48 hours. On rare occasions, this same virus may be transmitted directly from birds to humans, but is not believed to ever be transmitted from one infected human to another.

immunosuppression A compromised state of the immune system due to age, chemical exposure, genetic aberration, radiation, or infection that results in a relative inability to generate a full, multipronged response to invading organisms or toxins.

Immunosuppression occurs frequently during and after cancer chemotherapy, as a result of HIV and other infections, and at the extremes of life (newborns and the very elderly, in which it is sometimes referred to as "immune senescence").

incubation period The time from initial exposure to a disease-causing agent (not necessarily an infectious agent, since toxin-induced diseases also have an incubation period) until the onset of particular symptoms.

Incubation periods vary widely and may be characteristic of certain diseases. For example, the incubation period of smallpox (from exposure to onset of rash) is approximately 13 days, much longer than most viral infections.

influenza A diverse group of RNA-containing viruses that share in common two surface chemicals—hemagglutinin and neuramidase—that assist in viral binding to, and entry into, mammalian and avian cells. The virus may cause the *disease* "influenza" (in humans or primates) or "avian influenza" in birds.

Influenza transmits easily from human to human in most cases as an aerosol, so that one infected individual is capable of infecting many others. The virus also has a high propensity for mutation, which accounts for new forms of influenza disease suddenly causing massive epidemics as occurred in 1918. Fortunately, most mutations of the virus are unsuccessful in infecting humans.

isolation The separation from the rest of the population of individuals thought to have been exposed to a communicable infectious illness, *or* who are at high risk for exposure to an infectious illness.

Isolation is typically employed to protect individuals from contracting serious illness rather than for the sole purpose of preventing their infecting others; it should be distinguished from ***quarantine*** (q.v.).

Japanese encephalitis A viral disease of birds and pigs that frequently spreads to humans through mosquitoes. It is mostly found in China and Southeast Asia, where approximately 50,000 cases are reported per year. Mortality rate in humans is about 30%.

Koch's postulates A series of requirements to prove the infectious (i.e., disease causing) nature of an organism, named after the famous nineteenth-century German bacteriologist Robert Koch. The requirements are:

- The bacteria must be present in every case of the disease.
- The bacteria must be isolated from the host with the disease and grown in pure culture.
- The specific disease must be reproduced when a pure culture of the bacteria is inoculated into a healthy susceptible host.
- The bacteria must be recoverable from the experimentally infected host.

While there are some limitations to the utility of these postulates (e.g., some organisms, such as the one that causes syphilis, may be difficult to grow in pure culture), they have served remarkably well for over 100 years in experimental microbiology.

Lassa fever A viral infection found mostly in West Africa that is characterized by abdominal pain, facial swelling, chest pain, diarrhea, and generalized weakness and may progress to massive internal bleeding. Because of the extraordinarily high concentration of the virus in the blood of human victims, Lassa is an extremely contagious disease and the highest possible barrier precautions must be in place when handling or caring for a patient with this disease.

Lyme disease A disease of humans and wildlife mammals caused by the *Borrelia borgdorfei* bacterium. Symptoms and signs are multiple and protean and may involve the brain, heart, and other organs of the body. Without prompt treatment with antibiotics, the disease may become chronic. It is transmitted primarily by the deer tick to humans.

necropsy Synonym for autopsy.

Newcastle disease A viral-caused disease of domestic fowl and other birds that is almost always fatal, even before birds show classical signs of the disease, which typically involves the nervous system. A vaccine is available, but very expensive.

nucleic acids The individual chemical components of DNA and RNA, usually paired with a second nucleic acid to form the helical structure of DNA. Guanine, thymine, cytosine, adenine, and uracil make up the vast majority of nucleic acids, and since they are found in greatest abundance in the nucleus of the cell, their name derives from that fact.

pandemic A very widespread disease—usually meaning that the disease is occurring in multiple countries or continents. The classical example is the 1918 influenza pandemic that affected at least 20% of the world's population and killed at least 2% to 5% of victims.

However, in more recent times, AIDS has been characterized as a pandemic as well—not because of the speed with which it spreads or kills, but because of the existence of AIDS cases in humans in virtually every country of the world.

pathogen A microorganism (bacteria, virus, or fungus) that causes disease in some host. Many pathogens are host-specific, whereas others can cause disease in a wide variety of species.

PCR Polymerase chain reaction. A laboratory technique where an enzyme (called a "polymerase") is used to make thousands or millions of copies of single pieces of DNA (a similar technique may be applied to RNA as well).

This technique is extremely useful for early diagnosis of disease because small amounts of the DNA unique to a pathogenic organism can be detected quickly and characterized very specifically, often within hours or days, well before standard culturing techniques yield useful results.

Peromyscus maniculatus Commonly known as the "deer mouse," this tiny rodent (or its close relatives) is the natural reservoir of hantavirus in the Americas.

pneumonia Any inflammation of the lungs (sometimes also called "pneumonitis"), but most typically a disease caused by infection by bacteria (e.g., pneumococcus), virus (e.g., influenza), or fungi (e.g., coccidiomycosis).

The prognosis of pneumonia in humans depends on the age and general health of the patient, the causal organism, and the availability of specific treatment. Many dozens of organisms are known to cause pneumonia, and some have been employed as biological weapons agents (e.g., anthrax, plague, and tularemia) because of their high mortality or morbidity rate.

prion A term coined to describe a new *pro*teinceous *in*fectious particle that has the property of being transmissible (i.e., infectious) from one host to another, replicating, and causing disease symptoms, yet possessing no DNA, RNA, or other nucleic-acid containing genetic material.

The prion was first described by Professor Stanley Pruisner of the University of California, San Francisco School of Medicine. Originally, Prusiner was derided as a kook, because the existence of a disease-causing protein that could also replicate *without* the presence of genetic material completely upended the basic paradigm of molecular biology described by Watson and Crick in 1953. Pruisner was later awarded the Nobel Prize in Medicine for his discovery. Prions are the cause of several severe dementia diseases in humans (Creutzfeldt-Jakob disease and "new variant Creutzfeldt-Jakob" disease), as well as mad cow disease in bovines, scrapie in sheep, and similar illnesses in large cats that have consumed prion-infected animal material.

protozoa Single-celled organisms that, unlike bacteria, possess a nucleus. Examples are amoebas, cryptosporidia, and toxoplasma. The latter two organisms are well-known for their ability to cause severe disease in immunosuppressed humans, but only mild disease in immunocompetent hosts.

quarantine The enforced isolation of individuals known (or strongly suspected to be) ill with infectious disease that is of a communicable nature (c.f. ***isolation***).

RNA Ribonucleic acid: a nucleic acid molecule similar to DNA but containing ribose rather than deoxyribose. RNA is formed upon a DNA template. There are several classes of RNA molecules. They play crucial roles in protein synthesis and other cell activities:

- Messenger RNA (mRNA) is a type of RNA that reflects the exact nucleoside sequence of the genetically active DNA. mRNA carries the "message" of the DNA to the cytoplasm of cells where protein is made in amino acid sequences specified by the mRNA.
- Transfer RNA (tRNA) is a short-chain type of RNA present in cells. There are 20 varieties of tRNA. Each variety combines with a specific amino acid and carries it along (i.e., transfers it), leading to the formation of protein with a specific amino acid arrangement dictated by DNA.
- Ribosomal RNA (rRNA) is a component of ribosomes. Ribosomal RNA functions as a nonspecific site for making polypeptides.

SARS Severe acute respiratory syndrome: a *description* of symptoms and signs that heralded the recognition of a new disease caused by a previously undescribed type of ***coronavirus*** (q.v.) in 2002. The actual reservoir of the virus remains unknown, and the disease spreads poorly from person to person, yet it carries a mortality rate of approximately 8%.

St. Louis encephalitis A viral disease of birds that can be spread to humans by mosquitoes and tends to be relatively mild as compared to equine encephalitis viruses that find their way into human hosts.

stroke Damage to a portion of the brain or spinal cord due to the sudden obstruction or rupture of a blood vessel supplying that area of the brain. Typically only one side of the brain is affected with each stroke, potentially resulting in loss of muscle or sensory function on one side of the body. Also called "cerebrovascular accident."

syndrome A syndrome definition is a combination of signs and symptoms. In its simplest form, signs are what a doctor finds upon examining the patient. Symptoms are what the patient complains about. Thus, "flu-like illness" is a syndrome of high fever, cough, muscle and joint aches, headache, and sometimes swollen lymph nodes and skin rash. Note that a syndrome is not a "diagnosis" but rather a description of the patient that assists the physician in reaching a diagnosis.

toxin A poisonous or noxious substance that is either part of a cell (including a plant cell or microorganism), secreted by a cell, or a combination of both. Toxins are, by definition, "nonliving" but are produced by living organisms. Examples include ricin (produced by the castor bean), botulinum toxin (produced by the organism *Clostridium botulinum*), and mycotoxins produced by some fungi.

Interestingly, the disease caused by the diphtheria organism (now rarely seen in the United States due to widespread vaccination) results from a toxin secreted by the bacteria and not due to invasion of the bacteria into tissues or organs.

USAMRIID U.S. Army Medical Research Institute in Infectious Diseases is located in Fort Detrick, MD and is devoted to diagnosis, medical treatment, and development of prophylaxis against particularly dangerous infections, such as might be encountered by soldiers deployed overseas, or biowarfare agents. USAMRIID does not develop, produce, or test biological weapons, in compliance the Biological and Toxin Weapons Convention of 1975.

variola A virus containing double-stranded DNA and the cause of the disease smallpox. Variola and the other members of the Orthopox family of viruses are the largest known viruses and can barely be seen with a high-quality, ordinary light microscope. Variola infects only humans in nature, although in experimental conditions in laboratories, macaques and monkeys have been infected with the organism.

VEKTOR The Russian (formerly Soviet) State Research Center of Virology and Bacteriology, located in Koltsovo, Russia, approximately 40 kilometers from the Siberian city of Novosibirsk. VEKTOR is one of the two official World Health Organization repositories for smallpox and contains the world's largest BIOSAFETY level 4 laboratory where active research on smallpox and other extremely dangerous organisms is conducted. The director of VEKTOR since its inception in 1980s has been academician Lev Stepanovich Sandakhchiev.

virus Microscopic (generally less than 100 nanometer in size) infectious agents that depend on other cells (bacterial, mammalian, or plant) in order to replicate and spread. By definition, viruses are classified by the type of genetic material they contain (DNA, RNA, either in single- or double-stranded form) and also by their appearance under the microscope. On occasion, they are also classified by their mechanism of transmission (e.g., "arboviruses" are those spread by insect vectors from one host to another).

yellow fever A mosquito-borne (*Aedes aegypti* mosquito) illness of humans and primates, mostly found in West and Central Africa. The disease is characterized by inflammation of the liver; hemorrhage may also occur. There is no treatment, and mortality is in the range of 10%; however, an effective vaccine is available and quite safe.

Yersinia pestis ("plague") The bacterial organism that is the cause of multiple forms of plague (pneumonic, bubonic, septicemic) and circulates naturally among many species in the wild, especially rodents, marmots, ground squirrels, and prairie dogs. The disease "plague" is endemic to the southwest United States and Central Asia and Southeast Asia; it appears sporadically in Africa and on the island of Madagascar.

zoonotic disease An infection that is usually found most commonly in wildlife and may on occasion be transmitted to humans. Insects transmit many zoonoses, but direct transmission from animals to humans is possible in some cases from consumption of animals (e.g., trichinosis).

INDEX

absenteeism rates, 187–188
active surveillance, 184, 190
acute fatality rate, 58
adult respiratory distress syndrome (ARDS), 42, 43, 53
Aedes japonicus, 14
aerosols, 27, 108
  definition of, 117, 247
  influenza as, 117
  smallpox as, 110–111
air conditioning systems, 86, 87
Albert Einstein Medical School, 8
Alzheimer's disease, 247
amino acids, 248
animalcules, 124
anthrax, 137–138, 140
  bioterrorist attack scenario for, 149–152
  carriers of, 18
  hardiness of, 174
  mortality rate from, 122–123, 148, 165
  in New York City, 176–178
  obtaining, 156
  particles of, 243
  Sverdlovsk outbreak of, 109–110
  2001 attacks of, 146–147, 172, 182–183
  as zoonotic disease, 32
antibiotics, 248
antibodies, 27, 66–67, 95n.5
antigens, 206–207
Appert, Nicolas, 69–70
Aral Sea, 96–97, 100–102
Aralsk smallpox outbreak
  cause of, 107–110
  knowledge gained from, 110–111
  origin of, 100–102
  reporting of, 104–106
  ring containment for, 103–104
  and spread of disease, 102–103
ARDS, *see* adult respiratory distress syndrome
arenaviruses, 43, 248
Asnis, Deborah, 2, 3, 17
attenuated live virus vaccines, 210–211
avian influenza, 5, 219–228
awareness tools, *ix–x*

bacteria, 248–249
  carriers of, 18
  increasing benignness of, 115–116
  smallest known, 10
  unidentified, 175
  see also specific bacteria
Bahe, Merrill, 38–40, 45, 50
Betrayal of Trust (Laurie Garrett), *vii*
biofilms, 87–90, 249
biological warfare, 138–159
  and classical rules of diagnosis, 146–148
  and different strains of pathogens, 153–155
  feasibility of, 156–159
  pathogenic bacteria for, 140
  pathogenic viruses for, 141
  and physicians' knowledge of agents, 142–146
  with plague, 153–154, 156–157
  and principle of diagnostic parsimony, 155–156
  reasons inhibiting, 157, 172
  and reload phenomenon, 152–153
  during Revolutionary War, 137, 138
  with smallpox, 158–159
  Soviet facilities for, 106–108, *see also* Aralsk smallpox outbreak
  threat list for, 138–142
  threat of, 188n.1
  time factors in, 149–152

biological warfare (*continued*)
toxins for, 138, 139
see also bioterrorism
Biosafety levels, 9, 20n.1, 149
bioslime, 87–89
bioslime communities, 88, 92
biotechnology, 242–243
bioterrorism, 241–243
diseases suited for, 147–148
hypothetical scenarios of, *see* hypothetical scenario(s)
investigating for, 13
perceived threat of, 172
physicians' experience with, 147–148
protection against, *see* Project BIOWATCH
Biowarrior (Igor V. Domaradskij and Wendy Orent), 160n.3
bipeptides, 78
bird flu, *ix,* 219–228
birds, viruses spread by, 15
Bisenova, Bayan, 100–102, 104–108
Bisenova, Sakijan, 102, 110
Black Death, 140–141
Botox, 139–140
botulism, 139
bovine spongiform encephalopathy (BSE), 69–81, 249–250
cause of, 71–73
and prion-based diseases, 70–71, 73–81
prion protein responsible for, 78
Bravata, Dena M., 203n.1
Bronx Zoo, 4–6, 8–9
brucellosis, 170
BSE, *see* bovine spongiform encephalopathy
bubonic plague, 9, 154
bunyaviruses, 43, 49, 250
Burgasov (biological weapons worker), 109, 110
Burkhart, Mike, 51
burn rate of diseases, 63
Butler, Thomas, 179, 180, 191

case definition, 26
castor bean plant, 138–139
CDC, *see* Centers for Disease Control and Prevention
cell-mediated immune response, 212
Centers for Disease Control and Prevention (CDC)
and flu vaccine, 213, 215
and Legionella pneumophila, 83
plague expertise of, 154
public health department responsibilities listed by, 189
and SARS outbreak, 26, 28, 29
and shoe-leather epidemiology, 135
and Sin Nombre virus, 44–48, 50, 51, 54
as smallpox repository, 111
and threat of avian flu, 241
and West Nile virus outbreak, 3, 6–8, 10, 11, 13, 16, 19
centripetal rash (smallpox), 98–99
chance, 8
Chilean cholera epidemic, 121–122
China
pigs in, 204
SARS in, 22–25, 30–31, 239–240
cholera, 60, 124–126, 140
Chilean epidemic of, 121–122
conditions enabling, 123
London outbreak of, 124–126
Peruvian epidemic of, 120–121
spread of, 120
treatment of, 120–121
chronic wasting disease, 80–81
City of Lubbock Health Department, 179–180, 188n.2, 189, 191, 193
CJD, *see* Creutzfeldt-Jakob disease
clinical surveillance systems, 190
Clostridium perfringens, 139
cold-adapted influenza virus, 210
communication, 17
accuracy of, 202
hotlines for, 185–186
by local public health officials, 238
between physicians and public health officials, 169
political roadblocks to, 239
during SARS outbreak, 26, 29
during Sin Nombre hantavirus, 54
and suppression of SARS information, 21, 22, 25, 30–31
conformations (prions), 79
coronaviruses, 31, 32, 36, 250

coronavirus urbani pneumonitis, 31, *see also* severe acute respiratory syndrome (SARS)
Corvids, 1–2
cowpox, carriers of, 18
Creutzfeldt-Jakob disease (CJD), 70–78
  connection of prion to, 80
  isolation of, 77
  spread of, 75–76
  symptoms of, 71
  theories about, 74–75
Crimean-Congo hemorrhagic fever, 141
crows, 1–2, 4
cryptosporidiosis, 126–133, 186, 187
  costs associated with, 130
  diagnosis of, 129
  surveillance for, 131–133
  and water turbidity testing, 130–131
CURED diseases, 168

Danzig, Richard, 152
Darwinian principles, 115–116
data collection
  from absenteeism rates, 187–188
  creating methods for, 135–136
  from hotlines, 185–186
  importance of negative data in, 11
  from pharmacy sales, 186–187
  see also disease surveillance
data mining, 184, 186
dead-end hosts, 65–66
deer mice, 50, 52, 53, 255
Department of Environmental Conservation, 2
diagnostic parsimony, principle of, 155–156
differential diagnosis, 5
diffuse infiltrate, 25
diphtheria, 143–144
direct fluorescent antibody test, 90–91
disease cycle, prevention of pandemics and, *ix*
diseases
  burn rate of, 63
  easily prevented, 167–168
  extinction rate of, 63
  lifestyle, 183
  naming of, 240
  pathogen strains and differences in, 153–155
  prion-based, 70–71, 73–81
  reportable, 169–170
  reproductive rate of, 34–35
  risk factors for, 64–65
  severity of, 58–59
  untreatable, 165–167
  viral, 29
  zoonotic, *see* zoonotic diseases
  see also specific diseases
disease surveillance, 183–188
  active vs. passive, 184–188
  for cryptosporidiosis, 128, 131–133
  Minitel-based, 184
  national system for, 176
  in Project BIOSENSE, 173
  for Sin Nombre hantavirus, 54
  by veterinarians, 18
  by zoos, 4
DNA, 250
  amplification of, 30
  in flaviviruses, 7
  radiation damage to, 82n.1
DNA-based vaccines, 211–212
Domaradskij, Igor V., 154, 160n.3
Dorrell, Stephen, 72
DPT vaccine, 144, 159n.2
drug addicts, 145

E. coli, see Escherichia coli
Eastern equine encephalitis (EEE), 5–6, 251
Ebola, 18–19, 22, 250–251
  fragility of, 119
  isolation of those infected with, 63
  spread of, 119
  as zoonotic disease, 32
EEE, *see* Eastern equine encephalitis
EIS (Epidemic Intelligence Service), 46
elk, chronic wasting disease in, 80–81
El Niño, 55
Emerging Infections (Joshua Lederberg and Robert Shope), *vii*
emus, 6
encephalitis, 2, 3, 251
  due to West Nile virus, 4, 7, 15
  viruses causing, 12

encephalitis (*continued*)
  see also specific types, e.g.: St. Louis encephalitis
Environmental Protection Agency (EPA), 173, 174, 177, 178
enzymes, 251
EPA, *see* Environmental Protection Agency
epidemic curve, 32
Epidemic Intelligence Service (EIS), 46
epidemics, 60, 251
  definition of, 59
  overreaction to, 35
  and removal of source of disease, 126
  see also specific diseases
epidemiologists, 12
epidemiology
  definition of, 251
  false beliefs in, 122–123
  and physicians' training, 135–136
  shoe-leather, 133–135
equine encephalitis, 251
Escherichia coli (E. coli), 208–210
Europe
  BSE disease in, 71, 72, *see also* bovine spongiform encephalopathy
  linkages between public health and clinicians in, 171n.5
evolutionary biology, 116–123, 251
  and cholera, 120–122
  and influenza, 117–118
  and smallpox, 116–117
  and vector-borne diseases, 118–120
extinction rate, 60–61, 63

FADDL (Foreign Animal Disease Diagnostic Lab), 9
filoviruses, 43
filtration process, 127, 128
flaviviruses, 7, 10, 43, 251–252, *see also specific viruses*
flocculation, 127, 128
flu, *see* influenza
FluMist, 210
fluorescence, 27
FMD, *see* foot-and-mouth disease
fomites, 108
food-borne illness, 69–70, *see also* bovine spongiform encephalopathy
foot-and-mouth disease (FMD), *ix,* 18, 57–58, 167–168
Foreign Animal Disease Diagnostic Lab (FADDL), 9
forensic pathology, 165
Four Corners (New Mexico), 37
Four Corners pulmonary syndrome, 246
France, Minitel system in, 184
Frist, Bill, 188n.1
future of public health, 237–246
  and bioterrorism, 241–243
  and needs of current public health system, 243–245
  and possible pandemic-causing pathogens, 240–241

Gallup Indian Medical Center, 38, 39
Gambusia affinis, 16
Garrett, Laurie, *vii*
genes, 252
genetic engineering, 252
genome, 252
genomic sequencing, 13
Gerberding, Julie, 30
germ theory, 124, 126
Giuliani, Rudolph, 6
gold, cell internalization of, 216n.2

hantaviruses, 48–49
  as not being a pandemic disease, 60
  total U.S. cases of, 54
  see also specific types
hantavirus pulmonary syndrome (HPS), 59, 246, 252
health surveillance and awareness system, integrated, *x*
hemorrhagic fevers, 18, 32, 56n.3
hemorrhagic fever with renal syndrome (HFRS), 49
hemorrhagic smallpox, 111, 113
Henderson, D. A., 100, 109
hepatitis C, 7, 67
HFRS (hemorrhagic fever with renal syndrome), 49
highly pathogenic avian influenza, 252
HIV, 20n.3, 22, 67, 238
hogans, 50
hotlines, 185–186

Houston Health and Human Services Department, 178
Houston tularemia alarm, 178–179
HPS, *see* hantavirus pulmonary syndrome
human-induced environmental diseases, 84, *see also* Legionella pneumophila
humic acid, 175
hypothetical scenario(s), 218–236
  of anthrax as bioweapon, 149–152
  of avian bird flu, 219–228
  of bioterrorist attack, 228–236
  of foot-and-mouth disease, 167–168
  of influenza, 168, 204–205
  of smallpox as bioweapon, 158–159
  of SYRIS use, 195–202

ICUs, *see* intensive care units
immunocompromised people, 59
  and cryptosporidiosis, 128
  home health hazards for, 92
  Legionnaire's disease in, 92–93
immunologic tolerance, 216n.1
immunosuppression, 252–253
  following nuclear radiation, 98
  and Legionnaire's disease, 84
  and West Nile virus, 12
incubation period, 253
index cases, 56n.1
  for Ebola/HIV, 22
  finding, 22
  from long ago, 12
India, plague outbreak in, 239
infections
  extinction rate of, 60–61
  opportunistic, 142
  physicians' limited knowledge of, 146
infectious disease specialists, 142–143
influenza, 253
  control of, 117–118
  FluMist vaccine for, 210
  fragility of, 117
  highly pathogenic avian, 252
  increase of mortality rate from, 116
  1918 pandemic of, 118
  potential pandemic of, *viii*
  reproductive rate of, 34
  vaccine for, 207–208, 213–215
  variants of, 118
information
  sharing of, 17, 26, 29, 54, 169
  suppression of, 21, 22, 25, 30–31, 239–240
insect-transmitted viruses, 7, *see also specific viruses*
Institute for Viral Preparations (Moscow), 111
intensive care units (ICUs), 148, 166
intentional infections, 13
isolation, 63, 253

Jahrling, Peter, 112
Japanese encephalitis, 253
Journal of Homeland Security, 4

Koch, Robert, 76
Koch's postulates, 76, 253–254
kuru, 74–75

Langmuir, Alex, 133–135
Lassa fever, 44, 254
law of unintended consequences, 93–94
Lawrence Livermore National Laboratory, 175
Lederberg, Joshua, *vii*
  and letter to Lev Sandakhchiev, 112–113
  on pandemics, *x*
Legionella pneumophila (Legionnaire's disease), 68n.2, 83–94
  emergence of, 84
  in immunocompromised persons, 92–93
  intermittent exposure to, 92
  and law of unintended consequences, 93–94
  means of contracting, 91–92
  membrane structure of, 86–87
  source of pathogen for, 85
  testing for, 90–91
  transmission of, 85–86
Lev Berg, 100–101, 105, 108
lifestyle diseases, 183
Liu Jianlun, 24, 25, 31
lockjaw, 145–146
Lubbock County plague vials, 179–181
luck, 8–9

Lundgren, Ottilie, 182
Lyme disease, 17, 254

Mad Cow disease, *see* bovine spongiform encephalopathy
Maimonides, oath of, 170–171n.2
major histocompatibility complex (MHC), 216–217n.3
malaria
  control of, 119
  early theories about, 124
  increase of mortality rate from, 116
mathematics, 62
McNamara, Tracey, 4–11, 13, 17–19, 143
measles, 34, 35, 59
medical disciplines, 56n.2
medical investigators, 164
medical surveillance programs, *x*
Meselson, Matthew, 109–110
Metropole hotel (Hong Kong), 21, 24, 25, 31
MHC, *see* major histocompatibility complex
miasma, 124
microbes
  naturally occurring, *ix*
  scientists' knowledge of, 175
microencapsulation, 242–243
Milwaukee cryptosporidium outbreak, 127–133, 186, 187
Minitel system, 184
Monath, Tom, 112
Moscow News, 110
mosquito-borne viral disease(s)
  increase of mortality rate from, 116
  survival of, 118–119
  West Nile virus as, 5, 6, 12, 14–16
  yellow fever as, 133
mutations of viruses, 118

Napoléon Bonaparte, 69, 70
National Academy of Sciences (NAS), 109, 112
National Electronic Disease Surveillance System (NEDSS), 203n.3
National Security Council (NSC), 173, 174
National Veterinary Services Laboratories (NVSL), 8, 10
National Wildlife Health Center, 16
naturally occurring microbes, *ix*
natural reservoir
  for hantaviruses, 49–50
  for SARS, 36
natural reservoirs, 65–67
Navajo Nation, 41, 45, 48, 51, 52, 55
necropsy, 254
NEDSS (National Electronic Disease Surveillance System), 203n.3
negative data, 11
Newcastle disease, 5, 254
The New England Journal of Medicine, 145, 146
New Mexico Department of Health, 40, 43, 45, 48, 90
new variant CJD (nvCJD), 70
New York City
  anthrax in, 176–178
  West Nile virus outbreak in, 1–20
New York City Department of Health, 3, 4, 177–178
New York State Department of Environmental Conservation, 5
New York State Department of Health, 3
The New York Times, 2
North Korea, smallpox and, 114
NSC, *see* National Security Council
nucleic acids, 254
nvCJD (new variant CJD), 70
NVSL, *see* National Veterinary Services Laboratories

oath of Maimonides, 170–171n.2
Office of the Medical Investigator (OMI) (New Mexico), 39, 41–44, 47
"one disease" perspective, 19
"one medicine" concept, *x*
oocytes, 127
opportunistic infections, 142
Orent, Wendy, 160n.3
organisms
  reproductive rate of, 34–35
  scientists' knowledge of, 175
outbreaks, 57–60

Paine, Thomas, 138
pandemics, 254

definition of, 27, 59–60
occurrences of, 238
possible pathogens causing, 240–241
particulate samplers, 173–174
passive surveillance, 184, 185, 190
Pasteur, Louis, 70
pasteurization, 70
pathogens, 254
pathologists, 56n.2, 164–165
PCR, *see* polymerase chain reaction
PEEP (positive end-expiratory pressure), 28
Peromyscus maniculatus, 50, 255
pertussis, 144, 145
Peruvian cholera epidemic, 120–121
Peters, C. J., 52
Pezzullo, John, 35
pharmacy sales data, 186–187
physicians
amplification of instructions to, 245
bioterrorism experience of, 147–148
infectious disease knowledge of, 141–146
in public health system, 244
public health system knowledge of, 161–163
training of public health system officials vs., 163–165
training of scientists vs., 135–136
uses of time by, 169
plague, 140–141
as biological weapon, 153–154
carriers of, 18
dead-end hosts of, 66
Indian outbreak of, 239
Lubbock County reported loss of, 179–181
natural reservoir for, 65
obtaining, 156
transmission of, 41, 181–182
Turkmenistan outbreak of, 155
in Western United States, 39
as zoonotic disease, 32
plaque (on teeth), 89–90
plaques (from BSE), 80
plating out process, 205
Plum Island, 9, 20n.1
pneumonia, 67–68n.2, 255, *see also* Legionella pneumophila
pneumonic plague, 154
polymerase chain reaction (PCR), 30, 174, 176, 177, 254–255
positive end-expiratory pressure (PEEP), 28
principle of diagnostic parsimony, 155–156
prion-based diseases, 73–81
destruction of prions causing, 77
emergence of, 70–71
isolation of, 77
lack of treatments for, 73
species-specific nature of, 78–79
spread of, 75–76
symptoms of, 73
prions, 70, 73, 75, 79–80, 255
Project BIOSENSE, 173, 175
Project BIOSHIELD, 173
Project BIOWATCH, 172–188
and active/passive disease surveillance, 183–188
and anthrax in New York City, 176–178
"false positives" in, 175–176
major flow of, 174
particulate samplers for, 173–174
and plague vials in Lubbock County, 179–181
and tularemia in Houston, 178–179
uncompleted phases of, 176
and usefulness of data, 181–183
protozoa, 255
Prusiner, Stanley B., 75, 78, 80
public health officials
decision making by, 243–244
training of, 164
transferring information to, 183
uses of time by, 169
public health system, *vii,* 161–170
and easily prevented diseases, 167–168
failure factors in, 168–170
future of, *see* future of public health
lack of linkage in, 176
Langmuir's contributions to, 133–135
need for, 162–163
needs of, 243–245
physicians' knowledge of, 161–163
real-time, Internet-based communication in, 26

public health system (*continued*)
recent significant failure of, 163
statistical basis of, 126
training of physicians vs. officials in, 163–165
and untreatable illnesses, 165–167
working relationships in, 19–20
purity of culture, 205–206

Q fever, 141
quarantines, 63–65, 255–256

rabbit fever, *see* tularemia
rabies, 17
radiation, 82n.1, 98
Rapid Syndrome Validation Program (RSVP), 188n.2, 191–193
recombinant synthesis, 208–210
Reed, Walter, 133
reload phenomenon, 152–153, 156
reporting
approval processes for, 36
legally mandated, 169–170, 171n.3
and Milwaukee cryptosporidiosis outbreak, 132
Minitel system for, 184
by physicians, 169
of smallpox, 99–100
via RSVP, 192
Web sites for, 26
reproductive rate of organisms, 34–35
retrospective studies, 94n.1
retroviruses, 7
reverse transcription-polymerase chain reaction, 13
rheumatoid arthritis, 216n.2
rhinoviruses, 27
ricin, 138, 139
Rift Valley fever, 141
ring containment vaccination, 99, 104
risk acceptance, *vii–viii*
risk factors (for diseases), 64–65
RNA, 256
in flaviviruses, 7
radiation damage to, 82n.1
Romania, West Nile virus in, 12, 20n.2
RSVP, *see* Rapid Syndrome Validation Program

Sandakhchiev, Lev, 111–113, 259–261
SARS, *see* severe acute respiratory syndrome
SBDSSs, *see* syndrome-based disease surveillance systems
scenarios, *see* hypothetical scenario(s)
Science magazine, 34
The Secret Life of Germs (Philip Iterno), 13–14
seed cultures, 205–208
SEIR model, *see* susceptible-exposed-infectives-recovered model
severe acute respiratory syndrome (SARS), 21–36, 256
case definition for, 26
central Web site for, 29
first appearance of, 22
identification of, 27–32
reporting of, 26, 29
spread of, 22–25, 33
suppression of information on, 21, 22, 25, 30–31, 239–240
symptoms of, 25
syndrome surveillance program used with, 32–36
treatments for, 28–29
severity of disease, 58–59
shoe-leather epidemiology, 133–135
Shope, Robert, *vii*
signs (of disease), 26
Simpson, Gary, 40–44, 46–48, 50–52, 54, 55, 56n.4
Sin Nombre hantavirus, 37–56
control of, 53
data collection for, 43–45
and El Niño phenomenon, 55
first deaths from, 38–40
as good example of disease surveillance and containment, 54
identification of, 41–42, 48–52
naming of, 52–53
new cases of, 45–47
precautions against, 51
pre-epidemic cases of, 55
temporary name for, 42
"skin popping," 145
"slate wiper" diseases, 5
SLE, *see* St. Louis encephalitis

smallpox, 96–114, 141, 142
Aralsk outbreak of, 97, 100–111
as biological weapon, 97–98, 109–111, 158–159, 243
dead-end hosts of, 66
extinction rate for, 61
global eradication campaign for, 98–100
hardiness of, 117
identification of, 147
increase of mortality rate from, 116–117
intentional introduction of, 159n.1
newborns' immunity to, 66
physicians' limited knowledge of, 146
project for eradication of, 97–100, 111–112
in repositories, 111–114
spread of, 108–109
sustainable outbreaks of, 62–63
unofficial repositories of, 113–114
Snow, John, 124–126
sonication, 206
Soviet Union
biological weapons program of, 160n.3, 241–242
diphtheria epidemic in, 144
pneumonic plague weaponized by, 154, 156–157
smallpox used by, 97, 98, *see also* Aralsk smallpox outbreak
Special Pathogens Branch (CDC), 47–48, 50, 52
St. Elizabeth Medical Center, 84
St. Louis encephalitis (SLE), 6–8, 10, 11, 256
Stanhope, William, 236n.1
Staphylococcus enterotoxin B, 139
Stewart, William, 170n.1
stroke, 2, 3
supportive care, 165
surface expression, 211
surveillance, *see* disease surveillance; syndrome-based disease surveillance systems
susceptible-exposed-infectives-recovered (SEIR) model, 62–63
sweating sickness, 94n.1
symptoms, 26
syndrome-based disease surveillance systems (SBDSSs), 189–202
advantages of, 35–36
categories of, 190
in Lubbock County, Texas, 180–181
and outbreaks with animal sources, 190
RSVP as, 191–193
for SARS, 32–36
SYRIS as, 193–202
syndrome definition, 26, 256
Syndrome Reporting Information System (SYRIS), 188n.2, 193–202
case study of, 195–202
as improvement over other SBDSSs, 193–194

Tchaikovsky, Pyotr Illich, 125
Tempest, Bruce, 39, 40, 42, 43, 53, 56, 246
testing, problems/mistakes with, 29–30
tetanus, 144–146
Texas Tech medical school, 180
thermophiles, 86
Tierno, Philip, 13–14
toxins, 256–257
toxoid vaccines, 144
toxoplasmosis, carriers of, 18
trailers, 50
training
of physicians vs. public health officials, 163–164
of physicians vs. scientists, 135–136
of veterinarians, 18
Trichothecene nycotoxin, 139
triclosan, 94n.3
tripeptides, 78
tuberculosis, 216n.2
tularemia, 140
Houston alarm for, 178–179
lethality rate of, 147–148

unintended consequences, law of, 93–94
University of New Mexico, 44, 45, 51, 52, 90
U.S. Army Medical Research Institute in Infectious Diseases (USAMRIID), 10–11, 257
U.S. Navy ships, 152
USAMRIID, *see* U.S. Army Medical Research Institute in Infectious Diseases

vaccination, ring containment, 99, 104
vaccines, 204–215
 from attenuated live viruses, 210–211
 diphtheria, 144
 DNA-based, 211–213
 DPT, 144, 159n.2
 increasing introduction of, 68n.2
 for influenza, 207–208, 213–215
 for pathogenic bacteria, 140
 for pathogenic viruses, 141
 from recombinant synthesis, 208–210
 from seed cultures, 205–208
 for smallpox, 98
 for toxins, 139
 toxoid, 144
van Leeuwenhoek, Antonie, 95n.4
variola, 257, *see also* smallpox
variolation, 137
vector-borne diseases
 controlling, 120
 Ebola as, 119
 survival of, 118–119
vectors, 49, 65
VEKTOR, 111–113, 257
Venezuelan equine encephalitis, 141
veterinarians
 as front line of defense, 17–18
 in public health system, 244–245
 relationships between public health and, 19–20
 as separate medical branch, 143
veterinary pathologists, 18
viral diseases, 29, *see also specific diseases*
viruses, 7, 257
 attenuated, 210
 categorizing, 10
 coronaviruses, 31, 32, 36
 families of, 43
 flaviviruses, 7
 hantaviruses, 48–49
 increasing benignness of, 115–116, 122–123
 as life-forms, 75
 mutations of, 118
 naming of, 49, 240
 retroviruses, 7
 RNA-containing, 7
 sizes of, 10
 see also specific viruses
Vozrozhdeniye Island, 106–108, 110

Ward, Tigi, 180–181
Washington, George, 137
water-borne disease(s)
 cholera as, 120–122, 124–126
 cryptosporidiosis as, 126–133
Western equine encephalitis, 251
West Nile virus, *ix,* 1–20
 "acuteness" of, 67n.1
 animal deaths from, 15
 at Bronx Zoo, 4–6
 in crows, 1–2
 early prevention efforts against, 6–7
 first NYC human cases of, 2–4
 humans infected with, 16, 17
 identification of, 11
 luck factors in identification of, 8–10
 measures taken against, 16
 physicians' experience with, 147
 spread of, 11–15, 65
 and veterinarians as front line of defense, 17–18
 and working relationships among agencies, 19–20
WHO, *see* World Health Organization
working relationships between agencies, 19–20
World Health Organization (WHO)
 daily bulletins of, 27
 oral hydration program of, 121
 and pandemic flu summit, 213
 and SARS outbreak, 21, 23–30, 33
 and smallpox eradication project, 97–100, 111–112, 114

Yates, Terry, 52
yellow fever, 133, 257
Yersinia pestis, 257, *see also* plague

Zelicoff, Alan, 32–35, 113, 188n.2, 191, 203n.2, 236n.1
Zhdanov, Victor, 98, 99
zoonotic diseases, 9, 17, 18, 32, 258
 on CDC "highest risk" list, 190
 severity of, 119
 on threat list, 141–142